HEIRS OF LONDON

HISTORICAL REGENCY ROMANCE & COZY MYSTERY COLLECTION

JOYCE ALEC

Heirs of London

Text Copyright © 2021 by Joyce Alec

All rights reserved. This book or any portion thereof may not be reproduced or used in any manner whatsoever without the express written permission of the publisher except for the use of brief quotations in a book review.

This book is a work of fiction. Names, characters, places and incidents are either the product of the author's imagination or are used fictionally. Any resemblance to actual persons, living or dead, or to actual events or locales is entirely coincidental.

First printing, 2021

Publisher
Love Light Faith, LLC
400 NW 7th Avenue, Unit 825
Fort Lauderdale, FL 33311

LOVE LIGHT FAITH

Receive a FREE inspirational romance eBook by visiting our website and signing up for our mailing list. Click the link or enter www.LoveLightFaith.com into your browser.

The newsletter will also provide information on upcoming books and special offers.

LONDON STRANGER

HEIRS OF LONDON BOOK ONE

London Stranger

Text Copyright © 2020 by Joyce Alec

All rights reserved. This book or any portion thereof may not be reproduced or used in any manner whatsoever without the express written permission of the publisher except for the use of brief quotations in a book review.

This book is a work of fiction. Names, characters, places and incidents are either the product of the author's imagination or are used fictionally. Any resemblance to actual persons, living or dead, or to actual events or locales is entirely coincidental.

First printing, 2020

Publisher
Love Light Faith, LLC
400 NW 7th Avenue, Unit 825
Fort Lauderdale, FL 33311

1

The carriage bounced over an uneven part of the road and Juliet winced, gritting her teeth as she held on to the strap. The many hours she had spent in the carriage were beginning to take its toll and Juliet did not know how she was meant to endure much more. Her body ached and she was weary and exhausted. It was all very well for her father, who had chosen to hire a horse so that he might ride the last stretch to London, and her companion—one Mrs. Grey—was sound asleep in the opposite corner of the carriage, her mouth ajar as her dark grey head bobbed with every jostle of the carriage. Juliet could not even think of sleeping at present, even though she was thoroughly exhausted. Their last inn, whilst pleasant enough, had not had the softest of beds and Juliet had spent the night tossing and turning whilst, again, Mrs. Grey slept soundly and without complaint. It had all been most irritating.

It will be worth it, she told herself, thinking of London and society and all that came with it. *Once you are back in London, it will all be worth it.* A small smile captured her mouth as she thought of what awaited her. Last Season, she had made her debut and had enjoyed her time in London, being introduced to various gentlemen and ladies, conversing with them, dancing with the gentlemen, and trying to make herself known amongst the *beau monde*. Her Season had not lasted as long as she had hoped, however, for her companion had become gravely ill and, once she had improved enough to travel, they had all returned to her father's estate so that Mrs. Grey might continue her recovery there.

Juliet prayed that this year, she would be able to stay in London for the entirety of the Season.

"Whoa there!"

The carriage, much to Juliet's astonishment, suddenly began to slow. She frowned and looked out of the window, wondering why they were doing so. London was still some distance away and they certainly had not arranged to take any respite in between, not unless her father's horse required it.

Unable to see anything of interest, Juliet waited as the carriage came to a complete stop, astonished to hear her father's loud voice calling up toward the driver. Wondering what it was he had discovered, Juliet opened her carriage door without hesitation, but the driver jumped down from his perch and then came toward her at once, his face flushed from the heat of the sun.

"My lady, the master has stopped us," the driver told her as the other servants climbed down to join him. "He states that it is best that you remain in the carriage, however. He gave no instructions to say you should join him."

"Hurry up, man!"

Juliet winced, hearing the firmness in her father's voice. The driver dipped his head and then hurried away, leaving Juliet and Mrs. Grey to sit—or sleep on—in the carriage.

Frustration lit Juliet's soul. Why had her father demanded such a thing? Surely he knew just how difficult it was to sit in the carriage for a long period. Questions burned in her mind as she heard the murmur of low voices drifting toward her, her brow furrowing as she strained to listen through the open carriage door. What was it they had discovered? And why must she remain in the carriage? Had they discovered something that would put her 'delicate constitution', as her father so often called it, at risk? Irritation grasped a hold of her heart and Juliet glanced toward Mrs. Grey, noting that the lady slept on, seemingly all the better now that the carriage had stopped. With a small sigh of exasperation, Juliet climbed out carefully and stood on the grassy verge, permitting herself a long stretch as her muscles began to complain about what she had been doing. The thought of climbing back into the carriage was not one she relished and thus Juliet was quite determined to make the most of this opportunity.

"Juliet!"

The moment she came into view, the horses still between herself and her father, the Earl of Lansbury immediately began to rail at her.

"I gave specific instructions that you were to remain in the carriage."

"I am aware of that, Father," Juliet replied calmly, "but I need to take a short walk. It has been a rather difficult journey and I am tired."

Her father glared at her, his dark grey eyes fixed to her face, but Juliet ignored him entirely. The earl might have a good deal of bluster, but it never amounted to anything. No doubt she frustrated him entirely by refusing to do as he asked, but on this occasion at least, Juliet felt entirely justified.

"Do not come near," the earl said after a moment or two. "Juliet, I beg of you to listen to me, even though a father ought never to have to beg anything of his child." Clicking his tongue, he looked back at Juliet steadily, waiting for her answer, and something in his gaze caught Juliet's attention.

"Yes, Father," she said slowly, looking at him carefully and wondering at the dark frown on his face. "What is it that you have discovered?"

The earl blew out a breath and looked away. "It is best you do not know, Juliet."

"Please, Father," she said, a tremor running through her at the clear upset in her father's face. "It is something truly terrible?"

Again, her father did not immediately answer, his gaze still fixed on a point in the horizon. "It appears, Juliet," he said eventually, "that some highwaymen have been along this road."

All of Juliet's determination and eagerness washed away in an instant and she could almost feel the color draining from her cheeks. Without even meaning to do so, she took a small step to her right, horrified to see the outline of a man lying on the ground behind her father. His eyes were closed and his skin grey. It was clear that there was no life left within him.

Putting out one hand, Juliet leaned on the carriage itself for support, hearing the horses whinny nervously as she turned away. She ought not to have come out of the carriage. Her father, seeing clearly that his daughter was overcome, came closer to speak to her over the horses' backs.

"Highwaymen?" she whispered, and the earl nodded, his mouth in a tight line. "How can you be certain?"

"I cannot be certain that it was, but what other reason would someone have to discard people by the side of the road without any of their jewelry left on them?" the earl asked bluntly. "As I have said, Juliet, I think you should have remained in the carriage. What you have observed already is more than enough. This is not a sight you ought to see."

Juliet wanted to argue, wanted to state that she was quite all right and that he did not need to mollycoddle her, but she could not deny that even the small glimpse of what the highwaymen had left behind had turned her stomach. With a tight nod, she turned back to where she had come from, although she did not instantly climb back inside. Instead, she kept one hand on the door, breathing hard and forcing the fright out of herself. She would not give in to it, not when they were so close to London, and surely no highwaymen would attempt to do anything given just how close they were to the city.

Except they have clearly been at work in this very spot, she said to herself, sickened at the thought. *It is not as safe as you might have hoped.*

Whilst Juliet had heard stories of highwaymen and knew that the tales were, for the most part, quite true, she had never permitted herself to linger on such stories whenever they had set out to travel, knowing that she was well protected by her father's staff. But now to hear that they had almost driven past those who had been attacked by highwaymen and had lost their lives because of it made things all the more real to her. She felt sick, breathing hard so that she would not cast up her accounts by the side of the road. There was more mettle in her than this, surely.

"My lady?"

She turned to see the driver returning.

"We are to make haste to London," the driver told her gently, his kind face telling her that he knew she was feeling quite ill at ease. "Might you climb back inside?"

Juliet nodded and accepted his hand, climbing back into the apparent safety of the carriage and letting out her breath slowly, feeling it rattle out of her as she tried to grasp a hold of her courage. Sitting back down, she waited for the driver to close the door, only for him to step away quickly as the earl suddenly appeared.

"You are quite all right, Juliet?" he asked, showing her more compassion than usual. "I know such things are distressing but just be glad that you did not see anything too grotesque."

This did not help her nerves in any way, making her stomach twist in a most alarming fashion. "There is no hope for any of them?"

The earl hesitated. "Not for two of them, the poor devils," he said, his face holding a good deal more anger than Juliet had expected. "The third is still breathing and, whilst in a great deal of pain and distress, has life left within him. I have done what I can for them. A young lad came near to us as we were discussing what to do and I have sent him back to the nearest village to fetch those who might be able to not only remove the bodies but bury them also. He will also bring whatever country doctor he can find, just in case the third can be saved."

Juliet swallowed the nausea that rose in her throat. "Then we are to stay here at present?"

"*I* shall," the earl replied firmly, "but you are to carry on to London. You and Mrs. Grey—" he glanced at the sleeping woman before he continued, a slight flicker of mirth in his eyes now. "You are both to set yourselves up in the townhouse and make certain that you are both settled and rested. We will not go out into London until either the morrow or the day after."

Had they not found such a dreadful sight and had Juliet's stomach not been battling to keep a hold of itself, Juliet might have argued with her father that she could very easily go out into society come the morrow, but given just how ill she now felt, she lapsed into a quiet agreement of silence.

"And there is one more thing," the earl said quietly, speaking now very seriously indeed. "There was a letter in the gentleman's pockets, Juliet. The one who still breathes. I should like you to take it back to the townhouse with you."

Juliet's head lifted and she stared at her father, who was nodding encouragingly.

"You mean to say that you looked through their clothes?" she asked, a little repulsed. "Why would you—?"

"The driver did so," the earl replied, interrupting her. "And I had him do so in order to make quite certain that it *was* highwaymen and not some other thing. It confirmed to me that yes, it must have been highwaymen who had done such a dreadful thing, given that everything of value is gone from them. It was only by chance that I discovered this note and, whilst I have not yet read it, I think it would be wise to take it back to London in case it yields something of importance. I do not know if this gentleman will ever recover and if he does not, then who will ever know of it?" A flare of anger burned in his eyes and he looked away for a moment, his hand whitening as he pulled the letter out from his pocket. "Recall, Juliet," he said, looking back at her and clearly keeping his voice constrained with an effort, "that we do not know the name of that man, or of those who lie dead."

Juliet nodded, reaching out to take the letter from her father without any further hesitation, realizing what he meant and why the letter might be of such great importance. Those who had perished at the hands of the highwaymen were, at present, entirely without name or identity. The people from the nearby village might know them, if they had passed through, but if they did not and if the third passed away also, then it would be nothing but three unmarked graves. Families would be left bereft, uncertain as to where their beloved son or husband or brother had gone. It was up to Juliet and her father to do the very best they could for them.

"I thank you, Juliet," her father said gently before closing the carriage door. "Now, off to London with you. And do not stop until you reach the townhouse."

She nodded. "Yes, Father," she promised, looking down at the letter in her hand and then glancing across at Mrs. Grey, who was still sound asleep. With a jolt that made no difference to her companion, the carriage moved away again, jostling Juliet hard as she looked steadfastly out of her window, refusing to turn her head for fear of what she might see out of the opposite window. Her hands tightened on the letter she held, her breathing uneven as she fought rising nausea. Looking down at the letter, she caught her breath before having to suck in air desperately, horrified at the roiling of her stomach. She could not cast up her accounts here, not when her father had told her not to stop until they reached London. But as she glanced back down at it again, Juliet felt a horror begin to creep over her skin, her heart pounding and her fear growing steadily.

The letter was flecked with blood.

∽

IT WAS a sennight before Juliet felt ready to step out into society. After the journey to her father's townhouse, Juliet had grown all the more weary and tired, finding that there had been none of the exhilaration she had hoped for in returning to London. Instead, she had taken to her bed and had rested for some days, whilst her father fretted that she would become just as ill as her companion had been last Season and that they would have to return to his estate before the Season had even begun.

This, however, had not been the case. Juliet had increased her strength daily and had finally managed to push all thoughts of highwaymen and the horrors they had witnessed from her mind, leaving her only to push aside a straying memory or two whenever they came to her.

The letter, however, had been very little help. Her father had opened it almost the moment he had returned to London, only to discover that there was nothing within. Juliet had taken it from him with a frown, turning it this way and that but discovering that it was entirely empty. Her father had muttered about throwing it in the fire but, for whatever reason, Juliet had kept it in her bedchamber, as though it might yield its secrets to her if she could only wish for it hard enough.

"Let me see you, then."

Juliet blushed as she walked into the drawing room, seeing her father waiting for her. He waggled a finger and Juliet turned slowly, praying that he would be satisfied with her gown for the evening.

Thankfully it appeared he was *more* than contented.

"You look very lovely, my dear," he said kindly. "That gown was an excellent choice for your first ball of the Season."

Juliet smiled back at her father, thinking him to be a very kind gentleman in his way. He had never expressed any great fondness for her but, in his own way, made certain that she realized she was of importance to him. Whilst he preferred to bury himself in business, read a great many books, and take long, solitary walks, Juliet found herself desperate for company, for conversation, and for laughter with friends and companions. Mrs. Grey did not provide such things, although Juliet was very grateful for her indeed. This evening, she might be able to reacquaint herself with one or two of the other ladies whom she had met last Season. That, she was sure, would help her re-establish herself in society.

"You will be careful to do all that Mrs. Grey says," the earl continued, his tone now a little more firm. "Everything she insists you do, you do without question or hesitation. Is that clear?"

"Yes, Father," Juliet replied quickly, aware that, whilst she might find Mrs. Grey's presence a little irritating at times, she was only there to ensure that Juliet behaved with all propriety and that gentlemen, too, treated Juliet with the respect she deserved. Whilst Juliet was all too aware of the presence of rogues and rakes within society, she had not met any as yet and that, certainly, was not a source of disappointment to her. Some young ladies wanted nothing more than to be introduced to such a gentleman, but Juliet was not one of them. She wanted to find herself a sensible, kind-hearted gentleman that would suit her very well. That was both her own and her father's intention for her this Season and Juliet wanted very much to fulfill it.

"And you will inform me of any gentlemen of note, Mrs. Grey," the earl continued as Juliet's companion nodded quickly. "Particularly if they seem interested in my daughter. She must be protected."

"I quite understand, my lord," the lady replied, curtsying quickly in evident deference. "I will make sure to do so."

Becoming frustrated with her father's evident unwillingness to hurry them to the carriage and, instead, to talk with them both about what his expectations were—expectations that were already very well established, given that Juliet had heard them many times before—she gave her father a pointed look.

He understood it immediately, a small smile spreading across his face and making his dark grey eyes twinkle.

"Yes, yes, we shall depart," he said with a wave of his hand that instructed Juliet to make for the door. "I shall, of course, be there to make certain you are welcomed by the host but, thereafter, I do intend to find the card room just as soon as I can."

Juliet smiled up at her father as she passed him, feeling no concern whatsoever that he would be seeking out the card room. He was not a father who had ever shown great concern for his offspring. There had been a great concern for her older brother, of course, given that he was the heir, but now that he was wed and settled, her father had shown no great interest in Juliet's future. No doubt he expected her to find someone suitable, but there was no need for him to be involved in any great detail, hence why she now had Mrs. Grey as her companion. Hurrying to the carriage, Juliet climbed inside carefully, making certain not to wrinkle her gown.

"A very fine evening this is to be, I am sure," Mrs. Grey said, sitting down with a small sigh. "And plenty of eligible gentlemen."

Juliet laughed. "I will be happy just to reacquaint myself with those I met last Season," she said as her father joined them. "That will suit me very well." Her hands tightened in her lap as the carriage pulled away from the house, a knot of excitement squirreling into her belly. A sudden thought came to her and she looked at her father. "Have you heard anything from Mr. Johnson?" she asked, having been told the name of the man who had taken on the responsibility of caring for the third man they had found, as well as the burial of the other two.

Her father shook his head. "There is very little change," he replied, a hint of sorrow in his voice. "The third man hovers between consciousness and unconsciousness, eating very little and having said nothing at all." After a moment, he reached across and patted Juliet's hand. "But you must not think of that now. London is waiting for you and you shall be at the very heart of all there is to enjoy."

Juliet nodded and returned her gaze to the window. The horror of what she had seen, the fear of the highwaymen, and the dreadful thoughts that had filled her mind for so long no longer troubled her to the same extent. In fact, she was able to push them aside without any great difficulty given the excitement of what was before her. Her first ball of the Season. It was, as Mrs. Grey had said, sure to be a very fine evening, and Juliet could hardly wait until they arrived.

∽

"I THANK YOU." Juliet smiled briefly at their host and then turned to Mrs. Grey, aware that both she and her father were now waiting for her.

"You did very well, Juliet," Mrs. Grey murmured as the earl cleared his throat, looking all about him and paying Juliet very little attention. "Lord Fauster is well known for making some uncomfortable and disconcerting remarks at times, but I presume that he did not say anything of note to you?"

"Nothing at all," Juliet replied happily. "His wife appeared to be keeping a sharp eye on his behavior and his words, however." She smiled as Mrs. Grey chuckled, making their way together toward the ballroom, her anticipation building with every step. "I do hope that all will go well this evening."

"You have your dance card?" Mrs. Grey asked, her blue eyes turning to Juliet with a sudden worry dancing in them. "You have not forgotten to tie it around your wrist?"

In answer, Juliet lifted her arm and allowed Mrs. Grey to see the dance card dangling from it, the silk ribbon slipping over her glove as she did so.

"I am glad to see it," Mrs. Grey replied as two footmen opened the ballroom doors for them so that they might walk inside. "For I am quite certain, Juliet, that you shall have your dance card filled very soon."

"I do hope so," Juliet said, walking into the ballroom and clasping her hands together with the sheer joy of being back in society. The orchestra was playing, some couples were dancing a quadrille, and all around her were small groups of guests conversing together. Overwhelmed with the sheer joy that filled her at being back amongst it all, Juliet let out a sigh of contentment, pausing in her steps for a few moments simply so that she might look all about her.

"Yes, yes, it is all quite wonderful," Mrs. Grey said, laughing as she grasped Juliet's elbow gently. "But come, we must make our way through the crowd and find someone that we are acquainted with."

"But of course," Juliet replied happily, following Mrs. Grey. It did not take long for them to discover an old acquaintance and, very soon, Juliet was talking cheerfully with one Lord Stevenson, one Lady Richmond, and one Miss Swettenham, whose mother stood only a few steps away, keeping a sharp eye on her daughter. Soon afterwards, she had Lord Stevenson asking to sign her dance card and, with a nod of agreement and a heart filled with delight, she gave him her consent. Within the hour, Juliet found herself practically surrounded by old acquaintances and, just as Mrs. Grey had hoped, her dance card filled completely. Smiling and laughing, Juliet felt her heart lift free of the remaining strains of fear and worry that lingered there, finding herself filled with a great happiness that chased all adverse emotions away. She was back within society, back in London, and there was nothing to take that joy away from her.

2

"Might I have the pleasure of introducing my daughter to you?"

Duncan cleared his throat but forced a smile to his face. "But of course, Lord Haskett," he replied, forcing some sort of warmth into his voice as the older gentleman beamed at him, before turning to beckon a young lady over toward him. "I should be very glad indeed to become acquainted with her."

"Capital!" Lord Haskett exclaimed as a young lady with soft brown eyes and ringlet curls falling gently over her shoulder came near. She was, Duncan had to admit, rather pretty but he did so very much hate being forced into considering a young lady simply because of her outward merits. A lady's title and dowry were important, of course, but he would not be forced into considering a lady just because he might find her beautiful.

"My dear, might I introduce the Earl of Strickland," Lord Haskett said, gesturing toward Duncan. "Lord Strickland, this is my daughter, Miss Sarah Poole."

"My very great pleasure, Miss Poole," Duncan murmured as he bent low into a bow. "I do hope that you have found this evening to be enjoyable thus far?"

Miss Poole nodded, her smile big and bright and lighting up her features completely. "It has been very lovely indeed," she said, her voice not at all as quiet as Duncan had expected. "Although I do wish for some dancing. I always like a bit of dancing, Lord Strickland."

He smiled back at her although inwardly thinking that he would prefer a quiet evening given that there were balls almost every evening at present. Balls where he would be hounded by young ladies or their mothers in the hope of him striking up an interest in one of them. "You are fond of dancing, then, Miss Poole?" he asked, and she nodded fervently. "Is there anything else that you enjoy?"

This seemed to stump Miss Poole for a short time, and she considered this question for so long that Duncan began to wonder if she would ever answer him at all. Lord Haskett said nothing but rather smiled down at his daughter fondly, making Duncan think that he was well used to his daughter's long silences.

"I can only say, Lord Strickland, that dancing is my very favorite pastime," Miss Poole announced in a rather dramatic fashion. "I may read upon occasion or do other such activities that are expected of young ladies, but to my mind, there is nothing better than being out amongst society and enjoying the company and conversation of others." She smiled and a gleam came into her eye. "Particularly when one is able to make *new* acquaintances."

This did not make Duncan smile, however, for he could hear the gentle flirtation in the lady's voice and could see the fluttering of her lashes as she looked back at him. He was not at all inclined toward Miss Poole, just as he was not at all inclined to any young lady who sought him out in such an obvious fashion.

"Indeed, Miss Poole," he replied in a somewhat firm voice, wondering how to extract himself from the conversation without appearing rude. "I am sure that there are a good many gentlemen and ladies within the *ton* that will be glad to make your acquaintance, Miss Poole. This is your first Season, is it not?"

"It is," Miss Poole replied, blushing now at the apparent compliment Duncan had given her. "You are very kind to say such a thing. In fact, I—"

"I should be glad to introduce you to any of my acquaintances," Duncan interrupted, quickly grabbing the attention of Lord Jennings, who was meandering across the room without any obvious intention. "Ah, Lord Jennings," he continued loudly, as Miss Poole looked at him with astonishment—although it seemed that her father was quite delighted given the broad smile settled on his face. "Might I introduce you to a new acquaintance of mine?"

Thankfully, Lord Jennings appeared to be more than willing to do as Duncan asked, coming toward them at once and bowing to Miss Poole after greeting her father. Duncan quickly introduced them both and then, his duty done given that he knew Lord Jennings would be able and willing to converse with Miss Poole for some time, he excused himself quietly.

A long sigh escaped him as he crossed the room, praying that he would not be greeted by any other gentleman or lady wishing to introduce him to their daughters. He had endured quite enough already, and he had only been back in London for a sennight. Unfortunately for Duncan, it was well known that he was the richest earl in all of England, whose wealth outstripped even the Marquess of Longbridge. This was not a truth that he had shared with anyone but rather one that his own mother had been very delighted to express to all who would listen, in the hope that this would encourage Duncan to find a suitable wife.

It had done the exact opposite, however. Instead of encouraging him toward a particular lady, he had found himself doing all he could to avoid the young ladies that sought him out. They wanted his attention solely so that they could have the chance, as they saw it, to wed a gentleman with a great deal of money so that they could live in such a way as to satisfy their every indulgence and whim. It was not because of his own character that they had any particular interest but rather that they saw only his title and his fortune—and those sorts of young ladies meant very little to Duncan.

"Good evening, Lord Strickland."

With a small groan, Duncan turned around expecting to be met with another young lady being presented to him for, indeed, it seemed as though this evening's gathering was filled with debutantes, but much to his relief, it was none other than Lady Richmond, whose eyes were dancing with mirth.

"You are not trying to escape from anyone, are you?" she asked as Duncan gave her a wry smile. "My husband is nearby somewhere, and I am sure he would be able to steal you away to a game of cards or some such thing, if you are already struggling."

"You know of my difficulties," Duncan muttered, a little darkly, "and yet I believe you mock me."

Lady Richmond only laughed, not at all influenced by his irritated expression. "I know very well what such a situation is like, Lord Strickland," she reminded him, one eyebrow lifted. "Do you not recall that I had a very great dowry which, it seemed, the *ton* in its entirety knew of?"

Duncan let out a heavy breath. "I do," he said, still frustrated with the eagerness of Lord Haskett to introduce his daughter to him. "And yes, you well know what such a struggle is like." Throwing up his hands, he shook his head. "But it was easier for you, was it not? Your father, seeing what occurred, sought out a gentleman or two who had no need of your dowry." He arched one eyebrow, recalling how his friend, Lord Richmond, had found himself quite caught up with the lady and had been unable to even go an hour without mentioning her.

"That is true, I suppose," Lady Richmond replied dreamily. "Lord Richmond is a most exceptional gentleman."

"And now you are quite contented," Duncan said as Lady Richmond smiled back at him. "But I am struggling desperately to find a young lady that has no awareness of who I am or what I have. It seems as though they all come to London with the full knowledge of the gentlemen within society who are the wealthiest and, therefore, the most eligible."

"You did not decide to linger in the continent, however," Lady

Richmond murmured, a flicker of interest in her eyes. "I had thought you had meant to reside there for the year."

Duncan hesitated. After last Season, he had left for the continent almost at once, thinking that he would remain there for some time until everything that had irritated and frustrated him about the Season had washed from him. "I found it unbearable," he said hoarsely. "The heat. The company—or the lack thereof."

"And this is better?"

A wry smile tipped Duncan's lips. "Perhaps I hoped things would have changed this Season—even just a little. But it seems, thus far, that I have been entirely mistaken."

For a few moments, Lady Richmond said nothing, studying Duncan with a rather thoughtful expression. Duncan frowned, wondering what it was Lady Richmond was thinking, only for her to smile softly at him.

"If it is any comfort, I could introduce you to a lady that I am certain has no knowledge—or interest—in your wealth," she said, surprising him. "I know that you are rather tired of being introduced to various young ladies, but I am certain that she will be rather refreshing."

Duncan frowned hard as he considered what was best to do. Lady Richmond was quite correct—he did *not* want to be introduced to any further ladies who would look at him with greedy eyes but, at the same time, if she had no awareness of his fortune, would that not be exactly what he sought?

"Come now, you cannot refuse after complaining as you have done," Lady Richmond laughed, slipping her arm through Duncan's and beginning to walk across the room, with Duncan having no other choice but to join her. "Besides which, you must know that Lord Richmond and I care a great deal about your welfare. I would not introduce her to you if I thought her to be in any way unsuitable."

Aware of this, Duncan nodded and glanced at her. "I should prefer to go and find a card game," he said, a little brusquely, but Lady Richmond only smiled and looked away, evidently thoroughly resolved to do as she had suggested. Duncan gave himself up to her determined spirit, permitting her to take him to a quieter part of the room where a young lady was speaking with another, two older ladies near to them. Lady Richmond waited until one of the young ladies and her chaperone or mother, whoever she was, turned away, before quickly stepping forward to greet the remaining young lady.

"Ah, good evening," Lady Richmond said, letting go of Duncan's arm as she bobbed a quick curtsy. "Good evening, Mrs. Grey, Lady Juliet."

A trifle interested given the lady's title, Duncan stood mute as the conversation continued without him although he did not miss the older lady, Mrs. Grey, quickly assessing him as he stood tall, his hands clasped behind his back.

"I do hope you will allow me to introduce a friend of mine, Lady Juliet," Lady Richmond said quickly, turning back toward Duncan. "I claim him as my friend, you understand, even though he was dear friends with my husband first."

Duncan could not help but chuckle at this, noting now the young lady looked at him with curiosity flickering in her eyes. She was, he considered, rather pretty. She had very dark hair, with gentle curls brushing her temples, and, from what he could see, blue eyes that appeared to be flecked with gold. A delicate oval face, gentle sloping nose, and full lips added to his consideration of her beauty, although he did not allow himself any further thoughts given that he knew very little about her.

"This is the Earl of Strickland," Lady Richmond continued, gesturing to him. "Lord Strickland, might I present Lady Juliet, daughter to the Earl of Lansbury." She smiled at the older lady, who was waiting patiently for a further introduction to be made. "And her companion and chaperone, Mrs. Grey."

There was no immediate flare of recognition in Lady Juliet's eyes. She did not catch her breath, smile with delight, and curtsy beautifully, before batting her eyelashes at him, as so many other young ladies had done. Rather, her expression remained quite open as she curtsied, looking back at him without any hint of awareness as to who he was.

"I am very glad to make your acquaintance, Lord Strickland," she said, her voice quiet and calm. "Are you in London for the Season?"

"I am," he replied, ignoring the very broad smile on Lady Richmond's face, evidently rather pleased with herself for her choice of young lady. "And you? Is this your first Season?"

The young lady blushed. "No, it is my second," she replied, clearly a little embarrassed that she might have given the impression of being a debutante. "Last Season, however, I had to return home a little early due to an illness."

Duncan's interest stirred. "I hope you recovered well."

"It was not I who was unwell but my companion," she replied quickly, gesturing to Mrs. Grey. "I thank you for your concern, however."

"As do I, Lord Strickland," Mrs. Grey added, a glimmer of appreciation in her eyes. "I was disappointed that, for my sake, Lady Juliet had to return to her father's estate, but she would not hear of me returning alone."

This caught Duncan's interest, for if such a statement was true, then it spoke very highly of Lady Juliet's character.

"There is no need to make mention of such things," Lady Juliet interrupted briskly. "Lord Strickland, what of your estate? Where do you reside?"

Duncan smiled to himself, daring a glance toward Lady Richmond, who now looked all the more delighted with herself. It was very clear that Lady Juliet had no knowledge of him whatsoever and Duncan had to admit that he was glad Lady Richmond had been proven correct. Quickly, he told her about his estate, some distance north from London. She asked him some further questions about it and showed a genuine interest in all that he said. Much to his astonishment, Duncan realized that he was actually enjoying this particular conversation, even though he had not expected to.

"My mother, Lady Strickland, resides in the Dower house," he finished, a little offhandedly. "Some might consider her residence there a little premature since I myself am unwed, but it was for the best." A small, rather sad smile graced his lips. "I believe she found my father's absence very difficult."

A look of astonishment grew on Lady Richmond's face, leaving Duncan rather embarrassed as he realized what he had said, wondering why he had found himself speaking so openly with a young lady he had only just been introduced to.

"I can quite understand," Lady Juliet replied without any sign of embarrassment. "My own dear mother passed some years ago and I still feel her loss very greatly. Even if I see something that I know she loved very dearly, it brings an ache to my heart."

Duncan blinked and nodded, not quite certain what he ought to say next. He had never once spoken of his late father to any of his new acquaintances and why he had done so now, when Lady Juliet was still only a stranger to him, he simply could not say.

"Lady Juliet!"

Duncan half turned, seeing a young lady, a gentleman, and another older lady approaching. Recognizing them and seeing that it was quite apparent that they wished to speak to Lady Juliet rather than to him, Duncan quickly took his leave.

"It was very good to meet you, Lady Juliet," he said quickly. "I do hope that we will meet again soon."

"As do I," Lady Juliet replied sweetly, before turning her attention to her approaching acquaintances. Lady Richmond took her leave and together, both she and Duncan stepped away from the lady.

"You need not look so superior," Duncan muttered as Lady Richmond beamed with obvious pleasure at her success. "Yes, you did very well indeed, Lady Richmond. It was a new experience, I feel, to speak to a young lady who knew nothing of me."

Lady Richmond arched one eyebrow and looked at him. "And is that why you mentioned your mother in such a way?" she asked, clearly still surprised at what he had said. "I did not think that you would ever speak with such frankness to a new acquaintance."

"Nor did I," Duncan admitted ruefully. "Yes, I was quite astonished with myself, Lady Richmond, but I am sure it is simply because I am unused to having conversations with young ladies who are not doing all they can to have me take notice of them."

This made Lady Richmond laugh, catching the attention of her husband, who had been busy conversing with their host.

"I see you have stolen my wife away, Strickland," Lord Richmond grinned, coming to join them. "She looks very pleased with your company, however."

Chuckling, Duncan shook his head. "Lady Richmond insisted that I was introduced to a particular young lady who, it seems, has no knowledge of my vast fortune and eligibility."

Lord Richmond's brows rose. "Oh?"

"It went very well," Lady Richmond gushed, taking her husband's arm. "You will have to make certain that he asks her to dance at the next ball."

Duncan was about to protest that he could very well make certain of such a thing himself, only for Lord Richmond to say the very same thing to his wife, patting her hand with a tenderness that spoke of the great affection he had for her. Duncan lapsed into silence, a slight tug of jealousy in his heart as he watched his friend. It was not that he despised the friendship and the obvious affection between Lord and Lady Richmond, but rather that he was beginning to wonder if he would ever find such a thing for himself.

"How long shall you linger this evening?" Lord Richmond asked, looking up at Duncan. "Are you soon to tire of the lack of good company?"

Duncan chuckled. "If you are asking if I intend to make my way to White's this evening, then I can assure you that I fully expect to do so. It is not far from here, so I have already sent my driver home. I will either walk or hail a hackney."

"Then I may very well join you," Lord Richmond replied, daring a glance at his wife, who, much to Duncan's relief, did not look at all put out. "I shall look forward to hearing all about this new acquaintance of yours."

∼

HAVING DECIDED to walk the short distance to White's—mostly so that he might have a few moments of quiet in between what had been an evening of conversation and laughter and now would be a few hours of merriment—Duncan considered the young lady he had met earlier that night. Lady Juliet appeared to be just as Lady Richmond had described her. She was unaware of his wealth and quietly interested in his situation, and asked no particular questions about his fortune or made any attempt to discover whether or not he was seeking a wife. There had been no flirtation, no longing glances, no overt displays of interest. Rather, she had behaved very properly, and Duncan found himself all the more glad for it. It had been a relief to speak to her, even if he had been a little too open with what he had said.

"Hoy! You there!"

The shout came from nowhere and Duncan stopped dead, his eyes searching the streets, the dim lamps giving very little light to him. Taking a few steps forward, he tried to see where the shout had come from, when suddenly something came crashing down behind him.

Right where he had been standing.

For a moment, Duncan could not breathe. Turning slowly, he saw someone dart out in front of him, pick up whatever object it was on the ground, and then hurry off with it, giving him no opportunity to discover what it was or where it had come from. A sudden scrape to his left had him starting in surprise, but he could not work out where it had come from or what had made it. In fact, he was still rather dazed about what had happened, realizing, with horror, that had he been hit by whatever the object had been, he could easily have been knocked to the ground either unconscious or worse.

"That was a very near miss," he muttered to himself, hurrying forward on somewhat shaky legs as he made his way along the pavement. Quite what had been going on around him, he had no idea, but he thanked his lucky stars that he had not been injured.

Within a few minutes, Duncan was within a few yards of White's. Letting out a long breath of relief, he hurried toward the entrance and stepped in through the door held open for him by the footman.

"I did wonder whether or not you were coming," Lord Richmond cheered, only a few steps away from the door. "Goodness, what happened to you?"

Duncan frowned, looking down at himself. "What do you mean?"

"You look rather pale," Lord Richmond said, snapping his fingers at the footman so that he might have another brandy brought. "And there is, if you will forgive me for saying it, a good deal of dust on your shoulders." He moved around behind Duncan. "And, indeed, your back."

Shrugging out of his jacket, Duncan handed it to another footman with a request that it be brushed clean. A little embarrassed, he accepted the brandy from Lord Richmond and took a sip.

"Something occurred as I was walking here," he said, by way of explanation. "I think I must have been caught up in a ridiculous escapade by some foolish street urchins or some such thing."

Lord Richmond's eyes widened. "You were not hurt?"

"No, not in the least, although I might well have been," Duncan replied, quickly explaining all that had occurred before taking another sip of his brandy. The fright which had taken a hold of him at the realization of what he had narrowly avoided finally began to dissipate.

"Perhaps you should tell me about Lady Juliet instead of thinking of this most unfortunate encounter," Lord Richmond said with a sudden smile. "It would certainly take your mind from your troubles."

Duncan chuckled and gestured for Lord Richmond to find a seat for them both. "I do not think I have very much to say about her," he said with a wry smile. "She was pleasant enough, certainly."

"And beautiful, I believe," Lord Richmond said over his shoulder as he found them both a quieter corner of White's so they might discuss things without being forced to raise their voices too loudly. "That must have caught your notice."

Duncan shrugged and settled himself down in his seat, feeling the last of his fright disappear entirely. "As I have said, it was most refreshing," he said determinedly. "But that is all I shall say about her at present."

Lord Richmond chuckled. "Very wise, very wise," he said with a grin. "It is not as though everyone can be as I, finding myself deeply in love with a lady the moment I set eyes upon her."

"Indeed not," Duncan agreed, picking up his brandy glass and bringing it to his lips. Letting the heat of it spread through his chest, he rested his head back and closed his eyes for a moment. It had been both an interesting and tiring evening and now Duncan found himself quite weary. Perhaps he would not linger here for long after all.

3

Before she knew it, a fortnight had passed and Juliet found herself enjoying London society more and more. She was often asked to dance and did not struggle to find conversation or acquaintances but, as yet, there was no gentleman that caught her attention. And, it seemed, none that were particularly interested in her either. Yes, she had enjoyed some afternoon calls and yes, she had often been sought out at a ball so that her dance card might be scrutinized by a gentleman but, as yet, no one appeared to be eager to continue developing an acquaintance with her.

Mrs. Grey had told her not to worry and Juliet was doing her very best to obey. Part of her began to grow anxious over this lack of interest from other gentlemen, but she did not allow herself to continue on in such thoughts. Instead, she was determined to enjoy the Season without restraint, although she silently prayed that she would have at least one gentleman eager to court her by the month's end.

"And what do you think of Lord Strickland?"

Juliet meandered slowly through the London streets with Mrs. Grey beside her. "I am not certain whom you mean, Mrs. Grey."

"Yes, yes, you are!" Mrs. Grey exclaimed, looking up sharply at her. "The gentleman who was introduced to you at the evening soiree. Lady Richmond introduced him. He has asked you to dance upon occasion, I think."

Juliet searched her memory and then instantly recalled whom Mrs. Grey meant.

"Oh yes, I do recall," she said as Mrs. Grey smiled. "The Earl of Strickland, is it not?" She considered him carefully, spying a bookshop ahead of her and wondering if Mrs. Grey might be persuaded to go in to peruse it for a short time. "Yes, he is..." Nothing came to mind as she thought of him. "He is handsome, certainly, and can converse well." That could be said about any number of gentlemen who called upon her, but Juliet did not want to say such a thing to Mrs. Grey, given that the lady was clearly eager for Juliet to have more than a little interest in this gentleman.

"Well," Mrs. Grey said excitedly, "I have heard that he is a gentleman of great wealth. They say that he is richer than the Marquess of Longbridge, if you can believe it."

Given that Juliet had no notion as to who the Marquess of Longbridge was or just how much wealth that gentleman had, this did not make much of an impact.

"He has every young lady in London flocking to him," Mrs. Grey continued, sounding rather pleased, "and yet he has been seeking *you* out upon occasion, has he not?"

Juliet laughed, although this stole away some of the eager excitement that was so visible on Mrs. Grey's expression.

"I hardly think that a dance or two and a few minutes of conversation mean that he has any more interest in me than any other," she told her companion. "And to be truthful, Mrs. Grey, I do not think I have any real interest in him either. Wealth does not make a gentleman any more eligible than another, I think."

Much to her surprise, Mrs. Grey laughed heartily at this remark, as though Juliet had said something mirthful.

"I think you are one of the very few young ladies who would say such a thing, my dear," she said as a slight flush of embarrassment crept into Juliet's cheeks. "Every other young lady seeks out a gentleman of both high title and excellent fortune. In fact, the greater his wealth, the more eligible he becomes."

"Well, not I," Juliet declared, despite the touch of embarrassment she felt. "If he is able to provide a comfortable situation for both himself and me, then I will be most content with that." Wanting to change the subject entirely, she gestured toward the bookshop. "Might we step inside for a short time?"

Mrs. Grey nodded at once. "Yes, of course," she said, much to Juliet's relief, glad that Mrs. Grey was not about to insist that they remain out of doors so that they might meet any particular acquaintances. "But only for a short time, Juliet. I should like to go to Gunter's."

Now it was Juliet's turn to laugh. "So that we might meet any eligible gentlemen present?" she asked as Mrs. Grey shot her a knowing look. "Thank you, Mrs. Grey. I shall be glad to attend there with you, of course."

∽

THE BOOKSHOP HAD THAT WONDERFUL, almost inexplicable smell that Juliet had come to love so much last Season. It reminded her of old books, of quiet corners and whispered conversations, making her smile with gentle delight as she followed Mrs. Grey inside. There was a peace here that could not be found in any other part of London and Juliet had come to relish it. Last Season, she had found it a quiet haven, where she might peruse for as long as she wished, her thoughts wandering from one thing to the next.

"Pray do not leave the shop without coming in search of me, Juliet," Mrs. Grey warned, and Juliet nodded. "But I will leave you to your searching."

Juliet smiled and turned away, glad that Mrs. Grey had remembered just how much Juliet liked to be alone in such a place as this.

The bookshop appeared rather quiet, devoid of other patrons, although this did not disturb Juliet at all. Picking up a novel, she opened it to the first page and looked at both the title and the author, before beginning the first chapter. It was, she discovered, a little dull and, after a few moments, she set it back down again on the shelf.

He has every young lady in London flocking to him.

Why such a remark by Mrs. Grey should come back to her now, Juliet could not understand. She had no need to think of Lord Strickland, no need to even consider him at present. Yes, he had asked her to dance and yes, she had conversed with him on a few occasions, but Juliet did not think that such an acquaintance would come to anything. It irritated her somewhat that Mrs. Grey considered her to be so fickle as to want to wed someone with a vast fortune and title, without ever considering his character and temperament. It was true that, whilst she would be glad to have a husband who could provide for her comfortably, she did not require one who had more wealth than almost anyone else in England. Besides which, she considered, picking up another book and opening the cover, she did not know very much about Lord Strickland at all. He had told her a little about his mother and his estate, but aside from that, what awareness did she have about his character? Was he a kind gentleman? Or was his temper inclined to flare at any moment?

"You did not succeed with Strickland."

Juliet looked up, looking all about her and wondering if she had heard Lord Strickland's name or if it had only been her thoughts confusing her with another matter.

"That is hardly my fault," came another voice, low and quiet in the apparent hope that they would not be overheard. "My aim was true. He stepped forward when we did not expect it."

The first voice came again and Juliet's heart began to pound furiously, realizing that she ought to move away but fearing that, if she did so, she might be overheard.

"I need him removed," said the first, clearly a lady of quality speaking. "You know very well why it must be done."

"And as I have said," the second voice said, sounding now a little irritated, "it was unexpected that he moved in such a way. Otherwise I would have succeeded."

"But that is the second time you have failed," said the first voice, clearly now quite angry with the second. "How long am I to wait?"

There came no reply from the second person and Juliet turned slowly to move away, her whole body rippling with a tension she could not push from herself. A mixture of fear and embarrassment plagued her as, on gentle feet, she began to take slow steps back toward the front of the shop. Her mind was swirling with terrified thoughts, wondering if what she had overheard could be true. Was someone attempting to injure Lord Strickland? And for what purpose?

"Ah, there you are." Mrs. Grey emerged from another part of the bookshop, coming toward Juliet quickly. "Have you found something you wish to purchase?"

Juliet did not immediately answer, her mouth going dry as she stared at Mrs. Grey, too overcome with horror to speak. What was she to do? Should she linger, waiting for those who had been speaking to emerge so that she might identify them? Or should she hasten from the bookshop out of fear that they would see her pale cheeks and realize that she had overheard them, and then bring her into their dark plans?

"You look a little unwell, Juliet," Mrs. Grey said, frowning. "Perhaps we ought to return home. Gunter's can wait."

"No, no, of course not," Juliet managed to say, forcing a smile to her lips that barely lifted the corners of her mouth. "Here, I have found something I should like to purchase. And then, of course, we can make our way to Gunter's." She tried to speak in her normal voice, but she could tell that Mrs. Grey was not entirely convinced, given the searching look in her eyes.

"Are you quite certain you are well, Juliet?" Mrs. Grey asked, quietly, putting one hand on Juliet's arm. "You look a little overcome."

Hearing a noise coming from behind her and fearing that the two perpetrators would soon be upon her, Juliet shook her head and, her book still in her hand, made her way to the proprietor. The purchase was quickly made, with the bill being sent to her father, although Mrs. Grey still watched her with a growing sense of concern.

"To Gunter's, then?" Juliet asked brightly, turning to look at Mrs. Grey and, to her horror, noting a lady and a gentleman emerging from where Juliet herself had been standing only a few minutes before. "It sounds like an excellent idea, Mrs. Grey." She did not wait for her companion to speak or to agree but rather hurried toward the door at once, leaving Mrs. Grey to follow after her in a state of great confusion.

Once outside, Juliet did not stop to even catch her breath but turned in the direction of Gunter's and continued along her path with quick steps. Mrs. Grey caught up with her after only a few moments, but the hand on Juliet's arm told her that she was not about to go any further without some sort of explanation.

"Something has occurred, has it not?" Mrs. Grey asked as Juliet turned to face her, her heart still pounding furiously. "What is it, Juliet?"

"We must keep walking," Juliet replied tightly. "I will explain all, Mrs. Grey, but we *must* hurry on."

For a moment, she feared that Mrs. Grey would refuse, but then her companion nodded and began to walk again, albeit at a slower pace.

"Well?" Mrs. Grey asked quietly. "Did someone say something to you, Juliet? If there was a gentleman within making some sort of inappropriate advances, then I do not think I can permit you to wander through a bookshop alone again."

Juliet shook her head. "I would have much preferred it if it was something such as that, Mrs. Grey," she said unsteadily, dread still burning through her. "I have overheard something that has greatly concerned me."

Mrs. Grey's eyes widened. "Indeed?"

"In the bookshop," Juliet clarified. "There were two others present speaking in rather hushed tones. I did not mean to eavesdrop, of course, but I confess I did so without being aware of it."

"That is not of any particular concern to me," Mrs. Grey said firmly, clearly not at all bothered that Juliet had heard something not meant for her ears. "What was said?"

Feeling a little off balance, Juliet took a moment to catch her breath before she spoke, steadying herself inwardly. "I am sure that what was spoken of was to do with Lord Strickland," she said slowly. "From what I heard, it seems as though they are quite intent on…injuring him rather severely."

Mrs. Grey gasped, her steps slowing all the more. "Are you quite certain?"

"I am," Juliet replied, swallowing hard. "The words were harsh and direct, with the lady appearing more than a little angry that the task had not yet been fulfilled."

"The task?" Mrs. Grey asked as Juliet shuddered.

"The task of having Lord Strickland removed, whatever that means," she said, her voice tremulous. "I could not say whether they meant to have him gone from London or…" She could not bring herself to finish, the horror of even the thought shaking her to her core.

"I see," Mrs. Grey said softly, clearly not needing Juliet to explain any further. "Then we must, of course, speak to Lord Strickland about what you heard, Juliet."

Juliet blinked, looking at her companion quickly. "Do you think that is best?"

"Of course it is," Mrs. Grey replied practically. "He must know that there is a particular danger dancing around him and you, my dear Juliet, must be the one to inform him of it. Whether he believes you or not does not matter. You will have done your duty at least."

Juliet nodded, Mrs. Grey's words bringing a calmness to her heart. "Very well, Mrs. Grey," she said quietly. "Although quite how to go about such a conversation, I have not the faintest idea."

"You will manage," Mrs. Grey replied confidently. "And let us hope that Lord Strickland takes your words with all seriousness else who knows what shall happen?"

4

"And have you danced with any young ladies of note?" Duncan resisted the urge to roll his eyes. "If you are asking me whether or not I have sought out Lady Juliet, then I can assure you that I have not," he said firmly. "We have danced on occasion and I have enjoyed conversation with her certainly, but as yet, I do not have any intention of pursuing anything further."

"And why would that be?" Lady Richmond asked as her husband chuckled quietly. "She is, as you have said, a refreshing change from the other young ladies of the *ton*."

Duncan hesitated, not quite certain how to express his seeming inability to even consider what he might do as regarded Lady Juliet. These last few days, he had found himself thinking of her very often and realizing just how much he enjoyed being in her company, but he also noted the fact that she showed such little interest in his excessive wealth. However, doubts had begun to creep into his mind for, surely by now, she would have heard all about his fortune from other acquaintances. Was she, perhaps, pretending that she cared nothing about it in the hope that he might continue her acquaintance with her? Given the fact that Duncan had been surrounded with young ladies who wanted nothing more than to claim him as their own for the sake of his wealth, it was now proving difficult to think of Lady Juliet in any other light.

"You cannot explain, I see," Lady Richmond said gently. "I will not press you, then. Although I shall say that I will be very glad to discuss any such matters with you should the time come."

Relieved, Duncan gave her a quick smile. "You are most discerning, Lady Richmond."

She laughed, turning away from both him and Lord Richmond. "And you are most complimentary, Lord Strickland."

Duncan smiled to himself and watched her walk away, turning his head to catch Lord Richmond doing the very same—save for the fact that *he* was watching the lady with a clear and obvious affection.

Duncan sighed.

"That is it, you see," he said plainly. "You care for Lady Richmond very deeply. She cares for you. I have spent many hours wishing for something akin to what you share with your wife, but it has always felt very far out of reach, given my circumstances."

Lord Richmond's brows rose, perhaps a little surprised at the openness with which Duncan had spoken, but Duncan did not regret saying such words. Instead, he merely shrugged and shook his head to himself, blowing out a long breath as the conversations around them continued to flow.

"And you do not think you could find such a thing with Lady Juliet?" Lord Richmond asked after a moment or two, appearing a little confused. "She is quite lovely in every sense, with a sweet and gentle character." Seeing Duncan's sharp look, he grinned broadly. "My wife has been making gentle enquiries," he said, by way of explanation. "She is quite set on the lady."

"I see," Duncan replied with a small smile. "Whilst I admit that I might very well be able to have a relationship with a young lady such as Lady Juliet, I am beginning to worry that she is just the same as every other."

Lord Richmond frowned. "In what way?"

Trying to find the words to express his thoughts, Duncan paused for a moment, thinking quickly. "It will have been told to her by now that I am a gentleman of some means," he said carefully. "What if her lack of interest in my wealth now comes from a desire to make herself all the more desirable to me?"

"That would make her very deceitful, certainly," Lord Richmond responded at once, "but the only way to make certain of such a thing would be to remain a little longer in her company. Perhaps show a little more interest than you are at present." His broad smile made Duncan wince, irritated that his friend knew him so well. "I think that you have been considering her for some time, Strickland, even if you do not wish to admit it."

Duncan made to answer but then his gaze snagged on someone of interest. They were not looking at either Duncan or Lord Richmond and certainly did not show any intent of coming toward them. But regardless, their presence at the ball made a deep frown form across Duncan's forehead, his brows knotting together as a grimace pulled at his lips.

"Good gracious!" Lord Richmond exclaimed, giving a half-turn in the direction Duncan was now looking. "Whatever have you seen that would make you frown so?" A grin split his features as he leaned closer. "Is it that you have seen Lady Juliet being led from the dance floor with another gentleman?"

Duncan's frown did not lift even for a moment.

"It is Lady Ridgedale," he said slowly as the smile instantly fell from Lord Richmond's face. "I am surprised to see her here. I thought her mourning period would not yet be over."

Lord Richmond glanced toward the lady, the same dark look appearing on his own features. "I knew she had returned to London, but I did not think she would so quickly reintroduce herself to society," he said with a shake of his head. "That being said, given what I know of Lady Ridgedale, I do not think that the lady would have waited for any longer than was required of her before doing so."

Duncan snorted with disdain, thinking that he would prefer to remain as far from the lady as possible. "Lord Ridgedale did not choose his bride well."

"He did not," Lord Richmond agreed starkly. "But he would not be the first to have his heart captured by a beautiful face and an apparently welcoming heart."

"To the point that he did not listen to any of the whispers that ran through society about her?" Duncan asked, a hard line forming around his mouth. "The number of times I have had to..." He did not finish his sentence, shaking his head with the memories of the unfortunate lady before turning his gaze away from her. "You know what her character is like."

"I do indeed," Lord Richmond muttered. "A grasping, cruel creature who seeks only her own good."

Duncan bit his tongue not to say more, recalling the many times that Lady Ridgedale had attempted to make her way into his favors. The idea, he presumed, had been that she might become his mistress and, in doing so, would gain some financial freedom of her own. Her husband, he knew, had not at all been inclined to purchase his wife fripperies or jewelry or any such thing and Lady Ridgedale had chafed against his seeming lack of desire to spend his wealth. Of course, Duncan had made it quite plain that he was not the sort of gentleman who toyed with other men's wives and although Lady Ridgedale had used all of her charms against him, he had remained entirely disinterested.

Then had come the anger.

"She dislikes me intensely, I am sure," Duncan commented quietly. "She must be back in London in the hope of securing another husband."

Lord Richmond shook his head. "From what I understand, I believe she has enough wealth to keep her in good standing," he said, surprising Duncan. "Lord Ridgeland kept his wealth far from his wife whilst he lived but left her a significant portion in his will."

One shoulder lifted in a half-shrug. "That is what I have heard, of course. It may not be true."

"Regardless," Duncan remarked, turning away from the lady entirely. "I have no desire to remain anywhere near her. Might we take a—oh."

His embarrassment at turning so swiftly and almost walking directly into another young lady's path was multiplied all the more when he realized that the young lady in question was none other than Lady Juliet. Covering his embarrassment with a quick bow, he straightened and tried to smile.

"Good evening, Lady Juliet, Mrs. Grey," he said quickly. "Do forgive my haste." He made no explanation as to why he had been behaving so and, instead, waited for them to speak.

Thankfully, Lady Juliet did not appear to be at all embarrassed over his evident mistake.

"Good evening, Lord Strickland. Good evening, Lord Richmond," she said, curtsying quickly. "I am sorry if I have prevented you from making your escape from something." Her eyes twinkled with good humor and, despite himself, Duncan found himself smiling. "I shall not stand in your way any longer, however." Making a small sidestep, she gestured for him to move past her, but Duncan shook his head, as Lord Richmond chuckled.

"It is quite all right," Lord Richmond said promptly. "It was only that we thought to go in search of another brandy, so you have not interrupted us at all."

The next few minutes were spent in general conversation, with Duncan fully aware of the glances that Lord Richmond was sending toward him in a most regular fashion. It was quite clear that he expected him to ask Lady Juliet if she wished to dance and yet the obvious way in which he was doing it made Duncan rather embarrassed.

"Lady Juliet," he found himself saying, suddenly desperate to do so simply in order to stop Lord Richmond from behaving in such an overt fashion. "I do hope you have some remaining dances on your card? I would very much like to peruse it, if I may?"

Lady Juliet smiled and handed it to him without another word, although Duncan was rather surprised to see that most of the dances were taken. In fact, the only two remaining were the quadrille, which was due to happen within the next few minutes, and the country dance. Sighing inwardly, he wrote his name in both spaces, knowing that it would be foolish not to do so. Two dances would not be noticed by anyone, given that other gentlemen were doing the very same. Lord Jennings, he noticed, had written his name down for both the supper dance and the cotillion, making him wonder if the gentleman had a penchant for the lady. After all, the supper dance meant that he would spend a little more time in Lady Juliet's company, making certain to sit with her once the dance was at an end. A twinge of jealousy spread through Duncan's heart although he dismissed it quickly enough. There was no need to feel such things when it came to Lady Juliet. He would be satisfied with the quadrille and the country dance.

"I thank you," Lady Juliet murmured, taking a small step closer to him as Mrs. Grey quickly began to engage Lord Richmond in conversation. "However, Lord Strickland, there is something I must ask you. Something that you will, I am sure, think is both unusual and very forward."

Taken aback by both her words and her secretive tone, Duncan cleared his throat and gave her a small smile. "But of course, Lady Juliet," he said, as though such a request was to be expected and hiding his very great confusion. "Whatever it is you wish to ask, I will be happy to listen."

"I thank you," she replied with such a look of relief spreading across her face that Duncan immediately began to wonder what it could be that she wanted to discuss with him. "I will also assure you that Mrs. Grey is fully aware of what I am to ask and is in agreement with it." Taking a moment, she looked to her companion and then back to him, her face now flushed as she continued to speak. "I must ask you, Lord Strickland, if you would be willing to call upon me at your earliest convenience." Her face flushed all the more as words began to trip over each other in their eagerness to be spoken. "It is not at all because I wish you to show me some sort of attention, nor is it in any way a manipulation to force you into my company, but rather because there is something of the greatest importance that I must share with you."

Duncan did not quite know how to respond. From the color in the lady's cheeks and the way her gaze continued to dart from one place to the next, he could tell that she felt very awkward indeed but, to his mind, he could not be sure that she spoke the truth.

"I am certain that you will think me very improper and rather rude, Lord Strickland," Lady Juliet continued, her eyes now fastening themselves to his as though through sheer effort she might be able to convince him. "I know this request does appear to be for my benefit, but I assure you that it is not." For a moment, her eyes left his and turned to the right and then to the left, as though afraid someone would overhear her.

"Then speak of it now," he said with a small frown. "Why could you not speak of it now to me, Lady Juliet?"

She shook her head, closing her eyes. "I cannot," she breathed, opening her eyes and looking at him steadily. "It is too dangerous."

The word shot through him with sudden force, making his frown deepen as he watched her, seeing the concern in her eyes and wondering if there was any possibility that she was telling the truth. The usual doubts rose in his mind, making him believe that, most likely, she was just as every other young lady of his acquaintance and was doing whatever she could to manipulate him into showing regard for her, even with the outward appearance of being entirely disinterested in his wealth. Yet there was something in her voice and expression that spoke of warning and a true concern for him that he could not simply turn away from.

"Mrs. Grey," Lady Juliet said, turning quickly to her companion and, in doing so, interrupting the conversation between her and Lord Richmond. "Pray forgive the interruption but I must ask you to express to Lord Strickland the urgency behind my request."

Mrs. Grey lifted her chin and looked sternly back at Duncan, making him feel as though he were a young boy being chastised by a governess.

"Lady Juliet is doing all she can to protect you, Lord Strickland," Mrs. Grey said firmly. "I am well aware that you might suspect ulterior motivations in her request, but I can assure you it is not so. I give you my word, such as it is, that there is a true desire to help you, although as yet, of course, you are entirely unaware of your need for it."

Duncan blinked in surprise and cleared his throat, finding himself a little more convinced by Mrs. Grey's demeanor than he had expected.

"Very well, Lady Juliet," he said slowly, aware of Lord Richmond's curious expression. "I will call upon you tomorrow, if I may?"

Lady Juliet let out a long breath of relief and nodded, her smile returning and making Duncan fear that he had made the wrong decision.

"I thank you, Lord Strickland, for your willingness to trust me," she said as Duncan inclined his head, unwilling to state that, as yet, he had not fully done so. "I know it must be most unusual to hear a request such as this."

Duncan cleared his throat, fully aware that he would have to explain everything to Lord Richmond once the lady had departed. "I understand, Lady Juliet," he replied without being fully convinced of her words. "Tomorrow afternoon, then."

"Tomorrow afternoon," she replied, making to take her leave, only for their dance then to be announced. With a question in her eyes, she looked back at him and Duncan found himself a little uncomfortable, holding out his hand to her and wondering at his own state of emotion.

Why did he feel such a sense of nervousness, simply because it was now their turn to dance together? Was it because of what he had just agreed to? Had he just allowed her some great victory that would then bring her a great benefit but mortify him completely? Part of him still feared that he would call upon Lady Juliet tomorrow and find that her important news was of no significance whatsoever. The *ton* would, no doubt, hear of his visit to her and, given that he was now to dance with her twice this evening, would then go on to whisper that his interest in the lady was rather marked. A cold hand grasped his heart as he stepped out with Lady Juliet, but he forced himself forward. He could not refuse to fulfill his dance with her now.

"I can tell that you are having some difficulty in believing what I have said, Lord Strickland," came Lady Juliet's quiet voice, making Duncan look down at her in surprise. A small, sad smile crossed her lips as she held his gaze for a moment.

"You must fear that I am doing all I can in order to gain your attention for my own purpose," she continued, practically speaking every word within his heart as though she could see it without any difficulty. "I am sure that you have had many a young lady attempt to manipulate you so and thus, I shall not hold such sentiment against you." They came to join a set and he let go of her arm, turning to bow toward her as she curtsied.

"But my words are true," she murmured, her voice low enough so only he could hear. "And I will prove it to you come the morrow." Her eyes were practically glowing with determination now, holding to his with such force that Duncan could not look away. He felt his heart soften just a little, felt the anxious thoughts begin to leave his mind as he looked back at her, finding himself somewhat comforted by her manner and her words of conviction.

The music began and there was nothing further for him to say. Following the steps of the dance, Duncan allowed himself to continue to puzzle over Lady Juliet, finding his thoughts quite taken up with the lady. Dare he permit himself to believe her? Dare he hope that she might be speaking the truth? *And what will that change within your own heart if it is proven so?* said a quiet voice in his head. *Will you think better of her? Will you permit yourself to consider what might flourish between you, if only you would let it?*

It was not a question Duncan could immediately answer, finding it such an unknown situation that he did not know what to think. But somewhere deep within him there ignited a tiny flame of hope. A flame that Duncan knew Lady Juliet might either encourage or blow out entirely, depending on what she said to him the morrow.

He would have to simply wait to know what she would do.

5

"If you continue to pace, then your father will be most displeased at having to replace the carpet."

Juliet did not even glance up as Mrs. Grey spoke and thus, missed the twinkle in the older lady's eye. She was nervous beyond expression, anxious that Lord Strickland would not attend as he had said, fearful that he would give in to the clear belief that she was not as she made out to be. There had been such an apparent distrust in his expression and his words last evening that Juliet knew there would be a great deal of difficulty in convincing him to call on her. Trying to explain to him that there was a great seriousness in her request had been a struggle and even now, Juliet was not at all convinced that he not only believed her but would do as she had asked.

"He will call," Mrs. Grey said gently. "You need not be so anxious, Juliet."

"He may not," Juliet replied quickly. "I saw the distrust in his eyes, Mrs. Grey. I saw that he did not want to do as I asked. Had I not turned to you, then I am quite certain he would have refused."

Mrs. Grey let out a small sigh. "But he agreed in the end, did he not?" she said, setting her needlework down. "And he is a gentleman who keeps his word, I am sure of it."

Juliet did not say anything to either agree or disagree, continuing to pace up and down the drawing room, worrying her lip as she did so. She had danced twice with Lord Strickland last evening but neither dance had been one of enjoyment. Instead, she had found herself lacking conversation, unable to find anything particular to say, and Lord Strickland himself made no effort to converse with her at all either. It had been two somewhat awkward dances and Juliet had found herself both frustrated and upset over the matter, wishing she had been able to convince Lord Strickland without any great effort and yet fully understanding why he did not trust her so.

"He thinks me eager to impress him in any way I can," she said, rather sadly. "I am sure of it, Mrs. Grey. He believes that I have told him this in order to urge him to my father's townhouse which will, of course, be noted by someone in the *beau monde*."

"He will attend you, just as he has said," Mrs. Grey interrupted, before Juliet could continue. "Stop your anxious thoughts, Juliet. It will do you no good."

Juliet opened her mouth to say that she could not help it, but before she could do so, a scratch came at the door.

A scratch that had Juliet's heart leaping wildly, her hands pressing to her lips for a moment as Mrs. Grey called the butler to enter.

"Lord Strickland, my lady," the butler murmured, handing Juliet his card and returning to the door. "Shall I have refreshments brought?"

"Juliet," Mrs. Grey hissed, beckoning her toward a chair. "Juliet, do hurry."

It was with leaden limbs that Juliet walked toward a vacant chair, standing in front of it as though she had only just risen from it. "If you please," she said to the butler, her heart hammering furiously as he nodded and then stepped back out into the hallway for a moment, ready to bring in Lord Strickland. He had come, then.

He *had* attended her, just as he had agreed and just as Mrs. Grey had stated. Now all that remained was for her to tell him precisely what she had overheard, showing him that she had spoken the truth in her request.

Lord Strickland came into the room with his head held high, his shoulders set, and a rather grim look settled into his expression, as though he was quite convinced that she would immediately be disingenuous. Juliet curtsied quickly as he bowed, struggling to put a smile on her face as she lifted her eyes to his.

Lord Strickland's gaze was hard, his lips pulled thin and a coolness in his eyes that told her he was not at all convinced as yet.

"I thank you for calling," Juliet said, a little breathlessly. "Please, do sit down, Lord Strickland. The butler has just now seen to some refreshments. They will be here momentarily."

Clearing his throat, Lord Strickland gave her a tight smile. "I should prefer that we discuss whatever matter it is that has brought you so much concern, Lady Juliet," he said, his eyes fixed to hers. There was ice within the blue orbs, a clear and apparent disbelief that anything she had to say would be of any true interest.

"Very well," she told him, finding her mouth now dry as she tried to find the words to express to him what it was she had overheard. "It was some two days ago, Lord Strickland. I was in a bookshop with Mrs. Grey, merely perusing the books and without any real interest in any of them." She could see his brow furrowing and knew that he must now believe her to be telling him nothing but a foolish story. "This is of significance, I assure you." Taking in a breath, she let it out again slowly. "Mrs. Grey was in one part of the shop and I in entirely another. There was, as you might expect, a quietness there that is not often found in any other part of London and thus, enjoying that silence, I continued to meander without any true intention."

Lord Strickland sighed and sat back in his chair a little more, brushing back his fair hair from across his forehead. "Indeed," he said in a dull, bored voice. "And in what way does this relate to me?"

"If you would but listen without interruption, then I believe you would find out."

Juliet blinked in astonishment at Mrs. Grey, whose sharp words had shot across the room and hit Lord Strickland directly. Mrs. Grey was frowning fiercely, her eyes sparkling with a clear anger that Juliet was surprised to see. There was no immediate response from Lord Strickland, who appeared to be just as astonished as Juliet, although he cleared his throat and sat up a little more, a touch of color coming into his face. Juliet found herself struggling to find the right words to say next and was all the more relieved when the door opened and a tea tray was brought in. It gave her a few moments to gather herself and to consider what she was to say next.

"I thank you," she murmured as Mrs. Grey offered to pour the tea, leaving Juliet to finish what she was saying. "Yes, Lord Strickland," she continued, finding a fresh boldness beginning to fill her. "This does relate to you entirely, for as I was in the bookshop, in the quieter part of it, I overheard two people talking." Taking in a deep breath, she lifted her chin a notch and looked back at him. "They spoke of you."

The change that came into Lord Strickland's expression was immediate. His eyes flared and he leaned forward in his chair, his eyes now searching her face. "Indeed?"

"They spoke of you in a manner that has me quite convinced they intend to do you a great deal of harm," Juliet continued, managing to tell him, almost verbatim, what had been said. "In short, Lord Strickland, whilst I cannot be entirely convinced as to what it is they intend to do, I am entirely certain that you are in great danger."

Lord Strickland did not say anything for some minutes. In the silence, Mrs. Grey handed Juliet her teacup, leaving her to sip at it as Lord Strickland remained sitting quietly, his eyes now staring blankly at something on the wall behind Juliet's head, his face paler than before.

"And you are sure that they spoke of a failure?" he said abruptly, turning his eyes to Juliet once more. "They said something about having failed already?"

Frowning, Juliet tried her best to recall the exact words. "I believe the lady in question, whoever she was, told the fellow that he had failed. He then expressed to her that it was not his doing, as his aim had been true but that you had stepped forward unexpectedly." Seeing the color drain all the more from Lord Strickland's face, Juliet glanced toward Mrs. Grey, who was now watching Lord Strickland with a growing concern. "Does that mean something to you, Lord Strickland?"

The gentleman nodded slowly, his hands tightening together as he clasped them in his lap. "It does, Lady Juliet," he said hoarsely. "In fact, I must now apologize to you for refusing to believe that you had anything of true significance to tell me. I can see now that this is of the greatest importance and, had you not told me of it, then I would have continued on believing that what occurred was nothing more than an accident and that I was simply in the wrong place when such an event occurred."

Not at all sure as to what he was referring, Juliet held back the questions on her lips and waited for him to say more, glancing toward Mrs. Grey, who looked back at her with the same confused expression. There was clearly more to this situation than she had expected, with Lord Strickland seemingly aware of something she was not. Whether he would share it with her, Juliet did not yet know, although she was fully aware that he had no need to do so.

"Lady Juliet, do you think you would be able to recognize the voice of either the gentleman or the lady again, should you hear them?"

Juliet thought hard, her brows furrowing. "I wish I could tell you that I would do so without struggle, but the truth is I am not at all sure I would succeed," she said honestly, seeing the disappointment on his face. "I was, as you might imagine, quite horrified to hear such things and, to be truthful, quite afraid that I would be discovered. The thought of what might occur should they find out that I had overheard their plans was quite terrifying and I made my way to Mrs. Grey's side as soon as I could. Thereafter, we departed the bookshop."

"We might have lingered in order to watch those who departed from the shop, certainly," Mrs. Grey added in, as though she anticipated that Lord Strickland would make such a remark. "But it is as Lady Juliet has just said. We had to ensure that she was not noticed in any way, that she was kept safe given what she had overheard."

Lord Strickland nodded, one hand now rubbing his chin. "I shall not berate you for that, Lady Juliet," he said softly. "You could easily have been threatened also, had you not done such a thing."

"Then you believe the threat to be real?" she asked, surprised at the strain that was in her voice. "You know there to be significance in what I overheard?"

Nodding, Lord Strickland dragged his gaze to hers. "An incident occurred some days ago," he said slowly. "I was walking from a soiree toward White's. The distance was not far. However, as I walked, I heard a shout. A shout that had me stop dead for a moment or two, before I decided to continue on my way." He paused, then closed his eyes. "Something came flying toward me and would have hit me hard, had I not been already out of its path," he continued, his explanation now showing her precisely why he had gone so very pale after what she had related to him. "Someone's aim was true indeed, but I moved forward just in time."

Juliet caught her breath, realizing now why he had been so horrified with what she had said.

"At the time, I took it to be nothing more than an accident, believing myself to be very fortunate," Lord Strickland continued, running one hand over his eyes. "I can see now that I was more than fortunate. That was meant for me."

"Would it have thrown you to the ground?" Mrs. Grey asked quietly, and Lord Strickland nodded. "Knocked you senseless?"

"I believe it would have, yes," he told her as Juliet bit her lip, hard. "I do not know what their intention is, or why they seek to injure me so, but I am very grateful indeed to you for your willingness to inform me of this, Lady Juliet."

"But of course," she said quickly. "Lord Strickland, there must be more that I can do. I might not be certain that I would recognize the voice again, but I am very sure that the lady who spoke was one of the *beau monde*." She picked up her teacup and took a long sip, praying it would steady her nerves a little. "You are in danger; I am quite sure of it."

"And why they would wish for me to be struck down so, I cannot yet understand," he added, half to himself. "I do not know why..." He trailed off, then looked up at her sharply. "It is, in fact, the second occasion that has troubled me this Season."

Juliet stared at him, her hand trembling just a little as she set her cup down. "The second time?"

"The first occurred on my way to London," Lord Strickland told her, his eyes now wide with evident understanding and concern. "I had thought to take my carriage to London, rather than to ride, and had told my servants and the proprietor of the inn I was residing in of my intentions. However, on the morning I rose, I changed my mind, choosing instead to ride on ahead and allow my carriage to follow after. It was not until my driver made it to London and to the townhouse that I discovered it had very nearly been ambushed by highwaymen."

In an instant, the vision of what she had seen trapped Juliet in a flurry of horror and fright. She reached for her teacup blindly, bringing it to her lips and closing her eyes as she swallowed, not allowing her mind to be overcome with the reminder of what she had seen. Bile rose in her throat and she took another sip, before setting her teacup back down again. When she turned to Lord Strickland, she saw him looking at her with a mixture of both confusion and concern written in his eyes.

"It is only that, as my father, Mrs. Grey, and I made our way to London, we came upon a scene of such vile cruelty that even the thought of it turns my stomach, Lord Strickland," she said hoarsely. "The highwaymen, as you say, were behind this particular attack, according to my father."

Lord Strickland said nothing for some moments before

lowering his head and running one hand across his forehead. "Then mayhap it was nothing more than that," he said quietly. "If there are highwaymen at work, then it cannot be an attack on myself personally, as I first thought, terrible though it may be."

Juliet tried to push her memories of that day far from her, shuddering slightly as she did so. "Whether or not it was, my main concern at present is that you are in great danger from an enemy as yet unidentified," she said, forcing herself to return to the task at hand. "What is it that can be done?"

Lord Strickland frowned. "You need not concern yourself with this matter any longer, Lady Juliet," he returned, obviously a little surprised that she evidently expected to do just that. "You have informed me of it, for which I am very grateful, but you need not continue with the burden of it."

"Oh, but I must!" Juliet exclaimed, surprising herself at her vehemence. "It may very well be that I am able to identify the voice of those speaking, Lord Strickland, and besides which, you cannot face this alone."

"I—I shall speak to Lord and Lady Richmond, of course," he said, floundering just a little. "I should not like to put you in any difficulty, Lady Juliet."

A small flare of anger lit her soul and Juliet found herself frowning heavily, her eyes narrowing just a fraction as she looked back at Lord Strickland. Was he truly trying to protect her in some way? Or was there more to his disinclination than there appeared?

"Lord Strickland, it would be wise to allow Lady Juliet to assist you in some small way," Mrs. Grey said gently. "She was, as she has told you, the one to overhear this particular conversation and, whilst it might seem difficult to her at present to know whether or not she could identify the voices again, it may be that, in helping you resolve this matter, she *will* be able to do so, thus saving you a good deal of difficulty."

There was not an immediate agreement from Lord Strickland but rather a clearing of his throat and a small, jerky nod that did not state anything particular. The flame that had lit itself in Juliet's heart began to grow all the hotter, making her brow furrow deeply.

"If you believe that I am asking such a thing in order to pursue you in some sort of ridiculous fashion, then I can assure you I am not at all inclined toward you," she stated loudly, her words sharp and filled with anger. "I fear that your reluctance to accept my help is due only to your concern that I, like many other young ladies, seek to force myself into your affections. Is that not so?" Holding her head high, she arched one eyebrow and saw him turn his head away, realizing that she had been correct in her assumptions. "Then might I take this opportunity, Lord Strickland, to state quite clearly that I care nothing for your fortune, for your great wealth, and for all that such a thing might mean to a young lady of quality. I have no great desire to wed a gentleman with a vast fortune, for I have already determined that I shall be quite content with a husband who is able to provide for us both comfortably, but without a great deal of excess."

Lord Strickland lifted his head and tilted it to the left, eyeing her as though she were a creature of interest that he had never seen before, as if she were a brightly colored bird that he wanted to study a little longer. Juliet's blush rose in her cheeks, but she did not look away from him, keeping her gaze steady and holding her tongue before she said anything more.

"Is that so, Lady Juliet?" Lord Strickland murmured, disbelief flickering in his eyes and an edge of mockery in his words. "Then you are one of the most unusual young ladies I believe I have ever met, for what else must one seek in a husband if not a decent fortune and excellent title?"

Juliet's hand curled into a fist, finding Lord Strickland, in this moment, to be most dislikeable. "I think, Lord Strickland, that a gentleman's character speaks more of him than what he possesses," she replied tightly.

Lord Strickland's slightly sardonic smile began to fade as he kept her gaze, only for him to then drop his head back into his hands and let out a small groan.

"Very well, Lady Juliet, very well," he said, abruptly rising to his feet and looking down at her with evident superiority. "That is not to say that I entirely trust your motivations, but I suppose that I must use whatever assistance I can gain in this situation." He bowed stiffly, first to Mrs. Grey and then to her. "I thank you for speaking with me. I should take my leave now as I am sure you will have a good many other gentlemen seeking to call upon you this afternoon."

Juliet was forced to rise to her feet in haste, looking at Mrs. Grey, who was watching Lord Strickland with a sharp eye, her lips flattened and her brows low over her eyes. It appeared that she, too, was just as displeased with his response to Juliet as she was, although she was much too polite to say so.

"Good afternoon, Lord Strickland," Juliet said, keeping her tone even and calm as she curtsied. "I do hope you have an enjoyable evening, whatever it is you are doing."

"I am to attend Lord Courthaven's soiree," he said with a quick look toward her. "And you will be in attendance also, I believe."

"Perhaps we might speak to Lord Richmond then," Mrs. Grey added as Juliet felt anger flare up within her cheeks at his manner, finding that he appeared to believe himself to be quite superior to her, as though he was quite certain that what he thought of her was entirely true. "Good afternoon, Lord Strickland."

Bowing at the waist, Lord Strickland turned on his heel and took his leave, quitting the room at once. Juliet flung herself back into her chair, sighing heavily as she shook her head, both relieved and frustrated with the meeting.

"Lord Strickland took your words with all seriousness at least," Mrs. Grey said, sitting down and reaching for the teapot. "On that account, you must be glad."

"I am," Juliet replied begrudgingly. "It is only that I wish he would not consider me to be just as every other young lady of his acquaintance seems to be."

"You can hardly begrudge him that," Mrs. Grey replied calmly as she beckoned for Juliet to hand her the teacup so that she might refill it. "Consider what his situation must be like at present. Many gentlemen would find themselves greatly pleased with such attentions, seeking even to take advantage of their situation. However, Lord Strickland has not done so, it seems. Instead, he has tried his best to behave with all propriety."

Juliet tossed her head. "I will not permit that as an excuse for his own lack of good manners," she said firmly, making Mrs. Grey laugh. "He spoke very harshly to me, Mrs. Grey."

"But he has agreed to your assistance, has he not?" Mrs. Grey pointed out, and Juliet sighed and nodded, her anger beginning to dissipate. "In time, he will come to see that you are not the sort of young lady he believes you to be."

"Well, I do believe that he should be more gracious for my assistance, rather than accepting it begrudgingly," Juliet muttered, taking a sip of her tea and finding it to be quite satisfactory. Lord Strickland's pompous demeanor was most disconcerting. After all, she had already warned him. She had done her duty. After another deep breath, she felt a little more herself.

Still, she feared that if she did not continue to help him, then the worst might occur. And if something dire did happen to him, she would feel a great burden of guilt. She *had* to assist him, even if he did not like the idea. "I do appreciate your willingness to permit me to be involved in such a way, Mrs. Grey," she finished as the older lady smiled back at her. "I am quite certain that Father would not approve, however, should he come to know of it."

Mrs. Grey's smile grew and her eyes twinkled, as though she had some great intention behind all of this, making Juliet's brows flicker into a frown for a moment.

"I am sure it will all come about right in the end," Mrs. Grey answered mysteriously. "And you will certainly have made an impression upon Lord Strickland, Juliet."

Juliet's frown deepened. "I have already made it quite clear that I have no particular interest in him, Mrs. Grey," she said slowly, praying that her companion did not think that Lord Strickland would suit her. "Surely you cannot think—"

Another scratch at the door came and Juliet found her question cut short, with the butler announcing that she had another gentleman caller. Pushing aside her frustration about Lord Strickland, Juliet forced a gentle smile to her face and rose to her feet, ready to greet her guest. For the time being, at least, she was going to have to play the part of an eligible young lady of the *ton*, unburdened by any other thoughts and glad to converse with whatever gentleman came to call.

And then I shall see Lord Strickland again this evening, she reminded herself as Lord Rivers came into the room, bowing toward her. *Let us hope that he is in better spirits than this afternoon.* This thought brought a warm smile to her face which served only to delight Lord Rivers, who beamed at her in return. Juliet gestured for him to sit down and sent for a fresh tea tray, preparing herself for what might feel like a very long afternoon indeed.

6

Walking into the drawing room, Duncan took a deep breath and forced his hands to uncurl, aware that his nails had been pressing hard into his palms. This was nothing more than another soiree, he told himself, trying to find a calmness that had eluded him ever since he had left Lady Juliet's presence. The revelation of what she had overheard had come as something of a shock for he had never once expected to hear such a thing. The incident that had occurred a few days ago, the night he had narrowly missed being struck, now came to him in a fresh light. It was not a mere accident, it had not been something that he had only just narrowly avoided. It had been deliberate, determined, and sure. Whoever was responsible had wanted to injure him severely and they had almost succeeded.

"Good evening, Lord Strickland."

Jerking slightly with the surprise of being pulled from his own thoughts and addressed in a loud manner, Duncan quickly covered his reaction and bowed toward his host. After a few minutes of genial conversation, he was directed to join the rest of the guests, who were spread out through the house, it seemed. The library, the drawing room, and the music room were open to them all. Lord

Courthaven owned one of the best townhouses in all of London and was not shy in showing off all that he possessed.

"I thank you," Duncan murmured, before turning to make his way toward the waiting footman, taking a brandy from his tray and then meandering across the room in the hope of finding someone to converse with. Someone who would not press their daughter upon him or make mention of their eligible sister.

Unfortunately, he was not to have what he desired.

"How wonderful to see you, Lord Strickland."

Duncan groaned inwardly, forced to greet Lady Montague. She had long been acquainted with Duncan and had attempted to foist first her eldest daughter upon him and, now that she was wed, was trying to do the same with her second.

"Good evening, Lady Montague," he said with not even a hint of enthusiasm in his voice. "And how do you fare this evening?"

"Very well, very well indeed," Lady Montague said, beckoning to someone who stood behind Duncan. "I do hope you remember my daughter, Miss Winters?" She smiled brightly up at him as the young lady came to join her mother with another young lady in tow. "And her friend, Miss Johnson." This last introduction was said with much less fervor, with Lady Montague clearly displeased that her daughter had chosen to bring her friend into Duncan's company.

"Yes, yes, of course," Duncan replied, having met both young ladies before. "Good evening, Miss Winters, Miss Johnson. I do hope you are both enjoying the evening."

Both girls blushed and looked at each other, a giggle escaping from Miss Winters' lips as she darted her gaze up toward him.

"I am so very glad you recall our acquaintance, Lord Strickland," she said, practically cooing at him as she spoke. "I have only just returned to London with Mama and have been very much looking forward to greeting you again."

I cannot say the same, Duncan thought to himself, clearing his throat gently and trying to find something to say. He had no eagerness to encourage the young lady and certainly did not want to say anything that might give her the impression that he, too, had been hopeful of acquainting himself with her again.

"I am sure that there are a good many gentlemen who would be eager to reacquaint themselves with you, Miss Winters," he said, seeing the spark fade from her eyes. "And you also, Miss Johnson."

"You are too kind, Lord Strickland," Miss Johnson giggled, her cheeks still warm. "We must hope that *you* are one of those gentlemen."

Irritation rose in Duncan's chest, but before he could say anything, someone drew near to him, catching his attention—and it was with relief that Duncan bowed toward her.

"Ah, good evening, Lady Juliet," he said as the three other ladies turned toward her with equal expressions of frustration and disappointment. "I had hoped to see you this evening."

Those words seemed to have a great and terrible effect upon the young ladies, as well as upon Lady Montague. They all turned toward him with wide eyes, and he was certain he heard a gasp come from one of them. Lady Juliet, on the other hand, remained quite serene, smiling at him gently although it did not quite reach her eyes.

"Good evening, Lord Strickland," she said, before greeting the ladies in turn. "I do hope that you have all been enjoying this wonderful evening. Does not Lord Courthaven have the most wonderful townhouse?"

There were murmurs of agreement but nothing that could constitute a conversation. In fact, it did not surprise Duncan at all when Lady Montague took her leave of them both, dragging her daughter and Miss Johnson along with her.

Lady Juliet watched them depart with a look of surprise forming slowly across her face, her eyes widening gently and her eyebrows lifting. "Did I say something wrong?" she asked as Mrs. Grey, who had been staying a few steps away, moved a little closer although she did not seem to find any need to speak or interrupt her charge. "I did not mean to drive them away." Her eyes turned to his. "It is only that I thought you might be struggling to converse with someone such as Lady Montague, given her reputation."

Duncan gave her a half-smile. "You know of her reputation, then?"

Lady Juliet laughed and, much to his surprise, Duncan found himself smiling, the sound ringing through the air around him and seeming to warm it. "Yes, indeed," she said brightly. "For it is well known amongst the *ton* that she has done all she can to encourage both her daughters to wed as best they can. I am sure," she continued with a wry smile, "that you have been one of the gentlemen she has sought out?"

"I have been, yes," Duncan replied with a chuckle. "Lady Montague first attempted to encourage me toward her eldest daughter, although I made it very clear indeed that I was not at all interested in continuing an acquaintance with her."

"She is wed now, I think?" Lady Juliet asked, and Duncan nodded. "And I must now presume, therefore, that she is pushing her second daughter toward you?"

"Indeed," Duncan replied with a shake of his head. "I am grateful to you for coming to join our conversation. I am afraid I was already floundering."

Lady Juliet laughed softly and Duncan's smile remained quite fixed in place, making him realize that he had perhaps misjudged Lady Juliet from the first. This afternoon's conversation had ended badly, even though he had felt quite justified in his lack of willingness to engage her support any further. Now, however, he felt a little awkward given that she had come to aid him in such a fashion.

"I should apologize, Lady Juliet, for speaking to you in what I believe was a somewhat insulting manner earlier this afternoon," he said slowly. "I have been uncertain of your motives and yet, even when you told me the truth of them, even when you made it quite plain that you were doing all you could to help me with a very difficult matter, I remained reluctant. I apologize for that."

One shoulder lifted, her blue eyes glinting with gold. "Then might I surmise that you believe my intentions are not to pursue you in the hopes that you might court me?" she asked bluntly. "Or is there still that suspicion within you?"

"I will be honest with you and state that it has not entirely left me as yet," he said truthfully. "But in time, I hope it will dissipate completely, perhaps once our acquaintance grows."

"I hope that also," she replied calmly with a small smile. "Although, I must let you know that I do not feel the need to persuade you that I am true of heart. You can either accept me for my willingness to help, or you can turn me away. It will not make a difference to me either way. I feel no need to prove myself to you."

Duncan was surprised by her forwardness, and he watched as Mrs. Grey's eyes widened in astonishment and disapproval at Lady Juliet's words. He could not hold back a smirk. Her willingness to speak her mind made him respect Lady Juliet all the more.

Lady Juliet continued, "Now, if you will excuse me, I think I shall take a small turn to the library. I have heard that there are some excellent books in our host's library, and I should like to see them for myself." She bobbed a quick curtsy and made to leave but Duncan held out a hand, surprising them both at his action.

He took a breath, wondering at what he had done and why he had done so. With a quick smile, he spread his hands. "Perhaps I might join you, Lady Juliet?" he said as Mrs. Grey smiled on in approval. "The library may not be of particular interest to me, but I am sure that your company will save me from any further conversations with others such as Lady Montague."

Lady Juliet did not immediately accept him, as he had expected. Instead, she looked back at him steadily for a few moments, clearly thinking about what he had suggested. Mrs. Grey said nothing, although, from the way she bit her lip, Duncan was quite certain that she would have encouraged her charge to accept him, should she be willing to speak.

"Very well, Lord Strickland." Lady Juliet's voice was soft, her touch on his arm very gentle indeed, although from her expression, she still appeared a little uncertain. Quite as to why, Duncan did not know, although he was glad that she had accepted him.

Together, they walked from the drawing room and toward the library, following the footmen who stood to attention at various points along the hallway in case a guest should need them. Mrs. Grey came only a step or two after them, making certain to remain close by for the sake of propriety.

"You are reluctant to be seen in my company, Lady Juliet?" Duncan found himself asking as they made their way into the library.

Her smile was brittle. "Not reluctant, I assure you," she replied tightly. "But rather I find myself praying that such attentions will not be noticed by the *ton*, Lord Strickland."

"Oh?"

Again, her eyes met his only to dart away. "It is well known that you are a gentleman who does not seek out any particular company. You have shown no interest in any young lady of your acquaintance. Whilst we must be in each other's company in order to make certain of your safety, I think we must also be wise in just how often the *ton* sees us in such a fashion. Otherwise suggestions will be made, and rumors will run wild. I do not wish for such a thing."

It was as though she had struck him hard across the face, although Duncan could not help but chuckle to himself. He had been so very afraid that she was the one determined to be in his company, eager to push herself into his affections and attentions in any way she could, only for him now to realize that she had no such desire whatsoever. In fact, it sounded as though she disliked even the idea of such a thing.

"Whatever you have said to make Lord Strickland laugh so, I must hear it." The jovial voice of Lord Richmond drew near to them before Duncan could respond and he turned to his friend at once, glad to see both him and Lady Richmond coming to join them. Lady Juliet also appeared relieved, for she greeted Lady Richmond fervently, striking up a conversation almost at once.

"It is of no importance," Duncan replied with another quiet

chuckle as Lord Richmond eyed him suspiciously. "Lady Juliet is excellent company, that is all."

"I am glad to hear it," Lord Richmond replied, glancing toward the lady. "Although I am surprised to see you so contented, given that you stated quite clearly that you did not think you would be eagerly pursuing her company."

Duncan hesitated, his smile fading. He had not yet told Lord Richmond about what Lady Juliet had seen, nor had he said anything about the threat that he now felt hanging over his head. Was now the time to do so?

"There is something you are not telling me," Lord Richmond stated, a grin spreading across his face. "If you have changed your mind, then please, do inform me at once so that my wife and I might gloat about such things together."

"I am afraid no gloating can take place as yet," Duncan replied as the two ladies continued to talk, with Mrs. Grey watching on. "But before I tell you everything, perhaps we might..." Seeing a footman, he caught his attention and quickly sent him off in search of a brandy for both himself and Lord Richmond.

"It is something rather serious, then," Lord Richmond said slowly, eyeing Duncan with concern. "Although quite what Lady Juliet has to do with it all, I cannot imagine."

Lady Juliet, clearly overhearing him, turned toward Lord Richmond with an enquiring look on her face, one eyebrow lifted gently. "You are speaking of me, Lord Richmond?"

Lord Richmond inclined his head, clearing his throat as he lifted his gaze back to Lady Juliet, clearly embarrassed by what she had overheard.

"It is only that Lord Strickland was about to tell me something of significance," he said, keeping his voice a good deal lower than before. "I was merely wondering aloud what it could be that involved you, Lady Juliet."

"I see," she replied, tilting her head just a little. "Well, I presume Lord Strickland is to tell you?"

A little embarrassed, Duncan took the brandy brought to him by the footman, only to catch his arm. "Where is the one for Lord Richmond?" he asked, with the footman then immediately apologizing and hurrying away again. Aware that Mrs. Grey, Lord and Lady Richmond, and Lady Juliet were looking at him, Duncan waved a hand and took a small sip of his brandy. "Please, go ahead, Lady Juliet." His lip curled and he looked down at his brandy, a trifle confused.

"Is something wrong, Lord Strickland?" Lady Juliet asked, taking a small step forward. "Is there—?"

"No, no, it is quite all right," Duncan replied, taking another sip and giving her a small smile. "It was only that I thought this brandy tasted a little...unusual, but I am sure I was just being foolish. Lord Courthaven always has the very best, and I should not like to complain."

This seemed to satisfy Lord Richmond, who turned back to Lady Juliet, looking at her expectantly.

"If you are quite certain," Lady Juliet replied cautiously, before quickly explaining to Lord and Lady Richmond what she had overheard. Duncan watched as their expressions changed from joviality to horror, turning to look at him with wide eyes.

"Thus, Lady Juliet and I shall find a way to discover the truth about this particular lady," he said, lifting the brandy to his lips again. "Although what we are to do next, I cannot imagine."

Lord Richmond frowned hard and made to say something, but the footman interrupted him with his own glass of brandy. Taking it quickly, Lord Richmond brought it to his lips and took a sip, before shaking his head in Duncan's direction.

"It is quite as you would expect," he said, gesturing to Duncan's brandy. "Whatever is wrong with yours, it is not the case with mine."

Duncan opened his mouth to answer, only for a sudden pain to slice through his stomach, before another sharp pain ran across his forehead. Rubbing at it hard, he gave himself a slight shake in order to regain his composure, only for the pain to come yet again.

"What is wrong, Lord Strickland?" Lady Juliet asked as the

others looked at him in surprise, evidently seeing the grimace that he could not hide from his expression.

"Nothing is the matter," he lied, his stomach tightening with another stab of pain. Pressing one hand to it for a moment, he straightened and gave Lady Juliet a quick smile. "I am—"

He could not finish his sentence, squeezing his eyes shut as the pain in his head doubled. Whatever was the matter with him? Thinking to throw back the rest of his brandy in the hope that it might ease whatever trouble was going on within him, he lifted the brandy glass to his lips, only to be stopped by a loud exclamation.

"Lord Strickland!" Lady Juliet reached for him, tugging the brandy glass from his hand before he could drink it. "Wait a moment."

He looked at her, confused, wincing hard as another pain shot through his head, his stomach still tight and sore.

"Did you not just say that someone is attempting to injure you in the most severe manner?" Lady Richmond asked, speaking very slowly indeed but a look of realization beginning to sweep across her features. "What is wrong, Lord Strickland?"

Duncan shook his head, then squeezed his eyes tightly shut as another stab of pain ran through his head. "Nothing," he muttered, not wanting to appear in any way foolish. "My head is a little painful, that is all. My stomach..."

"And this has only affected you after you had taken some of your brandy," Lady Juliet remarked, looking down at it and then back at him. "Lord Richmond believes there is nothing wrong with his, whereas you believe that it tastes a little unusual."

Frowning hard, half from the pain and half from trying to understand what Lady Juliet meant, Duncan rubbed one hand across his forehead. "I am mistaken, I am sure," he said but Lady Juliet shook her head, then handed the glass to Lord Richmond.

"If you might, Lord Richmond," she said as he reached to take it from her. "If there is any difference, I presume you will notice."

Lord Richmond nodded, his expression grim. Taking the

smallest taste of Duncan's brandy, he screwed up his face and shook his head.

"There is something very odd about that," he said, looking toward Duncan. "That might very well be why the footman brought us one glass and then the next. So that they could be certain you could have *this* particular brandy."

Lady Juliet took the glass from Lord Richmond and held it in her hand, lifting it a little higher so that she might scrutinize it. Her lips pursed as she studied it carefully. The pain in Duncan's head slowly began to lessen, as did the cramps in his stomach, and he stood up straight again, his frown remaining in place.

"I cannot imagine what would have occurred had you taken all of it, Lord Strickland," she said slowly, looking up at him. "I am certain that someone has placed something within your brandy in order to bring you pain and suffering."

Blinking hard and feeling sweat break out across his forehead, Duncan pulled out his handkerchief and dabbed it away. "You believe that someone has deliberately placed something in my brandy?" he asked, looking around the room as his heart began to pound furiously. "Someone present this evening?"

"I believe so," Lord Richmond said, and Lady Richmond's eyes widened in astonishment. "It appears that Lady Juliet has been quite correct in her considerations yet again, Lord Strickland. If you had decided to throw back the entire measure of brandy, then I cannot imagine how ill you would have become."

A sudden shudder passed through Duncan's frame as he looked at the brandy in Lady Juliet's hand, glad that the pain was fading all the more. He found himself taking in a deep breath, gazing into her eyes and finding himself more than a little relieved that Lady Juliet had seen danger in the brandy glass where he had not.

"They must be here this evening," Mrs. Grey interjected, catching everyone's attention. "And we must speak to the footman who brought you the brandy."

Duncan nodded slowly. "That would be wise," he agreed,

looking all about him. "Someone must have made certain that I was given a particular glass."

Lady Juliet let out a heavy sigh. "There are so many guests, however," she said, her lips pursing for a moment as she looked all about her. "Just how are we meant to discern who it could be, given that Lord Courthaven has invited so many guests this evening?"

"We cannot," Lady Richmond answered, shaking her head. "There are too many of them. What we must do, therefore, is seek out the footman that served your brandy, Lord Strickland. Do you recall him?"

Trying to remember, Duncan fought for clarity. "I did not pay much attention," he replied, a little awkwardly. "However, I am sure that if I saw him again, I would recall him."

"Then you must look about the house at once," Mrs. Grey said firmly. "Take Lady Juliet's arm, Lord Strickland, and make your way around this room and, thereafter, to the hallway, the music room, and then the drawing room." She gave him a firm nod as though all was decided. "I will attend with you, of course."

Duncan blinked rapidly and then, seeing the urgency of the situation, offered Lady Juliet his arm. She accepted it at once, her hand tight on his arm as they turned and walked together. Nothing was discussed, no words were said, but rather they walked in silence, looking not at the guests but at the footmen that stood around the room. Some were making their way from one guest to another, trays of refreshments in their hands, whereas others stood quietly to one side, waiting for a summons from one of the guests or to fix their attention to some duty or other.

"Are any of them recognizable?" Lady Juliet asked, her voice low. "None of their faces spark any awareness?"

"None," Duncan replied, frustrated with his own lack of alertness. "To be truthful, I do not often pay great attention to the servants or the like." He gave her a rueful smile. "Mayhap I should do so in the future."

"If you are to be poisoned in a brandy glass, then yes, I should think you ought to," Lady Juliet replied with a small smile, glancing up in his direction. "Perhaps we should go to the music room? He might be there?"

Duncan suddenly caught his breath, his eyes catching sight of one particular footman. A footman that was, he noticed, now quickly making his way from the room, glancing behind him in Duncan's direction.

"There," he said, keeping his voice low although he did not miss Lady Juliet's swift intake of breath. "I believe that is he. Come now, Lady Juliet. We must catch him."

7

Juliet stumbled after Lord Strickland, her hand tight on his arm. She had feared that Lord Strickland would be unable to identify the correct footman but now, it seemed, he had recognized him. Lord Strickland walked quickly, making his way through the guests without hesitation and, no doubt, gaining attention from some of them. She did not allow herself to be embarrassed by this, however, making certain to do just as he asked her, her heart pounding furiously as they followed the footman.

She had felt herself growing all the more anxious as she had slowly begun to realize the truth about Lord Strickland's brandy. What would have occurred if he had drunk the full glass, she was not at all sure, although she had begun to question whether it was merely injury that the as yet unknown lady now sought for Lord Strickland.

"There, he has gone away from the library and is making his way through the house," Lord Strickland said hoarsely as the footman's strides quickened all the more. "Lady Juliet, I should leave you and—"

"Mrs. Grey remains behind us," she said hastily, not wanting him to even consider for a moment for fear that he would take his eyes from the footman. "Please, Lord Strickland, we must hurry. Go after him. We will come after you."

This appeared to make all the difference for Lord Strickland did not so much as glance behind him to make certain Mrs. Grey was following. Rather, he simply let go of her arm but continued to stride after the footman, making his way past the drawing room and hurrying down the hallway. Juliet went after him without hesitation, Mrs. Grey joining her now, as Lord Strickland shouted aloud in an attempt to stop the footman from hurrying away.

"You there! Stop!"

The footman turned his head and looked back at Lord Strickland, his eyes widening with fear. He stared for a moment, making Juliet wonder if he would remain where he was as Lord Strickland had asked—only for him to turn on his heel and break into a run. Lord Strickland did so also, hurrying after him and leaving Juliet and Mrs. Grey to catch up. Juliet's heart began to burn as they rushed forward, knowing what would occur should the footman disappear below stairs. They would lose him for good, unable to simply make their way to the servants' quarters and demand to see all the footmen present.

The footman disappeared through a door and Lord Strickland went after him, only a moment or two behind.

"There!" Mrs. Grey exclaimed, hearing a loud shout. "He has him now, I am sure."

Juliet did not reply, her heart still pounding furiously as they hurried in through the door, only to see Lord Strickland standing in front of the footman, who now appeared to be utterly terrified of the consequences that Lord Strickland might bring. There was a small fire in the grate, candles lit on almost every surface and a few small tables set about the room. It took Juliet a moment to realize that they had entered a small parlor which, she presumed, had been prepared for any of Lord Courthaven's guests who wished to play cards. Perhaps some gentlemen would do so later in the evening.

"It was you who gave me that brandy, was it not?"

Lord Strickland's voice spread out across the room, shattering the silence and making the footman step back from him, his hands held up in a defensive gesture.

"There is no need to deny it," Lord Strickland continued, his voice hard. "You did not expect me to be able to come after you in such a fashion, I presume, given that I was meant to be in so much pain that I would either be already on my way to my own townhouse, or unconscious from it all, is that not so?"

The footman's eyes were huge, his face as pale as milk as he took another step back, his eyes drifting to something to his right. Juliet frowned hard, noticing at once that there was another door there. Clearing her throat, she caught Lord Strickland's attention and gestured toward it.

"And there is no need to attempt to escape from me again," Lord Strickland continued, making his way to the second door and leaving Juliet and Mrs. Grey to stand in front of the first. "I will have the truth from you, in any way I can."

"You may as well speak it," Juliet told the footman quietly. "There will be consequences piled upon your head if you do not."

"That is what he said," the footman groaned, seeming now to shrink before them as his way of escape was quickly cut off by Lord Strickland. "If I did not, then I would have my employment here brought to a swift end. I wouldn't get any references. I *need* my position here, my lord." His eyes flew to Lord Strickland, as though he might understand. "What else was I to do?"

Juliet saw Lord Strickland frown, feeling her stomach twist furiously within her.

"Then it was not a lady, as we thought," Mrs. Grey said quietly, and Juliet nodded.

"It must have been the gentleman I heard speak," she said, reminding her companion of who she had overheard in the bookshop that day. "As you might recall, I spoke of two that were present."

"What did this fellow look like?" Lord Strickland demanded, his tone giving no leeway for the footman to avoid the question. "When did he approach you?"

The footman dropped his head. "I will lose everything I have here if I tell you," he said hoarsely. "I have done as he asked but if I speak of it—"

"If you do not speak of it, then it will be all the worse for you," Lord Strickland interrupted harshly. "You may have caused me a great deal of agony by your actions and, whilst you were threatened into doing such a thing, you are still responsible. I must know."

Juliet held her breath, her fingers pressing together in front of her as she watched the footman lower his head, his shoulders slumping.

"The servants' entrance is at the back of the townhouse, as you would expect," he said, speaking in a dull voice as though he had given up and lost all hope. "I was making my way back inside when a fellow stepped out of the shadows and grasped my arm. I didn't know what was happening, until I felt the tip of a knife at my throat."

A chill ran over Juliet's frame as she heard Mrs. Grey catch her breath. It seemed that the people responsible for this attack on Lord Strickland were ruthless and determined, ready to do whatever was necessary to gain what they required.

"He told me that I was to watch for you, Lord Strickland," he said heavily. "That I was to put a vial into your brandy. That is all I know. I have been keeping a close watch on you since the moment you arrived, fearful of what I must do and yet knowing there was no other choice for me but to do it."

Lord Strickland laughed harshly. "You mean to say that you did not know anything about what the vial contained?" he asked, as though he could hardly believe what was being said. "That you were unaware of the consequences?"

"I did not!" The footman lifted his head and turned to face Lord Strickland, his voice holding more determination than before. "I swear to you I did not. But the man threatened me with such violence and with the loss of my employ that I had no other choice.

If I am thrown from this house without reference, then what future is there for me?" His voice broke and, despite herself, Juliet felt a swell of sympathy pulling through her heart. "I had hoped to become a butler one day. But if I did not obey, then even my position as footman would be taken from me."

Nothing was said for some moments with the quiet crackling of the fire being the only sound. Juliet looked toward Lord Strickland, who was watching the footman with hard eyes, his jaw working furiously and his eyes narrowed. She did not want to tell him what to say or what to do but silently prayed that he would realize, as she had done, that this footman had not been eagerly participating in the attack upon his life. She could well understand the fear that must have entered the man's heart upon hearing that everything he knew, everything that was a security for him, would be pulled away in a moment.

"The vial."

Lord Strickland's words were quiet and filled with a wrath Juliet could well understand.

"The vial," he said again, a little more loudly. "Where is it?"

The footman stared at Lord Strickland for a moment as though he was entirely unaware of what the man was saying, only to give himself a slight shake and begin to fumble about in his pockets. Juliet caught her breath as a small, clear vial was brought out and handed directly to Lord Strickland, making her heart quail for a moment as she saw Lord Strickland open the top and take a sniff, wrinkling his nose as he did so.

"It appears you have failed in your task," he said, looking back at the footman. "I am meant to be grievously ill now, am I not?"

Again the footman spread his hands. "I do not know, my lord," he said helplessly. "I have no knowledge of what was in that vial, nor did I even imagine what the consequences might be. Instead, I simply did as I was asked."

"Then how was this fellow—the one with the knife to your neck—meant to know that you had succeeded?" Lord Strickland asked as the footman's eyes widened. "How could he be certain that you had done as you were instructed?"

The footman stared back at Lord Strickland without answering, leaving Juliet to glance from Lord Strickland to Mrs. Grey and back again, quickly coming to the very same conclusion as they, given the expressions of understanding on their faces.

"Then he is present this evening," Juliet said softly as Lord Strickland nodded tersely. "That is the only way he could be certain of the success of it all. He would be watching closely, making sure that you did as you were instructed and thereafter, watching Lord Strickland for the after-effects of imbibing whatever is within that vial."

The footman dropped his head. "I am sorry, my lord," he muttered heavily. "I did not know what it would do to you, but I couldn't allow myself to be removed from my position here."

"I believe you," Juliet found herself saying as Lord Strickland turned to her, his eyes narrowed. "It does not excuse what you have done but it can certainly bring a little understanding as to why you did such a thing." Glancing at Mrs. Grey, she found herself frowning suddenly. "Given that there is someone here expecting you to have collapsed to the ground, Lord Strickland, I do not know what would be best to do."

Lord Strickland moved away from the second door and came toward them, not even glancing at the footman.

"You are dismissed," he barked, and, like a small, terrified child, the footman scrambled away, his head held low and his whole body seeming to shrink as he passed them. Juliet wanted to say something of comfort to him but knew she could not.

"You are correct, Lady Juliet," Lord Strickland said slowly. "There will be someone present who will be looking for something to occur with me. Something that they can then congratulate themselves upon, in the belief that they have managed to achieve their aim."

"But you are not as they expect," Mrs. Grey pointed out. "You are quite well. Juliet was quickly able to discern the cause of your pain and thus, you drank nothing more from the brandy."

"The brandy which will, I am sure, have been disposed of by now," Juliet added, knowing that Lord and Lady Richmond would not simply have held it back for them.

Lord Strickland rubbed at his forehead. "I could continue on as I am and, in doing so, prove to the person responsible that I am not unwell as they had hoped. Or..." He trailed off, tilting his head and twisting his lips for a moment, his brow furrowing hard. "Or I could make quite certain that they believe that they have achieved what they wish, in the hope that either yourself, Lady Juliet, or Mrs. Grey, or Lord and Lady Richmond are able to identify the gentleman present who has been carefully watching me."

"That seems like an impossible task," Mrs. Grey remarked, sounding anxious. "There are so many guests."

"Therefore, with a brandy in my hand, I shall walk from one room to the next, slowly and with great care," Lord Strickland continued, warming to his plan. "We shall walk together, in fact. Lord and Lady Richmond can watch carefully, for surely the person responsible will have to join me in whatever room I step into, simply to make certain that I am drinking the poisoned brandy."

"And to watch for your reaction," Juliet added slowly, her eyes widening just a little. "It is certainly an idea, Lord Strickland, but what if it does not succeed?"

"It is better than doing nothing," Lord Strickland replied with a lift of one shoulder. "If I remain as I am, then the evening's plan will have failed and the gentleman will only try again, albeit in an entirely different manner. Is it not best to try and discover them now?"

Juliet nodded, finding agreement in his planned actions and, thus, she found herself walking back along to the library, her hand again on Lord Strickland's arm and Mrs. Grey behind them. Lord Strickland walked purposefully, his intentions determined, and Juliet could not help but feel a little anxious. Anxious that she would not be able to do as he hoped in watching for anyone who might take great notice of Lord Strickland's health, that she would fail in her playacting when it came to Lord Strickland's feigned illness. That nothing would come of it and that they would have to depart this evening without having any awareness of who was behind it all.

"Strickland!"

Lord and Lady Richmond were still in the library, the glass of offending brandy still sitting on the small table to Lady Richmond's right. They looked with wide eyes toward Lord Strickland, clearly hoping that he had found success in his endeavors with the footman.

"I must have another brandy," Lord Strickland murmured, having quickly told Lord and Lady Richmond of their intentions. "But I cannot be seen to have requested it."

"No matter," Lord Richmond replied, handing his own, half-drunk glass to Lady Richmond before quickly catching the attention of a footman and requesting another one. He gave Juliet a small smile. "You have done very well this evening, it seems, Lady Juliet," he said kindly. "I do hope Lord Strickland is grateful to you for what you have done."

Heat rose in her cheeks. "He has been, of course, very grateful," she said, fully aware that Lord Strickland was beside her, "but that is not of importance at present. We must begin to make our way from the library and then to the drawing room. We cannot linger for too long."

Lord Strickland cleared his throat and nodded, waiting until Lord Richmond had been given another glass of brandy, and then reached for the glass of poisoned brandy, which was sitting on the table, waiting for him to do so. With a small clearing of his throat, he took the brandy from Lord Richmond and then handed him the poisoned one, which was then swapped with the one Lady Richmond held.

"I will make certain to have this removed," Lady Richmond said quietly as Juliet looked on. "The gentleman will not be watching us, and certainly will not take any notice of a lady who sets down a glass upon a footman's tray."

"It could be any gentleman," he said as Lord and Lady Richmond nodded fervently. "They will, we hope, come to join us in whatever room we attend, wanting to make quite certain that I have drunk whatever concoction they believe is in this glass."

"And when it comes time for your dramatic illness, then we shall all watch carefully for those who hurry toward you," Mrs. Grey remarked, but Juliet shook her head.

"No," she disagreed. "We must watch for whomever it is that lingers behind, staying away from it all but making certain to watch it without fear. They will not rush forward, not wanting to be seen, but will, I think, remain a little further away."

Lord Strickland looked at her steadily for a moment or two before he smiled, making the heat in Juliet's face rise back up in an instant.

"You are very wise indeed, Lady Juliet," he said quietly. "Then yes, you and Mrs. Grey will remain close to me, watching those who draw near, but Lord and Lady Richmond, might you do as Lady Juliet has suggested?"

They agreed without hesitation and thus, there was nothing to do but begin to carry out their plan. With a small smile placed gently on her lips, Juliet took Lord Strickland's arm and, together, they began to walk.

"I fear, Lady Juliet, that your eagerness to remain quite unacknowledged by the *beau monde* will not be successful today," Lord Strickland murmured as they walked together. "I am aware that you did not want to be noticed, did not want the *ton* to believe that I am showing a particular interest in you, but I fear that it may be too late now."

She did not quite know what to say to this, looking at him for a long moment before finally allowing herself a small smile.

"I think that my desires are not what is of the greatest importance at present, Lord Strickland," she told him, suddenly very aware that there would be many of the guests watching them walk together, having forgotten entirely about the rumors that would then be spoken about them both should she linger in his company. It seemed of such little consequence now that she knew the truth. "We must try to do all that we can in order to keep you safe from those who wish to harm you." Her brows furrowed. "Might I ask if you know what is within that vial?"

Lord Strickland shook his head. "I do not," he said honestly, "but it is offensive to smell, certainly. I shall, of course, ask an opinion of someone who might identify it better than I, but I cannot make any particular guess at present."

"It is all a little frightening, in one way," Juliet admitted. "To know that there is someone within the *beau monde* who is desperately trying to injure you in some way must be rather horrifying."

"I do not know why they would wish to do such a thing," Lord Strickland told her with a shake of his head. "I do not believe that I have ever done a great wrong to anyone." A grimace tugged at his lips. "Unless you count the many young ladies I have evidently sorely disappointed due to my lack of interest in them—and their mothers also."

Juliet could not help but smile, her worries alleviated for only a moment. "I hardly think any of them would wish to injure you so."

"You have not met all of them," he retorted, making her laugh as they walked into the music room. "But yes, I shall agree with you on that point, at least. I do not believe that there is any real threat from any such young lady *or* her mother. Although who else it might be, I cannot imagine."

Juliet hesitated. "Might I ask if there is someone within your family line who would inherit, should the worst happen to you?" Her question burned on her lips, her heart pounding furiously as she began to worry that she had insulted him by asking such a question. "I am not trying to suggest that there could be someone within your family line responsible, only to make the suggestion that—"

"It is a wise question," Lord Strickland interrupted, making her catch her breath with relief. "Pray, do not worry." His brow furrowed as they continued to walk slowly through the room, with Juliet entirely unaware of the many glances that were being sent in their direction, given just how much she was focused on Lord Strickland. He did not speak for a few more minutes but, when he did so, there was a heaviness about his words that spoke of a troubled heart.

"There is a cousin who would inherit," he said eventually. "But I have made certain that, due to my significant wealth, none within my family—my extended family—are left without. He is wed, settled in a fine house, and has borne two children already. He has an excellent living and, from what I understand, is very contented. I have never once thought him eager to claim the title, for he has shown no such interest."

"I see," Juliet murmured, relieved to hear such a thing. "Then we must surmise that there is someone set against you for entirely their own purposes."

Lord Strickland sighed heavily. "Purposes that I do not, as yet, fully understand," he replied, taking another sip of his brandy before making for the door. "Shall we make our way to the drawing room?"

She nodded, feeling a slight tension rising within her. "It is there that you will...?"

Glancing across at her, Lord Strickland nodded, a glimmer of a smile playing about his mouth and a warmth in his eyes that she had never seen there before. "There, we shall begin our little performance, Lady Juliet," he answered, lifting his brandy glass as though to toast their success. "Let us hope that something remarkable will come from it."

8

Duncan let out a groan as he lifted his head from the back of the chair where he had been resting. The butler immediately began to apologize for disturbing him, but Duncan shook his head and beckoned him in.

"Lady Juliet, Mrs. Grey, and Lord and Lady Richmond are settled in the drawing room," he told Duncan, who nodded quickly and then immediately winced. Last evening's fall to the floor, accompanied with whatever effects had lingered due to the poisoned brandy he had drunk, had left him with a rather painful head.

"I will join them at once," he said, rising from his chair. "Refreshments have been brought, I presume?"

"Yes, my lord," the butler murmured, and Duncan rose from his chair and made his way to the door which the butler held open for him. "Excellent," he said, garnering a small smile from the butler. "Now, recall that we are not to be disturbed until their time here is at an end."

The butler inclined his head. "But of course," he said quietly as Duncan nodded and then strode along the hallway to the drawing room.

Stepping inside, he was immediately greeted by Lord and Lady Richmond, Mrs. Grey, and Lady Juliet, who all rose to their feet at once with equal words of concern flying from their lips as he entered.

"I am quite all right," he assured them, a broad smile spreading across his face at the concern in each and every face. "Did my acting last evening convince even you?"

Lady Juliet flushed just a little, looking away from him as she sat back down. "I think you did very well last evening, Lord Strickland," she replied as the others took their seats again. "Everyone was very concerned for you, certainly."

"And the fact that they had to practically lift you to your carriage was an excellent addition," Lord Richmond grinned, clearly no longer as concerned about Duncan's state of health. "You did very well indeed."

Duncan chuckled and rose to pour himself and Lord Richmond a whisky.

"I have had enough of brandy for the moment," he quipped as he handed a glass to Lord Richmond. "And please, Lady Juliet, you are more than welcome to pour the tea for yourself and the other ladies." Sitting down, he let out a long, contented sigh, looking with a sense of great gladness and relief toward Lady Juliet. "Might I say again, Lady Juliet—for I do not believe that I made it particularly clear last evening—that I am profoundly grateful to you for your wisdom and insight. Had you not made the association between the striking pain in my head and the brandy, then I am sure I would not have noticed at all and certainly would have drunk the full measure, simply so as not to appear rude."

Lady Juliet smiled back at him, although her face held a little more color than usual. "You are most welcome," she said softly.

"You did very well, Lady Juliet," Lady Richmond replied, making Lady Juliet look down at the floor with evident embarrassment. "And I believe, Lord Strickland, that your performance last evening has brought us a little insight."

This piqued Duncan's interest almost at once. "Oh?"

"There were three gentlemen who went after you and Lady Juliet as you made your way through the house," Lord Richmond said, his expression now grave. "We could not be sure of their motives and, indeed, some might have been entirely unaware of their actions, but the three gentlemen all stood at the back and watched what was occurring, although all with equal expressions of horror."

"Which might very well have been nothing more than an act, just as yours was, Lord Strickland," Mrs. Grey said quietly. "Might I ask the names of these gentlemen?"

Lord Richmond nodded. "Of course. There was the Earl of Redford, Viscount Haverstock, and Viscount Brookmire."

Duncan frowned. "I do not believe I am at all acquainted with the latter," he said slowly, searching his memory. "The Earl of Redford is a well-established acquaintance, however, and Viscount Haverstock I have known since last Season."

"And neither of them hold any grudge against you?" Lady Richmond asked as Duncan shook his head. "Then I suppose we must consider all of them."

"I suppose we must," Lady Juliet agreed quietly, studying Duncan with a careful eye. "Although how are we to surmise if they have anything against you, Lord Strickland?"

No one said anything for a moment and then, much to Duncan's surprise, Lady Richmond flew from her chair, her eyes bright and her hands clasped together.

"You must do it, Lady Juliet!" she exclaimed, beginning to pace up and down before them all. "Do you not see? You have been seen on Lord Strickland's arm. Everyone noticed it last evening and, no doubt, the *ton* will be speaking of it today. Therefore, it would be natural for his name to come up in conversation between you and whoever else you wish to discuss it with…say, Lord Haverstock or Lord Redford."

"Yes, indeed," Mrs. Grey said, sounding much more enthusiastic than Lady Juliet appeared to be. "You are meant to be introducing yourself to as many eligible gentlemen as possible." Her eyes slid toward Duncan. "Neither of those gentlemen are wed, I hope?"

"No, they are not," Duncan replied, feeling himself rather unsettled by such a suggestion and how quickly Mrs. Grey was agreeing to it. "But to push Lady Juliet forward in such a manner—"

"All you would have to do," Lady Richmond interrupted as though she knew what Duncan would say to protest, "is to acquaint yourself with each gentleman in turn. No doubt, they will mention your acquaintance with Lord Strickland and, should they do so, you must shake your head and sigh, stating that you found him to be *most* disagreeable, although you were flattered by his attention —or some such thing."

Lady Juliet blinked rapidly, the color gone from her cheeks. "And you hope that this will encourage them to speak openly about Lord Strickland?"

"Enough to give us an idea as to whether or not they think well of him, yes," Lord Richmond said as his wife beamed at him, clearly delighted with his quick agreement. "It may mean that you will have to entertain their acquaintance a little longer than perhaps you might wish to, but I am sure that, in time, you will be able to garner an opinion about their thoughts toward Lord Strickland."

Duncan shook his head. "I do not think that such a burden is particularly fair to Lady Juliet," he said firmly. "Yes, she may have alerted me to this particular danger, and she has already saved me from a great deal of pain, but to ask her to do more seems entirely unfair."

Lady Juliet did not appear to hear him. "And it might very well be that I recognize the voice of either the Earl of Redford or Viscount Haverstock from the bookshop," she said, looking up at Lady Richmond with a hint of excitement in her voice.

"Lady Juliet." Duncan rose from his chair, commanding the room with his presence. Lady Juliet's smile faded as she turned to look at him, the light fading from her eyes. "Lady Juliet, whilst I have agreed for your input in this matter, surely you cannot be asked to do this." He looked around the room, half expecting Mrs. Grey and Lord Richmond to agree with him, but neither of them did so. "You have your own Season, do you not? You are meant to be enjoying all that London has to offer you and instead, you are sitting here, trying to come up with a solution that will be of aid to me rather than to you." He found himself frowning hard, trying to express to her exactly how he felt. "I am more than grateful for all that you have done thus far, but pray do not turn away from your own responsibilities for my sake."

The room grew silent as everyone turned toward Lady Juliet. She was looking at him with a glimmer of something yet unexpressed in her eyes.

"I will not have you pushed into this for my sake alone," he finished, sitting back down and feeling a little embarrassed that he had spoken so decisively in front of the others. "Pray understand, Lady Juliet, I seek what is best for you."

"As I do for you," came the quiet reply. "As much as I appreciate your concern for me, you must know that I put such a threat toward you far above my own need to find a suitor and enjoy the Season." A tiny smile tugged at her mouth and Duncan found himself suddenly transfixed, unable to look away from her. "Mrs. Grey is in agreement with my desire to be of aid to you, Lord Strickland, and given that I am the only one who could possibly identify the gentleman based on his voice alone, it is not as though I could simply turn around and refuse to be of help to you."

Lady Richmond let out a small, contented sigh and looked at Duncan with a softly lifted eyebrow. He knew very well what she was trying to say, telling him that he would not find another creature like Lady Juliet, no matter how hard he searched, and yet Duncan did not even permit his thoughts to turn in that particular direction.

"Then I am greatly in your debt," he said quietly. "Are you quite sure I cannot convince you?"

Lady Juliet laughed softly, tilting her head in an almost bird-like fashion. "I am quite certain you could not," she replied as the tension in the room suddenly dissipated. "Your life is of much greater importance than a few weeks of the Season." One shoulder lifted. "Besides which, I am sure that I will have plenty of time left to enjoy dancing and courting and the like, once you have made certain of your safety."

Duncan swallowed hard, nodding toward her but finding his heart suddenly pained at the thought of Lady Juliet being courted by another gentleman. Quite why he should have such a thought, he did not know, nor could he understand why it would bring him such displeasure. Quickly, he thrust it away from him entirely, leaving him to turn his mind back to the situation at hand.

"Very well," he replied, a trifle gruffly. "Then I suppose there is nothing for it but to wish you well, Lady Juliet."

"I shall be sure to inform you the moment I hear anything of interest from either gentleman," she promised, reaching for her teacup and giving so sign of intending to leave. "And you will linger here, I presume? Giving the impression that you are very ill indeed?" Seeing him nod, she gave a small shake of her head. "That is three times now that you have been in danger, Lord Strickland. Mayhap you ought to remain in your townhouse more often."

This made Duncan laugh, although he did not miss the frown that appeared on Lord Richmond's face.

"Three times?" Lord Richmond repeated, frowning. "I thought there was only the night after the soiree and then last evening."

Lady Juliet waved a hand. "Forgive me," she said with a rueful smile. "I forgot that the highwaymen were *not* something to consider."

"Highwaymen?" Lady Richmond repeated, and Duncan was forced to explain all that had occurred.

"My father and I came across a most dreadful scene the day we made our way to London," Lady Juliet added quickly, her color draining away just a little. "We have no knowledge of those who were left for dead, save for an empty letter that my father insisted we take with us in the hope that it might contain something that would be of assistance. It was not until we returned home that we discovered it empty. Two of the men attacked have been buried, and one, from what we have heard, still lingers between life and death. But," she continued with a small shrug, "it is not a particular consequence for Lord Strickland, given that it has happened to others."

"Besides which, I was lucky enough to avoid it," Duncan added hastily. "I rode rather than taking my carriage. Had I been in my carriage, then I might well have been stopped."

"But you were not," Lord Richmond replied, a frown still lingering on his brow. "Because you were riding rather than being in your carriage."

Duncan let out a snort. "Because of the skill of my driver," he answered honestly. "Even if I had been within the carriage, I believe from what was told to me thereafter that my driver managed to evade the highwaymen, although he may not have driven so wildly had I been inside."

"And what day was this?" Lady Richmond asked, looking from one to the next, her brows lifting in surprise as both Duncan and Lady Juliet spoke of the same day.

Silence ran across the room as Duncan's gaze slowly returned to Lady Juliet. He had never expected that they would have made their way to London on the very same day.

Lady Juliet frowned, biting her lip for a moment. "Did your driver mention whether or not he passed anyone else on the road?" she asked slowly, looking at him with a small frown flickering across her brow.

"He did not mention it," Duncan answered honestly. "Might I ask why?"

Shaking her head, Lady Juliet did not immediately answer but then, glancing at Mrs. Grey, expressed her thoughts. "It is only that I have always wondered about that strange letter," she said quietly. "I do not know if I have mentioned it to you before, Lord Strickland, but my father recovered a letter from one of the... unfortunate souls that had been struck down by the highwaymen." Her brow furrowed all the more. "I have it back at my father's townhouse for he requested I take it back with us—but to my surprise, when it was opened, there was nothing written inside."

Duncan did not quite understand what she meant. "The letter was without any words written inside it? And no name on the front?"

"None," Lady Juliet replied. "I have kept it, of course, for it is a question that does not yet have an answer. The reason I ask about your driver is to know whether or not he passed any other carriage on the road. Or if he, too, saw the same scene as my father."

"I did not ask him," Duncan repeated, spreading his hands. "I certainly can do. In fact..." Rising, he made his way to ring the bell. "I will send for him at once and see what he says."

~

It took only a few minutes for the driver to arrive, looking rather anxious as he stepped in through the door.

"You are not to be corrected or berated, George," Duncan said hastily, not wanting to upset his driver. "It is only that I must ask you something about the day we arrived in London."

The driver nodded, his hands tight together in front of him as he cleared his throat. "Yes, my lord?" He glanced nervously about the room before looking back at Duncan.

"There were highwaymen set waiting for you, were there not?" Duncan asked, and the driver nodded. "And you managed to avoid them. Tell me," he continued as the driver shuffled his feet, "was there anything else—anyone else—that you noticed?"

The driver frowned. "What do you mean, my lord?"

"Lady Juliet," Duncan explained, gesturing to the lady, "came to London on the very same day. Her father and driver stopped to help some who had, it appeared, been attacked by highwaymen but who had not managed to escape as you did. She wishes to know whether or not you saw them also."

A dark frown crossed the driver's face. "My lord, there *was* another carriage by the side of the road," he said slowly. "The horses were gone. I didn't see if there was anyone inside and, given the threat, I had no other choice but to keep going. I could not stop."

Lady Juliet sucked in a breath and Duncan frowned heavily, looking toward her. It meant that the highwaymen had, most likely, attacked the carriage before Duncan's had arrived, and then, for whatever reason, had disappeared before Lady Juliet's had driven by.

"I do not blame you, of course," Lady Juliet said quickly, speaking to the driver. "You had to make sure of your own safety. Of course you could not stop."

"Thank you, my lady," the driver replied, keeping his eyes low as he looked at Duncan, as though expecting him to say something entirely different. "I did what I thought was right."

"It was the correct course of action," Duncan replied honestly. "Thank you, George. You can return to your duties now."

The man looked thoroughly relieved and made his way from the room without hesitation. Lady Juliet sat back in her chair as the others simply looked at each other, perhaps all wondering as to what this might mean.

"Is there a possibility," Mrs. Grey said slowly, "that the highwaymen were waiting for you, Lord Strickland?"

"No," Duncan said quickly, "that cannot be. They attacked a carriage before attempting to do so to my own. That is precisely what I would expect."

"But they did not succeed," Lady Juliet said softly. "Why, then, should they disperse? Surely they would linger to take on the next carriage? The one that I was in?"

Duncan shook his head. "I do not think it means anything," he said firmly. "It is an unfortunate event, certainly, but perhaps not one that is in any way related to the ongoing situation as regards my safety."

"I would not be so quick to ignore it," Lord Richmond replied solemnly, surprising Duncan. "Let us not throw it from our minds entirely. We must consider all possibilities and, in fact, Lady Juliet, I should very much like to see this letter of yours. The letter that bears no mark." His lips quirked. "It is interesting, certainly."

Lady Juliet smiled at him and Duncan felt his heart twist in his chest, dropping his gaze to the floor so that he might hide whatever emotion threw itself into his expression.

"I should be very glad to," he heard Lady Juliet say. "Thank you for your willingness, Lord Richmond."

Duncan cleared his throat, finding himself speaking before he even had any reasonable thought. "I should like to see it also." A little embarrassed, he shrugged. "That is, if you do not mind."

Ignoring the broad grin that spread across Lord Richmond's face, Duncan waited for Lady Juliet to speak, more than relieved when she accepted his offer without hesitation.

"I would be more than glad to show you," she said, looking reassured. "Thank you, Lord Strickland. Would tomorrow be suitable?"

"More than suitable," he agreed, surprised at the fervor in his voice. "I look forward to seeing it, Lady Juliet."

Mrs. Grey rose to her feet. "And now we should take our leave," she said briskly, although Duncan did not miss the knowing gleam in her eye. "You will be present this evening, I presume?"

"At Lord Whittaker's ball?" Duncan asked, and Lady Juliet nodded, her eyes suddenly darting away from his, pink in her cheeks. "Yes, I shall be in attendance."

Lady Juliet threw him a quick smile. "Until this evening then, Lord Strickland. And I shall make certain to speak to both Lord Redford and Lord Haverstock."

Recollecting what she was to do that evening, Duncan felt the smile fade from his face, the warmth in his heart fading slightly. "Yes, of course," he said, bowing as the ladies bobbed a quick curtsy. "Until then, Lady Juliet."

9

Juliet took a breath as she stepped into Lord Whittaker's ballroom. It was a large, spacious room that was already filled with guests. The hubbub of conversation and laughter rang all round her and yet she felt nothing but anxiety. She had a duty to perform this evening rather than simply enjoying herself.

This afternoon's meeting had gone quite well, all things considered. What had been most disturbing to her, however, was the fact that she had felt strange stirrings within her heart toward Lord Strickland. He had been behaving more warmly toward her than ever before and the resistance she had felt to being often in his company—for fear of what the *ton* would say—was no longer a concern. It was as though she simply did not care, wanting now to discover who was behind this disgusting desire to attack him in such a way and why. She recalled just how ill he had appeared when he had drunk some of the poisoned brandy, how her heart had slammed furiously into her chest with fright as she realized what had taken place. It had been in that moment that she had cared nothing for what the *beau monde* would say. Her only concern had been for Lord Strickland. In fact, the more time she spent in his company, the more her concern for him grew.

"Recall that your father is present this evening, Juliet," Mrs. Grey murmured, and Juliet nodded. "He will expect to see you dancing."

"I will," Juliet promised. "Although I am sure he is only here for the game of cards that will take place later this evening." She glanced toward her companion, who could not hide her smile. "He has asked me about whether or not I have had any particular interest from any gentlemen of the *ton* although he did not appear to be all too eager to hear the answer." She smiled fondly at the thought of her father. "He does try to be interested, Mrs. Grey, but I believe he is quite certain that I shall make a decent match entirely without his help."

"For which we should be very grateful," Mrs. Grey replied firmly. "Else I do not think you would be at all able to help Lord Strickland as you are doing at present." Her eyes narrowed just a little as she studied Juliet. "Although it may yet turn out just as your father hopes."

Heat rose in Juliet's cheeks, but she did not answer her companion. It was clear that Mrs. Grey had hope, if not expectation, that Juliet might yet make a match with Lord Strickland and, try as she might, Juliet could not push such a thought away. They had only been acquainted for a short time, but in these last few days, there had grown the beginnings of an intimacy between them which Juliet could not deny.

"Now," Mrs. Grey continued briskly. "Let us consider how we are to introduce you to these two gentlemen. I, unfortunately, am not yet acquainted with either and thus—"

"Perhaps I could be of aid, then."

Juliet's blush deepened all the more as she turned to see Lord Strickland bowing toward them both. She dropped into a curtsy, lingering for a moment longer in the hope that her face would not be so red by the time she rose.

"Good evening, Lord Strickland," she murmured as he smiled at her. "You think to introduce me to Lord Redford and Lord Haverstock?"

"Indeed," he replied with a twinkle in his eye. "I cannot introduce both at once, of course, but perhaps one at this present moment and one later this evening? That would mean that there should be no difficulty in continuing an acquaintance with either."

Juliet nodded. "That would be most helpful, Lord Strickland," she answered as Mrs. Grey watched with a small smile spreading across her face. "We were only just wondering what we were to do in order to ensure an introduction."

Lord Strickland inclined his head. "Might I be so bold as to be the first to write my name upon your dance card, Lady Juliet?" he asked, surprising her. "I should not like to introduce you to Lord Redford without having taken at least one of your dances, else he will think it very strange indeed."

Quickly handing it to him, Juliet watched Lord Strickland closely as he wrote his name in two separate spaces. "You think the earl will wish to dance with me?" she asked as Lord Strickland handed it back to her. "Upon only our first introduction?"

"I fully expect him to ask you to dance within the first few moments," Lord Strickland laughed as he offered her his arm. "He is the most incorrigible flirt, I am afraid, although he means nothing by it. He is not a rogue or a scoundrel, but rather one who simply enjoys behaving in such a fashion with the young ladies of the *ton*. Thus, it was important for me to make certain that I stole the very best of dances from him, so that he could not take them from me."

She did not know what to say to this, finding his change in demeanor almost overwhelming. No longer was he pushing her back, frowning and shaking his head at even the thought of having a prolonged acquaintance with her. Rather, he was seemingly eager to have her in his company and was now speaking as though he wanted nothing more than to linger there. Was it an act? A staged performance, set out to ensure that both the earl and Viscount Haverstock were aware of his supposed interest in her, so that they might speak of him to her without hesitation? Or was there any truth within his actions?

"He is not too far," Lord Strickland murmured as Mrs. Grey fell into step beside Juliet. "I am sure he will catch my attention without me even attempting to speak to him. He is that sort of gentleman."

Juliet did not know what Lord Strickland meant, only to hear a loud voice calling his name, seeming to boom across toward them. Blinking in surprise, she looked up at Lord Strickland and saw him grin.

"It is as I have said, is it not?" he murmured to her, before turning toward a small group of guests who were, by now, all turning toward her.

"Lord Redford," Lord Strickland called as they approached. "Good evening. It is not like you to shout so loudly. Is something the matter?"

This made the earl laugh, his small eyes crinkling so much they looked almost entirely closed. He was a larger man than Lord Strickland, both taller and broader than he. The foppish clothes did not hide his paunch but there was a jolliness to his expression that warmed Juliet's heart toward him almost in an instant.

"I could not help but exclaim at the sight of you with a beautiful young lady on your arm," the earl said beaming, turning his gaze to Juliet. "Whatever have you done, my lady?"

Juliet did not know what he meant, stammering awkwardly as she tried to reply. "I—I have done nothing, my lord," she replied, only for Lord Redford to guffaw with laughter.

"You have done something, certainly," he said with a broad smile and a wink in her direction. "Do you not know that Lord Strickland has never once shown any interest in any young lady of the *ton*? And now here he is, walking with you through the ballroom. Most extraordinary."

Juliet blushed but Lord Strickland took the opportunity to

quickly make introductions, freeing Juliet's arm and allowing her to curtsy.

"I am *very* pleased to make your acquaintance," the earl said, still smiling at her. "I must ask if your dance card is available to me, Lady Juliet, for there must be something about you that has captured Lord Strickland so, and I have to discover it for myself."

"You are much too kind, Lord Redford, but I can assure you there is nothing at all such as you have described within me," she replied, slipping off her dance card and handing it to him. "Lord Strickland is merely being a gentleman, that is all."

Lord Redford did not appear to believe this, guffawing loudly as though he knew all too well that Juliet did not speak the truth. With a twinkle in his eye, he held her gaze for a moment before dropping his attention to her dance card.

"Now, you can hardly expect me to believe such a thing when I can see from this that Lord Strickland has taken the supper dance," he said, writing his name with a flourish. "Although I shall take your first waltz, if I may?"

She smiled at him, rather glad that Lord Strickland had warned her about Lord Redford's flirtatious nature. Was he the sort of gentleman who would want to injure Lord Strickland in some way? And if so, for what reason? The man seemed much too jolly to want to harm anyone and yet Juliet knew that such demeanors could be an outward appearance only. However, she had to admit that there was something very likeable about the gentleman, finding her smile remaining steady as he continued to speak.

"I look forward to dancing with you, Lady Juliet," he said with a small bow as he handed her back her dance card. "Although I shall confess to being rather jealous that Lord Strickland has stolen the supper dance from me."

"No doubt you will find many other young ladies willing to step forward and offer you *their* supper dance, Lord Redford," Lord Strickland answered dryly. "Just so that you are not too disappointed."

Lord Redford chuckled at this remark, no hint of malice or annoyance in his expression.

"I hope you have noticed the arrival of one Lady Ridgedale, Lord Strickland," Lord Redford said suddenly, the smile on his face beginning to fade as a new seriousness came into his eyes. "She has not spoken to you as yet?"

"No," Lord Strickland replied, a tightness coming into his expression, his lips flattening and his jaw working for a moment. "She has not greeted me, and I have no intention of doing so either."

Juliet did not know what to make of this, a little confused as to who Lady Ridgedale might be and why she appeared to be so entirely disagreeable to Lord Strickland. Keeping her questions to herself for the moment, she dropped her gaze to the floor, making sure to show no particular interest.

"That is a wise choice," came Lord Redford's reply. "I think much of the *ton* are a little wary of her and it would not do your reputation any good to be seen in her company."

"Given just how much she clearly dislikes me, I do not think that such a thing shall ever occur," Lord Strickland replied firmly. "But I thank you for your concern, Lord Redford."

Lord Redford nodded sagely. "But of course," he said, only for the music to strike up for the next dance, leaving him to turn bright eyes toward Juliet.

"Ah, it is our waltz, Lady Juliet," he stated, holding out one hand to her. "Shall we take to the floor?"

∽

Much to Juliet's relief, Lord Redford was an excellent dancer. She had no difficulty remaining in step with him and he appeared almost effortless, gliding around the floor with ease as he maintained a conversation with her.

"Lord Strickland did not tell me just how proficient a dancer you were," Lord Redford said with a broad smile on his face. "You must have many excellent qualities, I am sure."

Juliet laughed, becoming a little more used to the gentleman's many—and seemingly continuous—compliments.

"Lord Redford, there is merely an acquaintance between myself and Lord Strickland, I can assure you," she said warmly. "Besides which, I confess that I do not know the gentleman very well at all as yet." Keeping her smile in place, she tilted her head just a little as he twirled her around. "Is there anything untoward about him that I ought to know?"

Lord Redford chuckled, his hand holding hers a little more tightly. "Indeed there is not," he said with seeming honesty. "There is nothing that I can think of that would make Lord Strickland lacking in your eyes. You should take great pride in knowing that you are the first young lady he has ever shown any particular interest in, which speaks very highly of you, I am sure."

Again, he returns to complimenting me, Juliet thought to herself, a little irritated that he would not say anything more about Lord Strickland. "You are too kind, Lord Redford," she murmured as the dance came to a close. "Then there is nothing you would warn me of? Nothing that I might come to discover about Lord Strickland that would push me from him?" She sighed heavily as he bowed, curtsying beautifully toward him. "I should not like to continue in our acquaintance only to discover something much too late."

Lord Redford's smile faded and, to her relief, he appeared to be a good deal more serious. "Please, Lady Juliet," he said, offering her his arm so that they might return to Mrs. Grey, "have no fear. Lord Strickland is just as he appears. He is not a rogue or a scoundrel. He has nothing in his history that would bring you any sort of pain. In fact, I believe him to be one of the very best gentlemen of my acquaintance." Reaching across with his free hand, he patted hers gently as it rested on his arm, as though they were very old friends. "You need only to know how he behaved with Lady Ridgedale to be sure of that."

Juliet blinked, tilting her head up toward him. "I know nothing of Lady Ridgedale," she said in a slightly plaintive tone. "Is that someone of importance?"

Looking down at her, Lord Redford made to speak, only to stop himself and shake his head. "You must speak to Lord Strickland directly," he said firmly. "It is not my story to tell, but I can assure you, that he was more than wise in such an acquaintance."

"That is a relief to know," Juliet murmured, her mind filling with questions as to who this Lady Ridgedale might be and precisely why she was so important to Lord Strickland. "Thank you, Lord Redford."

He grinned at her, the twinkle back in his eyes almost at once. "It was wonderful to dance with you, Lady Juliet," he told her. "I do hope that I might have the pleasure of doing so again very soon."

THE SUPPER DANCE was quite wonderful. To be in Lord Strickland's arms seemed, to Juliet, to be the most delightful thing in all the world. It was not as though they had not danced before, but something had changed in their acquaintance—as well as within Juliet's own heart.

"Lord Redford said too much, then, and Lord Haverstock too little."

Juliet looked up into Lord Strickland's eyes and saw him frown, silently praying that anyone watching would not think that he was displeased with her dancing.

"Lord Haverstock danced the cotillion," she reminded him gently. "And there is not much opportunity to speak as one might do in the waltz."

The frown lifted just a fraction from Lord Strickland's face. "Of course," he said, his eyes turning back toward her as the corner of his mouth lifted. "I was expecting too much from the first meeting, I think."

Juliet searched his blue eyes, looking for any sign of discontent within them, worried that he had thought her something of a failure in her endeavors. But there was none there, and for that, she was grateful. Once more, she was struck by the handsomeness of his features for, when he smiled, his face transformed entirely. Light came into his eyes, his brows lifted, and there was no longer any heaviness about him. Juliet could not help but smile back in return.

"You were studying me," Lord Strickland murmured as the dance ended and he released her gently. "Is there something you wish to ask me?"

Juliet curtsied quickly, hoping to hide her embarrassment. She could not very well tell him that she had been thinking just how handsome he was, or just how much his expression changed when he smiled.

"Well?" he asked, a teasing note in his voice as he offered her his arm. "You will not say?"

A little frantic to find an answer, Juliet looked away. "It is only that I was thinking about Lord Redford," she said, scrambling to find any sort of explanation. "He spoke very highly of you." Lord Haverstock, on the other hand, had not said a word about Lord Strickland, although he had spoken well to both her and to Lord Strickland when it came to conversation. Mrs. Grey herself had thought both gentlemen to be just as she would have expected, although had remarked that a little more might come from either gentleman upon further acquaintance.

"Lord Redford speaks well of everyone," Lord Strickland remarked with a small smile. "He is known not to speak poorly of those he is acquainted with, unless they have, of course, behaved in such a poor way that the entirety of the *beau monde* recognizes it."

Juliet was about to ask whether or not Lady Ridgedale was one such person, only for Lord Strickland to offer her his arm and lead her on through to the refreshments in the dining room, where tables and chairs sat waiting for them. Mrs. Grey, ever present, remained nearby, sitting next to Juliet as Lord Strickland showed her to a table.

"If you will permit me?" he asked, and Juliet nodded her thanks as he poured them all some wine. Looking at the many dishes, he quickly served both Juliet and Mrs. Grey and then himself, whilst other guests joined them at the table. Juliet felt herself becoming quite contented with how the evening had gone. This was more than delightful for her, to be sitting in Lord Strickland's company and enjoying a pleasant meal and excellent conversation. The threat that surrounded Lord Strickland no longer seemed to be of great importance, no longer felt as significant, even though she knew it to be so. These few moments were more than a little satisfying and Juliet felt herself sigh with a renewed sense of happiness.

"If you will excuse me for a few minutes."

Lord Strickland sent her an apologetic smile and rose from the table. Thinking nothing of it—for it was not the done thing to give a reason to excuse oneself—Juliet turned to Mrs. Grey and continued their conversation.

"The only other gentleman we must introduce ourselves to, if we can, is Lord Brookmire," Mrs. Grey remarked with a lift of one eyebrow. "I am aware that Lord Strickland is not acquainted with him in any way, but it might well be wise to be introduced to him regardless."

"Indeed," Juliet agreed thoughtfully. "Although it would seem very strange to me to have a gentleman eager to bring pain and suffering to Lord Strickland if he is not even acquainted with him. What purpose would he have?"

Mrs. Grey frowned, taking a small sip of her wine before setting it back down. "From what you said, it appears that the gentleman in question, whoever he might be, is doing all of this at the behest of a lady of the *ton*," she said slowly. "What if there is some sort of agreement between that lady and himself? Might it be then that he is hoping to receive some sort of benefit from her rather than having anything specific against Lord Strickland himself?"

A loud, raucous laugh caught Juliet's attention before she could answer and, turning her head, she saw Lord Redford guffawing loudly at some remark another at his table had made. Lord Haverstock sat near to him and there was nothing akin to enjoyment on his face but rather a look of tired acceptance. With a small, knowing smile, she turned back to Mrs. Grey. "That is a wise suggestion," she admitted as Lord Redford finally subsided. "I do wonder if—"

"Lady Juliet?"

A footman came toward them, bowing quickly but speaking with such sharpness that Juliet was a little taken aback.

"If you and Mrs. Grey would join me at once, Lord Strickland is in need of your assistance," the footman said quietly, so that none of the other guests would overhear. "This way."

There was not any suggestion as to what particular assistance Lord Strickland required but Juliet, with a glance toward Mrs. Grey, rose quickly and followed the footman, noting, with dismay, that Lord and Lady Richmond were following after them.

"Do you know what is the matter?" Lady Richmond asked as she fell into step beside Juliet. "What has happened to Lord Strickland?"

"He has fallen down the staircase," the footman replied, turning toward them for a moment, clearly having overheard their conversation. "I directed him to the gentleman's retiring room and I believe an incident occurred as he made to return to the drawing room."

Juliet's heart began to pound as she stared at the footman, with Lady Richmond's hand tightening on her arm. She could not take another step forward, suddenly dreadfully afraid of what she would find.

"Is he badly injured?" Lord Richmond demanded, one hand slipping around his wife's waist as they all came to a stop, horrified to hear such news. "Whatever happened?"

"He has asked for us," Mrs. Grey said quietly, "so he must be at least conscious."

The footman nodded. "I think it would be best if you spoke to him yourself, my lord," he said, clearly eager to hurry them along. "He was most specific and demanded that I did not inform my master of his injuries either."

"Then let us hurry at once!" Juliet exclaimed, her legs weak but her eagerness to see Lord Strickland for herself growing within her. "Please." She gestured for the footman to lead them on and, with a swift nod, he turned and continued walking along the hallway back in the direction of the ballroom. Her heart in her throat, Juliet hurried after him, her mind filled with dread as she wondered in just what state they would find Lord Strickland.

10

Making his way from the retiring room, Duncan allowed himself a small smile as he thought of returning to Lady Juliet. She was, much to his surprise, becoming more and more important to him with every moment spent together, to the point that he was struggling to even consider what his life would be like without her company. But that was within his future, he supposed, for given that his acquaintance with Lady Juliet had come about simply because of what she had overheard and her seeming eagerness to do all she could to help him, it was reasonable to expect that their acquaintance would fade once the matter was at an end. Was that something he wanted? Musing to himself, Duncan did not see a shadow suddenly step out from behind him, did not feel the hands pushing hard at him until it was almost too late.

He reacted at once. One hand shot out, his body twisting as he flailed backwards, trying to find something—anything—to hold onto. His hand grasped onto clothing and he managed to pull himself forward, with the fellow behind him gasping for breath as they fought.

"Unhand me!" Duncan exclaimed, his voice echoing through

the otherwise empty hallway, but there was no immediate effect. The man snarled, his face and expression a blur as Duncan fought to regain control. Pain shot through Duncan's stomach as the man punched him hard, one leg slipping down onto the first stair and his ankle twisting painfully.

"You may have escaped thrice, Strickland, but you will not escape again."

With a hard shove, the man freed himself from Duncan's grasp and pushed him back, hard. With a cry, Duncan found himself stumbling forward, hurtling down the staircase without managing to catch himself. His hands flew out in front of him, but it was not enough to stop him from falling, finding almost every part of his body burning with pain as he tumbled to the floor.

"My lord!"

A voice drew near to him as Duncan tried to recover himself, realizing, dazedly, that he was no longer falling. Everything ached, his head pounding furiously as he tried to breathe at a steady pace, making every attempt to work out where he was.

"Did you fall?" said the voice, a gentle hand settling upon his shoulder. "Can you rise, my lord? I will fetch another footman to be of assistance to you."

Realizing that it was a footman, Duncan slowly attempted to sit up, finding his head aching all the more as he lifted it from the cold floor, his arms shaking slightly as he did so. It took a great deal of effort but, eventually, he was able to stand. Another footman joined them, helping Duncan to make his way across the hallway as he fought to clear his vision. He could not put his full weight on his right leg, his ankle still burning painfully.

"There is a small parlor here, my lord," said the first footman, sounding more than a little anxious. The two footmen helped him into the room, settling him into a chair although Duncan could not help but groan as he sat down. The second footman hurried around the room, lighting candles and wondering aloud whether or not they ought to light a fire in order to keep Duncan warm. Duncan closed his eyes and murmured no, leaving both footmen to look at each other, wondering what they were to do next.

"Shall I send for a doctor?" said the first as Duncan opened his eyes. "I should also inform the master, I—"

"Do not do so," Duncan bit out, hardly able to speak, such was the pain coursing through him. "I must see Lord and Lady Richmond, and Lady Juliet also."

The second footman hurried off the moment Duncan had finished speaking, leaving the first to continue to question what he could bring and what he could do for Duncan. Reiterating that there was no need to bother the master of the house and stating that a whisky would suit him very well indeed, Duncan placed his head back against the chair and let out a long breath, trying to unsuccessfully blow away some of his pain. The footman pressed a whisky into his hand and then stood there anxiously, clearly very concerned for Duncan's health.

You may have escaped thrice.

The words the man had shouted before he had successfully managed to throw Duncan down the staircase echoed around his mind. Three times? That made very little sense to him, for he could only recall the time he had avoided the object thrown at him and thereafter, the incident with the poisoned brandy. What could have been the third?

"Lord Strickland!"

The door to the parlor flew open and four figures hurried in one after the other.

"Lord Strickland, are you quite all right?" Lady Juliet cried, hurrying toward him, her eyes wide with fright. "You fell down the staircase?"

Lord and Lady Richmond were just behind her, their faces etched with worry.

"I did not fall," Duncan replied, shifting his weight from one side of the chair to the other, wincing as he did so. "I was pushed."

A gasp of astonishment pulled itself from the assembled group as the two footmen stood by the door, glancing at each other.

"You saw the person in question?" Lord Richmond demanded before turning on his heel to look at the two footmen. "Did either of you?"

Duncan closed his eyes and took in another long breath, very aware of the pain that was beginning to settle in his ribs, his ankle, and the side of his head. "I did not," he replied heavily. "I was taken by surprise and in the struggle, did not see the gentleman's face clearly."

"I saw nothing, my lord," the first footman replied, his eyes flaring with obvious fright. "I heard a commotion and hurried to the bottom of the staircase, where I saw Lord...Lord..."

"Lord Strickland," Lady Richmond reminded him and the footman nodded, gesturing toward Duncan.

"I saw Lord Strickland lying at the bottom of the staircase but neither heard nor saw anything more."

Duncan, who had expected as much, nodded carefully so that he would not compound the pain in his head. "I did not think there was anyone else present," he said as Lady Juliet dropped into a chair, Mrs. Grey following suit. "This gentleman, whoever he was, remained above stairs once I had fallen. I am sure he has returned to the ball now."

Lady Juliet closed her eyes and ran one hand over her forehead, clearly distraught. "It could not have been Lord Redford or Lord Haverstock," she said quietly as Lady Richmond sent the footmen away for something to eat and drink for them all, given that they had been required to leave the dining room so quickly. "They were both sitting near to us during your absence."

Duncan held her gaze, seeing the paleness of her cheeks and wondering just how he appeared at present. "Then we have only one gentleman left to consider," he said somberly, glad that both footmen had left the room so that he might speak openly. "A gentleman that I do not know and have never once been acquainted with."

Lady Juliet nodded as Lord and Lady Richmond sat down, their faces still etched with concern.

"Viscount Brookmire," Mrs. Grey murmured as Lady Richmond nodded. "I do wonder, Lord Strickland, if it is not Lord Brookmire's dislike of you—for whatever reason—that presses him into action, but rather the lady's promise of reward."

"It very well may be," Duncan agreed heavily, feeling his heart quail just a little. There was so much that he did not understand, so much that he could not make sense of, and it felt as though he was on the threshold of a great and terrible danger that he could not fully anticipate. "Whilst I will not go into the details of what occurred, what I will mention is that this particular fellow, whoever he is, shouted something about my escaping from him *three* times, along with the promise that I should not manage a fourth time."

Lord Richmond let out a hard laugh. "Then it seems you have proved him wrong," he said with a grimace. "But three times?"

Lady Juliet caught her breath. "The highwaymen," she spoke as everyone turned toward her. "I did wonder if there was something more to the fact that you and I had both come to London on the same day, having both seen the efforts of the highwaymen, as well as the fact that they attempted to attack your carriage but, being unsuccessful, did not linger to attempt another upon my carriage also."

A frown creased Duncan's brow, bringing with it a fresh stab of pain. "You mean to say that you believe the highwaymen sought only me?" he asked doubtfully. "That cannot be so, given what occurred to the unfortunate souls that your father discovered."

This brought a look of confusion to Lady Juliet's expression, her eyes narrowing for a moment as she looked at the floor, her lip caught between her teeth.

"Perhaps there is something of more significance to that strange letter than we have first thought," Lord Richmond suggested. "You are to study it tomorrow, are you not?"

"I am," Duncan replied, hardly daring to hope that such a thing might be. "Although quite what I am to discover from it, I cannot imagine given that Lady Juliet has already studied it at length."

Lady Juliet took in a deep breath and let it out slowly, her eyes still flickering from one place to the next, apparently still struggling to connect what had been said by the man who had attacked Duncan with what she now believed.

"I should return home," Duncan said, trying to shift himself out of the chair and finding the pain too great to move too much. Embarrassment raced through him as he reached for his brandy, clearing his throat awkwardly. "I do not think it is necessary to alert Lord Whittaker to what has happened, however."

"I have sent for refreshments to be brought," Lady Richmond reminded him. "I think it would be best if you ate something before you even *try* to make your way to your carriage."

Duncan hesitated, then nodded. "Very well," he agreed, aware that there was now a slight tremble taking a hold of his frame as he sank back into the chair. "I will wait."

As though they had been waiting for him to say such a thing, the door opened and the two footmen returned, laden with refreshments which they set down carefully for the small, assembled group.

"What else might we fetch for you, Lord Strickland?" one asked as they stood to attention. "What is it that you require?"

"I would like to know if Viscount Brookmire is present this evening," Duncan replied, and the two footmen glanced at each other. "That is all I need at present." He gave them both a curt nod. "You will have plenty of other duties this evening and I will be quite recovered in a short while, I am sure of it. Pray do not feel the need to linger or to inform Lord Whittaker of this situation. There is no need to trouble him given that the rest of the evening has gone as well as it has."

The two footmen nodded, promised that one of them would return with news about Lord Brookmire, and then swiftly departed, leaving Duncan to look around the room at the others, seeing their severe expressions.

"Then it must be Lord Brookmire," Lord Richmond said heavily. "And the highwaymen must have been the first attempt to injure you."

"It may not even have been highwaymen," Lady Juliet murmured, tilting her head and looking at him with questions burning in her eyes. "It could have been a mere pretense, set up to appear as though it were such a thing but intent solely on injuring you."

Mrs. Grey cleared her throat gently, catching their attention. "It may very well be that they wished to remove your life from this world entirely, Lord Strickland," she said as the others simply sat quietly, in obvious agreement. "You must take a great deal more care now, I believe. If you had fallen harder, if you had…" She trailed off and looked away, her face pale. "It could have been a great deal worse."

"But it was not," he answered, refusing to let any fear take a hold of his heart. "And whilst I will not be grateful for the pain that now lingers, I am glad that there is now very little doubt as to which gentleman it was that attempted such a thing."

"Lord Brookmire," Lady Juliet murmured as everyone else nodded. "Then, if we are aware of it, the question now comes as to what we are to do next?"

Duncan's lips twisted. "Indeed, Lady Juliet," he agreed softly. "Just what are we to do?"

∼

THE FOLLOWING AFTERNOON, Duncan's ankle was a little better, but he was still unable to walk without support. The rest of his body burned with pain no matter how he sat or stood. It had been difficult to rise from his bed and to have to request help from his staff had been somewhat embarrassing. However, after dressing and eating a hearty breakfast, he felt a good deal better.

You have escaped thrice.

Those words had not left him. They had been spoken with anger and vehemence, making him realize—as Mrs. Grey had said herself—that he was in a good deal more danger than he had ever anticipated. Lord Brookmire, if it was he who was doing such things, appeared to be more than a little furious that Duncan had thus far managed to escape from severe injury—or worse. That thought had been a sobering one. If his life was to be taken from him, then what was the purpose behind it? His cousin was the one who would take the title and Duncan was more than certain that there was no such dark vehemence within the man.

Unless I have been mistaken about that, he mused to himself, sitting down rather heavily in an overstuffed chair in the drawing room, letting his body relax against the cushions. The footman set out a stool for his ankle and Duncan nodded to him, gesturing to him that he might leave him now. Closing his eyes, he let his mind return to his cousin. Did he know him so little? Was there a hidden eagerness within him that would go so far as to take Duncan's life from him simply to gain the title? Try as he might, Duncan simply could not find it in his heart to believe it.

"My lord, you have visitors."

Duncan did not even open his eyes. "Of course," he murmured, trying to find the strength to push himself to his feet. "Show them in at once." With an effort, he opened his eyes and put his hands on the arms of the chair, about to attempt to push himself to his feet, when Lady Juliet stepped into the room and let out a startled exclamation.

"Lord Strickland, pray do not," she said, hurrying toward him. "You are still in pain, are you not?"

Gratefully, Duncan sank back down into his chair as Mrs. Grey and Lord and Lady Richmond came in after Lady Juliet. "You can tell as much simply by looking at me, Lady Juliet?" he asked, a small smile tugging at his lips. "Do I truly look that terrible?"

Lady Juliet hesitated, then smiled, although her eyes still lingered on him. "You are a little grey," she answered honestly. "And the way you set your jaw made it quite apparent that you were in a little difficulty." She sat down, smoothing her skirts as she did so. "Besides which, there is no need for any ceremony," she finished. "Not when we know what you have endured."

"Indeed," Lord Richmond muttered, tilting his head as he looked at Duncan. "You are a little recovered, at least?"

"I am still in some pain, but I can walk, at least," Duncan replied with a wry smile. "Although I thank you for your assistance last evening, Lord Richmond." Lord Richmond had been required to help Duncan to his carriage, which had been most embarrassing, but, much to Duncan's relief, had been achieved without either of them being spotted by any other guests.

Lord Richmond waved a hand, dismissing Duncan's thanks. "Now, this letter, Lady Juliet," he said as maids came in to set out tea and cakes for them all. "Did you bring it with you?"

Lady Juliet nodded and quickly extracted it from her person. "Here," she said, glancing from Duncan to Lord Richmond, as though uncertain as to whom she was to give it to. "As I have said, there is nothing within it."

Seeing Lord Richmond gesture that she ought to give to Duncan rather than to himself, Duncan again attempted to rise so that Lady Juliet would not have to do so, only for her to hurry across to him in a flurry of skirts, a sharp look in her eye. With a murmur of thanks, Duncan took it and then sat back down, whilst Lady Juliet asked if she might pour the tea. With a nod, Duncan looked down at the letter, seeing the flecks of blood that stained the outside. His stomach turned over. It was not that the blood itself made him feel so, but rather the thought of what had happened in order for it to occur in the first place. Grimacing, he turned it over and saw the broken seal, lifting it first and then spreading the letter out.

It was just as Lady Juliet had said. There was nothing written there, nothing that he could see at all. His heart sank. Whilst he had known that Lady Juliet had stated very clearly that there were no words written there, part of him had hoped that there would be something present that he could distinguish, something that she had missed.

But there was not.

"Might I?" Lord Richmond asked, getting up to take the letter from Duncan's outstretched hand. "There is nothing there, then?"

"Nothing," Duncan replied heavily, before smiling gratefully at Lady Juliet as she set a teacup on the small table beside him. "It is exactly as Lady Juliet has said."

"Which is to be expected," Lady Richmond said dryly. "Were you hoping for something else, Lord Strickland?"

Duncan allowed a heavy sigh to pass through his lips. "I do not know what I was hoping for, Lady Richmond," he said honestly. "To know that the highwaymen were not merely a group of men set on doing harm to anyone they could but, instead, that they were present solely to bring harm to me has made my mind and heart very heavy indeed."

"I can well understand that," Lady Richmond answered gently. "It is very strange that one of the men in the carriage before you was attacked in such a cruel fashion, however, if they were only waiting for you."

"Perhaps it was meant to be proof that they *were* highwaymen," Lady Juliet suggested with a frown. "Although we shall know more soon, I hope."

Duncan's brows rose. "Oh?"

"My father has been in correspondence with a Mr. Johnson," she said, by way of explanation. "It is he who has been taking care of the third man we found, who was, I believe, barely alive when they found him." Her lips turned downwards, her eyes glistening as memories returned to her. "He was also responsible for burying the two others."

"A good man," Lord Richmond rumbled as Duncan nodded. "And you say that he has been in correspondence with your father?"

"Yes, that is so," Lady Juliet replied with a small, sad smile. "My father was greatly troubled by what we discovered and has, I believe, been quite hopeful that the third man, whoever he is, will recover to the point of being able to not only say what occurred but perhaps describe those who attacked him. The letter was on his person also, although my father is unaware that I have it still. I know that my father wishes to know the moment the unfortunate soul is able to speak without restraint or difficulty."

A new admiration rose in Duncan's chest for Lord Lansbury. "That is very good of your father."

"Mr. Johnson wrote only this morning to state that the man has begun to recover somewhat," Lady Juliet continued, sounding quite relieved. "He was, for some time, between life and death and we were not certain that he would recover. But now, it seems, that he is well on the way to recovery and will soon be able to tell us a little more, once he has recovered his strength."

Duncan nodded slowly, rubbing his chin for a moment. "Then we might be able to discover something more about these highwaymen very soon," he said hopefully. "I cannot be certain whether or not this man's description of those who attacked him will bring anything more to light, but we can certainly make sense of why he was carrying such a strange letter."

"Might I ask if there is knowledge of this man's name?" Lady Richmond asked, and Lady Juliet began to frown hard, looking toward Mrs. Grey. "I presume he was so grievously injured that, as yet, he has been unable to say more than a word or two."

"I—I believe he did," Lady Juliet said slowly as Mrs. Grey nodded. "My father told me of it this morning. I cannot be certain, but I believe it was one Mr. Ayles?" She looked again to Mrs. Grey, who twisted her lips for a moment and then confirmed it.

"Yes, I believe that was correct," she said quietly. "A Mr. Ayles. We know nothing more, however. The poor fellow has been unable to say more than a word or two, apparently, given his lack of strength."

Duncan stared at Lady Juliet, his heart thundering furiously as he felt all of his strength beginning to drain from him. It could not be. It could not be.

"Lord Strickland?"

Lady Juliet was watching him now, her brow furrowing as she

leaned forward in her chair, looking at him carefully, clearly aware that there was something troubling him.

"Is something wrong, Strickland?" Lord Richmond asked as Lady Richmond and Mrs. Grey looked on, clearly perplexed. "You look as though you have had a great shock."

Duncan closed his eyes and forced himself to speak. "You said a Mr. Ayles, Lady Juliet?" he asked, opening his eyes to see her nodding, her blue eyes wide with astonishment. "Are you quite certain?"

"I believe I am, yes," she replied anxiously. "Why, Lord Strickland? Is that man known to you?"

Nodding, Duncan felt an ache rise in his heart, horrified to realize that the man who was now recovering from a great and severe attack was, in fact, well known to him.

"Mr. Ayles, if it is one and the same, is my cousin," he said slowly, aware of the gasps of astonishment that came from almost every quarter. "Mr. and Mrs. Ayles live in the country, in a very pretty little house. Mr. Ayles has excellent employment and both he and I have kept in correspondence over the years, although it is not entirely regular." He shook his head, reaching for his teacup as though that might help push aside his shock a little more. "My own cousin. I—I cannot imagine..." Swallowing hard, he looked up at them all. "I must go to him at once."

There was a short silence before Lord Richmond spoke up, shaking his head. "You cannot, Strickland, not when you are still recovering yourself," he said decisively. "Believe me, I well understand the desire to go at once, but if he is only just able to speak a few words, then he will not have the strength for some days to enter into conversation."

Lady Juliet nodded. "Mr. Johnson is doing all he can for him," she said earnestly. "He will write to my father the moment that there is any improvement. I am sure it will be only a few days—perhaps a sennight—before things will improve."

Duncan shook his head, ignoring the stab of pain that flashed through his head. "I must go at once."

"You cannot," Lord Richmond said sharply. "You must recover first, Strickland."

"And I am sure that Lord Brookmire believes that he is gone from this world," Lady Richmond said gently. "There is no immediate threat."

Lowering his head for a moment, Duncan passed one hand over his eyes. He was battling hard against the desire to call for his carriage and to leave at once, discovering the location of where his cousin was from Lady Juliet herself. And yet, given that he was struggling with a good deal of pain still, he knew in his heart that it was wise for him to wait.

"What if Lord Brookmire hears that my cousin is recovering?" he asked hoarsely, looking up at them all. "The letter too—why was my cousin carrying such a thing? Who was it for? What might it mean?"

There was no immediate answer. His friends looked back at him with a gentle frown on each of their faces. They could not give him the responses he sought, could not tell him what he wanted to know.

"We will hear from Mr. Ayles himself very soon, I am sure," Lady Juliet said gently, clearly trying to encourage him. "He will be able to give you the answers you seek."

"And in the meantime?" Duncan asked, speaking more sharply than he had intended. "What am I to do? Sit here and recover whilst I worry about my cousin?" Squeezing his eyes closed, he ran one hand across his forehead. "What of his wife? His children? Are they now living alone, uncertain and afraid as to where he is gone?"

"I cannot answer that," Lord Richmond said quietly. "And by all means, write to her if you wish it, but I cannot advise that you travel when you are still recovering. Lady Juliet will tell us the moment news comes from Mr. Johnson and we will travel together to speak to your cousin."

"Or even have him brought to London, if he is well enough," Lady Juliet suggested, and Duncan let out a quiet groan, wishing that he was just as strong and able as he usually was. Had he not been thrown down the staircase last evening, then he would have been able to walk without difficulty and could have traveled to see Ayles without hesitation.

"Very well," he said eventually. "But there must be something more we can do in the meantime."

"Of course there is," Lady Juliet said firmly. "I will be introducing myself to Lord Brookmire."

Duncan's eyes flew to hers, a protest burning on his lips.

"I am aware that you will tell me there is a danger in acquainting myself with him, but it will be quite all right," Lady Juliet continued, sounding quite determined. "It may be that something he says or someone he is acquainted with will catch my attention."

"And I will be with her, of course," Mrs. Grey added as Lord and Lady Richmond nodded.

Letting out a long breath, Duncan spread his hands. "It seems it is all agreed on, then," he said without any sense of contentment. "I am merely to stay here and do what I can to recover in the meantime."

Lady Juliet smiled at him gently. "You may use your time to consider the letter," she suggested, as though she could see his frustration and wanted to help. "There is mayhap a secret there that the rest of us have not yet discovered."

With a twist of his lips, Duncan nodded. "Very well," he said as the others looked on with evident relief in all of their expressions. "And you will inform me the moment your father receives word from Mr. Johnson?"

With a nod, Lady Juliet held his gaze. "Of course, Lord Strickland," she said. "Of course I will."

11

"How very good to meet you." The knot of anxiety that had settled in Juliet's chest did not depart from her but rather grew in strength as she curtsied, lifting her gaze to Lord Brookmire as she forced a smile to her lips. Lord Brookmire appeared to be rather bored with such an introduction, for he did not show any particular interest in greeting her and there was not even a pleasant smile on his face as she looked back at him.

"And are you in London for the Season, Lord Brookmire?" she asked as the other guests around her quietly kept to their own conversations. "Or do you intend to go elsewhere during these months? I have heard that Bath is quite lovely during the summer and some of the *ton* make their way there."

Lord Brookmire's lip curled as though she had asked the most ridiculous question. "Of course I shall remain in London," he said as Lady Thornton stood by Juliet's side, having been the one to introduce them both. "There is much more enjoyment to be found in London than in Bath." He snorted, his eyes flashing with what appeared to be a good deal of mirth. Mirth that came at Juliet's expense.

Instantly, Juliet felt a swell of dislike rise in her chest, but she forced her expression to remain entirely devoid of such a feeling.

"Then you must tell me what you enjoy the most about London, Lord Brookmire," she said, desperately hoping to find a way to continue the conversation despite his apparent boredom at being introduced to her. "I confess that I very much enjoy the theater, although I have not been very often."

Lord Brookmire let out a long and heavy sigh, as though he was greatly irritated with her conversation already. "The theater is pleasant enough," he said with a wry smile. "But there is often very poor company to be found there." He eyed her in a most unpleasant manner and Juliet found her anger beginning to burn. Whatever he was trying to imply, it was not anything kind.

You must do what you can, for Lord Strickland's sake.

Steeling herself, she put a small smile on her face and kept her voice light. "Then might I ask, Lord Brookmire, what occasions do you consider hold the best company?"

This question appeared to intrigue him and, much to Juliet's relief, he stood silently for a few moments with an evident attempt to think of an answer.

"I suppose I should say a dinner party," he replied eventually. "For then one can choose one's company directly and not be forced into conversation with those one would rather avoid."

Rather than abating her frustration with his reply, Lord Brookmire's response only added to it. Juliet clenched her hands hard, the nails cutting into her skin as she forced herself to remain precisely where she was, and held back the sharp response she wanted to fling at him. Whether or not he was being deliberately rude, she did not know, but there was nothing about this gentleman that made her want to remain in his company for even a moment longer. She could not think of anything to say, her mind filled with nothing but anger as she looked up at him, seeing the arrogant smile on his face, as though he knew the precise effect he was having upon her.

"Oh, you must excuse me," Lady Thornton cried, cutting

through the growing tension between Juliet and Lord Brookmire. "I must go and speak to Lady Sheffield."

"But of course," Mrs. Grey murmured as Juliet managed to smile and thank her, seeing the dark glance that was sent Lord Brookmire's way and finding herself rather satisfied that Lady Thornton was just as displeased with him as she was herself. Clearing her throat gently and wondering just how she was to turn the conversation to Lord Strickland, Juliet tilted her head and studied the gentleman again, relieved that she had managed to take the edge off her anger.

"And might I ask—" she began, only for a tall, slender lady dressed in a dark blue gown to walk past Juliet and stand directly in front of Lord Brookmire, greeting him as though Juliet and Mrs. Grey were not present.

"Lord Brookmire," she heard the lady say. "Good evening." Her words were sharp, tense—like fiery darts that were being flung one after the other. "Might I ask what occurred last evening? I thought that you—"

"It appears I am to take my leave," Juliet said loudly, not allowing the lady's rudeness to simply interrupt her in such a fashion. "Do excuse us, Lord Brookmire."

She made to turn away, but then the lady in question turned her head sharply and looked at her directly. A coldness about her pierced Juliet instantly, and even when the lady smiled there was no flicker of warmth in her gaze.

"Do excuse me," she uttered with a false brightness, as though she had only just realized what she had done. "You were in conversation with Lord Brookmire, were you not? Forgive me, my dear, I was not even aware."

Juliet did not know what to say to this, for surely the lady would have noticed the two ladies that stood directly in front of Lord Brookmire.

Lord Brookmire cleared his throat. "Might I introduce Lady Juliet, daughter to the Earl of Lansbury," he said quickly, as though eager to have such a conversation ended as he gestured to the lady. "And Lady Ridgedale."

Finding the introduction rather abrupt, Juliet hesitated for a moment before curtsying quickly. "How very good to meet you," she murmured, a little awkwardly. "Pray, excuse me. Our conversation was almost at an end."

Lady Ridgedale laughed and shook her head, although Juliet did not miss the coldness that lingered in the lady's eyes. "Nay, it was nothing of importance," she said, turning a little more toward Lord Brookmire. "A foolish matter, truly."

Mrs. Grey touched Juliet's elbow, murmuring something to her, and Juliet, grateful for the excuse, simply shook her head. "I must excuse myself," she said quietly. "I do hope you both enjoy the rest of the evening." She turned to her chaperone, who led her across the room, making certain not to even glance back at Lord Brookmire and Lady Ridgedale. Her irritation at their behavior, her anger at Lord Brookmire's rudeness, and her intense dislike of their characters rolled up into a tight ball within her, her breathing faster than usual and her hands still curled up into fists.

"You did very well, my dear," Mrs. Grey murmured as they came into the company of Lord and Lady Richmond, who were both talking to another young lady and her mother. Juliet remained to one side for a few moments with Mrs. Grey, making certain not to interrupt the conversation but rather to wait until there was an opportune moment for her to join them. It also gave her the chance to calm herself somewhat, to take in long breaths and to let her hands relax as she blew out some of her ire.

"They were both exceptionally rude," she said, only just managing to keep her voice low as Mrs. Grey nodded, clearly just as unhappy as she at the behavior exhibited by Lord Brookmire and Lady Ridgedale.

"Quite what Lady Ridgedale thought she was doing by interrupting us both in such a manner, I cannot imagine," Mrs. Grey huffed. "And to pretend that she did not even realize we were speaking to Lord Brookmire is utter nonsense, I am sure."

"Indeed," Juliet replied as Lord and Lady Richmond ended their conversation and came quickly to join Juliet and Mrs. Grey. "I found myself most upset with them both."

A smile settled upon Lord Richmond's face as he approached, evidently overhearing her. "You have been upset by something, Lady Juliet?" he asked as Lady Richmond's face filled with concern. "Then let both my wife and me restore your good spirits."

Juliet found herself smiling despite herself. "You are both very kind," she said honestly. "Lord Brookmire, on the other hand, was one of the rudest gentlemen I believe I have ever met. His manner and his conversation were both ill-judged and rather insulting at times."

"Only for us then to be interrupted by another lady, who came to stand directly in front of Juliet in order to speak to Lord Brookmire," Mrs. Grey said with a shake of her head. "Can you imagine it? She claimed she did not see us both, but I can hardly believe that."

Lady Richmond laughed and settled a hand on Juliet's arm for a moment in a comforting gesture. "That does sound quite awful. I presume Lord Brookmire said nothing about Lord Strickland?"

"I did not even manage to mention him," Juliet replied with a sigh. "Lord Brookmire was clearly entirely unwilling to speak with me for long, although I must say he appeared more than eager to converse with Lady Ridgedale."

The moment she mentioned Lady Ridgedale's name, the smiles fell from both Lord and Lady Richmond's faces. With a quick glance toward each other, they then turned back to Juliet, who was looking at them with great confusion as to why they appeared so altered.

"Did you state that Lady Ridgedale was in conversation with Lord Brookmire?" Lord Richmond asked, a dark frown coursing across his brow. "That they appeared to know each other?"

"There was not any need for introduction, if that is what you mean," Juliet replied, still not fully understanding why they appeared to be so interested in Lady Ridgedale. "I thought her most discourteous, however, for as was said, she simply strode in front of Lord Brookmire and spoke to him as though Mrs. Grey and I were not present."

"Goodness," Lady Richmond murmured, looking at her husband with wide eyes. "We should inform Lord Strickland of this at once."

Juliet frowned, then looked to Mrs. Grey before returning her gaze to the Richmonds. "I do not understand," she said, spreading her hands. "Lady Ridgedale's connection to Lord Brookmire is worthy of note?"

Lord Richmond nodded. "Indeed it is," he said quietly, his eyes sliding from the right to the left and then back again, as though he was afraid of who might overhear him.

"It has not been just young ladies that have sought out Lord Strickland's attention, you understand," Lady Richmond said delicately, and Juliet quickly realized what she meant, a swirl of embarrassment heating her cheeks. "Lady Ridgedale was also very interested in a...connection of sorts, even though she was wed to Lord Ridgedale."

"I see," Juliet replied, wishing the color would dissipate from her face. "Is Lord Ridgedale not a wealthy gentleman?"

Lord and Lady Richmond exchanged glances.

"He *was* a wealthy gentleman," Lord Richmond replied quietly. "Lady Ridgedale is now a widow. When he was alive, I believe he was not overly generous toward his wife and Lady Ridgedale chafed against such restraints. Therefore, she sought out an intimacy with Lord Strickland in the hope that he would give her what she wished for the most—some wealth of her own."

"Whether that be in jewelry, in gifts, or in other small favors," Lady Richmond added quickly. "Lord Strickland, of course, refused to even countenance such a thing."

"Which," Juliet interrupted, realizing the reason for their interest, "did not please Lady Ridgedale at all."

Lady Richmond nodded. "I believe she was very angry and deeply frustrated," she said quietly. "I know that the rumor is that she has gained a good deal of wealth from her husband's passing, for it seems that he made provision for her in his will."

"Meaning that she has no need to make any sort of connection with Lord Strickland—or any other," Juliet added slowly, to which Lord and Lady Richmond nodded. "She has the wealth she now requires." Her frown deepened again as she saw the same discontent flickering in Lady Richmond's eyes. "Yet you believe that there might be something of importance in her acquaintance with Lord Brookmire?"

Lord Richmond let out a long breath. "It may very well mean nothing, but it does interest me that there is a connection between her and Lord Brookmire," he said with a small shrug. "She was, as I have said, very angry and upset with Lord Strickland for refusing to give in to her supposed charms and, in his refusal, denying her what she so desperately wanted from him."

A note of fear struck Juliet's heart. "And do you believe that she might have held onto such anger?" she asked, and Lady Richmond began to nod. "And that, in all that she felt, she then decided to punish Lord Strickland in some way?"

There was silence for a moment as Lord and Lady Richmond considered her question. Then, with a small sigh, Lord Richmond spread his hands. "It is a possibility," he conceded, "and not one that I have considered before when, in fact, I should have done. Lady Ridgedale is a vindictive, spiteful creature who has no regard for the opinions or considerations of others."

"And she has the wealth to ensure that it is not she who is involved in any way," Lady Richmond added. "If Lord Brookmire has been promised something from her, whether that be payment in either coin or favors, then he is the one responsible for attempting to injure Lord Strickland. But behind it may well be Lady Ridgedale."

Juliet took in a long breath, feeling herself shudder, her eyes closing tightly as she fought to control the panic that suddenly took a hold of her. She had been so close to Lady Ridgedale, so near to the very person that might be the one responsible for all that had happened to Lord Strickland. "Then what do we do?" she asked, opening her eyes to see Lord Richmond frowning darkly. "Might we speak to her this evening?"

"I do not think that would be wise," Mrs. Grey said, speaking for what was the first time. "You ought not to do such a thing, Juliet, for fear of arousing her suspicion. After all, it was quite clear to her that we thought her most improper in her manner. She will not expect us to return to her company again."

"It may very well be that such an outcome is precisely what she wanted," Lord Richmond replied grimly. "We can do nothing this evening. We must speak to Lord Strickland and, thereafter, decide what it is we shall do."

"I would agree," Lady Richmond said, with Juliet feeling it best to do whatever they considered right, given just how much they knew compared to her. "And the sooner he knows, the better."

Juliet pressed her lips together and darted a quick look toward Mrs. Grey. There was a rather bold suggestion in her mind and whether or not she dared to speak it aloud, she was not yet sure. Would Mrs. Grey concur? Or would she be upset at such an idea?

"Might I suggest," she began, choosing her words with great care and finding her heart quickening just a little, "that if it is of such great urgency, we take our leave from here and call upon Lord Strickland?" Seeing the look of surprise that jumped onto Mrs. Grey's expression, Juliet continued quickly before her chaperone could interrupt. "Surely we must inform him just as soon as we can? And, thereafter, we will need to form a plan of what we are to do next."

"It would be wise," Lord Richmond agreed slowly. "What say you, Mrs. Grey?"

Juliet held her breath, her gaze swiveling toward her chaperone, who sighed and shot her a rueful look.

"Very well, but I must have Lady Juliet returned to her father at the proper time," she said, somewhat reluctantly. Lord and Lady Richmond nodded and turned to take their leave, but Mrs. Grey put a hand on Juliet's arm.

"You must be careful, Juliet," she warned firmly. "I have been, perhaps, unwise in permitting you to behave in this fashion thus far, but I will state that it comes from a desire not only to aid Lord Strickland but also to see a match created between the two of you. A match that, I believe, is still possible. However, I fear that the danger that encircles Lord Strickland is beginning to pull you in also and, in that, perhaps I should insist upon removing you from it."

Juliet's heart lurched. "Please, do not," she said urgently. "Mrs. Grey, I cannot even imagine leaving Lord Strickland in such a situation, not when there is more I can do. I know you have been not only understanding but also more than willing to step outside of what one is expected to do during the London Season, and for that I shall always be very grateful indeed."

Mrs. Grey's lips twisted, and she studied Juliet for some moments. "Do you care for Lord Strickland?"

The question was not only blunt but rather direct and Juliet felt embarrassment flood her soul as she dropped her gaze to the floor.

"I do care for him," she said softly, knowing that it was best to be honest with her chaperone, even if it was deeply discomfiting to do so. "I, of course, wish him to be free from Lord Brookmire and whoever else is involved, but once the matter is at an end, I cannot help but wonder..." She trailed off, unable to finish the sentence and praying that her chaperone would know what she meant.

"Then I am satisfied," Mrs. Grey said with a broad smile, surprising Juliet somewhat. "For I am quite certain that Lord Strickland has hopes similar to your own, my dear."

Juliet's eyes flared. "Truly?"

Mrs. Grey laughed and patted Juliet's arm. "Let us just wait and see what happens," she said, turning Juliet toward the door. "But I am very sure indeed that Lord Strickland will not simply thank you and turn from your acquaintance—which will, of course, make a good many people very happy indeed."

. . .

"Lord Strickland?"

Juliet stepped into the room, relieved not only that Lord Strickland appeared glad to see them all but that he was looking a good deal better than before.

"Please, do not rise," Lord Richmond said with a chuckle. "Your ankle?"

"Recovering," Lord Strickland replied, although his eyes lingered on Juliet's face. "You have something of importance to say to me, mayhap? It is not that I am not glad to have evening visitors since I am confined here for the present, but this is certainly not a usual occurrence."

"Indeed, it is not," Juliet replied, sitting down carefully. "It is that I have met someone that Lord and Lady Richmond believe to be of importance." Her gaze slid toward Lady Richmond, who was sitting down carefully. "Lord Brookmire, I must say, was *not* particularly gentlemanly and I certainly did not enjoy conversing with him."

Lord Strickland grinned, his expression amused as his eyes lit up. "No?"

"And that was without even mentioning your name, Lord Strickland," Mrs. Grey remarked, her eyes twinkling. "I must admit that I, too, found him very rude, for some of his remarks were..." She broke off, shaking her head. "He was not at all the sort of gentleman I would ever permit Lady Juliet to acquaint herself with. Although the lady in question was all the more improper."

Juliet watched as Lord Strickland's smile faded. "And which lady might that be?"

She took a breath. "Lady Ridgedale," she said quietly, seeing how the astonishment at her statement caused Lord Strickland's eyes to flare wide. "She interrupted the conversation—such as it was—between myself and Lord Brookmire without any hesitation, and then attempted to profusely apologize, pretending as though she had not been aware of my presence."

"Which," Mrs. Grey added thoughtfully, "might well have been the case, given just how determined she was to speak to Lord Brookmire."

Pressing her lips together for a moment, Juliet leaned forward in her chair, looking earnestly at Lord Strickland. "Lord Richmond has told us of her attentions toward you, and how you rebuffed them," she said hastily, seeing how Lord Strickland opened his mouth in what was perhaps an attempt to say precisely that. "Might it be that her dislike of you now could push her to such cruelty?"

Lord Strickland said nothing for some minutes. In fact, the entire room fell silent as everyone within it watched him, waiting for him to give his opinion on what Juliet had suggested. Eventually, he let out a heavy sigh and raked one hand through his hair, which made it fall at random, burning like gold in the candlelight.

"It may be," he said as Juliet's stomach lurched. "The vehemence of her anger at my refusal is something that I shall never forget."

Lord Richmond rose to his feet, walking across the room to pour brandies. "Then we have a connection between Lord Brookmire and Lady Ridgedale which makes sense," he said as Juliet nodded. "What must we do next?"

Lord Strickland shook his head. "I do not know," he answered, before reaching for the letter that Juliet had left with him earlier. "We might have to wait until my cousin recovers himself before anything further can be done." Another sigh left his lips. "If only I knew why my cousin carried such a letter with him. It might then—"

His words trailed off as something seemed to occur to him, and he held the letter to the candle by his side. For a moment, Juliet thought he was to burn it, but then realized that Lord Strickland was, apparently, warming the page.

"Good gracious."

Lord Strickland's whisper tore through the room like a thunderclap. With a gasp of astonishment, he rose to his feet, holding out the letter toward Juliet.

"Look!"

She took it from him, a little confused, only for a gasp of astonishment to leave her lips as she saw, for the first time, words appearing on the page.

"How can this be?" she whispered as Lord and Lady Richmond rose to come toward her, their eyes wide as they looked at the letter. "How did it come about?"

Lord Strickland ran one hand through his hair, letting out a long breath as he moved back toward his seat, his leg still paining him too much to remain standing. "It appears that my cousin was afraid for his life," he said heavily as Juliet began to read the letter. "He used this technique—one that he and I used upon occasion during our childhood—in order to ensure that what he wrote was kept secret from anyone who might come across it. No doubt he intended to send it to me once he arrived in London, without having to come to speak to me in person, fearful of what would occur if he did so and yet desperate to make certain I was safe." Closing his eyes, he let out a groan. "I should have remembered that this was what we used to do as children. It was something my grandfather showed me. A childish game but one that we both loved."

Juliet shook her head. "You did not know it was he that had sent it," she said hoarsely, her whole body burning with the shock of what she had just read. "How could you know that your cousin was coming to speak to you?" Her eyes returned to the paper. "His poor wife…"

"I pray he will recover," Lord Richmond said firmly, "so that he might return to his wife and children. He sounds, Strickland, a very courageous man."

"He is."

Juliet shook her head, looking at the paper again and reading the words. The words that told them so much and now filled her with horror. "'Lady Ridgedale seeks to end your life,'" she read aloud. "'Do not ask me yet how I know such a thing, but it is true. My own life has been threatened, but I cannot leave you to face your doom without making you aware of it.'" Letting out a long breath, Juliet looked up at Lord Strickland again, seeing the grief and upset on his face. "A very courageous man, Lord Strickland."

"He knows all, it seems," Lord Strickland replied, rubbing one hand across his forehead. "I need to speak to him."

"You may well be able to soon," Mrs. Grey said, pushing hope into her voice. "Only a few days and then…"

Juliet saw the hope in Lord Strickland's eyes but knew that was all it could be. Hope. Hope that his cousin would recover enough to speak of all that he knew, to tell him everything about Lady Ridgedale.

"I must meet with Lady Ridgedale," Lord Strickland murmured, and Juliet's audible gasp echoed around the room. "There must be something I can say to her, something that I can do that will make her say—"

"It is not wise," Lord Richmond interrupted. "If you plan anything specific with Lady Ridgedale, then she might very well make use of such an opportunity."

"An opportunity to do you harm," Lady Richmond finished as Juliet nodded fervently. "You must be wise in this, Lord Strickland."

It was not as Juliet had hoped. She had expected him to come up with some sort of resounding plan, had hoped that he would know precisely what to do now that they had discovered Lady Ridgedale's involvement with Lord Brookmire, but it seemed now that it was not to be.

"Perhaps," Mrs. Grey murmured quietly, "we might meet again come the morrow. This must be something of a shock for you, Lord Strickland."

He looked up, his eyes searching Juliet's face rather than responding to Mrs. Grey.

"This is a rather improper request, Mrs. Grey," he said quietly. "But might I have a few moments with Lady Juliet? I swear I shall only speak with her, but I must make some things quite clear." Slowly, his eyes turned to Mrs. Grey and, as they did so, Juliet felt her heart slam hard into her chest. Her breath hitched as she glanced to her companion, utterly astonished when Mrs. Grey nodded.

"A few *moments*, Lord Strickland," she said firmly as she rose from her chair. "I will be just outside the door."

Juliet did not know what to do or say, her hands tightening on the arms of the chair as the room emptied, save for herself and Lord Strickland. What was it he wanted to tell her? Certain that he could hear the thumping of her heart, Juliet dropped her gaze to the floor, pressing her lips together hard.

"Lady Juliet."

Lord Strickland's voice was quiet and gentle, holding a tenderness she had never once expected to hear.

"You have already become far too involved in this matter," he continued as she slowly lifted her eyes to his. "There is nothing more you need do. It is entirely at an end now. I have discovered the truth, I am sure of it, and for your own safety, I must urge you to step back from me—from this."

Juliet shook her head, a sudden fear clutching at her heart. "I do not wish to, Lord Strickland."

"But you must," he declared, rising from his chair in spite of the obvious pain he was in. "You have done more than enough, Lady Juliet. Return to the joys and the delights of the Season, rather than wasting your time with me. I wish only to protect you, to push you back into the life you ought to have been enjoying thus far here in London."

Now she rose also, coming a little closer to him and feeling tension rippling down her spine as she looked at him. His eyes held such warmth and yet such desperation that, for some moments, she could not look away.

"I cannot," she answered quietly. "I *will* not."

Lord Strickland dropped his head and let out a long breath, sounding more than a little frustrated. "Why?"

Lifting his head, he looked back at her steadily, waiting for an answer that she was not certain she could give. How could she explain the desperate urge to remain by his side? How could she express all that she felt when she could not even fully understand it herself?

"Why, Lady Juliet?" he asked again, taking another small step forward so that he was only a few inches away from her. "What is it that will keep you here with me?"

"You."

The word seemed to rip the room apart, making her chest tighten and her eyes widen with the shock of what she had said. Breathing heavily, she stared up into his face, feeling her whole body tingle with both embarrassment and the awareness that what she had said could not be taken back. Lord Strickland did not respond, nor did he seem surprised, his eyes holding hers with a gentleness that Juliet could practically feel emanating from him.

"Lady Juliet?"

Mrs. Grey's voice broke through the swirling of Juliet's frantic thoughts, her quiet words forcing Juliet to look away from Lord Strickland and toward her chaperone.

"We must depart," her chaperone said, taking a few steps into the room. "Come now."

Juliet nodded, looking back at Lord Strickland and feeling her face burn with embarrassment. He had said nothing to her since she had given that one, single exclamation and she had no knowledge as to what he was thinking at present.

"Good evening, Lord Strickland," she murmured, bobbing into a curtsy and dropping her gaze. Turning back toward the door, she made to follow Mrs. Grey out of the room, only for Lord Strickland to catch her hand.

Astonishment flared in her chest as he took her hand in his and lifted it to his mouth, heat running from her hand to her arm until it coursed all through her as his lips touched the back of her hand. His eyes held a good deal of unspoken emotion and yet Juliet was too afraid, too uncertain, to ask him what he felt.

"Good evening, Lady Juliet," he murmured, lowering her hand from his mouth but still holding it tightly, his fingers gently pressing hers. "And might I thank you for your honesty. It..."

Letting go of her hand with seeming reluctance, he smiled at her again. "It has brought my heart a great deal of joy."

Uncertain as to what to make of this but finding that she was, for some reason, smiling back at him with a great sense of happiness flooding her, Juliet held his gaze for another few moments before unwillingly turning back toward the door so that she might take her leave. But the smile did not leave her face and her heart did not lose its joy for the rest of the evening until, finally, she fell into a wonderful, delighted slumber.

12

Duncan could not remove Lady Juliet from his thoughts. He spent half the night tossing and turning, the echo of her voice spinning around his mind, the memory of how she had looked as she had spoken filling his thinking until he gave himself up to it, allowing his heart and mind to open entirely toward her and, for the first time, thinking about what she might one day be to him.

It had been clear that she had not intended to speak in such a way, had not meant to be as honest with him as she had been, and yet he was glad indeed that she had done so. Whilst she had not expressed it fully, he was certain now that there was a desire within Lady Juliet's heart that was much akin to his own. For whatever reason, he wanted nothing more than to be in her company, to linger there and to have her as a part of his life. He did not think that he would have any satisfaction in continuing on without her and certainly, there was no eagerness to depart from her in any way. He had only said such a thing to her for her own safety, wanting to make certain that she felt no obligation toward him when there was none. What he had discovered instead was that there was more than just a determination for determination's sake. Rather, there was clearly an eagerness to remain near to him. She *wanted* to be by his side, wanted to do all she could to bring this matter to an end so that…

Duncan frowned. So that they might continue their acquaintance without hinderance? So that they might then consider what the future could hold for them both? Slowly, his frown lifted as he realized that this in itself was precisely what he wanted. He was almost desperate to find that happiness and contentment that had eluded him for so long. No longer would he have to worry about what wicked scheme would next be thrown at him, no longer would he have to try and consider what he was to do next. In fact, he would not even have to worry about which young lady he would be forced into conversation with next, not when he had Lady Juliet.

A smile spread across his face and he sat back in his chair, resting his head and allowing a sense of contentment to fill him. He would ask Lord Lansbury for his permission to court Lady Juliet and, thereafter, would allow himself to finally consider a future that he had never even felt was anywhere near his reach before.

A scratch at the door alerted him to the butler's presence, drawing his thoughts away from Lady Juliet for the time being.

"Come in."

Sitting up straighter and relieved that his body was a little less painful today, Duncan waited until the butler stepped into the room, reaching for the letter that the butler held out to him on a silver tray.

"Might I fetch you something to eat, my lord?" the butler asked, but Duncan shook his head.

"No, I am quite all right at present," he said, turning the letter over and noticing the seal, aware of how his heart leapt wildly in his chest. "Was there any requirement for me to reply quickly?"

The butler shook his head and Duncan dismissed him so that he might read the note from Lady Juliet in peace. Would she speak of last evening? Would she give further explanation as to what she had said? With a broad smile settling across his face, he opened the note and read the page eagerly, only for his heart to slow suddenly, his smile fading to an astonished expression.

Your cousin has regained some strength, the note said. *It seems he has insisted on returning to London. He will be here this very afternoon, brought to my father's townhouse. Pray, join us if you have the strength.*

That was all it said. There was no more, no expression of hope that they might be able to speak again privately at another time, no reiterating of what she had said last evening, but Duncan did not even permit himself to feel any disappointment. Instead, his anticipation instantly began to build.

He pushed himself from his chair and limped toward the door, throwing it open and forcing himself back toward his bedchamber with as much haste as he could. There was no time to waste. He would have to dress and prepare himself to call upon Lady Juliet in the hope that he would be present for his cousin's arrival. Once more, he felt his heart fill with gratitude toward the Earl of Lansbury, grateful that the gentleman was the sort of man who would not simply stand aside whilst other men lay injured. Quite how he would explain to Lord Lansbury what had happened to his cousin and his knowledge of it, Duncan was not yet sure, but for the moment, that did not matter. All he wanted was to see his cousin again and to, finally, hear all that had taken place these last few, dreadful weeks.

∽

"Lord Strickland."

Lady Juliet practically breathed his name as he limped into the drawing room, rising quickly and making her way toward him, one hand outstretched. Whether or not she meant for him to take it, to kiss it as he had done last evening, Duncan was not certain, although, of course, he was more than eager to do so.

"Lady Juliet," he replied, embarrassed when she caught his arm and made to help him to a chair. "I am quite all right, I assure you."

She laughed softly and tilted her head so that she might look him in the eye a little better. "Your face is quite grey and there is a good deal of strain written upon it," she told him with a knowing smile. "Do not think that you can hide the truth from me, Lord Strickland."

He grimaced but allowed himself to chuckle as she twinkled up at him, only just realizing that they were alone. Once he had sat down, he looked back at her as she settled herself into a seat near to him, finding himself most contented to be in her company again.

"Mrs. Grey?" he inquired, and her cheeks burned a sudden, hot red.

"She is just about to join us," she said, looking away from him as though embarrassed that he had noticed. "We will wait for refreshments until Lord and Lady Richmond arrive, however, if that is suitable for you?"

He nodded, not wanting her to feel any sort of mortification that her chaperone was not yet present but rather eager to make the most of such an opportunity.

"I am glad that we have a few moments with which to speak, Lady Juliet," he told her, seeing how she looked back at him tentatively. "After last evening, I have been quite unable to remove you from my thoughts. They have swirled furiously all night, filling me with regret that I did not respond to you when you spoke to me last evening."

Her gaze molded to his, a hope burning within her blue eyes as one dark curl fell forward across her cheek, as though everything within her was eager to hear what he had to say.

"Had I the wits, I would have told you, Lady Juliet, that I am more than delighted at your desire to remain so close to me," he said honestly. "It is more than I could have ever hoped for. The truth is, I find myself eager for this matter to be at an end, not only for my own safety but also to give me the freedom to consider what I might now wish to pursue."

A small, flickering frown danced across her brow. "What you would wish to pursue, Lord Strickland?"

A smile spread across his face before he could prevent it.

"Indeed, Lady Juliet," he answered gently, leaning a little closer to her. "To consider my future. To consider what it is I now hope for, what I might be eager enough to seek out."

"Oh." Her color faded to a gentle pink, adding to her beauty. Duncan smiled delightedly at her, feeling his heart warming all the more to the idea of being closer to her than ever before.

"Would you be amenable to such considerations, Lady Juliet?" he asked hopefully. "Once this matter is resolved, I had thought to speak to your father, to determine whether or not he might be willing to allow me to court you."

Her eyes dropped to her hands that she now clasped so tightly in her lap, but Duncan did not miss the broad smile that spread across her face, the way that her cheeks warmed a little more. Settling back in his chair with a sigh of contentment, he waited for her to speak.

"I think, Lord Strickland, that I would be very glad of such a thing," she answered after a few moments of quiet. "In fact, it would make my heart very happy indeed." Finally, she looked back at him, her eyes glowing, her smile dazzling him, and Duncan felt his contentment grow all the more.

"Wonderful," he found himself saying, as though he had been searching for the right words but had been quite unable to find more than one. "Then let us hope, Lady Juliet, that this will soon all be behind us so that we might consider the future together."

∽

"I SHALL LEAVE YOU, OF COURSE."

Duncan made to rise but the earl gestured for him to remain sitting.

"You will have many questions to ask of your cousin, I am sure," Lord Lansbury continued as he made his way to the door. "Had it not been that I have many pressing matters of business, then I would have remained a little longer, but as things are at present…"

He shrugged but Duncan could not help but feel a great deal of relief.

"I thank you, Lord Lansbury," he replied gratefully. "You have shown my cousin great kindness and, had it not been for Lady Juliet and I being so acquainted, it might have been some time before I came to know of his presence here in London."

The earl nodded and smiled toward his daughter who, much to Duncan's delight, was sitting in a most demure fashion, looking back at her father with a small smile gracing her lips. She said nothing to him, did not give a hint that there might have been more to her acquaintance than Lord Lansbury knew, but instead simply watched her father depart. The moment he left the room, however, Duncan felt relief wash all across the room, flooding each and every person as they sat a little more easily in their chairs.

Ayles, however, did not look as relieved as Duncan might have hoped. In fact, he had been rather shocked by the appearance of his cousin when he had first arrived, taking in the man's pale face, the dark shadows around his eyes, and the way that he had been helped into a chair by not one but two footmen. It had been a struggle for him to remain sitting straight, for Duncan had seen the strain ripple across his cousin's face, but he had been silently proud of such determination.

"Please, Mr. Ayles, do not feel you need to sit on ceremony any longer."

Lady Juliet's voice was kind, making Duncan wonder if she, too, was aware of the struggle that Mr. Ayles was currently enduring.

"Sit back, if you wish," she continued kindly. "I can see that you are fatigued and, after what you have endured, there is no shame in resting a little."

It took a moment but Ayles eventually did as she suggested, sitting back with a sigh and resting his head on the back of the chair.

"You are very kind, Lady Juliet," he rasped, his voice thick with tiredness and pain. "Very kind indeed." Slowly, his gaze returned to

Duncan's, giving Duncan the impression that his cousin was desperate for a moment to speak to him alone.

"I received your letter," Duncan began, seeing how his cousin's eyes widened. "Although I only discovered the truth of it yesterday."

Mr. Ayles smiled painfully. "I had hoped that it would remind you of what we did as boys, whenever our fathers had reason to call upon each other," he said as Duncan nodded. "Then you know you are in danger?"

"I do," Duncan replied, noting how Ayles' eyes went around the room. "But Lady Juliet was the one to overhear it being spoken at the first. She informed me of it, and with Lord and Lady Richmond's help, we have surmised that it is Lady Ridgedale who wishes to bring harm to me." Seeing his cousin nod, Duncan leaned forward in his chair. "Might I ask how you discovered it?"

"I received a note," Ayles replied, his voice still hoarse. "She requested to know whether or not you were returned from the continent, although gave no indication as to why. I did not respond to her, however, for there was something about the note that did not sit well with me." He shifted a little in his chair, a grimace pulling at his mouth. "I soon received another, which was, in its tone, a good deal more demanding. I did respond to that one, telling Lady Ridgedale that I was not at all certain of your plans." Shaking his head, he closed his eyes. "It was then that she came to call upon me."

There was a moment or two of silence.

"You mean to say that Lady Ridgedale called upon you to speak to you about Lord Strickland?" Lady Richmond asked, breaking the quiet. "What was she asking you about?"

Ayles' lips tipped in a wry expression. "There was the belief that I might wish to take on the title," he said heavily. "Lady Ridgedale made it quite plain that she thought very poorly of my cousin and insisted that I should be much better suited to such a thing. I believe she was quite astonished when I refused."

"You are a good man, Ayles," Duncan murmured, but Ayles shook his head.

"I should have written to you of her visit almost at once," he said softly. "Then you would have been aware of it. But I believed her to be quite foolish—almost, perhaps, a little mad. And thus, I dismissed it. It was not until I received another note from her, warning me away from speaking to you of her visit and her intentions, that I realized the truth."

"That she fully intended to remove me from this earth," Duncan muttered, and his cousin nodded. "You could not know, of course, that she held a great deal of anger toward me." Seeing his cousin frown, he quickly explained all that Lady Ridgedale had sought from him and how he had refused time and again, leaving her to become rather furious with his lack of agreement.

"And her anger has become so great that she wishes to take on some sort of revenge," he finished as Ayles' eyes widened with shock. "I did not expect it, of course, and had it not been for Lady Juliet, then I might well have succumbed to one of her schemes."

Ayles blew out a long breath and ran one shaky hand across his forehead. "I wrote to you," he said heavily. "I wrote many a letter, but I did not receive a reply. Afraid that my letters were being stopped by someone as yet unknown, I took leave of my wife and children and made my way to London in the hope that you would be there for the Season." A wry smile lifted one side of his mouth. "As I said to Lady Ridgedale, I was quite uncertain as to whether or not you would be in London this year. But I went in the hope that you would be present and that I might warn you of her intentions."

"But you were prevented from doing so," Lady Juliet added as Ayles' turned his head toward her. "Highwaymen?"

Nodding slowly, Ayles frowned hard. "I believed them to be, yes," he said slowly. "Although one did not appear to be so. He stood behind as the other three men attacked me, as well as the other men within the carriage." His voice became thin with anger, his eyes narrowing as he looked away from them all, his gaze fixed to the floor. "We were all left for dead and, indeed, I believed myself to be so."

"Except," Duncan said quietly, "I do not think it was highwaymen, Ayles."

His cousin looked up sharply. "No?"

"No," Lord Richmond said, getting up from his chair in order to refill brandy glasses. "We believe it now to have been Lady Ridgedale's intention to prevent you from reaching London. Someone must have been watching all that you were doing, Mr. Ayles. Someone must have prevented your letters from reaching Lord Strickland. And someone, knowing of your intentions to come to London, made every preparation to stop you."

"All on Lady Ridgedale's orders," Duncan muttered darkly. "And I believe I know precisely who it was."

His cousin sucked in a breath, his eyes wide. "Then you are able to prevent them from injuring you further?"

"More than that," Duncan replied, a flare of anger burning in his chest. "I have every intention of making quite certain that their plans come to nothing but failure, Ayles. It is time that the truth is made known in its entirety. And I have just the way to do it."

∼

"Might you take my arm?"

Lady Juliet nodded but did not smile and Duncan could feel the tension radiating from her.

"It shall all be well," he assured her as best he could, taking in the seriousness of her gaze as she looked up at him. "Nothing can go wrong this evening."

"But it may still be that..." She swallowed hard but did not finish her sentence, slipping her hand under his arm.

"All will be well," he said again in an attempt to reassure her. "All I need do is make certain that Lord Brookmire hears what I have to say. He will not attempt to injure me here, not in front of so many patrons."

Lady Juliet let out her breath slowly, nodding as she did so. Her eyes roved around the drawing room as though searching for those who might step out to attack him at any moment.

"You must try and smile, my dear lady, else no one here will think you glad to be in my company."

This brought a lightness to her expression that had not been there before, her lips quirking gently. "And surely that must apply to you also, Lord Strickland?" she asked as he grinned at her.

"I have no difficulty in expressing my delight in having you on my arm, Lady Juliet," he replied truthfully. "In fact, I shall be very glad indeed to walk about this room with you next to me. I shall not care one whit if anyone remarks upon it, for I am glad to be beside you."

This made her expression light up and Duncan smiled back at her, seeing the happiness in her eyes despite the tension that she must still surely feel.

"Then shall we make our way to what is certainly the loudest group of gentlemen and ladies that are present this evening?" she asked, tilting her head just a little. "They will, no doubt, be more than willing to listen to what you have to say and, in a short time, will spread it throughout everyone in this room."

Duncan laughed and patted her hand with his free one, fully aware that Mrs. Grey would remain close by, just as she was at present. "Very good, Lady Juliet," he said, beginning to walk across the room, his limp only slight as he pushed aside any pain that came with each step. "Then let us begin our plan."

Making his way slowly toward the large group and quickly spotting at least one gentleman he was acquainted with, Duncan bowed quickly and greeted him, being quickly welcomed into the group. Introducing Lady Juliet and fully aware of the knowing glances that were quickly shot between one lady and the next, he listened for a few moments to the amicable conversation, before managing to inject himself into it.

"Speaking of matters of interest," he said, quickly commanding the conversation, "I have only just discovered something that has greatly distressed me."

This, of course, caught almost everyone's attention and Duncan was left with a most attentive audience who all watched him with interest flickering in their eyes.

"My cousin—one Mr. Ayles—has only just written to me to inform me that he has been attacked on his way to London," he began as one or two ladies let out a startled exclamation. "He was left for dead but has, thankfully, begun to recover." Taking a small step forward, he leaned in a little more, keeping his voice low. "He states that he has something of great importance to tell me but that he cannot write of it, such is its seriousness."

"Good gracious!" one lady exclaimed, her eyes wide. "Whatever shall you do, Lord Strickland?"

"I am to go to him tomorrow afternoon, of course," Duncan replied as murmurs immediately began to rise from those within the group, speaking to each other about what he had only just revealed. "He is too unwell to travel to London and thus I am to make my way to an inn named 'The Owl and the Hound' which, I have been informed, is not too far from London. Less than a day's travel, I believe."

Lord Miller cleared his throat, his expression grave. "I do hope that you find him recovering well, Lord Strickland," he said. "Is there any suggestion as to what this dire news might be?"

Duncan shrugged and shook his head. "No, I have very little idea," he lied. "But I am eager to find out what it is, of course."

"Then might we wish you every success," said another young lady who then immediately shot a dark look toward Lady Juliet, which Duncan did not miss.

"I thank you," he replied, before excusing himself and, taking Lady Juliet with him, he stepped away from the group.

Lady Juliet swallowed hard, looking at him. "Do you believe it is done?"

With a quick look over his shoulder, Duncan nodded, chuckling at the sight of the ladies already removing themselves from the cluster of gentlemen so that they might all talk together.

"I believe all is as we had hoped," he told her. "Within the hour, Lord Brookmire shall know of it."

"And then, Lady Ridgedale," Lady Juliet murmured as he nodded. "Let us hope that they will act as you expect, Lord Strickland."

There was not even a flicker of doubt in Duncan's mind. "I have no doubt that they shall," he said firmly, pressing her hand lightly. "And then, my dear Lady Juliet, we shall have other things to speak of." Smiling at her, he saw her blush and the light that burned in her eyes. "A great many other things indeed."

13

"Juliet?"

Juliet lifted her head from her book, which she had not quite managed to read even though she had been staring at the page for at least ten minutes. "Yes, Mrs. Grey?" she asked, her anxiety growing steadily as she saw the look in the lady's eyes. "Is something the matter?" Closing the book, she rose to her feet.

Mrs. Grey shook her head. "All is well," she said gently. "Your father is aware that you are to spend the afternoon with Lord Strickland. He is already gone from the house so will not miss your prolonged absence. However," she continued as Juliet pressed one hand lightly to her stomach, "I continually question myself as to whether or not I am doing the right thing as your chaperone, Juliet. I know that you care for Lord Strickland, but he is right to suggest that you step back from this." Her eyes searched Juliet's face. "I have permitted more than perhaps I ought to have done already and I could not bear to have you placed in any sort of danger." Looking away, she sighed heavily, clearly troubled. "Might you not wait here for his return? I could not imagine having to tell your father the truth, should you be injured."

Panic began to clasp a hold of Juliet's heart. "I must be present," she said, stepping forward. "How can I stay at home when there is such a moment at hand?" Trying to express herself as best she could, she gave a small shake of her head. "I cannot linger here, hoping and wondering as to what is occurring. I have to be a part of this."

Mrs. Grey's lips twisted, her eyes thoughtful. Juliet knew that all that her chaperone had said was quite right, for she had given Juliet a good many more freedoms than other chaperones would ever have done. And yet there still lingered this desperation to be with Lord Strickland, to be beside him when the moment of his freedom came.

"You care for Lord Strickland, Juliet?"

"I love him!"

The words flung themselves out from her, but Juliet felt no shame in speaking them. There was no embarrassment, no sense of mortification. Rather, she felt relieved, as though she was glad to have said them to Mrs. Grey.

"You care for him greatly, then," Mrs. Grey murmured, rather thoughtfully. She said nothing for some minutes as Juliet remained precisely where she was, her stomach tightening with anxiety. It all rested on Mrs. Grey and her decision, for Juliet could not simply set out with Lord Strickland without her.

Mrs. Grey sighed. "Against my better judgment, I shall permit it," she said eventually as Juliet closed her eyes with relief. "Come, then, we must have you dressed and ready for Lord Strickland's arrival."

"Thank you, Mrs. Grey," Juliet breathed, a slight weakness catching her limbs. "Thank you, with all of my heart."

THE DRIVE to the inn did not take as long as Juliet had expected. Lord Strickland explained that he had chosen one just on the outskirts of London but near to where the supposed highwaymen had attacked the carriage. Very little had been said on their journey and, from the tight expression on Lord Strickland's face, Juliet knew that he was somewhat apprehensive, praying that all should go as he hoped.

"There is a private parlor waiting for us all," Lord Strickland murmured as the carriage came to a stop. "Lord and Lady Richmond may well be waiting for us already."

Juliet nodded and accepted his hand as she climbed out of the carriage, holding his gaze for a few moments and seeing the glint of steel in his eye. A shiver ran through her as she waited for Mrs. Grey to descend, her anticipation turning to nervousness. Within a few minutes, they had stepped inside the gloomy inn and been directed toward the private parlor, which, much to Juliet's surprise, was very finely decorated indeed.

"You have arrived, then." Lady Richmond rose from where she had been sitting by the window, a bright smile on her face. "I am quite certain that all shall go as planned, Lord Strickland, for the news of your cousin's attack and the supposed secret that he is to tell you has gone all around London at great speed."

"I believe even our servants were speaking of it," Lord Richmond grinned, clasping Lord Strickland's hand in a welcoming gesture. "And, as per your suggestion, I am able to confirm that Lord Brookmire and Lady Ridgedale were in discussion last evening for some time." He grinned as Juliet looked at him in surprise. "Do you believe Lord Brookmire will come alone? From what was overheard, I myself do not think it likely."

"With my presence expected here also?" Lord Strickland replied as Juliet sat down by Lady Richmond. "No, I highly doubt it. I think that Lady Ridgedale will see it as her opportunity to avenge the injustice she has long borne within herself and will arrive with Lord Brookmire."

Another shudder ran through Juliet's frame as she thought of what Lady Ridgedale intended for Lord Strickland. It was not as though she believed she would succeed but the intent alone was horrifying.

"Then all we can do at present is wait," Lord Richmond said, sitting down with a satisfactory sigh escaping him. "Thankfully, they have quite delicious meals here, should you wish it, although I must hope it will not be of long duration."

"I must hope so also," Lord Strickland replied, turning to look at Juliet before he sat down. "The sooner this matter is at an end, the better."

~

IT WAS some time before anyone came to speak to them. The scratch at the door made Juliet start violently, her eyes widening as a servant came in and quickly spoke to Lord Strickland. When he left, Lord Strickland drew in a long breath and looked at them all.

"Lord Brookmire and Lady Ridgedale are here," he said quietly. "My servant recognized them both."

Juliet clutched the arms of her chair. "So what are we do to?"

Lord Strickland smiled at her. "Remain where you are, with Lady Richmond and Mrs. Grey," he said calmly. "Lord Richmond and I will greet whoever steps through the door and, be quite assured, Lady Juliet, they will bring you no harm." His smile remained in place, encouraging her. "Recall that they believe me to be traveling here this afternoon and thus now expect me to arrive much later in the day. The innkeeper will direct them to the room that is supposedly held by Mr. Ayles, which is connected to this private parlor." One shoulder lifted. "No doubt they will hope to ambush me upon my arrival but, if it goes as I have hoped, they will be the ones taken by surprise."

Juliet swallowed hard and nodded, glancing to Mrs. Grey, who looked very anxious indeed. For some minutes, there was not a single sound amongst them. Lord Strickland and Lord Richmond were standing by the door, whilst she, Lady Richmond, and Mrs. Grey remained where they were, each looking equally nervous.

"Thank you *very* much."

Lady Ridgedale's voice was quite clear as it came from behind the door.

"I am sure Mr. Ayles is expecting us," she continued, clearly dismissing the servant who had directed her. "I thank you."

The door opened and Juliet's heart began to pound furiously, her hands gripping the arms of the chair with great force. Lady Ridgedale walked confidently into the room, only to stop dead as she caught sight of Juliet, Lady Richmond, and Mrs. Grey. Lord Brookmire came in afterwards, letting out a loud exclamation just as Lord Strickland shut the door hard.

"I am certain that you were not expecting me, Lady Ridgedale," he said, his voice filling the room as Lady Ridgedale gasped and clutched at her chest, turning around swiftly. "You thought I should arrive later, did you not?"

Lord Brookmire took a step back, his voice filling the room. "Strickland," he boomed, although Juliet noticed the paleness of his cheeks. "I—no, you are quite mistaken. Lady Ridgedale and I..."

"What is it that you are doing here?" Lord Richmond asked as he stood by Lord Strickland. "I believe you said, only a few moments ago, Lady Ridgedale, that Mr. Ayles was expecting you." One eyebrow lifted. "Mr. Ayles, unfortunately, is not here."

Silence rang around the room for some minutes as Lady Ridgedale and Lord Brookmire struggled to find an answer to Lord Richmond's question. A glance was thrown between them although neither of them said a word. Juliet dragged in a breath, lifting her chin and forcing herself to speak.

"I overheard you and Lord Brookmire speaking, Lady Ridgedale," she said, her voice shaking rather than being filled with the confidence she had hoped to project. "You have set yourself against him."

"As he set himself against me!" Lady Ridgedale screamed, her anger at being discovered suddenly seeming to set herself alight. "When I needed his assistance, when I was desperate for his help, he refused me."

"As he had every right to do," Lady Richmond replied calmly. "You were a married woman, Lady Ridgedale. Your dislike of your husband's frugal ways were nothing to do with him."

Lady Ridgedale's face was scarlet with ire, her eyes narrowed with hate. "Lord Ridgedale knew what I had done," she hissed furiously. "Lord Ridgedale heard of Lord Strickland's refusal and he punished me for my actions. *Punished* me." She shook her head, her lip curling. "He never once laid a hand to me, but he refused to give me *anything* I asked for. Kept at home, occasions forgotten, with no company but my own?" She sliced the air with her hand, her whole body shaking with evident rage. "And it was all because of Lord Strickland."

"It was all because of *you*," Lord Strickland replied mildly. "You made such choices, Lady Ridgedale. I will not take any responsibility." Pushing himself away from the door, he took a few steps toward her. "But what you have done to my cousin and attempted to do to me will not be tolerated."

Lady Ridgedale narrowed her eyes all the more. "It is what you deserve," she hissed furiously. "Nothing less." Her eyes turned to Lord Brookmire. "Brookmire, do what you must."

Juliet's hand flew to her mouth, fearing what Lord Brookmire intended to do, only for the gentleman to take a small step away from the lady, his hands raised and a look of fear wrapping across his expression.

"I cannot, Lady Ridgedale," he said haltingly. "To do so would be most foolish indeed."

Lord Strickland tilted his head. "Then you admit that you have been in league with Lady Ridgedale?" he asked quietly. "You have been doing her bidding?"

Lord Brookmire, it seemed, was not a gentleman with a good deal of mettle. He began to stammer, stepping back from them all with his hands lifted and his eyes wide.

"I—"

"Say nothing, Brookmire," Lady Ridgedale demanded furiously. "You shall not say a word."

Lord Brookmire swallowed hard, his strength clearly ebbing from him as he realized just how much danger he was now in. Lord Strickland and Lord Richmond both wore equal expressions of fury, their eyes narrowing all the more as they watched him, their arms folded and their stance strong.

"She—she promised me that all my debts would be paid," he cried, stepping back from them once more, only for his back to hit the mantlepiece, rendering him unable to walk any further away. "As well as..." he swallowed and looked away, "as well as other favors." His eyes rose to Lord Strickland's. "I did what I had to. I have barely anything left."

Juliet sucked in a breath. "Then you were the one who attempted to attack Lord Strickland on the road to London," she said quietly. "Who missed a second attempt in London in the darkness of the night. Who put a vial in his brandy, who threw him down the staircase?"

Lord Brookmire shook his head vehemently. "I did not do all that you have said," he cried, as though such an admittance would somehow relieve him of his guilt. "I was not the one who employed those men to attack Mr. Ayles. I did not put the poison in his brandy." He dropped his head. "I was to remain to make certain of his demise, yes. The other claims you have put to me, however, I will not deny."

Juliet looked at Lord Strickland, whose brow was raised.

"Then it was you, Lady Ridgedale," he said softly, a chill running down Juliet's spine as he spoke. "You were the one who hired rogues to attack my carriage."

She laughed harshly. "Not only you but to watch for Mr. Ayles," she replied, as though proud of what she had done. "If that meant stopping every carriage on the way, then so be it." She shrugged. "Although I should not have paid them so handsomely, given that your cousin still lives." Her gaze sifted to his. "He does *live*, does he not?"

"Your threats mean nothing any longer," Lord Strickland told her quietly. "You have admitted to everything, Lady Ridgedale. And you, Lord Brookmire, you weak, insufferable man, I have nothing but disgrace to heap upon your head."

Reaching back toward the door, he rapped upon it sharply, and much to Juliet's astonishment, four men came into the room. Men that Juliet did not recognize.

"Mr. Ayles will return to his family, where he will live out the rest of his days in safety," Lord Strickland continued as Lady Ridgedale lifted her chin and looked at him with a supercilious smile on her face as though, in some way, she had won. "What a rumor Lord and Lady Richmond will have to tell back in London, about how they found themselves in the very same inn as Lord Brookmire and Lady Ridgedale—which will be all the more shocking given that you were discovered in the same room on the premises." He shook his head in an almost pitying fashion, ignoring the smirk on Lady Ridgedale's face. "And, due to your shame, you will choose to depart from here and make your way to the continent, where you will settle for the rest of your days." Leaning forward, he glared hard at Lady Ridgedale and Juliet was satisfied to see the smile drop from her face.

"It is at an end, Lady Ridgedale," he said quietly. "Your victory has been snatched from you. You shall not be satisfied."

Lady Ridgedale opened her mouth to speak, only to close it again, silence her only response. The hard look was still in her eyes, the anger clear in her expression, but Juliet knew that there was nothing but defeat left for her now. The matter was quite at an end and everyone present in the room knew it.

"I shall not go," Lady Ridgedale hissed, but Lord Strickland held up one hand.

"Yes, you shall," he stated calmly. "By force or by intention, you *will* board the boat and you will not return, Lady Ridgedale. For I fully intend to tell everyone in the *ton* precisely what you and Lord Brookmire have done. You will never again be welcome in society. You will never be able to even lift your head. And that, Lady Ridgedale, are the consequences that will follow you for the rest of your life."

It was some minutes later that Juliet, Mrs. Grey, Lady Richmond, and Lord Strickland stood outside the inn. Juliet felt rather dazed, as though the entire world had shifted beneath her feet, and yet, with it came such a sense of freedom that she wanted to laugh aloud.

"It is done," Lord Strickland said softly, his hand slipping about Juliet's waist as he pulled her lightly toward him, despite the fact that they stood with Lady Richmond and Mrs. Grey. "It is over."

"It seems so," Lady Richmond replied with a small smile. "I am sure that Lord Richmond and the others will make certain both reach their destination very safely indeed."

Lord Strickland's smile was a little tight. "Indeed," he said with a small shake of his head. "Wealth, it seems, has some benefits." He said nothing more but looked down toward Juliet, who did not want to ask him what he had been required to do to find such men. "The consequences, I feel, were appropriate."

"*More* than appropriate," Mrs. Grey replied firmly. "You have been fair, Lord Strickland. More fair than others might have been."

"I would agree," Juliet said softly. "And now there is nothing for you to do but recover yourself."

"And to return my cousin to his family," he reminded her, turning toward her a little more as Mrs. Grey and Lady Richmond began to speak quietly, leaving them both to face each other without interruption. "Thereafter, Lady Juliet, I should like to speak to your father."

Her heart quickened. "My father?"

"I cannot imagine my life without your presence in it," he told her, his voice quiet so that only she could hear. "I have such a relief flooding over me that it opens up the entirety of my life all over again—and I do not wish to return to it as it was. I want you to be as you are now, as you have been these last days. To be beside me, to be often in my company, and for me to share my innermost thoughts and hopes with you." He frowned suddenly, looking away as though embarrassed. "Perhaps I have spoken out of turn. Perhaps you do not feel as I do."

The urge to reassure him was on her in a moment. "I feel just the same, if not more," she said, one hand pressed lightly against his chest as he looked down at her, hope burning in his eyes. "Truly, Lord Strickland. My fear has been that our acquaintance will end and that I shall no longer be in your company as we have been these last days. But to know that it is not so, that you seek the very same as I…" Her smile began to spread slowly across her face, her heart racing as he captured her hand where it rested against his heart. "It is more wonderful than I could ever have imagined."

Lord Strickland drew in a long breath. "Then in a few days, I shall seek an audience with your father, Lady Juliet," he murmured, lifting her hand to his lips and kissing it gently. "So that we do not have to face that fear that has captured both of our hearts, it seems." His smile began to grow steadily, a relief and a happiness in his eyes that had been absent for so long. "Thank you, Lady Juliet, for all you have done. I do not think I could have survived this Season without you."

EPILOGUE

"Lady Juliet."

Juliet rose from her chair and held out her hands to Lord Strickland. "It went well?"

"Your father was most amenable," he told her, much to Juliet's relief. "But I confess that I did not ask him only to court you, Lady Juliet."

Her hands caught his, squeezing them gently as she looked up into his face. "Oh?"

He smiled at her and Juliet's heart lifted with anticipation. "Throughout this ordeal, I have found you a constant," he told her. "You have remained steadfastly by my side, determined to do all you can to help me and making quite certain that I would not be lost to the cruelty of Lady Ridgedale. You have shown an entire disregard for my life of wealth and instead sought to know me just as I am."

"And what I have found has been wonderful," she told him, glad beyond measure that Mrs. Grey had left them alone for a few moments. "You have become very dear to me indeed, Lord Strickland. I confess that there is a love for you within my heart that has grown with every moment I have been in your company. I—"

He held up one hand, silencing her.

"If I might," he murmured, his hand now slipping around her waist. "I want to tell you, Lady Juliet, that my heart now belongs to you. I have never met any lady such as you and I am certain that I shall not do so again. How can I let you go now? How could I turn away from you when my heart yearns for you, when it cries out for you?" His other hand tugged from hers so that he might pull her a little closer and Juliet's heart soared to the skies, her anticipation and hope mounting with every second. "I love you, Lady Juliet. I want not only to court you, but to marry you." The words fell from his lips directly onto her heart, making her want to cry out with joy. Her hands went around his neck, her head tipping back so that she might look into his eyes.

"If you will ask me, Lord Strickland," she murmured, her eyes dancing, "then I shall give you my answer."

A wry smile pulled at one corner of his mouth. "Will you marry me, Juliet?"

She sighed contentedly as his head began to lower. "My dear Lord Strickland," she replied, filled with a happiness that she had never felt before, "what answer can I give but to say yes?"

∼

STOLEN HEART

HEIRS OF LONDON BOOK TWO

Stolen Heart

Text Copyright © 2020 by Joyce Alec

All rights reserved. This book or any portion thereof may not be reproduced or used in any manner whatsoever without the express written permission of the publisher except for the use of brief quotations in a book review.

This book is a work of fiction. Names, characters, places and incidents are either the product of the author's imagination or are used fictionally. Any resemblance to actual persons, living or dead, or to actual events or locales is entirely coincidental.

First printing, 2020

Publisher
Love Light Faith, LLC
400 NW 7th Avenue, Unit 825
Fort Lauderdale, FL 33311

PROLOGUE

It had been a very wet day indeed and Colin was not particularly impressed by the spring showers. He had intended to go out into the fields and assist with the planting but it seemed that the weather had not been in his favor. Shaking his head to himself, he made his way back to his small but comfortable living room and sat down by the fire. He was shivering inadvertently as though he could still feel the rain pouring down upon his head and running in cold rivulets down his back. Returning to the house, he had been glad that the fire he had left banked was still warm and had quickly added more wood to it so that it burned quickly and heated the room. His wet things were still drying, steam rising from them as the fire's blaze warmed them all the more. Picking up a glass, he poured himself a small measure of brandy, knowing that he had very little left, and sat down in his comfortable chair by the fire.

Sighing, he let out a long, slow breath. As much as he might complain about the weather, he did enjoy his life here in Scotland. Having been born only a short distance from this house, he knew this land well. His brother, Arthur, now worked alongside him to make certain that the crops did well and that there was enough income to keep them and their small farm sustained. It had been a difficult few years and Colin did not know whether or not he would have had as much success had it not been for his brother. Closing his eyes, Colin rested his head back and let himself settle into a comfortable peace. The day was at an end and perhaps the rain would have stopped by the time morning came.

A sudden, sharp rap at the door startled him and, cursing, he looked down at his glass and discovered that most of his remaining brandy was now on his trousers. His only servant had the afternoon and evening free today, meaning that it was Colin's responsibility to open the door and greet whoever stood there on the step. With a curse, he rose to his feet and made his way to the front of the small house, flinging open the door with every intention of berating whomever it was that had come to disturb him.

Instead of finding his brother or one of the workers standing there, however, there was a small, wiry man who looked up at him through rain-splattered spectacles. Behind him, in the gloom, Colin could see a coach and horses, which explained why the man in front of him was not entirely bedraggled.

"Are you Colin Montgomery?"

Colin blinked in surprise. "I—I am," he said, before remembering his manners and stepping aside so that the man might come in. "Do I know you?"

The man stepped over the threshold and looked about him, as though assessing the condition of the house where Colin lived. This irritated Colin somewhat but he remained silent, standing steadfastly between the man and the rest of the house, his arms folded and his eyes narrowed.

"You *are* Colin Montgomery?" the man asked again, looking up at Colin with a slight air of puzzlement. "It has taken some time to find you."

"I am Colin Montgomery," he replied, his irritation growing. "My brother is Arthur Montgomery. I can fetch him if you want someone else to confirm the truth of my identity." One brow lifted but the man cleared his throat, clearly unwilling to do anything Colin had suggested.

"Your father was George Montgomery, your mother Alice Montgomery?"

"Yes."

Colin wanted to demand to know why this man was here, asking such questions, but held his tongue, seeing that this fellow had every intention of asking his questions repeatedly until he received his answers.

"You have lived here for some years, I believe?"

"I have," Colin replied tightly. "The farm here belongs to both myself and my brother."

The man let out a small laugh which only made Colin frown all the more. Was the man laughing at his way of life? At the quality of the house around him? His hands balled into fists but he remained quiet, forcing himself to keep his irritation and frustration contained.

"Well, if we might sit down, Mr. Montgomery," the man said after a few moments of assessing Colin's features, "I have some news for you which I think will be something of a surprise." One side of his mouth lifted in a half-smile. "It will, I believe, change your life entirely. This farm will have to go to your brother."

The irritation that Colin had felt so strongly fled in an instant. "What do you mean?" he asked, a cold hand at his heart. Was the man about to state that, for whatever reason, he was going to be forcibly removed from his home? That the farm would no longer be his to care for? His mind began to whirl with thoughts as he tried to recall what he might have done in order to gain such a punishment.

"Mr. Montgomery?" the man said again, although his tone was a little more gentle now as though he realized the fears that were plaguing Colin. "Is there somewhere we can sit down?"

It took Colin a moment to realize what he had asked and, therefore, a minute or two before he finally led the fellow back to his small sitting room. Gesturing for him to sit in the more comfortable seat, Colin sat down in the other, forgetting entirely to offer the man any sort of refreshment. Instead, he fixed his eyes upon the man as he sat down, heard him clear his throat, and noticed, for the first time, that a small sheaf of papers was held in one of his hands. His heart began to pound furiously as a light sheen of sweat formed across his brow.

"Mr. Montgomery," the man began, lifting his head to look at Colin directly. "There has been a death in your family."

Colin's shoulders slumped. "I have no family to speak of, save for my brother," he said slowly. "My father and mother have both passed away."

The man arched an eyebrow. "And your father's brothers and their families?"

All the more confused, Colin leaned forward in his chair. "My father had no brothers."

"In that, you are entirely mistaken," the man cried, looking greatly shocked. "Are you trying to state, Mr. Montgomery, that you have no awareness of your father's status? Of his family?"

"None," Colin replied, a little surprised by the man's excited tone. "I know that my father's parents were not at all pleased at his choice of a bride. Therefore, he decided to move to Scotland with her and bring up his family here." One shoulder lifted. "I have never had any meeting with my father's parents, if that is what you are asking, nor should I wish to."

To Colin's immense astonishment, the man rose to his feet in a sudden, agitated state. He began to walk about the room, muttering to himself as he threw the occasional glance toward Colin, as if he could hardly believe what he had heard. Colin felt an increasing need to defend himself, to state that he fully supported his father's decision, one that he had never had any need to question. They had been a very contented family and he missed both his parents a great deal.

"My goodness, my goodness!" the man exclaimed, throwing his hands high in the air. "Then this will be all the more astonishing to you, Mr. Montgomery!"

Colin rose to his feet. "Perhaps you can explain it to me then, sir," he said, forcing a fierceness into his voice that finally seemed to catch the man's attention. "I don't even know your name as yet."

This seemed to quieten the fellow, for he nodded, muttered once more to himself, and then stopped pacing. Facing Colin directly, he spread his hands wide, with one still clutching the papers.

"Mr. Grey, at your service, Mr. Montgomery," he began with a small bow. "Now, as for the reason for my visit, I should explain from the start, I believe." Taking in a deep breath, his eyes flashing with evident excitement, he cleared his throat and snapped his heels together. "Mr. Montgomery, your father was the third son of the Marquess of Lindale," he said as Colin's mouth dropped open in astonishment. "I do not fully understand the details, but for some reason, your grandfather did not give his third son his inheritance. Indeed, I believe that he did not make mention of his third son even in his will."

Colin blinked and, closing his mouth, tried to clear his whirling thoughts. "That is because my father chose to marry my mother," he said slowly. "A lady who must have been considered far below him."

Mr. Grey nodded in evident understanding. "Your father, then, despite being disinherited, was still the third son of Lord Lindale."

"Yes, yes," Colin murmured, still trying to take in all that had been said. "I understand. But what does that have to do with me and your visit here?"

Mr. Grey's eyes flared with evident amazement. "You clearly have very little idea of this at all," he said with glee. "Well, Mr. Montgomery, the second son of the Marquess of Lindale did not marry or have any children," he continued. "The first son wed and married but produced only daughters." A frown flickered across his brow. "The second son passed away only six months ago, which was when the search for you began. However, within that time, the Marquess of Lindale himself has *also*, regrettably, passed from this life to the next." Taking in a deep breath, he gestured toward Colin. "Therefore, the title now falls to...well, to you."

Staring wide-eyed at Mr. Grey, Colin felt his whole body freeze with a coldness that he had never once experienced before. It was then followed with a flush of heat that had him gasping for breath, his hand clutching at his heart as Mr. Grey's smile faded away. The little man moved toward him as though he feared he was about to faint.

Colin waved him away, then reached for his glass and his decanter of brandy. Rather than being careful with the measure he used, he poured it liberally into his glass and then threw it back in one gulp.

Catching his breath, he looked at Mr. Grey steadily, forcing himself to concentrate. "Are you trying to suggest, Mr. Grey, that I am now the Marquess of Lindale?" he asked, and Mr. Grey nodded fervently.

"Yes," Mr. Grey explained, speaking with great slowness so that Colin could take in all that was being said. "Mr. Montgomery—or, as I should refer to you, Lord Lindale—you now hold the title of the Marquess of Lindale."

Colin closed his eyes tightly, his heart beginning to roar within him. He had never once considered himself to be anything other than what he was. The son, he believed, of an ordinary, hard-working man who had made a reasonable living for his wife and his sons. And now to discover that his father had been a great deal more? That was almost too astonishing to believe.

"Lord Lindale?"

It took Colin a few moments to realize that the fellow was referring to him, shaking his head heavily before passing one hand over his eyes.

"You have an estate, Lord Lindale," Mr. Grey continued as though this were quite a regular conversation. "Your brother also, although, of course, it is lesser in size and in fortune than your own. Both are ready and prepared for you both, with a full complement of staff. There are a good many details which need to be considered, of course, and the solicitors will be ready to discuss your fortune, your finances, and the like with you, but for the moment, all that needs to be done is for you to make your way to your new estate." He held out the papers toward Colin, who found himself taking them, his fingers numb, his eyes unseeing as he looked down at them, trying to work out what it was that was written there, but his head was so filled with a great many thoughts that he could barely put them into order.

"I will leave you for this evening," Mr. Grey said, a broad smile settling across his face as he reached to shake Colin's hand, although how Colin managed to lift his hand to accept it, he was not quite certain. "But I will return in the morning and perhaps we might discuss the details a little more."

Colin blinked rapidly and tried his best to nod and say something that was comprehensible but found himself only stammering, which made Mr. Grey chuckle, his expression no longer somber but one of great delight.

"Good evening, my lord," he said, bowing low and seeming to be filled with a newfound respect which Colin did not think he at all deserved. "I will return tomorrow."

Colin nodded but did not move, one hand still holding his empty brandy glass whilst the other clutched the papers Mr. Grey had given him. He was not even aware when the fellow left the room, nor when the front door closed again. All he could think of, all he could see, were the papers in front of him that held his new title.

It seemed that no matter how he felt or what he wished, he was now the Marquess of Lindale.

Setting down the papers on the table to his left, Colin poured the last of his brandy into his glass and took another sip, savoring it a little more this time. He would have to give up his farm, he realized, his heart aching as he considered it. He would be expected to go to his estate—but to do what? He had very little idea of what it meant to be such a highly titled gentleman.

"And I shall have to marry," he muttered, raking one hand through his brown hair, another shock running through him. Titled gentlemen would be expected to keep the family line consistent, for fear that it would pass on to a distant relation—such as it had done now.

Blowing out a long breath, Colin shoved his fingers through his hair one more time. "The Marquess of Lindale," he muttered to himself, still too overcome to believe it. "I will have to tell Arthur."

Shaking his head, Colin threw back the rest of his brandy and picked up the papers once more.

"The Marquess of Lindale," he said again, the name still strange on his lips. "I am the Marquess of Lindale."

1

"My lord, you have a visitor."

Colin smiled and nodded, ignoring the uncomfortable prickling that ran down his spine as he rose to welcome his guest. The last months had been very trying indeed but, now established as the Marquess of Lindale, Colin had nothing other to do but to throw himself fully into the role.

"Thank you," he said to the butler, before recalling that there was no need or expectation for him to thank the staff. The butler did not say a word, however, but stood respectfully to one side as another gentleman walked into the room.

Colin's stomach twisted. He had met Viscount Castleton last evening at his very first outing into society and had, somehow, managed to arrange for him to call today. He had been worried that Lord Castleton would either deliberately forget their arrangement or would, in turning up, laugh at what Colin had to say to him but, either way, Colin knew he could not continue on through society without making some sort of friendship. He only hoped that Viscount Castleton would understand.

"Good afternoon, Lord Lindale." Lord Castleton bowed smartly, his sharp brown eyes assessing Colin quickly as he rose.

"Thank you for coming," Colin replied, gesturing to a vacant chair and sitting back down in his own once his guest had made his way there. "I do appreciate it."

Lord Castleton chuckled. "You are the new Marquess of Lindale," he said as Colin made to get out of his chair to pour them both a brandy, only to recall that his butler was still present and, thus, ought to be the one to do it. Gesturing to his servant, he settled back in his chair and waited for the fellow to do so.

"An excellent brandy," Lord Castleton grinned, seeming to be quite at ease in Colin's company.

Colin grimaced, comparing the brandy he held in his hand to the brandy he had been used to drinking when he had been nothing more than a simple farmer. These last few months, he had been required to become accustomed to a good many things, including the fact that the very best of brandies was no longer well out of his reach.

"You do not think so?" Lord Castleton asked, evidently seeing Colin's grimace. "Or is it that you prefer a good whisky?"

Colin hesitated, then murmured to his butler that there was nothing further at present and that he was not to be disturbed. Waiting until the servant left, he turned back to face Lord Castleton, fully aware of the questions that were beginning to appear in the gentleman's eyes.

"Lord Castleton," he began as the gentleman took a sip of his brandy. "Last evening was my first outing into society, which I am sure that not only you but many others were aware of." His lips pulled into a small scowl as he recalled the many whispers that had followed his entrance. Had he made such a fool of himself that the *ton* would now be doing nothing other than speaking of it? "You were, I am glad to say, pointed out to me as an excellent gentleman and one who might be able to help me."

Lord Castleton's brow lifted. "Indeed?" he remarked, looking rather pleased. "I am glad to hear that my reputation is based on character rather than wealth."

Colin nodded, choosing not to mention that he had been

forced to demand such suggestions from his butler, who had, with great reluctance, managed to do so without too much difficulty. Colin had been given the names of three gentlemen whom the butler considered to be those within society who might be willing to assist Colin in all that he intended to do. Knowing none within society whatsoever, Colin had been forced to introduce himself to Lord Castleton as well as to one or two others, even though he knew by now that such a thing was considered to be very rude indeed.

"I had hoped," Colin continued, a little reluctantly, "that you might be willing to assist me, Lord Castleton."

The gentleman sat forward in his chair, a look of interest growing in his eyes. "Assist you, Lord Lindale?" he asked, sounding both intrigued and pleased. "I should be glad to do whatever I can to help the Marquess of Lindale."

"That is precisely the problem," Colin answered, before he could help himself. "I am uncertain as to how much you are aware of, Lord Castleton, but I am not long in this position."

Lord Castleton tilted his head just a little. "You have been six months as the new marquess," he said as Colin nodded. "That is all that I know."

Dragging in air, Colin forced himself to speak honestly. He knew that he was taking a great risk in doing this, since he would have to tell Lord Castleton the truth about his background, his astonishment at becoming marquess, and the six months of difficulty he had borne in order to prepare himself for becoming a gentleman of the *ton*. But what other choice did he have? He had no one else in London to turn to, no one else that he might ask for aid. He had taken the word of his butler and now hoped that he would not fail because of it.

"I have been told that you are trustworthy, Lord Castleton," he began slowly. "That what I am about to say to you will not be passed on to anyone else."

Lord Castleton frowned, the smile fading from his lips. "I do hope that this is nothing...untoward," he said hesitantly, and Colin shook his head fervently. "We are not very well acquainted as yet, Lord Lindale. Are you quite certain—?"

"It is *because* we are not very well acquainted that I have to speak to you about this," Colin replied hastily. "I have no other friends or acquaintances here in London."

This seemed to surprise the gentleman greatly for he lifted his brows in great astonishment as he looked back at Colin.

"You are, of course, wondering how such a thing could be," Colin continued with a small, wry smile. "If you will let me, I would be glad to explain."

It took a moment but eventually, Lord Castleton nodded and sat back a little more in his seat, watching Colin carefully.

"My father was the third son of the Marquess of Lindale," Colin began. "But for reasons I will not go into, he was disinherited. He moved to Scotland with his wife and set up home there." Spreading his hands, Colin's lips tipped in a rueful smile. "I did not know that I had two uncles on my father's side, nor that my grandfather was a marquess until some months ago."

Lord Castleton caught his breath, his eyes widening. "Indeed?"

"It is as I have said," Colin continued, quickly explaining the rest of the story. Lord Castleton continued to sit in evident astonishment, his eyes growing rounder still as Colin related how he had been forced to give up his farm, and, along with his brother, make his way to his new life as the Marquess of Lindale.

"My brother, Arthur, also inherited a great deal of money and land, and has chosen to stay in his estate for this summer," he finished. "He has a pretty little wife already, although they did not marry until a few months ago." A small smile lifted his lips as he thought of Marianne, who had followed Arthur from Scotland in order to take her place as his wife. "She was engaged to a farmer, only to find herself now a wife of a gentleman."

"Good gracious," Lord Castleton murmured, one hand at his chin as he stared back at Colin, clearly almost too overwhelmed with surprise to comment further. "That is…"

"The most ridiculous story, yes," Colin replied with a shake of his head. "I have no friends here in London, Lord Castleton. I am still trying to understand the *ton* and my place in it. The most pressing thing that has been set on my shoulders lately, by my solicitors and my advisor—the Mr. Grey I spoke of—is that I should establish myself in the midst of the *beau monde* and look to take a wife."

"So that you can quickly establish a family line," Lord Castleton remarked, nodding. "That is understandable."

Colin sighed inwardly. Yes, it might be understandable but it felt, yet again, as though he were throwing himself headlong into a whirlpool. He had no desire to marry, not when he was only just becoming used to the fact that he was a marquess rather than just a farmer. But over and over, he had been reminded of the fact that he was yet unmarried and needed to establish himself completely by finding a wife and producing an heir—something that apparently seemed to be very simple indeed for those in the nobility, whereas Colin himself preferred to choose a bride with great care and consideration.

"I will confess myself very much surprised by what you have said, Lord Lindale," Lord Castleton remarked after a few moments. "And you have told me all of this for a purpose, I suppose?"

Nodding, Colin cleared his throat, feeling a sense of embarrassment settle over him. "As I have said, Lord Castleton, I know no one here in London. Given that my father was disinherited, I have not spent time in the upper echelons of society." He chuckled wryly. "Six months ago, I was nothing other than a simple farmer, only to find my world entirely altered in less than a few minutes."

"And you need assistance to help guide you through the *beau monde* and its tempestuous sea?" Lord Castleton asked, one eyebrow lifting.

"I need..." Colin hesitated for a moment, trying to work out the best way to say what he required without sounding foolish. "I need a friend, Lord Castleton. Someone who will be able to understand my situation but will not speak to others of it. Someone who will be able to assist my steps as I fumble about here in London." One shoulder lifted in a half-shrug. "It is a lot of responsibility, I know, and I am sure I must have surprised you in not only inviting you here but then expressing all of this without so much as a—"

"I am greatly honored!" Lord Castleton interrupted, his eyes bright as he smiled back at Colin. "I should thank whoever recommended me also, for their consideration of my character is something I very much appreciate."

It was as though a great weight rolled from Colin's shoulders as he looked back at Lord Castleton and saw the contentment in his expression, the evident delight in being asked to do such a thing. "You are speaking truthfully, Lord Castleton?" he asked carefully, wanting to make certain that the gentleman was not being forced into an agreement whilst praying inwardly that he could trust the man. If he appeared in society this evening only to have everyone know of his background, of his hurried entrance into nobility, then he would know that he had failed in attempting to find a suitable acquaintance. Lord Castleton would *not* be the gentleman the butler had believed him to be.

Lord Castleton settled one hand over his heart, a look of seriousness coming into his eyes. "Lord Lindale, I confess that I am not only deeply gratified to hear that my character has been considered in such a good light, but also that I am very pleased indeed to be asked such a thing," he declared as Colin nodded slowly, doing all he could to believe him. "Your story is quite remarkable! Little wonder that you were forced to introduce yourself last evening."

Spreading his hands, Colin shrugged. "I have no acquaintances here," he said ruefully. "But I certainly do not want everyone to know why that is."

"Of course not, of course not," Lord Castleton nodded, agreeing quickly with what Colin had said. "I quite understand. You need not worry. You have taken a risk in speaking so to me, I understand, but it will not prove to be your downfall. I swear to you that I shall not breathe a word of what you have said to me."

"I am very grateful," Colin answered, only just realizing that his heart had been beating very quickly. "Very grateful indeed, Lord Castleton."

"And you will need me to introduce you to both gentlemen and ladies," Lord Castleton continued with a broad smile. "Something I shall be very happy to do. No doubt you will find your invitations to balls and soirées and the like greatly increasing."

A chuckle escaped from Colin's lips before he could prevent it. "Indeed, Lord Castleton, I have found myself overwhelmed with invitations so far," he said as Lord Castleton grinned. "The ball was one of the first I accepted, based solely on the advice of Mr. Grey, who has returned to London to continue with his work here. Since then, I haven't—have *not,*" he corrected, a little embarrassed, "I have not accepted any other. I do not know which is best to accept and which to ignore."

Lord Castleton nodded. "You do not ignore invitations but write that you send your regrets," he said as Colin listened eagerly, feeling not as though he were being taught by a stern teacher but rather as though he were being given very sage advice which he wanted eagerly to remember. "If you wish, you might have the invitations brought here and I can assist you with which to accept?"

"An excellent idea," Colin replied gratefully. Getting to his feet, he was about to make his way to the door so that he might fetch the stack of invitations himself from his study, only to veer to his right and tug at the bell pull.

"It is not something I am used to as yet," he said, coming to sit back down and seeing Lord Castleton's bemused glance. "I thought I would go and fetch the invitations myself, but..."

Lord Castleton chuckled. "But then you remembered that your butler would be most upset if you did so," he replied as Colin grinned. "You must have found these last few months rather trying."

Colin made to answer, but then a scratch at the door alerted him to the presence of the butler. Quickly calling him in, he explained what he wanted and the butler disappeared again.

"It has been very tiring," he found himself saying as Lord

Castleton listened with interest. "To be truthful, I did not want to give up my farm. I had spent so many years there with my brother, doing all we could to build it up, to make it profitable." He shook his head, his heart aching for the little Scottish home he had built for himself, knowing that he would never be able to return to that way of life. "I had to sell it."

"That must have been difficult for you."

"My brother did not seem as sorrowful as I," Colin replied, remembering how Arthur had practically danced around the room as he had taken in the news that he was, in fact, a wealthy landowner from an aristocratic family. "He was more than glad to make his way to my estate. We traveled there together and he stayed with me for the first month. We had to deal with a lot of papers and to gain an understanding of our holdings and what was expected of us." A small laugh pulled from his lips. "Although being a farmer and being a marquess both bring similar responsibilities in one way."

Lord Castleton lifted a brow. "Oh?"

"When I was a farmer, I worked the land with the other men we hired each day to work for us," Colin explained. "As a marquess, I am still to manage and oversee the land, I am just not supposed to ever become as involved as I would like."

Lord Castleton grinned. "You cannot put your hands in the soil," he remarked as Colin nodded. "Although I am sure your knowledge of farming will be a great benefit to your estate."

"I am very blessed that it is already so profitable," Colin replied truthfully. "My brother's estate is also doing very well. Arthur writes that he has enjoyed taking on these new responsibilities, although he has the additional benefit of his wife now with him."

"Something that you are yet to find," Lord Castleton chuckled as Colin smiled ruefully. "Have no fear, Lord Lindale, you will find many a gentleman in your position. Not all the ladies of London are as beautiful as they seem." His smile faded as he held Colin's gaze steadily for a moment. "There will be an increasing amount of interest in you. As the new Marquess of Lindale, and a marquess yet unmarried, the many young ladies of the *ton* will be eager to establish themselves as your wife."

Colin's mouth dropped open and Lord Castleton chuckled loudly.

"But they do not know me," he spluttered as the butler came back into the room. "They only know my title and nothing more."

"That will be more than enough," Lord Lindale replied, and Colin shook his head, raking one hand through his hair as his heart began to quicken all the more. "To know that you are titled, wealthy, and unattached will mean that the ladies of the *beau monde* will begin to press themselves into your acquaintance. Mothers will be eager to introduce their daughters. Widows will seek you out. It is important, therefore, that you treat all alike without making any preference—true or otherwise—obvious to anyone. Some you might establish a basic acquaintance with, whereas others you should only be introduced to but then greet as infrequently as you can."

Letting out a long breath, Colin gestured for his butler to leave them again, only to stop him and ask for their brandy glasses to be refreshed. After he had done so, the butler quit the room again, leaving Colin to stare down at the large stack of invitations that had been brought in on a silver tray. His head began to swim with heavy thoughts as he considered each one. He did not know whom to accept, and whom to write to with his regrets. And if he could not know such a thing as that, then how was he to be aware of which young ladies he ought to entertain in conversation and which he ought to turn from as soon as he could?

"You need not look so worried," he heard Lord Castleton say. He forced his gaze up from the letters and saw the gentleman grinning broadly, as though he found Colin's confusion entertaining. "You will do very well indeed; I am sure of it."

"You will help me?" Colin croaked, and Lord Castleton nodded, his grin still fixed in place as he reached for the first of the invitations.

"Gladly," came the reply. "Now, let us look at these and decide what you are to attend next." He gestured for Colin to pick one up also, his eyes then roving over the invitation he himself held. "This one you can send regrets to. Lord McKinley may be a Scottish baron but he is not to be considered good company for a marquess such as yourself." His nose wrinkled. "He imbibes far too much and his soireés are always very poor indeed." Setting the invitation aside, he gestured to the one Colin held. "And you?"

"A Lady Forsythe," Colin answered as Lord Castleton's eyes lit up. "To an evening soireé?" His eyes flicked over the date. "Goodness, it is tonight!"

"And not too late to reply and accept," Lord Castleton replied swiftly. "I am to be in attendance also and therefore, I think it would be an excellent occasion for you."

Colin nodded, glad that Mr. Grey had already made certain that all of his new clothes had been purchased in advance of him arriving in London. "Very well," he agreed, aware of a knot of tension that settled in his stomach. "I will write to her immediately."

"Good," Lord Castleton replied, looking quite satisfied. "And now to go through the rest."

Colin grimaced but reached for the next one anyway. Sighing, he resigned himself to an afternoon of going through his invitations and responding to them appropriately. He would not think about this evening for fear that it would make him all the more anxious. He was sure that, with Lord Castleton to help him, he would soon be able to make his way through society without *too* much difficulty.

2

"Will you please sit still, my lady!"

Ellen twisted her lips as her maid tugged at her hair for another moment before deftly pushing in another pin. It had been a rather painful procedure to have her hair set in such a delicate style, but Ellen knew that she had to make the best of impressions this evening. Her father, of course, would not be attending.

"I apologize if I spoke out of turn, my lady," the maid murmured, pushing in the final pin and then stepping back to examine Ellen's hair. "It is only that the master was quite specific about your appearance this evening."

"I am sure he was," Ellen replied, a little tightly. "My father is very eager that I should appear quite at my ease this evening." She grimaced and immediately, her reflection took on a most improper expression. No, that would not do. This evening, she could only nod and smile, regardless of what was said or what might be whispered about her.

"There," the maid replied, stepping a little further back still. "I believe you are quite ready, my lady."

Ellen looked at her reflection for a little longer, taking in the way her lady's maid had made certain to show off her red curls to their very best advantage. There were a few brushing her temples, with the rest pulled back to the top of her head in gentle twists. The curls ran freely from where they had been captured, moving gently as Ellen turned her head this way and that. A few seed pearls had been placed here and there and Ellen was certain she saw a glimpse of green also.

"Your emerald pins, my lady," the maid said, as though she knew precisely what Ellen was looking at. "It will bring attention to your eyes."

Ellen smiled tightly, knowing that her father wanted her to appear at her very best this evening in the hope that she might secure some interest from a gentleman or two. Perhaps they might seek to court her. But, without being pessimistic in her outlook, Ellen was quite settled on the fact that such a thing was very unlikely to occur. Gentlemen of the *ton* might dance with her, converse with her, and seem to give every impression of enjoying her company—and mayhap they did—but they would never consider courting her. Not when there were still rumors and whispers flying through London about her family.

"I should hurry, miss," the maid said gently, pulling Ellen carefully from her reverie. "Lady Sayers will be waiting for you."

Ellen nodded and rose, brushing her hands down her skirts, even though there was not a single crease in them. "Of course," she said practically as her maid handed her the reticule she was to take this evening. "And you are certain I look well?" It was the first trace of nervousness that Ellen had allowed to creep into both her voice and her questions, but the maid merely smiled and nodded reassuringly, before turning her head away and leaving Ellen to walk from the room without her.

∼

"You look very well this evening, Ellen."

"Thank you, Aunt," Ellen replied as Lady Sayers smiled back at her reassuringly while they waited in line to greet the host. "I do hope that..." She swallowed hard, forcing her anxiety back down into the depths of her heart. "I do hope that all goes well this evening."

"I am sure it will," Lady Sayers replied firmly. Ellen glanced at her and tried to draw courage from her aunt's formidable presence. Her aunt had always been a tower of strength, particularly in times such as these, and the fact that she had willingly offered to come to London and escort Ellen through society and the Season had meant a great deal not only to Ellen but to her father also. "And if they speak ill of you, then you need have no doubt that I shall do all I can to make certain that such whispers are immediately brought to an end."

Ellen nodded and took in another long breath, seeing that they were next in line to greet their host. Lady Forsythe, a widow of considerable means, and her son, Lord Forsythe, stood together, greeting the guests one at a time. Fixing a smile to her face, Ellen curtsied and spoke quietly and briefly to them both, thanking them for their kind invitation which, she knew, would not have been proffered by everyone within the *ton*.

"There, you see?" Lady Sayers told her, her eyes flashing as she took Ellen's arm, walking into the drawing room and looking all about her as she did so. "It went very well indeed, did it not?"

Letting out her breath slowly, Ellen nodded but did not say anything. To greet her hosts was one thing and, given that they had invited her to be present this evening, she did not think that they would have any difficulty in accepting her. It was the other guests present, however, that brought a good deal of anxiety to Ellen's heart.

"Good evening, Lady Sayers."

Ellen turned her head quickly as a lady greeted her aunt, although Ellen herself did not know who she was.

"Good evening, Lady Brittain," Lady Sayers replied quickly, curtsying. "How very good to see you again." Without hesitating, she turned to Ellen. "Might I introduce my niece?"

Lady Brittain's eyes flickered with awareness, although she smiled kindly at Ellen as she curtsied.

"Lady Ellen Rowe, daughter to my brother, the Earl of Grantown," Lady Sayers finished as Ellen rose. "And Ellen, this is Lady Brittain, a very dear friend of mine."

"And are you enjoying the Season this year, Lady Ellen?" Lady Brittain asked as Ellen's heart continued to quicken, fearful that Lady Brittain might turn away from her entirely or make some remark about what had occurred last Season. "I know it has only been a week or two but still, there have been a good many occasions already."

"I—I have only attended a few," Ellen replied quickly. "But yes, they have all been very enjoyable indeed."

Lady Brittain frowned, looking back steadily at Ellen as though she had only just seen her. "I suppose there will be those in the *beau monde* who consider the rumors from last Season to still be of great importance," she said as a flush of embarrassment rose in Ellen's cheeks. "I can assure you, Lady Ellen, that there is no belief within my own heart as regards the rumors of your father. Whenever I decide to throw a soireé of my own, I shall make quite certain to have you join us."

"That is very kind of you, Lady Brittain," Ellen managed to say, heat pouring into her cheeks as she bobbed yet another curtsy. "I very much appreciate your consideration."

Lady Brittain waved a hand as though it meant very little. "They are nothing more than rumors—and spurious ones at that!" she exclaimed as Ellen nodded fervently. "Your father might well be in financial difficulty, but whether or not that is true is nobody else's business but his own. And the suggestion as to how he came to be in such difficulties are quite ridiculous."

"I am sure that Ellen is glad you are so willing to dismiss such things, Lady Brittain," Lady Sayers said hastily. "Now, do tell us about your son. How does he fare?"

This made Lady Brittain launch into a great explosion of words, telling Lady Sayers all about her son, Lord Brittain, and the fact that not only had he wed last Season but that his wife was now in her confinement and they were all very much hoping for an heir. This, certainly, distracted her from any further remarks on Ellen and her father's situation, which greatly relieved Ellen. She listened without much attentiveness, wondering which of the other guests in the room might be so inclined to believe what was being said of her father.

A heavy sigh left her lips. She could not say precisely when such rumors had started, for she had not yet made her debut when her father had first gone to London for some important business. It had only been the year of her first entrance to society that she had learned of the whispers about him. It had not been through her father's explanation either, but rather the cold, cruel words of a lady of the *ton*. Ellen could still remember the chill that had come over her, the shock that must have been written on her face as those around her either laughed, sneered, or looked away in embarrassment.

Ever since then, the whispers had grown to rumors and Ellen had been forced to confront her father about them. He had told her, in no uncertain manner, that a particular gentleman had, unfortunately, taken a great deal of money from him. Land as well, for he had been forced to sell portions of land in order to clear whatever debt it was that he owed. Worst of all, Ellen had learned, this gentleman had been considered a friend of her father's, and he had not realized that the whole scheme had been nothing more than a ruse. Ellen did not know the details of such an arrangement but had been both angry and sorrowful over what her father had endured.

When Ellen had asked her father why he did not make known what this gentleman had done, so that the *ton* would know of it, he had simply shaken his head before rubbing one hand over his eyes, looking older than Ellen had ever seen him before. It seemed that, to pre-empt any such action by her father, this gentleman had gone on to spread rumors throughout London as to why her father was now in financial difficulty—and that it was as a result of his gambling, his drunkenness, and his penchant for visiting certain houses of disrepute.

The gentleman had shown her father a diary with a whole host of rumors, whispers, and gossip within it—although Lord Grantown had been unable to determine which were true and which were entirely false. What had made it all the worse, according to her father, was that the gentleman had shown him a small key and stated that, until he decided otherwise, such secrets and whispers would be kept hidden away, but that, at any time, they might all be brought to light. With great glee, the gentleman had declared that those whose names were written within this book would, of course, say whatever he wished them to for fear that he might reveal what he knew. Ellen had seen her father's shoulders slump as he had explained the situation to her. With such force behind him, he had known that there was no recourse but to accept the situation as it was. He had to endure the rumors and the lies, for it was only his word set against it.

This had all been told to Ellen in a calm manner, with her father stating, quite plainly, that nothing could be done and that, therefore, they would have to endure until the rumors died away. Ellen had pressed her father for the gentleman's name repeatedly until, finally, her father had given it to her. He had only done so in the knowledge that the gentleman in question had passed away and that, therefore, nothing could be done. But, of course, the rumors had continued and her father was unable to escape from them. Ellen had been affected also, for now many in the *ton* thought very poorly of her father and, therefore, very poorly of her. Had it not been for Lady Sayers and her determination that Ellen should continue on regardless and return to London for the Season, Ellen was quite certain that her father would have kept them both back at his estate.

If only I could find the diary, she thought to herself as Lady Brittain continued to speak of her son. *Then I might be able to prove to the ton that the rumors were nothing more than spurious lies. I might be able to show that the late Marquess of Lindale was a cruel, vindictive gentleman who stole from my father.*

Her jaw worked for a moment as she fought the anger that bubbled up within her. *Most likely, he stole from others also.* Of course, neither she nor her father had ever spoken to anyone of Lord Lindale's part in all the rumors and financial difficulties that now swirled around their family name—save for Lady Sayers, of course. They could not do so for fear of what might occur, and even though Ellen had suggested they speak of it now that the gentleman had passed away, her father had absolutely forbidden it.

"And we must include you also, Lady Ellen."

Ellen was brought back to the conversation, her cheeks no longer hot from the embarrassment that Lady Brittain's remarks about her father had brought.

"I should be very glad to be included," she replied quickly, even though she had very little idea as to what Lady Brittain was saying. "You are very kind to think of me."

Lady Brittain made to say something more, only for her eyes to flare wide as she looked over Ellen's shoulder, her breath catching at the sight she was taking in.

"Can it be?" she whispered, one hand reaching out to grasp Lady Sayers' arm. "Yes, I believe it is!"

Resisting the urge to turn around and look at whomever Lady Brittain was speaking of, Ellen kept her tone steady. "Is there someone there of importance, Lady Brittain?"

"Yes, yes, indeed," Lady Brittain hissed, her hand still tight on Lady Sayers' arm. "I was introduced to him only yesterday but now it seems he is to join the soireé this evening also." She smiled brightly at Ellen, who attempted to appear interested whilst wondering just when they might extract themselves from the lady.

"It is the new Marquess of Lindale," Lady Brittain said softly.

Ellen caught her breath, her eyes flinging themselves toward Lady Sayers, who looked just as astonished as she now felt. Her heart began to hammer furiously in her chest as the name repeated itself over and over in her mind.

Lady Brittain continued heedlessly, not at all aware of the effect her words were having on Ellen. "He has come with Viscount Castleton, it seems. They must be well acquainted, then, although I confess I am a little surprised, given the difference in their titles." She shrugged and then continued, her voice holding more and more excitement with almost every word she spoke. "I think he would be an excellent gentleman for you, Lady Ellen. You are the daughter of an earl after all!"

"A slightly disgraced daughter of an earl," Ellen muttered, before giving in to the urge to turn around and moving just a little so that she might stand by Lady Sayers instead of in front of her. Her eyes sought out the gentleman in question but, given that there were so many of them all around her, she could not tell which one she was meant to be studying. Her chest tightened painfully as Lady Brittain cheerfully pointed him out, her gaze finally landing on the gentleman and her heart burning furiously with an anger that she knew he did not fully deserve.

The new Marquess of Lindale was a little younger than she had expected, given that the deceased marquess had lived many years. Was it his son? She frowned, recalling that her father had told her that the man had no son. A cousin, then?

"I thought the title would have passed to the Marquess' brother," she found herself saying, and Lady Brittain nodded fervently.

"Well," Lady Brittain replied in a most eager voice. "It seems that Lord Henry Montgomery, the prior marquess' younger brother, did not have any children of his own before he passed away. Therefore, the title went to a distant relation of the marquess, I believe. *That* gentleman."

A little calmer now, Ellen looked carefully at the gentleman and allowed herself to study him. He was tall, with broad shoulders and a strong back, but yet there was a reserve to him that she had not expected. Those with high titles, such as a marquess, usually made their way through society with great ease and confidence. There was usually an inordinate amount of pride in themselves, as though they deserved the praise, respect, and almost reverence of those beneath them, but she did not think that would be the case with *this* particular marquess.

An idea came to her mind almost immediately. What if she were to acquaint herself with the marquess? Would there then be any possibility of her making her way into his home, perhaps by way of a visit, and thereafter, beginning to search for the late marquess' diary? She could not simply ask him to do so, could not simply demand that he give her what she asked. For all she knew, the diary might well have been destroyed, or be amongst the marquess' possessions back at his estate.

But would it be worth trying?

The answer was with her in an instant. Of course, any opportunity to do so would be worth attempting. It would mean that she would have to pretend to be interested in the marquess' company, that she would have to give the impression that all was well. He could not know of the diary or that she considered the late marquess responsible for the difficulties with her father at present. That would all depend, however, on whether or not he would be willing to greet her also. He might consider her to be unworthy of his attention.

"I think I should like to be introduced," she said quietly as her aunt shot her a sharp look. "You said you were acquainted with him, Lady Brittain?"

Lady Brittain nodded eagerly. "I should be glad to introduce you, Lady Ellen," she said, looking to Lady Sayers, who nodded her agreement. "Come now, let us do so whilst he is not surrounded by other guests. I am sure he will be very soon, for there is a great deal of interest in his arrival in London."

Pasting a gentle smile on her face and completely ignoring the anxiety that swirled about her soul, Ellen allowed Lady Brittain to lead her toward Lord Lindale. When he looked toward her, she felt her stomach twist with a mixture of nervousness and anger. She took him in as Lady Brittain quickly made the introductions, making first Lady Sayers known to him and then Ellen. His eyes were a light brown and filled with what Ellen took to be curiosity, although there was still a reserve about him that spoke of perhaps uncertainty or a lack of confidence—which was rather surprising, given his status. She had to admit that he was handsome, with his warm eyes, square jaw, firm lips, and broad shoulders.

"Lord Lindale," she murmured, dropping into a curtsy. "How very good to meet you."

3

"Your first sennight has gone very well indeed," Lord Castleton declared, and Colin nodded, a small smile spreading across his face. "You have been introduced to a great many gentlemen and ladies, you have accepted *many* invitations, and found yourself a gentleman whose attention is very often sought out."

"That is true, certainly," Colin admitted, finding that he was not as pleased as his friend over the latter remark. "Although I do not think that anyone wants my company solely for myself." He grimaced as Lord Castleton laughed.

"You mean they wish you there so that they might foist their daughters upon you or introduce you to their sister or cousin," he replied as Colin nodded fervently. "Or because they believe that you might be willing to spread a little of your fortune around at their game of cards?"

"I have avoided that so far," Colin replied as Lord Castleton chuckled. "I understand the game, certainly, but I am not confident enough to include any coin."

"That is wise," Lord Castleton replied, nodding. "But I am afraid that, with your title such as it is, there will be those in the *ton* who are eager only for your company simply because of your fortune, your status, or the fact that you are, as yet, unwed." He lifted one shoulder. "It is to be expected."

Colin sighed and ran one hand over his eyes. He had expected that coming to London and joining the *ton* would be difficult, but he had not thought it would be so very intricate and complex. Save for Lord Castleton, he did not feel as though he knew any other gentleman or lady very well indeed and was not at all certain that anything they spoke of had been of benefit to either himself or to them.

"They will not speak honestly or openly to you," Lord Castleton warned, getting up to help himself to Colin's brandy. "That is not something you should expect."

"I find that very strange indeed," Colin replied truthfully. "When I worked on the farm, we all spoke the truth to each other, without hesitation. Now I find myself in a place where the very opposite happens."

Lord Castleton shrugged and took a sip of his brandy. "It will take a little getting used to, I am sure," he answered, as though it was not anything of consequence. "It seems as though everyone in London is talking of you."

Colin rolled his eyes. "They talk about me because I am a marquess, with wealth and title, as you have said," he stated as Lord Castleton chuckled. "And because I am not *quite* as proper as they might expect." He had been all too aware of the differences in speaking between himself and other members of the *ton* this last sennight. There were times where he had simply stood and listened to what had been said, worrying that he might speak improperly and make a fool of himself otherwise.

"That may be so, but I would suggest that makes you something of an enigma," Lord Castleton continued airily. "They want to know more about you, want to discover all they can about you."

Again, Colin did not take this with the same delight that Lord Castleton expressed. He had found the attention of the many young ladies that had been thrust into his company very difficult indeed. He had not known quite how to react, although he had strived to make conversation with them, certainly. They had seemed to think everything he had said was quite marvelous, had laughed at him and fluttered their eyelashes in what he thought was meant to be a very becoming manner. Of course, he had not found it so but evidently, he was meant to delight in all the attention that had been bestowed on him.

"It would be easier for you if you simply chose one lady and then decided to court her," Lord Castleton suggested, and Colin shuddered violently at the very thought. "That would be one way to remove their attention from you, although you would soon find that there would be others seeking you out thereafter."

Colin frowned. "Others?"

"A potential mistress," Lord Castleton replied, as though it was something that Colin ought to have expected. "Many married gentlemen seek one out, particularly when they are in London and mayhap their wives have remained at the estate with their children." He shrugged. "It is not for me to say whether it is appropriate or not, but it is not something that I myself would choose."

"Nor I," Colin replied fervently. "I hope I would not be as selfish a gentleman as that."

Lord Castleton smiled but said nothing.

"I have appreciated all of your help so far, Lord Castleton," Colin continued, a little more meekly. "I do not think that I would have been so accepted into society had you not been of such great assistance."

"I am only grateful that you were willing to ask me," Lord Castleton replied. "Now, you must tell me whether or not there are any particular young ladies that have caught your interest."

"None," Colin stated firmly. "None whatsoever." Part of him wished that he had been like Arthur, his brother, and had already had a sweetheart before the title had been given to him. Then finding a wife would not have mattered. He would have already been wed and, regardless of her status, they would have found a way together.

Now, not only did he have to attempt to fit in amongst the gentry, he also had to try and work out what sort of young lady would be suitable for him as his wife. He did not want a young lady who would laugh at his past, who would mock him for the farmer he had once been. Nor did he want a young lady who would think too highly of herself in relation to him, who would always consider herself a little better than he. And certainly, he did not want to wed a lady who cared only for his title and his fortune.

"I think you shall have to host a dinner party soon," Lord Castleton said abruptly, surprising Colin entirely. "Or an evening soireé, whichever is preferable."

Colin blinked rapidly, surprised at just how nervous and anxious he felt at the suggestion. "But I know nothing about dinner parties."

"You have already been to one," Lord Castleton reminded him. "And I am to have one next week, which, of course, you are to attend also." He shrugged. "It is simple enough."

The idea still sent waves of anxiety through Colin, but he forced himself to take a deep breath and tried to think sensibly. He could not put off such things for the rest of the Season. This was something that would continue to be expected of him for the rest of his life, for even when he was wed and settled back at his estate, there would be all manner of such occasions for him to host.

"Very well," he said uneasily. "You will have to tell me which of the *ton* I am to invite."

"Excellent!" Lord Castleton exclaimed, looking quite delighted at the prospect of helping Colin host such a thing. "You will need a mix of both gentlemen and ladies, young and old." One brow lifted. "Shall we make a list now?"

∽

COLIN FROWNED HARD. "THAT ONE," he said, gesturing to the painting that hung on the wall in front of him. The footman stepped forward and carefully lifted it from the wall to the floor, leaving a blank space where it had hung. Colin grimaced. He had not liked that painting ever since he had stepped into this house and, in an attempt to make it feel as though he actually lived here rather than resided in another person's home, he had decided to alter the décor just a little.

"My lord?"

One of the footmen frowned as he looked down at the painting in his hand.

"There is something present here, my lord."

Colin moved toward him. "Oh?"

"I cannot say what it is, my lord," the footman replied, setting the painting down against the wall. "But it might be worthy of note."

Bending down, Colin looked at the back of the painting and noticed, much to his surprise, a small brass key that was, for some reason, attached to the back of the frame. Rather than pick it up, however, he simply looked all about him for somewhere the key might go. He found himself studying the wall, the table with the various trinkets upon it, and any other nook and cranny that might hold something important but could see nothing.

"It does not look very significant," he muttered, half to himself. Shrugging, he rose to his feet. Given that he was soon due to attend Lord Castleton's house party, Colin knew he had very little time remaining before he would need to prepare himself to leave. His valet would, most likely, be already waiting for him. "Well, I should say to put the painting as it is with the key into the study for the time being. I will examine it further later on."

The footman nodded and lifted the painting again, making his way toward the study and leaving Colin to scrutinize the blank wall that now stared back at him. He had very little idea of what to place there instead but, given that he had every intention of making this townhouse feel a little more like his own, there was no particular rush to find anything to replace the painting he had just moved. It was not as though any other person would see it.

"Good evening, Lord Lindale."

Colin bowed quickly, trying desperately to remember the lady's name. "Good evening," he answered, his mind screaming at him that it could not recall her title or how he ought to address her. He looked to the lady's mother, quickly remembering that she was Lady Fassington. "Good evening, Lady Fassington," he said, seeing the older lady smile. "You are both enjoying the evening so far?"

"Lord Lindale, we have only just arrived," the young lady laughed as a flush of embarrassment soared into Colin's cheeks. "But yes, if you are seeking a compliment then I should say that we are *very* much enjoying being in your company again."

"I assure you, I am searching for no such thing," Colin replied fervently, praying that the heat would soon dissipate from his face. "It does look to be an excellent evening, however." He could not think of what else to say, looking down into the young lady's face and seeing her simpering smile and fluttering lashes, and finding his heart twisting in his chest. He did not want this flirtation, this overt interest in him. Why could they not simply talk to him without any other motive?

"Tell me, Lord Lindale, about your estate," the young lady said, her eyes flooding with genuine interest. "Is it very far from London?"

Clearing his throat and feeling relieved that he could talk easily about this particular topic, Colin quickly began to describe his estate. He talked of the distance it was from London, the extensive grounds, the fishing that he had only just come to enjoy, and the wide-open spaces of the gardens that brought him so much pleasure. Much to his surprise, the young lady did not look at all pleased by his remarks. Rather, she began to frown, her lips pulling into a thin line. What was it he had said that displeased her so?

"That is all very well, Lord Lindale," she said tightly, "but what is the *manor house* like?" She sighed and spread her hands. "I am interested in the gardens and the river, of course, but I should much prefer to know the rooms that are contained within." Another sigh left her, but this one was more dreamlike, as though she were building a picture in her mind that he could not quite make out. "Do you have more than one drawing room? And is the ballroom quite magnificent?"

Colin hesitated, wondering whether he ought to oblige her with all that she sought or if he should speak the truth to her. In the end, he chose the latter, for given that he could not yet recall the young lady's name and that he disliked her manner toward him, he did not think there was any need to encourage whatever it was she hoped for when it came to their acquaintance.

"I do not really recall," he told her, still wishing he could remember her name so that he might address her directly. "I believe I have only set foot once in the ballroom and, if I am honest, I spent most of my time either in my study, in the library, or out of doors." He lifted one shoulder in a half-shrug. "The gardens, fields, and rivers are of much more importance to me, you understand."

This did not please the young lady at all, for she lifted her chin and stared at him hard, perhaps thinking that he was speaking this way purposefully in order to dissuade her from considering the estate any further.

"That sounds quite marvelous, Lord Lindale."

He turned his head and saw yet another young lady drawing near to him, accompanied by an older lady who was, he noted, watching him with sharp eyes. She smiled at him for a moment, but the expression soon returned to a watchful one, as though she suspected he might do something very terrible indeed.

"I thank you," he replied, looking at the second young lady now as his mind began to tear across the various names he had learned only last week. Who was she? "That is kind of you to say."

The young lady smiled at him again and then bobbed a quick curtsy in the direction of the first young lady and her mother. "Lady Fassington," she murmured, rising quickly. "Miss Wainwright. Good evening to you both."

"Good evening," Miss Wainwright replied, now looking rather

put out that she was no longer the only one talking with Colin. "You are…" She hesitated, tilting her head to one side. "It is Lady Ellen, is it not?"

"It is," the second young lady replied with a warm smile, although Colin felt the sting of Miss Wainwright's words. Had she deliberately pretended not to recall Lady Ellen's name for one reason or another?

"And," Lady Ellen continued quickly, "you recall my aunt, Lady Sayers?"

"But of course," Lady Fassington said hastily, clearly eager not to allow her daughter to make any sort of misstep. "Good evening to you both. We were just discussing Lord Lindale's estate. He was telling us of the fields and the rivers that he so clearly enjoys."

Lady Ellen turned back to Colin and looked at him, her eyes a vivid green. He took her in for a moment, seeing the way her red curls seemed to glow bronze in the evening's fire and candlelight. She had high cheekbones and full lips, making her rather pretty, although he felt as though there was something sharp in her gaze which detracted a little from her loveliness. It was as though she were hiding something from him, as though she did not think well of him but had not yet spoken of it to anyone.

"My father's estate grounds are also very lovely," she said with a small smile. "Although it is not always the right weather to enjoy them."

"Indeed," Colin answered quickly, not wishing to remind her that he had not yet been at his estate for even a year and so could not remark upon such a thing himself. "There is much to be done within the house itself also, of course."

"Oh?" Miss Wainwright took a small step closer to him, her eyes now fixed to his as they blazed with an interest he was sure was put on solely for his benefit, to puff up his pride that she was hanging on every word he spoke. "And what might that be?"

Colin shrugged, feeling a little uncomfortable with Miss Wainwright's closeness and her prying questions. He did not want to answer her for fear of giving her a little more encouragement in their acquaintance but knew that it would be rude of him not to do so.

"It is the same as must be done here in London," he said, glancing over Miss Wainwright's shoulder and seeing Lord Castleton throwing his head back in laughter at some remark that had been made. It did not look as though his friend would be able to come and rescue him from this particular difficulty any time soon. "The previous Lord Lindale has left the house just as he wished it. Therefore, I must take the opportunity to look through all that has been left behind, all that sits on the tables and hangs on the wall, to see whether or not I wish it to remain." He hoped that such an explanation was clear and, with a small smile, spread his hands. "I do not always care for certain things, you understand."

The two young ladies nodded eagerly, clearly wanting to make quite apparent that they understood all that had been said.

"For example, only this afternoon, I had a few paintings removed from the walls," Colin continued, seeing that Lord Castleton had finally glanced in his direction, only for a broad grin to settle across the man's face. Colin frowned hard in the hope that his friend would understand and come near to him, perhaps ready to enter the conversation at once, but Lord Castleton merely shrugged, laughed, and turned away entirely.

"Is something the matter, Lord Lindale?" he heard Miss Wainwright say and, glancing at her, realized that his frown had been noted by them all. Embarrassment flared in his chest and he let out a small laugh, trying desperately to think of some excuse.

"There is nothing the matter, no," he replied desperately as Lady Ellen raised one eyebrow and looked back at him steadily, clearly waiting for his explanation. "It is only that I remember..." He hesitated for a moment before, finally, his mind settled on one thing that might be a reasonable excuse. "I was thinking of the small key that I found at the back of one of the paintings this afternoon."

This seemed to be an excellent excuse for both the young ladies let out a small exclamation of surprise, which made Colin nod fervently, holding onto the excuse all the more. "It was only a small key and, truth be told, my footman was the one to discover it," he continued, speaking with a good deal more ease now. "It had been placed at the back of the painting and secured there."

"Goodness!" Miss Wainwright exclaimed, her eyes wide with apparent interest. "And you do not know where it came from or what it might open?"

"I do not," he told her with a small smile. "A mystery, it seems."

"And there was nothing around you that might be opened by the key?" Lady Ellen asked, her voice holding a slight hardness that surprised him. "Nothing that you considered to be a hiding place, for example?"

Spreading his hands, he looked at her. "I looked but there was nothing I could see," he answered, surprised at the fierce look in her eyes. "It is of very little interest to me at present, however. I will continue to decorate the house as I see fit and perhaps, in time, I will discover where it is to go."

"And where is the key now?" she asked, before Miss Wainwright could speak. "Have you kept it somewhere safe?"

A chuckle escaped him, for it was clear that this story brought a good deal more interest to both the young ladies than it had ever done to him. "No, I have simply had the painting and the key placed in my study for the moment. I do not much like the painting, I confess. I fully intend to replace it with one that is much more to my preference."

Miss Wainwright lowered her head but looked up at him from under her lashes, a slight pink to her cheeks. "I should be glad to advise you, should you ever require it," she said softly as Lady Ellen looked away quickly. "I do know a little about art and the like. I have taken a great many pains to improve myself these last few years."

Colin stiffened but thanked her, his smile fading quickly as he realized that no matter what he said, it appeared that Miss Wainwright would do whatever she could to suggest a furthering of their acquaintance. It was rather obvious, of course, but he found himself all the more reluctant to accept her. He did not like the flirtation or her forwardness. But, of course, he could not say so. He had to find a way to extract himself without insult.

"That is very kind of you, Miss Wainwright," he said, grateful that Lord Castleton had, in his own way, prepared Colin for situations such as this. "Should the need ever arise, I shall know precisely whom to turn to for advice."

This made Miss Wainwright blush and, for a moment, Colin feared that he had said the wrong thing and that he had somehow given the impression that he was eager for her company but, much to his relief, he quickly realized that he had done no such thing. He was all the more grateful when the dinner gong sounded, and their conversation was brought to an end.

"Ah!" he exclaimed, turning toward the door where the line would form. "And now we are to dine, it seems." Turning back to Miss Wainwright, he inclined his head to her before doing the very same to Lady Ellen. "Thank you both for your company and conversation."

They both murmured a reply, although Miss Wainwright's cheeks were still pink and her smile still lingering, whereas Lady Ellen looked away quickly and showed no sign of interest in him in any way whatsoever. That, Colin had to admit, was something of a relief and, turning toward the line, he made his way there quickly so that he would not hold the other guests up. There was a good deal he had to take note of this evening so that his own dinner party, in a few days' time, would go just as well as this.

And I have invited Lady Ellen and Lady Sayers, I think, he thought to himself as he found his place. *But not Miss Wainwright and Lady Fassington.* The thought made him smile as he waited in line, his heart lifting just a little. It would be far easier to have at least one young lady there who would not openly share her flirtations and show such eagerness to further her acquaintance with him. And given how Lady Ellen had spoken and appeared this evening, Colin was quite certain he could depend upon her for that.

4

Ellen smiled as warmly as she could as she curtsied toward Lord Lindale, her heart hammering furiously in her chest as she did so.

"Good evening, Lady Ellen," he said, smiling at her. "I am very glad you could join me this evening."

"But of course," she answered as Lady Sayers watched on approvingly. "I am very glad to be present." That part, certainly, was very true indeed and, seeing other guests now coming to stand behind her, Ellen quickly took her leave and hurried a little further into the room.

"I think Lord Lindale is a very interesting gentleman," her aunt murmured, and Ellen nodded quickly, not wanting to speak openly about what she herself thought. "I know you do not want to associate with him a great deal, but I do not believe that he is anything like his late uncle."

Ellen sighed and looked away. "I do not think we can make such a judgment as yet, Aunt," she told Lady Sayers, whose eyes fixed to Ellen's for a long moment, studying her carefully. "I will reserve my opinion of him until I know him a little better."

Lady Sayers paused for a few moments, then lifted one

shoulder in a half-shrug, looking away from her niece. "You may be right," she said quietly. "But it is an honor to be invited this evening. You will note that Miss Wainwright was not included, it seems."

This made Ellen smile, for the way she had seen Miss Wainwright speak with Lord Lindale had made a lasting impression upon Ellen herself as well as, she was certain, Lord Lindale.

"She will be disappointed," Ellen replied as Lady Sayers laughed. "I am quite sure that she was desperate to make herself known to him."

"I am sure that she was," Lady Sayers replied with a small smile. "Although perhaps he did not appreciate her forwardness."

A wry smile tugged at Ellen's lips. Miss Wainwright had made her interest in Lord Lindale more than apparent, for she had done very little save for batting her eyelashes at him, smiling appreciatively, and doing all she could to hold the conversation to herself without allowing Ellen to share it. Not that Ellen had found much disappointment in such a thing, however, for she had been much too busy considering the painting and the small key that he had mentioned. When Lord Lindale had first mentioned it, she had felt every part of her freeze in place, a buzzing in her ears as she realized that he might well have found the very same key that the late Lord Lindale had taunted her father with. The key that would reveal the hiding place of the diary.

That was why she was very glad to be present this evening. She had every intention of making her way to Lord Lindale's study at some point in the evening, in the hope of discovering the small key and studying it. Quite what she would do thereafter, she did not know, but she prayed that the key itself might be an answer to the many prayers she had whispered over the last few months. Perhaps it would open a drawer, or a hidden space where she might be able to discover the late Lord Lindale's diary—although she would not have long to search through Lord Lindale's study itself.

Or perhaps Lord Lindale has found the diary already, she thought to herself, knowing she was taking a great risk in even considering doing such a thing. *But how can I know?*

Biting her lip, Ellen wondered whether or not she ought to mention such a thing to Lord Lindale, only to shake her head to herself. To do so would be to tell Lord Lindale about the sort of man his uncle had been and, if he did not know of the diary, then he would think her very rude indeed to insult the gentleman in that way. And if he *did* know of the diary, then he had no real need to tell her of it himself. Mayhap she might mention the key to him, to see whether or not he had ascertained what it might open.

She sighed and looked back toward the gentleman in question. Her aunt was right. Lord Lindale did appear to be an excellent gentleman, who spoke with such contentment about his estate that he appeared to be very grateful for it all. Ellen had to confess herself a little surprised that he had not spoken at length about the many rooms of his estate or the size of his ballroom, or made any other remark such as that, but had instead spoken of the grounds, the rivers, and the fields that surrounded it. He was not as she might have expected but that did not mean that she knew his character well enough to consider him to be either a kind or an amiable gentleman.

"You are looking very thoughtful, my dear."

Ellen looked up sharply, seeing her aunt watching her and realizing that she had become quite lost in thought. "I apologize, Aunt," she said hastily. "I was thinking about..." She shook her head. "It is foolish to consider Father and his difficulties at present but there is a certain struggle within my heart that comes simply from standing here within this house."

"Of course there is," Lady Sayers said, as though she had fully expected Ellen to say such a thing. "But we cannot judge the present Lord Lindale by the behavior of his late uncle." She looked across at him. "I confess I was a little surprised when you first sought an introduction, but I believe you were wise to do so. After all, to hold a grudge would not be wise."

Ellen nodded and smiled but did not say anything in response, not wanting to lie to her aunt but, at the same time, unwilling to state the truth. She had not garnered an introduction to Lord

Lindale simply so that she might heal whatever rift had been between her family and his, but rather in the hope that, somehow, she might get her hands on the late Lord Lindale's diary and, therefore prove to the *ton* that the rumors were entirely untrue. That would, of course, bring a little embarrassment and shame to Lord Lindale himself, but Ellen did not need to think of that. There was no requirement for her to do so, particularly when she cared very little about the gentleman in question. Besides which, it would only be a small amount of what her father had been forced to endure.

"He is handsome," Lady Sayers murmured, looking at Ellen with a slight gleam in her eye. "And you the daughter of an earl."

"I could never even *imagine* such a thing, Aunt," Ellen declared, quite taken aback that Lady Sayers would even make such a remark.

Although, the thought of spending more time with Lord Lindale did spark an unexpected quickening of her heart.

Ellen quickly dismissed her own thoughts. "Father would never condone it. Could you imagine how he would feel if I were to take up with the relation of his enemy?"

Lady Sayers tutted and shook her head. "I am sure that your father would see the wisdom in such a match, regardless of Lord Lindale's connection to his late uncle. If you wished to try for him, then I would have nothing but encouragement for you."

"I am surprised to hear you say so, Aunt," Ellen replied, speaking honestly. "I would have thought you would have discouraged such a relationship."

Her aunt shook her head. "You must understand, Ellen, that my sole purpose is, at present, to find you a suitable match and to make sure that, as best I can, the rumors about your father do not cling to you. If Lord Lindale is a suitable gentleman—and he most certainly is—then I see no difficulty in presenting him to you. Although, of course, we must be assured of his character first."

Ellen was now the one to shake her head firmly, wanting to make one thing very clear to her aunt. "Aunt, I could never even consider him," she said adamantly. "I have already stated that there is a struggle within my heart to even be present here, and whilst you might hope that such a struggle will, in time, fade away, I am quite certain it will not."

Lady Sayers sighed at this and looked away, clearly frustrated but willing to accept what Ellen said, for which Ellen was deeply grateful.

"Ah, and there is the dinner gong," Lady Sayers remarked, looking toward Ellen again. "Shall we go through? I confess I am looking forward to seeing what is presented this evening."

"As am I," Ellen replied, making her way to join the line. "As am I, Aunt."

∼

SLIPPING AWAY from the drawing room and the many delightful activities going on within it was a lot easier than Ellen had expected. Lord Lindale had clearly put a lot of thought into what this evening would hold, for there were not only cards for those who wished to play, but also music and dancing. Part of the room had been cleared so that there was space for a few couples at a time and, of course, the younger ladies present were eager to step out with Lord Lindale, who managed to oblige them. Murmuring to her aunt that she needed a few minutes—an excuse that her aunt understood to mean the retiring room—Ellen quit the room quickly, praying that her absence would not be missed by her aunt should she take longer than expected. Lady Sayers was deep in conversation with another lady, however, and Ellen hoped that the conversation would distract her aunt for long enough to keep her unaware of when Ellen returned.

Her breathing was coming quickly as she made her way through the house, seeing the occasional footman or maid passing her. They all inclined their heads, but none asked where she was going, given that it would be more than a little improper for them to do so. Glancing over her shoulder, she was relieved to see the staff making their way elsewhere, perhaps below stairs or to the drawing room itself, leaving her free—at least for the moment—to explore.

The first room she opened was the library. Closing the door quickly and wincing at the noise she made, Ellen hesitated and turned around again, praying no one was watching her.

Her shoulders dropped with relief. There was no one present.

Making her way across the hallway, she tried the next door, and much to her delight, found herself peering into what was clearly Lord Lindale's study. There were more than a few candles lit, meaning that she was easily able to see about her, although she picked one up carefully in order to help her with her search. Making sure to close the door behind her, Ellen took in a long breath and looked all about.

The study was not as tidy as she had expected. Having been in her father's study more than once, both here in London and back at the estate, she had always thought that a gentleman would keep his private space very neat indeed—but it was not so with Lord Lindale. There were all manner of things placed together in piles, as though he had looked about the room and decided what he did not like and had, therefore, set them all aside together.

And then she remembered what he had said about attempting to change the furnishings about the house and it all quickly made sense—although certainly he should have instructed footmen to remove such items if he had decided against them.

"The painting," she murmured, looking all about her. There were papers lying in piles on almost every surface, small ornaments sometimes atop them, and as she gingerly made her way across the room, she saw books set in great stacks upon the floor. Clearly, Lord Lindale was in the midst of a very thorough cleaning or he simply was a most untidy fellow indeed.

And then, she saw it.

Her breath hitched as she caught sight of a painting set on the floor, leaning against the wall. It was of a great and terrible sea, dark clouds pouring down upon it. Walking on legs that were beginning to shake, Ellen made her way across to it and, setting her candle down carefully, bent down to look at it. Leaning it forward, she searched eagerly behind it, looking into the frame as best she could, but much to her disappointment, found nothing at all.

Her heart sank. She was just about to set it back against the wall when she noticed another painting, one that was now hidden behind a great pile of books just to her right. Had she not moved the first painting, then she might not even have noticed it.

My aunt will be looking for me soon, said a warning voice in her head. *I must hurry.*

She contemplated what to do for a moment. The books were stacked very high and to lift one book at a time did not seem like a wise recourse, given her lack of time. Thus, she reached out and took a hold of the top of the frame, yanking it with all of her might.

The books came crashing forward, toppling over in a very noisy fashion. Ellen winced and turned about, her heart in her throat as she waited to see if anyone had overheard the noise and would come to see what had occurred. What would she say then? What excuse could she make that would be a satisfactory explanation as to why she was in Lord Lindale's study without his explicit permission?

Her skin crawled as tension climbed up her spine, her heart beating so loudly she was certain that the sound of it filled the room—but no one came to the door. Turning back to the painting, she quickly set it down against the first, leaning it back so that she might study the back.

There!

A glint caught her eye and she reached out at once, her fingers closing over the small key. Holding it in her hand, she looked down at it and felt her heart swell with relief.

But what was she to do now?

Her sense of victory deflated in an instant as she looked about the room and knew that she had no time to search for what it might open. The room was in too great a state of disarray and, besides which, she was already very late. Her aunt might come to look for her if she did not return soon, and then what would happen?

Her hand tightened over the key and, before she could think of the consequences of what she was doing, she had slipped it into her pocket and made her way back to the door. Opening it as quietly as she could, she stepped out slowly, seeing no one about. Closing it behind her, she set her shoulders and made her way back to the drawing room without hesitation.

Stepping inside, Ellen was greatly relieved when her aunt merely glanced at her and then nodded, before turning back to her conversation. Evidently, the length of time she had been absent had gone entirely unnoticed by Lady Sayers.

But what are you to do about that key?

A sudden thrill of horror ran down Ellen's spine as she realized she had not stopped to put the painting back where she had found it. Instead, she had left it leaning against the seascape and all the books had been left on the floor.

She swallowed hard, making her way slowly back to where she had first been seated. Feeling someone's gaze settling upon her, she glanced up—only to see Lord Lindale looking back at her.

Her heart leapt into her throat, but she forced herself to give him a quick, demure smile before looking away again. He had not seen her enter the room again, had he? Her skin prickled with the awareness of his gaze as heat raced through her frame, making its way up into her cheeks.

"Lady Ellen, might you care to dance?"

She looked up with relief, seeing Lord Castleton holding out one hand to her as he bowed low.

"I would be delighted," she replied quickly, greatly relieved that he had stepped forward and taken her from Lord Lindale's view. "I thank you, Lord Castleton."

He smiled and she accepted his hand, rising from her chair and seeing her aunt give an approving nod. Without daring another glance at Lord Lindale, Ellen made her way toward the other dancers, all too aware of the small brass key that was still sitting in her pocket.

5

Colin frowned. He had not set foot in his study since yesterday afternoon and now, having come back to it this morning, he was quite certain that something was wrong.

Yes, the room was very untidy indeed, but he had needed, at the very least, one room in the house to feel like his own and, therefore, had set his mind to the task. Focusing on his study and his bedchamber, he had set aside all the things he did not care for, although as yet, he had not asked the footmen to remove it.

He would need to do that today.

Looking at the stack of books that had tumbled onto the floor, Colin allowed his frown to deepen. He was certain that it had not been that way last night, although it might have toppled on its own. His gaze moved to the left and he suddenly realized that the painting that had been behind the books, the one of the estate, the one he had removed from the hallway, was no longer there. Moving toward the pile of books, he bent down and began to pick them up one after the other. Seeing the back of a painting leaning against another, he pulled it forward carefully, looking at it.

His breath caught. It was the one he had removed from the hallway, the one of his manor house. Why was it sitting so?

"The key!"

His hand scrabbled for it, running along the back of the frame, only for him to realize that it was gone. Closing his eyes, he let out a long breath and sat back on his haunches.

The key had disappeared.

"Perhaps it has fallen," he said to himself, rising to his feet and looking all about him. He was about to start stacking things himself to clear the mess about him, but then remembered that he had staff waiting to serve. Despite the urge to do it himself, he rang the bell, and within minutes, footmen were beginning to clear the room of all the detritus that had gathered. They were under strict instructions to search for a small key as they did so, but as the room slowly emptied, Colin became more and more convinced that it would not be found.

Within the hour, he was standing in the study, which was now rather sparse, his hands on his hips and his brow furrowed.

"We did not find any key, my lord," the butler said as he stood in the doorway. "I am sorry."

"It is not your fault," Colin replied swiftly. "Have those things given away to some worthy cause. I will find other furnishings in time."

The butler nodded before asking if he might fetch anything more for Colin but was then dismissed, leaving Colin to stand alone in his study. Over and over he questioned where the key might have gone, whether or not it had simply disappeared into a nook somewhere, only to remember the toppled stack of books and the placement of the painting itself.

"Someone was in my study last evening," he said aloud, the thought sending a shiver down his spine. "Someone who has taken the key."

The door flew open and Colin was about to exclaim loudly and berate whichever servant had chosen to break apart his reverie without so much as a knock, only to see Lord Castleton step inside.

"I come to congratulate you on the success of your dinner party last evening," he cried, flopping down into a chair and tilting his head at Colin. "You are pleased with how it went, I hope?"

Colin blinked quickly, trying to align his thoughts and answer the question. "Yes, yes," he stammered, still lost in his considerations about the key. "It went very well."

Lord Castleton lifted one eyebrow and regarded Colin with a quizzical expression. "You are still a little overcome, perhaps?" he asked with a small smile. "Too much brandy last evening?"

"No, not in the least," Colin retorted, having always determined that he would never become the sort of fellow who lost his senses in a cloud of liquor. "It is only that…" He trailed off and looked back to the side of the room where the painting had been, only to shake his head. "You will think it a ridiculous suggestion, but I am certain that someone came into my study last night and took something from it."

Lord Castleton did not laugh as Colin had expected. Instead, he appeared to be rather concerned.

"I am aware that you will tell me that the study was in complete disarray and that I cannot be sure of that," Colin continued, running a hand over his eyes. "But I am quite certain that it is so."

"And what has been taken?" Lord Castleton asked, his eyes grave. "Something of importance?"

Colin shrugged. "It must be," he said slowly. "I told a few of my acquaintances that I had found a small key placed at the back of a painting that I wanted to remove from the house. The painting I had placed here in my study, along with all the other items that I wanted to remove. When I came in this morning, I discovered a stack of books tumbled to the floor and that particular painting in a different place. The key was gone."

Lord Castleton's brows rose. "Are you quite sure?"

Nodding, Colin spread his hands. "I had the footmen clear the study of all the things I want removed," he said, casting an eye over the room. "They did not find it. And I have no other explanation for how such things were moved other than the fact that someone else must have been in my study last night."

Letting out a long breath, Lord Castleton rose to his feet. "You did not lock the room?"

"I have never done that before," Colin replied as Lord Castleton blew out a second long breath. "I did not think I would have to."

"It would be wise to do so from now on, even to make certain that none of your staff enter without your permission," Lord Castleton replied grimly. "Do you have any idea as to who might have taken it or why? You said that you told a few of your acquaintances about this key."

A little irritated with himself and his foolishness, Colin nodded. "I told the story first to Miss Wainwright and Lady Ellen, if I remember correctly," he said, trying to recall. "And then, since it was of such interest to them, I repeated it to some others, simply so that I would have something to say."

Lord Castleton nodded slowly, looking very thoughtful. "And were any of those you spoke to about this key present last evening?" he asked as Colin's eyes widened. He thought hard, trying to recall, and eventually managed to remember.

"I know that Lady Ellen was present—and, in fact, I saw her slip back into the drawing room after a short absence," he said as Lord Castleton listened carefully. "There was also Miss Brooks, although I did not notice whether or not she quit the room at any stage."

"There might well be a simple explanation for her short absence," Lord Castleton reminded him as Colin began to pace quickly up and down the room. "And do not forget that either of those ladies—in fact, any that you have told of this key business—might well have spoken of it to others. Perhaps one of them took it from your study."

"But for what reason?" Colin asked, throwing up his hands. "It is a key. A key that opens something, but even I do not know what."

"And have you asked your staff?"

"I have," Colin answered, still pacing. "The butler does not know a thing about it."

Lord Castleton nodded and then shrugged. "The only thing you can do is to befriend Lady Ellen and Miss Brooks a little more and attempt to discern, somehow, whether or not either of them have your key." A frown flickered across his brow. "Miss Brooks I know a little about, since she is the daughter of a viscount and is, I will confess, someone I have considered. Lady Ellen, however..." He trailed off, looking at Colin for a moment. "There are some rumors about her father that have never truly disappeared. I believe that is why many gentlemen, whilst they are contented to dance and converse with her, will never give her any further consideration."

Surprised, Colin stopped pacing and looked back at his friend. "But she is the daughter of an earl, with what I am sure is an excellent dowry," he said as Lord Castleton nodded. "And she is quite lovely too."

Lord Castleton's smile was present in an instant. "She has caught your attention, then?"

"No, no," Colin replied hastily. "Nothing like that. I only meant that I was surprised that the rumors about her father have affected her so much."

"Again, it is the way of things here in London," Lord Castleton replied with a shrug. "Rumors cling to the entire family, regardless of whom they are about." He walked to the door. "Well, then, shall we go?"

"Go?" Colin replied, puzzled. "Where do you intend to go?"

"To call upon Miss Brooks and Lady Ellen, of course," Lord Castleton laughed. "It is soon to be time for afternoon calls. I will wait in the drawing room with a measure of your most *excellent* brandy whilst you finish changing." He cast a sharp eye over Colin which told him that he was not suitably dressed for such a thing as afternoon calls. "I am sure both young ladies will be very glad to see you."

"To see us both," Colin retorted, a nervousness clinging to his stomach that he tried to brush away but could not. But he admitted that there was wisdom in Lord Castleton's suggestion. With a sigh, he made his way to his bedchamber and rang his bell. He was, it seemed, about to become all the better acquainted with both Miss

Brooks and Lady Ellen. He only hoped that his efforts would not be in vain.

∼

"Thank you for allowing us to call upon you, Miss Brooks, Lady Templeton." Colin bowed toward them both, fully aware of the deep crimson blush that flooded Miss Brooks' cheeks. "I do hope you enjoy the rest of the afternoon."

Taking his leave, Colin felt a deep sense of frustration growing within him. Lady Templeton had been the one to speak, whereas Miss Brooks had barely said more than a word. She had been a little more talkative when she had been in the company of others but since this afternoon, she had been so very quiet that it had irritated Colin with every moment that passed. How was he meant to ascertain anything of importance from her when she would barely speak a word?

"That did not go particularly well," Lord Castleton acknowledged as they stepped back toward Colin's carriage. "She was quieter than I have ever seen her."

"That does not mean she did not take the key," Colin replied, climbing inside. "Perhaps her silence came from a sense of guilt."

"Mayhap," Lord Castleton agreed as the carriage pulled away. "But now we go to Lady Ellen, in the hope that she might be a little more forthcoming."

"Quite what I am to say to her, I do not know," Colin replied, still frustrated with Miss Brooks' lack of communication. "I can ask her the same questions as I asked Miss Brooks, but if she says very little, then I am just as much in the dark as I am at present."

Lord Castleton grinned. "But you will have furthered your acquaintance with both young ladies," he said with a chuckle. "And that cannot be considered a bad thing."

Colin sighed and shook his head. He had no interest in such things at present. All that mattered to him now was trying to find the key and discover why it had been taken.

It did not take long for them to arrive at the Earl of Grantown's townhouse and, much to Colin's relief, they were shown in very quickly. Lord Grantown was not present, they were informed, but Lady Sayers and Lady Ellen would be glad of their company. Clearing his throat, setting his shoulders, and lifting his chin, Colin walked into the room with Lord Castleton following behind. Lady Ellen and Lady Sayers rose at once to greet them and Colin smiled, bowed, and said the usual words of greeting. But all the while, he paid close attention to Lady Ellen, who, for the most part, appeared to be quite at her ease.

"We very much enjoyed your dinner party last evening, Lord Lindale," Lady Sayers said, once tea had been ordered. "That was your first evening occasion, I believe?"

"Yes, it was," Colin replied with a smile, trying to ignore the tension that was growing within him. "I was a little anxious, but all went very well indeed, for the most part." He allowed a slight frown to flicker across his forehead, casting a quick glance toward Lady Ellen, who merely reached for her teacup so that she might take a small sip.

"I enjoyed it very much," Lady Ellen said, not asking him what he might mean by such a statement. "The music and the dancing were very enjoyable indeed. "

"I am very glad to hear it," Colin replied, and for a few minutes more, the conversation moved to general things. Growing more and more frustrated with himself that he was not able to think of what to say that might provoke a reaction in Lady Ellen, Colin sipped his tea and forced himself to keep a pleasant expression.

"I should say, however," he heard Lord Castleton say, "that not all was pleasant for Lord Lindale last evening. He believes that someone had been inside his private study during the occasion—although, of course, it most likely was one of the staff."

Colin straightened, looking at Lady Ellen and seeing the slight widening of her eyes as she looked to Lord Castleton.

"Good gracious!" Lady Sayers exclaimed as Colin nodded in what he hoped was a saddened manner. "Have you questioned your staff thoroughly, Lord Lindale? I hope the item was not of great importance or value?"

Colin spread his hands. "In truth, Lady Sayers, I am only at the very beginning of considering my late uncle's many effects," he said carefully. "I am, at present, removing some ornaments and furnishings in order to replace them with some of my own. I believe that whoever took this particular item must have thought that I would not miss it given that there are so many things at present that are to be discarded."

"That is truly terrible," Lady Ellen murmured. Colin turned his head to look at her, his eyes fixing to hers. Lady Sayers continued to express just how sorry she was to hear that such a thing had occurred and suggested ways to make certain that his staff could be trusted, but all the while, Colin continued to look steadily at Lady Ellen. Two spots of color came into her cheeks, but she held his gaze without flinching. Was it because she feared that she was about to be discovered? Or rather that she was a little self-conscious over his attentions?

"Lord Lindale, I must hope that you find the culprit soon," Lady Sayers continued, forcing Colin to look back at her and take his attention away from Lady Ellen. "You must be able to trust your staff."

"You are quite correct, Lady Sayers," he replied, rising to his feet as he became aware that they had already overstayed their visit. "I do hope that I will be successful. In fact," he continued as Lady Ellen rose also, "I have every intention of discovering the truth, no matter how long it will take me."

Lady Sayers nodded and smiled. "That is very wise indeed, Lord Lindale," she said as he bowed to take his leave. "And thank you for calling. Thank you also, Lord Castleton. We have been very glad of your company."

Colin smiled and turned to Lady Ellen. "I do hope to call again another time, Lady Ellen," he said, looking directly into her eyes and seeing the way she blushed a little more. "Thank you for allowing me to visit."

Lady Ellen nodded and curtsied, although there was no smile on her face as she rose. "But of course," she said quickly as Lady Sayers watched with a delighted smile crossing her face. "Thank you, Lord Lindale."

Colin bowed once more and then made his way to the door, with Lord Castleton following him. Deep within his heart, he felt a small sense of satisfaction begin to replace his frustration. There was something about Lady Ellen that was of interest to him, something about her manner that made him all the more suspicious that she might have been the one to step into his study and take his key.

"Well," Lord Castleton murmured as they returned to the carriage. "I would say, in my opinion, that the conversation with Lady Ellen was a good deal better than with Miss Brooks, although neither young lady said anything of particular interest."

"You noticed her manner, then?" Colin replied as the carriage door was closed. "There was a slight anxiety about her, I thought."

"As did I," Lord Castleton replied as the carriage pulled away. "I hope you did not mind that I spoke of what had occurred. I thought it would be a way to encourage a response from Lady Ellen."

Colin chuckled, no longer feeling any sort of tension or frustration. "I think you achieved that, certainly," he replied as Lord Castleton grinned. "Although I did wonder if her flushed cheeks came from simply my study of her."

Lord Castleton shrugged. "It may have done," he agreed, "but I would certainly encourage you to continue an acquaintance with the lady. That is the only way you can decipher the truth."

Nodding, Colin sat back against the squabs and let out a contented breath. It had not been the disappointing afternoon he had expected and thus, he felt more than a little satisfied. All he had to do now was continue to meet with Lady Ellen in the hope that, somehow, she would give something away and he would be able to discover the truth about the key.

6

"It seems as though Lord Lindale is interested in furthering his acquaintance with you, Ellen."

A tremor ran through Ellen's frame and she prayed her aunt had not noticed. Lord Lindale had called for three days in a row and she had managed to avoid him thus far today by insisting that they come out to Hyde Park for a walk in the sunshine, rather than linger over afternoon calls. Lady Sayers had not been particularly pleased by the suggestion, but Ellen had been dogged in her determination and, therefore, she now found herself in the park, in the bright afternoon sunshine, as a feeling of dread began to settle over her.

"You are quite determined to refuse him, should he seek anything more?" Lady Sayers asked when Ellen did not immediately reply. "I do not know why you would be so persistent, Ellen. He is a perfectly respectable gentleman by all accounts and would suit you very well. Besides which," she continued with a wave of her hand, "it appears that he cares nothing for the rumors that still whisper through London about your father and that is certainly a mark in his favor."

"I am sure it is, Aunt, but I am not even thinking of considering him," Ellen replied firmly. "The knowledge of what his uncle has done to Father is too much for me to bear."

"Then perhaps you ought to speak to him of it," Lady Sayers suggested. "I am sure he will not understand why you refuse him, should it come to it, and you will need to give him an explanation."

Ellen looked sideways at her aunt, not quite certain what to make of such a remark. "I should inform Lord Lindale that his uncle made up rumors about my father?" she queried, and Lady Sayers shrugged. "You forget, Aunt, that there is no evidence of such a thing, save for my father's word. I do not think that Lord Lindale would accept my statement without questioning it excessively."

"Be that as it may," Lady Sayers replied swiftly, "you will have to consider what it is you will say to him by way of explaining why you do not wish for his company, should he ask to court."

"I do not think I shall," Ellen replied, ignoring the slightly panicked beating of her heart. "Father would not accept him."

Lady Sayers frowned at this remark, giving Ellen the impression that she had not thought of such a thing. Continuing along the path, Ellen tried her best not to let her aunt's words strike any sort of fear or worry into her heart. The truth was, she had begun to feel a good deal of worry the very moment Lord Lindale had come to call on her some days ago. She had not known why he had come and had told herself that it was simply a gentleman calling on a few of his guests from the previous evening, to make certain all had gone well for them. But when Lord Castleton had mentioned that Lord Lindale had discovered someone had been in his study and had taken something of his, she had felt herself slowly begin to sink into the floor.

Her stomach had knotted, her heart had begun to thump furiously in her chest, and her hands had grown clammy as she had attempted to sip her tea nonchalantly. The way Lord Lindale had looked at her made Ellen believe that he suspected she had been the one to do so—and she had begun to panic. Remembering how he had watched her as she had returned to the drawing room, she had found herself eager to say something, anything, that would give her the right kind of excuse for what he had seen. But she had, instead, forced herself to remain mostly silent, giving nothing away and allowing Lord Lindale's sharp gaze to continue to penetrate into her heart, unearthing the guilt that lay there.

The key, of course, was still in her possession—although quite what she was to do with it now, Ellen had very little idea. She had studied it carefully but had soon come to realize that it told her very little. A sense of frustration and foolishness had begun to grow within her heart and had not left her for some time, for there was nothing for her to do save to keep the key safe and wonder, fruitlessly, what it might open.

Although, she had conceded to herself, at least it meant that Lord Lindale did not have the key himself. He could not use it to open whatever it was meant to, could not discover the diary himself. If he did, then Ellen did not know what he might do with it, although she considered that there was a very real possibility that he might dispose of it entirely. That was the last thing she wanted.

"You are not listening to me, Ellen."

Hearing the sharpness in Lady Sayers' tone, Ellen looked up quickly at her aunt. "I apologize, Aunt," she said swiftly. "I was thinking of Lord Lindale, that is all."

"It seems you will have to do more than just think," Lady Sayers answered, a slight twist of mirth in her voice. "It seems as though you will have to greet him this afternoon, despite your attempts to avoid him."

Ellen caught her breath as she lifted her head, only to see Lord Castleton and Lord Lindale speaking to a young lady and her chaperone. She recognized the lady at once as Miss Brooks, and the chaperone, in fact, to be her mother, Lady Fassington.

"We do not need to interrupt their conversation," she said hastily, praying that they would not be noticed. "We can turn around and make our way back to the carriage, can we not?"

Lady Sayers laughed softly. "It is a little too late, my dear. Lord

Castleton has already seen us and has mentioned it to Lord Lindale. To turn away now would be seen as very rude indeed."

Ellen let out a long sigh, the protest on her lips dying away as her aunt smiled broadly in welcome, with Lord Castleton being the first to turn toward them both.

"What luck we have," Lord Castleton said as he bowed toward Lady Sayers and then to Ellen. "I believe Lord Lindale was just on his way to call upon you, Lady Ellen, and now here we see you coming alongside us in the park."

"Indeed," Ellen replied, trying to force a smile to her lips but failing entirely. "It is very fortunate."

Lord Lindale finished his conversation with Miss Brooks and Lady Fassington and, taking his leave of them, turned quickly toward Ellen and Lady Sayers. Ellen did not miss the way his eyes flashed with evident pleasure, a smile across his lips as he bowed to them both.

"How wonderful," he said, grinning at her. "I was to call on you, Lady Ellen, but it seems as though fate has entwined our paths this afternoon." He offered her his arm. "Might you care to walk with me for a time?"

There was no easy way to refuse him, even though the last thing Ellen wished to do was take his arm. Glancing at her aunt, she saw her give a small yet determined nod, her eyes a little narrowed as she shot a quick glance toward Lord Lindale before looking back at Ellen.

"Yes, of course," Ellen found herself saying, even though she had no particular wish to walk with him in such a fashion. "Thank you, Lord Lindale. You are very kind."

Stepping forward, she took his arm quickly and they began to walk together, leaving Lady Sayers and Lord Castleton to fall into step behind. For some moments, nothing was said, and Ellen felt her stomach twist this way and that, as though she were in a tumultuous storm. She had not yet had any opportunity to converse privately with Lord Lindale, given that Lady Sayers had always been present in the same room, so quite what he might say to her, Ellen had very little idea.

What if he mentions the key? she asked herself, feeling her heart quicken. *What will you say then?*

"A pleasant afternoon, Lady Ellen."

"Yes, very pleasant." Her words were too quick, her voice sounding much too tight to give any impression that she was enjoying his company. She could feel his eyes resting down upon her but did not look back up at him, instead choosing to keep her eyes fixed to the path ahead.

"And might I ask what social occasion, if any, you are attending this evening?"

Finally, she looked up at him. "An evening soireé," she said with a small smile that felt both false and hurried as she returned her gaze to the path. "Lord Whittington is to be our host."

"How fortunate," he said, and she looked up at him in surprise at the sense of happiness in his voice. "I am to attend the very same. I shall have the pleasure of being in your company twice in one day."

She could not summon the same enthusiasm. "It appears so, Lord Lindale," she answered softly. "How very fortunate are we both."

A chuckle answered her response and Ellen's cheeks flared with heat. Was he laughing at her? She prayed not.

"I believe your sense of eagerness is a lot less than my own, Lady Ellen," he told her as Ellen's embarrassment grew. "But that does not matter to me. I shall continue to be in your company, until I can determine…" He trailed off, leaving his sentence unfinished and, in turn, making Ellen's heart quicken all the more as her breath hitched. She swallowed hard, daring a glance up at him and seeing the determination in his expression. There was a hardness about his jaw now, a tightness that had not been present before. Dare she ask him what he meant? Or was it better for her to remain silent?

"Determine?" she said eventually, hoping that her voice was steadier than she felt. "Determine what, Lord Lindale?"

His gaze met hers, flecks of gold and copper dancing around in his dark brown eyes. "Determine what I am to do with you, Lady Ellen," he said, his voice low but his words giving no sense of clarity to what it was she now asked. "There is more to you than I believe you wish anyone to see, is that not so?"

"I do not know what you mean," she answered quickly, quite certain now that he believed that she had stolen the key from him. "I am just as you see me."

A small chuckle left his lips. "I hardly believe that, Lady Ellen," he answered swiftly. "I believe that you hide a great deal from everyone, including, mayhap, your aunt. Does she know that you slip away from her from time to time?"

"I do not do such a thing," Ellen retorted, even though she felt a curl of guilt settle upon her heart. "I am only ever absent from her when I am required to do so by...by..."

Lord Lindale's brow rose, a mocking tone in his voice. "When you are required by your own determination, Lady Ellen?"

"When I am required to do so by the determinations of my own body, Lord Lindale," she retorted, heat pouring into her face. "If you are referring to your awareness of my return to your drawing room on the evening of your dinner party, I can assure you that I simply made my way to the retiring room and then returned." It was, of course, not at all proper to speak of such things, but given the evident suspicion in Lord Lindale's voice and the sharpness of his gaze, Ellen felt as though she had no other choice. Besides which, she might find that speaking in such a manner would embarrass him and could, in turn, throw him from his discussion.

She was quite mistaken, however.

"I see," he answered without so much as a flicker of embarrassment in his gaze. "You can understand my considerations, Lady Ellen, given that you were the only one I noted returning to my drawing room, as well as the fact that I had mentioned the key to you already."

"Key?" Forcing an innocent curiosity into both her voice and her expression, she looked up at Lord Lindale with wide eyes, seeing how he frowned as he looked back at her.

"Very good, Miss Lindale," he replied with a twist of his lips. "If you are doing all you can to prove to me that there is nothing about this missing key that interests you, then I must say you are doing very well indeed."

A flood of anger poured into Ellen's veins and she looked back at him, a stray curl flying out from underneath her bonnet and dancing around her temple. "Lord Lindale, there is no need to speak to me so," she told him, rather primly. "I do not know what it is that you are referring to, although I will say that I recall the key you spoke of. To suggest otherwise is a little insulting."

This brought a dark frown to Lord Lindale's face, his brows now low over his eyes and a slight gleam of confusion in his eyes as he looked back at her. Ellen said nothing more, darting a look toward him now and again but otherwise remaining quite silent.

"If something about this key interested you, Lady Ellen, then I should like to know of it," he told her after a few moments of silence. "Rather than keeping such things to yourself, I would be glad to know of the reasons for your interest. As it is, I know very little." One shoulder lifted. "I do not like being stolen from, however. That is most unfair and, to my mind, quite wrong."

The quietness in his voice seemed to add more guilt to her soul than his harsh words had done. There was a willingness, it seemed, on his part to listen to what she had to say, but Ellen could not trust him to believe her, should she do so. After all, she would be speaking ill of his uncle, attempting to explain to him all the wrongs that his uncle had done—and with the late Lord Lindale not present any longer to defend himself. The chances of his believing her were very slim, and Ellen could not take the chance.

"There are many things in this world that are both unfair and entirely wrong, Lord Lindale," she found herself saying, a coldness in her voice that she had not intended to be present but was there regardless. "This is only a small matter; would you not say?" She threw him a withering glance, knowing full well that she was, in addition to answering him in her own way, doing all she could to remove any sort of guilt from her heart also. "There are matters of much greater importance, matters that affect the life and the situation of any one person as they attempt to make their way through London."

Lord Lindale did not immediately answer this remark, although she could feel his gaze settling on her for some moments. Eventually, he let out a long breath and, much to her surprise, reached across with his free hand and patted her fingers.

"We are to remain as we are, then," he said, sounding fatigued. "You will not say anything to me and I, it seems, must remain with my suspicions. Although, Lady Ellen, should you wish to change your mind and speak honestly with me, I should be very glad to listen."

"I have nothing to say," she answered quickly, so that she would not leave him with the wrong impression.

"And I am sorry for whatever difficulties you speak of," he continued as though he had not heard her. "These matters that are of greater importance to you, the ones that affect you so. If I can do anything to assist in their dispersion, then you will speak to me."

It was not a question but rather an offer of his assistance—which Ellen simply could not understand. How could he, in one moment, tell her almost outright that he believed her to be guilty of taking his key and then, in the next, offer to do whatever he could to help her? It simply did not make sense.

"I will look forward to seeing you this evening, Lady Ellen," Lord Lindale finished, turning her around so that they could wait for Lady Sayers and Lord Castleton to catch up to them. "Perhaps we will be able to continue our conversation for a little longer there."

Ellen kept her mouth closed but looked up at him steadily, seeing the look in his eye and feeling her heart begin to quicken all over again. He still was convinced that she had taken the key and her denials, it seemed, had done very little. What was she to say?

Was she to tell him the truth and hope that he would understand? Or was she instead to continue to remain silent and hope that he would turn his suspicions to another?

And what am I to do about that key?

"I hear that we are to join you at the soireé this evening." Lord Lindale smiled as Lady Sayers and Lord Castleton reached them, having been only a short distance behind. "I look forward to seeing you both again."

Lady Sayers smiled brightly and thanked both Lord Castleton and Lord Lindale for their company. Ellen did so also, although for whatever reason, she found it rather difficult to lift her head and look into Lord Lindale's eyes, even though she forced herself to do so, fearing what he might think of her otherwise. Lord Lindale looked back at her directly, a small, curling smile pulling at one side of his mouth as though he could tell just how difficult she was finding this.

"Until this evening, then," he said with another small bow. "Good afternoon, Lady Ellen. I have very much enjoyed your conversation and your company and look forward to it again this evening." With another swift inclination of his head, he straightened and smiled at them both, no trace of either anger or frustration evident in his expression. "Good day."

"Good day," Ellen murmured as both gentlemen turned on their heel, leaving Ellen and Lady Sayers to stand and watch them for a moment.

"My goodness," Lady Sayers murmured as Ellen let out a long breath. "It seems quite obvious to me, my dear. Lord Lindale has a certain interest in you."

"I do not hold the same fondness in my heart," Ellen responded quickly, wanting the eagerness to fade from Lady Sayers' eyes. "Come now, Aunt, I find myself getting a little weary. Might we return to the carriage?"

This seemed to strike a great anxiety into Lady Sayers, for she immediately took Ellen's arm and began to walk swiftly back toward the carriage, as though she thought Ellen might faint at any moment.

"I am just a little fatigued from the sun, Aunt." Ellen laughed, pushing aside any thought of Lord Lindale and the conversation she had endured with him. "I am not about to swoon or any such thing."

Lady Sayers glanced back at her worriedly before shaking her head. "All the same, we should return quickly," she said, "so that you might rest before dinner and then the soireé." Her eyes twinkled as some of the worry left them. "Although it appears Lord Lindale will be very glad to see you again, even if you are not delighted to see him."

Ellen sighed inwardly but did not respond to her aunt's teasing. Lord Lindale, she wanted to say, had his own motivations for speaking to her and none of them verged on anything like a genuine interest. Her heart dropped to the floor as she realized that, should she tell Lord Lindale the truth about the key and the diary, he might very well drop his feigned interest in her all at once and her aunt would, of course, then question why such a thing had occurred.

Guilt swamped her again and she shook her head to herself, letting out a long breath as they came to the carriage. She had been so certain of herself before, so glad that she had managed to find the key and take a hold of it, but now she felt more foolish than ever. Somehow, she had managed to give herself away to Lord Lindale and, despite having the key, had no idea as to what it might open. Yes, she prayed and she hoped that it was the diary of the late Lord Lindale, but it was a hope and not a certainty. What if Lord Lindale found the diary regardless? What would she do then?

"I should have made you return home sooner," Lady Sayers fussed as they both sat in the carriage. "You look rather pale, Ellen."

"I am only a little tired," Ellen reassured her, fully aware that her pale cheeks came from nothing more than her encounter and her consideration of what Lord Lindale had said. "I will be back to myself once we have rested and dined."

"I do hope so," Lady Sayers replied with a shake of her head. "I should not like you to miss this evening's soireé."

"Nor should I, Aunt," Ellen lied, silently thinking to herself that there would be nothing she would like better than to avoid Lord Lindale's company for another evening. "I am sure it will be a very enjoyable evening indeed."

7

Watching Lady Ellen was becoming something of a habit, Colin realized. He watched her whenever he came to call. He watched her when they were at a social engagement together. He could think of nothing other than Lady Ellen and the thoughts were becoming all the more intense.

After this afternoon's conversation, Colin was all the more convinced that Lady Ellen was the one who had taken his key. He had practically asked her as much yesterday afternoon and whilst she had, of course, pretended to know very little about what he was saying, Colin had not been convinced. Something in her manner, something about her voice, had told him she was not speaking the truth.

And yet, he had to confess that something she had said continued to plague him. She had spoken of difficulties, of struggles that she considered to be of greater importance than his present circumstances.

"You look as though you are deep in thought instead of enjoying the *many* interesting sights that are all around you."

Colin grimaced and lifted his brandy glass to his lips for a moment before replying to Lord Castleton.

"I am thinking of Lady Ellen," he said by way of explanation. "I am quite certain that she has the key."

Lord Castleton shrugged. "I would agree with your assessment, given what you have told me, but what is it you intend to do?" He tilted his head. "Ask her outright?"

"I have all but done so," Colin replied, a little frustrated. "She denies it completely."

"As you would expect," Lord Castleton replied as the music for the next dance began to play. "Therefore, you must think of another way to discover the truth."

Colin looked at him. "She said something that has intrigued me," he said slowly. "Might you be able to explain to me what she meant?" Briefly, he told Lord Castleton of the conversation and what Lady Ellen had said.

"But surely you must already know?" Lord Castleton replied with a frown. "Do you not recall? I told you already that there are some rumors about her father that have never quite faded away. She has to endure the difficulties that come with that, even though I am sure that such rumors are nothing more than idle gossip."

In a flash of awareness, Colin recalled precisely what Lord Castleton had said. How he had told Colin that many gentlemen would be contented to dance and converse with Lady Ellen but that none would ever consider her for matrimony, given the whispers about her father.

"What are the rumors exactly?" he asked, not able to recall whether or not they had spoken of them already. "Are they very terrible indeed?"

Sighing, Lord Castleton waved a hand. "They were much more severe last Season. It was said that Lord Grantown had lost a good deal of his fortune and had been forced to sell some of his lands in order to pay for his debts. Of course, no one wishes to consider the daughter of a gentleman such as that, but what made things all the worse was that the reasons given for his financial difficulty were..." He hesitated, looking away for a moment as he searched for the right words. "The rumors suggested that Lord Grantown had spent his coin on things such as gambling and houses of disrepute."

Colin recoiled.

"But they were and are only rumors, of course," Lord Castleton said hastily. "Many in society have questioned it, of course, which is why I believe Lady Ellen is still mostly accepted, although I doubt she will find an excellent match."

"That seems unfair," Colin replied, a line forming between his brows as he considered what Lord Castleton had said. "The rumors affect her father, not her."

"And as I have informed you, that is the way of society," Lord Castleton replied with another wave of his hand. "Nothing can be done, unless you would consider marrying her yourself."

Much to Colin's surprise, the retort that came to his lips was not one that he allowed himself to speak. The idea, he supposed, was not an entirely poor one, for Lady Ellen was certainly very lovely to look at, although he did not know much about her character save for the fact that she could be very obstinate indeed.

And untruthful, he told himself, putting a wry smile on his face as Lord Castleton chuckled. *With, evidently, a few secrets to hide.*

Sighing to himself, he shook his head. "I do not know what to do when it comes to Lady Ellen," he confessed. "I am sure that she has taken the key."

"Then might I suggest a simple solution?" Lord Castleton interrupted with a weary smile. "Endear yourself to Lady Ellen. Encourage her attentions. And then, when the time comes, mention that you have found a small box which you are *certain* can be opened by the small key. Say how distressed you are that you cannot find it and make certain that she knows that this box is kept in your study." He put a hand on Colin's arm. "Then throw a ball and wait to see what occurs." With a small smile, he gestured to the guests around them. "But do not permit yourself to consider the matter any longer this evening, Lord Lindale. You are here at the ball, with many young ladies already making eyes at you, and it seems that you are entirely unaware of their presence."

Colin cast a quick glance around him and saw that there were more than a few young ladies who were, as Lord Castleton had said, casting longing glances in his direction. His lip curled, although he had to admit that Lord Castleton's suggestion was a wise one indeed.

"You cannot tell me that you are not at all inclined to dance," Lord Castleton chuckled, slapping Colin on the shoulder. "Come now, find a little enjoyment in your celebrated status, Lord Lindale. Not very many gentlemen are given such an opportunity."

Sighing to himself, Colin was about to rake one hand through his hair in frustration, but stopped himself as he recalled just how long it had taken for his valet to prepare him for this evening.

"You might be able to dance with Lady Ellen also," Lord Castleton suggested, his eyes straying to someone just over Colin's right shoulder. "She is here, at least." One eyebrow lifted. "You might start your feigned interest in her this very evening."

"Where is she?" Colin turned about at once and saw her standing only a short distance away, with Lady Sayers next to her. Turning back to Lord Castleton, he grinned, feeling his spirits lifting a little more.

"I shall do just that," he replied, pulling out his own little dance card and praying that Lady Ellen would accept him. "Do excuse me, Lord Castleton."

Lord Castleton grinned, nodded, and turned away, leaving Colin to make his way toward Lady Ellen. He saw the moment she caught sight of him approaching, for her eyes flared wide, her cheeks lost their color, and she immediately turned herself away just a little, making it quite clear that she had no eagerness to be in his company.

That did not dissuade Colin. What Lord Castleton had suggested had begun to settle firmly in his mind and, since he had to admit that the idea was a good one, he was all the more eager to begin such a plan.

Waiting until the conversation between Lady Sayers and

another lady had been brought to a close, Colin stepped forward and bowed.

"Good evening to you both," he said as Lady Ellen looked at him with a sharpness in her gaze. "I do hope you have found the ball enjoyable so far?"

"Very much," Lady Sayers replied with a warm smile. "Although I do not think I can speak for my niece." She turned to Lady Ellen, who was now facing him. Lifting her eyes to his, he was surprised to see a flicker of defiance within her emerald eyes.

"Might I beg you for your dance card, Lady Ellen?" he asked, bowing low. "I do hope you have not found them all taken at once, for I should dearly like to have at least one dance this evening."

Lady Ellen did not answer him but the suspicion in her eyes was more than apparent. She did hand him her dance card without complaint, however, and he took it at once, rather glad that there were very few names written there already. It meant that he could take both the cotillion and, after a word to confirm with Lady Sayers, the waltz. Handing it back to Lady Ellen, he smiled at her and, as though she had always intended to do so, Lady Sayers quickly greeted someone passing her, allowing Colin to have a few minutes to converse with Lady Ellen without being overheard.

"I do hope these dances are to your liking, Lady Ellen," he said, smiling at her although his smile was not returned. "I look forward to accompanying you to the dance floor." He did not tell her that he had been forced to spend many hours practicing all the various dance steps until he was able to dance them all without hesitation, or just how nervous he still became at each dance in a social setting.

And yet, there was something about being able to have Lady Ellen in his arms that sent another flurry of nervousness through him, although he did not allow himself to ponder it or let it pervade through him any more than it had already done.

"You are quite incorrigible, it seems," she replied, looking up at him with a calmness in her eyes that Colin did not quite believe to be genuine. "But yes, both dances are more than suitable, Lord Lindale. I thank you."

"I simply cannot keep myself from your company," he replied, just as Lady Sayers turned back toward them. "I look forward to our first dance, Lady Ellen." With a sharp bow, he turned away, a small yet satisfied smile spreading across his face.

∽

THE COTILLION CAME to an end and Colin bowed low, relieved that he had remembered every single step and had managed to execute them without hesitation or mistake. Lady Ellen curtsied graciously and then took his arm as he turned them back toward where Lady Sayers would be waiting.

They had said very little during the dance—which was just as well, given just how much Colin had been forced to concentrate. But Colin was still very well aware of the tightness about Lady Ellen's features, of the way her eyes darted to his upon occasion only for her to look away again suddenly. A tension between them continued to grow every time they were together, and Colin prayed that perhaps the desire to rid herself of such tension would be the cause of Lady Ellen's confession, should it ever come.

"Good gracious!"

Lady Ellen stopped suddenly, her head swinging sharply to the right as she saw something he had not taken note of. After a moment, he glanced there also, only to see a gentleman he did not know leering down at the young lady on his arm. The lady in question was attempting to remove herself from his grip but was not able to do so, for whatever reason.

"Excuse me, Lord Lindale," Lady Ellen said swiftly. "I must go to her aid at once."

Colin did not hesitate. "But of course," he said but rather than departing from her and allowing her to step toward the lady in distress, he walked with her toward them. Lady Ellen's steps were hurried, her hand tight on his arm and her concern for the lady more than apparent.

"Who is the gentleman?" Colin asked as Lady Ellen dropped her hand from his arm. "Do you know him?"

"Lord Drake," she said, her voice hard. "A rake and a drunkard."

There was no time to say more, for the gentleman and lady were just ahead of them now. Colin saw Lord Drake's hand on the lady's arm, realizing that he had her captured tight against him and would not allow her free. His heart began to slam hard into his chest. Was Lord Drake really about to press himself upon the lady without her consent? Whilst Colin had not been long in society, he knew all too well the damage that could be done by the gentleman's behavior.

"Lord Drake!" he said loudly, catching the man's attention. Putting his hand on the man's arm, he tried to stand between him and the young lady, who was gasping with fright. Lady Ellen did so also so that the young lady was between them. As Colin held Lord Drake's arm, he felt Lady Ellen do the same, putting her hand out and beginning to push down hard.

To anyone watching, it would have appeared that they were both merely standing very close to Lord Drake, perhaps encouraging him to be a little more careful as he led the young lady from the floor. However, with a grunt, Lord Drake finally let the young lady go and she stepped back, her face white and one hand rubbing at her wrist where Lord Drake had held it.

"I will accompany Lord Drake to the card room, perhaps," Colin said, and Lady Ellen nodded, quickly taking the arm of the young lady. "Miss...?"

The young lady glanced up at him. "Miss Archibald," she said breathlessly, her eyes still wide with fright.

"Miss Archibald, Lady Ellen will take good care of you, I am sure," Colin continued, still holding tightly to Lord Drake. "Do excuse me."

He turned and began to lead Lord Drake toward the crowd of guests. Some, of course, had watched everything that had taken place and Colin could not be sure what they were thinking. Lord Drake, for whatever reason, had become very compliant and, despite the fact that he was not acquainted with Colin, was evidently very willing to allow him to take him wherever he wished.

"The card room," Colin muttered, practically shoving Lord Drake through the door. "Enjoy yourself, Lord Drake."

Lord Drake turned and looked at Colin, a small frown flickering between his brows.

"I have more dances," he said, slurring his words just a little. "Miss Archibald..." Fumbling, he pulled out his own dance card, the one gentlemen used to write down which young ladies they were to dance with and in what order, and began to stare down at it, swaying slightly as he attempted to focus his gaze on it.

"You have done enough this evening, I think," Colin replied, deftly pulling the dance card from Lord Drake and turning away. "Go, Lord Drake. Play some cards and drink some brandy. There is no need for you to dance any longer."

Whether or not it was sheer confusion as to what Colin was doing and why, or if it was the liquor that gave Lord Drake such a lackadaisical attitude, Colin did not know, but when he glanced over his shoulder, he was satisfied to see Lord Drake wander into the card room a little further, looking all about him in a somewhat stupefied fashion.

"Good gracious, whatever happened with Lord Drake?"

Lord Castleton joined him practically the moment Colin returned to the ballroom, evidently having been waiting for him to do so.

"You saw it, then?"

"I believe many people did, although Miss Archibald should suffer no ill consequences given how quickly both you and Lady Ellen stepped in."

Colin shook his head. "I would not have noticed her plight had it not been for Lady Ellen," he replied, looking through the crowd. "Do you know where she has gone?"

Lord Castleton looked a little surprised. "Lady Ellen?"

"Yes." Colin felt a deep urgency to make certain that she herself was all right, as well as finding himself rather admiring her awareness of others and her willingness to step in. "Is she with Lady Sayers?"

"She is," Lord Castleton replied, gesturing to his right. "Last I saw, she was speaking with Miss Archibald and Miss Archibald's mother, Lady Trevelyan."

Nodding, Colin made his way slowly through the crowd of guests, his heart beating a little more quickly than before. Finally, after some minutes, he caught sight of her.

Lady Ellen was standing with her hand still on Miss Archibald's arm. She was speaking quietly to the young lady, whilst Lady Sayers was in conversation with another lady, whom Colin took to be Lady Trevelyan. As he watched, not wanting to interrupt, he saw Lady Trevelyan reach out to grasp Lady Ellen's hand, clearly indebted to her for what she had done.

Colin waited for some minutes, his eyes fixed on Lady Ellen. There was a kindness in her eyes that he knew was real. What she had done had proven it to him. For so many days, he had thought of her in less than generous terms given that he believed her to have stolen from him, but now he realized that there was a good deal more to her character than that. She had seen a lady in distress and had not hesitated to go to her, heedless of what might happen to her. He had to admire her for that.

"Lady Ellen," he murmured, moving forward after Lady Trevelyan and her daughter had moved away. "Are you quite all right?"

Something shifted in her expression, something minute that he could not quite make out.

"I am," she told him, giving him a small smile that did not quite reach her eyes. "Thank you for your assistance, Lord Lindale."

"I would not have noticed her had it not been for you," he replied as Lady Sayers murmured something to Lord Castleton, who nodded gravely. "You have saved her reputation, from what I understand."

Her smile became fixed and a deep sense of sadness came into her eyes. Her head dropped for a moment and she looked away. "It is easier to see those who might be in difficulty when you yourself have endured such a thing, Lord Lindale," she told him, her eyes still held away from his. "Rumors and whispers and gossip do a great deal to those who do not deserve it." Finally, she lifted her chin and looked back at him, her sadness lingering in her expression still. "I could not allow that to happen to Miss Archibald. It is both unfair and deeply damaging. I am only relieved that you managed to relieve Lord Drake in the way you did."

Colin blinked for a moment, then inclined his head, one hand against his heart. "As I have said, I would not have noticed save for you, Lady Ellen," he replied softly. "You are quite remarkable, I think."

"No, I am just a little more aware than others may be," she replied as her aunt moved to join her. "No doubt, had things continued as Lord Drake wished, Miss Archibald would have found herself quite ruined and forced, perhaps, into matrimony with him." She shuddered. "He is naught but a selfish, arrogant fool."

Lady Sayers murmured something, but Lady Ellen did not detract anything she had said.

"I quite agree with you, Lady Ellen," Colin replied swiftly. "I must once more express my gratitude and my admiration." He inclined his head. "I shall leave you now until the time comes for our waltz. Do excuse me."

8

"Ellen?"

Looking up from her book, Ellen quickly made to rise to her feet at the sight of her father standing in the doorway, but he quickly gestured for her to remain where she was.

"I thought to come to speak to you, since I did not have the opportunity to sit with you at breakfast," he said, coming a little further into the room and sitting down heavily in a chair opposite her. "I hear that you were involved in a small fracas last evening."

Ellen lifted one eyebrow. "It was hardly a fracas, Father."

He chuckled and the small flickering tension in Ellen's heart quickly disappeared. "Indeed, I am only teasing you. But I did hear that you were quick to intervene in what could have been a very poor situation for one Miss Archibald?"

She nodded, wondering from whom he had heard it. "Lord Drake was a little inebriated," she said with a shake of her head. "Poor Miss Archibald had already had to endure a dance with him but was then unable to escape from him." Frowning hard, she saw her father's expression change from mirth to anger. "He was, I am sure, about to pull her into his embrace without so much as a single thought as to where he was or what it might do to her reputation. I am only glad that I was able to reach her in time—and that Lord Lindale behaved as he did also." Her frown lifted for a moment as she considered Lord Lindale, fully aware that he had conducted himself in a manner that not only had surprised her but that she had been very grateful for indeed.

"Yes," Lord Grantown said slowly, tilting his head just a little as he studied his daughter. "I did also want to mention what I have been hearing about Lord Lindale." He gave her a small smile, but Ellen felt a sudden flood of tension, worried about what her father would say. "Lady Sayers has spoken to me about his interest in you, Ellen. I would not like to hold you back from any considerations of him."

Ellen shook her head. "Father, I could not," she replied quickly. "He is the nephew of the late Lord Lindale, who treated you with such cruelty that we are still feeling the effects of it now."

"But he is *not* his uncle," her father replied softly. "I do not bear the man any ill will."

Ellen's lips twisted. "I cannot understand that, Father," she protested. "Our family name has been disgraced because of his family. How, then, could I consider a match with such a gentleman?"

Her father spread his hands. "I am not my brother," he reminded her. "Your late uncle was a fool. He gambled and was inconsiderate when it came to his wealth. Does that mean that I, too, am a fool? That I, too, must behave as my brother has done?"

"No," Ellen said quickly, "for you are of very different characters. But surely, Father, you can see that—"

"From what Lady Sayers has said and from what you yourself have stated also, a clear difference is evident between Lord Lindale's character and that of his uncle," Lord Grantown interrupted. "It would be foolish of me to push you from him simply because of who his uncle was."

Taking in a deep breath, Ellen shook her head. "But you were friends with Lord Lindale," she pointed out. "You believed him to have a good character. But then, in the end, it became quite apparent that he did not. He used your friendship for his own gain and treated you very ill."

Shaking his head, Lord Grantown let out a long breath. "Again, that does not state that the new Marquess of Lindale will be anything like his uncle," he said softly. "I can understand your concerns, my dear, but it would be unwise to discard him. He is a marquess, after all, and would be a very suitable match. He would be able to provide for you for the rest of your life and you could establish the family line together." Sitting forward, he put his elbows on his knees and clasped his hands together, looking at her earnestly. "Do not ignore his interest on my account, my dear Ellen. I have made my position clear to you and I want you to feel no guilt whatsoever. Do you understand?"

Ellen nodded but did not immediately reply. Her father's words ran around her mind and as much as she wished to push them away—for they were rather unsettling—she knew she could not simply ignore them. She was expected to marry, of course, but never once had she thought that Lord Lindale would be someone she ought to consider. Until last Season, the entirety of society was open to her but now, thanks to the late Lord Lindale, everything had changed.

"Now, if there are others that pursue you, then that is entirely a different matter," Lord Grantown continued, still speaking with great gentleness. "I am aware, of course, that the rumors about me are still hindering you and for that, I am sorry."

"That is no fault of yours, Father," Ellen replied quickly, not wanting him to feel any guilt whatsoever. "That is all the cause of the late Lord Lindale. I only wish..." She hesitated for a moment, her mind going back to the small key that she had hidden in her room. "I only wish that there was something I could do about the entire situation, so that you might be restored to your full place in society."

Lord Grantown smiled sadly. "I believe that is gone from us

forever, my dear. But I am determined to accept the situation, despite how much I dislike it."

"Might I ask, Father," Ellen said, a trifle tentatively as her father rose to his feet, "are our finances, at present, better than last year? Are you quite certain we can remain in London?" Swallowing hard, she spread her hands. "If you would find it preferable to return to the estate, then I would go without protest."

"You are very good," her father replied wearily. "But you are not to worry about such things. I am sure that, in time, all finances will be as they once were. Although," he added with a hint of sadness in his eyes, "you should make certain to thank both your aunt *and* your uncle for your Season in London. They were very insistent that they contribute financially toward it, even though I did my best to refuse." He put one hand on the door. "I was not meant to inform you of that, of course, but..." He shrugged, smiled, and quit the room, leaving Ellen staring after him in shock.

Her aunt and uncle had paid for her Season? She could hardly believe it. Lady Sayers had never once said a single thing and although she was greatly appreciative of their kindness, it reminded her all the more of her father's difficulties.

Suddenly, the key became even more important to her. She had spent so many days just wondering what it was she ought to do, and just how she could find out what it opened and whether or not the diary would be present within.

You could accept Lord Lindale's court, said a small voice in her head. *In doing that, you might have greater access to his townhouse.*

"But a chaperone with me at all times," Ellen muttered to herself, rubbing one hand over her eyes. But within her, she felt a fresh determination to find the diary, to make it known the sort of gentleman Lord Lindale had been when he was alive and the cruel trick he had played on her father, whereby he had taken great amounts of money from him and blackmailed her father into remaining silent.

"I could," she mused aloud, "show a vague interest in Lord

Lindale for the present. And once I have discovered the diary, there will be no requirement to remain in his company."

A small sense of satisfaction settled within her heart. It would be easy enough to do so, given that Lord Lindale appeared to be determined to linger in her company, although whether or not he intended to court her, Ellen was not quite certain. She was sure that he believed her responsible for the loss of his key, but was there any more to his interest in her than that?

Her smile grew as she thought of how he had spoken to her last evening, at the look that had come into his eyes as he regarded her. She was quite certain that any continuation of their acquaintance would lead to an increased intimacy between them and, thereafter, perhaps a courtship, for they could not simply continue to be in each other's company without any true indication of what was intended between them.

Of course, should he ever be led to propose, there was no requirement for her to accept him. She could easily refuse and certainly had every intention of doing so, provided she had the diary.

"I doubt he will want to linger in my company once he discovers the truth about his uncle," she said to herself, making her way toward the window so that she might absentmindedly look out at the quiet street below. Taking in a long breath, Ellen set her shoulders. She would continue to protest her innocence to Lord Lindale but would, however, accept his interest in her, regardless of his reasons for doing so, and would return it with interest of her own. It would be solely to find the diary in Lord Lindale's townhouse, of course, but he did not need to know such a thing. Resolved, she walked away from the window and picked up her book once more. This evening's soireé would be the perfect opportunity for her to show the very beginnings of interest in Lord Lindale. Who knew what would follow after that?

"I must tell you something, Aunt," Ellen murmured as they smiled and nodded at various other ladies and gentlemen, before coming to a stop in a quieter part of the room.

"Oh?"

Ellen smiled at Lady Sayers. "I have considered not only what you have said but also what Father has suggested and, therefore, have decided that I will be accepting of Lord Lindale's attentions. No longer will I try to hide from them or do all I can to convince myself that it is not something that I want. Rather, I will look at the possible match with a practical eye and realize that, as my father has said, Lord Lindale is not his father or his uncle. He is his own man and therefore, it would be wise for me to be considerate in my judgments."

Ellen had thought that her aunt might cry out in astonishment, look wonderfully relieved, or clap her hands in delight. However, much to her surprise, her aunt gave no reply but instead placed both hands on her hips and narrowed her eyes as she looked back at Ellen, perhaps a little less than convinced at her words.

"This is not at all what I expected, Ellen," she said, eyeing her with suspicion. "What is the truth behind such a decision?"

Spreading her hands—and hating that she was not about to tell her aunt the truth—Ellen looked back steadily at Lady Sayers. "Father has made it very clear that he has no need for me to wed anyone this Season. However, he has also stated that I am not to ignore Lord Lindale just because of who his uncle was. In addition, he has reminded me that I am, unfortunately, viewed in a poor light by many, given the rumors about my father. I will not pretend that I do not enjoy the conversation and the offers to dance, but I am well aware that there has been no further interest from any other gentleman save for Lord Lindale." Her hands fell to her sides as the words she spoke pierced her heart for, even though she had no real intention of considering Lord Lindale, she found the truth of her words to be very painful. "I would be foolish to ignore the attentions of a marquess."

Lady Sayers held her firm position for a few moments more,

and then let her hands slip to her sides as a tiny smile plucked at the corner of her mouth.

"I see," she replied softly. "I am sorry for your predicament, Ellen, for I know that you have a good many emotions when it comes to Lord Lindale, but I think it would be wise to do as your father suggests." Her smile grew and a twinkle came into her eye. "Besides which, it is not as though your father is pushing you toward a baron or baronet. He is suggesting that you consider a *marquess*, Ellen. One that, I am sure, almost every young lady in the *ton* is aware of at present."

Ellen's smile became fixed. She had not considered that. The *beau monde* would be very well aware of Lord Lindale and it would certainly be remarked upon should he begin to show her a little more attention. Was she prepared for that? Little doubt that the rumors would come flying up around her again, for the *ton* would make certain that Lord Lindale knew every single one of them. There would be those who would speak of her father with cruel and harsh words, in the hope that such information might cause Lord Lindale to turn away from her entirely. Was that something she was ready for?

"Ellen?" Lady Sayers put a hand out toward her niece. "You have gone a little pale."

Giving herself a small shake, Ellen looked up at her aunt and nodded, her smile no longer as certain. "I am quite all right, Aunt," she promised. Her gaze traveled over Lady Sayers' shoulder, landing on the very gentleman of whom she had only just been speaking. "It is only that Lord Lindale has arrived."

Lady Sayers turned her head sharply before looking back at Ellen, a broad smile on her face. "So he has," she said as Ellen managed to quieten her frantically beating heart. "Should you wish to greet him?"

"Not yet," Ellen replied, not wanting to rush toward him practically the moment he came into the room. "In a few minutes, Aunt."

Lady Sayers nodded but the excitement in her eyes was more

than apparent. It appeared that Ellen had managed to convince her although that did not make her feel any sense of happiness.

"It appears as though you are not going to have to wait for too long," Lady Sayers murmured, casting another glance over her shoulder. "It seems as though he is about to approach you."

Ellen swallowed hard, surprised at just how nervous she felt. She was, of course, merely playing a part, for the only reason she was to show any interest in Lord Lindale was so that she might find the diary. For whatever reason, she still felt a swirl of apprehension in her stomach as Lord Lindale came toward her, dropping her eyes and bending into a quick curtsy as she did so.

"Good evening, Lady Ellen, Lady Sayers," Lord Lindale said, looking quite delighted at seeing them both. "And how are you both this evening?"

"I am very well," Ellen replied as Lady Sayers nodded. "And glad to see you also, Lord Lindale."

The words seemed to have a startling effect upon Lord Lindale, who looked back at her sharply, a small line forming between his brows as he studied her. A faint blush caught her cheeks and she dropped her gaze, fearing that she had been a little too forward.

Lord Lindale cleared his throat abruptly, then smiled. "I thought to take a short walk through St. James' Park tomorrow afternoon, Lady Ellen," he said as Ellen slowly lifted her gaze back toward him. "No doubt you have other engagements already, but if you do not, then perhaps you might like to join me?" He looked to Lady Sayers. "With your permission and your attendance also, of course."

Lady Sayers laughed. "My dear Lord Lindale, I pray you do not even think for a moment that I would refuse you." she said, before looking pointedly at Ellen. "Ellen? What say you to Lord Lindale's request?"

Ellen looked into Lord Lindale's brown eyes and saw the question there. He was waiting for her response, and Ellen knew that this moment would be the one that would change her acquaintance with him for good. Taking in a deep breath, she set her shoulders and placed a delicate smile on her face.

"Thank you, Lord Lindale," she replied, aware of the knot of tension that now tightened her stomach. "I would be glad to join you. I should like it very much indeed."

9

Colin smiled as Lord Castleton entered his study.

"Good afternoon, Castleton," he said, waving his friend to a chair. "I cannot welcome you in for too long, however, for I am to take a visit to St. James' Park within the hour."

Lord Castleton lifted a brow. "Oh?" he asked, splashing a little brandy into a glass before he sat down. "And why might that be?"

"Because," Colin replied, surprised at the slight wave of nervousness that washed over him, "I am to walk with Lady Ellen." Refusing to immediately look up at his friend for fear of the shock he might see on Lord Castleton's face, Colin finished sorting out one or two papers before he finally did so. Lord Castleton did not look at all shocked or surprised, however. In fact, he merely took another sip of his brandy and then shrugged, as though it made perfect sense for Colin to do so.

"Ever since the ball with Miss Archibald, she has appeared a little warmer toward me," Colin continued. "Last evening, she expressed a gladness to be in my company again and I took the opportunity to ask her to join me for a short walk." He lifted one shoulder. "I have taken your suggestion to heart."

"So it seems," Lord Castleton said, a grin finally spreading across his face. "You are aware, of course, that the *ton* is now beginning to speak of your interest in Lady Ellen?" He chuckled and raised his glass. "It did not take them long but after the ball, it has already become clear to them that you consider her very highly."

A streak of either fright or awareness ran down Colin's spine. "That was certainly quicker than I anticipated," he replied slowly, "but what else can be done?"

"You must be very careful indeed not to toy with the lady," Lord Castleton warned. "I will confess that I spoke quite hastily, Lindale. Whilst the idea I have given you might well be considered wise, I should remind you that any attention you show to a lady cannot be quickly and swiftly removed for fear of what that will do to her reputation. If you are to continue along this path, then soon you will need to consider courtship. That does not mean that you should be forced into matrimony, of course, but that any connection between you will have to be brought to a careful end, should you discover that she *has* taken your key."

Colin's eyes flared but he said nothing.

"You do not find that a particular concern?"

"I do not," Colin replied slowly. "I have considered what it might be like to wed Lady Ellen. Yes, I believe that she has taken the key from me, but if she has not and my attentions toward her continue, I find there to be no particular difficulty there. I have seen her kindness and her determination to protect others from what she has been forced to endure."

Lord Castleton nodded slowly, his expression thoughtful. "You speak of Miss Archibald."

"I do."

His friend let out a long sigh and finished the rest of his brandy. "Lady Ellen has struggled, certainly," he said quietly. "But do not lose sight of what it is you are seeking in all of this. You seek the truth. You want to discover the key. And you must prepare yourself for what might follow when you do so."

THOSE WORDS RANG around Colin's head as he climbed out of his carriage and stood at the entrance to St. James' Park, thinking that the day was very fine indeed. Lord Castleton was correct, of course. There *was* a concern over what the *ton* might say as regarded his attentions toward Lady Ellen, particularly given the rumors about her father. He would have to be very careful if the time came to end any increased intimacy between them.

And yet, the idea of courting Lady Ellen, of increasing his acquaintance with her and finding a new intimacy with her, was not an unpleasant one. Ever since he had seen her with Miss Archibald, he had begun to view her in an entirely new way and part of him was very eager to know her a little better. In fact, whilst he was quite determined to follow the plan that Lord Castleton had suggested, there was certainly a lack of willingness on his part—as though part of him wanted to refrain entirely. It made very little sense and Colin shook his head to clear his thoughts, hearing the sound of wheels coming along the road behind him.

Turning, he saw another carriage approaching and, within a few minutes, both Lady Sayers and Lady Ellen had come to join him. He took in Lady Ellen, finding her to be very lovely this afternoon. Her green eyes sparkled with vitality and her smile appeared to be genuine.

"Good afternoon," he said, bowing quickly. "Thank you for joining me."

"Not at all, Lord Lindale," came the reply. "I am glad to do so this afternoon. The day is very lovely, is it not?"

After a few words of welcome and conversation with Lady Sayers, Colin offered Lady Ellen his arm and she took it without hesitation. Lady Sayers stayed behind a few steps and, after a moment, Colin began to walk into the park with Lady Ellen on his arm.

"How are you this afternoon, Lady Ellen?" he asked, feeling as though he were already struggling for conversation as a tightness came into his chest, his heart beginning to quicken already. He knew what he had to say during this conversation, knew what sort of trap he had to set down before her, and yet somehow maintain an easy conversation.

"I am well, I thank you," she replied, glancing up at him before looking away again. "How do you find London, Lord Lindale?"

He shrugged. "It is certainly more interesting than I thought. It has taken some time for me to settle into the townhouse. Finding that strange key and then, only yesterday, I discovered a wooden box in my late uncle's study, which, I am sure, will be opened by that key." Sighing heavily, he shook his head. "Alas, I—"

"I know it is your first Season in London," Lady Ellen interrupted, surprising him with the hastiness of her words, as though she did not wish him to speak of the key any longer. "That must be rather difficult."

It was not something they had discussed before, for there had never been any particular intimacy between them. They had talked of general things but never once of his first foray into London society.

"Forgive me," she said quickly, making Colin realize that he had not answered her in some minutes. "I should not have asked. Of course, that is an entirely personal matter and—"

"Please, forgive me," Colin interrupted quickly, looking down at her. "I was only thinking of how to answer." He gave her a wry smile as she smiled up at him. "It has been very strange, Lady Ellen. You will not find it so, of course, since you have always had this particular way of life, but it was not that way for me."

"I have heard that you were given the title only some months ago," Lady Ellen replied, sounding very interested. "My father knew your late uncle, of course."

"Of course," he repeated, knowing that the gentlemen of the *ton* were mostly acquainted with each other. "Unfortunately, I did not."

Her head twisted toward him sharply. "Oh?"

Colin hesitated, wondering whether or not he should express the truth to her or if he should hide it from her. Would she think less of him if he told her the truth?

"I was not even aware that my father came from a noble family,

Lady Ellen," he said, speaking with great slowness for fear that he would make the wrong decision in telling her such a thing. "When Mr. Grey—that is, the gentleman who has done a great deal for me and who was tasked with finding me when my uncle passed away—when he discovered me, it was utterly astounding."

"Goodness!" Lady Ellen exclaimed, although there was no sense of disdain in her voice but rather surprise and great interest. "Then this all came as a great shock?"

"A very great shock," he agreed.

"I should never have thought it," she replied, a little more quietly. "Your manner and your speech—in fact, everything about you speaks of a gentleman who has always been brought up in such a life."

Colin chuckled. "It has been a difficult few months with a great deal to take in, for both myself and my brother," he told her as her eyes widened, now fixed on his, perhaps unaware that he had a younger brother. "My brother has also inherited a great deal of wealth and has set himself up in his estate with his new bride." He smiled softly, thinking of Arthur and the way he had reacted to the news of their improved circumstances. "He has found it all quite wonderful, I should say. Indeed, he took to the training and the study and the requirements made of us as gentlemen much easier than I. He has thought it all quite marvelous and has moved into his new situation with an ease that I regret I do not have."

Lady Ellen laughed, her eyes dancing. "I think I should like to meet him," she told him, making Colin smile as his sense of worry that she would think less of him began to fade away. "He sounds very different in his character to you." She turned a little more toward him suddenly, her steps coming to a sudden stop. "That is not to say, however, that I find your character at all lacking."

Colin looked down into her eyes, seeing the worry there and finding himself chuckling. She had made something of a misstep, but he was not at all insulted.

"You need not worry," he told her as she searched his face with wide eyes. "I am not upset by such a remark. Indeed, my brother *is* very different from myself and I am sure he would be glad to meet you also."

Lady Ellen stood for another moment or two before she nodded and began to walk again, her cheeks still very red. Colin found himself smiling as he walked alongside her, almost glad that such a thing had happened since it had given him an opportunity to see her concern for him.

"I think you have done very well thus far, Lord Lindale," Lady Ellen said quietly after a few moments. "You have everyone in society speaking well of you and it seems as though every young lady wishes to be introduced to you." Her smile became a little shy as she darted a quick look toward him. "I suppose I should consider myself very fortunate to be in your company."

"Not at all," he said, shaking his head. "I find that I do not like all the attentions you speak of." Grimacing, his brows knotted together. "In fact, I find them to be a little irritating at times."

"Irritating?" Lady Ellen responded, sounding very surprised. "I thought gentlemen were very eager for such attentions."

"I speak only for myself," Colin replied swiftly. "But there is a falseness in many an acquaintance that I do not much like."

Lady Ellen went silent for a few moments, then looked up at him tentatively again. "A falseness, Lord Lindale?"

He waved his free hand. "Young ladies who seek my attention in the hope that I might consider them, without having any interest in my character, my past, my family...nothing of significance. All they care for is my wealth and my title and that is not enough for me." Realizing that he was speaking very freely, Colin paused for a moment, worried that he was talking too openly to her.

"That is both admirable and distressing to hear," Lady Ellen replied after a few moments. "To know that you have such intentions is very impressive, but to hear that you have come into society and recognized such falseness so quickly is rather troubling."

A small shrug lifted Colin's shoulders. "It is as I have found it."

"Then perhaps I should be all the more appreciative of your request for me to join you this afternoon," Lady Ellen replied, although she turned her head away and lowered her gaze, so that he could only see a few stray curls brushing at her temples, her eyes hidden from him. Colin did not immediately reply, not quite certain what to make of what she had said and thinking that perhaps it might be best to remain silent for a short time.

"Tell me," he said after a few minutes of quiet. "You must have found difficulties within society also, surely?"

She looked up at him sharply. "What can you mean?"

"I have heard of the rumors," he said without any embarrassment or hesitation. "I know that you have struggled, and I am sorry for it. It is, of course, another part of society that I have had to learn about, and it does not make me at all glad to hear it."

Lady Ellen frowned, her own brow furrowed somewhat, but after a few moments, she sighed and shook her head. "Many within society like nothing more than to gossip and spread untruths," she said heavily. "My father has been caught up by them and the whispers have spread. It was at its worst last Season, but it still remains during this Season."

"For what it is worth, I promise that I have no eagerness to either listen or believe such things," he stated, making Lady Ellen look back at him again with slightly widened eyes. "Financial affairs ought to be a private matter, surely? And rumors are nothing more than that—mistruths that are spread by malicious tongues. They are worth nothing."

"That is exactly what I think," Lady Ellen responded with such a great ferocity that Colin could not help but smile at her, despite the seriousness of their conversation. "They have done a great deal of damage to both myself and my father and yet there are very few within the *ton* who would even *consider* the possibility that there might be nothing but falseness within those words."

Colin's smile faded and his brows furrowed as he considered what Lady Ellen had said. "Could you not confront the person who began such rumors?" he asked, and Lady Ellen looked up at him suddenly, a fire burning in her eyes that Colin had not noticed before. "I know that I am new to society and, perhaps in my own foolish way, entirely ridiculous when I make such a suggestion, but there must be a way to counter this gossip." Looking down at her, he searched her face. "Unless there is some reason why your father could not do so."

Lady Ellen was silent for many moments. In fact, Colin began to feel rather awkward, suddenly worrying that he had suggested something that was so preposterous that Lady Ellen was now trying to find a way to thank him for the idea but to say, rather gently, that she did not think such a thing was possible.

"In some cases, Lord Lindale, there might be the possibility of doing as you have said," she eventually replied, a tightness about her voice that spoke of frustration and a deep, unresolved anger. "However, in this particular circumstance, such a thing can never take place." She tore her eyes away from his, her lips in a thin line, her hand on his arm now holding a little more strongly than before.

"I am sorry to hear it," he replied, truly feeling a sense of sorrow over her difficult situation. "Would that there was something I could do to assist you, Lady Ellen."

Again, her head twisted sharply, and she looked up at him, that fire burning in her eyes once more as heat poured into her cheeks. Colin did not know what to make of such a reaction, gazing back at her for a few moments before he cleared his throat and once more turned his head toward the path.

"There is not."

Her words were hard and angry. Colin forced himself not to immediately believe that it was *he* she held such fury toward. It made very little sense to think such a thing and he did not want to allow his mind to hurry to conclusions that were not at all practical.

"Although I am grateful to you for your willingness, Lord Lindale."

This took some of her anger from her voice and Colin glanced her in relief, before clearing his throat awkwardly once more.

"I am sorry if talking of such things has upset you," he continued, still feeling a great swirl of tension hanging like storm clouds over their heads. "I did not mean anything other than—"

"Please." Lady Ellen stopped suddenly, put her hand on his arm, and, turning to one side, looked up into his eyes. Colin stopped quickly, astonished to feel heat begin to travel up his arm as he gazed back at her. This interest he had in Lady Ellen was merely for his own benefit, he reminded himself. It was so that he could discover whether or not she had stolen the key—and, if she had, what she intended to do with it. To have any sort of emotion toward the lady was not required and certainly not expected.

"I am sorry. I have been speaking with frustration and anger," Lady Ellen told him, her openness surprising him all the more. "Forgive me. I should not have allowed you to see it."

"In heaven's name, why ever not?" he replied as Lady Ellen dropped her hand as well as her gaze. "Is it not the done thing? Is that another part of society I am yet to fully understand?"

"Indeed," Lady Ellen replied, a little more quietly. "Regardless, you did not upset me. Although I thank you for your concern."

"But of course," he murmured, offering her his arm which, after a moment, she took. And then, together, they continued to walk through the park, with their conversation turning toward other, more lighter things.

10

Ellen bit her lip as she looked at herself in the mirror. For whatever reason, these last ten days spent in Lord Lindale's company had not gone entirely as she had planned. There had not been any further opportunity to visit his townhouse and, whilst they had spent a good deal of time in each other's company, she had not found any way or opportunity to speak to him of his uncle or the possibility as to where the key might go. What was making things all the worse was that she was beginning to find herself, most unexpectedly, rather enjoying his company.

Indeed, this evening, a fluttering of excitement was in her stomach. Although Ellen tried to tell herself that such a feeling came merely from the fact that she was, at long last, to be in Lord Lindale's house again. She had not forgotten what Lord Lindale had said to her some days ago about the wooden box he had discovered. Was the diary to be in there?

"Are you quite ready, Ellen?"

She turned, just as Lady Sayers came into the room to smile at her. She had said very little about Lord Lindale since Ellen had agreed to spend more time in his company, but from the smile on her face and the knowing look in her eyes, Ellen suspected that she knew already what Ellen was beginning to feel.

That irritated her somewhat, given that she did not want to even have such feelings in the first place.

"A ball at Lord Lindale's," Lady Sayers said as Ellen smoothed her skirts and brushed out invisible creases. "Are you prepared, my dear? Might I say that you look very lovely indeed?"

"I thank you, Aunt," Ellen replied, not wanting to say anything in particular about Lord Lindale. "Shall we depart? We do not want to be tardy." She brushed one hand over the side of her gown and, despite the fact that she could not feel it, she knew very well that the key was settled deep within it. Suddenly awash with nervousness about what she intended to do, Ellen tightened her fists, praying that her expression remained calm as her aunt fell into step with her.

"Do you feel quite well, Ellen?" Lady Sayers asked as they walked together toward the carriage. "You look a little pale."

Ellen shook her head. "I am quite well, Aunt," she replied swiftly as the butler held the front door for them. "I am a little excited, certainly." She swallowed hard, pushing away the flurry of guilt that came with the idea of making her way back into Lord Lindale's study in the hope of finding the wooden box he had mentioned. "That is to be expected with any ball, I suppose."

"Mmm," her aunt murmured, saying nothing in particular but keeping a small smile on her face as they sat down in the carriage. Ellen said nothing more, her breath hitching as the carriage pulled away. Just what would this evening bring?

THE RUSH of exhilaration that came with stepping into Lord Lindale's townhouse brought a gentle rosiness to Ellen's cheeks. For some minutes, she forgot entirely about the key in her pocket and the intention she had of making her way to Lord Lindale's study, caught up with the excitement that only a ball could bring. It was, she had to admit, a little more intense this evening, although she could never admit that to anyone other than herself.

"Good evening, Lord Lindale."

Ellen curtsied as Lord Lindale bowed, his brown eyes flickering with what she hoped was happiness at seeing her again.

"Good evening, Lady Ellen," he said, having already greeted Lady Sayers. "I am very glad of your company this evening. I do hope that you enjoy every minute of tonight's occasion."

"I am sure I will," she replied, making to move away only for Lord Lindale to press his hand to her arm, stopping her suddenly.

"Might you put my name down for the waltz and the country dance, Lady Ellen?" he asked, keeping his voice quiet and dropping his hand almost at once. "I fear I shall be held back from seeking you out simply by the requirement I have at present to greet my guests." He smiled at her and Ellen felt a flush of heat climb up her spine as she nodded, dropping her gaze for a moment.

"But of course, Lord Lindale," she answered softly. "I would be glad to."

"The waltz and the country dance," he said again, as though to ensure that she recalled them both without difficulty. "I look forward to it, Lady Ellen."

"As do I."

Those words left her mouth before she could prevent them, and the way Lord Lindale's eyes flared spoke of both surprise and delight. Flushed, Ellen curtsied again quickly and followed after Lady Sayers, who was waiting for her only a short distance away.

"His interest in you has already been spoken of by the *ton*, Ellen," Lady Sayers remarked as Ellen joined her. "And it is not as though he is doing anything at all to hide it."

"I am aware of that," Ellen replied, the heat in her face still lingering. "But what can be done, Aunt? Should I ask him to be a little more discreet?"

Lady Sayers laughed and took Ellen's arm. "No, indeed not," she replied as they made their way toward the ballroom. "What I meant to suggest was that I believe that he will ask permission to court you very soon." Her smile faded. "I am a little surprised he has not done so already."

"It has been less than a fortnight, Aunt," Ellen reminded Lady Sayers. "Less than a fortnight of his attentions increasing toward me. Perhaps he is a little uncertain."

Or perhaps he still believes that I have the key and is waiting for me to say so before anything further commences, said a quiet voice within her and Ellen dropped her gaze for a moment, a deep disquiet settling within her heart. She could not lose her focus now, she told herself, trying not to be overwhelmed by Lord Lindale's remarks to her.

Whilst she might appreciate Lord Lindale's company, whilst she might find him charming and interesting and, were she honest, very handsome, she had to recall that her sole purpose for accepting his interest in her was to discover the diary of his late uncle. That she was doing all of this in the vague hope of freeing her father from the rumors that still bound him.

But would such a thing matter if Lord Lindale proposed to you? that same, quiet voice niggled at her, seeming to drown out the sound of the ballroom entirely despite the noise that surrounded her. *The rumors would have no effect then. You would be wed and settled. Your father would be able to retire to the estate without any further difficulty.*

"Save for his financial ones," Ellen muttered to herself, fully convinced that her father was still struggling with either debts or the costs of his estate at present. She shook her head to herself in an attempt to clear her thoughts and missed entirely the sharp look that Lady Sayers sent toward her.

"Lord Lindale has asked me to keep back the waltz and the country dance for him, Aunt," Ellen remembered to tell her. "Might you wait a moment until I write it on my dance card?"

Her aunt beamed at her and nodded, although Ellen did not remark further. Hastily slipping the ribbon from her hand, she felt in her pocket for a small pencil, only for her fingers to close over the small key that she had placed there.

A chill ran over her and she pulled her fingers away hastily, as though she did not want to be reminded of the task at hand.

"Here," Lady Sayers said quickly, handing Ellen another pencil—although quite where Lady Sayers had pulled it from, Ellen did not know. "Two dances, then?"

"Indeed," Ellen replied, finding that the country dance came first, and the waltz was much nearer the end of the evening. "I did not think there were any concerns on your part, Aunt?" She looked up at Lady Sayers, who was still smiling with evident delight.

"None whatsoever," Lady Sayers announced as Ellen handed her back the small pencil. "Two dances—and one the waltz."

Ellen smiled but said nothing, turning around to find herself quickly greeted by Lord Castleton, who then enquired if he might also steal a dance or two. Obliging him, Ellen handed him her dance card, only for another gentleman she recognized to approach. Within minutes, Ellen found herself surrounded by friends and acquaintances and, forgetting about the key entirely, began to enjoy the company and conversation that this evening was to bring.

∽

"You dance very well, Lady Ellen."

Ellen felt what was now her third blush creep into her cheeks, glancing up at Lord Lindale and seeing the warmth in his eyes as they made their way from the dance floor.

"You are very kind to say so, Lord Lindale," she replied, quickly dropping her gaze to the floor. "This evening appears to have gone very well thus far."

"It has," Lord Lindale replied, looking about him in a contented fashion. "I confess I was a little anxious, but it seems that Lord Castleton has been proven correct."

"Oh?" A stir of curiosity bubbled up within her. "What did Lord Castleton say?"

Lord Lindale laughed and shook his head. "He *berated* me, Lady

Ellen, if you can imagine it." The warmth in his eyes grew as he held her gaze for a few moments. "He told me that I was worrying incessantly and that it was doomed to fail if I continued in such a manner. He stated that all would go just as planned and that being fearful about what might occur was more than a little foolish." Letting go of her arm, since they were now near to Lady Sayers, he shrugged one shoulder. "It seems he was correct."

Ellen smiled back at him. "I can understand being a little anxious since this was the first ball you have ever hosted," she answered as Lady Sayers came forward to join them. "But I believe that Lord Castleton is wise in his counsel. There is nothing but pure happiness here this evening."

He tilted his head, something in his eyes making her heart quicken. "Even for you, Lady Ellen?" he asked softly, her breath catching at the intensity of his gaze. "Is that happiness present for you?"

She had no opportunity to answer, for Lady Sayers was with them in a moment, smiling brightly at Lord Lindale, who gave her a small bow.

"An excellent dance, I must say," Lady Sayers remarked as Ellen looked away from Lord Lindale, trying to calm her quickened heart. "This ball is most enjoyable, Lord Lindale. You are to be commended."

"I thank you." Lord Lindale bowed and then, with a small sigh escaping him, looked away. "I fear I must take my leave of you both," he said with yet another sigh. "I am next to dance with Miss Berkshire. But I look forward to our second dance, Lady Ellen."

"But of course, Lord Lindale," Ellen replied, smiling at him. "Until our waltz, then."

He smiled at her, looking at her for another moment or two before finally taking his leave. Ellen found herself watching him depart, her happiness growing in a manner she had never once expected. Lord Lindale was treating her in a way that no other gentleman had ever done before and she was falling into the delight of having his attentions curled around her. He made her feel such an array of emotions that she did not know how to react to them all, struggling to quieten the joyous beating of her heart and the anticipation that came with knowing she would soon be in his arms again.

"Oh, Ellen. There is a tear to your gown!"

Ellen's eyes dragged themselves away from the retreating figure of Lord Lindale, only to see Lady Sayers' horrified eyes resting on the bottom of Ellen's gown.

"Is there?" Ellen asked, frowning as she turned her head to look down. "Oh, so there is! I did not even notice such a thing occurring."

Lady Sayers frowned and shook her head. "Nor I," she stated, taking Ellen's arm and hurrying her away from the dance floor. "You are not due to dance the cotillion, I believe?"

Ellen shook her head. "No, Aunt."

"Then we will have your gown fixed in a few minutes, I am sure," Lady Sayers replied firmly. "Come. I know where to go."

Within a few minutes, Ellen found herself sitting quietly in a chair whilst a maid scurried about with a needle and thread, surveying the damage to Ellen's gown as Lady Sayers looked on. The room was not overly large but there were only three other ladies present, as well as Ellen.

"If you wish to wait for me, Aunt, I will make my way to you when I am ready," Ellen told her, aware of the sudden tightness in her chest as she spoke. "It will be only a few minutes, I am sure."

Lady Sayers hesitated, then nodded. "Very well, Ellen," she said, glancing down at Ellen's gown before looking away toward the door. "I will wait for you."

Ellen nodded and smiled, although her fingers twisted together as she watched Lady Sayers leave. There was an opportunity now at hand for her, for Lord Lindale's study was just a short distance away. They had passed it as they searched for the powder room and Ellen had felt a thrill of both horror and anticipation climb up her spine.

Letting out a long, slow breath, she closed her eyes tightly. Part of her wanted desperately to do as she had always intended but something else held her back. The way Lord Lindale had looked at her as he had taken his leave still lingered in her mind. The warmth in his gaze, the smile on his face, and his genuine eagerness to dance with her again sent a stab of guilt into her heart. Was she really about to trespass into his study once more in search of this box? Was that what she wished to do? Shaking her head to herself, Ellen passed one hand over her eyes, not seeing the startled look from the maid as she sewed up the hole in Ellen's gown.

It had all seemed so very clear to her only a few days ago. She had told herself she would entertain Lord Lindale's attentions so that she might find a way to return to his townhouse and find a place for the key. She had been single-minded in her determination and when he had told her of the wooden box, she had felt her heart quicken with the awareness of what such a box might contain. That had been her sole determination, her only interest. And yet, during the last ten days, it had faded away and lost a good deal of its strength. Something had shifted within her, something that she did not want to give name to for fear that it might overwhelm her.

Could she really take a hold of this opportunity and abuse Lord Lindale's kindness and generosity in such a way? Could she truly slip away to his study, step inside even though she knew she was not meant to be there, and then rifle through his things, seeking the wooden box he had spoken of? There had been no guilt whatsoever the first time but now, she was practically ensnared by it.

"There, my lady."

The maid rose and stepped back, looking down at Ellen's gown with satisfaction. "I believe that is restored."

Ellen glanced down and, much to her relief, saw no mark whatsoever left behind. "Wonderful," she replied as the maid blushed. "You are to be commended."

The maid curtsied and looked away and Ellen quickly took her leave, quitting the room and finding herself back out in the hallway once more. She glanced to her right, her eyes fixing themselves to the study door that was such a short distance away. Then, she looked to her left, seeing Lady Sayers in deep conversation with another lady. Neither of them glanced in her direction, seemingly entirely unaware of her presence.

Ellen's breathing became quick and fast as she made her way to the study door, looking surreptitiously over her shoulder but seeing neither footman, maid, nor even Lady Sayers coming after her. There was no one else about and she turned the study door handle at once, fully expecting it to be locked up tight.

It was not.

The door swung open silently and, before she could lose her nerve, Ellen stepped inside.

One hand fluttered to her chest as she looked all about her. There was only a single candle flickering gently on the mantlepiece, illuminating the desk before it. Part of her longed to reach out and take it, to search the room for this wooden box and to find out whether or not the late Lord Lindale's diary was contained within.

But she stayed her hand.

Letting out a long breath, Ellen pulled the key from her pocket and slowly approached the desk. This was one of her greatest trials, one of her most difficult moments of indecision. So much was at stake, so much for her to lose depending on what she did. And yet, the answer was very clear to her.

The key did not belong to her. She had stolen it from Lord Lindale, who had then gone on to prove to her that he was not at all the gentleman his uncle had been. The kindness, gentleness, and affection that he showed to her proved as much. Now that she knew him a little better, enjoyed spending time in his company, and even found herself looking forward to being with him again, Ellen knew that she could not simply begin to search a room that was entirely his. Nor could she keep the key.

"I am sorry," she said aloud, the sound of her own voice making her jump as she pulled the key from her pocket and stepping forward, setting it down on the desk before her. It sat there quietly, catching the light from the candle and sending a tremor all through Ellen's frame.

But she turned away from it quickly, as though fearful that she would pick it up again should she linger. Making her way to the door, Ellen took in a deep breath and steeled herself, knowing that she was doing the right thing but still finding it something of a struggle. Her mind screamed at her that she was giving away the only thing that might reveal the truth about her father, whilst her heart knew that she was doing what was right. Lord Lindale did not deserve her deceit or her disloyalty. A time might come when she could speak to him of what had occurred, of what his uncle had done, but she could not simply take what was not hers and force him to realize the truth. If he were to discover the diary, then Ellen prayed he would be willing to come and discuss it with her, so that she might have the opportunity to explain.

And if he does not?

Opening the door, Ellen crept out quickly and quietly, filled with relief that no one had seen her. Closing the door, she made her way back toward Lady Sayers, her head held high and a sense of pride filling her.

If he does not, then I must hope that our seemingly mutual interest in each other continues, she told herself, her heart still beating a little more quickly but, rather than fear or dread, now beating with a sense of relief. The burden was gone from her. The key had been returned. There was nothing more to hide from Lord Lindale.

"My dear, you look a little flushed."

"My gown is wonderfully mended," Ellen replied with a broad smile. "The maid has done an excellent repair."

"So I see," Lady Sayers replied, looking quite delighted. "Then shall we return to the ballroom? I know you will not wish to miss any further dances."

Ellen laughed and fell into step beside her aunt. "I should hate to miss any of them, Aunt," she admitted, and Lady Sayers chuckled. "But perhaps I am looking forward to one more than the others."

∽

A figure moved stiffly out of his chair, the darkness still casting a gloom over him. Stretching, he moved forward slowly to Lord Lindale's desk and looked down at it, his hands now sitting firmly on his hips.

"Good gracious," he murmured, reaching out to touch the small key that now sat there. "That is a surprise." Blowing out a long breath, he raked one hand through his hair. "Most astonishing indeed."

11

"**W**ell?"

Colin hurried into his drawing room, where Lord Castleton sat lazily by the fire, looking up at him with a slightly weary expression.

"An excellent evening, by all accounts," Lord Castleton replied, lifting his brandy glass in a toast. "I myself certainly enjoyed it."

"I am sure that is so," Colin replied, a little frustrated. "But my study. Did you see anything? Or anyone?" His stomach tightened furiously as he came further into the room, pushing the door shut behind him and making his way to a large chair that was opposite Lord Castleton. Eyeing his friend and fully aware that the gentleman had already indulged more than a little, he forced himself to sit quietly and refrain from demanding or asking any further questions. Whatever Lord Castleton wanted to reveal would be done so in good time, even if it meant that Colin himself had to exhibit a good deal of patience.

"Brandy?" Lord Castleton asked, but Colin shook his head no. "You have excellent brandy, Lindale. Excellent."

"I thank you," Colin replied, feeling his frustration growing as a tightness came into his chest that he could not reveal to Lord

Castleton. "Now, the study?" He gestured with his hands, spreading them wide. "Did anyone come into the room?"

Lord Castleton grinned. "Someone did," he said, and Colin caught his breath, feeling as though he had been punched hard in the stomach. Part of him had been desperately hoping that Lady Ellen would refrain from doing what he had set up for her, perhaps praying that what he felt between them was also reciprocated by her. His shoulders slumped as he looked back at Lord Castleton, wondering why his friend had such a ridiculous grin on his face.

"And it was Lady Ellen, I suppose," he said, and Lord Castleton nodded yet again, his smile still present. He and Lord Castleton had come up with an arrangement whereby either he himself or Lord Castleton would be sitting in the study in near darkness, ready to observe whoever might come into the room.

Evidently, Lord Castleton had seen the one thing that Colin had already known would occur. Why, then, did he feel so despondent? Surely he should be claiming some sort of great victory?

"It is not what you think, Lindale."

Colin lifted his head.

"Yes, it was Lady Ellen, I have no doubt about that, but she did not search your study as you feared."

"She did not?" Colin repeated, his eyes widening as his friend held up what could only be the small key that he had discovered some weeks before. "You—you mean to say that she replaced this?"

"She set it down on your study desk and, after a moment, quit the room entirely," Lord Castleton replied as Colin rose to take it. "For whatever reason, rather than use the opportunity to try and discover whatever it was she wanted, Lady Ellen chose to set the key down and leave it where it belonged."

Colin took the key from Lord Castleton, his eyes wide as he looked down at it. He could hardly believe she had chosen to return it, not when she had gone to so much trouble to take it from him in the first place.

"But why?" he asked, returning his gaze to Lord Castleton, who was looking inordinately pleased with himself, as though he had been the one to return the key rather than Lady Ellen. "Why would she do such a thing? Clearly this is important to her."

Lord Castleton shrugged. "I could not say," he replied slowly. "Although I might surmise that it is due to the fact that she has come to consider you in an entirely different light." Rising to his feet, he threw back the rest of his brandy and chuckled, slapping Colin hard on the arm. "It appears that the lady might be fond of you." Bidding Colin farewell, he made his way from the room, albeit with a somewhat unsteady gait, before closing the door behind him.

Colin sank down into his chair, looking down at the key and blowing out a long breath as he did so. Lady Ellen had done something so entirely unexpected that he did not know quite how to respond. To tell her that he knew she had taken the key and had, thereafter, returned it would only state, loud and clear, that he had given her various attentions in the hope of revealing the truth. It would not say that he had *genuine* affection for her, but would, instead, drive her away.

He sat bolt upright, his eyes wide as he stared across the room unseeingly. True affections? Was that what was within his heart? Had he truly come to care for her? Was that why he was now so very reluctant to state such things to her, for fear that she would remove herself from his company entirely?

She has come to consider you in an entirely different light.

Lord Castleton's words came back to him in a flurry, sending a tight spiral of excitement into Colin's stomach. Could it be that his friend was suggesting there was an affection within Lady Ellen's heart also? That she might have come to consider him in an entirely new light also?

Groaning, Colin sat forward and ran one hand through his hair. He had never been in this sort of situation before, had never found himself so confused and troubled, uncertain and yet thrilled that Lady Ellen had chosen to do as she had done. To set down the key, the key that clearly was important to her, and not go on to search his study, to seek out the wooden box that was supposedly discovered—that meant a great deal to him. But quite how he was meant to reveal that to her was another matter entirely.

∼

COLIN BOWED low and prayed that there was no expression of guilt or distrust on his face. "Good evening, Lady Sayers, Lady Ellen."

The two ladies curtsied beautifully and, as she rose, Colin was sure he could see a spark of either happiness or relief in Lady Ellen's eyes.

"Good evening, Lord Lindale," she replied as Lady Sayers murmured a few words of welcome. "Are you not dancing this evening?" She gestured to the other couples who were already making their way to the part of the room set aside for dancing, although Colin found no eagerness in his heart to join them.

"I may do so later on this evening, but for the moment, I am quite contented to stand here and converse," he replied, knowing that an evening assembly would permit him the time and the opportunity to do so. "And you, Lady Ellen? You are not dancing this evening?"

She laughed and there was a freedom in her expression that he was certain had not been there before.

"I have not been asked as yet, Lord Lindale," she replied teasingly. "But I confess that I am a little weary this evening."

He smiled at her, knowing that she referred to his ball and the many, many dances she had undertaken.

"Although I am certain I will have enough energy for one or two," she finished as his smile spread. "I do hope that you were pleased with last evening's ball, Lord Lindale. By all accounts, it was quite magnificent."

Giving her a small bow, he put one hand to his heart. "I am gratified to hear you say so, Lady Ellen," he replied truthfully. "I was contented with it myself, I have to say."

"It was *most* enjoyable," Lady Sayers interrupted, looking at him with a warm smile on her lips. "An excellent first ball for your Season, Lord Lindale."

Again, Colin bowed but continued to look at Lady Ellen, wondering how he was to have a private conversation with her without her aunt overhearing. If she did not care to dance, then he would struggle to find any other way to do so—although dancing was not often the easiest way to have conversation.

"Lady Sayers!"

It was at that moment that an older lady, wearing heavy drapes of fabric that presumably were meant to be some sort of gown, approached, looking only at Lady Sayers and ignoring both Lady Ellen and Colin entirely.

"Lady Humphries," Lady Sayers said and, whilst she did not move away from Lady Ellen, turned herself away from them both just a fraction. "How marvelous to see you again."

Lady Ellen smiled up at him whilst Colin silently thanked his good fortune that he had been permitted a few moments to speak with Lady Ellen alone.

"Lady Ellen," he began, a little awkwardly, for he knew what he wanted to say but found himself struggling to now find the right words to say it. "I should like to ask you if you would permit me..." He closed his eyes and shook his head, before opening them again and looking back at Lady Ellen, who was wearing something of a confused expression. Her green eyes were slightly narrowed, as though she feared that he was about to say something rather terrible.

"What I wish to say, Lady Ellen, is that there is a desire within me to speak to your father," he said, stumbling over his words. "But I should not do so unless you would be glad of it."

Lady Ellen's eyes flared wide and she put one hand to her heart. Her face filled with color and then drained away in an instant, making her appear a little unwell.

"Lady Ellen?" Colin said again, now silently calling himself all manner of names, given that he had clearly upset her somewhat. "I will not do so if you do not wish it, of course. I quite understand."

"Lord Lindale." Lady Ellen put up one hand, palm out toward him. "Might I ask what it is you wish to speak to my father about?" Her eyes fixed to his and in an instant, Colin realized his mistake.

"About courting you," he said hastily, aware now that she had gone such a strange color given that she was confused as to what he was asking. He had never mentioned courtship and thus, she had feared he meant speaking to her father as regarded her hand in marriage. "To arrange a courtship, Lady Ellen, that is all."

Her smile was a tiny one, but it was there, nonetheless. "I see," she said, a good deal more quietly. "Then yes, of course, Lord Lindale. You might speak to my father and inform him of my consent."

Colin swallowed hard, feeling a lightness about him that thrust every other weight from his shoulders. "Wonderful," he said, his voice rasping just a little. "That is truly wonderful, Lady Ellen."

Much to his surprise, she giggled and looked away, clearly delighted in his company and his request, which filled his heart all the more. All thought of the key fled from him and any thought he had as to speaking of it ran from his mind. All he wanted to do now was request to call upon Lord Grantown so that he might make his purpose clear.

"Good evening, Lord Lindale."

Having been about to carry on his conversation with Lady Ellen, Colin was a little irritated at the interruption but knew he could not let such irritation show in his expression. Clearing his throat, he masked his frustration with a genial smile and a small bow.

"Good evening, Lord Bradfield," he replied, recognizing the gentleman from a previous introduction. "How are you this evening?"

"Very well," the man replied, swaying slightly as he looked from Colin to Lady Ellen. "And Lady Ellen, how good to see you also."

Lady Ellen gave him a tight smile and bobbed a quick curtsy, murmuring a "good evening" but saying very little else. Colin frowned. Was there something about Lord Bradfield that Lady Ellen disliked?

"I see that you have been spending a good deal of time with this particular young lady," Lord Bradfield said, slapping Colin hard on the shoulder, which Colin accepted with gritted teeth. "Finally, a gentleman who will ignore the news of your father's poor character and financial ruin, Lady Ellen. How fortunate."

Lady Ellen's face flushed a deep, dark red but she said nothing. Her jaw tightened and she looked away, without even glancing toward Colin.

"I hardly think that such a remark is justified, Lord Bradfield," Colin said firmly, praying that the drunk gentleman would find something else to speak of other than Lord Grantown and the rumors about him. "Come now, there must be—"

"But then again, I suppose a *marquess* has more than enough of a fortune to take care of any particular difficulties," Lord Bradfield continued as though Colin had not said a word. "Although to align yourself with such a family, Lord Lindale, will bring its own concerns."

Colin closed his eyes and took in a long breath, doing all he could to steady himself before he responded. A growing anger settled deep in his chest and, given how Lady Ellen was still looking away, either angry or ashamed—or perhaps both—Colin knew it was his responsibility to respond fairly and in a way that defended the lady.

"There are those of us who believe that Lord Grantown has been unfairly punished by the *ton*," he stated, looking back at Lord Bradfield with a hard, furious gaze. "And regardless of that, I hardly think that your comments about Lady Ellen *or* her father are at all welcome at this present moment."

"But you surely must be aware of them all," Lord Bradfield said as Lady Sayers turned back toward her charge, clearly overhearing what was being said. "How can *you*, Lord Lindale, disregard such a thing?" He shook his head in a pitying manner. "*I* fear that you have ignored all you have been told and, for whatever reason, have chosen to pay attention to a lady that you ought to, instead, push far from you."

Colin's jaw worked furiously, and his hands curled into fists.

Breathe, he told himself, knowing that he had to contain this situation as best he could, without making others aware of it. *Control yourself.*

"Lord Bradfield, if you will excuse us, I believe our conversation is at an end," he said tightly, turning to Lady Ellen, who was now glaring at Lord Bradfield, her face still a deep, crimson red. "I will not have you speak in such a fashion. You are insulting both Lady Ellen and me, and your words are both unwanted and hostile. Do excuse me."

"What can you mean?" Lord Bradfield asked in a raised voice, grasping Colin's shoulder and hauling him back. It took every ounce of self-restraint Colin had to stop himself from physically responding, although he did shrug off Lord Bradfield's hand. "Your uncle was the one who informed us all of these rumors. Surely he must have told you of them. Why, then, would you go to the very lady whose father is so disgraced?" He laughed and shook his head. "You are foolish indeed, Lord Lindale."

Colin sucked in a breath, hardly able to believe what he had heard. His mind scrambled to make sense of it, seeing Lord Bradfield continuing to laugh and feeling every bone in his body beginning to quake.

My uncle?

His eyes turned to Lady Ellen, who had suddenly gone very pale and very quiet. Lady Sayers had one arm around the lady's shoulders, her own face dark with anger as she looked to Lord Bradfield.

"Remove yourself, Lord Bradfield," she stated, her voice holding more authority than Colin's ever had. "Else it shall be all the worse for you."

For whatever reason, something in Lady Sayers' voice made Lord Bradfield react. He stood straight for a moment, looking back at her, before he shrugged and stumbled away, clearly deciding that their conversation was no longer of any importance.

Colin let out a breath he had not known he had been holding.

"Lord Lindale," Lady Sayers began, but Colin held up one hand, shaking his head as he did so. Silence grew between the three of them as Colin turned his gaze toward Lady Ellen, who returned it without any sign of embarrassment, shame, or dismay. Her color had returned just a little and she looked back at him steadily, although Lady Sayers' arm still remained around her shoulders. The crackling tension seemed at great odds with the laughter and joviality around them, but Colin could not remove his thoughts from what he had just been told, could not think of anything other than that.

"It is true, then," he said, looking to Lady Ellen as he spoke. "My uncle was the one behind such rumors?"

Lady Ellen nodded but said nothing.

"And you have known this for some time?"

"Since my father informed me of it, yes," came the quiet reply. "I did not know that Lord Bradfield was aware of such a thing, however, although I presume that your uncle chose to inform him of these malicious rumors from the very first, given that he is such a gossip." This was all spoken with a great calmness that did nothing to quieten Colin's great upset. Instead, he shook his head and ran one hand over his face, realizing now why Lady Ellen had, at the first, been rather reluctant to improve her acquaintance with him.

"The key," he said abruptly as Lady Sayers' brow furrowed. "You took it in the hope of finding something that would prove my uncle's rumors to be nothing more than lies?"

Lady Ellen's eyes rounded and she did not immediately reply. There came a slight trembling to her lips, but when she spoke, it was clear and without hesitation.

"I did, Lord Lindale," she answered firmly. "I took the key from your study and returned it last evening. Although, I presume that, since you know I took it, you are also aware that I was the one to set it back in place?"

He shook his head. "I did not know for certain that it *had* been you, Lady Ellen," he responded, still swaying between anger and confusion. "I mentioned the box to you specifically, in the hope that you would—"

"That I would betray my guilt," she replied with a shake of her head. "That was the only reason for your supposed interest in me, then?"

Colin took a step forward and instinctively, Lady Sayers moved also, although Lady Ellen settled one hand on her arm, glancing up at her before looking back toward Colin.

"I will not deny that it was so at first, Lady Ellen," he stated coldly, "but that of late, my interest in you has become genuine. My affections have grown and, as such, I was inclined to forget about the matter entirely, save for the fact that I could not forget about the key and wonder what it might open. Why it was of such great importance to you." He shook his head, looking into her green eyes and finding his heart growing all the more despondent. "But you accepted my attentions in the hope of opening the box, did you not? The box I told you I discovered?"

"But I did not," she stated, a flash of anger in her eyes now. "I set the key down and left it there, ready for you to discover come the morning. I did not search your study, as much as I might have wished to."

Colin grimaced as Lady Sayers murmured something to Lady Ellen, which she completely ignored.

"And why did you do so, Lady Ellen?" he asked, only for Lady Sayers to interrupt.

"This has all come as something of a shock," she stated, quite loudly. "I am astonished at my niece's behavior, Lord Lindale. I did not know anything about this key or her intention to..." Trailing off, she passed one hand over her eyes. "Might you call tomorrow afternoon, Lord Lindale?"

"No." Colin turned back to Lady Ellen, his upset and anger still burning fiercely. "No, I shall not call. We shall take a walk through the park, Lady Ellen, and you will confess all to me. I must know everything. I must know *why* that key is worth so much to you." He bowed quickly toward Lady Sayers. "But perhaps, as you say, this is not the opportune moment. Good evening to you both."

And so saying, Colin stepped away from both Lady Sayers and Lady Ellen, without even bidding them farewell. His hands were still curled tightly, his anger smoldering like a fiery pit burning deep within him, and there was a fury that seemed to blaze through every part of his being. Why had he not known of this before? Why had he never heard that his uncle had been the one to throw such rumors through London about Lord Grantown? And why had Lady Ellen not simply told him as much?

Perhaps she feared your reaction.

At this thought, his anger began to quell itself slightly, making him realize that he was behaving in the very way that she might have predicted. She had, he recalled, set the key back down in his study and had not searched for the wooden box he had pretended to have discovered. A choice had been presented to her and she had chosen to do the more difficult thing of setting the key down and walking away from it, rather than finding whatever it was that might assist with her father's predicament.

Did that not say a great deal about how she considered him?

"Lindale?"

Colin stopped abruptly, his eyes focusing on Lord Castleton, who was looking at him with concern.

"You have walked across the length of the room without so much as looking up," Lord Castleton continued, stopping a footman and taking two glasses of whisky from the tray he held. Handing one to Colin, he continued to look at him steadily. "Whatever is the matter?"

Taking a gulp of his whisky, Colin let it settle in his stomach for a moment before he answered. "It seems that my uncle, the late Lord Lindale, was the one who spoke such rumors about Lady Ellen's father, Lord Grantown," he said harshly. "I pray that you did not know of such a thing?" He eyed Lord Castleton for a moment, only to see the shock ripple across the gentleman's face.

"I knew none of it, I assure you," Lord Castleton protested, one hand against his heart. "By what means did you discover this?"

Briefly, Colin related what had occurred, including, without embarrassment, how he himself had reacted.

"I see." Lord Castleton's brow furrowed, and he took a sip of his whisky, as though it might help him think a little more clearly. "That explains why she took the key, then, although she did not tell you what she hoped to find?"

"I did not give her the opportunity," Colin replied, now feeling a little guilty over his harsh reaction. "I am to walk with her tomorrow."

Lord Castleton nodded sagely. "Mayhap that is for the best," he replied as Colin threw back the rest of his whisky. "It will give you both time to consider what it is you wish to express to the other."

Colin let out a harsh laugh. "And here I was believing that I had every opportunity to go to Lord Grantown and ask for the honor of courting Lady Ellen," he said, a trifle bitterly. "I had every intention of doing so come the morrow, given that the lady herself encouraged me to do so." A sigh ripped from his lips. "Now, I do not know what to do."

There was a short silence. Lord Castleton, too, finished his whisky and then put one hand on Colin's shoulder. "Do you care for the lady, Lindale?"

Lifting his eyes, Colin nodded slowly. "I do," he admitted quietly. "I believe that I have a true affection for her. I did not expect to feel such a thing, but nevertheless, it has begun to grow within my heart."

"And what of this matter?" Lord Castleton asked, his hand dropping back to his side. "Does it change what you feel for the lady?"

Colin hesitated, then shook his head. "I want to know the truth," he said honestly. "I want to know what it is my uncle said and what he did. I want to know *why* he did such a thing. And I must discover what importance this key has. But," he continued with a small shrug, "even if I am given all the answers I seek, even if the questions are at an end and I am entirely satisfied, I shall still feel all that I do for Lady Ellen, I am quite certain of it."

Lord Castleton nodded, looking a little more contented than before. "Then I must hope that your discussion with her tomorrow is fruitful," he replied quietly. "And that you find the truths you so desperately seek."

"As do I," Colin replied heavily. "I must hope that I have not made things too difficult already and that my obvious anger did not turn her away from me." Raking one hand through his hair, he blew out a long breath, finding himself irritated by how strongly he had reacted to Lady Ellen when he had first discovered the truth. "I was not as calm or as considered as I ought to have been."

"Then tell her so tomorrow," Lord Castleton advised. "And be glad of her company. I am sure that once you have discussed it all, everything will come to rights, just as it ought."

12

Try as she might, Ellen could not rid herself of the memory of Lord Lindale's face when he had heard the truth from Lord Bradfield. There had been first astonishment and then a growing anger that seemed to sweep over him. His eyes had become hard, his jaw had tightened, and the way he had looked at her had made Ellen's heart begin to beat furiously.

Guilt had poured into her heart when he had spoken to her, when he had demanded to know if such a thing was true. She had managed to speak calmly, yes, but inside, she had been beyond afraid. When he had spoken of the key, when he had made it plain that he knew she had taken it, the look from her aunt had been one of deep dismay. It had cut Ellen to the quick and she had felt a deep sense of shame fill her. When Lord Lindale had taken his leave, she had forced herself to look up into Lady Sayers' face and had seen both shock and sorrow etched there.

Of course, there was no question of them lingering at the assembly rooms for the remainder of the evening. Lady Sayers had demanded that Ellen return home at once and, thereafter, Ellen had been forced to explain herself to both her aunt and to her father. What had made things all the worse was that, whilst her father stated that he well understood the intention behind what she had done, he was not at all in agreement with her choice to take the key from Lord Lindale's home. The disappointment in his eyes had crushed her spirit.

Ellen closed her eyes tightly, astonished to discover tears beginning to flow. When Lord Lindale had stated he would like to speak to her father, she had, for a moment, believed he had been speaking of marriage. It had only been when he had stated that he meant courtship that she had finally been able to take in a full breath—only to discover that it was not shock or dismay that had filled her at the idea, but rather a sense of joy and even anticipation. Now that seemed to be at an end. Lord Lindale had said that his feelings toward her had changed, that there was an affection for her within his heart, but she could not expect that to linger now. Not when he knew that she had not only hidden the truth about his uncle from him but had been the one to steal the key from his study.

"Ellen?"

She turned, dabbing at the corner of her eyes with her handkerchief.

"I am ready, Aunt," she said, making her way toward Lady Sayers, who stood, solemn faced, in the doorway. "Where are we to meet?"

Lady Sayers put one hand on Ellen's shoulder. "Your father received a letter this morning from Lord Lindale," she said quietly as Ellen's heart immediately began to pound furiously all over again. "He has requested that we meet him at St. James' Park, as we have done before. If we do not hurry, however, we will be late to our meeting with him and I should not like for that to occur." She smiled gently at Ellen, but Ellen did not return it, feeling her heart sinking to the floor.

"I am sorry, Aunt," she said softly, feeling tears burn in her eyes still and forcing herself to draw in a long breath so that they would disperse. "I know I have disappointed you."

"It is not I that you need to consider, but Lord Lindale," came the quiet reply. "He will need to hear your apology, Ellen. I do not know how he will react, of course, but it is best that you make your sorrow and regret quite plain—that is, if you truly feel such things."

"I do," Ellen answered fervently, and Lady Sayers nodded. "I am deeply sorry. That is why I put the key back. I knew it would be wrong to search through his things, despite my own desperation to help my father."

Lady Sayers put her hand on Ellen's back and ushered her toward the door. "Then say such words to Lord Lindale," she said encouragingly. "He may react in a way you do not expect."

~

SEEING Lord Lindale again sent such a shiver through Ellen that for a moment, she felt like turning tail and hurrying back to her carriage without hesitation. Whilst he was well dressed, formal in his appearance, and bowed to greet them both, there was none of the warmth in his eyes that she had come to hope for.

Clearly, he was still very upset and troubled by what she had done.

"Lady Ellen." Lord Lindale held out his arm to her and, a little surprised, Ellen hesitated for a moment before she took it. "Thank you for your willingness to join me this afternoon."

"We have many things to discuss, I am sure," Ellen replied as Lady Sayers remained a short distance behind. "But might I begin by expressing my sincere apologies for doing as I did?" She looked up at him earnestly, but Lord Lindale's face remained where it was, his eyes fixed to the path ahead. "I should not have taken the key from your study. To step into your domain and behave as I did..." She closed her eyes for a moment, wincing. "I had my reasons, but that does not make what I did right."

"No, indeed, Lady Ellen," came the hard reply. "It was not. I have been suspicious of you from the start. Miss Brooks was another whom I considered, but it soon became clear that she was *not* the one who had done such a thing." A small side glance came toward her. "But that does not mean, as I said to you last evening, that my motivation for showing you a little more attention than the other young ladies was also correct."

A little surprised, she looked up at him and saw some of the steel leave his eyes.

"I intended to find out whether or not my suspicions about you were correct," he said, a little more quietly. "But that soon began to change, Lady Ellen. I have found your company…enticing."

Her eyes flared. "Enticing?"

Lord Lindale nodded. "And by that, I mean that I have discovered an eagerness to be in your company that I did not expect. I have found myself thinking of you without realizing that you had even entered my thoughts. And soon, the key began to lessen in significance, and you became all the more meaningful to me." His eyes turned toward her for a moment. "I meant what I said, Lady Ellen. I have an affection for you that I did not either expect or desire. Despite what I have learned from Lord Bradfield, that will not change. However, I should like to know the truth from your lips, *including* the reasons that you took the key."

She swallowed hard, having never expected to hear such words from him. No longer was there anger in his voice but rather a gentle curiosity that seemed to lift a great weight from her shoulders.

"You have a great deal to forgive me for, Lord Lindale," she began meekly. "I have been most dishonest with you and have stolen from your house without your awareness."

"That is not something we need to dwell on," he replied swiftly. "Tell me *why* you sought the key, Lady Ellen. Tell me, if you know, *why* my uncle spread such rumors about your father." Turning to her for a moment, he stopped walking and held her gaze. "You already know that I am entirely unaware of my uncle's character. It does not sound to me as though he were an entirely generous man."

"He was a friend of my father's," Ellen replied, giving Lord Lindale a wry smile as his eyes widened in surprise. "They spoke of many things and were known to each other for many years.

However, from what my father has told me, it seems that Lord Lindale had intentions and plans of his own. Given that he lacked wealth, he wished to improve his standing through easier means than working hard at the land or finding other ways to develop his estate."

Lord Lindale frowned. "I have come into a great deal of wealth," he said slowly. "Do you mean to suggest that my uncle's fortune is not entirely his own?"

Ellen hesitated. "I cannot speak for anyone else," she said carefully, "but I know that my father has stated that Lord Lindale took money from him and then kept it as his own."

"Why did your father give it to him in the first place?" Lord Lindale's voice had become hard again, his eyes holding a frustrated look that Ellen knew revealed only a little of what he truly felt. "Surely there is some explanation as to why—"

"My father has never gone into the details of the arrangement with me, Lord Lindale," she interrupted hastily. "I believe it was something to do with an investment of sorts. My father believed that the money he gave to his friend would be returned to him with profit." Her eyes dropped to the floor. "My father even sold some of the land at our estate—again, because he believed it would be returned to him, having made some sort of profit. I cannot tell you, Lord Lindale, what the scheme was precisely, but I know that if you speak to my father, he might well be willing to inform you of it." Daring a glance up at him, she saw that he was frowning hard, lines forming across his brow. "I believe that my father was looking for a way to invest his own wealth, so that it might be swiftly improved. Instead of having his money returned, however, Lord Lindale kept it all entirely for himself and then began to spread rumors about my father so that he would not be able to state the truth." One shoulder lifted in a small half-shrug. "Even if he did tell the *ton* what had occurred, the gossip was already so rife that he was sure no one would believe him."

"And thus, you have been enduring such a situation," Lord Lindale added, and Ellen nodded. "The rumors that state your father is in financial difficulty are true, however, although the *beau monde* does not know the truth as to why that is."

Pain sliced through Ellen's heart. "That is it precisely, Lord Lindale," she told him, not quite managing to look up at him for fear of breaking down into tears. "The gossip and the whispers as to *why* my father has lost his wealth are all entirely untrue, however. He does not gamble or overly indulge in liquor and certainly does not..." She hesitated, not wanting to speak openly of the bawdy houses that had been mentioned by the *ton*. "He does not go to any social occasions save for ones he might consider to be worth his time. The *ton* know of this, of course, but it is more entertaining for them to spread the rumors and whisper about him all the more. Had it not been for my aunt's insistence that I return to London for the Season, I believe that my father would have remained at our estate this summer. And I can quite understand why he would have done so."

Nothing more was said for some minutes. They continued to walk along the path together and Ellen glanced behind her toward her aunt, but Lady Sayers was looking to her right, gazing out across the flowers and plants that adorned either side of their walk. She did not appear to be overly concerned about the conversation Ellen was having, even though Ellen herself was already feeling quite weary with all that she had expressed. Whether Lord Lindale would believe her, however, was quite another matter.

"I suppose that such transactions would have been recorded somewhere," Lord Lindale said eventually, his eyes shifting toward her for a moment before he looked away again. "If I were to speak to my solicitors, then I might be able to find them and confirm that such a thing occurred."

A slight flare of anger burned in Ellen's heart. "I am sure you will be able to *confirm* that what I have said is true," she said sharply as he let out a long breath. "Far be it from me to tell you what you ought to do next."

"You must understand, Lady Ellen," he said, a trifle more gently, "what you have told me is quite extraordinary. I want to know precisely what my uncle did and when. I shall speak to your father and ask him for the dates that such transactions were made. Thereafter, I shall speak to my solicitors and make certain that the money was settled into my uncle's account."

"And then?" Ellen demanded, her anger beginning to burn a little hotter. "Once you have discovered that I speak the truth, what are your intentions, Lord Lindale?"

The gentleman did not reply but instead ran one hand through his hair, unsettling it completely.

"I have told you the truth," Ellen continued, trying to keep her temper under control. "There is nothing more to it than that."

Lord Lindale looked down at her. "And the key?" he asked as Ellen's brow furrowed. "Why did you take it?"

Ellen closed her eyes for a moment, taking in a long breath as though she needed to steady herself entirely. She felt as though she had been speaking for an age, for the weight of what she had said thus far now sat heavily on her shoulders. This explanation, however, was required so that she might express to Lord Lindale the reasons for her own foolish behavior and that, she knew, would be a little more difficult.

"I should begin by expressing my sorrow, yet again, for taking something that did not belong to me," she said slowly. "When you told me of the key, my heart began to beat with such fervor that I could not help but make a plan to find the key and discover what it opened."

He nodded. "I am aware of that," he said, his voice gravelly. "But what was your purpose behind it?"

Pressing her lips together for a moment, Ellen began to explain. "When my father told me of the late Lord Lindale's actions, he also told me that your uncle had a small diary," she said as Lord Lindale's brows rose in surprise. "This diary was waved in front of my father's face as he was being mocked for believing and trusting Lord Lindale's words."

"I have never come across such a thing," Lord Lindale interrupted, although there was a small trace of interest now running through his words. "What was within this diary?"

Ellen's stomach tightened for a moment, praying that he would believe her. "Lord Lindale, your uncle stated to my father that the diary contained secrets about many others within the *ton*," she said softly. "He made it quite plain that those whose names were written within would do whatever he asked of them, for fear that their secrets would be made known. Therefore, when your uncle began to spread rumors about my father, there were those within the *beau monde* who had very little choice but to continue to spread such lies. They knew that if they did not, then Lord Lindale would use the secrets he knew against them." She glanced up at Lord Lindale and saw his shoulders slump. Evidently, he was beginning to realize the sort of gentleman his uncle had been. "I think that your uncle wrote the truth about my father as well as what he intended to do as regarded the gossip and rumor, into this diary," she finished, a flush of embarrassment beginning to creep into her cheeks. "I told myself that it was one of the only ways I could have the *ton* believe that my father was entirely innocent of these disgusting rumors. Therefore, I was determined to find it."

"And so you took the key."

She nodded, her face flaming. "I thought to search the study at the time," she replied, no longer able to lift her eyes to look up at him, such was her shame. "And, thereafter, when I took it with me, I thought to find a way to return to your townhouse and discover what the key opened. I prayed that the diary would be contained within."

"And that is why you accepted my increasing attentions toward you," Lord Lindale said slowly, and she nodded, her head lowering as regret piled itself upon her shoulders, adding to her burden. "Then we are both at fault, Lady Ellen."

Her head lifted in an instant. "Both?" she repeated incredulously. "Lord Lindale, I stole from you. I took something that was not mine with the sole intention of—"

"That does not matter," he interrupted, reaching across with his free hand to settle it atop hers, turning his head back toward her so that he might look into her eyes. "Your reasons for doing such a thing were well meant, Lady Ellen. You wanted to protect your father, to prove to the *ton* that he is not the gentleman they believe him to be. I will not say that it was right for you to do so, but I can understand your reasons. However, for my part, I was determined to force your hand, determined to have you reveal that you were the one who took my key. Therefore, I made it plain that I was interested in furthering my acquaintance with you, solely with the intention of setting up a small trap for you to walk directly into."

"The wooden box," Ellen said slowly as Lord Lindale nodded. "There is no such thing."

"Indeed," he replied heavily. "And when Lord Castleton informed me that you *did* return to my study and did not search for the box, but instead, returned the key, I could hardly believe what he told me." His steps slowed and he turned his head again to look down at her, his eyes searching her face as she finally met his gaze. "Why did you do such a thing, Lady Ellen?" he asked. "Why did you return the key, when finding the diary meant so much to you?"

She swallowed her first response and considered carefully how to reply. So many emotions swirled within her heart that to speak to him now, without hesitation, would not be wise. She had to speak with great deliberation but also with a great deal of honesty. Now was not the time to hide behind mistruth.

"Lord Lindale," she began, her heart pounding at the thought of speaking so to him. "The reason I returned your key was, in short, because I realized that it was wrong for me to have taken it. I should never have done so."

"But you would have been forced, instead, to speak the truth to me," he replied, and she nodded. "And yet you did not do so."

A small ache began to form in her heart, and she forced herself to be entirely honest with him. "Because I had come to believe that the diary might not be of such great importance any longer," she answered as he looked back at her in surprise. Turning her face away so that she would not have to look at him for fear of what would leap into his eyes, she continued quickly. "Because of these rumors, the *ton* do not see me as someone who is worthy of their prolonged time and interest," she said, a stab of sorrow in her heart. "I am greeted, spoken to, and, often times, asked to dance and, indeed, invitations to various events are not lacking. But that does not mean that any of those I am in company with consider my presence to be something they might wish to prolong." She winced, knowing that she was not speaking directly but was, instead, using words to make things a little less awkward for her to express. It did not seem to matter, however, for Lord Lindale was nodding fervently, as though he quite understood.

"Therefore," she continued, the ache in her heart growing steadily, "when it came to your attentions, a part of me began to hope that it might all be genuine. And that, in the end, became the sole reason for my actions in returning the key." Her words became a little quicker, flying from her mouth as though she were desperate to have them said without any real difficulty. "If there was no need to find the diary—and my father was quite insistent that I do nothing also, although he did not know about the key—then what need was there for me to continue to keep it?"

"I believe I understand, Lady Ellen," came the quiet reply. "You hoped that these attentions of mine might turn to courtship and, in turn, to marriage. Your own fortunes would be improved and—"

"It is not that I did not want to remove the rumors about my father from society," she said quickly, suddenly realizing that it sounded as though she thought of no one but herself. "But my father has been very insistent that I do nothing at all. He has told me repeatedly that if I am wed and settled, then there is nothing for him to do but return to his estate, contented. I—I wanted to see that contentment, Lord Lindale, and thus, I permitted myself to believe that such a thing might be within my grasp."

There came a short silence and Ellen's heart began to beat with such fervency that she was certain Lord Lindale could hear it. Closing her eyes, she took in a great breath and then opened them again, silently praying that he would not find her words too ridiculous.

"And might I ask, Lady Ellen," Lord Lindale said eventually, "should your future be as you have said, would you still wish to find this diary of my uncle's?"

Pressing her lips together for a moment, Ellen felt a tremor run through her frame. There was no certainty in what Lord Lindale had said but there was a hint of encouragement there.

"I will be honest with you, and state that such a future is one that I have come to hope for desperately," she said softly. "It was not only that hope that made me return the key, but rather the fact that my heart has become a little more engaged to you. I found that I could not continue with such deceit when my feelings were so very different to those that had resided within me at the start."

"And you know, I hope, that my affections for you still linger," he replied, his free hand once more reaching across to settle atop hers where it rested on his arm. "I have never spoken falsely when it comes to that. I have been angry, I have been deeply upset, but I have found my heart steady in what it feels. But you have not answered my question as yet."

She looked up at him, her heart now beginning to lift free of her regret and her shame.

"Would you be willing to set aside the need to discover this diary if I were to offer you the future that both you and your father have sought?"

The answer came to her lips in an instant, but she held it back for a moment or two, allowing herself to consider it carefully before she spoke. Studying her heart, she allowed herself to think of what a future with Lord Lindale might be like. She would have a great happiness with him, she was sure, but would the diary and the cruelty contained within it still bother her? Would she want desperately to find it?

"I returned the key, Lord Lindale," she said after a few moments. "I did so in the hope that I would forget about the diary entirely, if things continued to progress between us as I hoped. I would like to tell you that yes, I would be able to leave any thought of it behind, but I might well be mistaken. I might be fooling myself; I cannot say. But I can tell you that the intention, the desire to do so, is very much present within my heart."

Lord Lindale stopped dead, turned, and took both her hands in his. Ellen swallowed hard, seeing the gleam in his eye and finding herself not at all certain as to what he was feeling at this present moment.

"My dear Lady Ellen," he said, and her breath caught at such a tender expression. "Your honesty does you well. I am grateful for everything you have said. I should *very* much like to speak to your father, to not only confirm all that you have said, but to also ask his permission to court you. Thereafter, I should like to invite you to my townhouse—" his gaze slid toward Lady Sayers for a moment. "With your aunt, of course, so that we might search for my uncle's diary."

Ellen stared at him, a tingle running down her spine at the determination in his eyes. She could not quite believe what he had said, what he had offered her, and yet it was there, ringing its way into her heart and filling her with such joy and relief that she wanted to both laugh and cry at the same time.

"What say you, Lady Ellen?" he asked, coming a little closer to her and searching her face. "Are you still willing for me to speak to your father? And will you help me discover the whereabouts of this diary?"

"I will." Her voice was breathless, her words barely loud enough for him to hear, but the smile on his face told Ellen that he was more than delighted with her answer.

"Wonderful," he replied, lifting one of her hands to his lips and brushing a kiss across the back of it, sending a wave of heat crashing down over her. "Then might I suggest we return to your father's house?"

She did not move, her hand tightening in his. "You—you mean to speak to him this very afternoon?" she stammered, a little overwhelmed. "This very day?"

"Why not?" he asked, turning her back toward the carriage as Lady Sayers beamed with delight, having overheard every word of Lord Lindale's declaration. "I am filled with a great eagerness to make your father aware of my intentions and, I pray, to have his permission to court you, Lady Ellen. I want the *ton* to be aware of it also, so that I might stand by your side and show them just how proud I am to have you on my arm. That I do not believe the words that are spoken about your father. And, thereafter," he finished with a small smile, "I look forward to informing them of the cruelty of my uncle, of the tight grip he has held over some members of the *ton*, so that your father might be free of all vile gossip and vicious rumors, for the rest of his days."

Ellen did not know what to say. Her throat was aching, and tears pooled in the corners of her eyes. Lord Lindale had given her more than she had ever expected. He had not held a grudge. He had not thrown her aside when she confessed to stealing his key. Rather, he had listened to her, believed her, and was now determined to do right by her. And to know that a true affection resided within his heart for her was so overwhelming that Ellen could hardly believe it.

"What say you, Lady Ellen?" he asked, interrupting her tumbling thoughts. "Will we go in search of an audience with your father this very afternoon?"

A smile began to spread across her face as she nodded, almost too overcome with happiness to speak. "Yes, Lord Lindale," she replied, her voice wavering just a little with the rush of emotion that filled her. "Yes, let us do so at once."

13

Colin was quite determined. Having heard everything Lady Ellen had said, having heard the truth about his uncle from her lips, he was now filled with a great resolve to set such things to rights. It had taken some minutes for him to accept all that was said, for the truth of the matter was that he found her explanations to be quite overwhelming. To believe that his uncle held a diary of such cruelty somewhere within the house had been horrifying to hear and he had found himself struggling to take it in.

But, he had swiftly come to the realization that there was no need for Lady Ellen to tell any sort of mistruth. The way she had looked at him, with the tremor in her voice and the paleness of her cheeks, had been more than enough to convince him that she told him the truth. And what had come thereafter had been a swift desire to protect her, to help her, and to love her.

Love?

A small frown flickered across his brow as he sat in his carriage, making his way back to Lord Grantown's home. He had not considered such a deep emotion before, but the truth was, his affections for Lady Ellen were growing steadily and at such a rapid pace that such a feeling might well be settling within his heart. He had not expected to feel so much for her, but a deep sense of contentment was within him now, as though he were very glad that he did so. His brow furrowed as he thought of his late uncle. He had never met the man and had only seen a portrait of him, but to know the vileness of his character had struck hard at Colin's heart. He wanted to find the diary, wanted to discover precisely what his uncle had done, so that he might destroy it entirely and set the *beau monde* to rights about Lord Grantown.

"And any others," he muttered to himself, passing one hand over his eyes. To become the Marquess of Lindale had been a difficult enough trial in itself, but to know that his uncle had been so cruel, so arrogant and selfish, was yet another burden to bear. Silently, Colin determined that he should never follow in his uncle's footsteps. He would be the one to make right what was wrong so that such a thing might never happen again.

"Thank you for being willing to speak to me." Colin inclined his head and then sat down in the chair that Lord Grantown gestured toward. He studied the older gentleman for a moment, taking in his graying hair and noting the lines that had formed around his eyes and across his forehead. There was more than just age here. There was trouble and strife and trial. Colin winced inwardly. Just how much of the strain had been brought about by his uncle?

"I would like to speak to you, Lord Grantown, about my uncle."

The older man stiffened visibly, his eyes narrowing.

"Your daughter has told me as much as she knows," Colin continued quickly. "Do not berate her for it, however, for I had to know the truth. I am aware that you know of the key and her part in taking it from my house. There is no need for me to go into the details of that, save to say that I quite understand exactly why she did so."

"That is very generous of you, Lord Lindale," Lord Grantown began, but Colin shook his head.

"It is not at all generous of me, given what you have been forced to endure by the hand of my late uncle," he said firmly. "Lady Ellen tells me that there was a friendship between you both, at one time."

Lord Grantown sighed, rose to his feet, and went to pour a splash of brandy into two glasses, handing one to Colin. He did not resume his seat but began to pace up and down the room, clearly distressed.

"I do not want to speak overly ill of your uncle, Lord Lindale, given that you knew him so little, but it would be truthful to say that he and I were very good friends at one time. When he spoke to me of this investment, when he explained that his estate was in financial difficulty and that he required a little more funding in order to make the venture successful, I did not hesitate to give him what he required."

Nodding, Colin took a small sip of his brandy and let the warmth spread through his chest before he spoke. "And might I ask if you gave my uncle a vast amount of coin?"

Lord Grantown looked back at him with such a haggard expression that, for a moment, Colin feared he would be taken ill. Making to get up, he went to reach for the man, only for Lord Grantown to shake his head and hold out one hand.

"I have never told anyone the full amount," he said softly, making his way back to his seat and sitting down heavily. "As I have said, I was good friends with your uncle and believed every word he said. Why should I not? I had no reason to distrust him."

Colin leaned forward. "I will press you, Lord Grantown," he said solemnly. "I must."

Lord Grantown closed his eyes and let out a heavy breath. "I gave him half of all the wealth I had," he said, each word dragged out of him slowly. "I gave him some of my land, signed over by deed, with the reassurance that I would have it returned to me. It was sold, I believe. The owner, whom I have spoken to at length, has no knowledge of Lord Lindale."

Colin closed his eyes tightly, a flush of both embarrassment and anger washing over him.

"I could not purchase the land back again, of course," Lord Grantown continued, his shoulders slumping as Colin opened his eyes to look at the sorrowful gentleman once more. "Not enough was left for me to do so. Thus, Lord Lindale, the rumors you hear about my financial state are quite true. I have very little and am doing all I can to make certain that my estate is given all that it requires, even if I do not have very much left over."

"I am truly sorry," Colin replied, finding the flare of anger that had ignited his soul still growing within him. "My uncle was not the gentleman you believed him to be."

Lord Grantown shook his head and sighed, gesturing hopelessly toward Colin. "But that does not make me believe that you are of the same ilk, Lord Lindale," he said quietly, his green eyes alighting on Colin and holding his gaze steadily. "In fact, I believe that, given you knew very little of your uncle—from what my daughter has told me, you understand—you are entirely your own man."

"I am," Colin replied fervently. "And in that regard, Lord Grantown, I promise you that I shall find the sum you gave to my uncle and have it returned to you." He saw the man frown but leaned forward in his chair, wanting to convince him of it. "The land also, I shall make certain to purchase and return to you, Lord Grantown. I will not keep anything that you gave to my uncle in good faith. What he told to you about being without coin and lacking funds..." He shook his head, recalling the shock when he had discovered the great sum that was to be his. "I believe it was nothing more than lies, Lord Grantown. It appears that my uncle was entirely selfish, determined to make himself greater than any other, and at your expense."

For some minutes, Lord Grantown said nothing. Instead, he simply looked back into Colin's face as though trying to decide whether or not his words could be trusted. Wondering if he ought to say more, Colin chose to remain silent, holding Lord Grantown's gaze and waiting quietly.

"That is...a very generous offer, Lord Lindale," Lord Grantown said eventually, although his frown still remained. "It is not required of you, however."

"I am determined," Colin replied without hesitation. "I should also state, Lord Grantown, that Lady Ellen and I intend to find my uncle's diary, the one that I know he showed to you and which contains a great many secrets." His anger now began to turn to a solid resolve to do all he could to return this gentleman to society and to restore his fortune to what it had been before. The money that his uncle had taken from Lord Grantown was not money he wished to keep. It was stained with cruelty and injustice and Colin was determined not to claim it as his own.

"My daughter is to aid you in this?" Lord Grantown asked, looking a little surprised. "Even after what she has done?"

"More than that," Colin replied eagerly. "Lord Grantown, I wish to court your daughter. Our courtship will be solely aimed at soon becoming an engagement. I have found a deep affection for Lady Ellen within my heart and have found her courage and determination to remove these chains from you to be entirely admirable. I am resolved to consider her as a part of my future, but only, of course, if you will consent to it."

Lord Grantown blinked rapidly, clearly quite astonished at Colin's request.

"I am entirely sincere," Colin added, just to make certain that Lord Grantown knew he meant every word. "I care for Lady Ellen very deeply, Lord Grantown. I should like to court her with a view to matrimony."

Lord Grantown's expression changed in an instant. No longer did he appear to be the tired, careworn gentleman that Colin had seen at first. Instead, he practically threw himself from the chair, a broad smile spreading right across his face as he came toward Colin, one hand outstretched. Chuckling, Colin rose to his feet and took Lord Grantown's hand, which was shaken very firmly indeed.

"You cannot imagine just how happy I am to hear your request, Lord Lindale!" Lord Grantown exclaimed, his whole being seemingly alive with joy. "Of course, of *course* you have my blessing. I should never even consider refusing you." His smile suddenly faded and his eyes widened, his hand stilling. "That is to say, so long as my daughter…"

"I spoke to Lady Ellen before I even considered coming to you, Lord Grantown," Colin replied, grinning. "She encouraged me to speak to you in order to seek your consent."

Lord Grantown threw up his hands in delight. "Then all is settled!" he exclaimed, his expression brightening once more. "I am very glad indeed to hear it. Here, let me pour you another brandy."

Colin accepted the glass from Lord Grantown, feeling his heart lift with his own sense of happiness. It seemed, as Lord Grantown said, that all was now settled and that his future was bright.

"To you, Lord Lindale," Lord Grantown said, lifting his brandy glass high. "May you continue to strive to be the very best of gentlemen."

"May I strive to be the very best for your daughter," Colin replied, speaking from his heart. "To Lady Ellen."

Lord Grantown smiled. "To Lady Ellen."

14

Ellen stepped into Lord Lindale's study and found herself smiling as she looked all about it. It was certainly in better order than when she had first seen it, and there appeared to be a new décor which suited Lord Lindale very well indeed.

"Lady Ellen."

She turned and smiled at Lord Castleton, who had come in just after Lady Sayers and Lord Lindale. For the moment, Lord Grantown remained at home, although he would join them later should his business with his solicitors come to an end sooner than he expected.

"Good afternoon, Lord Castleton," she replied as he bowed. "You have come to help us in our search, then?"

He looked all about him, one eyebrow lifting. "Indeed, I have," he replied with a small shake of his head. "Although quite where we are to begin to look, I could not say."

"Not in here," Lord Lindale replied, smiling rather ruefully. "I have been through this room in its entirety, removing whatever I disliked and replacing it with what I prefer. I can assure you that there is nothing here that can be unlocked by the key."

Ellen looked at him. "The key?" she asked as he smiled at her. "You have it?"

"Securely," he replied, reaching into a drawer and pulling out a small piece of white cloth. Unfolding it, he revealed the key to her and then folded the cloth up again, before setting it in his pocket. "Although as I have said, I do not believe there is any need to search here."

Ellen sighed and moved toward Lord Lindale, seeing the smile on his face and returning it with one of her own. She knew that, regardless of whether or not they found the diary, she had a wonderful future with Lord Lindale. He had proven himself to be the very best of gentlemen, forgiving and understanding when he could easily have taken offence and turned from her for what she had done. His eagerness to resolve the issues between his late uncle and her father was more than commendable, making him all the more respected in her eyes.

"Shall we take a walk through the house?" he asked, offering his arm as though they were about to take a pleasant stroll through the gardens. "I cannot imagine where to look, but mayhap an idea will strike us as we do so."

Ellen laughed and accepted it but did not immediately hurry from the room. "Perhaps we might look at where you first found the key," she suggested, and Lady Sayers nodded her agreement, mayhap having been about to say the very same thing. "It would make sense for your uncle to keep the key near to where the lock was, surely?"

Lord Lindale's eyes brightened. "It would," he agreed, reaching across to press her hand as it rested on his arm. "An excellent suggestion, Lady Ellen. Come, then, let us go."

WALKING with Lord Lindale through his townhouse was something of a strange experience for Ellen. He was no longer simply Lord Lindale, an acquaintance, but rather Lord Lindale, her suitor. The gentleman she fully expected to soon become her fiancé and, thereafter, her husband. This townhouse was not a strange place to her. Rather it was one she looked at with fresh eyes, knowing that, come next year, she would be residing here with him instead of at her father's townhouse. The thought sent a shiver of delight all through her, which Lord Lindale must have felt, given the way he looked down at her quickly.

"My mind is filled with a great many thoughts," she said, answering his unspoken question. "All quite wonderful, I assure you."

Lord Lindale laughed, his presence beside her both exciting and comforting in equal measure. "I am glad to hear it, Lady Ellen," he replied as they made their way along toward where he had first seen the painting. "After all we have been through, after all the secrets and struggles that have come to light, I am very contented to know that you are as happy as I."

"It is impossible to describe how I feel," Ellen replied as Lady Sayers and Lord Castleton walked behind them, deep in conversation. "My heart has been so very full, Lord Lindale. You have been more than generous toward me."

"That is because I can do nothing else," he replied, making her blush. "My heart is yours, Lady Ellen. I am sure that you must be aware of that by now." For a moment, he tilted his head just a little, his eyes becoming more thoughtful. "I have told you things that I have spoken of to no other," he added quietly. "Lord Castleton has been a great help to me, but you have learned of the emotions within my heart, of the struggle I have endured in stepping into the role of marquess. There is a good deal more for me to share, of course, but for the moment, let me tell you just how grateful I am to you for all you have become to me. Your determination to aid your father speaks very highly of your love and your loyalty toward him."

Ellen's smile softened. Lord Lindale spoke from the heart and she greatly appreciated his honesty.

"Ah, here we are," he said, bringing their private conversation to a somewhat abrupt end. "As I have said, it was a painting that I did not much care for."

"One of your estate, was it not?" Ellen asked, letting go of Lord Lindale's arm and stepping forward, looking at the empty space on the wall as though it might offer her a clue as to where this diary could be. "You did not much care for it?"

Turning around, she saw him shake his head, a small, wry smile pulling at his lips. "It was, yes," he said, reminding her silently that she only knew such a thing because she had broken into his study and searched for the key. "I did not much like it, no. To be reminded of one's grandeur, of one's property, did not sit well with me."

Sighing, he gestured toward the wall. "But I do recall looking about me quickly in the hope of finding somewhere that the key might go but there was nothing obvious."

"Nothing?" Ellen asked, coming back to stand beside him. "Nothing at all?"

Lord Lindale sighed and shook his head. "There were a few trinkets, certainly, but nothing that held any space for a key. Besides which, it would be a little too late should any of them be what we are searching for, given that they have already been given away."

A small pang of fear ran through Ellen's mind, but she did not allow it to take hold.

"Then it must be elsewhere," she said firmly, refusing to even entertain the idea that it was gone. "The painting was of the estate, you say?" She tilted her head and looked toward her aunt, who was wearing a very thoughtful expression. "Is there anything else within this house that is related to your estate, Lord Lindale? Perhaps it might be hidden there."

For some moments, Lord Lindale said nothing. He considered what she had said, rubbing his chin thoughtfully.

"There are some things, certainly," he replied slowly. "Some have been removed or sent back to the estate, but I can assure you that there were none that had a keyhole anywhere. The only other thing I can think of that could be..." He trailed off, a frown flickering between his brows. "That is to say, I might well be mistaken but—"

"Do hurry up, man," Lord Castleton pleaded, making Ellen jump and then laugh as Lord Castleton grinned and threw up his hands in exasperation. "We are all waiting for your reply."

Lord Lindale laughed and apologized.

"It is only that I might be entirely wrong," he said, by way of explanation. "I do not spend a great deal of time in many rooms of this house, but I am certain that Mr. Grey—the gentleman who introduced me to my new status, such as it is—spoke very eagerly about a pianoforte that had been brought from the estate to the townhouse many years ago."

Ellen frowned. "For what purpose?"

"His daughters, I believe," he replied, a frown still marring his brow as he attempted to remember what had been said. "Lord Lindale's daughters were, of course, seeking husbands of their own during the London Season, albeit some years ago, and were, from what I understand, all very proficient on the pianoforte."

"But surely," Lady Sayers interrupted, "he could have purchased such an instrument from London?"

Lord Lindale shrugged. "I suppose he could have done so, but Mr. Grey told me that his daughters were most insistent that the pianoforte be brought from the estate to London. And thus, it was done."

Lord Castleton shook his head in evident disbelief that a man would do something so ridiculous, but Ellen considered the matter closely. "There might very well be something there," she suggested slowly, looking to Lord Lindale. "The pianoforte itself, I would suggest, might have nothing of particular note, but I do recall that some stools have a small storage box underneath the cushion."

Lord Lindale caught his breath, his eyes flaring wide. "You may be correct, Lady Ellen," he said as Lady Sayers smiled, her eyes dancing. "Shall we make our way to the music room? You do still have the key, Lady Ellen, do you not?"

She shook her head. "It is in your pocket, Lord Lindale," she reminded him. He shook his head wryly to himself and then, rather than offer his arm to her again, reached out to take her hand. It was a little overt given their company, but Ellen did not care in the least, finding her heart dancing with delight as she hurried alongside Lord Lindale, feeling his urgency with every step.

The music room was quiet and cold, seemingly solemn and peaceful in harsh contrast to their own quickened excitement.

"I do not often set foot in here," Lord Lindale said, as though apologizing for the quietness. "There is no fire lit unless I expect guests who might wish to join me here. As yet, that has not ever occurred."

Ellen laughed up into his eyes. "I do not think it shall be often required, given that I am not at all proficient," she told him as he let go of her hand. "But I can see that the instrument is very fine indeed."

"It is," Lady Sayers agreed as they all approached the pianoforte. The stool sat quietly in front of it, a small, rectangular-shaped piece that had red embroidered ribbon around the edge and beautifully patterned silk on top.

"I have never examined the stool," Lord Lindale said, his voice dropping low as though in reverence. "Does it have any sort of keyhole, as you suggested, Lady Ellen?"

She bent carefully and studied the stool, running her fingers over the edges. Her heart quickened—and then sank to the floor, for she could find no such thing at all.

"I do not think that—"

"Aha!"

Lord Castleton's voice was so loud that it seemed to bounce across the room, startling them all. Turning her head, Ellen saw Lord Castleton standing by the back of the pianoforte, gesturing to something she could not yet see.

"I knew Lord Lindale would do something such as this," he declared, as though he had known all along that the key would not open the piano stool but rather the pianoforte itself. "I am certain that he had this installed under his own instructions, rather than purchasing one with such a feature."

"What is it?" Ellen asked as Lord Lindale and Lady Sayers asked the very same question. Together, they hurried to where Lord Castleton stood, and Ellen's breath caught as she saw the small keyhole he was pointing to.

"A very well-hidden place also, I should think," Lady Sayers remarked, reaching out to touch it. "I would not have noticed it had you not seen it, Lord Castleton."

Lord Lindale turned toward Ellen, his eyes glittering with unexpressed excitement. "Should you wish to open it, Lady Ellen?" he asked her, pulling out the white cloth from his pocket and unwrapping the key. "It is for you to do."

Ellen reached out to take the key but found her hands trembling just a little. Her fingers closed around it and she looked up at Lord Lindale, seeing him nod.

"What if it is not the diary?" she asked tremulously. "What if it is nothing more than—"

"Then we will continue to look," he told her firmly. "But have no fear now, Lady Ellen. Look inside and tell us if it is what you have been searching for."

Ellen nodded and took the key a little more firmly, stepping forward to the pianoforte. Swallowing hard, she placed the key in the lock, discovering that it fit perfectly. Her heart was beating with such force that it felt as though it might come out of her chest, her fingers slipping on the key as she turned it.

There was only a moment's hesitation as the key turned fully in the lock and a small portion of the pianoforte began to pull back. Ellen held her breath as she swung it open, seeing the delicate hinge on one side.

"What is there?"

Lord Lindale's voice was thick with anticipation and, as Ellen bent down a little more, she saw a small, dark-covered book inside.

"I pray it is the diary," Lady Sayers murmured as Ellen reached out to take it, before making to hand it to Lord Lindale.

He shook his head.

"Pray, look inside, Lady Ellen," he said gently. "You must tell us whether or not it is what you are looking for."

Her mouth went dry as she opened the first page. She had no need to look further. Words were scrawled across the page, writing about some poor Lord Allan, who had gambled away his wife's diamonds without her knowledge.

Shuddering, she closed the book and looked up at Lord Lindale.

"It is the diary," she said softly, seeing how his eyes flared as he took it from her. "It is what I have been searching for."

His fingers brushed hers as he took it and Ellen felt her heart begin to quieten itself. There was both horror at what she had read and great relief that she had finally found the only thing that would bring her father respite from the gossip and whispers that had surrounded him for so long.

"What a relief," Lord Castleton murmured as Lord Lindale began to look through it, his face contorting with disgust. "Then all can be made right."

"All *will* be made right," Lord Lindale answered, snapping the book shut and looking directly at Ellen, his eyes blazing. "Everyone that is mentioned within this book will be informed of it, along with the promise that the diary itself shall be burned to ash. I will make quite plain that I am *not* the sort of gentleman my uncle was. I have no wish to continue along such a path and I will make that more than obvious to everyone." Reaching out one hand, he held it out toward Ellen, who took it at once. "And Lady Ellen, I will, by careful means, make certain that the *ton* are aware that the rumors were started by my uncle, for his own gain. I will not state everything, of course, but they will come to know of my uncle's disgrace. The wealth and the land will be returned to your father—indeed, I have already arranged to speak to my solicitors about the matter. Everything you and your father have lost will be restored."

Ellen swallowed hard, tears coming into her eyes as she looked up at Lord Lindale, her heart swelling with love for him. Lady

Sayers murmured something that Ellen did not hear, and after a few moments, she realized that it was only herself and Lord Lindale standing together in the music room.

"Lady Ellen, I cannot express my sorrow over what occurred with my uncle," Lord Lindale said, still holding the diary in one hand. "Would that I had known him even a little before he died. I might have been able to recognize his character for myself and done what I could to bring such cruelty to an end."

"No, Lord Lindale," she replied, stepping closer to him as he set the diary back down on the pianoforte. "None of this is your doing. In fact, you have not been required to do anything at all in order to resolve the situation. You have done so out of the goodness of your heart, out of a willingness to make certain that your uncle's wrongs are set to rights." She smiled up at him, aware that his fingers were now threaded through hers. "How could I remain cold toward such a gentleman? How could my heart not cry out with both gladness and overwhelming relief?"

His smile was tender. "I pray there is a little more than that within your heart, Lady Ellen," he said softly. "For I have every intention of marrying you."

Laughing, Ellen boldly reached up and settled one hand against his chest, feeling the steady beat of his heart. "Your heart speaks of a great affection for me," she answered him as he nodded. "My own is filled with love for you, Lord Lindale. I did not once expect to feel such a great, overwhelming emotion but it is there within me, growing steadily and with such force that I cannot do anything but express it to you."

Much to her surprise, Lord Lindale swiftly lowered his head and, before she could say another word, caught her lips with his in a firm kiss. She started violently and he began to pull away, only for Ellen to pull him back toward her. Her arms were about his neck, his hands at her waist as they shared their first, momentous kiss of love.

"When the time comes, will you accept my offer of marriage?"

he asked, his mouth only a breath away from her own. "You must know that I love you in return, Ellen. I love you desperately."

Her hands tightened gently about him and she closed her eyes, resting her forehead against his for a moment as she stood on tiptoe in order to reach his lips.

"I will say yes," she promised, laughing softly at his sigh of relief. "I love you, Lord Lindale, and I believe I always shall."

FINDING THE EARL

HEIRS OF LONDON BOOK THREE

Finding the Earl

Text Copyright © 2020 by Joyce Alec

All rights reserved. This book or any portion thereof may not be reproduced or used in any manner whatsoever without the express written permission of the publisher except for the use of brief quotations in a book review.

This book is a work of fiction. Names, characters, places and incidents are either the product of the author's imagination or are used fictionally. Any resemblance to actual persons, living or dead, or to actual events or locales is entirely coincidental.

First printing, 2020

Publisher
Love Light Faith, LLC
400 NW 7th Avenue, Unit 825
Fort Lauderdale, FL 33311

PROLOGUE

"Now, you do recall what is to happen, do you not?"

"Yes, Father." Marianne caught the slight smile pulling at the corner of her mother's mouth as she watched both Marianne and Lord Gillingham converse.

"Then repeat it back to me."

Sighing inwardly, Marianne settled her hands in her lap and looked directly back at her father. He had spoken to her of this at least five times already and she was fully aware of their plans. Why she had to hear it yet again, she did not know. It was not as though she had even the opportunity to forget it.

"My brother and his wife have just had their first child," Marianne said, speaking quickly. "However, due to the fact that you have no wish for me to miss the first part of the Season, you have decided to ask your sister, Lady Voss, to accompany me for the first two weeks of the Season. You will reside with my brother and, thereafter, will come to London to join both Lady Voss and myself."

Her father, whose brows had knotted heavily over his eyes, nodded slowly, although Marianne did not miss the look of concern that he shot toward his wife. Quite why he appeared so concerned about this particular situation, Marianne had very little idea.

"We may be three weeks with your brother and his dear wife," Lady Gillingham said as Marianne lifted one shoulder in a small shrug. "Your father believes that it will only be a fortnight, but I am inclined to believe that it will be a little longer than that, given the weariness that usually comes over him whenever we travel."

Lord Gillingham frowned, folding his arms across his chest. "If you speak in reference to me, my dear, I believe you are quite mistaken," he said firmly. "It is never a weariness within *me* that is of concern. It is always for you."

Marianne smiled to herself at the verbal sparring that followed, knowing full well that her parents had a great regard for each other, although her father could often be a little overbearing when it came to his concern for both his wife and his daughter. Her own thoughts turned to London and to the Season that was waiting for her. Excitement flooded her heart as she considered the dancing, the music, and the gentlemen that she would meet. Having made her debut last Season, this Season she was expected now to find a suitable match. Her father had made that very clear, which was why she was to be in London for the very start of the Season—so that she did not miss a single opportunity. *After all,* her father had said, *many a match was made in those early weeks. Why should it not be so for you?*

Marianne's smile grew as her mother rose, came toward Lord Gillingham, and reached up to kiss his cheek before ringing the bell. Her actions stopped Lord Gillingham's hurried monologue and, as Marianne watched, he reached for his wife's hand and brought it to his lips, their differences clearly brought to a swift end.

A gentle smile crossed Marianne's face. What she saw displayed before her was what she sought for herself. She did not want to make a match with a gentleman who was only *suitable* for her, but rather wished to find a husband who would treat her with the same gentle affection as she saw displayed here, between her mother and father. That, she was sure, was not something that many young ladies considered, knowing full well that it was often the gentleman's title and wealth that made him the most eligible, but for herself, she was quite determined that it would not be so.

"Lord Castleton will be present in London also, I am sure."

Marianne was drawn back to the present as she looked back at her father, seeing now that her mother had returned to her seat and had picked up her needlework.

"You remember Lord Castleton, do you not?"

Frowning, Marianne nodded. She certainly recalled Lord Castleton and had to confess, albeit only to herself, that she did not think well of him. Having been acquainted with her father, with his estate not far from Lord Gillingham's, he had often called to visit the earl, but had been rather dismissive of Marianne. She had thought him handsome but reserved, and whenever she had tried to converse with him, she had found her conversation brought to a swift end. Now that she thought of it, she could still see the look in his eye as he'd turned away from her to speak again to Lord Gillingham. He had been dismissive, cold, and entirely unlikeable. There was no eagerness in her heart to see him again.

"He is a little older than you, certainly," the earl continued glibly, clearly unaware of Marianne's inner considerations. "But I do not think that you should ignore him entirely, given that he is a well-respected and well-connected gentleman."

Marianne wanted to state aloud that she would *never* consider Lord Castleton, given how little she thought of him, but instead chose to remain silent. Her father did not need to know her thoughts as yet. Instead, she simply allowed a smile to catch at her lips, and thankfully was not required to answer further given that the maids arrived with trays for both Marianne and Lady Gillingham.

Lord Gillingham cleared his throat. "I should return to my study and finish with my matters of business," he said as Lady Gillingham looked up at him and smiled. "Which reminds me that I shall have to order a new seal for when we return to London. I am sure my other is quite broken." With a small shake of his head, he looked back toward his wife and smiled. "I will see you both at dinner."

Marianne nodded. "Very well, Father."

"And you will not forget what is expected of you when you go to London with my sister?" the earl asked, his expression suddenly dark. "You know the standards that are set. The propriety that is demanded of you."

A frown caught Marianne's brow as she looked up at her father, wondering at the strange expression on his face. "Of course, Father," she answered, a little hurt that he would ask her such a thing. "Why should you think that I would forget?"

Lady Gillingham tutted and shook her head, whilst Lord Gillingham did not reply but instead, with a sharp nod, turned on his heel and quit the room, leaving Marianne's question entirely unanswered. Marianne watched him leave, her frown only deepening as she did so. Her father had been very insistent that she remember everything that had been planned and now was asking her to recall what they expected of her during her time in London without them present. That was a little upsetting, however, and Marianne could not help but feel a sting of pain at his questions.

"Do not mind your father, Marianne."

Marianne glanced at her mother, who gestured to the tea tray with an expectant smile on her face. Sighing, Marianne nodded and rose, making her way to the small table where the tea tray sat, so that she might pour a cup for both herself and her mother.

"He does not mean to suggest that he fears you will behave improperly," Lady Gillingham continued as she watched Marianne carefully. "He is only concerned."

"Concerned about what in particular?" Marianne asked, her brow still furrowed. "We were all present in London last Season and I never once either said or did anything that would make him question me so."

"I am aware of that," Lady Gillingham replied softly. "I am sorry for his questions, Marianne. He is a little anxious about separating ourselves from you, I believe."

This brought Marianne some relief from her worries as she looked back at her mother for a moment, before reaching down to stir a little milk into her mother's teacup so that she might hand it to her. "I will be quite all right in London with Lady Voss."

"I am sure that I ought not to be speaking so," Lady Gillingham continued as though she had not heard Marianne, "but your father is not concerned for *you*, my dear, but rather for his sister."

"For my aunt?" Marianne replied, surprised. "What do you mean?" Picking up her own teacup and saucer, she returned to her chair and held her mother's gaze, seeing the lines of concern that had formed across Lady Gillingham's forehead.

"Lady Voss, as you know, has only ever had sons," Lady Gillingham said carefully. "She has not had any daughters to introduce to society, to watch over and to guide. Your father is concerned that she might be a little more nonchalant about such things than he would like."

Marianne laughed and shook her head. "I am quite sure that Lady Voss is fully aware of all that is expected from a lady by society," she said quickly, surprised when her mother did not instantly agree with her. "There can be no real concern there, surely?"

Lady Gillingham hesitated before she answered, her needlework, by now, entirely forgotten. "Just be aware of what is expected of you and do not rely on your aunt's judgment," she cautioned, making Marianne aware that her mother also shared the very same concerns as her father about Lady Voss. "Recall everything that was taught to you and how you conducted yourself last Season and I am sure that all will be well."

"Of course it will be, Mama," Marianne said, attempting to do all she could to reassure her mother. "I know what can occur if I do not do as society expects—and as you and Father expect. You can trust me. You can trust my judgment. I will not do anything foolish; I assure you."

Lady Gillingham seemed to relax just a little, for her shoulders dropped, the lines of concern began to fade from her forehead, and the look in her eyes softened.

"I am glad to hear it, Marianne," she said quietly. "Very glad indeed. But it will only be for two or three weeks, I hope. And then we shall join you in London and all will be well."

"It will all turn out just as you expect," Marianne agreed firmly. "And I am sure that you will have the most wonderful time with my brother and his family." Her heart squeezed for a moment. "I will miss seeing him and his new son."

Lady Gillingham took a sip of her tea, set the cup back down on the saucer, and smiled. "You will do so soon, my dear," she said gently. "All in good time, Marianne. All in good time."

1

There were so many familiar faces at the ball that James felt himself a little dizzy. Everywhere he looked there was someone he was already acquainted with, seemingly eager to greet him again. Young ladies curtsied to him and, whilst he bowed and smiled, there was no opportunity to make conversation, given that within a moment, there was someone else present also, looking to him with expectant eyes.

The first ball of the Season was, of course, a crush of guests but he had not expected to be so overwhelmed as he was at present. What was wrong with him? He had been looking forward to this moment, had he not? Why, then, was he finding himself so anxious?

"The card room is just to your left, Castleton," he heard someone say, turning his head to see an old acquaintance, Lord Wright, grinning at him. "I am on my way there now, should you wish to join me?"

James nodded and, saying nothing to any others, followed Lord Wright, relieved beyond measure when he managed to step out of the ballroom and into the long hallway that opened up to him. Lord Wright turned to the door on his left and it was opened for them at once by a footman, leaving Lord Wright and James to step inside.

"What a relief!" Lord Wright exclaimed as James resisted the urge to pull out a handkerchief from his pocket and wipe it across his brow. "There are far too many young ladies at the ball this evening." He chuckled and handed a glass of brandy to James, who accepted it eagerly. "And I have never once believed that I should say such a thing as that."

James took a sip of his brandy and then shook his head. "It is such a crush." he exclaimed, relieved now that he had come into the quiet of the card room. "I could not even say a word to an old acquaintance for, wherever I turned, there was another face eager to greet me."

"Something that not every gentleman would complain about," Lord Wright replied with a chuckle slipping from his mouth. "But yes, I quite understand your meaning. Although, that is entirely your own doing, Lord Castleton. I do not think I can hold a good deal of sorrow for you, I am afraid."

A frown marred James' brow. "My own doing?" he repeated, confused. "What do you mean?"

Lord Wright grinned, his eyes dancing. "Well, if you *must* be the richest viscount in all of London and if it *must* be known that you have purchased one of the best townhouses in the city, then what else can you expect but for the young ladies of the *beau monde* to come in search of you, in the hope of becoming your bride?" He chuckled as James grimaced, although James himself found no humor in what Lord Wright said. "It is not as though you could have hidden your wealth from the *ton*, however. No doubt, someone would have discovered it."

James said nothing in response to this. Between last Season and this, some investments of his had done very well indeed. Remarkably so, in fact. Of course, news of it had spread throughout all of England, it seemed, for almost everyone was aware of his good fortune. Perhaps it had been unwise of him to purchase another townhouse for himself, he considered, a little glumly. Regardless of his wealth, he certainly had no wish to be dragged into the company of particular young ladies who wanted him only for their own improved standing in society. That was not something that pleased him at all, even though he had to admit that it would be wise for him to consider matrimony this Season.

"And how does your friend?" Lord Wright asked, changing the subject entirely. "He was wed recently, was he not?"

"You speak of Lord Lindale?" James asked, and Lord Wright nodded. "Yes, he was wed to Lady Ellen. They are very happy indeed, from what I understand." He smiled to himself, recalling all that had occurred last Season. "I am very glad for them both."

"But of course," Lord Wright replied with a broad smile. "Why should one not be pleased for a gentleman such as that? He appears to be quite contented and, given the way he was thrust into the title, has done very well indeed, I should think."

"Yes," James agreed. "He has."

"It does put me in mind to consider matrimony," Lord Wright continued with a small shake of his head. "But there are so many eligible young ladies that one does not know where to begin."

James could not help but laugh at this, with Lord Wright grinning broadly, as though he knew he had made something of a foolish statement and was, in his own way, rather pleased with it.

"And what of you, Lord Castleton?" Lord Wright asked when James quietened his laughter. "Will you seek a bride this Season?"

The smile slid from James' face. "I am not certain," he answered, aware that such an idea had been in his own thoughts only a few moments before. "There are, as you have said, a good many eligible young ladies and I am not particularly inclined toward any of them as yet."

Lord Wright's laughter tore across the room, making a flare of mortification sear James' cheeks. Had he said something foolish?

"My dear Lord Castleton, this is only the first ball of the Season," Lord Wright exclaimed as James grimaced. "I am sure that, in time, one or two of them might appear to be a little more appealing to you, should you give them the opportunity."

"I suppose that is so," James replied tightly. He did not say anything more, finding Lord Wright's laughter somewhat insulting, although he realized that he had spoken unwisely. Whatever the reason, he had found this evening's crush to be a little too much, a little overwhelming. There had been no excitement in his heart, no happiness at being returned to the *ton*. Perhaps this Season was not to be one of enjoyment for him.

"I did not mean to mock you," Lord Wright said slowly, perhaps seeing the frustration that had melted into James' expression. "Only to state that your first impression of the young ladies here in London is based solely on this ridiculous ball and to suggest that it might not be wise to form any opinions of them as yet."

James shrugged. "I greeted Lady Catherine, Miss Newton, and Miss Dunstable," he said with a shake of his head. "I can assure you, Lord Wright, that none of them would interest me."

Lord Wright shrugged. "Then it is just as well there are so many others," he replied, his smile growing steadily once more. "And some that you have not as yet been introduced to."

"I do not think I should pursue a debutante," James replied quickly. "I feel a little too aged to do such a thing." Shaking off any final strands of embarrassment, he gave Lord Wright a grim smile. "I have been in London for many Seasons and, as yet, have not considered matrimony or given any real consideration to the ladies present. This year, I shall do so—but I shall not even *glance* at the debutantes." He shook his head, half to himself as he spoke. "It would be better for me to seek out a lady in her second or third Season, mayhap."

Lord Wright shrugged. "Whomever you chose, I am certain they will be more than willing to be in your company," he said, which only dulled James' heart all the more. "I would be astonished if you found anyone who was unwilling to be so."

James sighed and shrugged, finding that he had no desire to carry on such a conversation any longer. The concept seemed to weary him, to make him feel quite lackluster, as though this Season would hold no joy or interest for him.

It is only the first week of the Season and you are feeling so already? Giving himself a slight shake, James threw back the rest of his brandy and then looked around the room. "A card game or two might cheer me," he said aloud as Lord Wright grinned. "Should you wish to join me?"

"Very much," Lord Wright replied, spying a group of gentlemen whose game had only just come to a close. "Perhaps we might join them?"

James nodded and made his way across the room. Soon, he found himself in much better spirits, enjoying the conversation, the game, and the excellent brandy provided. All thoughts of matrimony, of young ladies, and of the Season itself flew from his head, leaving him very contented indeed.

∽

"I FEAR you shall have to venture out into the ballroom again, Lord Castleton."

James groaned aloud, swaying slightly where he stood. The card games had gone on for a very long time indeed and he had imbibed a little too much brandy. It had, at first, lifted his spirits and, as he had continued to partake, had found himself growing more and more jolly. The moment he rose from the table, however, he had found himself a little overcome, only realizing then just how much he had drunk.

"I think I shall return home," he answered as Lord Wright chuckled. "I have no desire to converse with anyone and certainly I do not think I can dance."

"I would not recommend you try," Lord Wright replied, slapping James on the back. "Perhaps returning home would be wise. I am sure that your carriage can be called very quickly, and you will find yourself back at your townhouse very soon."

James nodded and turned to thank the other gentlemen who had been playing with him, only to discover that one of them had fallen asleep in his chair, his eyes closed, his head lolling back, and his mouth a little ajar. With a roll of his eyes, and silently promising himself that he would never allow himself to be in such a state of disarray, James pushed the door open and stepped out into the hallway.

It was certainly quieter than the card room had been, although the sounds that came from the ballroom attempted to make their way through toward him, pushing their way through the door to make themselves known to him. James groaned aloud and ran one hand over his eyes, wishing that he had behaved with a little more consideration.

"My lord?"

The footman, who had been standing by the door, looked at him with a slight flicker of concern in his eye. "Might I help you with something?"

"No," James replied, shaking his head and then immediately regretting that he had done so. "I am quite well." His head swam and his vision remained a little blurred for some moments as he focused again on the door that led to the ballroom. Making his way slowly toward it, for he needed to concentrate on walking in a straight line so as not to embarrass himself further, James pulled it open and felt the noise of the ballroom hit him hard, as though he had walked into a solid wall. Stumbling back, his hand still on the door handle, James attempted to right himself before walking into the room, setting his shoulders as he did so.

The room itself seemed to be moving, packed as it was with the many, many guests within it. Quite how there was room for dancing, James did not know, but from the music that was now floating over the top of the crowd toward him, James presumed that such a thing was occurring somewhere. Grimacing—for the thought of dancing when he was in such a state made him recoil inwardly—he turned his attention to trying to find the door that would lead him from the assembly rooms back out toward where the carriages were waiting. He no longer felt any concern over the young ladies who attempted to catch his eye, ignoring them all entirely as he walked slowly through the crowd, being jostled and bumped by those about him.

"Lord... Castleton?"

Someone touched his elbow and he turned his head, stumbling back as he tried to turn around to see who had spoken to him. His eyes narrowed as he took in the young lady before him. He had very little idea as to who she was and certainly there was not even a flicker of recognition within his heart.

"Good evening," he muttered, dropping into a bow which took him some time to escape from. His head felt heavy, his bones seeming to weigh him down. "If you will excuse me, I—"

"You are back in London, then?"

James let out a long sigh, looking back at the blue-eyed young lady and taking her in once more. Still nothing came to him. She was naught but a stranger.

"I am," he said, aware that the young lady's chaperone—or mother, depending on who she was—had been standing listening to their conversation, such as it was, without saying a single word. "And—and you?"

The young lady frowned, her brow furrowing as she studied him. Her eyes were rather piercing, and James found himself eager to look away from her, finding that the intensity of her gaze was a little too much for him to take. Instead, he focused on the rest of her features, taking in her gentle sloping nose, high cheekbones, and oval face. Brown curls were trailing down from the back of her head, with one or two sitting gently on her shoulders. There was a gentle beauty about her, despite the sharp look in her eyes.

"You must know that I was in London last Season, Lord Castleton, even though we did not have the opportunity to meet," the young lady said after a few moments of silence. "I presume you were present also?"

"I was, yes," James replied, speaking rather thickly as he attempted to keep his composure. "But, as you said, we did not meet." Bowing again, he struggled to lift his head and, in finally managing to do so, stumbled forward and managed to knock into the young lady. She let out a yelp of surprise and pushed him away, causing James to sway to his right, struggling to keep his balance.

Reaching out to grasp at anything that might help him remain upright, James found himself hanging onto the young lady's arm, although her companion instantly grasped a hold of him also and thrust him back. Quite how he managed to stay on his feet, James did not know, but thankfully, he did not collapse to the floor as he feared.

"My most sincere apologies," he said as an urge to laugh began to build up within him. "I did not mean to knock into you so."

"I believe you are foxed, Lord Castleton."

The young lady's voice was thin, her eyes narrowed now with anger, and her cheeks flooded with color which, he was sure, only came from embarrassment at his behavior. Despite knowing that to laugh at his foolishness would only upset her further, James found the urge to do so unavoidable and, feeling it bubble up within him, let out a burst of laughter. The young lady looked all the more affronted, her eyes widening as she stared at him.

"I am sorry!" James exclaimed, the wide grin spreading across his face speaking against his words. "I do not think that—"

"Good evening, Lord Castleton," the young lady interrupted sharply. "I can see that coming to speak to you was foolish indeed. I shall not make such a mistake again."

She turned to her companion, who, with a glare in James' direction, then also turned about and led her charge away from James, their steps hurried as though they were desperate to remove themselves from his company. James, still finding laughter building up within him, turned away and, his smile still broad and fixed across his face, made his way through the crowd once more, still determined to return home. The incident with the young lady was instantly pushed from his mind as he focused solely on returning home, thinking that there would be nothing better than sitting in front of a small fire with a glass of whisky in his hand before finally retiring to bed. The young lady might have been insulted, yes, and certainly he had made a fool of himself, but at the very least, it would push her away from thinking him an eligible match and that, as far as James was concerned, was, in fact, a rather good outcome.

The first ball of the Season, he considered, finally managing to find his way out, had not been as bad as he had first thought. Perhaps it would be a good Season after all.

2

"Good morning, Marianne."

Marianne smiled at her aunt and sat down at the dining table, ready to break her fast. She had slept for a good many hours after the ball and now felt very refreshed indeed.

"Good morning, Aunt," she said as Lady Voss handed her a cup of tea that she had only just poured. "I do hope you rested well?"

Her aunt smiled, her eyes lighting up in much the same way as Marianne's father's did when he was truly happy about something.

"I did, I thank you," she replied as Marianne took a small sip of her tea and felt it warm all through her. "And you look very well this morning, I must say."

Marianne nodded. "I feel very refreshed, although I confess that one of my feet is a little bruised." Her smile faded as she recalled what had happened last evening. "That is my only disappointment."

Lady Voss grimaced. "I do hope it was not from that ridiculous Lord Castleton?" she asked, and Marianne closed her eyes and sighed. "The other gentlemen you danced with all appeared to be very careful with their steps."

"It *was* Lord Castleton," Marianne replied, opening her eyes to see her aunt frown. "I think he made a very great fool of himself last evening, although what upsets me all the more is knowing that he might very well have made a fool of me also, had you not been able to catch him."

"That is true," Lady Voss replied with a shake of her head as Marianne rose to set her plate with the various breakfasting foods awaiting her as her stomach rumbled gently. "I am very glad indeed that I was able to do so, Marianne, for I do believe he would have pulled you to the floor with him had I not done so."

Marianne said nothing as she took her plate back to the table, sitting down with as much gracefulness as she could. When she had first seen Lord Castleton, she had quickly made every attempt to catch his attention, so that she might write to her father and inform him that she had not only seen Lord Castleton but had conversed with him also.

Unfortunately, Lord Castleton had not appeared to recognize her, and when she had realized he was in a state of befuddlement, she had felt her heart sink to the floor. She had attempted to converse with him in the hope that he would recall her, but he had remained vague and disinterested. When he had stumbled into her, she had been so overcome with shock that, for a moment, she had not reacted. When Lady Voss had moved to pull Lord Castleton away, Marianne had broken out into a sweat, realizing just how badly such an incident might have affected her. She might have found herself lying prone on the floor with Lord Castleton atop her, and then all manner of difficulties would have followed.

"I confess that I do not think well of him," Lady Voss said firmly. "When he began to laugh, I was filled with such ire."

"As was I," Marianne agreed, a grim line pulling at her mouth. "Indeed, had I felt myself able to, I would have given him a stinging rebuke—but as it was, I did not believe that he would have listened to me at that time."

"I think that was wise," Lady Voss replied, reaching to pour herself a little more tea. "I do hope you will say something to him now, however. He is a friend of your father's, I understand? Surely he must know that to behave in such a fashion is not at all acceptable?"

Marianne let out a small sigh and lifted one shoulder. "I do not think that gentlemen give such things any consideration when they are in their cups," she answered as Lady Voss lifted her teacup to her lips. "But I certainly have no wish to return to his company again. After how he behaved, I should expect an apology at the very least, but I am doubtful that he will recall what he did."

Lady Voss sighed. "You are, no doubt, quite correct in your assumption, but I do not think that you should remain silent about the matter," she said, her manner reminding Marianne that her aunt was quite a determined character and certainly would not allow such a thing to go without apology. "The next time you happen to be near to him, I would state, without hesitation, that you are still waiting for him to rectify matters." She lifted one shoulder. "That would prove to you whether or not he recalls it."

"And if he does not?" Marianne asked, a smile tugging at her lips. "What should I do then?"

"Remind him of it!" Lady Voss exclaimed, as though it was without question what Marianne should do. "Demand that he apologize for being so thoughtless."

Marianne smiled at her aunt. Her mother, Marianne knew, would encourage her to remain silent about the matter and pray that Lord Castleton would speak to her of his own accord. If he did not, then it mattered very little. However, Lady Voss was quite the opposite, telling Marianne that she ought to make certain that Lord Castleton was not only aware of his actions but that he would apologize to her also. She herself was not quite certain what to do.

"My concern, Aunt, is that Lord Castleton does not know who I am," she said softly. "When I greeted him last evening, there was not even a hint in his eyes that he recognized me." Holding up one hand toward her aunt, who had been about to speak, Marianne shot her a quick smile. "I know that you will say he was befuddled by too much whisky or the like, but I am not certain that, even without it, he would know who I was. I confess I am a little surprised that he did not know me, given that we have been introduced and acquainted for some time, but regardless, I would feel all the more ashamed if I were to speak to him and have him look at me with that same confusion and uncertainty."

Lady Voss considered this for some moments, and then shrugged. "Very well, Marianne," she said after a while. "I shall leave this matter to your own judgment." She smiled kindly at Marianne, who allowed herself a small breath of relief as she picked up her teacup. "Despite Lord Castleton's ridiculous behavior, I should say that I thought last evening went very well indeed. You made a good many new acquaintances and greeted those you already knew."

"I did enjoy it," Marianne replied truthfully. "And are we still to step into town this afternoon?" Her heart quickened just a little as Lady Voss nodded, feeling her anticipation grow. "I am very much looking forward to being back in London again."

"I think a visit to a milliner and perhaps to Gunter's would do us both a great deal of good," Lady Voss replied as Marianne's smile grew. "Let us hope the weather stays fine for our outing."

∽

Much to Marianne's relief, the sun *did* remain in the sky, although there were also a great many clouds to hide its radiance from their view. It did not matter to her a great deal, however, for she was looking forward to being out amongst society again rather than having any great concern about the weather. Stepping out of the carriage, she let out a long, contented sigh as she looked all about her, recalling just how much she had enjoyed making her way through town during last Season.

"Where are we to go first?" Lady Voss asked, and Marianne considered the matter for a moment. "I am entirely at my leisure and would be glad to go anywhere you would like."

Marianne drew in another contented breath. "The bookshop?" she asked, and Lady Voss nodded. "I might purchase a new book for Mama, so that when she arrives, she will have something to read. You know how she likes to rest for a few days after any long journey."

Lady Voss smiled. "Indeed I do," she answered, directing Marianne toward the bookshop, which was only a short distance away. "And I think that is very thoughtful of you."

"No doubt they are very much enjoying the company of their new grandson," Marianne replied softly, feeling a small sense of sorrow in her heart that she could not be with them. "I am very glad for my brother."

"As am I," Lady Voss replied. "I recall how glad I was when my first son produced his heir. Of course, my husband was much more delighted than I, given the assurances that came with such an event, but I myself was rather taken with the child."

"As will Mama be," Marianne said, nodding and smiling to a few acquaintances as they passed. Marianne smiled to herself and tipped her face toward the sky for a moment, even though she knew she risked unsightly freckles by doing so.

"Marianne, look."

Her smile faded as she saw two gentlemen approaching her. They were talking rather rapidly, with the second shaking his head and the first nodding fervently, as though he were insisting on something. She recognized the second at once, realizing that it was none other than Lord Castleton who was drawing near to them both.

"Shall we go into the bookshop, Aunt?" Marianne said urgently. "I have no wish to speak to Lord Castleton in the middle of a London street."

Lady Voss made to say something, only to seemingly recall that she had promised Marianne that she would leave the matter entirely in Marianne's hands. "Very well," she said, turning on her heel and making her way toward the bookshop, Marianne walking with her with hasty steps, unwilling to wait for even a moment longer.

"Lady Voss?"

She froze, her eyes closing for a moment before she turned back toward the two gentlemen, aware of the tension that now flooded her being.

"Lady Voss!" the first gentleman exclaimed, now hurrying toward them both. "I do hope you remember me, else this shall make for a very awkward conversation indeed."

Marianne glanced up at her aunt, whose expression had gone from one of frustration to one of delight as the gentleman approached.

"Goodness, Lord Wright!" she exclaimed as Marianne forced herself to step forward to join her aunt, lowering her eyes so that she looked at the ground rather than up at Lord Castleton. She could not explain the embarrassment that filled her, given that it was Lord Castleton who had behaved so poorly, but for whatever reason, she simply could not bring herself to look at him.

"Lord Wright is a very dear friend of my *third* son," Lady Voss told her, turning to Marianne quickly, before speaking again to Lord Wright. "And you are in London for the Season? Can it be that you are still unmarried?"

Lord Wright laughed and Marianne dared a quick look at him, seeing the way his eyes danced and considering him to be a very jolly-looking fellow indeed. Steeling herself, she threw a quick look toward Lord Castleton, only for her stomach to twist furiously in a tight knot. He was smiling politely, looking at Lady Voss and then at Marianne for just a moment, and still there was not even a single flicker of recognition in his eyes. How could he not recall her? The last time they had spoken was only a little over eighteen months ago, when he had come to visit her father on some matter of business.

"I am still unwed," Lord Wright replied with a wry smile. "That may change during the course of the Season, however, for I am quite open to such a thing."

Marianne frowned, hoping that Lord Wright was not suggesting that *she* might be the one to change his mind about such a thing.

"Oh, do forgive me," Lord Wright said, striking his forehead with the heel of his hand. "I have been very rude indeed, have I not? Allow me to introduce my companion." He gestured to Lord Castleton. "Might I present Viscount Castleton? Lord Castleton, this is the charming Lady Voss."

Marianne was more than aware of Lord Wright's eyes upon her and she flushed as she waited for Lady Voss to make similar introductions.

"I am very glad to meet you," Lord Castleton said, accompanying this with a short bow. "Lord Wright clearly thinks very highly of you." Smiling at her, he then gestured toward Marianne. "And might we be introduced to your charming friend?"

Glancing up at her aunt, Marianne caught her gaze and then looked away once more, aware of the tension that was beginning to mount.

"I thank you, Lord Castleton," Lady Voss replied slowly. "I am a little surprised, however, that you require an introduction, Lord Castleton. Not only were you speaking to my *friend*, as you call her, but you are also very well acquainted with her."

Heat slowly rose in Marianne's chest as she forced herself to look back at Lord Castleton, seeing the slight widening of his eyes and realizing, to her disappointment, that he still had very little idea as to who she was.

"I—I must apologize profusely for my lack of awareness," Lord Castleton said, putting one hand to his heart. "Last evening, I am afraid I overindulged just a little."

"Indeed you did," Marianne said, speaking for what was the first time. "You almost dragged me to the floor, Lord Castleton. And then did not have the decency to apologize." The words tore from her lips despite her embarrassment, and as she finished speaking, she saw Lord Castleton's color begin to fade.

"I have nothing but apologies," Lord Castleton replied, inclining his head and then turning his gaze to Lady Voss rather than back to Marianne. "And you say we were already acquainted?" A look of confusion crossed his face. "If it was earlier in the evening, then I can only tell you—"

Marianne resisted the urge to stamp her foot. "My father is the Earl of Gillingham," she said loudly, interrupting Lord Castleton's attempt at an explanation. "You have called upon him many times, Lord Castleton. You have taken tea with us, have dined with us, and yet, the moment I see you here in London, you appear not to recognize me." She lifted her chin and glared at him, her embarrassment now turning to anger. "What is it that has removed knowledge of me from your thoughts?" Her hands were now planted firmly on her hips, all thought of those around her who might very well be witnessing all that she was saying gone entirely from her mind. "Or is it that you have never really noticed me at all?"

There was nothing but silence for some moments. Lord Castleton's eyes had widened, and for a moment, his mouth had dropped open, although he had the presence of mind to close it again very quickly thereafter. Marianne's aunt was looking rather pleased at all that Marianne had said, whilst Lord Wright was standing with an amused expression on his face as he turned toward his friend, clearly enjoying every part of Lord Castleton's discomfort.

"Lady Marianne?" Lord Castleton whispered eventually, before clearing his throat abruptly and closing his eyes. "Lady Marianne, you are quite correct. I did not recognize you."

"That," Lady Voss interrupted, "is *more* than apparent, Lord Castleton."

He dropped his head, spreading his hands. "I can give you no explanation for my lack of recognition, Lady Marianne, other than to say you have changed significantly since I last saw you. Other than that, it is entirely my own doing and my own failure that has permitted me to be so thoughtless. Last evening, I wanted nothing other than to escape from the ball, and to know now that I behaved in such an abominable fashion has brought me all the lower in even my own estimation."

Marianne considered this for a few moments, tilting her head and studying Lord Castleton. He gave every appearance of contrition, certainly, but the embarrassment still remained.

"If there is anything I can do in order to bring about reparations, Lady Marianne, then I shall be glad to do so." This was accompanied by a quick bow, although still, Lord Castleton did not look to her again. His head lifted, but he did not look into Marianne's eyes, perhaps all too ashamed of his behavior to do so.

"Well," Lady Voss said as Lord Wright began to chuckle, clearly still enjoying the situation immensely. "Now that we have had this discussion, Lord Castleton, we will consider the situation, and if there is anything for you to do that might aid Marianne, we will inform you of it at once."

Marianne settled her shoulders and spoke in a firm, clear voice that was laced with displeasure. "Although, Lord Castleton, should you again choose to deliberately make yourself as ridiculous as you were last evening, I would ask that you stay well away from me, so I am not to endure such foolishness from you again."

Lord Castleton finally lifted his eyes to hers and, deep within his brown eyes, she was sure she saw something akin to shame. But Marianne did not permit herself to feel any sort of sympathy for the gentleman and certainly did not regret anything that she herself had said. Instead, she simply turned to Lord Wright and ignored Lord Castleton completely, smiling at the other gentleman and wiping all frustration from her face at once.

"I am glad to make your acquaintance, Lord Wright," she said in a most genial manner. "Do forgive my outburst."

Lord Wright grinned, his eyes still twinkling. "Not at all, Lady Marianne," he said, bending into a deep bow. "Under the circumstances, I quite understand it. And certainly, if Lord Castleton has behaved in a manner that is entirely inappropriate for a gentleman, then you have every right to criticize him in such a fashion."

"I thank you," Marianne replied as Lady Voss smiled and murmured something similar. "Now, if you will excuse us both, we are off to the bookshop."

Lord Wright nodded and took a small step back. "But of course," he replied as Lord Castleton flushed a deep, crimson red. "Thank you for stopping to speak to me, Lady Voss, Lady Marianne. It has made for a very...interesting afternoon."

Marianne smiled back at him and turned on her heel, taking her aunt's arm once more and stepping away from Lord Castleton without hesitation. Lady Voss walked quickly, and once they were more than ten paces away from the gentlemen, immediately began to whisper to Marianne.

"You did very well, my dear," she said, keeping her voice low. "I am sure that Lord Castleton was not only astonished but also greatly embarrassed by his behavior. I am certain he will not behave so again."

Marianne nodded but did not reply. She waited until her aunt had pushed open the door to the bookshop before daring a glance over her shoulder. Lord Castleton had one hand over his eyes, shaking his head slightly as Lord Wright spoke to him, a broad smile still across his face. Marianne felt a small sense of triumph fill her as she walked into the bookshop and let the door close behind her. Lord Castleton, it seemed, had finally realized just how much of a fool he had been.

3

"I assume she will be present again this evening."

James grimaced as he walked alongside Lord Wright into Lord and Lady Austbridge's townhouse. "I am sure she will be," he muttered, still feeling a crippling sense of shame burning up within him. "And I am also just as certain that, this evening, she will do her level best to pretend that I am *not* present." He shook his head to himself, making no attempt to remove the frustrated expression from his face. "Not that I can blame her for such a thing, of course."

"No, you cannot," Lord Wright replied, no longer finding James' situation a laughing matter—much to James' relief. It had been more than a little irritating to have his friend find so much humor within the situation given just how mortifying it was for James himself. "Have you done anything to try to make amends?"

James lifted one shoulder in a half-shrug. "What is it you think I should do?" he asked as they made their way toward the receiving line. "I have written a long and honest letter to her, not only apologizing but stating that I still wait for her to inform me of what I can do by way of recompense. That I am still willing and determined to do whatever is required."

"And she has not responded to you?"

Shaking his head, James let out another breath. "No, she has not," he said quietly. "But as you have said, I cannot blame her for choosing to behave so. I must have embarrassed her greatly when I was in my cups, and to not even recognize her..." He ran one hand over his face. "Even now, I feel great shame over that particular incident."

"You have not told me *why* you did not recognize her," Lord Wright said, just before turning to greet their host and hostess. James followed suit, although he knew full well that Lord Wright would still be awaiting an answer when he had finished doing so. "Is there something about her that has changed so significantly that you did not do so?"

James' lips twisted as he tried to find a way to explain himself. Whatever he said, it would not make him appear in a particularly good light and he had to admit that there was a part of him that did not want to shame himself further.

"Lord Castleton?"

"You will not stop asking me until I tell you, is that not so?" James asked as they stepped into the ballroom. He had to raise his voice a little just so that Lord Wright could hear him. "The truth is, Lord Wright, I never took much notice of Lady Marianne. Yes, I dined with her and her family, and took tea a number of times, but she was always rather quiet and did not speak unless she was asked something specific."

"You mean to state that she behaved just as a young lady ought?" Lord Wright asked, his eyes widening in mock horror as he placed one hand against his heart. "That Lady Marianne did all that her parents asked of her in front of a guest?"

James' heart twisted painfully in his chest as he took in Lord Wright's expression and realized just how wrong he had been. "Yes, I suppose she did," he muttered, resisting the urge to pick up a brandy glass from a passing footman's tray. Should he do so, he would only throw it back so that he would not have to answer any further questions for at least a few moments. "Regardless, I did not pay her much attention. She is quite a few years younger than I, and given that I was more interested in business matters with her father than anything else, I did not feel any obligation to show even the slightest bit of interest in her."

"Then you were a little afraid that Lord Gillingham might consider you a suitable match?" Lord Wright asked, but James shook his head.

"No, I never had such a concern," he answered honestly. "It was just a consideration of my own thoughts, that is all."

Lord Wright said nothing in response to this, looking around the room and allowing James a few moments of respite. He did not like talking about his failings, did not like discussing *why* he had been so foolish with his lack of awareness of who Lady Marianne was. He certainly did not want to admit that the beautiful young lady he had seen before him, with her beautiful blue eyes framed by dark lashes, her delicate nose, and her tumbling, brown curls, had nudged a note of interest within his heart.

That had been before she had told him the truth of who she was, before he had felt such a great sting of shame and had felt himself burn with embarrassment. Now, every time he so much as glanced at her, he felt the very same thing wash over him again. It was not that he feared she would speak of what had happened to others, but rather that he was still all too aware of just how much of a poor impression he had made upon her.

"She is certainly not without beauty."

James grimaced, darting a sharp look at his friend.

"That is only my opinion, of course," Lord Wright continued airily, as though he knew precisely what James was feeling at present. "And I am certain that, despite yourself, you would admit to it also."

Refusing to dignify this with an answer, James snapped his fingers and beckoned a nearby footman toward them. Picking up a glass of whisky, he handed it to Lord Wright before taking one for himself.

"You are not about to get foxed again this evening, I hope?" Lord Wright said, his grin slowly returning. "You know very well that—"

"No, I shall not be doing so," James interrupted sharply. "But one glass shall not do a great deal of harm."

Lord Wright laughed and agreed that it would not be so. After taking a small sip, he then gestured to the other guests already in the room. "Do you think you will dance this evening?"

James considered for a moment. This ball, it seemed, was less of a crush than the very first one had been and, as yet, he had not been crowded by many young ladies who sought out his company. After his first sennight within London, it seemed that the *ton* had become used to his presence and, perhaps, there were a few other gentlemen who had arrived in London who were of better title than he.

"I might very well do," he said as Lord Wright chuckled. "I have not set foot on the dance floor as yet, have I?"

"No, you have not," Lord Wright agreed, a knowing look in his eye. "And I am sure that you would have many willing young ladies eager to accompany you."

"Then perhaps I shall," James replied, setting all thought of Lady Marianne from his mind and deciding instead that he would do all he could to have a good evening. "Do excuse me, Lord Wright. I think I shall go in search of a few young ladies to converse with."

Lord Wright inclined his head, a broad smile on his face as he gestured to his left, as though he were giving James permission to depart. With a chuckle, James stepped away, meandering slowly through the crowd and wondering just who he might choose to speak to first. Nodding at a few gentlemen and smiling at some young ladies who caught his eye, James turned to his right, only to come face to face with Lady Marianne.

The smile fell from his face in a moment. Lady Marianne and Lady Voss stood together in shock for a moment, before Lady Voss cleared her throat and then bobbed a quick curtsy.

"Good evening, Lord Castleton," she said tightly as Lady Marianne finally dropped into a curtsy also. "I hope you are well this evening?"

James swallowed hard and wondered if such a remark was meant to be a stinging reminder of his behavior at their last meeting. "I am very well, I thank you," he said, bowing. "And you?"

Lady Voss' smile was not a warm one. "I am very well, indeed," came the reply, although she said nothing more, glancing at her niece, who finally chose to speak.

"I thank you for your letter, Lord Castleton," Lady Marianne said, her chin lifting slightly and looking at him directly. "My parents are due to return very soon, and I am sure my father would like to speak to you again."

James did not know what to say to such a remark, clearing his throat and putting his hands behind his back. "I would be glad to speak to Lord Gillingham whenever you—or he—should wish it."

Lady Marianne sighed and closed her eyes for a moment. "Lord Castleton, I shall have to put my feelings toward you to one side, I believe. My father thinks very highly of you, I know."

"That is very generous of you, Lady Marianne," James replied, swallowing hard as heat began to climb up his spine. "But there is truly no need to do so. I—"

"Should you wish to join us for dinner?" the lady asked, interrupting him as her voice rose just a little. "Shall we say a sennight hence?"

Surprised, it took James a moment to respond. "You—you would wish me to join you all for dinner?" he asked, and Lady Marianne nodded, although he did not miss her impatient sigh. "Even after my foolish behavior?"

"Even still, Lord Castleton," came the sharp reply. "As I have said, I must set aside my own feelings for the sake of my father. I know that he would be glad to see you and to speak with you at length about whatever business matters have come to his attention of late. I recall that you both have spent many hours conversing over the last few years."

"That is true, Lady Marianne," James replied, rather humbled by her willingness to think of her father rather than her own disapproval. "I have found conversations with your father to be of great benefit."

"Then you will join us?" the lady asked, and James nodded. "Wonderful. I expect them to return to London very soon. After a few days' rest, they will be very happy indeed to return to society."

He nodded and thanked her again, their conversation coming to a somewhat stilted end. For a moment, the strangest thought came into his mind—the thought of asking her to dance, so that perhaps the tension between them might begin to shatter—but then Lady Voss smiled, excused them both, and bore Lady Marianne away before he could say anything more.

James let out a long breath and dropped his head, rubbing one hand across his forehead. That was not something he had expected and, were he honest with himself, he would admit that his consideration for Lady Marianne's character had risen significantly. It took a great deal of determination and selflessness to behave as she had done. A great deal of maturity also, he considered, dropping his hand and looking all about him. For a young lady who must be in either her first or second Season, there was a good deal of sensibility about her.

"Lord Castleton."

He was quickly thrust back into his present circumstances by the excited voice of a lady he recognized as Miss Hathaway. She stood with another that he did not know and, just a small step away, stood Miss Hathaway's mother. James sighed inwardly, recalling just how eager Miss Hathaway had been in her conversation with him some two nights ago at an evening soiree. It had been difficult to remove himself from her company.

"Good evening," he murmured, bowing low and resigning himself to having, once more, to endure a conversation with her and, no doubt, a dance. For the moment, it seemed, Lady Marianne could be nothing more than a brief interaction.

"And so, you are to join Lady Marianne for dinner?"

James grimaced as he studied his cravat in the mirror before turning to throw a hard glance at Lord Wright.

"You did not need to call upon me this afternoon solely to make certain I was going to attend," he said crisply. "I have already told you that I accepted her invitation and look forward to greeting Lord and Lady Gillingham again."

Lord Wright grinned, his eyes twinkling. "That speaks very well of Lady Marianne, does it not?" he said as James let out a long sigh with the hope that his friend would understand the frustration that now filled him. "Given just how poorly she thought of you, to then invite you to dine with her family is most extraordinary."

"It appears that Lady Marianne *is* a little extraordinary," James replied, hoping that this would satisfy Lord Wright. "Is that what you wish me to say? To admit?"

Pushing himself from his chair, Lord Wright picked up his brandy glass and threw the rest back in a single mouthful. "Yes, I think that is precisely what I wanted you to say," he replied with a small shrug. "You complain that you have been surrounded by young ladies who know of your wealth. They want nothing more than your fortune to claim as their own, is that not so?"

Resisting the urge to adjust his cravat, James lifted his brows and looked at Lord Wright. "Yes, that is so," he admitted as Lord Wright chuckled. "But what has that to do with Lady Marianne?"

"Because she is the very opposite of what you despise," Lord Wright explained, spreading his hands wide. "Do you not see? She does not seek to know you, as these other young ladies do. She does not want to be in your company, as so many of the other chits are eager to be. She is only doing so for the sake of her parents, I believe. Does that not tell you that she encompasses everything that you have sought? That you have hoped for?"

James' lips twisted as he considered what it was that Lord Wright was attempting to suggest. "That may be so," he replied slowly. "But that does not mean that I am at all *inclined* toward her."

Lord Wright shrugged one shoulder, although a half-smile

came to his lips as he did so. "That may be so at present," he replied, "but there is no need to think that it will always be so."

"That is entirely ridiculous!" James exclaimed, throwing up his hands. "She is entirely unwilling to even be in my company, as you well know, and is doing so only to please her father. Even if I were to consider her, there is certainly no promise that she will consider me."

"Then you are certainly willing to think of such a thing," Lord Wright replied with a chuckle. "That is...interesting."

James closed his eyes and bit back a hard retort, wishing that Lord Wright would remain silent about what James considered to be utterly foolish ideas. Were he to tell his friend the truth, he would state that he was already a little nervous about his dinner with Lord and Lady Gillingham and somewhat anxious about what his interactions with Lady Marianne would be like without Lord Wright suggesting such things. Things that would, most likely, swim around James' mind all through this evening.

"I shall leave you now," Lord Wright continued airily as James shook his head and let out a heavy sigh of irritation, which Lord Wright steadfastly ignored. "Do enjoy your evening."

"I am sure I shall," James replied firmly. "Good evening, Lord Wright."

∽

JAMES WALKED from his carriage and climbed the stone steps that led to Lord Gillingham's townhouse. His stomach was churning in a most disconcerting manner, and try as he might, he could not find even a modicum of calm. It was not the thought of seeing Lord and Lady Gillingham again that sent such nervousness through him but rather being in the company and presence of Lady Marianne.

He prayed that she had not told her father of his foolishness and his lack of recognition when he had first been introduced to her, for that would only add to his shame. And yet, James knew he could not blame her for doing so, had she decided to speak of it.

Rapping sharply on the door, James straightened his shoulders and found himself holding his breath with anxiety. The door did not open to him, however, and he had to let his breath out slowly, reaching up to rap at the door again. Frowning, he placed his hands behind his back and waited, beginning to fear that he had come to call on the wrong evening.

What was he to do? Glancing behind him, he saw his carriage still waiting and wondered if he should return to it. Frowning hard, he reached up to rap at the door for one final time, only for the door to creak open. Relieved, James let out a long breath and waited for the butler to open it to him, but only saw a pale-faced footman looking back at him.

"I—I believe I am expected," James said slowly as the footman pulled the door a little further open for him. "I am expected for dinner?"

The footman bowed and then spread his hands. "I am truly sorry, my lord, that there was no one present to greet you," he said, a little awkwardly. "Although I am afraid, I must inform you that I do not think there will be any dinner this evening."

Astonished, James stared at the footman, who once more lowered his head in an apologetic gesture. "And why might that be?" he asked, his forehead furrowed in consternation. "Am I no longer invited? Am I to be so poorly thought of that I am to be turned away from the door?"

The footman held up both hands, beginning to stammer. "No, no, my lord. N-no, certainly, it is not as you fear. I pray that you will permit me to explain."

James resisted the urge to throw back the request at once, glaring at the footman whilst anger and embarrassment thrust itself through him. Lady Marianne had, it seemed, told her parents of what he had done and thus, they no longer wished him to join them for dinner. Why they could not have written, he did not know, but perhaps it had been solely to mortify him much in the way he had done to Lady Marianne.

Hurried footsteps were heard as James waited for the footman to answer, and he turned to his left, seeing Lady Marianne coming toward him. He was about to demand why he had been thrown from the house, why the dinner had been cancelled, but something about Lady Marianne stayed his response. Looking at her, he waited until she came into the light, utterly astonished when she practically ran to him and grasped his hand with both of her own.

"Oh, Lord Castleton, you are come," Lady Marianne said as James looked down into her face and saw tears swimming in her eyes. His anger faded away in a moment, his upset disappearing as concern began to rise within him. "I am so relieved you are here."

"My dear lady," James replied, finding himself placing his other hand upon hers. "Is something troubling you? Has something occurred to upset you?"

She nodded, dropping her head and then sniffing indelicately. "It is my mother and father," she said hoarsely, her words torn out from her lips with evidently great pain as her face lifted to his, contorted with grief. "They left the house this afternoon and have not returned."

James' breath caught as he looked down into her eyes, panic rising in his heart. "What do you mean?"

"I mean," she replied, whispering now, "that my parents, Lord Castleton, are missing."

4

The day had gone very well indeed. Marianne had enjoyed a leisurely morning with her mother, who had risen about the same time, whilst her father had made his way quickly to his study. It had been a joy for her to have them back with her and, in particular, to hear the news of her brother. Lady Gillingham had still been a little fatigued, however, and had retired back to her bedchamber for the afternoon, whilst Marianne and Lady Voss had taken afternoon calls, and for a short while, had been amongst the other patrons at Hyde Park. Having returned early, Lady Voss had encouraged Marianne to prepare for dinner and thus, she had retired to her room without greeting her mother or her father. Lady Voss had done the same, given that she was residing with them at present, and they had both come together again in the dining room, expecting Lord and Lady Gillingham to meet them there.

"You are not anxious, I hope?"

Marianne turned her head from where she had been giving her reflection a final glance in the mirror above the fireplace. "Anxious?" she repeated as Lady Voss nodded. "Why should I be so?"

Lady Voss lifted one shoulder. "Because Lord Castleton has

treated you rather poorly," she said quietly. "Because he did not recall you, he embarrassed you, and, whilst he has apologized profusely, there can be no real desire for his company."

"But as I have said," Marianne replied tersely, "I am doing this solely for my father's benefit. I have not spoken to either my mother or my father of Lord Castleton's mistakes and certainly have no intention of doing so." She shrugged. "He has apologized, as you have said."

The truth was Marianne had found herself eager to hold a grudge. She had wanted to continue to ignore Lord Castleton as best she could but had known within her heart that to do so was very foolish indeed. Her father thought very highly of him and her mother, certainly, had no concerns about their acquaintance. She knew very well that her father would appreciate his company and conversation and therefore had decided to invite Lord Castleton to dinner regardless of how she herself felt about him. Lady Voss had congratulated her on her consideration but had also stated, on more than one occasion, that she would not have been so inclined and certainly would be more than willing to tell Lord and Lady Gillingham of what had occurred, should Marianne wish it.

Of course, Marianne had refused such an offer. She now suspected that her aunt was beginning to wonder if Marianne was thinking of Lord Castleton as an appropriate suitor, despite his foolishness, and she certainly wanted to dissuade Lady Voss of such a notion.

"There is nothing more to my request that he join us for dinner, Aunt," Marianne finished, speaking quickly. "I can assure you of that."

Lady Voss held Marianne's gaze for a long moment, then sighed, nodded, and turned away.

"Very well," she said, walking across the room in a somewhat restless manner. "Then I shall continue to think highly of you, my dear. I only wish that your dear mama might know of this also, so that she, too, might consider you in such a light."

Hiding a smile, Marianne took one final glance in the mirror as

Lady Voss murmured something more, which Marianne did not hear.

"Where is your mother?" Lady Voss said as Marianne turned around. "Lord Castleton will be here at any moment and I must confess, I am surprised that neither she nor your father has joined us as yet."

A small, flickering frown crossed Marianne's brow as she realized the time. "You are right, Aunt," she agreed, crossing the room to ring the bell. "I know they have been fatigued after their journey, but I would not expect them to be—"

She was interrupted by the door opening and a footman stepping inside, ready to hear what was asked of him.

"Might you inform me as to where my father is?" Marianne asked. "And my mother also? Are they not ready to join us?"

The footman frowned, glancing to Lady Voss and then looking back at Marianne. "My lady, I—I thought Lord Gillingham to be in his study and Lady Gillingham to be in her bedchamber. Do you wish for me to confirm that their presence is—"

"Yes, yes, go at once," Lady Voss said, flapping her hands as she hurried the footman away. "And return quickly. We are expecting our guest at any moment."

The footman nodded, a startled expression on his face, before he turned and pulled the door tightly behind him, leaving both Marianne and Lady Voss to wait patiently for his return. Marianne's frown had not dissipated. Rather, it only grew, for what was her father doing remaining still in his study when he knew that Lord Castleton was to join them for dinner? It did not make sense to her that he should be doing such a thing, and certainly her mother would not still be resting either.

"I am sure that footman is mistaken," Lady Voss said with a quick smile that Marianne knew was meant to encourage her not to worry. "Your father might very well be merely assisting your mother with something, or simply being in her company until she is ready to join us. You know yourself that she has been very fatigued since her return."

Marianne nodded but did not quite manage to return her aunt's smile with one of her own. "Of course, Aunt," she murmured, moving so that she might sit down in a chair, only to rise again given the worry that began to flood her. This was her parents' first social occasion since their return to London and, given that it was a quiet dinner, not something that she had thought would tax them. Both of them had appeared to be very grateful to her for such consideration and had, from what they had said, been looking forward to such an event. Perhaps she had been wrong. Perhaps they had been unwilling to show her the full extent of their tiredness and had instead chosen to give an appearance of contentment.

"Do sit down, Marianne," Lady Voss demanded as Marianne shook her head. "You are beginning to tire me out with your pacing. I am sure that they will be with us in a moment and then what good will your worry have done you?"

Marianne did not answer. Clasping her hands together tightly, she continued to meander about the room, unable to sit still and wait for the return of the footman. Lady Voss said one or two things more, but Marianne did not hear them. Instead, she silently prayed that all would be well—and that Lord Castleton might himself be a little tardy.

A scratch came at the door and Marianne froze in place for a moment, before calling for the footman to come in. He entered at once, but it was not only he who stepped inside. With him came her mother's lady's maid, who, Marianne noted, had wide eyes and a somewhat pale face.

Fear clutched at her heart all over again.

"My lady," the footman said slowly, glancing from Marianne to Lady Voss. "Your mother...Lady Gillingham, she has not returned from her outing."

Marianne's breath caught as she turned to the lady's maid, who was now beginning to tremble.

"Outing?" she repeated as Lady Voss sank down into a chair, no longer filled with hope. "What is it you speak of?"

The lady's maid shook her head. "I did not know what to do," she replied, her voice barely loud enough for Marianne to hear. "I knew that my lady was taking a short walk with your father, but given that she had not returned, I presumed that she had chosen to remain so a little longer. It is not my place to chase after the lady." Her eyes began to swim with tears as she looked back at Marianne, clearly distraught. "I am sorry if I have done wrong."

Marianne closed her eyes and tried to drag in air, feeling her whole body tight with both anxiety and fear. She wanted to try and reassure the maid so that the lady might think calmly and clearly and might be able to tell them of anything else that Marianne might need to know, but for the moment, she herself was struggling to know what to say.

"Did you say that Lord Gillingham took a stroll with his wife?"

Marianne's eyes snapped open and she looked at Lady Voss, who had now fixed a hard gaze to the maid. Her aunt's coloring was almost grey and there was a whiteness about her lips as she practically glared at the maid, as though she were the one responsible for such a thing.

"I—I did not see them leave, Lady Voss," the maid replied, still struggling to inject any strength into her voice. "All I know is that my mistress intended to take a short walk with her husband and asked me to have her dinner things prepared for her return."

"Then do you know?" Marianne asked, finding her voice and gesturing toward the footman. "My father, did he step out with my mother?"

The footman spread his hands. "I do not know, my lady," he said with a lowering of his head. "But I can confirm that Lord Gillingham is not in his study."

Marianne's breathing began to quicken as she looked to her aunt and saw the fear that had begun to creep into Lady Voss' expression. There had to be something she herself could do, something that she could say that would allow them to find the explanation as to where her parents had gone.

"The butler will know," she said quickly. "Send for him."

The footman nodded, leaving the quietly crying lady's maid

standing alone as he quit the room. Marianne said nothing to her, turning on her heel and beginning to pace up and down the room again, waiting desperately for the butler to attend them and tell her what he knew.

There must be some simple explanation, she told herself as Lady Voss closed her eyes tightly and balled up her hands. *They must be nearby, surely? Unless they have forgotten the dinner and chose to accept an invitation to...*

That idea made very little sense, Marianne knew. The lady's maid had said her mother had asked her to prepare her things for dinner. Her father had mentioned to Marianne only that morning how much he was looking forward to speaking with Lord Castleton again. Neither of them could have forgotten what was to occur this evening.

The door opened again, and Marianne turned her head, seeing the butler hurry inside.

"My lady." He bowed low. "I have not meant to be tardy to your summons."

"My parents," Marianne said quickly. "I do not know where they are gone."

The butler spread his hands and, with a sad shake of his head, looked back at her.

"My lady, I, too, have been wondering the very same," he said, making Marianne realize that the butler had been all too aware of Lord and Lady Gillingham's absence long before she herself had realized it. "I knew that they had stepped out for a short time but had expected their return long before now. I have not wanted to alarm you, but I have sent one or two of the staff out to walk the streets in search of them."

It was this that made Marianne finally slump into a chair, her legs feeling weak and her body tired as she tried to take in what the butler was saying.

"Perhaps I should have informed you sooner, my lady," the butler continued, spreading his hands and inclining his head. "I did not want to worry you, but the truth must be spoken now."

"And the truth is?" Lady Voss asked, her sharp tone ringing across the room as Marianne's heart twisted painfully in her chest.

The butler hesitated for a moment and then looked directly into Marianne's face. "The truth is that we do not know where Lord and Lady Gillingham are gone," he said. His voice was very quiet indeed, but his words sounded to Marianne like a thunderclap, filling the room entirely and sending such a jolt through her that she shuddered violently.

"They are still looking, my lady," the butler continued, clearly hoping that this would be of some relief to Marianne. "I am sure they will find something."

"And where did my father state that they were going to?" Marianne asked, aware of just how hoarse her voice was. "Did he not tell you?"

The butler shook his head. "I am not always privy to the whereabouts of the master," he said, which Marianne had to admit she was already well aware of. "He stated that he and Lady Gillingham were to take a short stroll before they returned to prepare for dinner. The carriage was not sent for, my lady, and I do not think that they intended to hail a hackney."

Marianne closed her eyes tightly, a knot of tension forming in her stomach. "And they appeared in good spirits?" she asked, opening her eyes to see the butler nodding. "They were not upset or sorrowful?"

"No, my lady."

Looking to her aunt, Marianne took in her ashen face and felt her own heart struggle against panic and fear. What was she to do now? Where might her parents have gone?

"My lady," the butler continued, now lowering both his head and his gaze. "What is it that we should do? Is there someone nearby who would know of the master's whereabouts?"

Marianne shook her head. Yes, they had those who lived nearby but she did not think that her father would simply call upon them without invitation. "This is not to be spread through London," she told the butler, taking in a deep breath and forcing herself to speak calmly. "Tell the staff that if any of them breathe a word about my parents' absence then they shall be removed from this house without hesitation and with no promise of a reference." She lifted her chin and saw the butler nod, clearly understanding what it was she was asking him. "Thereafter, we must look through the house. Into each and every room."

Lady Voss half rose from her chair, her eyes wide. "Do you think that you might discover them, Marianne? Somewhere here?"

"We must be quite certain that they are not present," Marianne replied, even though she knew in her heart that to hope for such a thing was more than a little foolish. Her father was not likely to be hiding in the parlor, for example, given that there was a dinner to attend. "Have one of your trusted staff make discreet enquiries to others who live on this street. They must be nothing less than discreet, however."

"I know just the person to do so," the butler replied, glancing back at the footman, who nodded eagerly, clearly willing to do whatever he could to help. "I shall oversee the staff at once, my lady."

"I thank you." Marianne gestured to Lady Voss. "We will return here within the hour. If nothing is discovered, then we shall have to think of what we will do next."

The butler nodded and, having been dismissed, quit the room at once. It was only then, once the door had closed behind him, that Marianne allowed herself to break down. The tears that had been held behind her eyes for many minutes were finally allowed to come freely, her hands covering her face as she sank down into a chair and began to sob.

Lady Voss was with her in a moment.

"You need not worry, Marianne," she said, even though there was a slight tremor in her voice. "I am sure that they will be found."

Marianne shook her head, dropping her hands from her face and quickly accepting the handkerchief that her aunt had given her. "I do not think so, Aunt," she said brokenly. "There is no reasonable explanation for their absence." Tears continued to flow as she hiccupped back a sob, dabbing at her eyes. "I do not think we will find them anywhere."

"Then where might they have gone?" Lady Voss asked, and Marianne shook her head mutely. "There must be some explanation! Someone will have seen them."

Marianne swallowed hard and closed her eyes tightly, stemming the flow of tears. "What if there has been some dreadful accident?" she whispered as Lady Voss patted her hand gently. "What if they are both...?" She could not bring herself to say it and her aunt shook her head firmly, clearly refusing to accept such an idea.

"Then the staff would have heard of it, I am sure," came her aunt's reply. "If there had been some horrific accident, if there had been something that had endangered both your mother and your father, then do you not think that the staff would know of it?" A tiny smile lifted the corners of her mouth. "After all, you have given clear instructions to the staff to remain silent about your parents' absence because you know full well that any such gossip will be gone from their mouths in an instant, if they are not checked. They would have heard of such a thing, had it occurred. I am sure of it."

Sniffing, Marianne nodded, relieved that she had managed to push the tears from her eyes. "I should help search the house," she said slowly as Lady Voss nodded and rose to her feet. "I cannot simply sit here and wait."

"I will join you, of course," Lady Voss replied as Marianne made her way to the door. "Let me ring the bell to order tea for us both within the hour. I am sure we will both require it."

Marianne nodded and slipped from the room without another word. Taking in a deep breath, she closed her eyes and forced her anxiety from her. She would not allow it to continue to control her, not whilst she had a task to fulfill. She was not about to allow the staff to search for her parents whilst she remained silent and inactive. Making her way along the hallway, she was suddenly greeted by the sound of voices. Wondering at them for a moment, her heart leaping wildly in her chest as she felt a surge of hope, she quickly realized that it was not her parents who had returned but rather Lord Castleton who had arrived.

It was not frustration that filled her, or upset, or dread. Rather, there came a great swell of relief, as though she was truly glad to have his company with them now, at this dreadful moment. Finding her steps quickening, Marianne hurried toward him, seeing the footman turn to glance at her before backing away. Evidently the butler had not answered the door and therefore, a passing footman had been required to do so, but Marianne did not care about such a thing as that.

Tears began to burn in her eyes again as she reached him, finding herself suddenly desperate to be enfolded in his arms, to be reassured and comforted.

"Oh, Lord Castleton, you are come," she breathed, fully aware of the tears that now began to burn in her eyes again. "I am so relieved that you are here." Her hand found his and, as she looked up at him, Marianne could see the shock in his eyes. But then, after a moment, he pressed his other hand to hers and held it there, clearly aware that she was deeply upset.

"My dear lady," he began, his voice low and his eyes fixed to hers. "Is something troubling you? Has something occurred to upset you?"

Marianne nodded but found that she could not look up at him for fear of breaking down into tears once more. Dropping her gaze and sniffing in a most improper manner, she paused for a moment so that she might speak without difficulty. "It is my mother and father. They left the house this afternoon and have not returned."

"What do you mean?"

She looked back up at him again, her vision blurring as tears crept into her eyes. "I mean that my parents are missing."

Lord Castleton's eyes flared wide and he stared back at her, clearly waiting for her to say something more but, as Marianne looked back at him, beginning to realize that there was nothing more for her to say.

"You have sent the staff to look for them?" he asked, and Marianne nodded. "And they have not discovered either Lord or Lady Gillingham?"

"No," Marianne whispered softly. "No, they have not." She swallowed hard and forced herself to continue, fully aware that he was still holding her hand with both of his. "I did not realize their absence until a short time ago." Briefly she related all that she had learned and all that she had asked to be done, finding Lord Castleton nodding fervently.

"That is wise," he told her as she shuddered violently, suddenly feeling very fatigued indeed. "But you must rest now. Come, I will return you to the drawing room."

Marianne shook her head. "I cannot," she said, her voice wavering. "I must look for my—"

"You must rest," he interrupted, before she could insist. "Your color is very bad, Lady Marianne, and I am concerned for your welfare. I am easily able to search in the rooms that you yourself intended to, if that would ease your mind?"

Marianne hesitated, then nodded. "I thank you, Lord Castleton," she whispered as he slipped one hand about her waist and held onto her hand with the other, leading her back the way she had come. "I do hope that you will not speak of this to anyone."

"But of course, I would not," he replied firmly. "I quite understand your trepidation, Lady Marianne. I will not say a single word to any of my acquaintances or to yours, should you so wish it."

"I think very few are aware of my parents' return to London," Marianne replied as Lord Castleton continued to lead her toward the drawing room. "I cannot have this news become gossip."

"I quite understand," he told her, letting go of her waist to open the door to the drawing room, before leading Marianne inside. "I should not like such a thing to occur either." Seeing the room empty, he led her further inside and placed her gently in a chair. "Your aunt?" he asked, before going across the room to fill a glass with a small measure of brandy. "Is she present?"

"She will be looking through the house also," Marianne replied, surprised when Lord Castleton pressed the glass into her hands. "She is deeply upset."

Lord Castleton nodded. "Understandably so," he replied softly. "Now, Lady Marianne, it would be my advice for you to drink what you can of that brandy. It will help restore you."

Marianne looked back into his face, his brown eyes filled with such sympathy and concern that she felt tears spring back into her eyes. He had been so kind to her thus far, so good to her, and she had thought nothing but ill of him these last few days. Her throat ached and she attempted to thank him but found that she could not.

His hand found hers and settled upon it for a few minutes.

"There is no need to say more," he continued, as though he knew what she was trying to say. "You will be quite all right sitting here for a short time? I think it best to go in search of Lady Voss and bring her here to sit with you also."

Marianne nodded and, with a trembling hand, lifted the glass of brandy to her mouth and took a tiny sip. Fire erupted in her chest as she swallowed it, feeling the heat spread through her and chase some of her tiredness and fear away.

"Good," Lord Castleton replied, a small smile on his lips which, in turn, rose to touch his eyes. "I will return just as soon as I have found her. It will not be for long that you sit here."

Marianne looked into his face for another long moment before he finally rose and made to take his leave of her. Marianne watched him make his way to the door, finding herself speaking his name just as he pulled the door open.

"Lord Castleton?"

He looked back at her at once, clearly ready to return to her should she wish it. "Yes, Lady Marianne?"

"I—I thank you."

His smile was immediate, spreading across his face and lighting his eyes gently. "But of course, Lady Marianne," came the quiet reply. "You are not alone in this. Of that, I give you my full assurance."

She managed a small but tentative smile back at him as he quit the room, before finally sinking back into the chair, resting her head back and closing her eyes.

You are not alone in this.

That was a small comfort to her, knowing that now, at the very least, she had both Lady Voss and Lord Castleton present to help her find out where her parents had gone. All she needed now was to find them and restore them to both this house and herself. To have them remain absent from her, without explanation or understanding, was not worth thinking about.

5

The evening had not gone well. James rubbed one hand down his face as he looked at his tired reflection in the mirror, realizing just how haggard he looked and knowing that it came from an otherwise sleepless night. His thoughts had been tormented and troubled for he had hated having to leave Lady Marianne and her aunt behind when they were both so distressed. And yet, there had been nothing else for him to do.

Lord and Lady Gillingham had not been discovered and, in fact, there had been no sign of their whereabouts. The servants had known nothing of their absence, the footman dispatched to the surrounding townhouses had returned with nothing of use, and the search of the house had yielded nothing of note. It was as though the couple had set foot outside and had disappeared into the wind, leaving no trace behind them.

Lady Marianne had been both greatly distressed and yet, in her own way, very calm indeed. She had managed to listen to his suggestions without interruption, had not broken down into sobs or hysterics. Lady Voss had said very little, her eyes filled with tears for a large part of the evening, but as yet, she had not come up with any other suggestions or ideas as to where Lord and Lady Gillingham might have gone.

James closed his eyes and let out a long, heavy breath. He wished that he had been able to come up with a reasonable suggestion, or had thought of something to say or do that might help Lady Marianne, but he had found himself quite lost. There appeared to be nothing further for them to do other than to send out a few servants into the ether of London in search of the lord and lady and pray that, somehow, they would be given some sort of hint as to where they had gone.

"My lord?"

James turned around, seeing his butler standing in the door. "Yes?"

"You have an urgent note, my lord. I thought to bring it to you at once."

Quickly, James beckoned him toward him and took the note, asking his butler to wait for a moment should it be something that he had to respond to. Breaking the seal and realizing just how quickly his heart was beating, James unfolded the letter and read it quickly.

His eyes closed for a moment and then he folded up the note.

"Have the carriage prepared," he said as the butler nodded. "And send my valet to my room. I am to visit Lady Marianne and Lady Voss."

"At once, my lord," the butler replied, evidently aware of the urgency with which James wanted to depart. "At once."

James nodded, watching his butler leave, before he made his way to the window and looked out, unseeing of the view below him. He let out another long breath, trying to calm his whirling thoughts. It seemed that Lady Marianne had been unable to sleep well either, for she had begged him to join her just as soon as he was able. The note had not said whether or not there had been any further progress in the search for her parents, but James had to wonder if it was so. Was that why she was eager for him to call?

"Lady Marianne." James bowed low as Lady Marianne came toward him, her hands outstretched.

"Lord Castleton," she said as he took both her hands in his, seeing Lady Voss looking away for a moment, as though she was a little embarrassed by her niece behaving so. "I want to thank you for calling upon us this morning, as well as for all your assistance last evening."

"But of course," James replied, pressing her hands gently. "I quite understand, Lady Marianne. I am only glad that I was present in order to assist you." He let go of her hands, turning to address Lady Voss. "Good morning, Lady Voss."

"Good morning." She turned her head back to look at him and he was struck by the change in her appearance. Her eyes were dull, her cheeks appearing sunken and her pallor almost grey. Clearly, she had spent a very disturbed night also. "Thank you for calling, Lord Castleton. I believe we need as much assistance in this matter as possible."

James cleared his throat, inwardly wondering what it was he could do to help further. "Of course, Lady Voss. I am sure that you and Lady Marianne must be finding this situation very difficult indeed."

Lady Voss closed her eyes and nodded. "We are," she said softly as Lady Marianne rang the bell, before gesturing for James to sit down. "It is deeply troubling."

"Then there has been nothing of note?" James asked, and Lady Marianne gave him a quick glance. "You have heard nothing? Discovered nothing?"

Lady Marianne exchanged a look with her aunt before she answered, spreading her hands. "It seems that my parents were seen climbing into a carriage," she said quietly. "One of the servants was told this by another who works for Lord Stockbridge, who lives a short distance away. When he was asked whether or not he knew who was within, the footman said he did not. Nor could he recollect very much about it."

"I can understand that," James murmured, just as the door opened so that the maids could bring in the tea tray. "There must be a great many carriages going about."

"And a footman would not notice any of them in particular," Lady Voss added, nodding to the maid, who quickly scurried from the room. "But, for whatever reason, we know now that Lord and Lady Gillingham went with someone else."

"And you have no thought as to why that might have been?" James asked, and Lady Voss shook her head. "They did not say to either of you that they had other plans?"

"I did not know they even intended to step out for a short walk," Lady Marianne replied, throwing up her hands in evident exasperation. "I hurried home and then quickly made my way to my room so that I might prepare for dinner. I did not meet them before then. I did not speak to my mother for I thought I would be in her company very soon later that evening." Her eyes began to swim with tears as she looked back at James, although she managed to keep her composure. "I would never disturb my father when he is in his study, unless there was no other choice. Thus, I had no knowledge whatsoever that they intended to leave the house for a short time."

"And they both were eagerly looking forward to the dinner with you, Lord Castleton," Lady Voss added as Lady Marianne nodded fervently. "Lord Gillingham, in particular, was very keen to speak to you again. I cannot think that they deliberately chose something other than joining both you and Marianne for dinner."

James frowned. "Then you believe that their joining this person in the carriage was not something that had been planned?"

"I would suggest it was not planned at all," Lady Voss replied firmly. "It was clearly just on the spur of the moment and mayhap, they did not think that they would be a prolonged length of time."

Accepting a cup of tea from Lady Marianne, James allowed

himself to consider what he had been told. Had Lord and Lady Gillingham climbed into that carriage willingly?

"There was no sign of difficulty when Lord and Lady Gillingham took to the carriage?" he asked as Lady Marianne hesitated, her cup halfway to her mouth. "The footman did not get the impression that they were forced inside?"

At this, Lady Marianne shook her head. "No, I do not believe so," she said softly. "That was not asked specifically, of course, but I could certainly have the footman asked again."

James shook his head. "I believe he would have noticed had there been anything of concern," he replied as Lady Marianne finally took a sip of her tea. "Then it must have been a friend that they joined? Perhaps they walked a little further than they intended and were offered—"

"No, that cannot be so," Lady Voss interrupted. "Lord Stockbridge does not live very far from this house, so it could not be so."

"Then might there have been a request for them to join whoever was in the carriage for a short drive?" James asked as Lady Marianne spread her hands. "I suppose the question then becomes who was it that was within the carriage?"

Lady Marianne nodded. "It might well be as you have suggested," she replied honestly, "but until we can know who it was within the carriage, we can only make suggestions rather than consider anything of true importance."

"And that will be practically impossible," Lady Voss replied with a sadness in her voice that James could only sympathize with. "If we are to do our best to keep this from the *ton*, then how are we to discover where they have gone?"

James straightened. "You do not wish to tell anyone else?" he asked, a little surprised. "Surely that would not be wise?"

Lady Voss shook her head. "It would send nothing but rumors and whispers all through London about Lord and Lady Gillingham," she explained as James frowned hard. "There were so few of his acquaintances that knew he was returned to London. If we tell all and sundry that they have disappeared, then what good will it do? It will only spread such whispers throughout the *beau monde* about them that, no doubt, people will begin to think ill of them. The whispers will turn to gossip, and all manner of things might be suggested. I cannot allow that to occur, not when I must care for Marianne and her reputation also."

Hesitating, James bit back his first response, realizing what Lady Voss meant. Personally, he would have suggested that they ask almost everyone they were acquainted with if they had seen Lord and Lady Gillingham, but in considering what Lady Voss had said, he now realized that such an idea might not be the best one. Lady Marianne had been seen chaperoned by Lady Voss and, for the moment, that could continue.

"Then you intend to hide this from the *ton* for as long as you can?" he asked, and Lady Marianne nodded. "Might I suggest that you tell one or two trusted friends, however? Only one or two who might then be able to assist and support you a little more?"

Lady Marianne took another sip of her tea and then looked back at him, her eyes clear. "I do not know anyone of that description," she answered with a faint, rueful smile. "Those I am acquainted with, even those I would consider to be almost friends, are not those who would keep such a thing secret."

"Then," James countered, "might I suggest that Lord Wright be told? He is a trustworthy gentleman and could be of further assistance to you, I am sure."

It only took a moment of hesitation before Lady Marianne nodded. "Very well," she said, just as there came a knock at the door. "If you believe him trustworthy and that he will also be of help, then I would be contented with you speaking to him." She then called for the footman to enter and he came in at once.

"This arrived for you, my lady," he murmured as James watched Lady Marianne pick up a small note, which bore a blank wax seal. Lady Marianne frowned, then dismissed him, before setting the note aside and picking up her tea, clearly aware that to read it now when he was present might well be considered rude.

"Lady Marianne," James said, choosing his words with great

care so that he would not offend her. "Might I suggest that you open that note at once?"

Lady Marianne looked a little surprised. "I do not think it will be anything other than a message from one of my acquaintances," she replied with a small shrug. "It does not need to be given my attention at this moment."

"If that were so," James replied swiftly, "then would it not have a seal pressed into the wax?"

It was clear that Lady Marianne had not noticed such a thing, for she turned the letter over at once and looked at it blankly, only for her breath to catch in a small gasp as she realized what he meant. James felt his heart quicken as she broke the wax and unfolded the letter, seeing how her hand pressed lightly to her heart as she read it. He kept back the questions that now dogged his mind, desperate to learn who had written the note and what it said but knowing that he had to give the lady time to read and absorb what had been written there.

"It—it has been written by my mother."

Lady Voss threw herself out of her chair and rushed across the room to where Lady Marianne was. Lady Marianne rose from her seat and handed the note to her aunt, who read it feverishly, before letting out a small moan. James did not know what to do, wondering if Lady Marianne would offer him the note or if he should ask to read it.

"Lord Castleton?" Lady Marianne looked toward him, and James pushed himself out of his chair, standing a trifle awkwardly as he looked back into her pale face.

"Yes, Lady Marianne?"

She held out the note. "If you would."

Taking it from her, he let his eyes scan the page quickly, reading each word with great haste before beginning to read it again for the second time so that he might make certain he had taken it all in.

"And you are sure this is from your mother?" he asked, and Lady Marianne nodded. "The writing is hers?"

"It is," Lady Marianne replied softly as he took a small step closer to her. "I am certain of it."

James shook his head and blew out a long breath, realizing that what he had read then must have come from Lady Gillingham. There was no question of it.

"Then what are you going to do?"

Lady Marianne just looked at him, her hands spread.

"You will do as she asks?"

"What else can I do?" Lady Marianne whispered as Lady Voss flopped into a chair, waving her hand in front of her face as though she was near to fainting. "My mother has requested that I find her emerald earrings for her. She does not state where she is or why she wishes to have them, only that I am to find them for her and have them prepared. That they should be with me when I attend Lord Worthington's ball tomorrow evening." Her hands spread wide. "What else is there for me to do, Lord Castleton, but to do as she asks?"

James ran one hand over his eyes as a knot began to tie itself in his stomach. Something was very unsettling, something that he was very troubled by, and yet there was nothing to state exactly what such a thing was.

"You have said that only a few people have known of your parents' return to London?" he said hurriedly as an idea suddenly came to him. "Not a great number?"

Lady Marianne nodded, taking back the letter from him before folding it up again and lowering her head as she did so. "Indeed."

"Then might you know who such people are?" James asked, taking another step closer to her so that he might grasp her hand, forcing her to look up into his eyes. "Do you not see, Lady Marianne? If we have a list of those who knew of your father's return to London, then we will be able to discern which of his acquaintances or friends we should consider."

His fingers tightened on hers and, after a long moment, Lady Marianne finally pressed them back.

"I understand what you mean," she said slowly as a faint light began to flicker in her eyes. "There is a little hope there, I think."

"We will have *something* to consider, at least," James replied as Lady Voss dropped her hand and sat up a little straighter. "And whilst I agree that there is nothing for you to do but to obey the request your mother has written to you, that does not mean that you should remain entirely in the dark as regards her whereabouts."

Lady Marianne lifted her chin and took in a long, steadying breath that seemed to quieten her upset a little. "You will help us, Lord Castleton?"

"You *know* that I will," he assured her, feeling a sense of determination grip his heart. "I will do all that I can to aid you in this, Lady Marianne. And I am quite sure that, very soon, we will be able to discover the truth about what has occurred. You will be reunited with Lord and Lady Gillingham again, very soon, I hope."

Lady Marianne nodded, sighed, and let go of his hand. "Then shall we make for my father's study?" she asked as Lady Voss closed her eyes tightly and leaned her head back against the chair. "I am sure he has written to a few of his acquaintances to inform them of his return to London. Perhaps he has had a few replies."

"That would be very helpful indeed," James replied as Lady Marianne made for the door. "Lady Voss? Do you wish to join us?"

With a great effort, the lady opened her eyes, grasped the arms of the chair, and pushed herself out of it. When James offered his arm, she took it at once, however, although a sense of grim determination seemed to come over her as she looked back at him.

"Of course I will join you," she stated with more firmness than he had expected in her voice. "We must discover the truth, Lord Castleton, just as you have said."

"And we will," he answered, injecting as much confidence as he could into his words. "I have no doubt, Lady Voss, that we will. It may just take a little more time."

6

Marianne took in a deep breath and lifted her chin, forcing a smile to her face that she did not truly feel. The last place she wanted to be this evening was at a ball where she would be expected to dance and to smile and to laugh, but there was no other choice open to her. If her mother had requested that she bring the earrings to the ball, then of course, she was required to do so.

"Do you think your dear mama will be here this evening?" Lady Voss asked as they walked into the ballroom. "I do hope so. I hope that she will be able to give us a clear explanation as to what has happened to her."

Marianne shook her head, her heart already fully prepared to accept the fact that her mother would *not* be present this evening. She did not expect to see her, did not expect that she would simply come close to Marianne and that all would be well. There was reason and purpose behind Lady Gillingham's letter and Marianne believed that, much to her upset, her mother was in a difficult situation. No, she would not be here this evening but, somehow, the emerald earrings would be taken from Marianne and secreted away for some purpose or other.

"You do not think that she will be here?"

"I do not believe so, Aunt," Marianne replied, even though her eyes quickly searched through the crowd for any sign of her mother or father. "Somehow, the earrings will be taken from me. Of that, I am quite certain."

Lady Voss' hope faded from her eyes. "I do wish that you could tell someone of what has occurred," she muttered, although Marianne quickly reminded her that she had both Lord Castleton and, she presumed, Lord Wright now able to help her.

Yesterday morning, Lady Voss had been of very little help as Marianne and Lord Castleton had searched through her father's study, with Marianne hating every moment of it. She had been required to do it, of course, but still, it had felt very wrong indeed to be rooting through her father's private correspondence.

Lady Voss had sat in a corner of the room and observed, one hand pressed to her heart and a deep sorrow written across her face. She had let Marianne and Lord Castleton search without interruption and when, finally, they had accumulated the replies their father had received, had shown no great interest in the list of names they compiled. It had been as though the shock was much too great for the lady and thus, she had become a shadow of her former self.

This evening, however, Lady Voss appeared to be a little more recovered, although Marianne feared that the determination to assist her in all that she was doing would fade within a very short time, just as it had done yesterday when she had accompanied them to the study.

"Good evening, Lady Marianne."

Recognizing Lord Wright, Marianne curtsied quickly as he bowed. "Good evening, Lord Wright."

"Lord Castleton has told me of your troubles," he said quietly as Marianne nodded. "I am sorry to hear of them."

"I appreciate your sympathy," Marianne told him as he greeted Lady Voss. "It was very fortunate that Lord Castleton appeared when he did. From what the footman told me, I believe he was a little insulted at first and might well have stormed from the house without knowing the truth of our difficulty."

Lord Wright nodded and smiled. "But of course," he replied softly. "I am sure that he has been of great help to you, Lady Marianne. I only hope that I can do something to assist you also."

Marianne smiled back at him, feeling her heart begin to lose a little of its sorrow. "Again, I am greatly appreciative of your willingness, Lord Wright. Has Lord Castleton shared the list of gentlemen and ladies who knew of my parents' arrival back in London?"

Lord Wright nodded again. "He has," he replied. "But it is only a short list, no?"

"It has four names," Marianne answered. "Those are the ones that we know my father wrote to, however." Spreading her hands, she gave him a rueful smile. "We cannot know if there are others that he wrote to also."

"Nevertheless, it is something that we can begin with," Lord Wright replied, speaking with more seriousness than Marianne had ever heard from him before. "Lord Castleton is, at this moment, seeing which gentlemen and ladies are present this evening."

Marianne allowed herself another smile. "That is very good of him," she answered, thinking very highly of Lord Castleton now and realizing just how much he was doing for her. "I presume, however, that most of them will be present?"

Lord Wright smiled back at her, albeit wryly. "Indeed," he said quietly. "And the earrings are still within your reticule?"

She nodded, her chest tightening for a moment as she remembered what she had with her. "Yes."

"Then make certain to keep them with you or with Lady Voss," Lord Wright replied as Lady Voss nodded. "But in the meantime, you must look as though this is merely another ball for you attend —and an enjoyable one at that." He inclined his head. "Might I ask for your dance card, Lady Marianne? I promise I shall not steal the best of your dances."

"I am not inclined to dance this evening," Marianne replied, although she took off her dance card from her wrist regardless. "And yet I suppose I must."

"If you do not wish the *ton* to ask why you are not doing so, then yes, I fear you must do so," Lord Wright replied with a wearied look about him. "I quite understand that there is no desire within you to find any enjoyment this evening, but there will be many watching you, I am sure."

A trace of alarm ran through Marianne's frame. "Watching me?"

Lord Wright glanced up at her from where he was writing his name. "As they always do," he explained, making Marianne realize he had not meant anything sinister by the statement. "There are many older ladies in particular who watch the young ladies as they dance and converse. I am sure that is all they enjoy."

He handed her the dance card and Marianne took it from him, seeing the cotillion and the country dance were both his.

"And here is Lord Castleton," he said, making Marianne turn her head to see the very gentleman approaching, although there was no easy smile on his face.

She dropped into a quick curtsy. "Good evening, Lord Castleton."

"Good evening." He bowed low and then looked expectantly at her dance card, which she still held in her hand. "Might I be as equally honored as Lord Wright?" he asked, and Marianne smiled at him, remembering that she was to give the impression that all was well. "I do hope there is space on your dance card for my name also."

"You shall only be the second, Lord Castleton," Marianne replied, handing the dance card to him. "Lord Wright told me that you were searching the ballroom for those on the list?" Swallowing the sudden ache in her throat, she took a moment to ask her question. "Are they all present?"

Lord Castleton finished writing his name and then shook his head. "Not all, no," he replied, looking back at her as he handed her the dance card. "Lord and Lady West are absent this evening."

She nodded slowly, biting her lip for a moment as she thought.

She did not see how Lord Castleton watched her, nor did she see the worry that etched itself across his features as he saw her considering matters.

"Then I suppose that would mean that Lord and Lady West do not have any knowledge of my parents' whereabouts," Marianne said slowly, slipping her dance card back onto her wrist without even glancing at it. "If they are absent, then they cannot do anything as regards the emerald earrings I still have in my possession."

"Perhaps," Lord Castleton replied, although by the slowness of his response, Marianne realized that she had made too quick an assumption. "They could easily dispatch someone else to fetch the earrings for them, if it comes to that. But," he continued with a small smile, "I have no real idea of what will occur when it comes to those earrings. You may very well be correct."

Marianne nodded but said nothing, wishing she knew precisely what was to happen. There was a great deal of anxiety within her and a fear in her heart that would not leave her, she knew, until the ball had come to an end.

"That is our dance, Lady Marianne," Lord Castleton said gently, interrupting her thoughts. "Of course, I have chosen two so if you would prefer to remain here at present, then I am more than contented to—"

"But of course, Lord Castleton, forgive me," Marianne said quickly, handing her reticule to Lady Voss. "I am to make all the appearances of happiness, am I not? To continue as though all is quite well." She smiled as brightly as she could and accepted the offer of his arm. "Shall we?"

THE DANCE WENT VERY WELL INDEED and, thereafter, Marianne found herself quite caught up in the evening. There seemed to be no time to even think of her reticule and the earrings within it, for if she was not conversing with someone, she was then dancing with another. It was as every other ball had been, save for the fact that she was continually looking about her and wondering whether or not the person drawing near to her might, in fact, be seeking the earrings.

"Again, it is our dance, Lady Marianne."

Surprised at the swell of relief that filled her heart, Marianne bobbed a quick curtsy toward Lord Castleton, once more handing her reticule to Lady Voss. "Our second dance, Lord Castleton," she commented as he smiled at her. "What is it to be? I confess I have not even looked as yet."

He cleared his throat and inclined his head, making Marianne wonder if she had embarrassed him by admitting to such a thing. "The waltz, Lady Marianne. I do hope that is satisfactory."

"But of course." They walked to the middle of the ballroom, ready to begin the dance and allowing Marianne a few moments of respite. "It is a relief to be dancing with you," she told him as he looked at her in surprise. "I have been dancing with all manner of gentlemen and none, save for Lord Wright, know of the pain in my heart and the troubled thoughts in my mind. I have had to play a part and, I confess, I have found it very wearying indeed."

Lord Castleton gave her a half-smile, bowed, and stepped forward to take her into his arms. Marianne went willingly although, much to her surprise, she felt her body tense just a little as he settled his hand at her waist. The music began and Marianne allowed him to lead her, settling into a rhythm of rising and falling as they traversed the floor. Marianne held Lord Castleton's gaze, looking up into his eyes and considering just how much her opinion of him had changed within such a short space of time.

"You are studying me, I think," Lord Castleton murmured as he continued to lead her in the dance. "It must be greatly displeasing for you to have me be the one to come to your assistance. I am sorry for that."

"But why should you think so?" Marianne asked, catching her breath as he twirled her quickly. Taking a deep breath to regain herself, she tried to understand his meaning. "I can assure you,

Lord Castleton, that I am very grateful to you for what you have done thus far, and for the support and the help you have given to both myself and Lady Voss."

"If only I had not been already in your disfavor, then I am sure that would have made things a good deal easier for you," he replied, grimacing. "I only hope that I can improve your opinion of me, Lady Marianne. Although, of course, I would aid you regardless."

Finally understanding what the gentleman meant, Marianne did the only thing she could and pressed his fingers tightly as he held her hand.

"Lord Castleton, I have already forgotten about all that passed between us prior to this," she told him truthfully. "That matters naught. The only things that I consider when it comes to you are your willingness and your sense in this matter. I can assure you there is nothing more that I bring to mind."

Lord Castleton did not say anything to her in response to this. They danced the rest of the waltz in silence, but Marianne was sure that he tugged her gently just a little closer to him as they danced.

"You are both forgiving and considerate, Lady Marianne." Lord Castleton's expression was sincere as he bowed low, their dance now at an end. "I am truly grateful to you for your selflessness and willingness to forgive."

Marianne took his arm and together, they walked back to where Lady Voss was standing, talking to another lady Marianne did not know. Her heart suddenly quickened as she began to wonder if this was someone on the list that Lord Castleton had put together.

"That is Lady Forester," Lord Castleton muttered quietly as they approached. "Your father did not write to Lord Forester about his return, as far as we know."

Her heart sank before a feeling of ridiculousness washed over her. Part of her had hoped that Lady Forester would be the one to take the emerald earrings and that, therefore, they would be able to demand answers from her—but that, she realized, would have been much too obvious.

"Ah, Marianne," Lady Voss smiled, looking a good deal brighter than Marianne had seen her in the last two days. "Might I introduce you to Lady Forester? She is a very dear friend of mine and has only just returned to London."

Marianne smiled, curtsied, and greeted the lady and, for a few minutes, the four of them passed conversation together. Eventually, Lady Forester took her leave and Marianne turned to her aunt.

"My reticule?"

Lady Voss nodded and slipped it from her wrist, handing it to her. Marianne opened it at once, feeling the urge to make certain the earrings were still there—only to discover that the small box she had placed inside was gone.

Her breath caught in her chest as she stared up at her aunt, whose smile then immediately fell to the floor.

"No," Lady Voss breathed as Lord Castleton frowned hard, stepping a little closer. "It cannot be."

"They are gone, I am sure of it," Marianne replied, her heart tearing at a furious pace in her chest. "Oh, Aunt, say you did not give my reticule to anyone?"

Lady Voss shook her head. "I did not," she said primly, only for her eyes to widen and a stricken look to come over her face. "That is to say, I may have done but it was only for a moment. A moment, I assure you!"

Marianne closed her eyes and let out a long breath. "Then who else had my reticule, Aunt?"

Lady Voss closed her eyes tightly, her lips thin and flat. "The footman offered me a glass of ratafia, and I thought to fetch one for you also. I—I set the reticule down on the table to my left so that I might pick up two glasses. That is all."

Lord Castleton clasped his hands behind his back, looking grave. "Might I ask how long it sat there for?" he asked as Lady Voss' eyes began to fill with tears. "I do not mean to blame you, Lady Voss, pray do not feel any guilt."

Lady Voss closed her eyes tightly and then let out a shuddering breath. "It was just to my left for a few minutes, I am sure of it," she said, her voice tremulous. "I did not mean to behave foolishly."

"I can see that you did not," Marianne replied, pushing her anger down so that she did not reveal it to her aunt. Lady Voss had clearly made an error in judgment and Marianne did not want her to feel any worse than she already did at present. To cause strife between herself and Lady Voss would not be wise. "But if it was to your left, then you must not have always been able to see it?"

"It was out of my sight for only a moment!" Lady Voss exclaimed, clearly distraught. "I thought nothing of it. I reached to set down your glass on another table and then turned to pick it up again. I am sure that no one could have done so." She opened her mouth again, only to close it, her eyes suddenly widening. "Although," she continued, her voice a good deal quieter now, "I am sure that the footman who was present had offered such refreshment to me this evening already. Perhaps on two occasions?"

Lord Castleton put a comforting hand on Lady Voss' arm. "I quite understand," he said in a calm voice that seemed to bring a quietness to Marianne's heart even though his words were directed toward her aunt. "Now, can I ask if you recall anyone who was near to you when you spoke to the footman? Did he himself linger? If he was already near to you earlier this evening, then that may be of importance."

Lady Voss squeezed her eyes closed again, her lips tight. "I—I do not know," she said eventually. "The footman lingered, certainly, but there may have been other guests near to me or passing by me, but I did not even glance at them."

Marianne frowned. "Mayhap we should find the footman in question," she suggested as Lord Castleton nodded in agreement. "It may be that he might be aware of those who passed by."

"Or has the emeralds, given that he has been close to your aunt this evening," Lord Castleton replied gravely. "What say you, Lady Voss? I am aware that there are a great many footmen present and certainly, it might be difficult to recall his face, but—"

"I will be able to find him," Lady Voss interrupted determinedly. "I have no doubt."

Lord Castleton nodded, throwing a glance toward Marianne, who allowed herself a tiny smile before looking to her aunt.

"Shall we take a turn about the room then, Aunt?" she asked, and Lady Voss nodded fervently. "And tell us the moment you recognize him."

"I shall," Lady Voss replied, before taking Marianne's arm and stepping out across the ballroom.

7

James walked slowly behind Lady Voss and Lady Marianne as the ladies made their way through the crowd of guests. It was most unusual to be looking for a footman rather than for acquaintances and the like, but this was, he supposed, a rather uncommon situation. He knew that Lady Voss was more than a little upset over her lack of wise consideration and he himself had to admit that he was irritated by it also. Most likely, the enjoyment of the ball had helped Lady Voss forget some of the severity of their circumstances and thus, she had not been as careful as she ought.

The realization that, in the few moments the reticule had been sitting by itself, someone had reached out to take it sent a flare of alarm through James, for he now understood that someone, somehow, must have been watching Lady Voss and, mayhap, Lady Marianne, very closely indeed. To know that the earrings were in the reticule would not have been a difficult assumption, for where else would a young lady keep such a thing? Whoever it was that had urged Lady Gillingham to write to request the earrings had taken note of Lady Marianne and Lady Voss' arrival and had waited for an opportunity since that moment.

Quite what they would have done if Lady Voss had *not* set the reticule down, James did not know. Would they have taken it by force? Snatched it from Lady Marianne's fingers before hiding themselves amongst the other guests?

"I do not see him anywhere," he heard Lady Voss say, her voice rather high and filled with a great anxiety. "This crush—it is too great. Too many people are present for me to be able to single out a single servant."

James let out a long breath and tried not to allow frustration to capture him. "I have a suggestion," he remarked as Lady Voss turned to look back at him. "Whilst it would be preferable to find the fellow this evening, in the hope that he might have what you seek, if we cannot do so, there is an alternative."

Lady Voss' eyes widened. "Yes?"

"We should simply return come the morrow," James replied, a little tightly given the irritation that now ran through him. "I will speak to Lord Worthington and will come up with some excuse as to why you wish to view all of his footmen. When you identify the one in particular, there will be an opportunity then to speak to him, to ask him what we wish to know."

Lady Marianne looked up at her aunt, her face still a little white. "What say you, Aunt?" she asked as Lady Voss closed her eyes tightly. "I know that you wish to find this footman, but we have now made our way around the ballroom three times and as yet, have seen no sign of him."

"And that may be deliberate," James added as Lady Voss opened her eyes. "He may now be hiding as best he can, to make sure that what we intend does not come to pass. If it *is* he who was somehow involved in taking the earrings from your reticule."

"It appears that I have very little choice," Lady Voss replied heavily. "I have been foolish, I know. I am very sorry indeed, Marianne." Turning to her niece, she took her hand and pressed it hard. "I behaved foolishly and now we are in a predicament where the earrings are gone, and we have very little idea as to where they are or what happened. I am truly sorry."

For a moment, James wondered if Lady Marianne would speak of the frustration that was within her heart, the frustration that he had seen in her expression when she had first heard from her aunt all that had occurred. But, after a moment, Lady Marianne sighed, shook her head, and then smiled briefly back at Lady Voss.

"Do not torment yourself further, Aunt," she said as admiration slowly began to build in James' heart. "It will do you no good. What has occurred is not something that we can change and thus, we must now consider what we are to do next rather than allow our minds to be filled with regret and other heavy thoughts."

Lady Voss nodded although James did not miss the gleam of tears in the lady's eyes. His consideration of Lady Marianne grew steadily, seeing how she set aside her own feelings and spoke with gentleness and understanding. Yet again, she proved to him just how generous she could be.

"Then I shall find Lord Worthington and will arrange something for tomorrow," he said, bowing low. "I do hope you enjoy the rest of the evening as much as you can, Lady Voss, Lady Marianne. Do excuse me."

Lady Marianne bobbed a quick curtsy in response. "Thank you, Lord Castleton," she replied quietly as he looked at her, seeing the softness about her eyes. "We are both very grateful to you for your help."

James nodded, smiled briefly, and stepped away, making certain to push all manner of feelings and emotions away. He had no time to consider the look in Lady Marianne's eyes as she had spoken to him, no time to think of just how wonderful he found her character to be. There was an arrangement to be made and James had to fix his mind solely on making it. Anything else could be considered later.

"Good afternoon, Lord Castleton."

"Good afternoon, Lord Worthington." Bowing, James quickly

stepped aside and allowed Lord Worthington to greet Lady Voss and Lady Marianne. They both smiled and curtsied, hiding their true emotions from the gentleman, whilst James himself knew that both felt rather anxious, given what had been said in the carriage they had shared on their way to visit Lord Worthington.

"I understand that you wish to look at each of my footmen, Lady Voss," Lord Worthington spoke, a broad smile spreading across his face as he spoke. "Something about one of them being able to tell you what you did with a particular item?" He glanced at James, who merely nodded and waited for Lady Voss to speak.

She nodded, her eyes darting from James to Lord Worthington as though she were afraid that the latter would not believe her explanation. "Yes, that is it precisely," she replied, speaking with great haste. "I set down my reticule last evening, just as your footman was serving ratafia. I do hope that he knows where I placed it."

Lord Worthington accepted this explanation without any sort of hesitation. "I quite understand," he said gallantly, before offering Lady Voss his arm. "Come, dear lady, and allow me to take you to the ballroom, where I have had the footmen assembled."

Lady Voss took his arm at once, although she threw a sharp look toward Lady Marianne, clearly expecting her to follow. James stepped forward and, following Lord Worthington's example, offered his arm to Lady Marianne, who took it after only a moment of hesitation.

"Do you think that we will be successful?" she whispered as Lord Worthington led the way, exclaiming loudly over the triumph of his ball the previous evening. "What if the footman is no longer present?"

"I am sure that he will be," James replied grimly. "A footman cannot simply toss aside his employment, not without good reason. I highly doubt that he will have been able to do so. No, we will discover him here and will have to ask him about what occurred last night. Whether or not he will inform us of such, particularly when his master is present, I do not know."

Lady Marianne's hand tightened on his arm for the briefest of moments. "I will be able to distract Lord Worthington, surely?" she said as James turned his head to look at her. "What I mean to say is that I can direct his attention elsewhere, which might, in turn, allow this footman to speak a little more openly."

Considering this for a moment, James nodded. "I suppose that would be a wise suggestion," he said, although he had to admit that the thought of Lady Marianne walking with Lord Worthington in such a manner as they were doing at present sent an uncomfortable tightness to his chest. "Lady Voss and I might be able to encourage a little more from the footman, should his master be... distracted, as you have suggested."

She glanced at him, gave him a quick smile, and then looked away. There was a deep sense of anxiety within her heart, James knew, and he could not blame her for it. The fact that both Lord and Lady Gillingham were still absent and had not returned was a great trial indeed and James only wished there was more that he could do to comfort her.

"And here they all are."

James walked into the ballroom to see the footmen all neatly assembled in a long line.

"Speak to whichever one you please, Lady Voss," Lord Worthington continued, letting go of the lady's hand and stepping back so that he might give her a small bow. "They are entirely at your disposal."

Lady Marianne gently removed her hand from James' arm and, with a quick look in his direction, moved directly toward Lord Worthington. Rather than watch her capture Lord Worthington's attention, James made his way to where Lady Voss now stood, seeing her look at the footmen assembled there and praying silently to himself that the one she recalled would still be present.

"Come, Lady Voss," he said, moving forward so that they might go a little closer to the first. "The moment you identify him, you must—"

"It is that one."

The exclamation that came from Lady Voss' mouth echoed around the room and James winced inwardly, closing his eyes as the words spun around the room, seeming to bounce from the walls and growing in intensity.

A laugh caught his attention and he turned his head to see Lady Marianne smiling up at Lord Worthington, who now had his back to them although one hand was lifted, gesturing to something on the wall. For a moment, James was transfixed, looking at the lady in question and seeing the brightness of her eyes, the delighted smile, and the slight color in her cheeks, and finding his own heart squeezing tightly.

"I am certain," Lady Voss said, dragging James' attention away from Lady Marianne. "That is the one who served me ratafia last evening."

James looked directly at the one servant that Lady Voss was indicating, noting to himself that the gentleman appeared to be a little paler than before. He stood just as a footman ought, however, a calm expression on his face, with eyes that fixed themselves to a point somewhere near to the shoulders of both himself and Lady Voss, although he looked beyond them as though there was something of great interest across the floor of the ballroom.

"The rest of you are dismissed," James said quietly, hearing Lady Marianne's gentle laughter and telling himself not to become distracted by it. "You there. Come forward."

The footman in question stepped a little closer whilst the others dispersed, clearly relieved that they were not about to be questioned by James.

"You served ratafia last evening," James said, and the footman nodded, not looking at either of them. "And you also took something from the reticule held by Lady Voss."

The footman did not immediately react but, after a few moments, his shoulders slumped and he dropped his head. "I do not understand, my lord," he replied, the very picture of compliance. "It is right that I served ratafia, but if you are accusing me of stealing, then I must express my innocence."

"Well, if you did not, then you arranged for someone else to do so," Lady Voss replied sharply, although James put out one hand, gesturing for her to keep her voice quiet so that Lord Worthington would not overhear. "You came near to me on three occasions, offering me refreshments. Were you hoping that I would set down my niece's reticule? And, when I finally did so, out of my own foolishness, you saw your opportunity?"

The footman remained precisely where he was and did not reply. James felt his stomach tighten with anger, but he controlled himself with an effort.

"You must know what is at stake here," he told the man, speaking with as much authority as he could muster. "If you value your position here, then you must be aware that to deny the truth will only result in you losing all that you have gained. And do not think that a reference will be given you either, for that, I am afraid, will not follow."

The footman lifted his head just a little and glanced at James, before looking away again. "I am speaking the truth, my lord," he said as James frowned. "Pray, do not threaten me with the one thing that I cannot afford to lose."

Lady Voss sighed and screwed her eyes closed, biting her lip as she did so. Clearly aware that she felt as though this discussion was not aiding them in the least, James took a small step closer to the footman, keeping his voice low and grave.

"What did they offer you?" he asked as the footman dared a glance up at him. "Or did they threaten you with something that you are now too afraid to speak of? Whatever it was, if you speak to us of it, then I can assure you that nothing else will occur. But if you continue to remain silent, then it will be all the worse for you. I can assure you of that."

A loud laugh came from behind James and he grasped a hold of the opportunity at once. "Do you not see that your master is, at present, quite distracted from all that is being said between us?" he said as the footman's head lowered just a little more. "It can remain so, if you wish it. Else it will have to be quite the opposite. I will call

Lord Worthington over and tell him that you have refused to give us the truth of the matter and will tell him all." He spread his hands. "I have no other choice. Lord Worthington is a fine acquaintance and he deserves to have the very best of staff."

"Please." The footman's head lifted, and James was astonished to see the fear that shone in the man's eyes. "Please, you have said enough, my lord. I have already endured enough."

Lady Voss put a hand on James' arm and stepped closer. "You mean to say that you have been threatened already?" she asked, no tenderness in her voice and no sympathy on her face but rather a good deal of eagerness that practically flowed from her. "What has been said to you?"

The footman let out a long and heavy sigh, pressing one hand across his forehead. "My—my mother is very unwell," he said quietly, his head still lowered. "For whatever reason, a doctor was sent to her and only recently, she has begun to make a recovery." Slowly, he lifted his gaze and finally looked into Lady Voss' face, although he still avoided James' glare. "I did not understand it although I was truly grateful. The medicine she has been receiving has helped her a great deal."

"And what has this to do with—" James began, only for Lady Voss to silence him with a slice of her hand through the air.

"Continue, please," she said, her tone a little more gentle as she looked up into the footman's face. "Your mother?"

The footman nodded, closed his eyes, and carried on with his story. "The medicine, however, stopped being brought for my mother," he said softly. "She began to return to the very same state she had been in before. And then, I received instructions."

A flurry of excitement flowed through James. "Instructions?"

"It was a letter," the footman replied dully, as though he had resigned himself to speaking the truth to them even though he had no desire to do so. "I was to take the emerald earrings from Lady Marianne. I did not know who she was or why I was to take them and so, I had to try and make certain that I recognized the lady. The letter said that she would have them on her person in her reticule. I confess that I was the one to take them, Lady Voss." His head lifted just a little and he looked at her, his lips pulling thin for a moment. "I can tell you that I am very sorry indeed for doing so, but I don't know if that will make much difference. I had no other choice."

"You *did* have a choice," James replied firmly. "You did not have to do so."

"But if I did not, then my mother would, most likely, slip away into death!" the footman exclaimed, speaking with more fervor than before. "If I did as I was asked, if I left the earrings where I was instructed to, then I would find the medicine for my mother returned to her."

Closing his eyes, James took in a long and steadying breath, finally realizing just why the footman had behaved so. "You mean to say that your mother has now received more medicine?" he asked, and the footman nodded. "You are sure of it?"

"I sent one of the young lads who works here to go and speak to her only this morning," the footman replied, finally looking into James' face. "She was given some last night. Someone came to the servants' entrance and she had it within an hour of me taking the emerald earrings from the reticule."

James blew out a breath, closing his eyes and shaking his head as he tried to take in all that he had been told. "I see," he replied tightly. "Then shall we say that you were forced into doing so?" He tilted his head and looked at the fellow again. "And what would you have done if you had not managed to procure them in the way that you had planned?"

The footman's face turned from white to scarlet. "I had other plans, my lord," he stated, without telling James what any such plans might have been. "I am not proud of what I have done, I promise you, but I had to do all I could to save my mother from her deathbed."

A sharp retort rested on the tip of James' tongue but, before he could express it, Lady Voss reached out and settled her hand on the footman's arm. Astonished, James was all the more taken aback when Lady Voss expressed her understanding and, to his amazement, had no evident anger toward the footman or his actions.

"I understand the reasons that you behaved as you did," Lady Voss said softly. "I will not hold your actions against you, and neither will Lord Castleton. Indeed, Lord Worthington himself does not need to know of this."

James wanted to say something entirely the opposite, but as he saw the relief begin to etch itself across the footman's features, he finally felt a small tug of sympathy for the fellow. "The note," he said as the footman looked back at him. "Do you know who wrote it? Anything about it?"

"I do not," the footman replied as James let out a frustrated breath. "It was simply sent to me one afternoon, that is all. Delivered by a street urchin." One shoulder lifted. "And the earrings were returned to the writer of the note in much the same way."

Stiffening, James narrowed his eyes just a little. "You were instructed to give the earrings to a street boy?" he asked. "Someone who could have simply run away with them?"

The footman nodded. "The lad was waiting for me, outside the servants' entrance," he replied as James frowned hard. "He took them and ran off without saying a single word."

"But the medicine was given to your mother, which means that the person who sought them was given them without any difficulty," Lady Voss added as the footman murmured an agreement. "You were, it seems, entirely successful." Letting out a heavy sigh, she turned back to James. "I think we have achieved all that we came to do," she said as the footman sent quick glances between Lady Voss and James. "Is there anything else you wish to ask?"

James shook his head, thinking to himself that they had discovered a good deal more than he had expected. "No, there is not," he replied, just as the footman cleared his throat gently, in order to capture their attention.

"I am sorry," he said as Lady Voss looked back at him. "Truly, I did not mean to cause you any distress or difficulty. I knew that what I was doing was wrong and I did not want to do it, but my mother—"

"I quite understand," Lady Voss replied with a kindness in her voice that James was quite astonished to hear. "You love your mother. The thought of her fading away was not something you could endure, particularly when you knew that medicine was there, ready to help her."

The footman nodded, his head lowering. "You are very kind, my lady," he replied as Lady Voss shot James a look. "Thank you."

With a deep breath, James shrugged one shoulder. "And I will not speak of this to Lord Worthington," he promised. "Your position here is safe."

The footman's head dropped a little lower as he thanked James profusely, clearly overwhelmed by all that had passed between them. James was about to turn away, only for something the footman had said to suddenly strike at him. With a quick breath, he turned back to the fellow, reaching out to grasp his arm hard.

"You said something about the servants' entrance, in relation to your mother," he said urgently as the footman nodded. "Does that mean that she is also in service?"

The footman's brows knotted together. "Yes, my lord," he replied as James' heart began to pound furiously. "She works in the household of Lord and Lady Stanfield."

James stared up into the man's face for a moment before finally letting go of his arm, his breathing still coming rather quickly as he looked back at Lady Voss. She did not seem to understand at first but, within a few moments, he saw her eyes flare wide. He gave her a small nod.

"I thank you," he said, before turning away from him, and, taking Lady Voss' arm, they made their way back toward Lord Worthington, who was, it seemed, still quite taken with whatever conversation Lady Marianne was sharing with him. His eyes were fixed to her, a smile pulling at the corners of his mouth and a brightness in his expression that James knew came from a keen interest in the lady. Not that he could blame Lord Worthington for feeling such a way, for even James had to admit that Lady Marianne was one of the most interesting young ladies he had the opportunity to know.

"Ah, Lady Voss," Lord Worthington said, turning toward them and looking behind James to where the footman had been. "Did you find out what you required?"

"I did," Lady Voss replied, putting a happiness into her voice that James knew was not at all genuine. "It appears that my reticule has been taken into safekeeping by one of my acquaintances. I am to go to her directly to fetch it." Her hand settled at her heart for a moment. "I cannot tell you how relieved I am, Lord Worthington. I thank you for your willingness and your assistance."

The gentleman bowed gallantly. "But of course," he said, before turning to Lady Marianne. "I do hope that I might be permitted to call upon you one day soon, Lady Marianne? I should very much like to continue our conversation."

James felt his heart twist in his chest as Lady Marianne smiled back at the gentleman, feeling such a strange sense of irritation settle there. Irritation that was directed solely toward Lord Worthington, even though James knew he had no right to feel any such thing.

"But of course, Lord Worthington," Lady Marianne replied as Lord Worthington took her hand and bowed over it. "I would be very glad to see you again."

This seemed to delight Lord Worthington greatly and he accompanied Lady Marianne from the room, talking as he went and leaving James and Lady Voss to follow after him.

"She plays her part well, does she not?" Lady Voss murmured as they made their way toward the front door. "Quite how she has such strength, I do not know."

A little confused, James looked back at Lady Voss. "What do you mean?"

"I mean that she has no real interest in Lord Worthington," Lady Voss replied with a small yet wry smile. "She is to continue on through society as she normally would, is she not? Therefore, to refuse such a gentleman would be out of the ordinary."

James said nothing but caught the knowing look in Lady Voss' eye but did not permit himself to acknowledge it. Following Lord Worthington from the room and back to the hallway, he found a sense of relief beginning to flood his soul as he thought about what Lady Voss had said. There was no real interest, then, between Lady Marianne and Lord Worthington. Rather, it was simply Lady Marianne doing what she could to maintain a happy, settled exterior that was expected of the young ladies of the *beau monde*. It was foolish indeed for him to have such relief within him and the reason for such a feeling was not something he wished to consider at present. There was a good deal more for him to think on, given the situation. To allow himself to think of all that he felt rather than what the footman had told them was not to be permitted for even a single moment.

"I thank you, Lord Worthington," he murmured, bowing as the gentleman bid them farewell. "You have been most understanding."

"But of course," Lord Worthington replied with a quick smile. "And it is good of you to speak to me on Lady Voss' behalf. I know that she is not particularly well acquainted with me and that to lose her reticule must have been of great embarrassment to her."

"You understand the situation perfectly," James replied, glad that Lord Worthington accepted his reason for being present with both Lady Voss and Lady Marianne. "Thank you again. Good afternoon."

Lord Worthington smiled but his gaze was once more fixed to Lady Marianne, who was now sitting in the carriage with Lady Voss, her profile displayed in the carriage window. "Good afternoon, Lord Castleton," he replied as James made his way toward the carriage. "And thank you."

8

"Thank you for joining us."

Marianne smiled at Lord Wright and then at Lord Castleton, trying her best to push aside her feelings of anxiety that seemed to swamp her every time she allowed her thoughts to fix on her parents. Being forced to behave in a manner expected by society was rather wearying and given that Lord Worthington had called upon her that very afternoon and had lingered for much longer than she had expected, Marianne found herself to be all the more fatigued. She was very glad indeed that she had no social occasion to attend that evening, although their planned discussion on her current situation was, she was sure, going to be somewhat taxing.

"But of course," Lord Castleton replied quietly. "The dinner was most excellent."

Marianne kept her smile fixed in place. "We would be glad to leave you to your port, gentlemen," she said, rising quickly from her chair. "Please do join us in the drawing room when you are ready."

"I—" Lord Castleton half rose from his chair, just as Lord Wright opened his mouth to say something. "Apologies, Lord Wright. What I was going to say is that I do not feel any need to stay behind with Lord Wright. I am aware that there is an urgency with these matters and given that we joined you both solely with the understanding of discussing them, I should be glad to come to the drawing room at once."

Lord Wright chuckled and pushed himself out of his chair. "Which was precisely what I intended to say also," he replied as Lady Voss rose from her seat. "I am sure we can enjoy a glass of port just as much in the drawing room as we can here."

Marianne hesitated, then smiled. "That is very kind of you both," she replied as she gestured to the footman to do as Lord Wright had suggested. "I thank you. Shall we adjourn, then, to the drawing room?"

Walking from the room and all too aware of the growing tension that had begun to cloud over her as she did so, Marianne made her way quickly to the drawing room, praying that a cup of tea might steady her somewhat. After yesterday's discussion with Lord Worthington, as well as his visit only that very afternoon, she had found herself growing a little weary of the fellow but had been forced to continue on in such a manner that showed nothing but delight. She prayed now that he would not seek her out again in such an eager fashion, not when she had so many other things to contend with. The thought of her parents struggling and afraid, wherever they were, left a chill rushing through her as a hand squeezed her heart painfully. She wanted desperately to find them, to know where they were gone, and to restore them to their home and to their life but, as yet, she felt as though she could do nothing at all. Lady Voss had, of course, told her all that the footman had said and whilst she was interested in hearing that the mother of said footman worked for Lord and Lady Stanfield, she knew that they were not included on the short list that Lord Castleton had compiled of those her father had written to in order to inform them of his return to London.

"So," Lord Wright said, taking the tray from the footman and setting it down before picking up a glass and pouring port for both himself and Lord Castleton, "Lord Castleton has informed me of all that this footman said to you, Lady Voss. It appears that the fellow was blackmailed and, out of sheer concern for his mother, did as he was asked."

"Indeed," Lady Voss replied as the maid brought in the tea tray and set it down before Marianne. "I felt a little sorry for him, I must confess. To not have the coin to pay for your own doctor and to, therefore, rely on the generosity of a stranger—only to have such generosity pulled from you and a heavy darkness thrown around your shoulders instead must be very dreadful indeed."

"Certainly," Marianne agreed quietly. "You are most understanding, Aunt. I am sure that the footman appreciated your consideration." She smiled at Lady Voss before handing her a cup of tea. "And I understand that the lady in question works for Lord Stanfield?"

Lord Wright's brow rose. "I did not know that."

"They are not someone we have named," Lord Castleton interrupted quickly. "But that being said, it does not mean that Lord Gillingham did *not* write to him."

Marianne took a sip of her tea and tried to calm her whirling thoughts. Part of her wanted to rush to Lord and Lady Stanfield's home and demand to know where her mother was but knew that to do such a thing would be very foolish indeed. Another part of her wanted to demand that they do all they could to find this street urchin, simply in the hope that he would then tell them where he had taken the emerald earrings. Again, she knew that was nothing short of ridiculous, for there were so many street children around that it would be near to impossible to find the right one. But she felt so weak and useless doing nothing other than *discussing* what they might do next, rather than actually taking steps to help with the search for her parents.

"Might you remind me of those you wrote down?" Lady Voss asked as Lord Castleton frowned and then pulled a small note from his inner pocket. "I confess I have already forgotten."

Lord Castleton cleared his throat. "Lord Gillingham might have written to more than those we found responses from," he said, as though they all needed reminding of such a thing even though it had been mentioned only a short time ago. "Lord Balfour wrote to Lord Gillingham, expressing his delight that they were both back in London and hoped that they would be able to meet for a card game very soon. Lord Augustine responded, on behalf of both himself and his wife, as did Lord Kingman. Lord Dowding was the final letter we discovered, which stated that he hoped to meet with Lord Gillingham very soon and suggested they meet at White's one evening." He folded up his note again and set it back in his pocket. "Aside from those names, we have no others. I have, of course, made certain to introduce myself to those I did not know and now am acquainted with them all."

Marianne took another sip of her tea and felt herself begin to sink into despair. "I do not know what else we are to do," she said, looking about at the others and seeing them look back at her, with Lady Voss' expression one of deep sorrow. "We appear to be rather lost."

"I would not say that," Lord Castleton replied quickly as Marianne's shoulders slumped a little more. "We have the lady who works for Lord and Lady Stanfield. We might ask her about her circumstance."

"And what will she say?" Marianne asked, exasperated. "She will say that she did not know where the medicine came from and that she is very glad indeed to have received it again. That is all."

"Then mayhap we should consider who might have known of the lady's illness," Lord Castleton replied quietly. "If I were to guess, I would suggest that Lady Stanfield would be the one to discuss such a thing with others of her acquaintance, rather than Lord Stanfield."

Lady Voss nodded her agreement. "It would most likely be the mistress of the house, certainly," she said slowly. "Therefore, does that mean that we should study who her close acquaintances are, to see if any of them are those we have on the list of names?"

Marianne closed her eyes. It all felt so very uncertain. She wanted to cry out that it seemed fruitless, that even if they *were* to surmise such a thing, it still meant a great many days of her parents missing from the house and from her life, without any real answers. Realizing that she was trembling slightly, Marianne reached forward and picked up her teacup, draining it quickly and forcing herself to remain quite silent. Lord Castleton, Lord Wright, and Lady Voss all looked at each other as Marianne set back down her cup, waiting for someone to respond.

"We could do so," Lord Wright suggested after some moments. "However, would you be able to befriend her, Lady Voss? Are you acquainted with her? I am sure that if you managed to turn the conversation to the matter of staff and the difficulties they present when they become ill, Lady Stanfield would, most likely, talk about her own trials. And she might very well be willing to discuss with you who else she has spoken to about it."

Lady Voss exclaimed eagerly that she would be more than glad to do so, leaving Marianne to sit quietly and consider what she herself was meant to do in the interim. She could not simply sit back and observe as her aunt did all that was required. There had to be something that she could do as well.

"You do not look pleased, Marianne."

Her head snapped up as she realized her aunt was speaking to her. "Aunt?"

"You look displeased," Lady Voss repeated as heat began to sear Marianne's cheeks. "I know this must be a greatly distressing situation for you and I am fully aware that I have made it all the more difficult, but if there is anything else you wish to suggest, then please, do share it with us, my dear." Lady Voss leaned a little further forward in her chair, her hands clasped tightly together. "Please, my dear. Say whatever you wish."

Much to her astonishment, Marianne felt a lump come into her throat. She had assured her aunt repeatedly that she did not hold a grudge against her for the situation with the reticule and had, in addition, told her of the struggles of her own heart and the despair that so often threatened to overwhelm her. How could she speak of her sense of hopelessness now, when they were so clearly doing all they could to help?

"It is only that I find myself..." Marianne shook her head, trailing off as she looked away, hating that tears were pricking in the corners of her eyes. She tried to speak but struggled to keep her composure, feeling as though she were being tossed about from one place to the next without anything secure to cling on to.

"This must be dreadful for you, Lady Marianne."

The kindness and the sympathy in Lord Castleton's voice only made Marianne struggle all the more to keep back her tears.

"If I had something else to suggest to you, something more that we might do, then I would do so without hesitation," Lord Castleton continued, his shoulders lifting for just a moment. "As it is, I have nothing further to offer you."

Marianne tried to smile. "You have done a great deal already, Lord Castleton," she said, her voice breaking with emotion. "Lord Wright, your willingness to help is greatly appreciated, by both my aunt and myself. Truly, I do not wish to give the impression that I am at all ungrateful. It is only that I cannot help but think of my parents and fear for them." She could not say more, for the ache in her throat grew much too great and her eyes clouded with so many tears that her vision was blurred.

"You have great strength," she heard Lord Castleton say as Lady Voss came across the room to sit by her, pressing her handkerchief into Marianne's hand. "Pray, do not fear expressing the truth of your heart to us. We cannot imagine just how painful this must be for you at present."

Marianne sniffed and dabbed at her eyes, managing to regain control of herself. "I thank you," she said hoarsely. "If we must speak to Lady Stanfield, then I will be glad to do so. It is better than having nothing at all to hand."

Lord Wright murmured something kind and Marianne gave him a watery smile. Taking a deep breath, she lifted her chin and set her shoulders, fully in control of herself again. "For the moment," she continued, "perhaps we—"

A knock at the door interrupted her and she hesitated, before calling the butler to enter. Bowing his head, he came toward her with a note in his hand, holding it out to her and apologizing for his interruption.

"I believe it to be of great importance, my lady, else I would not have interrupted you," he said, inclining his head. "Forgive me."

Marianne said nothing, turning the letter over and seeing, for what was the second time now, a letter that bore a blank seal. Her breath caught, her eyes widened, and she looked up sharply at Lord Castleton.

He recognized her shock in a moment.

"Who delivered it?" he asked with distress in his voice, throwing himself out of the chair and striding toward the butler. "A footman? A boy? It is much too late for the post, so who brought it to the house?"

The butler's eyes widened, and he began to stammer, clearly a little surprised at Lord Castleton's demeanor. "A—a servant, I believe," he replied, "although I could not tell you his standing."

"Had he transportation?" Lord Castleton bellowed, now hurrying toward the door. "A horse? Hackney?"

The butler shook his head. "I do not think so, my lord."

"Lord Wright."

Marianne barely had time to breathe before Lord Wright also rushed from the room, leaving Marianne, Lady Voss, and the butler together in silence, the air around them almost spitting and sparkling with tension. Marianne let her breath out slowly and looked to her aunt, who was still staring at the door.

"Another tea tray, I think," Marianne said as the butler cleared his throat, nodded, and picked up the now cold teapot and set it back on the tray. "Lord Castleton and Lord Wright will return presently. They are to be sent back in at once."

The butler, who had managed to gather himself very well indeed, inclined his head.

"But of course," he said as Lady Voss gave herself a slight shake, turning to look at Marianne with a clear hope of an explanation in her eyes. "At once, my lady."

Waiting until the butler had quit the room, Marianne then turned her attention to the letter. "It does not bear a seal, Aunt," she explained as Lady Voss settled one hand on her arm. "The first letter I received from Mama did not have one either."

Lady Voss' eyes widened with shock and then understanding. "You believe this will be from your dear mother?" she asked as Marianne broke the seal, feeling her heart beginning to race. "Goodness, now I understand why Lord Castleton hurried from the room."

"Indeed," Marianne murmured, unfolding the note, but to her surprise, she had no recognition of the writing contained within. "I do not think this is from Mama, however. Although..." She read the note quickly and felt her stomach tighten with both nervousness and anxiety. "It appears that there is something more I am to bring."

She handed the note to her aunt before settling her elbows on her knees and putting her hands to her forehead, closing her eyes tightly so that she would not permit the many dread-filled thoughts to overwhelm her.

"Good gracious," Lady Voss breathed as she read the note. "They state that you should be aware by now that they have Lord and Lady Gillingham with them at present. They thank you for the earrings and now request Lord Gillingham's seal?" She looked up at Marianne, who had dropped her hands now, letting out her breath slowly. "Why ever should they want such a thing?"

"I do not know," Marianne replied heavily. "But it will be for some nefarious purpose, I am sure." She closed her eyes again and drew in a long breath, attempting to steady herself. "I must hope that they are both well."

Lady Voss gasped, her hand tightening now on Marianne's arm. "They state that if it is not done, harm will come to your mother."

"Yes, I have read that threat," Marianne replied softly, just as terrified as her aunt was but refusing to let it take a hold of her completely. "I have no choice, of course."

"No, I cannot see that you do," Lady Voss agreed, her voice weak and tremulous. "Oh, my dear Marianne, I am so very afraid for them both."

Marianne could not speak, such was the ache in her throat. Closing her eyes tightly, she tried to find even a modicum of peace but found that she could not. There was nothing but fear now, clasping tightly to her heart and filling her with such dread that she felt she could not bear it. Bile rose in her throat as she recalled the final sentence of the letter, the words sticking to her mind as though they intended to remain there for good.

If you do not, then harm will be brought to your mother and to your father. Have no doubt about that.

Tears pooled in her eyes and Marianne let them fall, her distress more than she could bear. Lady Voss came near to her and wrapped an arm around her shoulders, but very soon, Marianne realized that her aunt was deeply upset also. How long they remained there for, Marianne did not know, but eventually, her tears began to subside, and she wiped them away with her aunt's handkerchief.

"We will succeed," Lady Voss said in her ear, clearly trying to find some determination, some strength that might encourage both herself and Marianne. "They will be safe, Marianne. You must believe that."

"I want only to have them safely returned to this house," Marianne answered, just as the sound of voices was heard coming from the hallway. "That is all."

Lady Voss rose, sniffed, and shook her head. "That is not all I seek," she replied, speaking with a little more firmness to her voice. "I want those responsible for this *outrage* to feel the full force of justice's wrath. To have to face the consequences that will be brought to them for what they have done. Whilst I want your mother and father returned, my dear Marianne, I also wish for judgment to fall upon the heads of the perpetrators. And it is that desire which gives me a little more courage, a little more determination."

Marianne found herself nodding, looking at her aunt and seeing the fire that had suddenly ignited in her eyes. For the first time, rather than merely upset or fear, she felt the first few flickering embers of anger begin to burn within her.

"You may very well be correct, Aunt," she said, just as the door opened for Lord Castleton and Lord Wright to return to their company. "And perhaps, in time, that desire will begin to fill my heart also."

9

Trying to find a stranger in the dark gloom of the London streets was not a particularly easy matter but James felt his steps pushed by a fierce urgency that ran all the way through him. Lord Wright had gone in the opposite direction, whilst he had hurried to his right. There were very few others about, for rogues and ruffians were far too numerous at this time. James did not allow such thoughts to pull him back, however, for his determination to catch whoever it was that had delivered the note was growing with every step. He dared not return to Lady Marianne without having *something* to encourage her by. He had seen the sorrowful look in her eyes, heard her words, and practically felt her discouragement and fear. There had to be something he could do or say that would bring her a little hope.

James' eyes narrowed as he saw a figure ahead of him. "You there! Stop!"

The man turned and, much to James' surprise, stopped dead as he approached.

"Did you just come from Lord and Lady Gillingham's?" James demanded, uncertain as to whether or not the man would tell him the truth. "I must know at once."

The man shrugged off James' restraining hand. "I haven't," he said, his voice gruff. "Get your hands off me!"

"I must find him," James replied, undeterred. "Has someone passed you? Another fellow?"

Grunting something unrepeatable about the nobility, the man turned around and made to go on his way, only for James to hold him back.

"Here," he said, fishing desperately in his pockets and finding a couple of coins to give to the man. "As I have said, I must know. I must know whether or not someone has passed you."

The man hesitated, turning the coins over in his hand and then putting one in his mouth, biting it hard to make sure it was genuine. Evidently satisfied, he gave another grunt.

"Young fellow," he said, his tone still dark. "Pushed past me, he did. Walking awful quickly like."

James' heart pounded. "When?"

"Not more than a minute ago," the man replied as James began to hurry away from him. "What's so important about him anyway?"

Choosing not to reply, James broke into a run—dangerous for the gloom of the London streets—his heart beating with growing anticipation as he looked for the fellow in question. Quite how far away he was from Lady Marianne's townhouse, he could not say, but at the moment, the distance did not seem to matter.

And then, he saw him.

Another shadowy figure was only a few yards ahead. The dim lantern light seemed to glow a little brighter as though eager to assist him and James' strength seemed to redouble as he ran after the fellow. His steps echoed loudly and, just as he reached him, the man looked over his shoulder. James heard his swift intake of breath as he put out one hand and grabbed at the man hard.

"You were just at Lord Gillingham's townhouse," he said, his words punctuated by gasps as he fought to catch his breath. "Where have you come from? Who sent you to Lady Marianne?"

The man began to struggle but James held on tightly, his other hand reaching out to grasp the man's other arm.

"I will hear it from you!" he exclaimed as the man let out a growl of frustration. "Who sent you with that note?"

"I don't know what you're talking about," the man protested, his voice hard and angry. "Let me go!"

James' hands tightened, strength pouring into his frame. "I will not," he grated, something within him telling him that this *was* the man who had taken the note to Lady Marianne. "Do you know how much pain the lady is in, because of your note? Do you know how much she struggles?"

The man's breathing was becoming faster and faster, his fear clearly growing as he fought James off, but James was not about to release the fellow. A vision of Lady Marianne's sorrowful face came back to his mind, lingering there as though it wanted to push him to further action, to demand that he do more to save her from such pain. Fighting back, James never once let go of the man, holding onto him for all he was worth despite the blows that came and the pain that followed.

"Tell me who sent you," he said, slamming the man back hard against the iron fence that ran along the side of the street, setting a barrier between the houses and the street itself. "I must know! I *will* know."

The man gasped, the breath slammed from his body as James held him there. "I have nothing to do with this lady," he answered, his breathing ragged now. "I just do what I'm told."

James felt something within him break, something that then filled him with a great and inexpressible relief. He *had* found the right man. All he had to do now was get him to say more.

"And who tells you what it is you have to do?" he gritted out, his words forced out between his clenched teeth as with every modicum of strength, he held the fellow there. "Tell me at once."

The man said nothing in response, a small groan escaping him as his hands lifted, trying yet again to free himself from James' grip. His efforts redoubled, James fought back, trying to hold the man in place as the fellow did everything he could to escape. James picked up more bruises, felt his body filled with yet more pain, and still he refused to let the man slip away. It was as though every part of him was filled with such a great determination that it forced him to act, forced him to cling on despite it all.

"I will hear it from you," James shouted, just as the man twisted violently, half throwing James to his other side. Pain shot through James' face as the man's fist connected with his cheekbone, but he refused still to let go. Staggering to his left, he managed to pull the man with him and, with a great effort, thrust him back against the railings once more.

They were both breathing hard now.

"Tell me and I shall let you go," he hissed, ignoring the throbbing in his head. "That is all you need do."

A hard laugh came from the man as he slumped back against the railings, clearly exhausted. "And I'll receive no punishment from my master if I do so, is that right?"

"He does not need to know," James replied, and the man laughed horribly. "Who will inform him?"

The man shook his head. "He will find out. He has ways of discovering everything and anything he wants. I dare not tell you."

"You *must*," James insisted as the fellow shook his head again before lowering it, his breathing still ragged as he slumped just a little more, perhaps overcome with fatigue. "Lady Marianne—"

"I value my position," the man retorted, no longer fighting back physically with James but instead simply refusing to tell him all that he wanted, choosing to retaliate with words. Words that stung James' heart and left him feeling more and more disheartened. "The master will know that I have spoken to you. Then what will he do?"

A slight tremor ran through the man's frame and James frowned, dropping one hand from the man's arm whilst keeping the other holding the man's coat tightly. Was the fellow afraid of his master? That did not bode well for Lady Marianne, if it was so.

"Do you not understand?" James asked, his tone a little more even now. "Lady Marianne has suffered a great deal of pain under your master's hand. He has done something so despicable that it is almost too much for her to bear."

"Then you must understand why I won't tell you anything," came the reply. "If he is as despicable as you believe him to be, why should I risk anything by speaking with you?"

James' frustration grew. He *had* to discover something from this man. He had to know the truth. "You can take a new position with me," he told him, beginning to feel desperate now. "I guarantee it."

The harsh, mocking laugh that tore from the man's throat sent a wave of embarrassment through James, even though he did not know why. "Do you think that he will not find me there?" came the reply. "New employment will do me no good. My master has warned us often of the punishments that will come with betraying him." Again, that tremor came, and James' brow furrowed all the more. "I have seen it happen once already and I dare not let it happen to me."

James shook his head in the darkness, his heart pounding with a great urgency. "Fear is no reason to stay."

"It is *every* reason," the man replied tightly. "I will tell you nothing. Now let me go."

"I can follow you," James replied, not doing as the man asked. "I could follow your steps."

"Then I would walk all night, until I was certain that you were gone," came the swift reply. "And I would tell my master the truth—that you were following me."

James did not allow the threat to affect him. "You do not know my name or anything about me," he stated, allowing a faint mocking tone into his voice. "That does not dissuade me."

The man was silent for a moment or two and then he began to speak. "I must presume that you are Lord Castleton," he said as shock ran through James' frame. "Either that, or you are Lord Wright. You have been seen often in the company of Lady Marianne and have been observed joining her for dinner on more than one occasion. This evening was one of those occasions."

A jolt pinned James to where he stood, his whole body tightening with a sudden fear. "How do you know such a thing?"

"The master watches the lady," came the reply. "He knows that you—Lord Castleton or Lord Wright—are assisting her in whatever way you can." He shrugged. "I was warned that you would be present this evening and told to be careful. That's all."

It was as though this man's master, the one behind it all, rose up higher than ever before in James' mind, a shadowy, ominous figure that observed everything and controlled everyone.

"You think that you are doing all you can to find him," the man continued as James' jaw worked furiously, a sudden, fierce anger filling him. "You think that *you* are the one in control." He shrugged. "You are not."

"You are afraid of him," James replied as the man said nothing. "That fear will not bind itself to my heart. I care for Lady Marianne. I will do whatever I can to restore her parents to her."

Lifting his shoulders in a small shrug, the man pushed himself away from the railings, even though James still held onto him with one hand. "Then I can wish you luck but nothing more," he said as James shook his head.

"That is not good enough," he stated as the man began to try and pull away from James once more. "I need to know something about your master. Something that will be of assistance to me in identifying him."

"And I have told you that I will say no such thing," came the harsh reply as the man tugged himself away. "Now let me go."

"I will, I will," James responded, his determination to discover something, *anything*, about this man beginning to rise up within him once more. "But you must tell me something. You do not need to be specific but—"

"I can't."

James shook the man hard, both hands now on either side of the man's coat. "I will not let you go until you do!" he exclaimed as the man began to growl with frustration. "If you do as I ask, then I will release you, turn around, and walk away. There need be nothing specific, I promise you."

It took a few moments but, much to James' relief, the man finally stopped fighting James off and stood quietly, his breathing now a little quickened.

"Is your master wed?" James asked, praying that the man would answer. "Does he have a wife?"

Silence met his words but James bit back the harsh retort that sprang to his lips, knowing that he needed to give the fellow a little more time to speak before he asked him anything further.

"He is not," the man said after a few moments, his voice low and his words dark and angry. "Now will you release me?"

James shook his head. "He is rich?"

A snort escaped from the fellow in front of him. "Of course."

"Does he enjoy society?"

The man tilted his head. "If you mean to ask whether or not he goes out and about every evening, then yes, of course."

James nodded, feeling a little more satisfied. "What does he want with Lord and Lady Gillingham?" he asked, finally dropping his hands from the man's coat and taking a small step back. "You must be aware that he has them somewhere."

There came no response and James let out a long breath, closing his eyes tightly and praying that the fellow would answer. He had to know something of importance, had to be able to return to Lady Marianne and tell her what he had discovered. This was of importance—of great importance—and James could only stand silently and wait for the man to choose whether or not he would reply.

"I—I will not lie and say we have no guests in the house at present," the man said after a few moments. "But I don't know why they have joined us."

"That is not good enough," James retorted, but the man only shook his head, his hands lifting in a defensive gesture as he took a small step back. "That is all I know."

"There must be something more," James said, finding it all the more terrifying to think that he was so near to discovering the truth and yet so far from it also. "Your master, what is it that he requires? What is it that he needs from them that he cannot gain for himself?"

"You said that I could come into your employ," the man said, startling James with the sudden change in conversation. "If you manage to succeed, if you manage to find a way past all of this and my master is…dealt the consequences of it all, then promise me I will have a position with you."

"I swear it," James replied, putting one hand to his heart. "You will have a place in Lord Castleton's employ."

Silence swirled around him and the man took another step back, leaving James to steady himself, knowing he could not follow, since he had given the man his word. He wanted to shout aloud that the man needed to say something more, needed to tell him the reasons for his master's actions, but to do so would only push the fellow all the further away, he was sure of it.

And then, the man came charging back, hurrying toward James as though the very devil himself was chasing him. His steps were hurried, his figure still cloaked in shadow and gloom as he moved toward James—only for something hard to slam into the side of James' head. He staggered to one side, his hand pressed hard against the side of his head, feeling the strength leave his frame.

"Just in case you decide to follow me," he heard the man whisper. "I—I'm sorry. But I can't risk the master finding out."

"Why?" The word was forced from James' lips as he sank to his knees, his other hand finding the coolness of the railings and clinging to them desperately, trying his utmost not to give into unconsciousness. "Why?"

The man took a step back, his hands raised once more as James fought to keep his vision clear, still looking up at him and trying to discern his features. "Because I must," came the reply. "But one thing I will say, Lord Castleton…" He trailed off for a moment and such was the pain in James' head that, for a moment, he thought the man had left him entirely. And then, out of the darkness, came a few words. Words that sent a spiral of hope through James, despite his pain and his weakness.

"My master needs more wealth. I am sure of it."

Nothing more was said. Nothing more came to James' ears and, as he tried his best to push himself up to standing, he felt himself sway violently as the pain redoubled in his head. And yet, with all the agony that pierced his head, he felt a sense of relief fill him. He knew now some things about the man behind this situation, the man who had taken Lady Marianne's parents. Surely, now, they would be able to surmise who such a fellow might be?

The sound of hurried footsteps made their way slowly into James' head and, wincing, he turned around to see someone else approaching. With a small groan, James lowered his head and squeezed his eyes closed, trying to push aside some of the pain.

"Castleton?"

Relief seared him. "Lord Wright?" he managed to say, just as the man came near to him. He heard his friend's swift intake of breath and let his lips curve into a wry smile.

"I did not find anyone and so thought to come after you," he heard Lord Wright say. "Goodness, whatever happened?"

"Let us return to Lady Marianne," James replied, finally letting go of the railing but immediately beginning to wobble. Lord Wright caught him, one hand about his waist as he helped James to step forward. "I have things I must tell her."

"And blood to drip all over her floors," Lord Wright replied grimly. "Very well, if you insist on returning, then I shall take you."

James closed his eyes as he walked, letting his friend lead him. A tiny hope flickered in his heart that somehow, with all that he had learned, he would be able to discover the truth about the man behind all of this so that, in the end, he would see Lord and Lady Gillingham restored to their lives and to their daughter. Yes, he had to admit that there was a small part of him that began to wonder whether or not he would be able to continue his acquaintance with Lady Marianne thereafter, whether she would be willing to consider his attentions despite all that he had done, but James forced himself to set such thoughts aside. Lady Marianne needed nothing more from him at present save for his help, his support, and his consideration.

He would ask for nothing more.

10

"Good gracious." Marianne leapt to her feet as Lord Castleton and Lord Wright returned to the room, horrified to see Lord Wright supporting Lord Castleton, who had a cloth pressed to the side of his head.

"I am quite all right," he said quickly, evidently seeing the horror leap into her eyes. "It was merely a—a tussle."

Lord Wright grimaced as he released Lord Castleton, who, swaying for only a moment, finally managed to take a few small steps before sinking down into a chair, closing his eyes tightly as he did so, pain flashing across his expression. "I am quite well."

"You do not look well," Lady Voss exclaimed as Marianne found herself walking nearer to Lord Castleton, although she was unsure as to what she ought to do to help him. "You were in some sort of exchange?"

Lord Castleton opened his eyes and looked back at Marianne, his hand still pressed to the side of his head, the cloth slowly staining pink. "I found the man who delivered your note," he said by way of explanation. "He wanted to make certain I did not follow him."

Marianne caught her breath, her eyes rounding. "You—you found him?"

"I did," Lord Castleton replied as Lady Voss rose from her chair and made her way to the door. "I have heard a little from him but nothing that confirms the name or the identity of his master. But, before you lose all hope, I assure you that what I *have* learned will be of great benefit, Lady Marianne."

She did not know what to say, sinking down onto a small stool beside Lord Castleton and reaching up to where his hand pressed the cloth to his forehead. A maid came in, practically unnoticed, with yet another cloth and a clean bowl of water sitting on a tray, which she placed down beside Marianne.

"My lady?" she murmured as Marianne turned to see the maid holding out one hand to her. A little confused, she quickly realized that it was the stained cloth she wished for and, after a quick explanation, took it from Lord Castleton, revealing the wound underneath.

"It will need to be cleaned," Lady Voss said as the maid hurried from the room. "And we will need further refreshments. I will return in a moment." She gestured to Lord Wright. "Lord Wright, might you pour a brandy for yourself and for Lord Castleton? I believe you will both require it."

Lord Wright murmured something that Marianne did not hear, finding herself picking up the clean cloth that the maid had left her and dipping it into the water.

"I am sure there is no requirement for *you* to do such a thing, Lady Marianne," Lord Castleton said hastily, and Marianne shook her head. "The maid might be better suited to—"

"This injury is because of me, is it not?" she asked, her hand shaking a little as she began to dab the cloth around the sharp, jagged wound in order to clean the blood from the side of Lord Castleton's face. "Had you not been chasing after that fellow, you would not have sustained such a thing."

Lord Castleton winced but did not jerk his head away. "I do not see it in such a light, Lady Marianne," he told her, his voice a little lower now. "It was entirely the man's choice to do as he did. He—he is afraid of his master."

Marianne's breath hitched as a swell of fear ran through her, but she refused to permit it to fill her entirely with trepidation. "I cannot thank you enough for what you have done, Lord Castleton," she murmured, not seeing Lord Wright settle himself in a corner of the room, practically as far away as he could get from them both. "Your generosity and willingness have gone far beyond anything I imagined. I am deeply distressed that you have been injured so."

She pressed the cloth gently to his temple again and he caught his breath, the wound still oozing. Her heart began to ache at the sight of it, feeling all the more responsible for what he had endured. Part of her wanted to ask him what it was he had found out, and yet another part of her wished to remain silent, to remain quiet as she cleaned the wound that Lord Castleton had suffered for her sake.

There was no longer even a hint of irritation within her heart toward him. Instead, that had been replaced with gratitude, with gladness, and with a deep sense of shame that she had ever thought so poorly of him in the first place. Lord Castleton's character was more profound, more magnificent than she had ever imagined, and yet only now was it being revealed to her.

"The note."

Marianne jumped as Lord Castleton's fingers touched hers where her left hand rested on the arm of his chair. When she looked into his eyes, she saw the intensity linger there, the way that he held her gaze with such fervor flickering there that she wanted to look away but found she could not.

"What did it say?"

Marianne shook her head. "It was nothing pleasant," she told him quietly, turning her gaze back to his temple so that she might concentrate on cleaning up his wound rather than looking into his eyes. "It was not written by my mother or my father. I believe that the first note was written by my mother solely as proof that she was still alive and well."

Rinsing the cloth in the bowl, she squeezed it out carefully and then continued with her task.

"They want now the seal that belongs to my father," she continued as Lord Castleton sucked in a breath. "I will be sent another note instructing me where to take it and when. I do not know why they wish for such a thing."

"I believe I do," Lord Castleton replied, astonishing her. "As I have said, I caught the man who delivered the note to your house. It appears that his master, whilst having the appearance of wealth—or, mayhap, having a decent amount of coin—seeks more."

Understanding came in an instant. "And you believe that my father's seal will be used to take what belongs to him and give it to this…this…nefarious person?" she asked, putting the cloth down and feeling herself begin to shake with a mixture of both anger and upset. "That is what they intend?"

Lord Castleton shifted slightly in his chair so that he could turn toward her a little more.

"I believe so," he told her solemnly. "There is more that I have learned but, for the moment, that is precisely what I believe to be the case. But we will discover this person, Lady Marianne, I have no doubt about that. From what I have been told, we may well be able to soon identify the gentleman responsible."

Marianne clutched at his hand, her heart beating furiously as she looked into his eyes and saw the quiet determination there. "Do you truly believe that, Lord Castleton?" she asked, her voice breaking as tears began to press into her eyes. "We will succeed?"

Lord Castleton nodded. "Yes, my dear. We will succeed."

∼

IT WAS two days after Marianne had received her note that she was then sent instructions for what to do with the seal. She had expected to be sent such a thing soon after the first had arrived, but it had not been as she had thought. The anxiety that had torn through her was, according to Lady Voss, quite deliberate. It was as though the person responsible did not want her to ever feel secure or in control of the situation. They wanted to remind her that they were to be obeyed without question or refusal and that nothing she felt or said made any difference to the situation.

Walking into her father's study sent a slight tremor through Marianne. This was her father's place, a room where she was not meant to set foot without him. She paused for a moment, taking it in and practically able to see her father sitting at his desk, looking up at her with a smile.

Her stomach twisted and her eyes threatened tears once more, but with an effort, she pushed them away and made her way to her father's desk.

His seal sat on the left-hand side of the desk and Marianne picked it up tentatively, looking down at it and feeling the weight of it in her hand. Turning it over, she frowned hard, seeing the cleanliness of it, as though it had never been used before. Her frown deepened and she tilted her head to one side for a moment as she considered it, before her heart suddenly quickened as she recalled something her father had said. Something that he had mentioned about his seal before Marianne had ever come to London.

Her breathing quickened as she rang the bell, looking down at the seal and finding her heart pounding furiously within her chest.

"My lady?"

The butler was there in an instant, his eyes wide with surprise as though he had not expected to see her in Lord Gillingham's study.

"My father's seal," Marianne said quickly, coming toward him. "It was replaced recently, yes?"

The butler hesitated, then nodded slowly. "Yes, my lady. Lord Gillingham wrote and requested a new one prior to his return to London."

"Then what became of the old one?" she asked, praying silently that it had not already been disposed of. "What was done with it?"

Again, the butler took a moment to consider and then, murmuring for her to wait a moment, made his way across the room to the desk. After another momentary hesitation, he pulled open one of the drawers.

"We did not know what the master wished to do with it," he said slowly, "and thus, it was kept here."

Marianne closed her eyes for a moment, a sense of relief and triumph filling her.

"It is," the butler continued in an apologetic voice, "rather broken, my lady."

"That is wonderful," Marianne breathed, opening her eyes to see the butler unfolding a simple white cloth that revealed the broken seal. With trembling fingers, Marianne picked it up and examined it, realizing that it was precisely what she had hoped. The seal itself was cracked from one side to the other, rendering it practically useless. Anyone who saw the seal in such a distressing fashion, whether by sight or on the back of a letter, would know instantly that something was wrong.

"When did the new one arrive?" she asked as the butler looked at her in evident confusion at such questions. "Was it before or after my father disappeared?"

"Before, my lady," the butler replied quietly, turning to pick up the new seal and turning it over, looking at it carefully. "But I do not believe that he has used this as yet."

Whatever disappointment had threatened to flood Marianne quickly disappeared. "Indeed?"

"There is no sign of use, my lady," the butler replied as Marianne held onto the old seal tightly. "I might be mistaken, however. I know that your father wrote some letters during the first few days of his return to London. It may have had light use which has not yet evidenced itself on the seal."

Marianne nodded slowly, thinking hard. "Regardless, this is very helpful indeed," she replied, silently praying that whoever she was to give this seal to would accept the explanations she wrote with it—that the old seal was to be replaced but that as yet, the new had not arrived. She could only hope that her father would say the same, should he be asked. "I will take this with me."

The butler inclined his head and did not ask her the many questions that she was sure that he wished to. "But of course, my lady."

"And remove the new seal," Marianne continued quickly. "Have it placed in my bedchamber and pray, do not allow any of the other servants see you do so."

Again, the butler nodded but remained silent, picking up the new seal and taking it from the room. Marianne folded the white cloth back up and held the old, broken seal in her hands in an almost reverent fashion. "Let us pray that this will do," she murmured, before walking from the room.

∽

"How are you feeling, Marianne?"

Marianne gave her aunt a quick smile, all too aware of the package that was, at present, settled within her pocket.

"I am quite all right, Aunt," she said as Lady Voss watched her with anxious eyes. "I will not pretend that I do not feel a little unnerved at present but that is to be expected."

Lady Voss nodded. "But of course," she said as Marianne drew in a deep breath, settling her shoulders as she did so. "To hear all that Lord Castleton said about what he had learned was, I admit, more than a little unsettling." She gave a small shudder, closing her eyes for a moment. "To know that this gentleman, whoever he is, has been *watching* you is very disquieting indeed."

Marianne's lips twisted in a wry smile. Whilst she had been glad to hear of all that Lord Castleton had discovered, horror had begun to creep over her as she realized just how much she had been observed. Obviously, this gentleman was using whatever resources were at his disposal to make certain of her movements, and now that he was aware that Lord Castleton and Lord Wright were assisting her, it made her feel all the more on edge. Lord Castleton had reminded her that she had to give every appearance of being entirely unaware of this, however, meaning that she could not look all about her, study various passersby intently, or look for any sign of someone observing her. She had to behave just as naturally as she could, despite such unsettling knowledge.

"At least we know now that we can discount Lord and Lady Augustine, as well as Lord and Lady Kingman," Lady Voss continued as Marianne nodded fervently. "What with that servant telling us that his master is unwed, we are now left with only two gentlemen to consider."

"Lord Balfour and Lord Dowding," Marianne agreed quietly. "Although I myself am not acquainted with either."

"Nor I," Lady Voss replied grimly. "But I very much hope that I will be able to speak to Lady Stanfield this afternoon and, thereafter, will be able to tell whether or not she herself is acquainted with either gentleman." She shook her head. "Although I would confess myself surprised if she had talked to either one about difficulties with one of her servants."

"She may have done," Marianne replied as the carriage drew up and came to a stop. "It depends, I suppose, on whether or not she is a lady inclined to such discussions, regardless of whom she is speaking to."

"You mean whether or not she is overly talkative," Lady Voss replied with a chuckle. "Yes, my dear, I suppose that is so."

Marianne smiled back at her aunt, grateful for a little levity before she stepped out of the carriage. The afternoon was very fine, and Marianne might have enjoyed their excursion, were it not for the fact that the only reason they had come to Hyde Park was solely to hand over the seal. Quite what would happen, Marianne did not know, but she had followed the instructions given to her in the note without question.

"It is very crowded," Lady Voss murmured as they began to walk slowly away from the carriage and in through the swarms of other ladies and gentlemen that were present. "How are we meant to discover the person we are to give the seal to?"

"I do believe that we have been asked to come here for precisely that reason, Aunt," Marianne answered, doing her best not to look to her left and then to her right but rather keeping her gaze straight ahead. "Given that there are so many people present, whoever comes to take the seal from me will be able to disappear into the crowd without difficulty."

There was no time for them to speak further on the matter for, within a few minutes, they were greeted by another young lady and her mother, who appeared to be very glad to see Marianne and Lady Voss. Marianne was quickly drawn into conversation about the most recent fashion plates, although, of course, she had no real interest in the matter whatsoever.

"And is your mother due to return to London?" Lady Gressingham asked, a pleasant smile on her face as her daughter, Miss Henway, stood quietly beside her. "I should be glad to see her again also."

Marianne stiffened but forced a smile, finding that talking about her mother was very difficult indeed—not that Lady Gressingham was aware of such a thing, of course.

"My brother and his wife have recently welcomed their first child," she told the lady, who let out a coo of delight. "My mother and father wished *very* much to spend a little time with them before they came to London, as you might expect."

"And your sister-in-law is well?" Lady Gressingham asked, and Marianne nodded. "I am very glad to hear of such a thing. That must be wonderful for them both. You will be very glad to have Lady Voss as your chaperone, I am sure."

Darting a glance up to her aunt and finding it all the more difficult to keep her smile fixed to her lips, Marianne nodded. "But of course," she replied. "We have rubbed along very well together."

Lady Voss began to speak then, talking about her own family and how she had never once had a daughter to accompany through the Season, thus relieving Marianne of the need to say another word. She lapsed into grateful silence, the sun beating down upon her.

Murmuring a gentle, "Excuse me," she turned to open up her parasol, only for a man to come near to her.

"Give me the item."

Marianne looked up at him, her hands still on her parasol. He was not an overly tall man and, from the look of him, appeared to be a gentleman given the cut of his clothes, but there was something about his manner that told her he was not so.

"Hurry," he continued gruffly as Marianne nodded, her heart beating a little more swiftly than before. "I am not about to wait."

The way he spoke held a gruffness that made Marianne all the more certain that he was *not* a gentleman of the *ton*. He might be wearing the clothes of such a person, but he was not at all trained in the way of speaking that she would have expected. Quickly, she pulled out the seal, which was now wrapped in brown paper and tied with string, but she did not give it to the man straight away. Instead, she held his gaze, studying his features and making certain that she would be able to recall him should she need to do so. "And who are you to give this to?" she asked, speaking with more boldness than she truly felt. "I know that you have been sent here by another."

The man said nothing, snorted, and, in one swift motion, snatched the package from Marianne's hand. She let out a small cry of astonishment, only for the man to turn on his heel and step away from her. Marianne could not follow, for to do so would be more than a little foolhardy and certainly would damage her reputation.

"Are you quite all right, Lady Marianne?"

She turned back to where Lady Gressingham and her daughter were standing looking at her, their eyes wide.

"It—it was only my parasol," Marianne stammered as Lady Voss' eyes widened in understanding. "I believe I almost accidentally struck that gentleman."

Lady Gressingham laughed and Marianne tried to do so also, her parasol now held above her head. "I am sure he did not mind," Lady Gressingham said as Marianne allowed herself a small smile. "It is one of the many difficulties that come with being a part of the fashionable hour."

"Indeed, indeed," Lady Voss murmured, coming to stand a little closer to Marianne. "And now we should continue our short promenade. We do not intend to stay for long, I confess." Leaning toward Lady Gressingham, Lady Voss lowered her voice. "I find the crush a struggle to bear."

Lady Gressingham gave her a sympathetic look. "I understand," she replied as Marianne bid good afternoon to Miss Henway, who had remained practically silent throughout the conversation. "Good afternoon."

The very moment that they stepped away, Lady Voss took a hold of Marianne's arm. "I take it that you no longer have the seal?"

"No," Marianne replied, glancing up at her aunt. "I do not."

"And you did not recognize the person who took it from you?"

"No," Marianne said again. "I did not. I do not believe he was a gentleman, however, even though he was dressed in such a way. The way he spoke was rather rough."

Lady Voss' inhaled sharply. "He did not injure you?"

"He did not," Marianne reassured her quickly. "I attempted to ask him some questions about what he was doing and who he was collecting the item for, but he did not answer me. Instead, he snatched it from my fingers, which was why I let out a small cry of surprise."

"I see," Lady Voss replied, her brow now furrowed with evident alarm and frustration. "Then it is gone, and we have nothing further to do."

"Other than to find Lady Stanfield," Marianne reminded her as Lady Voss grimaced, clearly eager to return home. "We know she is to be here this afternoon, do we not?"

"According to Lady Brightly, Lady Stanfield is always a part of the fashionable hour," Lady Voss replied, stopping for a moment to look out across the park and taking in the many patrons present. "Although quite how we are to find Lady Stanfield, I do not know."

"Perhaps I can assist with that," came a voice from behind Marianne, and she turned to see none other than Lord Castleton standing there, his eyes gentle and his smile lifting the corner of his mouth just a little. "Good afternoon, Lady Voss. Good afternoon,

Lady Marianne. Forgive me for interrupting you, but I could not help but overhear what you said, Lady Voss. I have, in fact, just left Lord and Lady Stanfield only some moments ago."

Marianne found herself grasping his arm, albeit in as surreptitious a manner as she could. "But the seal is gone."

"And Lord Wright is following him," Lord Castleton replied calmly. "We both saw it." His eyes searched her face. "You did not recognize him?"

"I did not have even a flicker of recognition," she replied as Lord Castleton nodded, clearly having expected as much. "He was not a gentleman, I do not think."

Lord Castleton nodded, then offered her his arm. "Pray, put it from your mind, Lady Marianne," he said encouragingly. "Now, shall we make our way to Lady Stanfield so that Lady Voss can speak to her as she hopes?"

"Indeed," Lady Voss replied eagerly. "The sooner I shall be able to return home from this crush, the happier I shall be." She grimaced as Lord Castleton chuckled, finally drawing a true smile from Marianne. "Did you tell Lord Castleton about the seal, Marianne? He should know of it."

Marianne hesitated, looking down at the ground for a moment before she spoke. "I did not give the man my father's seal," she said slowly, "but rather his old one which has since been replaced."

The lightness quickly left Lord Castleton's face. "You mean to say that you did not give them what was expected?" he asked as Marianne bit her lip. "That what they have asked for will not be given?"

"It *will* be given," Lady Voss insisted firmly. "But the seal will be broken and, therefore, anything that bears Lord Gillingham's mark will most likely be questioned by those who receive it."

"And I *did* write a note of explanation," Marianne added quickly. "I stated that the old seal was broken and that a new one is being delivered to my father very soon." Realizing that her hand was still on Lord Castleton's arm, heat climbed into her face and she kept her eyes from his. "I wanted to find a way to stop—or at the very least, cause difficulty for—the person who seeks to take whatever he wishes from my father."

Lord Castleton let out a long, slow breath and then, much to her surprise, reached across and patted her hand with his free one. "That was wise, Lady Marianne," he told her as her head lifted and her eyes caught the admiration in his gaze. "Something I would not have considered, if I were to tell the truth."

"I thank you, Lord Castleton," Marianne replied quietly. "I only hope that there will be no consequences for my actions."

He nodded, pressing her hand for a moment longer before he squared his shoulders and cleared his throat.

"Now, shall we go in search of Lady Stanfield?" he asked, and Marianne felt her heart lift just a little, relieved that he had been in such agreement with her chosen course of action. "I do hope that Lady Voss will be able to garner the information from her that we require."

"I am sure I will," Lady Voss replied with a clear, grim determination. "Come, then. Let us go."

11

Making his way a little further into White's, James sat down heavily in a large, overstuffed chair and closed his eyes. It had been a rather busy day and he had to confess that he was tired. The evening soiree had been an excellent evening, but he had found it near impossible to remove his gaze from Lady Marianne. The thought of White's had been a welcome one and when Lord Wright had suggested it, in the company of both Lady Marianne and Lady Voss, James had accepted at once.

"This should help you," Lord Wright grinned, handing him a glass. "You do look rather weary."

"I am exhausted," James replied, opening his eyes and accepting the glass from his friend. "But not, I presume, as fatigued as you, given how long you had to trail that gentleman for." His brow lifted as Lord Wright sat down in the chair next to him, noting how the smile faded from the gentleman's face.

"He was not a gentleman," Lord Wright replied, grimacing. "I am sure of that."

"That is precisely what Lady Marianne said also," James replied with a wry smile. "Something about the way he spoke told her that he was not a gentleman."

Lord Wright nodded, lifting the glass to his lips and taking a small sip. "Regardless, yes, I did manage to follow him," he said as James listened eagerly, hoping that Lord Wright would give him the answers he desperately required. "But it was not as you might have expected, Castleton."

The eagerness and expectation within James' heart began to fade in an instant. "Oh?"

"I followed the fellow to the road and saw him climb into a hackney," Lord Wright began. "I, of course, followed after him in a hackney of my own, paying the driver a great deal not to lose the fellow. However, as we continued driving, the hackney that bore this particular gentleman came to a sudden stop. As I looked out of the window, ready to pursue him, he crossed between the approaching carriages—a foolhardy venture, I thought, where he might well have lost his life—only to make his way to the other side." He shook his head, a darkness in his expression that did not bode well. "A carriage stopped for only a moment and he climbed inside. When I shouted at the hackney driver to follow after him, he shouted back that there was no feasible way for him to do so. There was no space on the road for him to turn and, if he had done so, then most likely there would have been a great accident."

"So, he slipped from you," James muttered, his spirits sinking low. "That is not your fault, of course."

Lord Wright shook his head and let out a long, frustrated breath. "I am irritated with myself," he told James. "I feel as though I should have leapt from the hackney and chased after the carriage with all of my might."

James allowed himself a quiet chuckle. "I hardly think that being knocked down by a carriage or the like would have been a wise decision," he said as Lord Wright shot him a rueful look. "You did what was best." He looked steadily at his friend. "And you did not recognize the carriage?"

Lord Wright closed his eyes and rested his head back against the chair. "It was a very fine one indeed, certainly, but such was my haste that I did not take in anything else."

"Again, that is not something you should blame yourself for," James replied firmly. "You did your very best."

"The man, however," Lord Wright continued, as though he had not heard James, "was someone I would be able to recognize again. He had a strange gait, for his left side twisted a little as he walked. He leaned more heavily on that side, although it did not prevent him from walking very swiftly."

James nodded. "That is good," he said as Lord Wright grunted, not accepting James' compliment. "I am sure that, should we be able to make our way into either Lord Dowding or Lord Balfour's home on some pretense or other, then we might be in luck and recognize the fellow."

A strange light came into Lord Wright's eyes as he leaned forward in his chair, looking at James intently. "Have you not heard?" he asked as James frowned. "Lord Balfour is to host a ball in a sennight. The invitations have already been sent out."

James' brow furrowed all the more. "Indeed," he said slowly as Lord Wright nodded. "I am only briefly acquainted with the gentleman, however. I am not certain I will receive an invitation."

"I am sure you will," Lord Wright replied in a frankly mysterious manner. "Although it appears that he does not, as yet, know Lady Marianne or Lady Voss." His brow lifted as James nodded slowly, acknowledging this. "I have suggested to him, however, that you would be most grateful if Lady Marianne were to be invited."

James' mouth fell open and it took him a moment or two to regain his composure. Lord Wright chuckled and sipped his brandy with a great sense of calmness about him, whilst James attempted to understand what Lord Wright had done.

"I believe he intends to acquaint himself with her by the end of the week," Lord Wright said as James closed his eyes and gave a small shake of his head. "She will attend the ball and, mayhap from there, something more will occur."

"I am astonished," James replied as Lord Wright took another sip of his brandy. "You mean to suggest that now Lord Balfour believes there to be—"

"It is hardly only Lord Balfour!" Lord Wright exclaimed, interrupting him. "Surely you must know that all the *beau monde* think there to be an interest in you toward Lady Marianne?"

Opening his mouth to protest this, James closed it again tightly, realizing that it made perfect sense for such a thing to be considered. After all, he had often been in Lady Marianne's company, they had dined together, and were often seen together out walking or the like.

"I know that your eagerness is only to help Lady Marianne through this most difficult time," Lord Wright said quietly, "but this is a consequence of such a desire. Although," he continued with a shrug of his shoulders, "I do not think that it is a *severe* consequence." A glimmer came into his eye, but James did not reply to such a statement, fully aware of what Lord Wright was suggesting. "Certainly not one that I would find particularly arduous."

Frowning, James looked away from his friend and across the room, considering what had been said. Of course, the *ton* would think such a thing but what about he himself? Did he have any true consideration for Lady Marianne?"

He nodded to himself, fully aware of Lord Wright's study of him. He knew full well that there was a great admiration and regard for Lady Marianne, but was there any more to his feelings?

"She does not think as poorly of me as she did before," he admitted aloud as Lord Wright grinned. "That is one consideration, at least."

"There is no shame in having any sort of affection for the lady," Lord Wright stated, as though James needed to be reminded of such a thing. "She is quite remarkable, and I can well understand such warm considerations."

Again there came the urge to protest but James restrained himself with an effort. There was no need to lie to Lord Wright, not when he already had such an obvious and evident understanding of James' emotions toward Lady Marianne. It seemed, however, that James himself was the one who was less than inclined to consider such things.

"There is no time at present to allow myself to think of what might be," he said as Lord Wright shrugged. "I will not allow myself to do so."

Lord Wright considered this but then shook his head. "I see no wisdom in that," he stated firmly. "Whilst Lady Marianne is in a great deal of difficulty at present and whilst you are doing your very best to assist her, there is no wisdom in refusing to permit yourself to even *think* of what you might hope for, when Lord and Lady Gillingham are restored." He tilted his head and looked at James. "For then, when the time comes, you will know precisely what it is that you seek, what you hope for, and what you wish to say to her."

The thought of speaking to Lady Marianne of such deep emotions gave James a start, sending a slight tremor though him.

"*And*," Lord Wright continued, a broad smile spreading across his face, "it will make certain that you have no overwhelming trepidation when the time comes!"

Flushing, James threw back the rest of his brandy. "I may consider it," he replied, giving Lord Wright the answer he hoped would then silence him on the matter. "But for the moment, I will continue to do what I can to find Lord and Lady Gillingham and have them returned to Lady Marianne." He shook his head. "I do not know whether or not there will be any consequences for Lady Marianne, given that she sent the broken seal, but I can only hope it will not be so."

Lord Wright's smile faded. "And did Lady Voss discover anything of importance from Lady Stanfield?"

"She did," James replied with a rueful smile. "She discovered that not only had Lady Stanfield talked to all and sundry about her cook becoming ill, she had spoken both to Lord Dowding and Lord Balfour about it specifically. Apparently, her husband was rather irritated with her for mentioning it, but the lady was most upset, for she thought the cook to be very proficient indeed." He shook his head, feeling as though they had been pushed back at almost every turn. "Of course, she is now greatly relieved that her servant is back to full health, although evidently she did not care enough about the lady to make certain that she received the doctoring she needed in the first place." He rolled his eyes. "Lady Stanfield believes it was only through her fervent prayers that the cook was restored, rather than anything else."

Lord Wright bit back a laugh, gesturing for a footman to attend them. "Then she is entirely mistaken, of course," he replied as James nodded wearily. "Not that Lady Voss could say a word to her about it."

"Indeed, she could not," James replied, just as another footman drew near, handing him a note. "Oh, do excuse me."

Frowning, he unfolded the unsealed letter and quickly read over the words. His heart slammed hard against his chest, his breath catching and his chest tight.

"Whatever is the matter?" Lord Wright asked as James rose from his chair, his whole body suddenly burning with both fear and urgency. "Is there something wrong?"

"It is Lady Marianne," James replied as Lord Wright also rose from his chair, his expression wiped of all good humor. "She has returned home from the ball to discover her butler unconscious, her footmen injured, and her father's study seemingly turned upside down. She has begged us to attend her at once." Hurrying from the room, he refolded the note and placed it in his pocket, his mind already whirring with a thousand thoughts. Just who would have done such a thing? And why would they do so?

She gave them the old seal.

Dread filled his heart as he recalled what Lady Marianne had told him. Had the person responsible for the kidnap of Lord and Lady Gillingham returned to the house in order to make certain that what lady Marianne had sent him was the only seal Lord Gillingham possessed? He swallowed hard, stepping out into the night and making his way to where Lord Wright's carriage waited. He could only pray that she had hidden the new seal somewhere within the house and that it had not been discovered. He did not want to think of what would happen, should it have been found.

. . .

"Lady Marianne."

The lady rose at once, the moment he and Lord Wright stepped into the room.

James had expected her to be upset, had thought he would see tears in her eyes, evidence that she had been crying and perhaps with Lady Voss comforting her, but it soon became apparent that Lady Marianne had not been doing any such thing.

Instead, there was an anger burning in her eyes, a hardness there that had not been present before.

"Thank you for coming, Lord Castleton, Lord Wright," she said, her voice steady and without any trace of either fear or upset. "I am grateful to you both."

"But of course." He bowed low, seeing Lady Voss rise to join her niece, who bobbed a quick curtsy. "Someone has injured your butler, then?"

"A few of the staff have been injured," Lady Voss said tightly as James saw a similar anger within her gaze also. "None severely, thank goodness. They are having their injuries treated at present."

James let out a long breath, shaking his head as he did so. "I am angry and upset on your behalf," he said as Lady Marianne lifted her chin. "Who could have done such a thing?"

She held his gaze for a long moment before she spoke. "The person who has my father and mother clearly came, or sent someone, to make certain that I was truthful in my words when I stated that there was no other seal," she said, her voice remaining steady and her expression calm. "I have removed the new seal, however, and placed it in another part of the house. It remains there still, much to my relief."

Letting out a long, slow breath, James studied Lady Marianne's face and wondered at her expression. She did not appear to be upset but instead seemed to be completely in control. However, there was a coolness about her expression that made him hesitate, made him wonder what it was she was thinking at present.

"I only informed a few people that I had handed over the old seal instead of the new," Lady Marianne continued. "I must hope that you did not tell any other, Lord Castleton."

Her brow lifted and James felt an arrow strike at his heart. His brow furrowed hard, his lips pulling thin as he returned her gaze.

"I do not know what you mean to imply, Lady Marianne," he said slowly, looking at her steadily, "but I can assure you that I told no one at all about this seal of yours. Why would I do so?"

She did not answer but looked instead to Lord Wright, the very same question apparent in her gaze. Lord Wright held up both hands in a defensive manner.

"I did not even know of it until Lord Castleton explained to me only some minutes ago, as we made our way here," he said truthfully. "I swear, Lady Marianne, I did not speak of it to anyone."

A flicker of anger burned in James' heart and he allowed it to ignite. "I hardly think that any of us present here this evening have had anything to do with what has occurred," he said, a little sharply. "There surely cannot even be the *suggestion* that any of us spoke to another about the seal. Why would we do such a thing? Do you not think that we are all fully aware of just how difficult and precarious this situation is at present?" He saw something in her eyes flicker and, with an effort, restrained himself from saying anything further. For some reason, Lady Marianne had, in her own way and for her own reasons, chosen to allow her anger to question his motivation, and that of Lord Wright and, perhaps, even Lady Voss.

It was understandable, he supposed, for she must be quite overcome with what had occurred, but still, he felt both a little insulted and frustrated at her question.

"I—I can see that, Lord Castleton," she replied, stammering just a little as the anger faded from her eyes and a deep uncertainty began to replace it. "I cannot understand why the person responsible for stealing my parents away would come in search of my father's new seal, however."

Lord Wright, who appeared to have managed to remove any sense of frustration or upset from himself in a matter of moments, let out a sigh and plopped down into a chair. "I would surmise, Lady Marianne, that your father might well have been the one to alert him—this person—to the fact that the seal that was given was not his new one," he said as James nodded. "Either that, or the gentleman is desperate for your father's seal, given what we believe he intends to do with it, and is not satisfied with simply your word that there is not a new one at present. Therefore, they came in search of it themselves."

"That would make sense," James agreed as Lady Marianne glanced toward her aunt, who gave her an almost imperceptible nod. "Is your father's study in great disarray?"

Lady Marianne gestured toward the door, although when she looked toward him, she did not meet his gaze even for a moment. "Allow me to show you," she said as Lord Wright pushed himself out of his chair. "Please."

James followed wordlessly after her, keeping his whirling thoughts to himself at present. Lady Marianne walked through the house, which was very well lit with a good many candles, until finally they came to Lord Gillingham's study. James frowned hard, seeing that the door itself was damaged.

"It was locked," Lady Marianne told him, as though she anticipated his question. "Whoever came here did what they needed to in order to make their way inside."

"And no one heard him?" James asked incredulously. "That damage would have made a good deal of noise, I am sure."

Lady Marianne looked over her shoulder at him, her eyes hooded. "The butler and then two footmen discovered him," she said softly. "And they paid the price for doing so. Recall, Lord Castleton, that the house was not as well lit as you see it at present and, indeed, most of the staff were below stairs, given that both Lady Voss and I were absent from it." One shoulder lifted. "I would have stayed at home, had I known that such a thing was to occur."

"I am glad you were not," James replied fervently as Lady Marianne entered the room. "For then you might also have found yourself injured." His mouth fell open as he stepped inside, shock catching at him as he stared all around the room, seeing the devastation that had been caused. Practically every item in the room was damaged in some way. Drawers had been flung to the floor, the contents spilling out from them, if they had not been tipped out entirely. Papers were strewn everywhere, and even a small set of drawers had been knocked entirely to the ground.

"Good gracious," Lord Wright murmured, coming in after James. "This is...terrible indeed."

"And you say they did not find the new seal?" James asked, and Lady Marianne shook her head. "You did not keep it here?"

"I did not," she told him, much to his relief. "I already had it removed from here and placed in another part of the house." Her brows knotted together for a moment. "I—I am not sure why I chose to do so, but regardless, it was done as I had asked."

"That showed both wisdom and foresight," Lady Voss said from where she stood in the doorway. "The person responsible for this will have had to return to his master to tell him that there was no new seal to be found."

"And that," James added, "might well hold back any plans that they have to use your father's seal for their own ends."

A gentle clearing of the throat caught everyone's attention and Lady Marianne turned quickly as a footman came into the room to stand near Lady Voss.

"My lady, I would not have disturbed you, save for the fact that a lad turned up at the door and told me to give you this." He held out a small note that was sealed with wax but which itself bore no mark. "Said I had to do so straight away."

James took a small step closer, his eyes narrowing as he fixed them to the footman. "This boy came to the servants' entrance?" he asked, and the footman nodded, his face a little pale in the candlelight. "Not to the front of the house?"

"No, my lord," the footman replied as Lady Marianne reached out to take the note. "He came to the entrance that I and the others use. Ran off into the night before I could ask him anything."

Lord Wright cursed aloud, only to flush red and then apologize for doing so. Lady Marianne did not say even a single word, however, breaking open the seal and unfolding the note.

Dismissing the footman, even though he had no right or authority to do so, James turned back to where Lady Marianne stood, seeing the slight trembling in her hands as she handed the note to Lady Voss. There was no anger in her expression now, no uncertainty, no lack of belief. Instead, she appeared to have returned once more to anxiety and fear.

"Goodness," Lady Voss breathed as she read the note. "The diamonds?" Her eyes lifted to Lady Marianne, who nodded. "You know where they are kept?"

Lady Marianne nodded slowly. "I do," she said, her voice no longer as determined as before. "I know where the Gillingham diamonds are. They are within this house."

"The diamonds?" James repeated, throwing Lady Voss a questioning glance before returning his gaze to Lady Marianne. "You are to take diamonds somewhere?"

Lady Marianne nodded, just as Lady Voss held out the note for James to read. He took it at once, reading it quickly and finding his brow furrowing hard.

"The Gillingham diamonds are a family heirloom," he heard Lady Marianne say as he read the note over again. "They are without price, for I do not believe that there was ever any intention of selling them given just how precious they are to our family. They are only worn occasionally, and it gives my mother great pride when she does so." Her eyes began to fill with tears, but she blinked them away rapidly as James handed the note to Lord Wright. "I was to be given them this Season. I was to wear them for the very first time. That is why they have been brought to London. It is solely for my benefit."

"And your mother or father must have told this particular gentleman, whoever he is, that they are here in London also," James replied grimly. "You are expected to take them with you wherever you go for the next few days, although quite why he is asking you to do such a thing, I—"

"It is so that this person might demand them from Lady Marianne at any moment," Lady Voss interrupted as James looked toward her, listening hard. "They are not going to tell her when the diamonds will be demanded, will not give her any warning as to when that might be. Rather, they will be taken when the person responsible decides."

"There is not time to have a false set made," Lady Marianne added, her voice now shaking just a little. "I have no time to do anything other than what they ask."

"And I would advise you *not* to do so, even if you had the choice," James replied firmly, coming a little closer to Lady Marianne. "To wear paste when they expect the diamonds might only bring injury to either yourself or to your parents. You must be on your guard."

Lord Wright cleared his throat, looking at James and then at Lady Marianne. "It is interesting that you are soon to receive an invitation from Lord Balfour," he said slowly as a prickle of awareness ran down James' spine. "His ball is only a few days away. I cannot help but wonder if both the ball and the diamonds might be connected in some way."

Lady Marianne gasped. "You mean to say that you believe Lord Balfour might be doing so deliberately?"

"I cannot say," Lord Wright replied, spreading his hands wide. "But certainly I did ask him to not only acquaint himself with you but to have you invited to his ball also and he did not show any sort of reluctance."

James bit his lip, another deep frown settling over his forehead. "That might only be because he would be very glad indeed to have a beautiful lady such as Lady Marianne at his ball," he said slowly as Lady Marianne caught his gaze. "We must not make assumptions—although, certainly, I would suggest that Lord Balfour's ball will give us an opportunity to discover whether or not it is he or Lord Dowding that is behind this, Lady Marianne."

"If it is either of them," she replied, lowering both her head and her gaze as worry flooded her expression. "What if there is another who is the perpetrator? One we do not know? One that has not, as yet, revealed themselves?" Tear-filled eyes looked back at James as Lady Marianne's lips trembled. "What if I do all that is required but do not receive my parents back in return?"

He did not hesitate but put out his hands and caught both of Lady Marianne's in his own. "We *will* be successful," he told her firmly as Lady Voss pulled out a handkerchief and dabbed at her eyes. "Regardless of whether it is at Lord Balfour's ball or somewhere else a few days later, you must believe that we will achieve the safe return of both your mother and your father. You know that we will all work tirelessly for such a thing."

"I—I know," she answered quietly, holding his gaze and squeezing his fingers gently. "I am sorry for suggesting that you might have spoken out of turn, Lord Castleton. I should not have done so."

"No," James agreed, allowing the corner of his mouth to flicker upwards. "No, you should not have done so. But I shall take no offence from it, Lady Marianne."

She swallowed hard but did not look away. "Then you are very good, Lord Castleton," she replied softly, before finally letting go of his hands and stepping back. "Thank you again for calling this evening. I do not know what I ought to do next, to be truthful."

James looked to Lord Wright who, not helpfully at all, lifted one shoulder in a small shrug.

"Have the room tidied," he told Lady Marianne, not certain what else to suggest. "And rest, Lady Marianne. You must rest."

Nodding, she went to stand by her aunt. "And the diamonds?"

James shook his head. "There is nothing for it but to do as is asked," he said honestly. "Find them. Take them with you whenever you set foot into any ballroom, drawing room, or assembly room. Either wear them or carry them on your person but pray, Lady Marianne, do not lose them. Do not set them down for even a moment."

She held his gaze whilst Lord Wright looked away and Lady Voss wiped her eyes once more, color in her cheeks now as perhaps she recalled the mistake she had made with Lady Marianne's reticule that first time.

"I shall do as you say," Lady Marianne replied, her voice now a little steadier than before and a gentle determination beginning to build in her eyes. "I apologize to both you and to you also, Lord Wright, for any suggestion on my part that you might have spoken of the seal to any other. That was not wise of me to even *think* and I am sorry for it."

Lord Wright put one hand over his heart and bowed low, a smile spreading across his face. "There is no need to apologize," he told her as James nodded. "Truly."

"Indeed," James replied, understanding that her concern and her worry had made her consider things that were not even remotely possible. "Now, recall that you will soon be introduced to one Lord Balfour and that, most likely, he will invite you to his ball very soon thereafter."

"And I shall accept," Lady Marianne said as James nodded. "I pray that we will find something there to prove whether or not he is the one responsible."

"If he is not, then we shall turn our attention to Lord Dowding," James added, and Lady Marianne frowned, lines forming across her brow. "You need not fear, Lady Marianne. We will find the person responsible."

For a moment, she did not answer him. And then, she nodded and closed her eyes. "And if it is not Lord Dowding either, Lord Castleton?" she asked, a faint tremor shaking her frame. "What then?"

The answer came readily to his lips. "Then we will continue regardless," he stated unequivocally. "Until we discover the truth and find Lord and Lady Gillingham. They will be returned to you, Lady Marianne, and you will be freed of this nightmare." Wishing he could reach out and embrace her, that he could clasp her tightly to him and assure her that all would be well, he satisfied himself with a lift of his chin as he held her gaze. "I can assure you of that."

12

It had been a sennight since Marianne had received the note about the Gillingham diamonds. A sennight since she had come home to discover her footman injured and in pain, her butler lying unconscious on the floor outside her father's study, and the study itself completely ransacked. The horror of what she had seen, the fear that had clutched at her heart as she had taken in the scene before her, had not yet fully left her heart. It still lingered there, returning to her thoughts upon occasion and with such swiftness that it threatened to take a hold of her completely.

"You have the diamonds?"

Marianne looked up as her aunt came into her bedchamber. "I do, Aunt," she said softly, gesturing toward the diamonds that had been set out before her on the dressing table. "I was to place them in my reticule but mayhap—"

"You must wear them this evening," Lady Voss interrupted, before Marianne could say anything more. "It is foolish to not have such beautiful things out on display. And, besides which, it will make it quite apparent to whoever is watching you that you are doing as you are asked."

Marianne pressed her lips together and nodded, turning back

to glance at her reflection in the mirror. She had worn the earbobs already but had never once placed the necklace around her neck, had never once shown the diamonds off in all their beauty. And yet, this evening, she had thought of doing so.

"It is a ball," Lady Voss said, picking up the diamonds and placing them around Marianne's neck, fastening them at the back. "You would not be out of place wearing these, I am sure. Besides," she continued, tilting her head and looking at Marianne, "they are quite magnificent on you."

Marianne allowed a small smile to creep over her lips. "I am sure that they would be quite magnificent on anyone," she replied, one hand reaching up tentatively to touch them. "And yet I am a little afraid, Aunt."

Lady Voss settled one hand on Marianne's shoulder. "As am I," she replied honestly. "I have been so every day you have set foot out of this house, upon every social occasion or afternoon tea we have gone out to join this last week. I have dreaded what might occur or what might happen to you, my dear." A sigh escaped her as she shook her head. "And that has been when you have kept the necklace out of sight. I confess my worry all the greater now that I know that you will have it around your neck—although I still believe that it is right for you to wear it."

Marianne looked once more at her reflection, feeling a knot of tension tighten in her stomach. "Let us hope that this evening reveals something to us," she said softly. "I only pray that my parents are still well."

"I am sure that they are," Lady Voss replied, but without any true conviction in her voice. "At the very least, my dear, we must *believe* that they are, for that will keep our spirits bolstered."

Closing her eyes, Marianne took in a long breath and steadied herself inwardly. "Then let us depart," she said, opening her eyes and rising from her chair. "Lord Castleton will be waiting."

CLIMBING OUT OF THE CARRIAGE, Marianne pressed one hand lightly to her stomach and stood for a moment, looking up at Lord Balfour's townhouse. She had been introduced to Lord Balfour some days ago and had found him quiet, respectable, and entirely genial—although, of course, she herself remained entirely suspicious of him. Knowing full well that appearances could be deceiving, she had not allowed herself to be flattered by any of his compliments but had, of course, placed a smile on her lips despite her own inward thoughts.

"Goodness, the street is very well lit this evening," Lady Voss noticed, coming to stand by Marianne. "Lord Balfour clearly wishes to impress his guests."

Marianne smiled at her aunt, lifting one shoulder. "Mayhap you are right," she replied quietly, looking at the footmen who stood on the stone steps, each holding their own personal lantern so as to guide the guests up toward the house. Two footmen were on either side of the stone steps, lanterns in their hands and the light shining out from them toward Marianne and Lady Voss. It gave Marianne the very pleasant feeling of being warmly welcomed into Lord Balfour's townhouse, encouraging her to step out of the gloom and into the light.

The carriage rolled away behind her, taken to another place until Marianne and Lady Voss required it, and Marianne smiled at her aunt. "Shall we go inside?" she asked, trying to find as much confidence and strength as she could. "Lord Castleton and Lord Wright will be awaiting our arrival." That thought was a very pleasant one indeed, Marianne had to admit, although she felt rather ashamed still of how she had behaved the night she had discovered that an intruder had broken into the house.

Her mind had turned to varying frantic thoughts, panic had broken out within her, and, by the time Lord Castleton and Lord Wright had arrived, she had found anger bubbling up within her and had, much to her shame, asked whether they had informed any other about her father's seal. The moment she had spoken those words, she had seen the shock jump into Lord Castleton's eyes. Shock which was then immediately followed by a clear and understandable anger that she would even think to ask him such a thing.

And then, when she had realized her foolishness, he had shown such understanding and consideration that she had felt guilt pile itself upon her heart. The kindness he had shown her thus far, his willingness to help, and his desire to do all he could to assist her had been forgotten by her in a moment, her anger and panic making her speak in such a foolish manner that she would not have blamed him had he chosen to step away from her for good. But he had shown yet more of the very same characteristics that made her think so well of him and, from how things had been between them these last few days, Lord Castleton had evidently forgotten the matter entirely.

Her heart quickened as they began to make their way toward the stone steps, and she thought of being in his company again. There had been a growing intimacy between them and as yet, she did not quite know what to think of it. The way he touched her hand, the way she felt the urge to rush into his arms...surely that spoke of something greatly profound? And yet, Marianne knew that now was not the time to consider such things, not when there was so much still at stake.

"You ridiculous fool!"

Marianne stopped suddenly, hearing a harsh voice crash through her thoughts, making her turn her head in the hope that whoever this particular person was referring to, it was not her.

"I am only trying to help you, my lord," she heard someone say, only for a figure to storm past both her and Lady Voss, making them take a few steps back in shock. The gentleman climbed the stone steps without any hesitation and, it seemed, without any awareness that she and Lady Voss were present.

"Well, I must say," Lady Voss said as one of the footmen came to make certain they were both well and uninjured. "That gentleman was *much* too rude for my liking."

Marianne brushed her fingers down over her gown, worried

that her stumble had wrinkled it. "Indeed," she murmured, glancing over her shoulder and seeing a man close the carriage door before making his way toward the horses. Her eyes narrowed as she took in the man's strange, lolloping gait, seeing how he leaned heavily to his left side.

Her mind screamed with a sudden, startling awareness and she caught Lady Voss' arm.

"Come in at once, Aunt," she said quickly, beginning to climb up the steps and half pulling, half encouraging her aunt to come with her. Lady Voss went with her at once, although her breathing was a little quick by the time she reached the top.

"My dear Marianne," Lady Voss said as Marianne practically thrust her aunt through the door and quickly handed the footman their invitation. "Is something the matter?"

Marianne looked all about her, not answering immediately. "I must find Lord Castleton," she said hurriedly. "And Lord Wright. That man, the one who came in before us—we must discover his name."

Lady Voss gestured to the receiving line. "I am sure that he is already there, waiting," she said as Marianne looked toward it but saw, much to her disappointment, no gentlemen lingering there alone. Those that were present were clearly wed to the lady they stood beside, or standing with their daughters instead.

"No, he is not here," Marianne replied as Lady Voss began to move toward the receiving line. "He must have gone straight past the receiving line and made his way into the ballroom."

Lady Voss turned to look at Marianne directly, her brow furrowed. "I do not understand why you are so eager to discover such a thing," she replied, her brows low over her eyes. "What is it that you must know about this fellow?"

Marianne glanced all about her, not wanting anyone to overhear. "The man who was with that gentleman, the one who went past us in such a rude manner, he..." She took in a quick breath, trying to keep her composure. "I am sure he walked with a heaviness to one side." Looking into her aunt's eyes, she did not see even a flicker of understanding. "Do you not recall, Aunt? The 'gentleman' that Lord Wright saw and followed the day that I had the seal taken from me walked in much the same way."

Finally, light dawned in Lady Voss' eyes. "You mean to say that—"

"Whoever that gentleman was, I am certain that one of his servants was the one who took the seal from me," Marianne replied quickly. "Lord Balfour cannot be the gentleman, which may very well mean that—"

"Lord Dowding," Lady Voss said, before Marianne could speak his name. "Unless it is some other gentleman that, as yet, we are entirely unaware of."

Marianne nodded. "Which is why we must be certain," she said fervently as a wave of urgency crashed over her. "What are we to do, Aunt? We cannot simply follow after him and ignore the receiving line. And besides, he will have, most likely, gone into the ballroom and will now be mixed into the crowd."

Lady Voss hesitated, then nodded to herself, as though she understood what it was she had to do.

"The footman," she said, turning back on her heel and hurrying back to the front door. "He was collecting the invitations as we came in. Surely he will know the name of the gentleman who rushed in before us."

Marianne's heart slammed hard into her chest as she followed her aunt, who approached the footman eagerly.

"Just before we arrived," she said as the footman inclined his head toward her, "there was a gentleman who came in at great speed. He was most rude to me and to my charge. I must know his name."

The footman cleared his throat, then looked down at the invitations he held in his hand. "Of course, my lady," he murmured as Marianne resisted the urge to pull the invitations from him and look through them herself. "There were two others who came after you, which means that…" He frowned, and then his expression cleared.

Marianne could not help herself. "Is it, mayhap, Lord Dowding?" she asked, only for the footman to frown again and look down hard at the invitation.

"No, my lady," he replied, clearly a little confused. "It was Lord Worthington." Looking up at Lady Voss, he settled the invitations again in his hands. "Might I be of any more assistance?"

"No, thank you," Lady Voss replied smartly, whilst shock flooded Marianne. "That is most helpful. I will speak to him at once."

Astonished at the sudden weakness that tore at her limbs, Marianne accepted her aunt's arm as they walked back together toward the receiving line.

"Then it is he," Lady Voss murmured as Marianne nodded, her throat beginning to ache with a sudden tightness. "What are we to do?"

Marianne could barely speak, such was the shock that crashed through her. Lord Worthington? The gentleman that she had thought so well of? The one who had asked to call upon her, who had shown such interest in her? Why, then, would he have done such a thing?

"Marianne?" Lady Voss' voice was filled with alarm. "Are you quite all right? You look very pale indeed."

Swallowing hard, Marianne forced herself to take in great gulps of air in an attempt to calm herself. "We must tell Lord Castleton and Lord Wright," Marianne replied, aware of the trembling that now took a hold of her frame. "They will know what is best."

"We could make our way to his home and release your parents!" Lady Voss exclaimed, making Marianne beg her to quieten her voice a little. "They can only be—"

Forced to stop so that they might greet Lord Balfour, Lady Voss made a great show of thanking him for his *very* kind invitation, whilst Marianne herself struggled to even find the right words to say, such was her inner torment. Lord Balfour did not seem to notice, however, given the effervescent greeting of Lady Voss and, in a few minutes, they were able to make their way into the ballroom.

And, just as Marianne had expected, Lord Castleton approached them practically at once.

"Good evening." He bowed low whilst Marianne stood precisely where she was, the urge to tell him what she had learned overpowering even her sense of propriety. "Might I say, Lady Marianne, you look enchanting this evening."

"I know who has my parents," Marianne blurted out, stepping closer to Lord Castleton and grasping for his hands, her whole body trembling violently. "I saw—I saw the man with the strange gait, just the way that Lord Wright described him. And when we spoke to the footman, he told us that the gentleman who arrived with that servant was Lord Worthington."

This did not seem to have much of an impact upon Lord Castleton, for he remained where he was for a few moments, studying her and saying nothing.

"Do you not understand?" Marianne cried, no longer having any requirement to keep her voice low given the noise in the ballroom. "Lord Worthington is the one who has been doing all of this."

Lady Voss put a restraining hand on Marianne's arm. "Let me explain," she said, taking a little more time to describe what had occurred and why they had reached such a conclusion. Marianne pressed her lips together and impatiently waited for her aunt to finish, seeing the way Lord Castleton's eyes flared as he understood what she meant.

"I see," he said gravely. "That would mean that the footman who took the reticule has been at his master's mercy. There was no need for Lady Stanfield to tell anyone of the ill health of her cook. No doubt Lord Worthington heard it from his staff, one way or the other."

"And thus, he was able to manipulate the footman into doing as he was directed, without pressing any suspicion onto himself," Lady Voss breathed as Marianne nodded. "He could not risk his staff being aware of what he was doing, for fear that one of them might speak of it to some others."

Marianne shook her head. "Some of his staff must know what is occurring," she said slowly. "If my parents are within his house, then—"

"We cannot think of that at present," Lord Castleton interrupted gently. "There are many questions, certainly, but for the moment, let us conclude that Lord Worthington is the one who will seek you out this evening to take the Gillingham diamonds."

"But I have no intention of waiting here and allowing him to do so," Marianne said as Lord Wright came over to join them, having just finished dancing the quadrille. "I must go to his townhouse at once and seek out my parents."

Lord Castleton's lips flattened, and a deep frown etched his forehead as he looked back at her. "But what if we are mistaken?" he asked quietly. "What if Lord Worthington has merely another servant who is similar to the one that Lord Wright saw?"

Marianne resisted the urge to stamp her foot in frustration, wanting to tell Lord Castleton that she thought his delay much too foolish and trying to find the words to explain her desperation.

"I believe you have discovered the identity of the person you believe responsible," Lord Wright interrupted, before she could say anything. "You say it is Lord Worthington?"

"It is," Marianne replied, quickly explaining what had brought her to such a conclusion. "I cannot linger here, not when I fear that my parents are being held at Lord Worthington's home."

Lord Wright hesitated, then looked toward Lord Castleton. "And we cannot simply make our way into his house," he said slowly. "Do you intend simply to march up to the door and demand to be allowed entrance, Lady Marianne?" It was a simple question that held no malice and yet Marianne felt her cheeks heat with embarrassment.

"There must be something we can do," she said, not answering the question. "Something that we can do that will help me to determine whether or not my parents are contained within his house."

Lord Wright and Lord Castleton exchanged glances but neither said a word.

"We must attempt, then, to catch him in the act of taking your diamonds, although quite how he will do so, I am yet to understand," Lord Castleton said, speaking slowly as though he wanted to make certain that he himself understood all that he said. "You are wearing them and all about you will see you with them. It is not as though you will simply remove them and hand them to whoever asks."

Lady Voss shook her head. "Indeed not!"

Marianne tried to calm her whirling thoughts, tried to quieten herself just a little so that she could think on what Lord Castleton had stated. "Where, then, would someone attempt to take the diamonds from me?" she asked as the others frowned. "It cannot be out in public, for there would be an uproar."

Lord Castleton's eyes brightened suddenly. "In your carriage!" he exclaimed as Lady Voss let out a startled exclamation. "It would be so very simple to have his carriage follow yours, ready to take back whichever fellow might sit in wait for you there."

"The man with the limp," Lord Wright suggested as Lord Castleton nodded. "If he is present, that would suggest all the more that he might be the one to do such a deed."

"In the dark and the gloom, you would be unable to recognize their face and would have very little opportunity to refuse," Lord Castleton finished, speaking urgently. "I am certain that is what he intends."

Fear began to cloud Marianne's heart, but she pushed it away with an effort. "And if that is the case, then what is it I should do to prevent such a thing from occurring?" she asked, and Lord Castleton shook his head. "Surely I cannot allow him to succeed."

"You must," Lord Castleton said urgently. "Lord Wright and I will follow after Lord Worthington, if it *is* he, and will make our way to wherever he goes."

"But I *must* be present when the time comes to hear the truth," Marianne protested. "I cannot simply return home and wait." She looked up beseechingly at her aunt, who, after a moment, nodded slowly.

"I would agree," Lady Voss said quietly. "If all goes as expected, then Lady Marianne and I will come after you also. We will make our way to Lord Worthington's townhouse."

Lord Castleton held up one hand. "It may be that he does not return to his townhouse," he said quietly. "Why do you not climb out from your carriage and into my own?" He hesitated, glancing toward Lady Voss. "Although, if you would prefer to return home and wait there, then Lord Wright and I will continue on to Lord Worthington's.

Marianne shook her head, inwardly refusing to even consider leaving Lord Castleton and Lord Wright to discover the truth. "Of course, we shall join you," she stated with confidence that came from nothing other than sheer determination. "And I will be there when Lord Worthington is proven to be the perpetrator."

Lord Castleton smiled at her and Marianne lifted her chin, looking back at him steadily.

"Very well, Lady Marianne," he told her quietly. "You will need courage and strength for what is to come, however. Do not fight off the man who seeks your diamonds. Give them to him meekly for then he will, most likely, leave your side just as soon as he is able."

"How will I know that all of this is to take place?" Marianne asked as Lord Castleton grimaced. "What if we are mistaken?"

"You will know if our assessment has been correct if Lord Worthington departs at the very same time as you and Lady Voss," he told her as Lady Voss nodded slowly, her face a little pale. "And, of course, if you still have your diamonds."

Marianne drew in a long breath and lifted her chin. "Very well," she said firmly. "Then let us do what we can to enjoy the evening."

Lord Castleton grinned and bowed low, holding out one hand to her. "Then might I request a dance with you, Lady Marianne?" he asked, and she slipped her dance card from her wrist and handed it to him. "I will do all I can to lift your spirits."

"I am sure you will do very well," she told him as he wrote his name down. "Thank you, Lord Castleton."

13

"Are you prepared?"

James looked down into Lady Marianne's eyes and saw the flicker of fear lingering there.

"Lord Worthington has been very attentive this evening," she said as they walked from the dance floor back toward Lady Voss. "He has called upon me on at least four occasions now, but I have never once considered it to be anything other than a gentlemanly interest." She paused and threw a glance up at him. "What if it was more than that?"

"I would suggest that it was," James told her honestly. "He wanted to watch you, to see how you fared. It also now explains how he knew that both Lord Wright and I were assisting you, given that we were both present when Lady Voss went to speak to his footman."

"He is a cunning gentleman, that is for certain," Lady Marianne replied, to which James could only nod rather grimly. "I will dance with him and inform him, somehow, that I am to take my leave with Lady Voss directly." She looked up at James a little anxiously. "Do you think he will follow?"

"I have no doubt about it," James replied fervently. "Come now.

Let us pretend that all is well. That will be the more difficult matter, I am sure."

~

"Has the carriage been called?"

James nodded, all too aware that Lady Marianne and Lady Voss had already departed. He had also seen Lord Worthington call for his carriage thereafter and had quickly followed suit, although he had made certain that his request was kept far from Lord Worthington's ears. His heart was pounding furiously as he saw Lord Worthington climb inside the carriage, seeing just how swiftly it moved off. Impatiently, he waited for his own to arrive, stepping out a little more and praying that they would not be tardy.

"Here."

James gestured the footman to step aside, throwing open the carriage door and climbing inside, with Lord Wright just behind him. The carriage had barely stopped moving before he rapped on the roof, having already instructed the driver as to what was to occur.

"Do you think it will be as you have predicted?" Lord Wright asked, and James nodded slowly. "Then we must make certain that we remain a little behind Lord Worthington, so that he will not—"

"I have already spoken to the driver at length about the affair," James interrupted, aware that he spoke tersely but finding such tension within him that he could not prevent himself from doing so. "All we need do is wait."

Lord Wright lapsed into silence as the carriage trundled along, leaving James to his own thoughts. He could think of nothing other than Lady Marianne, fearing that she might already be in a state of great terror. He could only pray that she managed to keep her composure, find her courage, and do as was requested.

Suddenly, the carriage came to an abrupt halt.

"My lord."

The driver appeared at the window, having jumped down from his seat.

"The carriage ahead of us has stopped," he said, speaking quickly. "There is another one ahead of that, but it has turned to the left and now it, too, has stopped."

James' heart began to thump furiously. "He has not seen us?"

The driver shook his head. "I don't think so, my lord. We are well back from it. It is just as well the roads are quiet this time of night."

Thinking quickly, James glanced to Lord Wright before he spoke. "Wait until the second carriage again begins to move away," he said quietly. "Prepare for Lady Marianne and Lady Voss to join us here. They will not be a moment, I am sure."

The driver nodded and James heard him climbing back into his seat. Moving to the other side of the carriage, he looked out of the window, trying desperately to find any sign of Lady Voss or Lady Marianne coming toward them. The moon shone as best it could, but with the clouds continuing to push themselves before it, James found it very difficult to see anything at all.

And then, he saw something shift.

"I am sure they are approaching," he said loudly, pushing open the carriage door and stepping out, hearing the sound of the carriage ahead of them already departing. "Lady Marianne? Lady Voss?"

His voice carried forward into the gloom and, much to his relief, two figures came toward him. Whether or not it was the light of the moon, James could not tell, but both ladies appeared to be very pale indeed.

Without having had any intention of doing so, James pulled Lady Marianne close to him, his breath coming out in a rush as he realized just how relieved he was to see her again.

"Lady Marianne," he breathed, feeling her hand grasping at his shoulder and aware of her head resting against his chest. "You are quite all right?"

She did not answer immediately, before finally lifting her head and looking up into his eyes, her expression hidden by the flickering moonlight. "I am," she replied as Lady Voss whispered for them to hurry up into the carriage. "It was as you had predicted."

James waited until Lady Marianne had climbed into the carriage before he followed suit, aware of his growing anger toward Lord Worthington. Pulling the door closed, he rapped sharply on the roof and instantly, the carriage pulled forward into motion.

"There was a man in the carriage," Lady Voss said, her voice tremulous. "He demanded the diamonds from Marianne. She, of course, gave them to him without question."

"But he did not leave the carriage immediately," Lady Marianne continued, her hand finding James' in the darkness as they sat next to each other, her fingers gripping his tightly. "There were some minutes between his taking the diamonds and his departure."

James scowled. "Lord Worthington had to wait for a short while so that no one could see what occurred," he said, heat spiraling up his arm from where Lady Marianne gripped his hand. "But we will follow him. We will find him out and we will restore all. Have no doubt about that."

Lady Marianne let out a long, heavy sigh and rested her head back against the squabs. "It was quite terrifying," she said softly as Lady Voss murmured her agreement. "I feared for my life. The threats he uttered when he demanded the diamonds made my very soul tremble."

James wanted to pull her close again but knew he could not. Not in the present company, at least. There would be time for such things later.

"But you did as was asked of you," he told her. "And that is all that matters. Now, when the time comes, you will be able to demand the truth from Lord Worthington."

"And not only that, you will be restored to all that you have lost," Lady Voss replied, her voice now very quiet indeed so that James had to strain to hear her. "I cannot wait for this entire business to be at an end."

THE CARRIAGE finally came to a stop and James was the first to look out of the window. His frown deepened. They had been in the carriage for a good deal longer than he had expected, which, to him, meant that they were no longer in the part of London where Lord Worthington's townhouse stood.

"Wait for a moment," he murmured, before pushing open the door and stepping outside.

His driver was already waiting for him.

"My lord," he said quietly. "The carriage is a little further along the street. I did not dare take the carriage any further for fear that we would be seen."

James clapped the man on the shoulder. "You did well," he replied. "Do you know which house they have gone into?"

The driver shook his head. "The tiger has gone ahead," he told James. "He will be back in a few minutes and will be able to tell you all."

And so it was that, within ten minutes, James found himself standing at the door of a house that he did not know and certainly did not recognize. Lord Wright was beside him, with Lady Marianne and Lady Voss behind them. His driver and tiger stood behind the ladies also, ready to make certain that no harm would come to them.

James swallowed hard. He did not want any ill to befall the ladies and yet had been unable to persuade either of them to remain in the carriage. What they would find within, he did not know, but their only plan at present was to make their way inside and demand the truth from Lord Worthington.

The door opened almost immediately after James knocked although it was merely a crack rather than being pulled back in welcome. Without hesitation, James put his shoulder to the door and pushed hard, surprising the person behind the door and forcing them to stumble back.

Both he and Lord Wright managed to make it inside and, with

Lord Wright preventing the older man from closing the door again, James held it open so that the two ladies could step inside also.

"Stay with him," James directed his driver, pointing at the white-haired man who had opened the door for them. "Do not allow him to go anywhere."

Lady Marianne stepped forward, her chin lifted as she looked at the white-haired man with narrowed eyes.

"Lord Worthington," she said firmly, no trace of fear in her eyes or her voice. "Where is he?"

The man swallowed but said nothing, only for the driver to murmur something under his breath which made the man's eyes narrow.

"The—the drawing room," he answered, flinging one hand out in the direction of the room. "Please, do not—"

James heard nothing more, his heart beginning to beat furiously as they made their way along the hallway toward the first door that the man had indicated. The house was not particularly well cared for, given the state of it, but he presumed that Lord Worthington had purchased this property for the sole intention of using it to keep Lord and Lady Gillingham in.

He stopped at the sound of voices, turning his head to see Lady Marianne's eyes flare wide.

"Allow myself and Lord Wright to enter first," he said as Lady Marianne reached for Lady Voss' arm. "Be bold, Lady Marianne. I am sure that, within a few minutes, you will find your parents returned to you."

Lady Marianne nodded. James allowed himself a lingering look, holding her gaze for a moment before he turned to the door. Taking a deep breath, he pushed the door open and walked inside.

The sight that met his eyes was a welcome one. There sat Lord and Lady Gillingham, looking entirely unharmed, if not a little thinner than he remembered.

"Lord Castleton."

Lord Gillingham was on his feet in a moment, just as Lord Wright stepped in behind him. And then, only a second later, there came a cry of delight as Lady Gillingham rose to her feet, her hands stretching out toward Lady Marianne, who ran past James toward her.

"Lord Worthington."

Ignoring Lord and Lady Gillingham's joyous reunion with their daughter and Lady Voss, James fixed his attention to the gentleman who, as yet, had not risen from his chair. In fact, he had remained perfectly still, although there was an expression of great astonishment rippling across his features, his face lit by the many candles that were all about the room.

"I believe, Lord Worthington, that you have been discovered." James took a few quick steps closer to the gentleman, seeing the glass of brandy in Lord Worthington's hand and feeling his anger begin to resurface. The gentleman was so arrogant, so filled with a sense of his own self-importance, that he had never once even considered that he might be found out. "You have taken Lord and Lady Gillingham, have kept them here, and have demanded various things from Lady Marianne, is that not so?"

"That is precisely as you say it, Lord Castleton," Lord Gillingham said, walking toward James as he stood directly in front of Lord Worthington. There was a tiredness about his stride, however—a fatigue that told James that Lord Gillingham had been in a state of distress for some time. He could only imagine all that had occurred and just how much hardship they had both had to endure. Lord Gillingham settled a hand on James' shoulder, gripping it a little more tightly than James had expected. "I believed that Lord Worthington intended to take us for a short drive, merely as an acquaintance who was very glad to know of my return to London." With one finger extended toward Lord Worthington, Lord Gillingham took another step forward, his face contorted with anger. "And instead, he took both my wife and me to this confounded place and refused to let us leave."

Before James could ask any questions, he felt a hand slip into his. Looking down, he saw Lady Marianne looking directly at Lord Worthington as she held tightly to his hand.

"You took them here by force," she stated, her voice trembling with what James could only think was anger. "You made certain they remained here, simply to gain what they would not give you willingly."

Lord Worthington shifted in his chair for the first time since James had walked into the room. Clearing his throat, he set down his glass of brandy and looked back at Lady Marianne, one eyebrow lifted.

"Did you know, Lady Marianne, that I asked your father for your hand last Season?" he said calmly. "And that he refused me?"

"For good reason," Lord Gillingham stated as Lady Gillingham and Lady Voss stayed behind them all, listening to all that was said. "You have very little coin, Lord Worthington. I have looked into your affairs. I have learned of your gambling, your debts, and your foolishness. I could never permit you to marry my daughter. You sought her for her dowry, for her inheritance." Lord Gillingham looked down at his daughter, his eyes holding fast to hers. "I did not tell you, my dear, because I did not want to trouble you."

"It would have made no difference to me if you *had* done so, Father," Lady Marianne replied, her chin lifting as she turned her head back toward Lord Worthington. "I trust your judgment. I know that you would have made the wisest decision."

"But I *needed* you," Lord Worthington hissed, one hand now reaching out toward Lady Marianne as though he intended to pull her toward him. "To be refused was..." He shook his head, his jaw working and his eyes narrowing. "I took what I required. I needed the seal. I needed the diamonds. The wealth that I required was going to be mine, one way or the other."

Lady Gillingham's voice came from behind them, quavering, and yet clearly the lady was determined to speak. "I had no other choice but to write that first note, Marianne. He needed to make certain that you knew we were alive and well. It—it was a test."

Looking behind him, James saw Lady Voss take Lady Gillingham's arm, clearly supporting her. "There is no fault on your shoulders, Lady Gillingham," he said quietly. "The seal, I presume, was for Lord Worthington to make certain that he could access whatever funds he could, pretending to be Lord Gillingham in his correspondence."

Lady Gillingham nodded, her eyes bright with tears. "And the diamonds—our priceless heirlooms—"

"Where are they, by the way?" Lord Wright interrupted, his brows low over his eyes. "Where have you put them, Lord Worthington?"

Lord Worthington tilted his head, looking at Lord Wright as though he were some sort of curious creature, and did not immediately answer. James began to search the room with his eyes, wondering where Lord Worthington had set such a precious item.

"They are on my person, actually," Lord Worthington said eventually, patting his breast pocket. "They are mine now, of course."

Anger burned furiously in James' heart and he took a step forward, making sure that Lady Marianne was behind him. "You are no gentleman," he stated as Lady Marianne squeezed his fingers tightly. "You think only of yourself. You attempted to take what was not yours to begin with, simply because you decided it was owed to you." His voice rose a little more, seeing the arrogant look in Lord Worthington's eyes. "Those diamonds are not yours to take. *None* of this was for you to claim." Taking another step forward, he let go of Lady Marianne's hands. "You will return the diamonds, Worthington. You will return them, or they will be taken back by force."

Lord Worthington's cocky demeanor began to fade in the face of James' wrath. He looked first at James, then to Lord Wright, Lord Gillingham, and then to James' tiger, who was standing by the door, making certain no one could either escape or enter.

"I will give you a few moments to consider," James finished as Lord Worthington swallowed hard, looking away from him. "Perhaps, Lady Marianne, you, Lady Gillingham, and Lady Voss might wish to return to the carriage?"

Lady Marianne looked up at him and, for a moment, James thought she might refuse. And then, with a small nod, she stepped away from him and went toward her mother, who clung to her tightly, her arm about Lady Marianne's shoulders.

"Take them to the carriage," James told his tiger, who nodded gravely. "The rest of us will join you shortly." With a long, lingering look toward Lady Marianne, he watched as she quit the room—but not before she turned her head to smile at him, a freedom and a joy in her eyes that he had never seen before.

It was the most beautiful smile he had ever seen.

EPILOGUE

Marianne drew in a long breath as she rose from her chair, finding herself a little nervous. Lord Castleton came into the room and bowed low, smiling warmly at her before glancing to the maid that sat quietly in the corner of the room.

"Lady Voss is sitting with my mother," Marianne said by way of explanation. "She is still a little fatigued."

It had been a little over a sennight since Marianne had been reunited with her parents and, whilst the trauma of their situation had been brought to an end, a deep weariness had captured both Marianne's father and her mother. Lady Gillingham appeared to be the worst affected and spent most afternoons resting in the library, with either Lady Voss or Marianne for company.

Lady Voss had continued to take Marianne to any social occasions she wished to attend, although Marianne had chosen to attend only a few and, of those, she had only lingered for a short time. The joy and the delight at being reunited with her parents were still mingled with a worry for their wellbeing and their ongoing fatigue. At least she no longer had any concerns over Lord Worthington, however.

The diamonds had been returned to her father and, from what Lord Gillingham had said, it seemed that Lord Worthington would not only be entirely disgraced but would never again be seen in society. Marianne did not want to ask what had occurred after she and her mother had left, but knew for certain that whatever had happened, whatever consequences had been placed upon Lord Worthington's head, they would be entirely just.

"How are you, my dear Lady Marianne?"

The tenderness in Lord Castleton's voice sent warmth all through her. He had called upon her every day thus far and she had begun to eagerly anticipate his visits. She had not wanted him to leave, for his calming presence had been both an encouragement to her as well as a balm to her disquieted thoughts.

"I am well, Lord Castleton," she replied as the maid turned herself all the more toward the wall, so that she would not be able to so much as glance in Marianne's direction. "Please, do come and sit down." She gestured to the chair next to hers but, to her astonishment, Lord Castleton reached out and caught her hand, his eyes roving over her face.

"I cannot," he said abruptly. "Lady Marianne, my heart has been begging me to speak to you of all that is contained within it. I have kept silent these last few days, seeking only your welfare and making certain that all is restored as it ought to have been. But with every day that I have left your company, I have found myself regretting my silence. Pray, tell me, will you listen to me now?"

Marianne caught her breath, her hand still in his and her own heart beginning to beat with a quickened rhythm. "Yes," she breathed, aware of just how close she stood to him. "Yes, Lord Castleton, of course I will."

"I will state that I have not spoken to your father as yet," he told her, his eyes searching her face. "If you prefer, I can—"

Lifting one hand, Marianne settled it on his chest, astonished at her own boldness and aware of the heat that crowded her cheeks. "Speak, Lord Castleton," she said softly. "Know that I am willing indeed to listen."

Lord Castleton let out a long breath that brushed lightly across her cheek, a brightness in his expression that spoke of both relief and happiness.

"My dear Lady Marianne," he began quietly. "I know that from the start of our acquaintance, we have met with some great difficulties, some great trials. And yet, throughout them all, I have discovered my admiration for you, my estimation of your character, growing steadily. You are the most wonderful of ladies. You have shown such strength, such determination, and such courage that I could not help but think highly of you. And from that has come a deep and genuine affection that..." He trailed off, swallowing hard for a moment as though he were searching for the right words. "A deep and genuine affection that has grown into a love for you that will not be restrained."

The words he spoke made their way directly into Marianne's heart. She smiled up at him, her fingers twining with his as she felt her heart free from the grief and the suffering that had pulled it down for so long. Now, there was nothing to prevent her from speaking just as honestly as he, from telling him the truth of her own affections, and from allowing herself to think of a future that might soon be realized.

"Lord Castleton," she replied as his free hand reached up to brush across her cheek, down her neck, and then to rest gently on her shoulder. "It is not only your heart that feels such astonishing things. I find that I, too, have begun to feel the very same affection, the very same love that you have spoken of."

Lord Castleton's eyes closed for a moment before a broad smile settled across his face. "How wonderful," he murmured, opening his eyes to look back at her. "Then I must hope, Lady Marianne, that you will permit me to speak to your father? That you will give me a little hope that I might be successful, should I come to speak to you again?"

Knowing precisely what he referred to and finding her whole being filled with joy at the prospect, Marianne looked up into his face and wrapped both arms about his neck. "I will give you more than hope," she replied softly as his head began to lower, drawing all the closer to her own. "My dear Lord Castleton, when the time comes, I shall give you my promise."

∽

THE DUKE'S TRUTH

HEIRS OF LONDON BOOK FOUR

The Duke's Truth

Text Copyright © 2020 by Joyce Alec

All rights reserved. This book or any portion thereof may not be reproduced or used in any manner whatsoever without the express written permission of the publisher except for the use of brief quotations in a book review.

This book is a work of fiction. Names, characters, places and incidents are either the product of the author's imagination or are used fictionally. Any resemblance to actual persons, living or dead, or to actual events or locales is entirely coincidental.

First printing, 2020

Publisher
Love Light Faith, LLC
400 NW 7th Avenue, Unit 825
Fort Lauderdale, FL 33311

PROLOGUE

"I was sorry to hear of the death of your wife."

Nicholas gave his friend a quick smile, although he did not reply.

"That was some time ago, I understand."

"A little over eighteen months," Nicholas replied, picking up his brandy and lifting it to his lips. He had been glad of a little company lately and having one or two acquaintances join him at his estate for a few days had lifted his spirits a good deal. That being said, he did not want to become melancholy and allow himself to dwell on the past and the pain that lingered there.

His brother-in-law, Lord Dewsbury, cleared his throat. "Have you intentions of returning to London at all this Season?" he asked, lifting one eyebrow as Nicholas frowned. "I know you have never been truly eager to involve yourself in society, but it might be a wise idea."

Nicholas threw the suggestion aside at once. "No, I have no intention of returning there," he replied with a firm shake of his head. "Throwing myself into society and into all that the *beau monde* does has never been something that entertains me."

Lord Dewsbury shrugged. "I quite understand," he replied with a nod. "My eldest, Frederica, is due to make her come-out this year."

Nicholas' brows rose. His sister, Lady Dewsbury, was ten years his senior, and thus it was almost impossible to believe that her eldest daughter was now ready to make her come-out. "Indeed?"

"I can hardly accept such a thing myself, but she is seventeen years of age now and has been eagerly anticipating her first foray into London society." Lord Dewsbury chuckled. "It has not yet been arranged as yet, however, for my dear wife…" He trailed off, his smile fading slightly as he looked at Nicholas. "My dear wife is due to enter her confinement soon."

Nicholas' mouth dropped open. He had never expected his sister to be with child again, not when her youngest child was now five years old.

"I am hopeful it will be a son," Lord Dewsbury continued, his voice still a little low. "Whilst I am always grateful to have been blessed with four daughters, I confess that I am eager for an heir."

"Most understandable," said one of Nicholas' other guests. "My hearty congratulations."

"And mine," Nicholas said quickly. "Goodness, Dewsbury, you have kept that close to your chest."

Lord Dewsbury shrugged again, although a glimmer of a smile pulled at his lips. "As I have said, Frederica is due to make her come-out this year, but we shall have to see what arrangements can be made. I have a companion for her but as yet, no one to chaperone her through London." He looked back toward Nicholas, his gaze a little firmer than before. "If you *should* think about returning to London, Ellsworth, then do send word to me."

Nicholas sighed inwardly, fully aware of what his brother-in-law was now suggesting. If he was to make his way to London, then *he* might be the one to guide Lady Frederica through London society. She and her companion could reside in his townhouse alongside him quite respectably, which would allow for her to have her come-out and her first taste of London society, whilst permitting Lady Dewsbury to remain at home for her confinement—and Lord

Dewsbury to remain with her. Nicholas knew that his brother-in-law cared deeply for his wife—a trait that he had always admired—and that he would not want to leave her side during her confinement, especially when they had three other daughters to care for.

But the truth was, Nicholas had no desire to go to London. He was quite comfortable here, and whilst he did miss the company his late wife had brought him, it was not severe enough for him to consider changing his circumstances at present.

Being a duke, he knew that the moment he stepped back into society, he would be met with eager smiles and expectant hands, all plucking at him so that he might join their company. He wanted none of that. He had no intention of marrying again at present and certainly, should he show his face in London, the expectation would be that such a thing was precisely why he had come in the first place.

"I—I will consider it," he said slowly as Lord Dewsbury grinned. "But there is no promise that I shall say yes, however. As I have said, I am quite contented here at present."

"It is very good of you even to consider it," Lord Dewsbury replied, picking up his brandy. "And I know that Frederica would appreciate it also."

Nicholas rolled his eyes, knowing very well that Lord Dewsbury was doing all he could to encourage Nicholas without being particularly overt about it. "You say you have a companion for her?"

"I do," Lord Dewsbury replied, having taken a sip of his brandy. "A young baroness. Her husband *also* passed away a little over a year ago but left her practically penniless. She was known to my wife, and thus I have already secured her as a companion for Frederica."

"You mean to say she resides with you at present?" Nicholas asked, and Lord Dewsbury nodded. "Does Frederica require a companion already?"

"It is better than a mere governess and certainly, Lady Foster has proven to be quite remarkable thus far. She has encouraged Frederica to continue to further herself in some ways and her refinements, in particular, have been much improved." He shrugged. "I want the very best for my daughter and Lady Foster, given that she has already been in society and has been wed also, knows precisely what is required of Frederica. I have had no concerns as regards Frederica's companion and am quite certain she will do very well indeed... should the time come."

Hoping that his brother-in-law did not think that he had been questioning his decision over hiring a companion for his daughter, Nicholas nodded quickly. "I am glad to hear it," he said, fully aware that Lord Dewsbury was still hoping that Nicholas might consider making his way to London for the summer Season. "I am sure that Frederica will make an excellent match and be very contented indeed."

Lord Dewsbury chuckled. "There is no urgent need for her to wed," he said with a wave of his hand. "The first Season, certainly, can be a time for enjoyment, for dancing and conversation. Her second, perhaps, might be the time to consider such things."

"You are a very understanding father," remarked another of Nicholas' guests as Lord Dewsbury smiled politely. "I am sure your daughter will do very well. All of society will think well of her."

So long as they are true in their attentions, Nicholas considered quietly. *The daughter of a marquess is a fine prize for any gentleman.* A note of unease settled into his heart and in that moment, Nicholas knew that he would, in fact, return to London for the summer Season, regardless of what he had just said to Lord Dewsbury.

Frederica had always been in his sphere, and he had seen her every year since her birth. Of course he would take her to London and, in doing so, would make quite certain that she did not fall foul of any of the nefarious gentlemen who would only pursue a lady in order to gain her dowry. Sighing inwardly to himself, Nicholas threw back the rest of his brandy and set down his glass with a thump. Despite his reluctance, his misgivings, and even his own desire to stay precisely where he was, it seemed now that he was to be in London this Season.

But only for Frederica's sake, he told himself firmly. *And then I shall return home without any particular intention of returning again.*

Satisfied, Nicholas rose from his chair and went to add another measure of brandy to his glass. No doubt Lord Dewsbury would be delighted to hear the news but, for the time being, Nicholas intended to keep news of his decision entirely to himself. After all, the summer Season was a good few months away and there was no particular urgency. He could only hope that, when the time came for him to re-enter society, he would have a little more eagerness than he currently felt at present. Else what sort of chaperone would he be?

1

"How wonderful to see you again, Uncle."

Nicholas winced as Lady Frederica greeted him, taking in her bright smile and realizing just how dull and staid he must appear compared to her.

"I am very glad to have you here," he said truthfully. "And how was the road? Was it very bumpy?"

Lady Frederica laughed and shook her head. "No, it was not," she answered, sounding all the more excited. "I was so very eager to arrive that it hardly seemed like very long at all."

Nicholas chuckled and made to say more, only for another lady to step into the house, a bag clutched in her hand. A little surprised, he stepped forward and made to take it from her, but the lady stepped back just a little, her eyes wide as she looked up at him.

"Forgive me," Nicholas said quickly, bowing at the waist. "I thought only to help you. I—"

"Oh, but this is my companion, Lady Foster," Lady Frederica cried, interrupting him. "I should have told you of her at once, I suppose, and certainly should have been much better at my introduction, but I confess that I am just so very excited to be here with you that all decorum has faded from me." She giggled but Lady Foster, Nicholas noted, did not smile in return.

"You shall not be able to make such mistakes when we are in society, Lady Frederica," she said, her voice quiet and yet holding a sense of authority that even Nicholas himself could feel. "Regardless of your excitement or eagerness, you must *always* maintain decorum." Turning her gaze back to Nicholas, she curtsied quickly, then lifted her chin. "Good afternoon, Your Grace. I am very glad to make your acquaintance and most grateful for the opportunity you have given me to reside here with Lady Frederica."

Nicholas bowed again, even though he had already done so, a little taken aback by the lady's demeanor. Her brown eyes looked directly back into his as he straightened, her auburn hair only revealed as she removed her bonnet and handed it to the waiting footman. With her willowy figure, high cheekbones, and full lips, Nicholas considered that she was something of a beauty, although quite in contrast with Lady Frederica's fair hair and green eyes.

"Good afternoon, Lady Foster," he replied, glancing toward Frederica for a moment and noting how she was now a little subdued, clearly taking what Lady Foster had said to heart. "As I have said just now to Frederica, I am very glad to have you both here. I am sure that we shall all get along very well."

Lady Foster's lips twitched, but she did not smile.

"Might I have the footman take your bag to your room?" he asked, a little surprised when she shook her head, her fingers clutching it even more tightly. "It is not your responsibility to unpack the carriage."

"I am well aware of that," came the reply, "but all the same, this is my particular bag and I am eager to keep it with me at present."

This was met with an understanding smile from Lady Frederica and Nicholas, who was now wondering just what was in the bag that was so very important, gave her nothing more than a quick nod before turning his attention back to Lady Frederica.

"Should you like to rest for a short time?" he asked as Lady Frederica smiled back up at him. "I can have your tea tray sent up?"

"No, indeed not. I am very eager to talk to you at length about society and what occasions I am to attend," Lady Frederica declared as Lady Foster smiled softly at her charge. "Might we do so at once?"

Nicholas chuckled, then offered her his arm. "At once, if you so wish it," he replied, beginning to lead his niece away. "The drawing room, then? I shall have to show you around the townhouse also, so that you know each and every room and—"

"Will you join us, Lady Foster?"

His niece stopped suddenly and turned her head, looking back at her companion. Nicholas frowned and felt a small niggle of guilt push into his mind as he, too, glanced at the lady, noting the way that her hands clasped tightly to her bag and how her eyes no longer held that gentle warmth that had been present only moments before. Had he made a mistake? He had not thought to include Lady Foster in his suggestion to Frederica, but then again, he supposed he ought to have done, given that she was not only Frederica's companion, but also a titled lady in her own regard.

"Forgive me, Lady Foster," he said with a small apologetic smile. "The excitement of seeing my niece again has quite overwhelmed me."

"You need not apologize," came the reply, although there was now a slight tartness to the lady's words. "Please, do go on. Frederica, I shall rest for a short while and then join you. Do excuse me, Your Grace."

"The footmen will show you where to go," Nicholas replied, a little embarrassed now at his own lack of consideration. Watching the lady depart, he cleared his throat self-consciously and then continued along with Lady Frederica toward the drawing room.

"Mama thinks Lady Foster the most wonderful creature," Lady Frederica began as Nicholas listened, choosing not to say a word at present. "She has brought vast improvements to my playing of the pianoforte, as well as my conversation. I do hope that such attributes will do well for me in society."

"I am sure that she has," Nicholas mumbled, hoping that he

might find a way to improve what he was certain was disastrous impression of himself to Lady Foster. "Did you say she was a baroness?"

Lady Frederica nodded eagerly. "Her husband died last year some time, I believe," she said quietly. "Baron Foster. I do not know much about him other than that the marriage was an arrangement between him and Lady Foster's father. I do not think that there was ever any animosity or the like between them, but certainly no particular affection." One shoulder lifted. "She has borne her grief very well, but unfortunately, she now appears to have to find employment rather than rely on anything that the baron might have left for her."

Nicholas shook his head. "That is unfortunate," he agreed quietly, realizing now that the lady must have been left with barely anything when her husband passed away. "And you find her most encouraging?"

"Very encouraging indeed," Lady Frederica replied as they entered the drawing room. "Do not think her odd that she would not let go of that particular bag. I believe it contains almost all her earthly goods and, as such, she has no desire for anyone other than herself to take it." She smiled up at him, although there was a small flicker of sadness in her eyes. "Lady Foster has endured a good deal, and I should very much appreciate it if you were kind to her."

"Of course I shall be," Nicholas replied, gesturing for Frederica to sit down in a nearby chair, which she practically flopped into, showing a little less decorum than Nicholas had expected—although, he considered, given that they were uncle and niece, he could forgive her for such a thing. "Shall I ring for tea?"

"Please," Frederica replied with a small, contented sigh. "How glad I am to be here. You are very kind to have offered to take me on, Uncle. I am very grateful to you." Something flickered in her eyes for a moment as she watched him sit down opposite her. "Mama is due to enter her confinement any day now. I thought I should have to wait until next Season before I was permitted to come to London."

"I am very glad to have you," Nicholas said truthfully. "Although I must beg of you *not* to attempt to encourage me in the direction of any particular young ladies. I have no interest in such things and wish to make that quite clear to you now."

Frederica nodded solemnly, her eyes a little wider than before as she watched him. "I quite understand," she agreed quietly. "Father states that I am not to consider anything other than enjoyment this Season. I appreciate his consideration for me. Many fathers, I know, would want nothing other than to find a suitable match just as quickly as they could for their daughters."

Nicholas nodded, admitting to himself that he thought rather highly of Lord Dewsbury in that regard. The conversation continued on for some time, with uncle and niece reacquainting themselves with each other as Frederica drank what appeared to be copious amounts of tea.

There were smiles on both their faces, and Nicholas found himself admitting that he was, in fact, beginning to look forward to the next few weeks. He had come to London with a certain lack of enthusiasm, but now that Frederica was here, Nicholas felt a good deal more contented. He was certain things would go well and that, in due course, Frederica would find herself delighted with all that society had to offer.

"You are to be presented at court in two days' time," Nicholas reminded Lady Frederica as she nodded fervently, although her smile faded and left behind a slightly fearful expression. "Thereafter, we shall attend your first ball."

This, he noted, brought back a brightness to Lady Frederica, although there was still a hint of worry over making her entrance at court.

"Might I ask which ball we are to attend, Your Grace?"

Nicholas looked up in surprise, realizing with embarrassment, that he had not noticed Lady Foster entering the room. Quite how long she had stood quietly at the door he did not know and Lady Frederica, given by how sharply she turned her head, had very little awareness of it either.

"Pray, do join us, Lady Foster," Nicholas said, rising to his feet as quickly as he could and gesturing the lady forward. "I can send for a fresh tea tray, if you would like?"

Lady Foster shook her head although she did sit down rather hastily, as though to suggest that she was still quite fatigued.

"No, I thank you," she replied, a small sigh escaping her as she sat. "The ball, however? It is to be Lady Frederica's first and I should like to make certain that she is fully prepared for it."

Nicholas nodded, aware of how Lady Frederica clasped her hands tightly together, her eyes searching his face as though she were filled with a desperate eagerness to know of what he spoke.

"I have a very good friend," Nicholas explained, after a moment. "The Marquess of Hazleton. Last year, he wed a very suitable young lady and now, this Season, they are both returned to London. I wrote to inform him that I was to be in London and gave him my reasons for doing so—namely you, Frederica—and soon received an invitation to his upcoming ball, with the assurance that it would be the perfect place to make your entrance into society."

Lady Frederica said nothing, swallowing hard and then glancing to Lady Foster.

"It sounds most suitable," Lady Foster replied, turning her gaze back to her charge and smiling at her in a most reassuring manner. "And you will have your very best gown—your very best *new* gown, I should say—for the evening."

"I think—I think I should like to rest now, for a short time."

Nicholas rose to his feet as Lady Frederica pushed herself out of her chair and made her way quickly to the door. Her head was held high and she walked with grace and poise but still, there was something about her demeanor that spoke of a sudden anxiety and tension. He frowned, watching her depart, just as Lady Foster rose to her feet also.

"I will go with her," she said, but Nicholas held out one hand.

"If you please, Lady Foster," he said, preventing the lady from quitting the room and going after her charge, "stay a moment."

Lady Foster's eyes flared but she nodded and then sat back down, clearly willing to do what he asked without question.

"Is Lady Frederica quite prepared for the London season?" Nicholas found himself asking as Lady Foster looked back at him with a steadiness in her gaze that already confirmed the answer to him. "You believe that she will not behave foolishly in any way?"

"I believe that Lady Frederica is nothing more than a little anxious at present, Your Grace," came the gentle reply. "She is certainly more at ease with you than she will be with others, but that is to be expected, given that you are her uncle and there is clearly a closeness between you."

Nicholas considered this for a moment, then nodded slowly. "I can still recall holding Frederica as a baby," he said softly, his gaze drifting away from Lady Foster as he spoke. "I was not particularly old myself, still residing with my parents and being quite overawed with this very small creature in my arms. My sister, who is now Lady Dewsbury, is ten years older than I but we have always made certain to remain a part of each other's lives. I have seen Frederica grow up and now wish only to make certain of her contentment and happiness during this Season."

When he finally looked back at Lady Foster, he saw, much to his surprise, that she was smiling at him. There was no hint of mirth in her smile but rather a quiet gentleness that spoke of a kindness and an understanding that he felt wrap around his heart.

"That is why she is so very comfortable in your presence, Your Grace," Lady Foster said after a few moments. "That is why she can trust you implicitly. She may be a little nervous about stepping out into society—for who would not be?—but she will soon be throwing herself into all that society offers her, although I pray that she will always act with decorum."

"Given how highly she has spoken of you, Lady Foster, I am certain that she will," Nicholas found himself saying, a little astonished when Lady Foster looked away, her head dropping slightly as a hint of color came into her cheeks. "I shall excuse you now. No doubt, you wish to go to Frederica to make certain she is quite all right."

"Indeed, I do." Lady Foster rose from her chair and bobbed a quick curtsy. "Do excuse me, Your Grace."

"But of course." Nicholas watched Lady Foster leave the room, taking in her hasty steps and the clear eagerness that was within her heart to find her charge and take care of her. He had no doubt that Frederica would be glad of Lady Foster's companionship and was quite assured that, within a few minutes, she would find her confidence restored. Settling back into his chair, Nicholas closed his eyes and let out a long, contented sigh. It appeared that this Season would go very well indeed.

2

Having left Frederica in the capable hands of her lady's maid, it was now Louisa's turn to prepare herself for this evening. Looking at her reflection in the mirror, Louisa took in the paleness of her cheeks and the smudges under her eyes.

She had not been sleeping well.

Returning to London had brought with it her own renewed difficulties, although she would not speak of them to anyone, given that her duty at present was to Lady Frederica. She had not expected to have any sort of struggle, yet walking through London or being driven through it as she sat in the carriage had brought a new sense of loss to her heart. The last time she had been present in London, it had been with the full knowledge that she was to be introduced to her betrothed, one Baron Foster. Her father, the late Viscount March, had not done particularly well in finding Louisa a suitable match but had seemed to settle on whichever gentleman was eager to wed. A baron meant a lowering of her status and, whilst she had found Baron Foster to be pleasant enough, there had never been any true affection between them. Indeed, Baron Foster had shown very little inclination toward anything other than a quiet friendship between himself and his wife, and thus Louisa had led something of a lonely life for the short time she had been wed.

A slight tremor ran through her as she recalled the day she had been told of his passing. That had been difficult enough to bear, made all the worse by the new Baron Foster—her late husband's brother—who had done very little for her save for tolerating her presence in his house for her mourning year. The will had meant very little to her.

She had been left a small sum, but had it not been for the kindness of Lady Dewsbury, Louisa was not at all certain she would have managed to survive for any length of time. To have been given the opportunity of companion to Lady Frederica had been kindness in itself and Louisa was determined not to fail the lady. Lady Dewsbury had hinted that, should things go well with Louisa, should she make an excellent match, then Louisa would be kept on in order to assist with the next daughter in line to come to London. For the moment, at least, her future was quite safe.

"Then you must forget your own difficulties," she told her reflection firmly. "You must set aside the memories of the past and think solely of Lady Frederica's welfare." Her chin lifted and her brown eyes seemed to darken with resolve. There was to be no opportunity for self-pity. Her entire focus was to be on Lady Frederica.

"My lady?"

There was a quiet rap on the door and Louisa called for the maid to enter.

"I am finished dressing Lady Frederica's hair, my lady," the maid said, bobbing a quick curtsy. "Might I now see to yours?"

Louisa opened her mouth to protest but immediately closed it again. It was not as though she could simply tie her hair into a chignon for something as elegant as a ball.

"Very well," she said after a few moments. "But I do not want anything ornate. I am to be the companion, that is all."

The maid nodded. "I understand," she murmured, before setting to work. Louisa closed her eyes as the maid began to brush through her auburn curls, a sudden lump coming to her throat as she recalled just how often she had sat at the dressing table as a young, unmarried lady eager to make a good impression on those about her. Those days were gone from her now, never to be discovered again, and yet whispers of memory still remained.

"Might I see what gown you are wearing this evening, my lady?" the maid asked as Louisa opened her eyes. "It is only to make certain that anything I might add to your hair will not clash with the gown."

Louisa gestured to the simple green gown that had been laid out for her. It was very fine indeed, for Lord Dewsbury had insisted that Louisa have one or two new gowns also, but certainly very simple in its structure and its color. The dark green seemed to fade into the shadows of the room—and that was precisely what Louisa wanted. She was a companion, not someone to be seen and taken notice of. To remain hidden, to step back into the shadows was what would be required of her.

"Thank you, my lady," came the quiet reply, and Louisa gave the lady a small smile.

"I am sure whatever you do will be quite lovely," she answered as the maid smiled a little self-consciously. "But, as I have said, do make it quite simple. There is no need for me to draw anyone's attention this evening."

The maid nodded but said nothing more, leaving Louisa to her thoughts. The room grew quiet and Louisa found her eyes closing once more, still drawn back into the memories of the past that threatened to wrap around her heart, if only she would give them permission.

∼

"Now, do not fidget so," Louisa warned. "We are to step inside, greet the host and his wife—recall that His Grace will introduce them to you—and thereafter, you walk in alongside your uncle and I will be just a step or two behind." She smiled as warmly as she could before reaching across and taking Lady Frederica's gloved hands in her own. "There is no need for nervousness, my dear. You will do very well, I assure you."

Lady Frederica did not appear convinced. She nodded tersely but as the carriage came to a stop, Louisa heard the quickening of Lady Frederica's breath and felt how her hands tightened on Louisa's own.

"Come now," the duke said, his voice filled with warmth as it resonated around the carriage. "You have already made your entrance at court, which, I might say, you did very well indeed. But that was surely the part that gave you the most anxiety? This ball is a mere trifle compared to what you have already achieved."

Louisa said nothing, looking across the carriage to Lady Frederica and seeing the way her charge closed her eyes for a moment, evidently doing whatever she could to calm her nervousness down. The lantern light was strong enough that it danced across Lady Frederica's features, allowing Louisa to observe her steadily, although she prayed silently that her charge would not give in to anxiety but would find her courage and her strength of character within her heart.

"I—I am quite prepared," came the sudden, if not rather weak, reply. "You say we are to greet the hosts first?"

"Just as we step inside, yes," came the duke's reply, his tone now one of sheer encouragement. "You will do very well, Frederica. Come now, show a little mettle. It is nothing other than a greeting and then stepping into the ballroom. The music will not stop when you do, those who are dancing will not so much as look at you." He chuckled and Louisa could not help but smile, feeling some of the tension that clouded the carriage beginning to fade away. "Shall we, at the very least, step out of the carriage? I believe the footmen are waiting."

Lady Frederica swallowed hard, opened her eyes, and squeaked her consent, before the duke stepped out of the carriage and then waited for Frederica to do so also. With a hopeful smile on her face, Louisa watched as Lady Frederica took in another breath and then moved to the carriage door, taking the duke's hand as she stepped out. Louisa followed soon after, taking the hand of the waiting footman before she, too, joined the duke and Lady Frederica on the steps that led to the townhouse.

"Lord and Lady Hazleton," Lady Frederica breathed as the duke offered her his arm, which she accepted gratefully. "Lord and Lady Hazleton."

Louisa hid a smile as she stepped up after them, fully aware that Lady Frederica had nothing to concern herself with. The young lady was quite ready for society, for she was fully prepared, knew precisely what would be expected of her, and, should she be asked, had learned every step of every dance that might take place this evening. All that she lacked was a little confidence and that, Louisa hoped, would come in time.

Within a few minutes, they all were in the townhouse itself, with the duke leading Lady Frederica toward the receiving line. It was not particularly busy as yet and within a few minutes, Louisa found herself being introduced to the Marquess of Hazleton and his wife.

"Might I also present Lady Foster," the duke said, gesturing toward Louisa. "She is the companion to my niece."

A small flush caught Louisa's cheeks as she curtsied, all too aware of what being introduced in such a way would mean. Most likely, the marquess and his wife would now think of her as the poor relation or friend who had no other choice but to fling herself on the mercy of others.

But that is what you are, she told herself sternly. *What does it matter if that is what they think? They would be quite correct in their assumption.*

"Thank you both for your kind invitation," she said aloud as Lady Frederica glanced toward her. "Lady Frederica and I have been eagerly awaiting this ball." She smiled at her charge. "Lady Frederica in particular."

Lady Hazleton laughed and held out one hand to Lady Frederica, who took it hastily.

"We shall become very dear friends, I am sure," she replied, no longer looking or addressing Louisa. "I am sure that you will make quite a mark upon society. By the end of the evening, the *ton* will be busy speaking of you, Lady Frederica, and remarking on just how lovely a creature you are. I have no doubt about it."

This brought a flush of heat to Lady Frederica's cheeks and Louisa glanced toward her charge, hoping that she would not let such words either frighten her all the more or encourage her to think a little too highly of herself in that regard. Thankfully, it seemed they did not, for Lady Frederica smiled, thanked Lady Hazleton, and then was borne away by the duke, leaving Louisa to quickly follow thereafter. She noted the way that Lady Frederica held onto her uncle's arm, seeing the tension in the lady's frame and wishing there was something more she might either say or do that would help encourage her.

"Shall we?"

The duke glanced behind him toward Louisa, who met his gaze for a moment and then dropped her eyes, just as two footmen opened the doors to the ballroom so that they might step inside. Lady Frederica murmured something that Louisa did not quite hear, but she did not look behind her toward Louisa at all. Instead, they all stepped forward as one through the door, and instantly, everything changed.

It was as though she had been thrown back into her own memories, hearing the laughter and music that flooded every corner and the buzz of conversation that ran through the midst of it. She had found herself quite overwhelmed when she had stepped forward as a young lady who had just made her come-out, so she knew precisely what Lady Frederica was feeling. Yet Louisa knew that Lady Frederica had a good many more advantages than she herself had and that, therefore, there was nothing for Lady Frederica to be concerned about. She was the daughter of a marquess, with a fine dowry and inheritance. There was a gentle beauty about her also, and, underneath that, a kind nature.

Many gentlemen would be willing to consider her, Louisa knew, although she would have to make certain that any gentleman eager to further his acquaintance with Lady Frederica was not eager for her company solely so that they might take advantage of her dowry and inheritance. That, at least, was where Louisa understood things a little better than her charge. She knew all too well that there could be scoundrels in amongst the *ton* and that appearances were not simply to be accepted as the truth of a person. A gentleman might appear quite charming but, underneath that, have nothing but dark and selfish intentions.

"Lady Foster?"

Louisa started in surprise at her name being spoken, only to realize that the duke himself was speaking to her, with Lady Frederica looking at her also.

"I apologize," she said quickly, a little embarrassed. "I was only thinking of..." She trailed off and shook her head. "It matters not. Lady Frederica? Should you wish to make your way around the ballroom?"

The duke held up one hand. "Wait a moment, Lady Foster. I had, just now, thought to introduce Frederica to a few acquaintances of my own. I did wonder if you would wish to join us or if you wished to stay here for a short while, until we returned?"

Louisa did not immediately answer, glancing behind her and realizing, with a small stab of shame, that she was no longer a true part of society. Given that she was nothing more than a companion—and a paid companion at that—there was no particular requirement for her to be introduced to anyone of importance. A few other companions and wallflowers were seated behind her, all gathered together in the same place as they watched all that went on about them rather than truly engaging in it.

"But of course," she said, aware of a tightness in her throat. "I will wait for you hear, Lady Frederica."

Her charge shook her head. "That does not seem right, Uncle," Lady Frederica insisted, speaking to the duke in that familiar manner that only family could. "If you are to make particular introductions, then surely Lady Foster should be present also, so that she is both acquainted and aware of them?"

Louisa smiled but shook her head. "There is no need to concern yourself on my account, Lady Frederica," she said swiftly, seeing the slight frown form between the duke's brows. "I am quite contented to wait here until you are returned."

The duke's frown grew steadily, his sharp blue eyes running over Louisa as though assessing both her and what Lady Frederica had said. Louisa swallowed hard and looked away, not quite certain what to do or say in response to Lady Frederica's exclamation. There was merit in her suggestion, certainly, but she was more than glad to do as the duke had asked.

"I—I suppose that would be wise," the duke said after a moment. "Lady Frederica is correct. Given that I am not always to be by her side, it would be good for you to be introduced to my acquaintances also." His lips tipped in a small smile as Louisa dared another glance up at him. She had not had much of an opportunity to take him in as yet, given all that had been happening these last two days, but from what she *had* learned, the duke appeared to be a gentleman who gave all things a good deal of consideration. He was, according to Lady Frederica, very kind indeed, given that he had been willing to chaperone his niece through the London Season without any seeming concern.

"Come."

Louisa nodded her agreement and began to follow the duke and Lady Frederica, her thoughts still on the duke. It was impossible not to notice the way that so many of the ladies of the *ton* looked at him, for there were a good many side glances, which were then swiftly followed with whispers, smiles, and gasps of excitement.

Silently, Louisa wondered if the duke had also agreed to come to London in order to pursue a match for himself, given that he would soon require an heir. From what Louisa understood, his first wife had died unexpectedly of a feverish illness, leaving him a widower. Of course, there was a requirement for him to marry again, but Louisa knew all too well that such a thing was not always one's first thought after the loss of one's spouse. Whilst she had not loved her husband and had not found much of a friendship with him either, there had been a contentedness about her situation that had been torn from her the moment he had passed from this earth. The companionship that had once been was gone in an instant, the security of knowing that she would not be left to fend for herself ripped from her. For her, there was no thought of matrimony at present. How could she do so when she had nothing to offer? She had no dowry, no inheritance, no coin of any kind. As a poor yet titled lady, she was destined to remain as she was at present, until, if she was blessed enough, she would be able to take what she had earned and live out the rest of her days quietly.

"Ah, Lord Ponsonby."

Louisa stayed a step or two behind the duke and his niece as he quickly made introductions.

"I am very glad to have the opportunity to present you to my niece," the duke declared, a broad smile on his face as he turned to Lady Frederica. "Lady Frederica, daughter to the Marquess of Dewsbury."

Lady Frederica curtsied beautifully, and Louisa smiled to herself, glad that the young lady had done so well.

"And Frederica, this is my dear friend, the Earl of Ponsonby," the duke declared as the gentleman bowed. Louisa looked at him as he rose, taking in the roundish features, the red cheeks, and the broad smile that settled across the man's face. It appeared that he was rather a jolly fellow, looking at Lady Frederica with a brightness in his eyes that spoke of a true gladness at meeting her.

"How very good to meet you," Lady Frederica murmured, before shooting a hard look toward her uncle. "I do hope that you are enjoying the ball thus far?"

A little surprised at the glare that Lady Frederica had shot toward the duke, Louisa frowned and wondered whether or not she ought to gently remind her charge to focus entirely on the gentleman that was being introduced to her, but given that Lord

Ponsonby was now engaging Lady Frederica in conversation, Louisa chose not to do so. Instead, she remained precisely where she was, her head a little lowered as she listened to all that was being said.

"I do hope you will permit me to look at your dance card, Lady Frederica?" Lord Ponsonby asked, making Louisa look up quickly. "I pray that I am the first to ask you so that I might have the very best to choose from."

Lady Frederica said something Louisa could not hear and then handed her dance card to Lord Ponsonby, who took it with an exclamation of delight. Lady Frederica, in the few moments that she had when Lord Ponsonby was looking at the dance card, leaned toward the duke and murmured something furiously in his ear, which, in turn, made the duke start and then turn to throw a somewhat guilty look in Louisa's direction.

She frowned, looking away from him and praying that her face would not flame with embarrassment. What was it that Lady Frederica had said?

"I—I should also make sure to introduce you to Lady Foster, Lord Ponsonby," the duke said, sounding a little strained as Louisa understood at once what Lady Frederica had whispered to him. "Lady Foster is companion to my niece."

Lord Ponsonby, who had just handed the dance card back to Lady Frederica, looked at Louisa with a somewhat startled expression, then quickly dropped into a bow. "Good evening, Lady Foster," he replied, managing to compose himself with an effort. "Forgive me. I was not even aware—"

"The fault is entirely my own," the duke interrupted with a wave of his hand. "Forgive me, Lady Foster. I quite forgot."

You forgot that I was present? Louisa thought to herself before smiling brightly at Lord Ponsonby.

"Good evening, Lord Ponsonby," she said quietly. "I am very glad to make your acquaintance."

The gentleman inclined his head and then turned to Lady Frederica. "The quadrille, Lady Frederica?" he asked as the dance was announced. "Shall we step out together?"

Louisa surreptitiously placed a gentle hand on Lady Frederica's back, pushing her gently forward as an encouragement. She knew very well that Lady Frederica would be nervous about dancing, anxiously worrying that she might put a foot wrong or cause a good deal of difficulty in some other way, but Louisa had no such concern. Lady Frederica had undertaken all the lessons that were required of her, and Louisa knew for certain that she would be able to dance without hesitation.

"Yes, yes, of course," she heard Lady Frederica say, her voice a little higher pitched, betraying her worry. "Thank you, Lord Ponsonby."

Louisa watched her charge depart with the gentleman, her heart lifting quietly at the sight. Lady Frederica would do very well in society this Season, she was quite certain of it. All that was required now was for Lady Frederica to find the confidence to move through society with self-assurance and grace.

"I—I can only apologize, Lady Foster."

Looking up at the duke in surprise, Louisa saw the way his brows knotted together as he threw a quick glance toward her.

"I should not have forgotten your presence," he continued, his voice a little more gruff than before. "That was both rude and inconsiderate. I apologize profusely."

Louisa allowed herself a small smile. "Please, do not concern yourself, Your Grace," she replied, finding herself all the more respectful of the gentleman. A duke who thought to apologize to a mere companion spoke well of his character, given that she was so much lower in status and situation than he. "I am sure that you were only thinking of Lady Frederica. It is quite reasonable for you to want to introduce her, and given our present circumstances have only been established for a short time, I hold no grudge against you for it is entirely understandable."

The duke looked down at her for a moment longer, his brown

hair dancing across his forehead as he did so. And then he smiled, chuckled, and shook his head.

"You are most understanding, Lady Foster," he said, although Louisa herself did not quite know why such a statement had made him chuckle so. "There are many in the *beau monde* who would not permit such a slight."

Louisa shook her head, a rueful smile on her lips. "You forget, Your Grace, that I am no longer a true part of the *beau monde*," she replied, speaking with more honesty than she had intended. "I was once as Lady Frederica is now, but that time has passed for me." Seeing the way his smile began to fade and a seriousness came back into his eyes, Louisa tried to laugh but the sound was brittle and harsh. "Besides which, I do not think that a mere companion has any right to complain about any such thing, Your Grace, especially not one who is as grateful for their circumstances as I."

The duke considered her again for a moment and a slight flush came into Louisa's cheeks at his scrutiny. A sharpness in his eyes made her feel as though he was looking directly into her soul to see whether or not she spoke the truth.

"You are grateful to be a companion, Lady Foster?"

"More than you can know, Your Grace," Louisa replied honestly and with great fervor. "I would be quite destitute without the kindness of Lord and Lady Dewsbury."

"Your husband left you with nothing?"

The question was sharp and to the point, and Louisa felt the sting of it bite against her heart.

"Whilst my husband had wealth, Your Grace, he did not think to add any part of it to my name in his will," she said carefully, not wanting to suggest that her husband had been deliberately cruel but rather only a little thoughtless. "There was no expectation of his passing, so I presume that it was not something he ever thought to do."

The duke grimaced but said nothing, looking out again at the dance floor as though he was desperate to keep his niece in view, to make certain of her safety throughout. Louisa stood quietly also, not feeling any need to speak any further about her late husband. There was a shared understanding between them, she supposed, of what it was like to lose one's spouse, but as yet, it had not been spoken of by the duke. There was no expectation on Louisa's part that he would do so either, but at the very least, she was grateful for his consideration of her.

"Do you not wish to dance also, Lady Foster?"

The question startled her, and before she could answer, a quiet laugh escaped her. The duke's expression was one of shock and Louisa found herself apologizing profusely, whilst attempting to hide her smile at the same time.

"I did not mean to laugh, Your Grace," she protested weakly. "It is only that such a thought is, if I am to be honest, a little ridiculous. For who has ever seen a companion having their dance card filled? Would not eyebrows be raised at the sight of a companion dancing with eligible gentlemen?" Her smile became a little sad, but she still continued on. "I do not think that even a single gentleman here would even *think* of asking such a thing from me. And why should they do so? I am not here for my own sake but rather for Lady Frederica's. And that is something I am more than contented with."

The duke's brows lifted as he studied her once more, his voice a low rumble as he responded.

"Are you truly contented with your circumstances, Lady Foster?" he asked as Louisa returned his steady gaze with one of her own. "In the very depths of your heart, do you not have even a single wish to step out with the other young ladies and dance with such gentlemen as Lord Ponsonby? You are still of marriageable age, and were it not for your lack of financial independence, you would surely be able to—"

"I am quite content," Louisa interrupted, only to flush furiously as she realized she had spoken over a duke. "Forgive me, Your Grace. I do not mean to speak out of turn, but my circumstances are not likely to change. I have come to realize just how grateful I should be for what I have been given and to think of or seek out more is not beneficial."

The duke harrumphed and said something under his breath that Louisa did not quite hear. Giving him a quick smile—which she was not certain he caught—she returned her attention to Lady Frederica, seeing that the dance was now about to come to a close. Whatever the duke might think, whatever he considered, Louisa knew in her heart that she was both grateful and contented with her circumstances.

Any hint of longing in her heart about returning to the dance floor, about making her way back into society, was swiftly quashed. There could be none of that for her now and Louisa was quite determined to make the best of what she had been given.

3

In the first fortnight since Lady Frederica had arrived, Nicholas considered that all had gone rather well. She had now attended balls and soirees, and this evening she was due to join Lord Ponsonby for a dinner party at his townhouse. Lady Foster, however, had also been invited and for that, Nicholas was not quite certain whether to be pleased or a little ashamed.

For whatever reason, he had struggled with Lady Frederica's companion. Lady Foster was quiet and reserved and said very little unless she was asked directly. There had only been a few occasions when she had entered into conversation with him, and when she had spoken, she had done so with directness. She was forthright when she wished to be but said very little at all other times. Nicholas was not quite certain what to make of her, although Lady Frederica appeared to be quite delighted with her and Nicholas had to admit that, thus far, Frederica had done all that he would expect of a young lady in her come-out. Evidently, Lady Foster had taught her well.

"Frederica," he said, glancing across the breakfast table at his niece, who was busy pouring herself another cup of tea. "Did you say that Lady Foster's husband was a cruel sort?"

Lady Frederica frowned. "No, I did not," she stated at once. "Lord Foster was not at all as you think him."

"But he did not leave his wife anything in his will, and it appears the new Lord Foster has not done so either," he replied, frowning. "Why, then, should he be considered in a good light?"

Waving a hand, Lady Frederica let out a small huff of breath. "Their marriage was an arrangement and I believe that Lord Foster wanted only to wed in order to produce an heir. There was companionship, certainly, but no affection or real consideration." She lifted one shoulder. "I have asked Lady Foster about her circumstances on a few occasions and she has spoken of her late husband with kindness, so I have no reason to think ill of him."

Nicholas' lips twisted. For some reason, it did not sit well with him that a young lady such as Lady Foster should be forced to remain a companion for the rest of her life. Given that she would not receive a substantial salary, the only thing she could do would be to continue to be a companion for many, many years until she had saved enough money to live quietly somewhere.

No opportunity would be given to her for a happier future. She would never again be able to search for a husband, to present herself as a suitable match. That would all go past her as the years went on and on, leaving her behind as Lady Frederica and even he himself moved on with their lives. Why this troubled him so, he could not say, but more often than not, he found his thoughts considering the lady.

"Her father was a viscount," Lady Frederica continued quietly. "She should have made a better match, I think, but given that her father was eager for her to wed, I believe that he did not consider such a thing to be of great importance."

"Indeed," Nicholas murmured, his brow furrowing all the more as he thought on Lady Foster. When she had laughed at his suggestion that she might wish to dance that evening, he had not known what to think. She had been quite right to state that companions did not do such a thing and that any gentleman of note would not even *think* of asking her, but that had, in some inexplicable way, pained him to hear her speak so. It seemed to him that neither Lady Foster's father nor her husband had cared much for her and had not once considered her welfare or the like. Yet, she held no bitterness or sorrow within her heart. It seemed that she was quite accepting of her circumstances, even though they were a good deal poorer than what she had enjoyed before.

"I do wonder if—"

He stopped himself just as the door opened and Lady Foster stepped through, smiling gently at them both before she took her seat at the table. Her auburn curls were pulled to the back of her head, brushing the nape of her neck as she leaned toward Lady Frederica to ask if she had slept well. Nicholas allowed his gaze to linger on her for a short time, seeing the brightness of her smile and the warmth in her gaze and thinking silently to himself that Lady Frederica was blessed to have such a considerate companion.

"I hope you are well this morning, Your Grace."

Realizing that he had been staring at her, Nicholas cleared his throat abruptly and gave himself a slight shake. "I am very well," he replied, pushing himself out of the chair. "I have business to attend to, however. I do hope you are both looking forward to dinner this evening."

Lady Frederica let out an exclamation of delight, her hands clasped tightly together at her chest. "I am *very* much looking forward to it," she replied as Nicholas allowed a smile to cross his face. "Lord Ponsonby is very kind to have invited us all. I think him an excellent gentleman."

"So long as you do not consider him *too* much," Nicholas warned, a wry smile on his face. "Lord Ponsonby may be a gentleman, but he is inclined to throw his attentions onto one young lady and then to the next, without any particular reason for doing so. Whilst he is generous and amiable, he is not someone you should consider, Frederica."

Lady Frederica did not look at all disappointed at this, as he had expected. Instead, much to his surprise, she let out a giggle and glanced to Lady Foster, who immediately dropped her gaze to her plate.

"I am already aware of such a thing, Uncle," she replied, her eyes twinkling. "Lady Foster has already indicated as much."

"Indeed?" Rather surprised, given that Lady Foster had only spoken to Lord Ponsonby on a few occasions, he gave the lady a long, hard look which made her cheeks flush with color. "And how could you know such a thing, Lady Foster?"

She lifted her chin and looked up at him, her gaze steady although her face was still a little pink. "I surmised as much, Your Grace," she answered calmly. "I have observed him and came to much the same conclusion. Although, I should say that Lady Frederica is already very well aware that this Season does not require her to find a match."

"I see," Nicholas replied, finding himself quite impressed with Lady Foster's deductions. "Then it appears you are very well guided, Frederica." He gave them both a small bow. "I look forward to seeing you again this evening."

∼

"You are very kind to have invited me. I thank you."

Nicholas smiled at his niece as she finished speaking to Lord Ponsonby, thinking to himself that Lord and Lady Dewsbury had a good deal to be proud of when it came to their daughter.

"You are most welcome," Lord Ponsonby replied, bowing over Lady Frederica's hand. "And I am glad to welcome you also, Lady Foster."

The way that he greeted Lady Foster was precisely the way he had greeted Lady Frederica, bowing smartly and speaking with the very same warmth. Nicholas watched this interaction with a small smidgen of guilt beginning to burn through his soul. He certainly did not treat Lady Foster with the same consideration as his niece, although perhaps things were very different for him given that

Lady Frederica was family and, therefore, his most important consideration.

Although that has not prevented you from forgetting to introduce Lady Foster on multiple occasions, said the small voice of his conscience, sending another stab of shame into Nicholas' heart. Lady Foster was just as much a part of the *ton* as any other, although, of course, being a companion, she was not looked at in the same way. For a moment, Nicholas wondered whether or not Lord Ponsonby might consider her as a potential bride, only to immediately dismiss the idea. Lord Ponsonby was, as Nicholas had already expressed to Frederica, a gentleman who sought out one lady after another, declaring himself to be quite in love with them all. He would not do for Lady Foster.

"Shall we?"

He offered his arm to Frederica, who took it at once. She looked practically radiant this evening, her eyes roving all around the room, her cheeks a little flushed, and a bright smile on her face as she looked from one person to the next. This was her first dinner party, and Nicholas was certain she would enjoy it.

"Ah, good evening, Your Grace." An older lady swept into a deep curtsy before he had the opportunity to catch sight of her features. "How very good to see you in London again. I had heard that you were returned but had not yet had a chance to greet you." She smiled at him, lines forming around her eyes. "I do not think you have ever been introduced to my daughter, however. Might I do so now?"

Nicholas, still struggling to recall the lady's name, nodded. "But of course," he said quickly as a young lady with startling green eyes and golden hair moved forward, sinking into a curtsy. The older lady looked remarkably pleased at Nicholas' agreement and gestured toward her daughter with one hand.

"Then might I present Lady Judith Witham?" the older lady said as the younger lady rose from her curtsy. "Judith, this is, as you are well aware, His Grace, the Duke of Ellsworth."

"How very good to meet you, Your Grace," came the soft reply as the emerald eyes looked directly into his. "I am honored."

Nicholas smiled a little self-consciously, still fully aware that he could not recall the name of the older lady. "I thank you," he replied, bowing. Addressing the older lady, he smiled at her also. "Are you both in London for the Season?"

"Yes, we are, as is my husband, Lord Prestwick," the lady replied warmly, relieving Nicholas of his lack of awareness of her title. "He is not present this evening, however. He has taken the evening to see to some important matters of business."

"Of course," Nicholas replied, realizing that he had not yet introduced Lady Frederica or Lady Foster. "Might I take this opportunity to present my niece to you?" He beckoned Frederica forward and she quickly dropped into a curtsy. "Lady Frederica, daughter of my sister and her husband, the Marquess of Dewsbury." Quickly introducing Lady Prestwick and Lady Judith, Nicholas then turned to Lady Foster, only for Lady Prestwick to let out a great exclamation.

"Lady Frederica, you must be close in age to my own daughter!" she exclaimed as Nicholas hesitated. "I am certain that there is an opportunity for a great friendship here. After all, you are both very refined young ladies and certain to have a great deal in common."

Lady Frederica smiled brightly, although from the slight lifting of her shoulders, Nicholas considered that she was, in fact, a little anxious and perhaps did not know what to say.

"I would certainly be glad to call upon you one afternoon, Lady Frederica," Lady Judith replied, seemingly quite eager to do as her mother had suggested. "It can be so very difficult to find a confidante during the London Season."

"I—I am very blessed with having Lady Foster as my companion *and* my friend," Nicholas heard Frederica say, seeing how she gestured to the lady who was still standing quietly beside him, apparently unnoticed and unobserved by their two new acquaintances.

"Indeed, I should also introduce you to Lady Foster, who is Lady Frederica's companion," Nicholas said hastily, before any further interruptions could take place. "Lady Foster, this is Lady Prestwick and her daughter, Lady Judith."

Lady Foster dropped into a curtsy at once although, much to Nicholas' surprise, Lady Prestwick did not return the gesture and her daughter merely bobbed a curtsy. Neither of them smiled at Lady Foster, although Lady Prestwick's eyes were fixed to her.

"Lady Foster, you are rather young to be a companion, are you not?"

The directness of Lady Prestwick's question brought a touch of embarrassment to Nicholas although Lady Foster answered without hesitation.

"I suppose that I may be, Lady Prestwick, but unfortunately, circumstances have required it of me," came the quiet, calm reply. "Lady Frederica is, however, quite wonderful. I have very much enjoyed being able to chaperone her through London thus far."

Lady Prestwick said nothing to this, however. She merely sniffed and looked away, as though Lady Foster's conversation was very poor indeed.

"Lady Frederica, you must *surely* play the pianoforte," Lady Judith said eagerly, coming toward her and, to Nicholas' surprise, looping her arm through Lady Frederica's, as though they were the very closest of friends. "And tell me, have you been to the new milliner's shop? It is quite delightful."

There was something of a gleam in Lady Prestwick's eye as her daughter bore Lady Frederica away from Nicholas, although he supposed that Lady Judith was, in her own way, simply doing all she could to make Frederica feel quite at ease. It was true that they were close in age and might very well become good friends, should they see each other often.

"Should you not be going after her?"

The harsh tone of Lady Prestwick's voice snapped Nicholas' attention away from Lady Frederica and back toward Lady Foster.

There was a tightness about Lady Prestwick's jaw as she practically glared at Lady Foster, who, after a moment, flushed a crimson red, excused herself, and scurried after Lady Frederica, her head bowed low.

A streak of anger wound its way through Nicholas' heart. He did not know why Lady Prestwick was speaking to Lady Foster in such a way, when there was clearly no need for her to do so. They were all together in the drawing room with only a small number of guests and this was, he considered, the type of situation where Lady Foster herself might be able to converse with others without having to continually stand next to Frederica. Besides which, it was not Lady Prestwick's place to speak to someone that she did not know.

"If you will excuse me," he said stiffly, turning on his heel and about to make his way from Lady Prestwick's side, only for the lady to pluck at his sleeve in a most audacious manner. Nicholas' jaw worked hard but he forced himself to remain calm and pleasant as he turned back toward the lady.

"Yes, Lady Prestwick?"

"I do hope that you will be willing to allow my daughter to call upon Lady Frederica soon," she said, sounding hopeful. "I am sure that a friendship will form very quickly indeed, given that they appear so alike already."

Nicholas did not think that there was any similarity between Frederica and Lady Judith since, as yet, he had no knowledge of the lady in question, but it would have been rude for him to say otherwise.

"But of course," he replied tightly. "Now, do excuse me, Lady Prestwick. I am sure we will converse again later."

The beaming smile that crossed Lady Prestwick's face did nothing to resolve the anger burning in his heart. Making his way across the room, he sought to find any sign of Lady Foster, wanting to reassure her that he did not think as Lady Prestwick did, wanting to make quite certain that she knew she had not failed in her duties.

There was no sign of her.

Seeing Lady Frederica and Lady Judith were conversing with another older lady that Nicholas recognized to be Lady Fotheringhill, he continued to scan Lady Frederica's surroundings, believing that Lady Foster would be nearby. His heart began to hammer in his chest as he realized she was not present, and in fact, did not appear to be anywhere in the room.

Just where has she gone?

It was not the fact that she had left Lady Frederica that concerned him—Lady Frederica was quite all right kept within the confines of the drawing room at present—but more the fact that try as he might, he could not see any sign of her. Not wishing to draw attention to himself, Nicholas cleared his throat gently and put his hands behind his back, wandering slowly around the edge of the room, keeping his expression calm and pleasant whilst, inwardly, he became more and more uneasy.

"Might I ask you," he said, coming to stand just beside one of the footmen, "whether or not any of the guests have quit the room for a short time?"

The footman looked back at him steadily, his face devoid of expression. "Yes, Your Grace," he replied quietly. "A young lady has stepped out for a short while."

Nicholas' heart slammed against his chest. "And where did she go?"

"I could not say, Your Grace," the footman told him apologetically. "It was only a few minutes ago, however, so I doubt that—"

Nicholas turned from the footman before he could finish speaking and hurried from the room, knowing that Lady Frederica would be kept quite safe in the company of Lady Judith and her mother. He had no doubt that Frederica would behave impeccably until his return, and for the moment, his only concern was for Lady Foster.

He did not know where to look. The hallway was lit with candles and Nicholas began to make his way slowly forward, knowing that, soon, he would have to turn to the left or to the right to continue on through the house. Surely Lady Foster would not have stepped away from the room for good? He could not imagine her calling for the carriage, nor indeed choosing to walk back to his townhouse. Both would involve quitting her duties with Lady Frederica entirely, and Nicholas knew that she was not the sort of lady to do such a thing.

A sudden sound caught his ears and he stopped dead, frozen in place as he listened hard. It came again and then, in the next moment, a figure stepped out from the left, just ahead of him. Nicholas started violently, only to see Lady Foster approaching. Her head was low—to the point that he knew she had not yet seen him—and her steps were slow.

"Lady Foster."

A small, strangled exclamation left the lady's throat as her head lifted, one hand pressing hard against her heart as she stared at him. And then, her shoulders slumped, and she shook her head.

"Forgive me, Your Grace," she said quickly, her voice sounding tight and strained. "I—I had to..." She did not manage to finish her explanation, for it seemed that words would not come to her. Instead, her head began to sink low again, her hands falling to her sides as her shoulders slumped. "I will return to Lady Frederica at once. Forgive me for failing in my duty to her, Your Grace. I can assure you it will not happen again."

"Failed?" Nicholas found himself striding toward her, his anger beginning to burn yet again as he recalled what Lady Prestwick had said to her. "Lady Foster, there has been no dereliction of your responsibilities here, I can assure you." His hands reached for her, but he stopped himself at the last moment, choosing only to press one hand to her shoulder for a moment.

"You have done nothing wrong, Lady Foster," he said again, realizing that the lady had stepped from the room in order to regain her composure. "I am truly sorry for what Lady Prestwick said to you. It was not her place to speak so."

Lady Foster did not look up at him, and for a moment, Nicholas feared that she would not speak to him, would say nothing against Lady Prestwick or what had occurred.

And then, slowly, Lady Foster began to lift her head and, when he looked down into her eyes, Nicholas realized that she had been crying. His stomach twisted, a heavy weight sinking into his heart as he saw the true depths of her distress.

"I am sorry," he said again, one hand now reaching out to lightly press her arm as she held his gaze. "Lady Prestwick should not have spoken so. Lady Frederica is quite secure this evening without your continued chaperonage. Indeed, that is why I have left her and come in search of you."

A small smile tugged at the corner of Lady Foster's mouth, but it disappeared in an instant, her brown eyes searching his face as she looked up at him for a few moments. Nicholas said nothing, standing there quietly with her and praying that she would see in his gaze that she was telling him the truth.

"It is all so very different."

His fingers tightened on her arm. "What do you mean?"

"I am not ungrateful for my position," Lady Foster continued, as though she had not heard him ask his question. "I am truly grateful to have been given such an opportunity by Lady Dewsbury. But to return to London and discover that I am no longer the social equal of anyone present, that I am to be considered lower than before, has been difficult." Her head dropped forward, her voice becoming something of a whisper. "I forgot myself, Your Grace. Lady Prestwick is right. I should have gone after Lady Frederica without hesitation. I should *know* that to do so is what is expected of me, rather than—"

"No."

Both hands now gripped Lady Foster's arms as another flare of anger lit Nicholas' heart.

"No, Lady Foster," he said again, trying to speak in a calm, even tone but finding that he could not. "There will be times when you are not expected to do as you have been before. There will be occasions when you are just as much as anyone else, when you do not have to continually consider Frederica. This evening is one such occasion." He waited until her eyes finally lifted to his, looking down into her face and seeing the way tears glistened in the corners of her eyes. His heart ached for her. "Do not allow Lady Prestwick's words to enter your heart, Lady Foster. Do not allow her to make you feel smaller than you truly are. You are quite wonderful, I assure you." He smiled at her and, after a moment, Lady Foster managed a small, wan smile back toward him, although, as she did so, a single tear slipped from the corner of her eye and ran down her cheek.

Nicholas pulled his handkerchief from his pocket, but rather than handing it to her, found himself pressing it lightly to her cheek, dabbing the tear away and hearing Lady Foster catch her breath as he did so. A sense of foolishness began to wash over him, but he did not stop nor pull himself away from the lady, continuing to do as he had begun before he finally stepped back, pushing his handkerchief back into his pocket once more.

"I do not think ill of you," he told her firmly. "You have done nothing wrong. This evening, you are to be just as any other. You are not to act as Frederica's companion. Instead, you are to be the guest of Lord Ponsonby, just as I and Frederica are. There is to be no shame or guilt placed on your head and you are not to accept any such feelings either." Dropping his other hand from her arm, he saw a brightness coming back into her expression that had not been there at the first. "Ignore Lady Prestwick entirely, if you wish it," he continued, a small shrug lifting one shoulder. "I know that I fully intend to do so, given what she has done."

"But Lady Frederica and Lady Judith—"

"Will *not* become firm friends," Nicholas interrupted, before she could say more. "I do not believe that Lady Judith would be a wise choice for a close companion. She appears to have dragged Frederica away, making it quite clear that she thinks they will do very well as the very closest of friends, but I suspect that Frederica herself thinks a little differently about the matter. However, Frederica is, as yet, too polite to say so." A wry smile tugged at his lips. "I shall have to find a way to teach her how to extract herself from unwanted company without appearing to be rude in any way."

"I am sure you will be able to do so," Lady Foster replied, although much to Nicholas' relief, there were no tears in her eyes any longer. "I—I should return to the drawing room."

He nodded, glancing over his shoulder. "As should I," he said with a small smile. "Should you like to accompany me, Lady Foster?"

Seeing the slight hesitation in her eyes, Nicholas was not surprised when she shook her head no.

"I think I should wait for a few minutes, Your Grace," she said, sounding apologetic as though she feared disagreeing with him. "If there were those who saw us enter the room together, then I fear what might be said of you." Her cheeks flared red, but Nicholas realized with a rush of understanding precisely what she meant.

"I understand," he replied with an inclination of his head as she looked away, clearly embarrassed. "Then please, go ahead of me, Lady Foster."

Her brown eyes flared, and her mouth opened as though she intended to protest, but Nicholas shook his head.

"I will insist, Lady Foster," he said, smiling. "Please, do go ahead of me. I am sure the dinner gong will ring very soon."

Her eyes settled on his for a moment, and with a small smile, she dropped into a quick curtsy.

"You are very kind, Your Grace," she said softly. "Your consideration for me is very much appreciated."

"I could not very well leave you to cry out here on your own now, could I?" he replied, a glimmer of a smile on his lips. "I did not want you to think poorly of yourself, to berate yourself over something that was nothing of importance."

"Then you have succeeded, Your Grace," she replied, making to walk past him. Stepping a little closer, she put one hand tentatively on his arm, her face lifted to his. "I thank you for your kindness."

"But of course." Nicholas smiled down at her and then permitted himself to watch her depart, turning around so that he might make certain that she managed to re-enter the drawing room without difficulty. His heart felt a little lighter now, his spirits lifted as he, too, slowly began to meander toward the door. Lady Foster, he prayed, would have a very enjoyable evening and would forget the difficulties that had come to her due to Lady Prestwick's inconsideration.

It was the very least she deserved.

4

"That looks beautiful on you."

Louisa smiled at Lady Frederica as she turned her head this way and that, allowing Louisa to look at the new bonnet from all angles.

"I think it would be an excellent purchase," she said as Lady Frederica removed the bonnet carefully, setting it down again so that she might scrutinize it a little more. "And the ribbon is certainly a good color, for it will bring attention to your eyes."

Lady Frederica laughed, although a faint hint of color came into her cheeks. "Do you think so?" she asked, picking up the bonnet again and letting the ribbons trail through her fingers. "You do not think it is too dark of a green?"

Louisa shook her head. "No, I believe it is quite perfect."

Lady Frederica sighed contentedly. "Very well," she said as Louisa smiled. "I will purchase it." Her lips tugged into a broad smile. "Although, what I *should* say is that the duke will purchase it for me." Her eyes twinkled. "Any bills are to be paid for by the duke and then repaid by my father. I know that both expect me to behave wisely, however, else I should be eager to purchase a good few things."

Louisa laughed, looking around the milliner's shop. "There are many lovely things here, certainly," she agreed as Lady Frederica's eyes lingered on her for a moment, a thoughtful expression spreading across her features. "I do not think they will think ill of you if you choose to purchase one or two other things."

Lady Frederica nodded and let her gaze drift about the shop. "Perhaps a new pair of gloves," she murmured as Louisa nodded. "But what about you, Lady Foster? Surely there must be something *you* would wish for?"

A little surprised, Louisa shook her head, a slight embarrassment warming her cheeks.

"There is nothing I need," she lied, knowing full well that her best gloves were in need of replacement but choosing instead to set aside such a thing given that she would have to use some of her saved coins in order to purchase them. Her face heated all the more as she wondered if Lady Frederica had seen her gloves last evening and had thought them a little ragged. "Tell me, was this the shop that Lady Judith informed you of?"

Thankfully, the change in conversation seemed to be enough to pull Lady Frederica away from discussing what Louisa might like to purchase.

"Indeed," she said, scowling. "I confess that I found Lady Judith to be very eager indeed to become well acquainted with me."

"Oh?" This did not surprise Louisa, for she had watched Lady Judith and Lady Frederica last evening and had seen the tightness that had slowly entered Lady Frederica's expression over the time they had all sat to dine. Lady Judith had been seated quite close to Lady Frederica and had seemed to want to engage her in conversation throughout the evening, despite the fact that there had been a good few other guests present also. After dinner, Lady Judith had slipped her arm through Lady Frederica's as the ladies had made their way back to the drawing room for tea and had then gone on to sit directly beside her, engaging her with conversation for the remainder of the evening. Louisa had watched quietly, noting how Lady Frederica had remained as amiable as she could throughout the evening and finding herself rather proud of the young lady.

"She is certainly as eager as can be to become a 'very close friend' to me," Lady Frederica remarked, looking a little put out. "I do not mean to be cruel, Lady Foster, but I found her much too eager to be so. After all, she does not know me very well at all, and neither do I know her."

"I thought you did very well last evening," Louisa remarked as Lady Frederica picked up a new pair of silk gloves and held them out to Louisa, who nodded approvingly without ever really looking at them. "I could tell that you were growing a little frustrated and upset, but I can assure you that it was only I who could have realized such a thing given that I know you as well as I do. To Lady Judith, I am certain that you appeared both amiable and agreeable."

Lady Frederica rolled her eyes and Louisa could not help but laugh, glad that there was no one else present in the shop with them.

"I do not think that I am inclined toward forming a strong friendship with Lady Judith," Lady Frederica said after a few moments. "She is much too forward, much too insistent. I believe that friendships are formed quite naturally and will not be pleasant ones if they are forced in such a manner."

"I believe you are right," Louisa agreed as Lady Frederica picked up a second pair of silk gloves and draped them over her arm, as though to compare the two. "There is no need to accept such a friendship if you do not wish it, Lady Frederica. That is entirely your choice and should not be demanded of you by someone else."

"I simply cannot understand why she was so terribly eager," Lady Frederica replied with a small shake of her head. "Unless it is that..." Her eyes widened and she stared at Louisa for a moment, who simply looked back at her steadily, waiting for her to finish her explanation. "Unless it is that she hopes, in forming a friendship with me, she might become better acquainted with my uncle."

"With the duke?" Louisa repeated, and Lady Frederica nodded, her eyes still a little wider than before. She opened her mouth to say that she did not think it would be so, only to realize that there *was* the opportunity for such a thing to be set in place. "That—that *may* be so, Lady Frederica, but do not permit yourself to worry. I am quite certain that Lady Judith sought out your company solely because she wishes to have a friend in London with whom she considers herself the social equal." One small shrug lifted her shoulders. "And if it is as you have suggested, then you lose nothing by keeping the acquaintance just as it is at present."

Lady Frederica frowned. "I do not like to be used so," she stated as Louisa nodded in understanding. "I am quite certain that what I now think might very well be the case. After all, the duke is unwed and has come to London for the Season. Many will think him quite eligible and will push their daughters forward in whatever way they can."

Louisa hesitated, a question forming in her mind that she was not certain she ought to ask. It was not her place to know the duke's business and yet there was a strong desire for her to know a few things more about the duke.

"Might I ask, Lady Frederica, if that *is* why the duke is in London?" she asked, a little tentatively. "Or is he present so that he might chaperone you?"

Lady Frederica laughed, shattering the strain that ran through Louisa's frame.

"The duke has no intention of marrying as yet," she said, waving a hand. "No, indeed, he has made that quite clear with me, so that I will not encourage him in the direction of any particular young ladies that might catch his attention." She laughed again and Louisa managed a small smile, feeling a strange sense of relief growing in her heart and yet being quite unable to understand why she should feel such a way.

"I do not think that the *beau monde* are quite aware of his reluctance, however," Lady Frederica continued, taking the two pairs of gloves and setting them over by the bonnet that she had chosen before returning to Louisa's side. "No, they have already been practically *pawing* at him." Her smile began to fade. "Surely you must have seen it?"

Nodding, Louisa chose not to remark further. The duke was almost constantly in the company of others and, indeed, there were always young ladies present with him. She had seen how they looked at him, had seen the eagerness in their eyes, their bright smiles, and the way that they dropped their gaze so that they might look back at him coyly from underneath their lashes. It was to be expected, she supposed, given that they were all eager for his company, hopeful that they might be the one to catch his attentions. But it seemed that they were all doomed to fail, since the duke had made it clear to Lady Frederica that he had no intention of marrying again any time soon.

"I suppose he will have to wed at some point, however," Lady Frederica continued, a little carelessly. "He will need an heir, but I do not think that such a thing concerns him at present."

"The duke has many years yet before he will need to produce an heir," Louisa replied quietly as Lady Frederica picked up a dark blue ribbon. "And I can imagine it must be very difficult indeed to traverse through society when there are so many eager for one's company."

Lady Frederica nodded solemnly. "Particularly when there are so many acquaintances who seek him out solely to throw their daughters or sisters toward him." She shook her head. "The duke has already stated that he prefers to converse with those who have no such intentions, although those are few and far between."

Louisa felt a slight blush tinge her cheeks but turned her head away so that Lady Frederica would not see it. She had not spoken at length to the duke on any particular subject, but the way he had come in search of her last evening, the way he had told her that he held her in high regard, told her of his awareness of her. He was, she was certain, one of the very few gentlemen in London who was actually aware of her presence, although she had to confess that she was very grateful indeed to Lord Ponsonby for inviting her to dinner. Silently, Louisa considered the duke's character and had to admit that, thus far, she thought very highly of him. It seemed that he was considerate, kind, and generous as well as being quite determined to care for Lady Frederica as best he could. It was almost painful to her to consider that those in the *ton* thought only of his title and his wealth when she herself knew there was a good deal more to him than that.

"What do you think of this?"

Louisa looked up as Lady Frederica held up a very pale silk ribbon, holding it close to her hair. Considering it, Louisa then shook her head, wrinkling her nose just a little and making Lady Frederica laugh.

"It would simply fade into your fair hair," she said practically, coming toward Lady Frederica and setting all thought of the duke behind her. "Choose one that is a little bolder."

"It would suit you very well," Lady Frederica commented, holding the ribbon closer to Louisa's hair and tilting her head as she scrutinized it. "It draws the eye."

Louisa laughed and took a small step back. "And what need have I for ribbons?" she asked as Lady Frederica's studious gaze flicked away for a moment. "Now, what of this one?"

The two ladies continued in conversation over the ribbons for some time, with Lady Frederica comparing colors that suited Louisa to colors that suited herself. In the end, Lady Frederica settled on four ribbons—including the very pale one which Louisa did not think suited her at all—as well as some new seed pearls which she might place in her hair as an added decoration. Satisfied, she declared that she was quite exhausted and so went to complete her purchases, no doubt making certain that the bill was sent to the duke. Louisa smiled to herself as she watched Lady Frederica, glad indeed that the young lady had such support from both her father and her uncle. Whether it was this Season or the next, she was certain that Lady Frederica would make an excellent match and Louisa could not be happier for her.

"Did you have an enjoyable afternoon?"

Louisa looked up toward the duke but saw that he was directing his words toward Lady Frederica, who was nodding eagerly.

"We went first to the milliner's shop and then for a walk through St. James's Park," she said as Louisa continued to eat quietly, glad that Lady Frederica had enjoyed their afternoon together. "I do believe, however, that we missed some callers this afternoon, given that we were out of doors."

There was no disappointment in Frederica's voice, and Louisa hid a smile, knowing full well that the cards that had been given to them both on their arrival back at the house had revealed names of gentlemen that Lady Frederica had no eagerness to consider.

"One was Lord Ponsonby," the duke said with a grin. "I think he is quite taken with you, Frederica."

Louisa looked up sharply, fearing that, without explanation, the duke would then encourage Louisa toward the very gentleman he had warned her away from only a short time ago, only to see the twinkle in his eye and to realize that he was teasing Lady Frederica.

"That is very…considerate of him to be so enamored," Lady Frederica replied with as much dignity as she could, "but I doubt that his interest will last long, given what you have said of his character."

The duke chuckled. "You recall that, then? I am glad." He glanced toward Louisa, his smile beginning to fade as though he had recalled something disappointing or upsetting. "And you, Lady Foster?"

Not quite certain what he meant, Louisa hesitated for a moment, then nodded slowly. "I—I certainly enjoyed the afternoon, Your Grace."

"Good." His smile returned. "And you have had no difficulties?"

Realizing what he meant, a relieved smile crossed Louisa's face. "No, none at all," she replied as Lady Frederica looked on, a confused expression on her face. "Any acquaintances that we met were very amiable indeed."

"I am glad to hear it," the duke answered. "Although I should mention, Frederica, that Lady Prestwick and Lady Judith called this afternoon. I took tea with them, of course, but Lady Judith was most disappointed not to see you." He tilted his head just a little and looked at his niece, as though eager to see whether or not she was disappointed to have missed the lady. "I did inform them that you had gone into town to the milliner's and wondered whether or not they had then gone out in search of you."

"We did not see them," Lady Frederica replied, glancing at Louisa, who again had to hide her smile as she knew the full extent of Lady Frederica's disinclination toward Lady Judith. "Might I ask, Uncle, whether you would mind particularly if I did *not* form a close acquaintance with Lady Judith?" Her eyes held a little anxiousness as she looked back at her uncle, her hands, which held her cutlery, hovering over her dinner plate. "I know she comes from a very respectable family and is very eager indeed to form a friendship with me, but I confess I am not at all inclined toward—"

"Nothing would please me more, Frederica."

The fervor in the duke's voice surprised Louisa and she looked at him sharply, only to see a grimace cross his face.

"I do not believe that one's title makes one respectable," he said as Louisa listened carefully to every word that was said, feeling a heat begin to spread across her chest. "If Lady Judith is anything like her mother, then it would be wise for you to keep only a mere acquaintance with her. I should not encourage an increased friendship between you, for I do not think it would be in any way beneficial."

A look of relief crossed Lady Frederica's face and for a moment, she slumped back in her chair, blowing out a long breath as she did so.

"I thank you," she said, before sitting upright again. "I found Lady Judith to be much too forward, as though she expected me to do all that she asked without hesitation. Whilst I was glad of her conversation, it did begin to grate on me just a little."

"Then you and I share the same feelings," came the practical reply. "Good. I am glad to hear it." He looked pointedly toward

Louisa. "It means that you will have very little engagement with Lady Prestwick in the future which, I think, is for the best."

Louisa smiled quietly at this remark, truly grateful indeed for his consideration.

"Did Lady Prestwick say something untoward?" Lady Frederica asked, and the duke lifted his hand and waved it dismissively. "Or am I not to know?"

"It is not of importance," the duke replied with a small smile. "Now, what did you purchase at the milliner's? I received their bill this afternoon and paid it promptly although I did not look over the items."

Quickly, Lady Frederica launched into a great description of what she had purchased and, in particular, the bonnet that she had also chosen.

"However," she continued, her voice faltering just a little, "I should like to give one of the pairs of gloves and two of the ribbons—and, in fact, the seed pearls also—to Lady Foster."

Louisa's chest tightened suddenly, her head lifting as she stared at Lady Frederica, who had gone suddenly very still indeed. Her heart was hammering furiously, waves of heat crashing over her as she began to shake her head.

"But of course," the duke replied easily. "That is a very wise thought, Lady Frederica, and something that I should have thought of myself." Gesturing toward Louisa, he caught her attention at once. "Lady Foster, if there is something that you require during your chaperonage of Lady Frederica, then please, have bills sent directly to me."

Louisa closed her eyes tightly, a wall of shame seeming to box her in. She knew she ought to be grateful, ought to be thanking the duke for his kindness, but, for whatever reason, it felt wrong for her to be accepting such a thing.

"I cannot," she whispered as Lady Frederica began to frown. "That is very kind of you both, but I am being paid for my duties and certainly do not wish to take anything more from you."

Lady Frederica glanced toward her uncle, and then leaned a

little further forward across the table. "But my dear Lady Foster, it is to be expected that you will have some expenses," she said quietly. "I knew very well that you would refuse any offer of such a thing before we went to the milliner's, which is why I should like to gift you the gloves, ribbons, and seed pearls." Clearly seeing that Louisa was about to protest, she held up one hand, clearly asking her to wait. "It is not charity, Lady Foster," she finished, as though she had looked into Louisa's heart and seen what was there. "Nor is it a mere kindness. It is a practical arrangement, given that you will, as the duke has said, incur expenses. And it is a gesture of the thankfulness that I have within me for all that you have done thus far."

Louisa shook her head and tried to find something to say that would protest gently against this kindness but found that she could not do so. Words failed her. She wanted to express some kind of sentiment, whether it was thanks or unwillingness, but found that neither would come to her lips. Fully aware that both Lady Frederica and the duke were looking at her, waiting for a response, Louisa felt all the more embarrassed. Finding her face flaming with heat, she abruptly rose from her chair, murmured an apology, and fled the room.

∼

"Lady Foster, might I join you?"

Louisa turned her head away from the window and looked over her shoulder, seeing the duke standing in the doorway. "Your Grace," she murmured as he walked into the library. "This is your house, Your Grace. I should not dare forbid you from anywhere." Turning toward him a little more, she looked up into his eyes, a good deal more steady within herself now. "Forgive me for leaving you and Lady Frederica," she continued, although she did not drop her gaze. "I would be glad to return, should you require it."

The duke shook his head. "It will wait a few minutes longer," he said quietly. "Tell me, Lady Foster. Is there something about the generosity that is being offered to you that does not sit well within your heart?"

Louisa closed her eyes, shame crawling through her. "I do not want to appear ungrateful, Your Grace," she said hesitantly. "I can only apologize if it seems to both you and Lady Frederica that I have behaved so."

The duke shook his head and Louisa dropped her gaze for a moment, relieved that he did not appear to be angry with her.

"You are overwhelmed, I think," he said softly. "Is that not so, Lady Foster?"

Unable to disagree, Louisa nodded. "It is, Your Grace," she said, almost meekly. "I am a companion, however. There is no need for me to have seed pearls, or ribbons, or other fripperies. It is very kind and generous of Lady Frederica to gift me such items but truly, Your Grace, I have no requirement for them."

For a few moments, the duke did not reply. Then, he began to wander through the library, coming nearer to her. Louisa's breath caught in her throat.

"You are a companion, yes, but that does not mean that there are no expenses to be considered, Lady Foster," he said, his tone commanding and yet gentle. "What if you should need a new gown?"

"I..." Louisa tried to answer him but found the words dying in her throat. The coins she had saved thus far would be rather badly depleted if she was forced to purchase a new gown for herself—and it seemed that the duke knew it.

"Gloves, ribbons, and seed pearls are of no significance, Lady Foster," the duke continued, not showing off his wealth in front of her but rather speaking honestly to her and without any prevarication. "Whether you *require* such things or not, it would be my honor to have them purchased on your behalf. You have done a great deal for Lady Frederica thus far, and I know that you will remain dedicated to her until she finds a suitable match. But," he continued swiftly, "that may be not until next Season, or the Season after that.

What then? Will you still be so reluctant to allow those who have hired you to purchase what you require?"

"I am not ungrateful," Louisa whispered, passing one hand over her eyes as confusion began to dwell in her heart. "They have done so much for me already and you, Your Grace, have been so involved in Lady Frederica's come-out. I should not like to impose myself on you also."

Much to her surprise, the duke stepped forward and, reaching out, boldly took one of her hands in his own.

"You have been left with very little, although none of it is your doing or your fault," he said quietly. "The opportunity for you to remarry is still available to you, is it not?"

"Of course it is not," Louisa replied, aware of the nervous tickle in her stomach as he continued to press her hand. "I am a companion."

"But there are still opportunities for you where you might converse and acquaint yourself with others in the *beau monde*," the duke said firmly. "For example, the dinner last evening was a perfect opportunity."

"My sole focus must be Lady Frederica," Louisa replied, a little helplessly. "I cannot be looking to my own needs."

The duke's fingers tightened on hers, his eyes searching her face as he fought to make himself understood. "You could do both," he said gently. "When there is time and occasion, then there is nothing wrong with taking up my suggestions, Lady Foster," he said quietly. "In fact, I would encourage it."

Louisa did not know what to say. She wanted to shake her head and disagree with the duke but found that she could not do so. There was such kindness and generosity in his words that she knew it would be more than rude to outright refuse. And yet, the thought of considering herself in such a manner went directly against all that she knew was expected of her by Lord Dewsbury.

"And you need not worry about Lord and Lady Dewsbury's opinion of you," the duke added, making Louisa start violently in surprise that he had spoken of the very thing that now lingered in her mind. "I will write to him and inform him of what I have suggested. I have no doubt that he will be more than contented."

"Your Grace," Louisa whispered, wishing she could find the words to express her gratitude, her reluctance, and her fear that even *allowing* herself to have such hopes would only bring about disaster. "I do not think I can do so."

"Yes, you can," he said firmly. "I will make sure of it. Do not allow Lady Prestwick's words to weigh down your heart. You should not have the opportunity of a safe and secure future taken from you, simply because your late husband forgot to add a few sentences to his will." He shook his head and smiled at her. "Do not torment yourself so. You may well have accepted your situation and be truly grateful for what has been offered to you—which I quite believe—but there are further opportunities waiting for you, should you only be willing to accept them."

Louisa did not know how to respond to this. She had come to London with a very clear understanding of what she was to do and what was expected of her. She would guide Lady Frederica through society for the months of the summer Season, and if no match was made, return to the Dewsbury estate with her. Thereafter, they would return to London for the following Season until Lady Frederica was wed and settled, after which Louisa would have to wait and see what would become of her. Yes, Lady Dewsbury had said she would require Louisa for her other daughters, but that would remain to be seen.

Now, however, the duke was opening up a door that she had never even considered before. Opportunities lay before her that she had never even dared to think of, and it was as though she were stepping into a strange land that held a good deal of unfamiliarity. If the duke was serious about his intentions to encourage her to step out into society on her own at certain times, then that meant there was a faint hope that Louisa herself might find a suitable gentleman to wed. That her life would not be as she feared—a struggle that continued on and on until the end of her days. It was almost too much for her to consider, overwhelming her thoughts until she could barely look at the duke.

"You are a titled lady," the duke murmured softly, his words almost a gentle caress. "You have no need to remain as a companion, Lady Foster. There are gentlemen in the *ton* who would be glad to know you."

"But I have nothing," Louisa whispered, her head dropping forward as she struggled to speak clearly, such was the ache in her throat. "I have no dowry. I have no inheritance or anything else to speak of. There are no heirlooms, no jewels, nothing of value that I can bring. I am only a baroness. What sort of gentleman would consider me?"

To her utter astonishment, she felt a gentle hand begin to lift her chin. Her breathing grew rapid as she looked up into the duke's face, seeing such a tenderness in his expression that she could not look anywhere else.

"My dear Lady Foster, do you not know that your character is of greater value than anything else you have mentioned?" the duke asked as tears began to form in her eyes. "Not every gentleman of the *ton* seeks a good dowry in any future bride. They may have more than enough wealth of their own." His smile was warm as he dropped his hand back to his side. "That is why it is important for you to have the opportunity to converse with those in the *ton*. Once they are acquainted with you, I am certain they will think just as highly of you as I do." Stepping away from her, he inclined his head for a moment. "I shall leave you now to consider," he finished, making his way to the door. "Shall I have the maids bring the rest of your dinner to you here?"

Louisa swallowed hard, nodding when she realized she could not speak, her throat constricted with emotion and her eyes brimming with tears.

"Very well," the duke replied with a smile still on his lips. "You will join us for the soiree this evening, I hope?"

Quite how she would prepare herself for the soiree when she still felt as shocked and as overwhelmed as she did at present,

Louisa was not quite certain, but still, she found herself nodding her agreement, which only made the duke's smile grow.

"Excellent," he said quietly. "Until later, then, Lady Foster." And with that, he opened the door, stepped out, and pulled the door closed gently behind him, leaving Louisa to stand alone inside.

She pressed one hand to her stomach and leaned forward slightly, her breathing ragged as tears began to fall from her eyes. The duke had proven to her that he was nothing but kindness itself, that he was considering her in a way that no one else had ever really done before. To offer her such a chance as this was almost more than Louisa could believe.

Putting one hand to her heart, Louisa steadied her breathing and pulled out her handkerchief to wipe her eyes. It seemed, then, that she was to be able to have a chance at a settled, contented future—a future she had never once expected to have again.

"Thank you, Your Grace," she whispered, saying the words that had struggled to leave her lips when he had been present, hoping that, somehow, even though they were no longer in the same room together, he would be able to hear her.

5

"Good evening, Your Grace." Nicholas bowed to the gentleman before him. "Good evening, Lord Wetherby," he replied as the gentleman glanced toward Lady Foster and Lady Frederica, who stood beside Nicholas. "Might I introduce my niece, Lady Frederica, and her companion, Lady Foster. Lady Frederica, Lady Foster, this is a good friend of mine, the Earl of Wetherby."

Lord Wetherby bowed low. "A pleasure to make your acquaintances," he said, a smile on his face as he rose. "I do hope that you are dancing this evening, Lady Frederica?"

Nicholas glanced at his niece, who quickly handed Lord Wetherby her dance card with a murmur of thanks. Lady Foster looked on, no hint of irritation or jealousy in her eyes but rather a gentle consideration of Lord Wetherby, as he wrote his name down on Lady Frederica's dance card.

"Lord Wetherby and I have known each other for some years," Nicholas explained as Lord Wetherby gave Lady Frederica back her card. "He is an excellent gentleman, I assure you."

Lady Frederica smiled, a slight flush in her cheeks that Nicholas knew was not from being introduced to Lord Wetherby but rather simply the excitement of being at the ball. "And are you in London often?" she asked as Nicholas saw yet another gentleman approaching them. "Or do you come here only for the Season?"

"I am here often on business," Lord Wetherby replied, "although I confess that the Season holds a good deal more excitement than at other times."

"Good evening, Lady Frederica."

Nicholas stepped back just a little, catching Lady Foster's eye and seeing her eyes twinkle as she smiled at him. His niece was, as he had suspected, doing very well indeed within society, for many gentlemen were eager indeed to greet her, converse with her, and dance with her.

"It seems as though there will be a good deal for you to do this evening, Lady Foster," Nicholas murmured, moving behind Frederica in order to speak to her. "I believe Frederica will have her dance card filled entirely very soon."

Lady Foster laughed and nodded. "I think you are right, Your Grace," she answered, turning her head to look at Lady Frederica, who was now conversing with both gentlemen. "But she is very sensible. She is not inclined to become overwhelmed by their attentions."

"Indeed, she is not," he agreed, his attention caught for a moment by something he had seen in Lady Foster's hair. A little surprised that he had noticed it, he gestured toward it off-handedly, fearing that otherwise she would think he had been staring at her.

"You have the seed pearls in your hair this evening, Lady Foster," he said, aware of how she blushed furiously at this remark, her hand going toward her hair for a moment, only to drop to her side. "I am glad that you were willing to accept them from Frederica. She did so want you to have them."

Lady Foster looked away, but a smile crossed her lips regardless. "She is very kind," she replied as a strange, swirling tension began to form between them. "As are you, Your Grace. I am very well aware that you were the one to pay for those particular items and I am very grateful to you for them."

"But of course," he said, wondering why he should feel such a knot forming in his stomach as he looked back at her. "I am very glad to have done so. Besides which, it was not a very great expense, given what Lady Frederica has chosen to purchase."

This made Lady Foster laugh and Nicholas could not help but chuckle along with her, glad when the tension between them dissipated.

"Good evening, Your Grace."

A familiar voice caught his attention and the smile on his lips faded almost at once as he saw Lady Prestwick come to join them, her daughter beside her. Neither of them looked particularly pleased to see Lady Foster, but both did curtsy in greeting—although whether or not that was directed solely at him, Nicholas was not sure.

"Good evening, Lady Prestwick. Good evening, Lady Judith," he replied, realizing quickly that neither lady had greeted Lady Foster. "You remember Lady Foster, of course?" He gestured to her, his eyes hard as he looked back at Lady Prestwick, who only glanced at Lady Foster.

"Yes, of course," she said, somewhat dismissively, whilst Lady Judith did not so much as look at the lady. "The companion." The sheer amount of disdain in both her voice and her features made Nicholas' anger burn furiously once more but, with an effort, he kept it contained.

"Good evening," Lady Foster murmured, glancing up at Nicholas. "I should make certain Lady Frederica is all right."

"She is quite contented," Nicholas replied sharply, stopping Lady Foster from stepping away from him and seeing her eyes flare with surprise. "As you can see, Lady Prestwick, my niece is currently engaged in conversation with others, else I am sure she would have been glad to join us."

"Of course," Lady Prestwick said as Lady Judith let out a long, pained sigh as though she had expected to gain Lady Frederica's attention almost at once.

"And I believe she is to dance very soon," Lady Foster added, although Lady Prestwick's nose wrinkled as though a mere servant had chosen to step into their conversation and spoken out of turn. "Lord Wetherby has asked for the quadrille, which is to begin in a moment."

Lady Prestwick looked to her daughter for a moment, before they both turned their gaze back toward Nicholas, although now there was nothing more than a smile on both of their faces. He grew uneasy, wondering at this sudden change in their demeanor.

"Do you enjoy dancing, Your Grace?" Lady Prestwick asked, and a tightness caught Nicholas' chest, realizing what it was that she was implying. "My daughter enjoys it very much."

"I do indeed," Lady Judith said breathlessly, her eyes shining as she looked up at him. "I think my favorite dance must be the quadrille, in fact."

Nicholas' brows began to tie themselves together in a frown as he realized the very dance Lady Foster had mentioned would soon be danced by Lady Frederica and Lord Wetherby was now the one that Lady Judith had mentioned.

"And I do believe it is about to begin," Lady Prestwick said as the dance was announced. Nicholas turned his head to nod to Lady Frederica as Lord Wetherby offered her his arm. "What a shame you have no partner, Judith."

Having no desire to dance with Lady Judith, Nicholas cleared his throat, bowed, and turned to Lady Foster.

"Shall we?" he asked, seeing the way her eyes flared with astonishment. "Do excuse us, Lady Prestwick, Lady Judith. As you can see, I have already arranged to dance the quadrille with Lady Foster." He put a smile on his face and leaned toward them, although inwardly, his heart was cheering wildly at how he had managed to pull himself away from an otherwise difficult situation. "It is an excellent way to make certain that all is well with Lady Frederica, although I am sure that Lord Wetherby will be nothing but propriety itself." Feeling the tentative fingers of Lady Foster settling on his arm, Nicholas inclined his head and stepped away from Lady Prestwick and Lady Judith, relief flooding his chest as he did so.

"Your Grace?"

The quiet voice of Lady Foster met his ears and he turned his head to glance down at her, seeing the shock in her expression.

"I apologize, Lady Foster," he said, coming to join Lady Frederica and Lord Wetherby as they stood together so that he and Lady Foster might make up the set. "I could not even abide the *idea* of stepping out with Lady Judith. Your willingness has saved me."

"But—but we are to dance?" she asked, her voice low as she stared at him, a look of terror on her face. "Truly?"

Nicholas looked all about him, seeing the other couples coming to join them on the floor. "Yes, I believe we are," he said, a little more gently. "That does not concern you?"

"It should concern you, Your Grace," Lady Foster replied, a slight hardness to her voice that he had never heard before. "What will be said of a companion stepping out with the master of the house?" Her eyes closed tightly for a moment, a paleness coming into her cheeks. "What will be said of me?"

Nicholas swallowed hard, the relief he had felt only moments before quickly leaving him. He had not thought carefully enough about what would occur should he do such a thing, he realized. Even such a simple thing as this would be enough to set tongues wagging. Whilst being a duke meant that he could ignore such remarks and scrutiny—for indeed, his reputation was beyond being harmed by mere gossip—the same could not be said for Lady Foster.

The music began and Nicholas dropped into a bow, his heart quickening as he realized his foolishness. Lady Foster had no other choice but to curtsy and then to step forward into the dance, her face still rather pale.

"I will make certain that you dance again this evening, with other gentlemen," he said, realizing that such an idea was his only solution to her present difficulties. "Then the *beau monde* will perhaps think less of this particular dance."

She did not reply to him and when the time came for him to take her hand, she looked away, her face suddenly flaming with color. Nicholas cursed himself under his breath, aware now that he had let his anger and frustration with Lady Prestwick and Lady Judith fuel his inconsiderate actions. There was nothing he could do, nothing he could say that would improve the situation as it now stood. He would have to finish the dance with Lady Foster and pray that, somehow, she would not gain the scrutiny of others.

"I am sorry," he murmured to her as the steps of the dance drew them closer again. "Forgive me, Lady Foster."

Her eyes found his and held them steadily for a few moments. And then, she turned away into her steps and did not look at him again for the rest of the dance.

Just what had he done?

∽

"How very kind of you, Your Grace."

Nicholas gave Lady Worthington a quick smile as he handed the dance card back to her daughter, Miss Drake.

"But of course," he said as the young lady blushed furiously, glancing down at the card to see where he had written his name. "I thought I should dance this evening, rather than remain at the side of the room as I usually do."

"Well, we are very glad of your decision," Lady Worthington replied as Nicholas fixed his smile in place. "Tell me, are you in London for the Season?"

Nicholas nodded, inwardly weary of the same discussion, the same conversation that came to him time and again. How much he longed to have something more to say, something more to discuss. But try as he might, whenever he spoke to any lady of the *ton*, they asked him the very same things.

"Yes, I am in London for the Season," he said as mother and daughter exchanged glances. "However, it is solely for the sake of my niece, Lady Frederica. She has made her come-out this year and has come to reside with me for the summer months."

The look of disappointment in Lady Worthington's eyes was immediate. "I see," she replied, her smile lackluster, clearly having hoped that he had come to London in order to find a bride. "Her father is the Marquess of Dewsbury, I understand."

"That is so," he replied, realizing now that news of his charge must have spread through the *beau monde*. "Her mother is currently in her confinement, and so I have been glad to have her reside with me. Her companion, Lady Foster, is with her at present."

Lady Worthington glanced at her daughter, a look exchanged between them that Nicholas could not quite make out. He had made certain that Lady Foster had danced with Lord Wetherby and then, a short time later, Lord Ponsonby. There had been a good deal of embarrassment on Lady Foster's part, but Nicholas had assured her that she had nothing to be ashamed of. The two gentlemen had only taken a slight nudge from him before they had asked Lady Foster to dance, and he was sure that, since he had done so at the first, they now presumed that such a thing was quite acceptable.

"Lady Foster is here as Lady Frederica's *companion*?" Lady Worthington asked, emphasizing the last word as though to make quite certain that she had heard Nicholas correctly. "I was certain that I saw her dancing with you, Your Grace."

Nicholas nodded, a small shrug lifting his shoulder. "Indeed," he said as nonchalantly as he could. "Lady Foster has endured the loss of her husband, and then a year of mourning which has been very difficult indeed. I think that a small kindness here and there can do a great deal to lift one's spirits, do you not?"

This, for whatever reason, seemed to relieve Lady Worthington a great deal, for a dazzling smile swept across her face as she nodded.

"But of course, that was very kind of you indeed, Your Grace," she said as her daughter began to smile once more. "How considerate of you. How generous to think of such a lowly companion in such a way. I am sure she was quite overwhelmed."

Stiffening, Nicholas gave a small smile to both ladies and then, after a few moments more, excused himself. He had thought this evening would be a very pleasant one, but from practically the moment they had entered, he had found himself irritated and angry, and then choosing to behave foolishly because of it. Now that he had done such a thing as standing up with Lady Foster, he had been forced to spend the rest of the evening doing all he could to prevent the rumors from flying around the ballroom and through the *ton*, although quite how successful he had been, Nicholas could not say.

"You have quite a thunderous expression on your face, I must say."

Nicholas stopped, seeing Lord Ponsonby grinning at him from a few steps away. Reaching for a glass of brandy from a footman's tray, he took a quick sip and tried to straighten his features.

"I am enjoying this evening immensely," he lied as Lord Ponsonby chuckled. "And you?"

Lord Ponsonby shrugged. "It has been very satisfactory, yes," he agreed, coming a little closer to Nicholas. "I have danced with many a young lady and found myself quite lost in their charms." His head tilted. "And that includes your charge, Lady Frederica."

"I am aware that you have a good deal of interest in Frederica, Ponsonby," Nicholas replied, a glimmer of a smile etching itself across his face. "But you must know that I will not, in any way, permit her to consider you."

Lord Ponsonby chuckled, his shoulders lifting. "I fear you know me much too well, Your Grace." His smile faded just a little and a more serious look came into his eyes. "But what of Lady Foster?"

A ripple of surprise ran through Nicholas' frame. "Lady Foster?"

"Well," Lord Ponsonby continued, "I have danced with her and spent many a minute conversing with her. She appears to have quite an amiable character, although I would say she is a little quiet, but certainly she is quite lovely in appearance."

Nicholas swallowed hard, a sense of unease beginning to flood him. "Lady Foster is just as you say," he agreed slowly. "What is it that you wonder about her?"

Lord Ponsonby shrugged again, a calculating look in his eyes. "I require a wife," he said practically. "You know very well that my nature is not one that lingers on one particular lady for any length of time. Therefore, I—"

"You mean to say you wish to wed a lady who will be contented with her marriage and permit you to do as you please," Nicholas interrupted, a curl of disgust tugging at his lip.

"Precisely," Lord Ponsonby replied, clearly missing the dark look in Nicholas' eye. "I know that Lady Foster is widowed. I am aware that she has been forced to become a companion rather than being able to attend London as a lady of quality in her own right. Therefore, I am certain that she would be very glad indeed to marry again and certainly would be more than understanding when it came to my..." Looking away, he hesitated for a moment as he tried to find the right word. "My interests."

The very thought of Lord Ponsonby wedding Lady Foster, only to then set her aside in favor of another, to treat her as though she mattered very little to him, brought such a fierce anger to Nicholas' heart that for a few moments, he simply could not speak. Lord Ponsonby's suggestion was, he supposed, quite reasonable to some extent and certainly made sense to Lord Ponsonby's way of thinking, but it completely removed all thought of what Lady Foster would feel to be in a marriage such as that.

"I think not."

Nicholas' words were tight and angry although, with a great effort, he managed to control himself so that he said nothing more. He wanted to rail at his friend, to state that there was nothing at all that would induce him to ever suggest to Lady Foster that there was a good match to be made with Lord Ponsonby, but instead, he remained quite silent.

Lord Ponsonby looked back steadily into Nicholas' face, then sighed and shook his head.

"You think my suggestion to be in very poor taste, I think," he remarked as Nicholas held his gaze without responding. "Or is it that you think so highly of Lady Foster that you could not imagine her wed to someone such as I?"

"Both," Nicholas replied tightly. "Lady Foster is a remarkable young lady who has already endured a great deal. To wed someone such as you, who has desires such as you do, would not be fair to her. I could not permit it."

Another heavy sigh came from Lord Ponsonby before he threw back the rest of his brandy. "It does not seem to me as though you would have to give permission, Your Grace," he said cautiously. "Lady Foster is, from what I understand, in the employ of Lord Dewsbury, who is Lady Frederica's father."

Nicholas' frown deepened. "That may be so, Lord Ponsonby, but they both reside with me. As much as you might desire to court Lady Foster and make her an offer of marriage in the hope that you will be able to continue along your life just as you please, I am afraid that she is most inclined to pay attention to the advice that *I* give her. And I will tell her the truth of what you have just said to me, should it come to it."

This made Lord Ponsonby frown hard, no trace of mirth or even amiability residing on his face any longer. "That hardly seems fair."

"Of course it is fair," Nicholas replied firmly. "Lady Foster should know the truth about any particular match that might be offered to her, so that she and she alone can make a wise and considered decision." He saw Lord Ponsonby's frown deepen and felt a sense of great satisfaction fill him. "After all, I am sure that you, as a gentleman of the nobility, would not wish to wed a lady who did not know the truth of your intentions." A small smile pulled at the corner of his mouth. "That would make you something of a rogue, would it not?"

"I suppose it would," Lord Ponsonby muttered, turning away from him. "You are very protective of the lady for someone who is only permitting her to reside under her roof."

"For the sake of my niece," Nicholas replied, refusing to allow

Lord Ponsonby to make any sort of derogatory remark. "Good evening, Ponsonby."

He did not wait but turned on his heel and strode through the crowd, his jaw working furiously. He did not see the way Lord Ponsonby's eyes narrowed, or how he watched Nicholas' departure until, finally, he could no longer be seen.

6

Louisa stepped into the bookshop behind Lady Frederica, looking all around her as she did so. A small sigh escaped her, a slightly wistful smile on her lips. How many times had she escaped into such a place when she had enjoyed her Season in London? Having been entirely unaware of what awaited her—for her father had only told her of her engagement a week before the first banns had been called—she had found moments of sheer delight in bookshops such as these.

She was very glad indeed that Lady Frederica had requested to visit and hoped that she, too, might have an opportunity to purchase a new novel. She saved as much of her income as she could, but surely she could afford a single new book.

"It is so very quiet."

"It is," Louisa agreed, keeping her voice low as Lady Frederica made her way to the first lot of shelves and began to look through the books there. "Peaceful, I think."

Lady Frederica looked back at her, a smile on her face. "Perhaps," she said softly. "It is certainly quite a contrast to the conversations at a soiree or even the hubbub of noise outside."

Louisa smiled and then came to stand by Lady Frederica. "You would not mind if I also…?"

"But of course," Lady Frederica replied, smiling warmly at Louisa. "I will make certain to stay close to you."

"I thank you," Louisa said, her heart full of contentment as she began to look at the books. Her fingers traced over the spines, her heart settled and her soul contented. The ball last evening had brought a good many difficulties with it, and she had struggled through it with as much grace as she could manage, but now, finally, her mind seemed clear of all the troubling thoughts that had run through it. After the duke had practically pulled her onto the dance floor, she had found herself more embarrassed than she had ever thought possible, only for him to attempt to remedy the situation by forcing two other gentlemen to step out with her onto the dance floor whilst he made certain to chaperone Lady Frederica.

Having been quite certain that a good many of the *ton* now knew precisely who she was and had noted that she had been taken to the dance floor by the duke, she had prayed silently that no one would begin to gossip about her. Lord Dewsbury, she knew, would not be particularly pleased to hear that there had been rumors spreading about the very person he had employed to supervise and chaperone his daughter.

Although you did enjoy dancing with the duke, did you not?

Everything in her rebelled at that thought, pushing it away and refusing to even consider it. No, she had not found a single modicum of enjoyment, she told herself sternly. It had been difficult for her to remember the steps of the dance, such had been her panic and fear, so of course she had not found any sort of pleasure in it.

But when he took your hand…

Shaking her head firmly to herself, Louisa ignored the quiet words that seemed to come from her very heart, words that were eager for her to accept them. The truth was, Louisa did not want to even consider such a thought, even though she knew very well that there had been moments last evening when she had been forced to catch her breath, when heat had risen in her cheeks, and when she had found herself unable to look anywhere other than into the duke's eyes.

Louisa allowed herself a tiny smile. She was being utterly ridiculous, of course, for she was a baroness and a widow at that, who was now forced to be a paid companion, rather than enter into society on her own merits. It was not as though she was someone a duke might even look at with any consideration. But he was very kind, very generous, and despite his thoughtlessness in taking her onto the dance floor, Louisa knew that he had meant to be considerate of her. That, at least, spoke well of his character.

"Did you hear what has been said of her?"

Louisa hesitated, her fingers on the spine of yet another novel. Turning her head, she saw that Lady Frederica was only a short distance away, although clearly not at all able to hear what Louisa was, at present, listening to. She could not see those who spoke but presumed that they were near to her somewhere, their presence hidden by the many shelves of books.

"I am surprised that the duke permits her to reside under his roof."

Louisa's heart stopped for a moment, her hand frozen in place as her stomach began to fall and swell like the waves of the sea. It was not as though she wanted to eavesdrop, and she knew very well that she ought to simply move away so that she could no longer hear what was being said. But the mention of a duke stayed her. There were not too many dukes in London, and certainly even fewer that the *ton* might speak of. Surely it could not be the Duke of Ellsworth that these two ladies mentioned?

"I think that he is doing so only to care for his niece," came the second voice, a twist of spite in their words. "I know that she, at least, is very respectable."

"But why should the daughter of a marquess be given such a companion?" asked the first, sounding both exasperated and disbelieving. "It is quite ridiculous, unless she is some sort of poor relation that they simply *must* take care of."

"Lady Foster, I—"

Louisa swung around toward Lady Frederica, her eyes wide and one finger to her lips. Her heart was pounding furiously now, her stomach swaying this way and that as nausea began to climb up her throat. The two ladies, whoever they were, were speaking of someone she knew very well—herself. Quite what they were saying, Louisa did not know, but the thought of revealing herself to them, or of Lady Frederica inadvertently disclosing their presence, was a terrifying one.

"Whatever is the matter?" Lady Frederica asked, her voice still mercifully low as she took a small step closer to Louisa, her hand reaching out to take hers. "Is there something wrong?"

"I am sure that Lady Frederica does not know of her companion's wrongdoing, else she would not be as friendly toward her," came the second voice, sounding very prim indeed. "It may be that neither she nor her father know of it. And what then? Is it not our duty to set the matter to rights?"

Louisa stared at Lady Frederica, seeing the shock ripple across her charge's face as she listened, her eyes wide with surprise and her mouth a little ajar.

"It is only a whisper as yet," came the first voice, speaking a little more slowly as though they wanted to give great consideration to what they were saying. "I have no doubt that it is true, for the lady appears to demand great things for herself, despite being a companion. Did you see how she stood up with the duke himself last evening?"

The second lady laughed cruelly, and Louisa closed her eyes, shame pouring into her. Lady Frederica's hand pressed hers a little more tightly, but it was a thin comfort.

"I cannot imagine what she has said or done in order to have the duke behave in such a way," came the reply. "Well, when I say I cannot imagine, that is not *quite* true. I am sure she has her wiles."

Heat rushed into Louisa's face at their implication, horrorstruck that these two ladies would not only think of her that way, but that they would also speak so about her to each other. She had known very well that there would be those from the *beau monde* who would pay great attention to the fact that she had danced with the duke last evening, but she had never once considered that the rumors that would follow would be something akin to this.

"Well, if she *did* have a part in the death of her late husband—perhaps so that she might get the position of companion and grow close to the duke—then I must say, I am not surprised if she manipulates His Grace also," stated the first lady firmly. "I do not think that Lady Frederica is aware at all of the matter, although perhaps she was a little surprised to see her uncle dancing with her companion."

Louisa caught her breath, her free hand now going to her mouth as she stared, unseeingly, into the face of Lady Frederica. A great and terrible trembling took a hold of her frame as she realized the truth of what was being said. These two ladies had, somehow, heard the suggestion being made that *she* had somehow been involved in—or was responsible for—the death of her late husband, Baron Foster. Quite why anyone would say such a thing was beyond Louisa, for she had been residing at home when her husband had met his death, but now it seemed that such a rumor was going to be spread throughout all of London. A hand pressed hard over her heart, squeezing it painfully as she fought off the edge of panic that threatened to overwhelm her.

"But Lady Frederica would have no recourse to argue, given that he is a duke and she only his niece," argued the second, pulling Louisa back into their conversation. "The poor child, she must be quite confused. I cannot imagine what she must have thought, seeing the duke standing up with her companion like that—and in the very same set also."

"Caught up in a situation she knows very little about," sighed the other, sounding as though she were greatly concerned for Lady Frederica. "If only there was something we could do."

There was silence for a moment and Louisa felt herself swaying just a little as a sudden and harsh weakness came into every limb. She clutched at Lady Frederica's hand with her other free one and felt the lady hold onto her tightly, one hand on her shoulder and the other still holding her hand. Louisa's eyes closed as she dragged in air, trying to take steadying breaths and find some way to reclaim a little strength in order that she might continue to hide herself away without revealing her presence to these two ladies. The last thing she needed at present would be to collapse and cause a scene of great distress, where the two ladies who were, it seemed, still speaking of both her and the duke would discover her and then add yet more nonsense to the rumors that they spoke.

"I am sure that we can do *something* for Lady Frederica," came the reply as Louisa forced her eyes open, looking into her charge's face and seeing just how white the girl had become. "We can attend to her, befriend her a little more, and certainly pull her away from her companion as best we can."

"Indeed," said the other, sounding quite eager. "If we have her in our company, there will be no need for her companion."

"And the duke will be *more* than willing to allow his niece into the care of ladies such as ourselves, I am sure." The lady sounded both contented and determined, leaving Louisa to wither away inside, feeling utterly wretched. "Come now, I am to meet Lady Brookhurst for tea at Gunter's and I should not like to be late."

"No doubt she will be *very* interested to hear all that you have learned," came the reply, as yet more dread filled Louisa's heart. "Very interested indeed."

Louisa remained precisely where she was, barely moving an inch as she listened to the two ladies quit the shop. They walked near to her as they passed and she flinched violently, fearing that they would discover her, but in the next moment, they had moved far from her and she heard their footsteps making their way toward the door. It was only then that Louisa permitted herself to relax just a little, looking into the wide eyes of Lady Frederica, who still held her hand tightly.

"What is to be done?" Lady Frederica whispered urgently as the bell sounded gently, alerting them both to the fact that the ladies in question had departed. "They cannot be permitted to say such things about you. They were spurious lies, all of them. To even imagine that you had something to do with the death of your late husband is... is..."

Louisa shook her head, her hand tightening on Lady Frederica's. "We should return to your uncle's townhouse," she said as Lady Frederica's lips flattened into an angry line, whilst she herself felt nothing but despair. "He must know of this at once." She drew in a shaky breath, her eyes closing again for a moment. "I—I should leave London. It would be best for you to have another companion, Lady Frederica."

"No."

Lady Frederica's eyes were now flashing with anger, but Louisa could only shake her head, knowing full well that, whilst Lady Frederica clearly felt some sort of loyalty toward her—which Louisa greatly appreciated—she was not thinking about what would be best for her and her reputation here in London.

"We should discuss it with the duke just as soon as we can," Louisa said quietly, taking in another long breath and settling her shoulders as she did so, feeling a little strength return to her. "I am sorry to pull you away from the bookshop so soon, but I do believe that it is of the greatest importance that we speak to the duke as soon as we can. He must know of these rumors."

"Rumors which are entirely false and should not even be given a *moment's* consideration," Lady Frederica replied, her voice a little louder than before, her fingers tight as she squeezed Louisa's hand. "I will not allow you to leave me."

Louisa gave her a small, sad smile. "You may have to," she said, as quietly as she could. "It may be for the best."

The anger was still buried in Lady Frederica's gaze, but she said nothing in retort, turning around so that she might lead the way from the shop. Louisa closed her eyes for just a moment, steadying herself before she followed Frederica. Stepping outside, she glanced all about her, as though afraid that within a few moments, everyone around her would begin whispering and throwing her sharp looks as they spoke these terrible rumors.

But there was nothing of the sort. Instead, the sun shone just as brightly as before, ladies and gentlemen made their way past without so much as glancing at her, but Louisa knew that it would not be so for much longer. She could not go to another ball, to another soiree or dinner party without having people speak of her. The rumors she had heard would soon be spread far and wide, and Lady Frederica's reputation—and possibly the duke's reputation also—would be damaged by her continued presence here in London. As she climbed into the carriage, Louisa's heart sank low in her chest as she began to prepare herself for what was to come. She would have to leave London, although where she would go, Louisa had very little idea. Perhaps Lord Dewsbury would be able to secure her a new position. She did wish that her father would allow her back into his home, but the viscount did not offer.

Mayhap the duke would show kindness to her in the way he had done before and make certain that she was not left to fend for herself. Everything possible had to be done in order to protect Lady Frederica, and Louisa was quite prepared to step away from her present circumstances if it was required of her. As much as she had come to care for Lady Frederica, as much as she had, for the most part, enjoyed being back in society, that would all have to be set aside. Lady Frederica's future was at stake, and Louisa knew she could not remain.

"It will all be all right."

Lady Frederica leaned forward and pressed Louisa's hand once more, a warm smile on her face which Louisa struggled to return.

"We will tell the duke and he will find a solution, I am sure," Lady Frederica continued confidently. "You will not have to leave London. I will not allow it."

Louisa said nothing, turning her head to look out of the window. She would miss Lady Frederica, of course, but she would also miss the duke's company. They had not had a good many conversations, but what he had shared with her thus far, what she had seen of his character, made her quite certain that she would find herself feeling a sense of loss when she was separated from him. It was very rare indeed to find a gentleman so compassionate and caring and yet the Duke of Ellsworth had managed to be so. She would not find his like again, Louisa considered, but at least she was glad that she had been given the opportunity to know him a little.

Closing her eyes, Louisa leaned back against the squabs and let the heaviness in her heart escape from her as she let out a pained sigh. It was all to come to an end, she was sure of that, and the thought was most distressing. But what else was there for her to do?

7

Nicholas was attempting to work through a particularly difficult piece of arithmetic in order to make certain that various expenses were precisely as they appeared and that nothing further had been added, when the sound of great exclamations and hurried feet met his ears. Losing his concentration entirely, he looked up from his desk and frowned, wondering what could have caused such fervor. It could not be from Lady Foster, he was sure, given that she was such a quiet and reserved lady, which meant that Lady Frederica was greatly upset about something.

"Uncle."

The door flew open and Lady Frederica practically flung herself into the room, her eyes almost wild as she hurried toward him. "Uncle, you must do something at once."

Nicholas blinked in surprise, looking behind Lady Frederica and seeing Lady Foster stepping quietly into the room. Her eyes held his for a moment before she lowered them and, from her demeanor, he was quite certain that something was troubling her also.

"Is something wrong?" he asked, looking back into Lady Frederica's eyes and seeing, much to his distress, tears now forming there. "Goodness, whatever is the matter?"

"It is Lady Foster," Lady Frederica cried, large tears now beginning to splash down over her face as she flung one arm out toward Lady Foster, who had seemed to shrink just a little as she stood in the doorway, her head lowered all the more. "You must do something, Ellsworth."

Nicholas did not know what to think. Looking from Lady Frederica to Lady Foster, he suddenly began to fear that Lady Foster had done something quite dreadful, something that had greatly upset Lady Frederica. The thought was only a passing one, however, for he knew Lady Foster well and was quite convinced that she could not do such a thing.

"Perhaps I should explain to His Grace what has occurred, Lady Frederica."

Lady Foster came forward and put a gentle hand on Lady Frederica's arm, her other hand finding her handkerchief and pressing it into her hand. "You are most distressed."

"As are you," Lady Frederica replied hoarsely, although she did turn so that she might sit down in a chair near to Nicholas' desk. "Quite how you are so calm, I do not understand."

Lady Foster gave her a small smile, although it was not one that reached her eyes. When she turned to look back at Nicholas, he saw nothing but distress in her expression—distress that he knew she was doing her level best to hide.

"Your Grace, I believe that it has come time for me to leave London," she began, and a wave of shock crashed into Nicholas, just as Lady Frederica let out a strangled exclamation.

"No, you cannot," she cried as Lady Foster turned toward her. "I will not—"

"It may be for the best, Lady Frederica," Lady Foster replied gently. "It may harm not only your reputation but the duke's reputation too, if I remain."

A stab of frustration pierced Nicholas' heart. "Can someone please explain to me all that has occurred?" he asked, aware that he was practically demanding this from the two ladies but growing all the more concerned with every minute that passed. "I do not understand a word that has been said thus far."

Lady Foster's face flushed crimson and she dropped her gaze, a murmured apology immediately on her lips. Nicholas closed his eyes for a moment, his jaw tight as he realized how sharply he had spoken to a lady who was clearly already distressed.

"My apologies, Your Grace," she said, speaking a little more quickly now. "As I have said, I believe that I should find another position just as soon as possible. It would not be wise for me to remain in London for I fear that my continued presence here will not only affect Lady Frederica's reputation amongst the *ton* but also your own."

"And why would that be?" Nicholas asked, glancing toward Lady Frederica and seeing how she dabbed at her eyes. "What is it you have done, Lady Foster?"

"She has done nothing!" Lady Frederica exclaimed, her eyes still glistening with tears. "Do you not understand?"

Lady Foster held up her hand toward her charge, quietening her almost at once.

"I—I have not done anything, Your Grace," she said, stammering just a little. "However, due to what I overheard this afternoon, I believe it would be best for me to remove myself from your house as soon as I can. Rumors will be already spreading through London and I could not allow them to injure both you and Lady Frederica."

A frown pulled at Nicholas' brows. "Rumors?" he repeated as Lady Frederica blew her nose indelicately. "What is being said?"

A sudden guilt slammed into his heart as he recalled just how foolish he had been in pulling Lady Foster out to dance with him the previous evening. He had done his level best to make certain that other gentlemen danced with Lady Foster, so that he would not have been the only one to do so and thus would have removed the interest and speculation of the *ton* somewhat.

Clearly, it seemed, he had not done enough. It was unusual, of course, for a companion to dance and certainly all the more so for them to dance with the gentleman their charge resided with, so evidently now, words were being whispered about them both and Lady Foster had decided to remove herself from London entirely, in order to protect Lady Frederica.

The stab of guilt became all the more painful and he winced, looking away from Lady Foster.

"Was it my actions?" he asked, looking up at Lady Foster and seeing her eyes flicker. "Last evening, I should not have used you in order to escape from Lady Judith. I am truly sorry and if that is all that is being said, then—"

"I overheard two ladies speaking, Your Grace," she interrupted, before he could say more. "It is suggested, it seems, that I was involved in some way with the death of my husband."

It was as though all the air had been pulled from the room, for when Nicholas tried to take a breath, he found he could not do so. His lungs began to burn and still, he heard Lady Foster's words go around and around in his mind, horrified at even the thought of such a dreadful thing.

"Not only that," Lady Foster continued quietly, "but they also believe that, in some way, I have manipulated you, Your Grace."

Nicholas finally managed to drag in air to his starving lungs. "Manipulated me?" he repeated, his voice hoarse. "Whatever do you mean?"

A tinge of red came into Lady Foster's cheeks but when she spoke, her voice was still very quiet indeed and held that same, familiar calmness that he knew so well.

"They suggested that I had coerced my way into this position," she said, her gaze no longer fixed to his. "And that in doing so, I intended to continue behaving in much the same manner, so that I might gain..." She closed her eyes, her lips pressing hard together for a moment. "So that I might gain favor from you, Your Grace."

It took Nicholas a moment to realize what she meant, but when the truth finally came to him, he felt both embarrassment and anger burning through him together. "You mean to say that they believe—"

"They said she was using her *wiles!*" Lady Frederica exclaimed, bringing yet another flush to Lady Foster's cheeks. "That her dancing with you last evening was entirely her own doing and that she practically coerced you into doing so."

"I see." Nicholas let out a long, slow breath and saw Lady Foster's shoulders slump. "These are nothing but rumors, however. There is no truth to them, of course."

Lady Foster nodded, but when she finally met his gaze again, there was a faint gleam of determination within them. "Your Grace, it is best for me to leave this household at once," she said as Lady Frederica let out another exclamation. "Lady Frederica might not be able to see it as well as you or I, given that we have seen the effect of gossip and rumor before, and therefore I cannot simply remain here and allow her to be so poorly affected."

Nicholas found himself shaking his head long before Lady Foster had finished. The thought of her leaving was one he could not abide, and seeing the determination in her gaze made *him* all the more determined to refuse her.

"That is not at all fair," he said firmly as Lady Frederica now took out her own handkerchief in order to wipe her eyes. "These are whispers, Lady Foster, nothing more."

"But they will grow," Lady Foster insisted as Nicholas rose slowly from his chair, feeling the need to walk around the room as though it might help his thoughts to order themselves a little better. "You know very well, Your Grace, that such rumors cling to those that they are about and, in doing so, damage those near to them also." She gestured toward Lady Frederica, who sniffed and shook her head. "It would not be right."

"What is not right, Lady Foster, is the fact that there are those amongst us who wish to speak of you in such a way," Nicholas declared as Lady Foster watched him closely. "Why they would have thought of such a disturbing rumor, I cannot imagine. It is most despicable."

"I agree," Lady Frederica declared as Nicholas chose, wisely, to ring the bell for tea so that his charge and Lady Foster might have a little refreshment in order to restore them somewhat. "I cannot have you thrown from London by those who, for whatever reason, have chosen to speak of you so."

"And you know very well that there has been no manipulation on your part, Lady Foster," Nicholas told her as she slowly sank down into a nearby chair, her head now lowered and her eyes fixed to her lap. "Last evening, I was foolish enough to use you in order to escape Lady Judith. That was not wise, and if I have contributed in any way to this difficult situation, I am truly sorry."

Lady Foster said nothing, her head low and a great yet invisible weight seeming to rest on her shoulders.

"I know that you want to leave London, but that will not solve your difficulties at present, Lady Foster," Nicholas told her, feeling a great urge to convince her to remain even though she clearly wanted to depart in order to protect them. "Those rumors will continue, Lady Foster. I doubt that you will be able to find another position easily."

He heard her catch her breath but still, she did not look up.

"It is my fault," he continued heavily. "I should not have done as I did last evening. If I had not done so then—"

"Then I am sure that the rumor of my involvement in my late husband's death would still have been spoken," Lady Foster said brokenly. "I do not know why such things are being whispered about me, Your Grace, but it must surely be deliberate." Slowly, her head lifted and when he looked into her eyes, Nicholas could see nothing but tears. His heart tore for her.

"I am sure that Lord Dewsbury would wish me to step away from my position at present," she continued dully. "I can write to him this very afternoon and attempt to do what I can to—"

"No!" Lady Frederica rose from her chair, her arms spread wide. "You cannot be pushed from London simply because of the cruelty of others, Lady Foster." she cried, clearly greatly distraught. "I have such a friendship with you that I cannot *bear* to have you removed from my side. I do not think that I should find the same with any other companion and to ask me to do without you is not something I can bear." She came closer to Lady Foster, who had, Nicholas noted, also begun to cry. Bending down, she put her hand on Lady Foster's. "You will have nowhere else to go, Louisa. I know that you will be quite lost, forced to struggle to make your way through society, through life, without anyone else to aid you. I cannot allow that, not when you have become so very dear to me. I will take on whatever difficulties I must if it will keep you here with me."

Lady Foster shook her head, her tears flowing freely. "I do not think your father or mother would agree," she said, but Nicholas took a small step closer.

"I would disagree, Lady Foster," he answered, taking out what was now the third handkerchief that had made an appearance within the short time they had been together and handing it to her. "Lord and Lady Dewsbury will be concerned, certainly, but they will not want you to be removed from your position simply because of these rumors. Rumors that are no fault of yours, I might add." Smiling at her and yet still deeply disturbed by what he had heard from her, he saw her finally look back at him. "Please, do not leave Lady Frederica to my sole care, Lady Foster," he finished, trying to inject a little levity into the situation. "I think I should do a very poor job indeed without your guidance and aid."

"And I do not want you to go either," Lady Frederica added, as though Lady Foster was not aware of such a thing already. "My uncle will write to my father and explain the situation. I am certain that he will not ask for your departure either."

Closing her eyes again, with tears still streaking down her cheeks, Lady Foster eventually gave a small nod. Lady Frederica threw her arms about the lady and also began to sob with evident relief, leaving Nicholas to stand quietly and with a good deal of uncertainty as to what he was to do next.

Thankfully, the scratch at the door announced the arrival of the tea tray and within a few minutes, both ladies were seated again, their tears eventually fading as Lady Foster reached to pour the tea.

"The question remains, however," she said after a few moments. "What is it that I am to do, Your Grace?"

Handing a cup and saucer to Lady Frederica, she then poured one for him also, whilst Nicholas continued to consider her question.

"I think," he said slowly, "that we must find who is speaking such dark and disturbing rumors into the ear of the *ton*." He saw Lady Foster's eyes flare wide with surprise, perhaps having expected him to say that they would simply continue on as they were and rebuff such rumors whenever they came. "How else are we to know who is speaking such things, and why?"

Lady Frederica nodded eagerly, clearly in agreement. "That way, you might be able to confront them—and could do so in a manner that alerts the *beau monde* to the fact that they were entirely spurious," she said as Nicholas frowned. "That is the only way you are ever going to be free of this, Louisa."

Noting that his niece now referred to Lady Foster as 'Louisa' rather than her formal title, Nicholas waited for a moment to see if Lady Foster would say anything but, much to his surprise, she did not. Instead, she simply nodded slowly, her eyes considering.

"It will be rather difficult to discover the truth, however," Nicholas added, not wanting to discourage them but rather to make certain that they were both aware of just how hard it might be to actually find the perpetrator. "There appears to be very little reason for such things to be said, as far as I can see."

Lady Frederica took a sip of her tea, much calmer now that Lady Foster had agreed to stay with them for the present. "It is clear that they wish to damage Lady Foster's reputation, although why someone would wish to do so, I cannot imagine."

"And it is well known that your late husband passed away," Nicholas added, knowing that he himself had spoken of it to one or two acquaintances who would have, in turn, passed on such information to others. "But I do not think that anyone is aware of precisely *how* he died, which makes it all the more ridiculous to suggest that you had anything to do with it."

Lady Foster closed her eyes, her lips tight for a moment. "My husband fell from his horse," she said quietly. "There was the suggestion that he had drunk a little too much, but I could not say whether or not that was true. I had not even seen him that day, for he and I kept largely separate lives." Her cheeks flushed for a moment as she opened her eyes, as though she expected Nicholas or Lady Frederica to think ill of her for having such a marriage. Nicholas said nothing, however, knowing all too well that there were many in the *ton* who had marriages of a similar kind to Lady Foster. It was often what occurred when a marriage was arranged. He had to confess that, whilst he and his late wife had certainly been a little more companionable than Lord and Lady Foster had appeared to be, there was less of a pull toward an arrangement when the time came for him to marry next.

"I can still remember when they brought him in," Lady Foster continued after a moment or two, her voice tight. "I knew in an instant that he was gone."

"Then the suggestion that you had any involvement in his death is based on nothing at all," Nicholas stated as Lady Foster nodded. "The person in question must know only that your husband has passed away and has used that fact for their malicious rumors."

Lady Frederica set down her teacup and saucer carefully. "That does not tell us why they would wish to do so," she said as Nicholas made his way to sit down back in his chair, his brow furrowed, and a great many thoughts whirled through his mind. "Why should anyone wish to damage Lady Foster's reputation?"

Nicholas spread his hands, a heaviness in his heart that he did not think would leave him for a long time. He had no immediate idea as to what he was going to do to help Lady Foster, no thought as to what he could do first.

"We will have to think on it," he said quietly. "That is all we need to do at present."

"And this evening, Your Grace, mayhap it would be best for me to remain here," Lady Foster said, reminding Nicholas that they were all meant to be attending Lord Millford's soiree. "I am sure that my presence will not be missed, and given that the rumors will have spread through society already, it might be best for you and Lady Frederica to be without me."

Nicholas hesitated, seeing the way Lady Frederica shook her head, but then chose instead to agree.

"If that is what you think is best, Lady Foster," he told her, seeing the flash of relief in her eyes. "But we cannot hide you from society forever."

Her smile was a little wan. "I am aware of that, Your Grace," she answered steadily. "But this evening, I think I will do what I can to regain my strength and my composure so that I am prepared for tomorrow."

"Tomorrow?"

Lady Frederica looked at him. "There is the dinner party we are to attend, at Lord Whitehall's," she reminded him. "A quiet group, at least."

"Indeed," he replied slowly. "And plenty of opportunities to make it quite clear that whatever has been said about you, Lady Foster, is quite untrue. The *ton* will know that I am utterly horrified by such rumors and that I have no consideration for them whatsoever. Have no doubt that you will have both myself and Lady Frederica by your side. You will not be left to fend for yourself."

For a moment, Nicholas thought she might begin to cry once more, for her eyes glistened and her chin wobbled. But after a moment, she simply held his gaze and managed a very small smile.

"I thank you, Your Grace," she said, her voice so weak he could barely hear it. "Thank you for your understanding and your willingness to help me. I do not know what else I would have done otherwise."

"But of course," he replied, a little surprised at just how protective he felt over her. "You are not alone in this. In that, you have my word."

8

"How are you this evening, Louisa?"

It would be foolishness itself to lie when Louisa knew that her face was pale and drawn and that there was no color in her cheeks.

"I am nervous, Lady Frederica," she acknowledged as her charge nodded in gentle understanding. "The soiree will go very well indeed, but I find that I am somewhat troubled by the thought that the rumors about me will make your situation rather difficult."

Lady Frederica waved a hand in dismissal. "I will be all right," she said firmly. "It is not as though I am required to wed this Season, and given that by next summer, there will be a whole host of other whispers and gossip, I am certain that everyone will have forgotten about you entirely."

Louisa knew that this was meant to be encouraging, but she wished desperately that she could do something that would mean Lady Frederica was not affected by these rumors at all. And yet, given what both she and the duke had said, it appeared that they were both determined to keep her both in London and by their side, refusing to step away from her when even she thought it best that they did so.

"And you must call me simply 'Frederica'," her charge continued. "I know I have taken something of a liberty in calling you 'Louisa', but I feel as though we have become much more closely acquainted these last few days." She smiled at Louisa, who, despite her anxiety, could not help but smile back at her. "Although if I am taking liberties, then you must dissuade me of the thought at once."

"No, indeed, I shall not do so," Louisa replied, reaching to take Frederica's hand. "You have been a stalwart, Lady Frederica. It is not every young lady who would show such determination and strength of character when faced with something like this." She let go of Lady Frederica's hand and then turned back to glance at her reflection in the mirror one last time, reminding herself silently to pinch her cheeks before she stepped into Lord Whitehall's townhouse.

"That is kind of you to say," Lady Frederica replied quietly. "But you think too little of yourself, Louisa. You are not just my companion. You have become my friend and someone that I value greatly. I could not bear to allow those rumors to push you not only from London but far from me also. If such a thing occurred, then I do not think I would ever see you again, and that would tear my heart terribly."

"And mine," Louisa agreed softly. "I have always been quite determined that I shall see you happily wed, Frederica, but I fear now that I might be the cause of difficulties in that."

Lady Frederica shook her head firmly. "It shall not be so," she said resolutely. "I shall be very happily wed when the time comes. As I have said, I am to give no real consideration to such a thing this Season, and by next year, I am certain that all will have been forgotten. You will find yourself in the church on the day I am wed, I am quite certain of it."

Louisa smiled, her spirits lifting just a little as Lady Frederica made her way to the door.

"Now, shall we make our way to the drawing room and see if the duke is waiting for us?" she asked, and Louisa swallowed her nervousness and followed quickly after her. "Let us make our way to Lord Whitehall's and prove to the *ton* that you are not about to hide away for the rest of the Season, no matter what they might say of you."

~

Louisa wished desperately that she had Lady Frederica's confidence. The very moment she stepped into Lord Whitehall's drawing room, she found herself lingering behind Lady Frederica and the duke, wanting to hide herself away from the sharp gazes of the other guests. It was not that she wanted to avoid them for her own sake but rather for the sake of Lady Frederica. Over and over, she berated her own foolishness in attending, fully convinced now that it would have been best to remain far from Lady Frederica, no matter what she or the duke had said.

"Good evening, Your Grace."

Louisa stayed where she was, still behind Lady Frederica and the duke as a lady she did not know presented herself to him.

"Good evening, Lady Worthington, and to you also, Miss Drake," came the reply as he bowed. "Have I presented my niece to you before? I am afraid I cannot recall."

"I do not believe you have," Lady Worthington said as Louisa kept her gaze low, not wanting to appear too obvious. It would be better for everyone if she remained as unobserved as possible.

"Then might I present Lady Frederica, daughter to the Marquess of Dewsbury," the duke said, before looking over his shoulder at Louisa. Her eyes flared as they caught his gaze, her heart beginning to slam hard against her chest as she caught his intention. She began to shake her head no, but it was much too late.

"And this is Lady Foster, companion to Lady Frederica," he continued, standing to one side so that she had a clearer view of the lady in question. Having no other choice, Louisa dropped into a quick curtsy, her eyes lifting to the lady's as she rose, for she did not want to be rude.

"Lady Frederica, Lady Foster, this is Lady Worthington and her daughter, Miss Drake."

"Glad to make your acquaintance," Louisa murmured as she curtsied to Miss Drake, who was looking at her with a flicker of interest in her eyes.

Lady Worthington's lip curled slightly as she looked back at Louisa. "Your companion, Lady Frederica?" she said, turning to the lady instead of directing the question to Louisa herself. "I am a little surprised that you have retained her."

Louisa's stomach dropped to the floor and she looked away, a crushing wave of shame threatening to overwhelm her.

"I cannot imagine what you mean, Lady Worthington," Lady Frederica replied, her tone cool and yet her words filled with curiosity. "I am quite contented with Lady Foster as my companion. Is there something that you wish to say that might otherwise be unbeknownst to me?"

Louisa swallowed hard, not quite certain whether she should say something or remain silent. One glance toward the duke told her that she should remain silent, for his brows were knotted tightly together and his jaw set hard. There was no need for her to defend herself or make any sort of remark, it seemed. Lady Frederica was quite determined to do so herself.

"I—I only meant to say that I am a little surprised at your *choice* of companion," Lady Worthington said, a slightly doubtful expression creeping across her face as she glanced toward her daughter. "I have heard one or two things being said about Lady Foster and—"

"I should hope, Lady Worthington, that a lady such as yourself, with such a high standing in society, would be loath to not only listen to but believe any such rumors," the duke remarked, sounding rather surprised. "At least, that was my expectation." When Louisa looked at him, she saw that his brows had risen and there was a look of great astonishment on his face.

This immediately seemed to have a very great effect on Lady Worthington, for she put one hand to her heart and began to blink rapidly, her mouth opening and closing for a moment as she looked to her daughter, who was beginning to go a very dark shade of red, her cheeks flushed already.

"I—I quite understand, Your Grace," Lady Worthington stammered after another few moments. "Of course, having heard such rumors, I quickly dismissed them as nothing more than whispers that deserved *none* of my attention." She gave Louisa a quick smile, although it did not reach her eyes and barely lasted more than a moment. "It must be *very* difficult for you indeed, my dear."

Louisa did not know what to say, looking back at Lady Worthington and realizing just how self-interested she was. In only a few seconds, she had changed her mind entirely, based solely on what she now realized the duke wanted to hear from her. It was not based on anything Louisa herself had done or said, but purely on whether or not Lady Worthington would remain in the duke's good graces.

"I appreciate your concern," she replied, seeing the duke's rather satisfied smile beginning to spread across his face. "I have the duke and Lady Frederica's very kind understanding, and that, I confess, has been more than a little helpful."

"But of course," Lady Worthington said with such warmth that had Louisa not known better, she would think the lady very generous indeed. "I quite understand. What a trial for you. How glad you must be that the Duke of Ellsworth stands by your side in this." She did not wait for Louisa to respond but instead turned to the duke, her hands now clasped together in an almost beseeching manner. "You are most understanding, Your Grace. What a generous spirit you must have."

"I am not at all generous, Lady Worthington," the duke replied quickly. "I am the sort of gentleman who seeks truth in all things, and I know for certain that these whispers are nothing other than falsehoods." He inclined his head, one hand pressed to his heart. "Although I am glad to hear that you also are willing to agree with me on that."

Lady Worthington murmured something and gave the duke

another smile before excusing both herself and her daughter and taking their leave of Louisa, Lady Frederica, and the duke.

"I fear that it will be much the same for the rest of the evening," Louisa muttered, passing one hand over her eyes and feeling her heart sinking low in her chest. "I am sorry that—"

"No, you are not to apologize," Lady Frederica interrupted, turning toward Louisa. "This is not your doing."

"Although I confess that I am not entirely willing to believe that Lady Worthington is as easily convinced of her mistake as that," the duke replied, snapping his fingers at the nearest footman, who quickly brought over his tray of refreshments so that they might each take a glass. "I do not like duplicitousness, and I fear it was rather plentiful during our discussion."

Louisa looked up at the duke and gave him a small smile. "It does not matter," she said quietly. "Whether she believes the rumors or not, she has stated aloud that she will not even *consider* them. That, at least, will make quite certain that she and her daughter and more than willing to continue her acquaintance with you both, which I confess I was a little anxious about."

"And why should I wish to continue an acquaintance with Lady Worthington and her daughter, Lady Foster?"

The duke's question sent a spiral of confusion into Louisa's soul. She looked back at him steadily, seeing the way his brow lifted and the corner of his mouth began to pull upwards also. Was he teasing her?

"I—" She could not find what to say. She had thought that Lady Worthington's daughter was of marriageable age and wondered whether or not the duke might wish to consider Miss Drake, but now it seemed that even the suggestion of that idea was considered ridiculous by the duke. Yes, Lady Frederica had informed her that the duke was not at all inclined toward matrimony as yet, but she had wondered whether or not being in London and in amongst society would have changed that particular determination.

"I shall tell you something, Lady Foster, that I do not want you to forget," the duke said, chuckling. "Come a little closer so that you might make certain to hear every word."

Warmth infused her cheeks as she took a small step closer, seeing how Lady Frederica smiled at them both, her eyes dancing with mirth.

"I shall tell you now, Lady Foster, that I have no intention whatsoever of even *considering* courtship and the like, not with any young lady of my acquaintance," the duke said, lowering his head as though he needed to speak some great secret into her ear. "Miss Drake may be a very lovely creature and her mother may be quite determined to do all she can to make an arrangement between us, but unfortunately, my determination will mean that she is certain to fail."

He lifted his head and a shiver ran down Louisa's spine at the look in his eyes. There were emotions there that she could not make out, did not *want* to make out. "I see," she said quietly, choosing not to even question why he was making such a decision. "I did not mean to imply anything, Your Grace."

"Of course you did not!" he exclaimed, stepping a little away from her now, a broad grin on his face. "But it is best for you to hear such a truth from me, Lady Foster, so that you no longer worry about my own particular acquaintances."

"I shall do so no longer," she promised as the duke chuckled once more, only for another gentleman to approach them, bringing their conversation to a swift end.

"Good evening," Louisa murmured, recognizing the gentleman to be Lord Blackdale, whom she had been introduced to at the start of the evening.

"Good evening to you all," he said, before turning his attention to Lady Frederica. "My dear Lady Frederica, might I be permitted to introduce you to my sister? She is only just over there." He pointed to a young lady who was looking across at them eagerly, although she was, it seemed, in the midst of a conversation with some others. "I do hope you will not mind, Your Grace?"

"Not at all," the duke replied, glancing at Louisa, who nodded quickly, knowing that it would be best for her to remain with Lady Frederica rather than stand with the duke and watch from afar. Tongues would wag all the more if they saw her standing with the duke in such a fashion.

"I would be very glad to meet your sister, certainly," Lady Frederica said as Lord Blackdale beamed at her in evident delight. "Pray, lead on."

Louisa stepped out after them both, making certain to keep a short distance away but remaining with her charge regardless. She did not want to be overt in her chaperonage but still wanted to make certain that, in all things and in all matters, Lady Frederica remained quite proper and respectable—even with someone such as she by her side.

∼

"And this is your companion?"

Louisa winced inwardly as Lady Frederica nodded, dropping into a curtsy and then forcing herself to lift her gaze to the incredulous-sounding young lady who had not yet introduced herself to Louisa.

"Good gracious, you simply *must* find another," cried the young Miss Devaney, who was the sister of Lord Blackdale. "Have you not heard all that is being said of her?"

Louisa held her breath, wanting to find a way to defend herself without too much difficulty but realizing that she could not do so under the present circumstances. If she spoke up, if she said anything aloud, then news of what she had said would be reported to everyone in the *ton* and, most likely, repeated rather inaccurately indeed.

The tension and the awkwardness that swirled around Louisa seemed to pin her into place, her head lowering as waves of embarrassment crashed over her.

And then, Lady Frederica laughed. The sound seemed to rip

apart the nervousness that swirled through Louisa's chest, making her look up in surprise.

"My goodness, Miss Devaney, you cannot be serious in your suggestions," Lady Frederica cried as Miss Devaney and the other young lady stared at her as though she had quite lost her senses. "I should not remove my companion from her position just because someone wishes to spread malicious rumors about her. To do so would be most unfair indeed."

"But they may well not be malicious," complained the first, leaning forward and speaking to Lady Frederica in low tones as though Louisa could not be permitted to overhear her. "What if they are true? After all, it is quite understandable that a young lady might seek the attentions of a duke in order to improve her position."

"And being a baroness is not a particularly high title, especially if one is widowed," came the sneering voice of Miss Devaney. "Come now, Lady Frederica, you are being foolish. You should find yourself a companion who will have no scandal whatsoever affixed to her name."

Tears burned in Louisa's eyes, but they were not tears of sorrow. Rather, they were tears that came from anger. Anger that they would speak of her in such a way when she was only a step behind Lady Frederica and well able to hear them, as well as anger that they would believe all that had been said of her without hesitation. She grew angry with the *ton* for throwing themselves eagerly into whatever rumors or whispers were spoken, grasping a hold of them with great excitement so that they might then go on to share the same falsehoods with others. If only there were others like the duke and Lady Frederica who were willing to throw such aspersions aside and instead focus entirely on what they knew to be the truth.

"I must ask, Miss Devaney, wherever did you hear such ridiculous rumors?" Lady Frederica asked, turning to Louisa and beckoning her forward. "I am certain that both I and my uncle, the Duke of Ellsworth, would be glad to know who told such lies to you, for, as I have said, they are nothing short of ridiculous. Indeed, whoever has spoken such things is, I think, attempting to severely damage my companion's reputation, and in doing so, is also muddying my own." She shook her head and placed one hand on Louisa's shoulder, bringing her a little more encouragement. "I should hate to think that there is someone within the *ton* who is set on injuring both the duke and me in some way."

Louisa lifted her chin and looked steadily into the eyes of Miss Devaney, seeing the way that the lady shrank back just a little as she looked at her. The shame and the embarrassment that had clung to Louisa's heart seemed to quickly dissipate, as though it no longer wanted to be a part of her soul and instead was replaced with an anger that filled every part of her. An anger that burned away her mortification and instead gave her a determination to discover the truth.

"The duke has been *very* kind," she found herself saying as the young ladies then turned to her, their expressions equal ones of surprise, as though they had not expected Louisa to speak. "He is fully aware of these rumors and has told me, quite firmly, that he does not believe them."

Lady Frederica nodded as though to confirm to the two ladies that Louisa was telling the truth, her hand dropping from Louisa's arm.

"And I am certain that he thinks very poorly of anyone who *does* listen to such gossip," Lady Frederica said boldly as the two ladies glanced at each other. "Might I ask you again, Miss Devaney, who told you of these lies? I should very much like to know, as, I am sure, would the duke."

Miss Devaney's eyes narrowed as she looked back at Lady Frederica, a slight frown flickering between her brow. For a few moments, it looked as though she would refuse to speak, as though she would keep quite silent and merely shake her head and step away from the conversation, only for her to sigh and then spread her hands.

"I am afraid I heard it from my brother," she said, looking Lady

Frederica directly in the eye. "I am sure that he will tell you from whom *he* heard it, if only you should ask him."

"I shall," Lady Frederica replied firmly. "I thank you, Miss Devaney. You have been very kind, and I shall make certain that my uncle knows of it."

This brought a slight smile to Miss Devaney's face, but Louisa could only shake her head to herself, thinking that it took a mere mention of the duke's name for Miss Devaney to consider what she had said. At the same time, however, she felt very grateful indeed for Miss Frederica's determination to discover the truth. At least now they had some sort of purpose in what they were to do next.

"I shall speak to your brother directly, I think," Lady Frederica said, glancing back at Louisa, who nodded her agreement and felt a new strength begin to fill her. "Do excuse us."

As they walked away, Louisa murmured a few words of thanks to Lady Frederica, who threw a quick smile in her direction. For whatever reason, she now no longer felt ashamed or embarrassed. Rather, there was a sense of frustration and upset burning deep within her and, with that, came a small flicker of anger that seemed to root itself inside her heart. There was a great injustice here. She had known that ever since the bookshop, but for whatever reason, it had not filled her with any sort of resentment before. That was not the case any longer. Now, she felt as though she no longer had to hide away, to keep behind the duke and Lady Frederica.

They have both defended you, she thought to herself as Lady Frederica led her through the drawing room slowly, clearly looking for Lord Blackdale. *They have publicly stated that you are not guilty of all that has been said of you. They have laughed at those who have said otherwise, have asked to know why such people would believe those rumors. You have been thoroughly defended. Why, then, should you shrink back? Why attempt to hide yourself away? Surely to do so is only to verify your guilt to others?*

"Lord Blackdale?"

Lady Frederica smiled tightly at Lord Blackdale, who had been speaking to another gentleman. Turning to greet them both, a somewhat surprised look on his face, he inclined his head.

"Lady Frederica," the gentleman replied, ignoring Louisa entirely. "How nice to be in conversation with you again so soon."

Louisa, a new strength now flowing in her veins, coughed quietly, catching both Lord Blackdale and Lady Frederica's attention.

"Lord Blackdale," she said, glad that her voice was as strong as she had hoped. "We have just come from speaking to Miss Devaney. She has told us that the rumors she heard about me came from your lips." She lifted her chin a notch as Lord Blackdale's brows lowered, his lips pursed in a slight grimace. "I should like to ask where *you* heard such things from."

Lord Blackdale cleared his throat, looking from Louisa to Lady Frederica and back again.

"That is something of an odd question, Lady Foster," Lord Blackdale replied after a moment. "I do not see why such a thing is relevant."

"Of course it is relevant!" Lady Frederica exclaimed as Lord Blackdale's brows rose in surprise. "That is why both she and I have come to speak to you. We are determined to find the source of these ridiculous rumors and put an end to them."

Lord Blackdale blinked rapidly and put his hands behind his back. "I see," he replied, no longer sounding as confident as before and certainly having no smile on his face any longer. "You believe that what is said about your companion is untrue, then?"

Lady Frederica placed her hands on her hips and glared furiously at Lord Blackdale. "The fact that you should even ask me such a thing, Lord Blackdale, is beyond ridiculous," she stated as Louisa forced herself to continue looking into Lord Blackdale's face, noting every single change of expression. "It is not that I *believe* that these rumors are nonsense, but rather that I *know* them to be. Therefore, I will ask you the very same as Lady Foster: just where did you hear such rumors from?"

For a few moments, Lord Blackdale said nothing. His eyes

jumped from Louisa to Lady Frederica and then, finally, to something—or someone—over Louisa's shoulder.

"If you truly wish to know—not that I think it will be of any importance to you—I heard the story from Miss Drake."

Louisa frowned. Miss Drake was Lady Worthington's daughter. She had said very little to Louisa herself or to Lady Frederica, in fact, and Louisa had always presumed that she was something of a quiet creature. Now to know that it was *she* who had spoken such rumors about her to Lord Blackdale came as something of a surprise.

"Miss Drake?" Louisa repeated, and Lord Blackdale nodded, his jaw working hard for a moment. "You are quite certain?"

"We *shall* go and ask her directly, Lord Blackdale," Lady Frederica said in a warning tone. "You are aware of that?"

Lord Blackdale's frown grew all the more. "I speak the truth, if that is what you are asking me, Lady Frederica," he replied darkly. "I shall not state that I am sorry for speaking it to my sister, however. It is quite usual for such news to be spread."

Louisa bit back her response, wanting to state to Lord Blackdale that there was nothing wise about spreading gossip, but chose, wisely, not to do so. Lady Frederica said nothing but turned on her heel and strode away from Lord Blackdale, leaving Louisa to follow suit—only to see the Duke of Ellsworth waiting for them.

Clearly, she realized, it was he whom Lord Blackdale had seen over Louisa's shoulder.

"You are both quite all right, I hope?"

Lady Frederica let out a long sigh. "I am quite well, Uncle," she said with a shake of her head. "I have discovered that Miss Devaney has heard of the rumors from her brother, Lord Blackdale. And therefore, both Lady Foster and I spoke to Lord Blackdale to discover who *he* had heard it from—and it appears the source is none other than Miss Drake."

The duke's eyes fixed to Louisa's, filled with a great and evident concern. "Indeed?"

"It seems that Lady Frederica and I have come up with an

idea...of sorts," she explained as the duke continued to study her, as though he expected to find a great deal of distress in her expression. "We are to follow the path of the rumor, to discover the source of it all. I personally cannot think of anything else to do and this evening's attempts, although they have only been of a short duration, have proven to be rather insightful thus far."

The duke considered this for a moment, then lifted one shoulder. "That is one way, I suppose, although it will take a good deal of confidence to speak of it in such an overt manner."

"And confidence is what we *both* have," Lady Frederica replied, looking to Louisa, who found herself nodding in agreement. "I am determined that the *beau monde* will know that neither you nor I, believe a single word about Lady Foster."

Louisa smiled a little ruefully as she saw the proud look in the duke's eye.

"I feel a good deal more...frustrated by this particular situation, Your Grace," she said honestly. "I am truly grateful to both you and Lady Frederica for what you have chosen to do in supporting me in this present circumstance. Therefore, I cannot shrink back and hide away from what is being said of me, since continuing to do so would make it appear as though I am guilty." She shook her head. "I know I am not. I had nothing to do with my late husband's death. I have not come to London in the hope of securing a better position for myself. I am contented and secure, happy to assist Lady Frederica in any way I can. The *ton* must see that within me, and I must do all I can to show it to them."

The duke's face split with a smile and Louisa's breath hitched as his warm gaze settled down onto her own.

"Remarkable," he said, looking for a moment to Lady Frederica. "You are quite remarkable, Lady Foster. To have such strength of spirit and such determination of heart when your circumstances have been naught but difficulty after difficulty quite astounds me. But I am very pleased at your resolve for I am sure that, should we continue on this path, you will very soon be able to find the person who has begun to whisper such rumors. And, in doing so, put an end to it entirely."

"It is all I can hope for," Louisa replied with a wry smile. "I thank you, Your Grace."

He shook his head. "There is no need for thanks," he replied as Lady Frederica smiled with evidently great satisfaction. A line formed between his brows as he frowned suddenly, his smile disappearing as quickly as it had appeared.

"Did you say that you were to speak to Miss Drake?" he asked, and Lady Frederica nodded. "I wonder, might you leave such a conversation with me?"

A little surprised, Louisa nodded. "But of course," she replied, seeing the confusion on Lady Frederica's face and feeling the very same within her own heart. "Is there some particular reason that you wish to do so?"

The duke hesitated, his eyes darting across the room as he thought. "It—it is only that I believe Miss Drake hides a good deal from our view," he said by way of explanation. "I am aware that she remains silent for much of the time that she and her mother converse with us, but I believe that she keeps all that she thinks and perhaps feels within herself. That does not mean, however, that she would not speak of it to anyone. It may be that Lord Blackdale has encouraged her to speak openly and that, therefore, she has done so."

"And you think you can do the very same?" Lady Frederica asked, sounding a little doubtful.

"It sounds as though *you* do not believe I can," the duke replied, laughing. "But yes, I believe there may be more to Miss Drake's awareness of the rumors surrounding Lady Foster than she might be willing to say to you both. If I can make her feel a little warmer toward me, then I hope that she might reveal a little more. That is all."

Louisa swallowed a sudden burning in her throat at the thought of the duke encouraging any sort of increased interest between himself and Miss Drake, aware that the very idea made her wince inwardly, but having no particular understanding as to why such a thing could be.

"If you feel certain that you can do so, then I am sure neither I nor Lady Foster have any objection," Lady Frederica replied as Louisa quickly forced a smile and nodded, wanting to be appreciative rather than expressing the strange upset that now filled her. "Thank you, Uncle."

"Thank you, Your Grace," Louisa added hastily. "I do hope you are successful."

A gleam came into the duke's eyes as a slow grin spread across his face. "I shall be *very* successful, Lady Foster," he replied with all the confidence of a gentleman who knew precisely what was required of him and was quite certain to achieve it. "Very successful indeed."

9

Nicholas bowed low toward Miss Drake and then smiled at her mother as he lifted his head.

"How excellent it is to have come upon you both this afternoon," he declared, all too aware of the fact that both his niece and Lady Foster were still sitting in the carriage a short distance away, no doubt watching all that he did. "This afternoon is very fine indeed, is it not?"

Miss Drake's smile was immediate, although she only murmured her agreement and then dropped her gaze in an almost coy manner.

"It is a *very* fine day indeed, Your Grace," Lady Worthington replied with such a fervent smile that Nicholas was a little overwhelmed by her eagerness. "And it is *very* kind of you to greet us so. I do hope that you were not at all insulted by our conversation some two days ago, at the soiree? I certainly did not mean to imply anything improper about your judgment when it comes to Lady Foster."

Nicholas did not reply for a moment, glancing toward Miss Drake, who was still looking away from him, seemingly quite determined not to speak a word to him. When they had last spoken all together, at the soiree, he had found himself considering quite why it was that Miss Drake remained so quiet. The little she *had* said had been quickly retracted with an apology and an evident determination to believe all that she had heard of Lady Foster could not *possibly* be true, although Nicholas himself had not been fully convinced.

It seemed to him that Miss Drake had already learned how to hide her true self behind a mask, a charade. So many of the *ton* did so and it was not a trait that Nicholas himself considered to be at all engaging. In fact, he disliked it with such an intensity that it was as though every part of him wanted to push it aside in order to reveal the true person beneath.

"I do not hold grudges, Lady Worthington," he said as a look of relief swept over the lady's face, and she dipped her head, her other hand clutching tightly at the handle of her parasol although, as yet, she had not opened it. "I am only glad that you now see Lady Foster in the same light as I. You must understand, surely, just how difficult this has been for her, for to have her reputation damaged in such a way—even though she is only a companion—is still very upsetting."

"Particularly when the rumors are all entirely untrue, of course," Lady Worthington said as Nicholas nodded gravely. "I do hope that you will be able to find a way to release Lady Foster from these rumors, so that she will not have to struggle for too long."

Nicholas allowed himself a small smile. "I believe I *have* found a way, Lady Worthington," he replied without so much as glancing at Miss Drake. "I shall not say what it is we intend, but I am fully determined to find the person responsible for such rumors and, in time, show their words to be precisely what they are—nothing but dark and dreadful lies that have been spoken out of spite and maliciousness." He shook his head and sighed heavily, allowing the suggestion that this pained him a great deal to be clearly seen.

"Then I wish you success," Lady Worthington said quickly as Nicholas allowed himself a glance toward Miss Drake, noting how she appeared to have gone a little paler in these last few minutes. "I am certain that your endeavors will bring great relief to both Lady Foster and to your niece." She smiled warmly at Nicholas, who was still watching Miss Drake from the corner of his eye. He inclined his head quickly, one hand on his heart.

"You are very kind, Lady Worthington," he said, in what he hoped was a convincing tone. "Now," he continued briskly, looking all about him, "this is a very fine day indeed. I think I shall continue on for a short while rather than return to my carriage." Looking to Miss Drake, he cleared his throat and offered her his arm. "If you would permit me to accompany you, that is?"

The look that came over Miss Drake's face was one that Nicholas could not quite make out. She glanced toward her mother, her eyes a little wider than before and the paleness in her cheeks now replaced with a deep crimson. Her hands tightened together in front of her as she clasped them there, showing white across her fingers and knuckles. Was she anxious about accepting his arm? Afraid? Nicholas could not quite say what it was she felt, but remained precisely where he was still, his arm held out and a look of what he hoped was curious confusion resting upon his features.

"My daughter would be *glad* to walk with you, Your Grace," Lady Worthington gushed, after her daughter said nothing. "Look now, just how you have overwhelmed her with your kindness. I know that she will be very happy indeed to be in your company."

"Please, Miss Drake," Nicholas murmured, his arm still offered to the lady, and, much to his relief, she eventually took it. They began to walk together contentedly along the path, with Lady Worthington, Nicholas noted, falling into step behind them rather than coming alongside either Nicholas or her daughter in order that they both might converse rather than be interrupted by the lady.

Nicholas smiled to himself, feeling already a great deal of satisfaction. He had managed to secure Miss Drake's sole attention and, with Lady Worthington clearly determined to encourage this particular acquaintance, he found himself feeling all the more confident.

"Tell me, Miss Drake," he said with as much warmth as he could muster. "Are you enjoying the Season?"

The lady glanced at him, her eyes wide as though he had asked her something greatly distressing.

"I—I am," she stammered quietly. "Do I give the impression that I am not, Your Grace?"

Nicholas chuckled, reached across, and patted her gloved hand as it rested on his arm. "No, indeed not, Miss Drake," he replied airily. "It is only a very simple question with nothing else meant by it, I assure you."

This seemed to be of great relief to Miss Drake, for the breath she let out and the way her hand loosened gently on his arm spoke of a lessening of tension. Nicholas permitted his smile to remain as they continued to meander along the path together, knowing full well that he wanted Miss Drake to become even more at ease if he was to speak to her of Lady Foster.

"And what has been your very favorite occasion thus far?" he asked as Miss Drake dared another glance up toward him. "I confess I am partial to a ball and Lord Ferris' ball was a very enjoyable one indeed." He looked at her and smiled. "Did you attend?"

"I did," came the quiet reply as their conversation finally began to flow. "I have enjoyed every ball that I have attended so far, although there have been some excellent dinner parties that I have been able to attend also."

"Ah, indeed, the dinner party," Nicholas replied with a chuckle. "I must say that I believe a *good* dinner party is entirely dependent on who is in attendance. I have been to a few where the conversation has been so very dull that I have found myself either eager to remove myself from the situation entirely or struggling to remain awake for the remainder of the dinner." He laughed again and, much to his relief, saw a small smile tug at Miss Drake's lips. "Whereas, if the host has chosen well, then the dinner party becomes a thing of great enjoyment, where there is wonderful conversation, excellent fare, and the very best of company."

"That is, I believe, the very best, Your Grace," Miss Drake

replied, although her voice remained quiet. "And I am glad to say that the dinner parties I have attended thus far have been just as you described."

"That is very pleasing, I am sure," Nicholas said warmly. "Might I ask which ones you have attended?" She did not need to know the reason for his question, of course, but Nicholas had begun to wonder just who was in Miss Drake's closest circle of acquaintances and friends. Perhaps he would not have to ask her about where she had heard the rumors from. Perhaps he would be able to surmise from what she said just who had spoken of Lady Foster. After only a momentary hesitation, Miss Drake began to speak of the dinner parties she had attended of late and, with further questions on occasion, Nicholas was able to understand that she was well acquainted with a few debutantes and, in particular, dear friends with one Lady Jennifer, who was daughter to the Earl of Kessock. Silently, Nicholas pressed that name into his mind, wondering if she had been in any way involved with those rumors. He had been introduced to her, of course, but that had been some time ago and, whilst he might occasionally dance with her, he did not know her well.

Although I do not know if she is aware of Lady Foster, he considered as Miss Drake continued, his lips twisting gently. *Although what could be her reasons for doing so?*

"I—I must also take this opportunity to add to my mother's apology for what she said of Lady Foster."

The words caught Nicholas' attention and he looked down sharply at the lady, noting the flush of crimson in her cheeks. "I beg your pardon, Miss Drake?"

"I know that I also made some remarks about Lady Foster," she continued, not quite looking at him. "Given that my mother has apologized, Your Grace, I feel that I should take the opportunity to do so also."

"I see," Nicholas murmured, a little taken aback. "I am sure that it must be very difficult not to listen to all that is whispered by others, Miss Drake. I cannot pretend that I have never once allowed myself to listen to gossip, to believe it without question. However, when such lies now influence not only Lady Foster, but also my niece, I must make certain that such whispers are quickly dispersed."

"I understand, truly," Miss Drake replied, appearing to speak with great genuineness. "That is why I am all the more embarrassed to have been so forthright and yet without any true understanding or knowledge of the situation. I am deeply embarrassed to have accepted the truth of what was spoken to me without hesitation."

Nicholas did not quite know how to respond. It was clear that Miss Drake was speaking honestly at this present moment, for her words were so fervent and the look in her eye so true that Nicholas felt he could not have even a single doubt about what she said.

And yet he could not forget the look in Miss Drake's eyes when she had first looked at Lady Foster, could not quite ignore the fact that she had done nothing but ignore Lady Foster from the very beginning of their acquaintance. If Miss Drake wanted solely to be in his good graces, then all she had to do was convince him of her genuine regret over what she had said, without meaning even a single word of it.

"If I might, I shall pass on your apology to Lady Foster," he said slowly as an idea began to form. "Unless you should wish to do so yourself? I know that Lady Foster is not inclined to hold a grudge and would be very grateful to hear such words from your lips." It was difficult to see the full extent of her expression, given the way that she continued to look forward so that he could only see her profile, but the hesitation that came after he had spoken told Nicholas that he was, perhaps, being far too easily taken in.

"I—I should be grateful if you would pass on my apology, Your Grace," Miss Drake said eventually. "You will understand just how embarrassing such a situation would be otherwise."

Nicholas' lips flattened for a moment as he realized just how close he had come to accepting all that Miss Drake had said without hesitation. "Indeed," he muttered, knowing full well that it was not the thought of her potential embarrassment that prevented Miss Drake from doing so but rather that she did not want to be seen by anyone in the *ton* speaking directly to Lady Foster when she had such a poor reputation. It was simply her way of protecting herself instead of showing a true sorrow over what she had said or done.

"I shall, of course, make quite certain that those I heard this rumor from know now that you and Lady Foster *and* Lady Frederica are determined to set things to rights," Miss Drake added with a wave of her hand, a slight sense of the dramatic overcoming her. "And I will inform them at once that I am not at all in agreement with how they now view the lady."

"Do you think these young ladies will listen to you, Miss Drake?" Nicholas asked abruptly, a little stuck in his anger at how Miss Drake had so quickly dismissed the thought of speaking to Lady Foster alone in order that she might apologize. "These are the young ladies who spoke to you of the rumors in the first place, I suppose?"

"Yes, yes, indeed." Miss Drake nodded fervently, but Nicholas was not finished.

"Then might I know who they were?" he asked, albeit a little sternly as all thought of being coy flew from his mind. Miss Drake, whilst appearing to be quite honest in her confession, showed no real genuine sorrow and Nicholas was irritated with himself for almost having accepted her words without hesitation.

"I should not like to say, Your Grace," came the tentative reply, as though she feared giving him such a response. "I am sure that I will be able to convince them of what you have expressed to me."

He grimaced and looked away, his silence more of a response than anything he needed to say.

"I do apologize," Miss Drake continued hastily. "But what I will tell you, Your Grace, is that I heard the very same story about Lady Foster from three separate acquaintances."

"That does not aid me in any way, Miss Drake," Nicholas replied, allowing a thin edge of anger into his voice. "As you might imagine, I had hoped to speak to the lady privately, to reassure her —much as I have you—that Lady Foster is *not* as the rumors have made her out to be. That the whispers that she is attempting, in some way, to improve her standing in society by being Lady Frederica's companion are nothing but malicious rumor. Can you not see just how necessary it is to quash such gossip?" He threw out one hand in a zealous gesture. "Lady Foster has already endured a great deal. She has lost her husband and been forced, thereafter, to become a companion when she ought to be in society in her own standing. Can you imagine, Miss Drake, what it must be like for her at this present moment?" Nicholas knew very well that he was speaking to her with a good deal of emotion and fervor rather than practicality, but the desire to now know precisely who it was that had spoken to her of these rumors—given that it was three people rather than only one—was now growing so quickly that it could not be suppressed.

"She has done a great deal for Lady Frederica and now to hear these ridiculous rumors has quite broken her spirit," he continued heavily. "For her sake and for Lady Frederica's sake also, I must do all I can to remove these rumors from her."

Miss Drake looked up at him, her eyes glassy and the color gone from her cheeks. "I—I have not thought of her suffering at such great depths before, Your Grace," she replied, her voice tremulous. "But still, I would feel…"

Nicholas turned to her, no longer walking but instead looking deeply into Miss Drake's eyes in the hope that his determination would be all the more obvious. She did not continue for some minutes but slowly, a deep red flush crept up her neck and into her face and she dropped her gaze, her head lowering just a little.

"Miss Hayward, Miss Applebaum, and Lady Christina," she mumbled as Nicholas let out a long breath of relief. "Pray, do not tell them that it was I who—"

"You have nothing to fear, Miss Drake," he assured her, interrupting her and speaking with what he hoped she recognized as gratitude. "I cannot tell you just how grateful I am to you. I will be nothing but discreet." Reaching out one hand, he waited for a moment before she placed her hand in his. Lifting it, he bowed over her hand but did not allow his lips to draw near to it for fear of giving her the wrong impression.

"Are you to depart from us, Your Grace?"

Nicholas let go of Miss Drake's hand quickly, then turned to her mother. He had almost forgotten that she had been walking behind them although, from the curious look in the lady's eyes, he presumed that she had been watching their interaction very closely indeed.

"I fear I must, Lady Worthington," he replied, gesturing back toward his carriage which was now some distance away. "I have some matters of business to study this afternoon before I am to step out this evening."

"And will we see you again, perhaps?" Lady Worthington asked as Miss Drake dropped her head, clearly a little embarrassed at her mother's forwardness. Nicholas cleared his throat, placing his hands behind his back as he did so.

"I will be present at the soiree this evening, certainly," he said pleasantly, fully aware that Lady Worthington was not speaking of that in particular but rather expressing a hope that he might set out with her daughter in much the same manner at another time. "Good afternoon to you both."

Lady Worthington's look of disappointment was quickly swept from her face as she dropped into a quick curtsy. "But of course, Your Grace," she said as Miss Drake once more lapsed into silence. "And good afternoon."

10

"Lady Foster?"

Louisa hesitated, a lit candle in her hand as she stood in the doorway of the library.

"Please, do come in."

"I did not mean to interrupt your solitude, Your Grace," she said quietly. "I do apologize. I only thought to fetch a book so that I might read for a short time."

He beckoned her in, and Louisa stepped forward, setting down her candle on a table near to the door. Her stomach was swirling like a restless sea, her skin prickling with awareness. There was nothing untoward about her being in the presence of the duke without any other company, given that she was a widowed lady and he a gentleman, but she herself felt all too aware of him. The duke was sitting in a chair by the hearth, whilst a small but ferocious fire burned in the grate. A glass of brandy sat on a table next to him and he appeared very relaxed, with one elbow resting on the arm of the chair and one foot propped up on the opposite knee. His eyes, darker than ever before, it seemed, were fixed to her and Louisa knew she was blushing furiously, grateful for the shadows that bounced around the room and hid her features from him.

"You could not sleep, Lady Foster?"

She gave him a small smile but did not sit down despite the gesture from him to do so.

"I have not yet retired, Your Grace," she answered, relieved that she had not changed into her night things before making her way back toward the library. "But I shall, very soon."

The duke nodded but said nothing more, his eyes still searching her face as though she had not yet revealed something to him, and he wanted desperately to discover what it was.

"Did you say that you recognized any of the young ladies' names that Miss Drake mentioned?" he asked, and Louisa frowned, trying to recall them. "A Miss Applebaum, a Miss Hayward, and a Lady Christina."

"I do not think I have ever been introduced to them, Your Grace," Louisa replied, having not even the smallest flicker of recognition in her mind. "You have, however?"

It was a question rather than a statement and the duke nodded, although the smile on his face was somewhat rueful.

"I do not think that I know them very well, however," he stated as Louisa studied him. "And I cannot imagine why any of them would speak ill of you in such a way. It is utterly disgraceful."

Louisa smiled softly, her hand resting on the back of a chair. "You are very good, Your Grace," she told him. "You are taking great care of both me and my reputation and for that, I am truly grateful."

He smiled at her, the darkness in his eyes shifting for a moment. "I think that you will have to stop thanking me, Lady Foster, else my sense of self-importance shall grow to much greater proportions than it ought," he said as a quiet laugh escaped her. "I will confess to you that I think very highly of all that you have managed to both achieve and conquer. You may feel as though you have dropped to a position of low standing, but should people know the truth of your heart and your character, I am certain that they would think just as well of you as I."

Louisa did not know what to say to this. She was, of course, very touched by his kindness, but at the same time, a little overcome by it. A good deal of respect was in his words, a sense of understanding and commiseration that she knew came from his experiences of losing his own wife.

Louisa decided to be bold.

"You have also endured a loss, Your Grace," she said, finally sinking down into the chair that stood opposite to him. "I will not ask you to speak of it, since I know the pain must still linger, but in that, we are united."

The duke said nothing for a few moments until, finally, he shifted his chair, his hands clasping together as he sat a little straighter. Louisa looked away, a little embarrassed and now fearing that she had said far too much and had spoken unwisely. Perhaps the duke did not want such reminders. Perhaps she ought not to have mentioned his past at all.

"I had great consideration for my wife."

The words left his lips with a great slowness, as though, even now, he was uncertain as to what he wanted to say.

"She was perfectly respectable, amiable, and genteel," he continued, a faraway look in his eyes as he turned his head away from Louisa, looking into the depths of the flame. "But unlike you, Lady Foster, I was not left practically penniless when my wife died. I have been left without children, as you know, but that will, I suppose, come in time." A small shrug lifted his left shoulder. "I must produce an heir."

There was silence as Louisa tried to take in what he had said, realizing now that the duke's first consideration when it came to his future was his family line and title. There was no mention of fondness or affection between he and the late duchess. That did not mean, of course, that he had not cared for her, but rather, that his first priority was the dukedom. For some reason, that sent a spiral of disappointment into Louisa's chest, although she simply could not explain why.

"But yes, I suppose I could express an understanding as to the pain that comes with such a loss," the duke continued after a few moments. "I feel it deep within my heart, Lady Foster, even though I choose not to be aware of it. There is a painful sting there, a continual, daily reminder that I am entirely alone."

Louisa pressed her hands tightly together, fully aware of all that the duke spoke of. She, too, felt that emotion, the way that she continually was aware of her isolation. If her husband had still lived, then she would have a good deal more security than she had at present. She might even now have a child or be in her confinement at least. That had all been taken from her the moment Lord Foster had lost his life.

"I do want you to be free of this, Lady Foster."

She looked up at him, her eyes searching his face as he spoke in an almost tender tone. Her heart quickened as they looked into each other's eyes, a warmth beginning to flood all through her.

"If only there was something more I could do," the duke continued quietly. "If there was a way for me to make certain that your standing was not only improved but that your future was also secure, I would do so."

"But why should you care about that?" Louisa found herself asking, not wanting to appear ungrateful but quite astonished at his words. "You have done so much for me already."

The duke let out a harsh exclamation. "What have I done?" he asked, spreading his hands. "Very little indeed."

"That is not true," Louisa leaned forward in her chair, her heart thumping furiously in her chest. "After these rumors, many, I am sure, would have found me another position, if not simply removed me from their household. Instead, not only have you been glad for me to remain, you have also done far more than was required of you in order to try and assist me further. There has been no need for you to do so and I feel greatly blessed indeed to be in your household."

The duke moved suddenly and Louisa, for a moment, thought that he might pull her from her chair. Instead, however, he stopped directly in front of her, his hand held out toward her. Quite certain that he could hear the way her heart thumped furiously, Louisa tentatively held out her hand, catching her breath when he grasped her fingers.

"We have both lost those we wed," the duke said, his tone husky. "But despite our similar circumstances, I have not found myself in any of the difficulties that, at present, surround you. I sympathize with your sorrow and your mourning, knowing all that you struggle with, but what I cannot imagine is what you must be feeling at present." His fingers tightened on hers. "To have people speaking of you in such a despicable manner, to state that you were involved in some way in the death of your husband..." He trailed off and shook his head, his jaw working furiously. "I cannot even think of what I would do or what I would say should someone even *suggest* that I was in any way involved in my late wife's passing."

"I may not show you the truth of how I feel, Your Grace, but I can assure you there are a good many emotions that I do not express. I feel anger. I feel frustration and deep, cutting sorrow. Pray do not think that I am something I am not."

The duke shook his head, a small smile pulling at the side of his mouth. "Whether or not you feel such things, Lady Foster, you express such a kindness of heart and temperance of spirit that I am in awe of. That is why I speak as I do. That is why I *act* as I do and that is why I want to see your situation improved, even more than might have been possible for you before these rumors."

Louisa found herself rising to her feet, overwhelmed entirely by the duke's sentiment. "Your Grace," she said softly. "I beg you, do not think so highly of me. There is nothing I require other than the position I already have. To be able to remain with Lady Frederica, to be as I am at present is all that I need, truly."

She looked up into his face and found the tenderness in his eyes burning straight through her. She could barely take in a breath, feeling his thumb running over the back of her hand and trying to understand what it was that she now felt. His head began to lower, and Louisa found herself leaning forward, not certain what was to happen but yet finding herself willing to discover it.

And then, he took a breath and stepped back.

"I should permit you to find your book, Lady Foster," he said, his voice gruff. "I wanted to make certain, however, that you are fully aware of the admiration I have for you and the determination within my spirit to make certain of your safe and secure future. That is a desire that shall not leave me, not until I see that you are contented and truly, *truly* happy. Only then will I myself feel a lifting of the burden I hold at present. Only then will I be satisfied."

Louisa could not speak, her breathing rapid and her pulse racing. She could not look away from him, could not seem to step away and do as he had said. The only reason she had come to the library in the first place was to find herself a new novel and somehow, within that, she had discovered herself quite lost in the duke's presence. It overwhelmed her, drawing her in and enfolding her in its embrace, to the point that she did not want—and did not seem to be able—to remove herself from it.

"Lady Foster," the duke said again, his voice still hoarse. "Please, know that I did not mean anything...improper in my behavior this evening. It is only that—"

"I have not even the smallest thought of that, Your Grace."

He smiled quietly, his gaze dropping away from her for a moment. "We have been flung together in this, you and I. I should never want to push you from either myself or this house. This place should be your security, this home your protection, and I will never permit myself to be the cause of shattering that."

"You do not," Louisa answered him quickly, knowing full well that he must now feel something of the confusion and the desire to remain, just as she did, and was seeking, in his own way, to reassure both her as well as himself. "And I believe you never shall, Your Grace."

He nodded, holding her gaze for yet another moment before finally shaking his head and stepping back. He gestured to the many rows of books that surrounded them, his shoulders slumping as though he felt defeated in some way. Or perhaps, she considered, he felt the very same sense of loss that now lingered in her own heart, as though something more could have been achieved should he have been a little more courageous.

"Please, find whatever book you came for," the duke murmured, before finally going to sit back in his chair, his hand snaking out to reach for his brandy glass almost at once. "I will not disturb you further."

Louisa watched him for a moment, all too aware that something had shifted between them, something new and wonderful beginning to grow, and yet knowing that she herself had very little idea of what that might be. "I believe I will retire now," she said, stepping away from the duke and leaving all thought of finding a book behind. "Good evening, Your Grace." There was no need to fetch a novel now, no need to allow herself to drift off into another story when she had a good deal more to consider herself. The duke smiled at her, his eyes still holding that same tenderness and consideration that she had been so startled to see only a few minutes before.

"Good evening, Lady Foster," he replied, his voice low and filled with warmth. "I do hope that, soon, you will find happiness and freedom again."

"As do I, Your Grace," Louisa replied, before quickly hurrying from the room.

～

"You look tired, Louisa."

Blinking rapidly and forced to cover yet another yawn with her hand, Louisa smiled self-consciously at Lady Frederica. "I do apologize," she answered as the carriage continued along the road. "I did not sleep particularly well last evening."

Lady Frederica frowned. "How could you do so when there is so much for you to consider at present?" she asked, clearly believing that Louisa's troubled sleep came from thinking of the rumors and the whispers that ran through London about her. "I must say, I hope that the duke is successful this evening."

Louisa lifted one eyebrow, trying not to blush at the mention of the duke. The last thing she needed was for Lady Frederica to think that there was, in fact, something more to her acquaintance with the duke than there was.

"This evening?" she asked as Lady Frederica shot her a sharp look.

"Indeed, did he not speak to you of his intentions?" Lady Frederica asked, looking doubtful. "I am surprised."

"I have not seen His Grace today."

"Oh." Lady Frederica's frown deepened. "Then I shall inform you. The duke intends to dance with each of the young ladies that Miss Drake mentioned. Thereafter, he hopes to have a conversation with each regarding the rumors about you, Louisa. There will come answers from all of them, of course, as to who has spoken to *them* of such a thing, but if he does not succeed, then I myself will step in and do the very same."

Louisa blinked rapidly, feeling a little confused. "You mean to say that both you and the duke will speak to these three ladies in the hope of discovering who has told them of the rumors?" Seeing Lady Frederica nod, Louisa pursed her lips for a moment, a sense of displeasure beginning to build. "And what am I to do?"

Lady Frederica's eyes widened in surprise, as though she had only just realized that Louisa herself did not have a part in this particular plan.

"I have no intention, as you know, of hiding away from the *ton* any longer," Louisa continued. "I should not like to simply remain silent."

"Then—then if you wish, you might speak to the ladies individually," Lady Frederica suggested, hesitating just a little as she spoke. "The duke is quite determined, of course, and he may have more success than you or I, given his status and the respect that such a title brings."

This was true, of course, but still Louisa felt the urge to act on her own behalf. "You are acquainted with all the ladies, I presume?"

"I am," Lady Frederica replied with a small shake of her head. "But I do not know them very well at all. I believe I have only had the very shortest of conversations with Miss Applebaum, but Miss Hayward and Lady Christina I have only spoken to during our introductions."

Louisa nodded slowly and looked out of the window as the carriage drew to a halt, taking them to St. James's Park as Lady Frederica had requested. They were to take a short walk through park before returning to the townhouse to prepare for dinner and then for the ball that was to take place that evening. The determination she felt to push aside the rumors herself had grown steadily these last few days. She would not hide away, would not stand back and permit the duke and Lady Frederica to fight on her behalf, not when she could do so herself. Yes, she might be merely a companion but that did not mean that she could not speak, could not be heard by others.

"Shall we walk?"

Louisa did not miss the hint of trepidation in Lady Frederica's voice and winced because of it. She knew all too well that to walk with Louisa by her side might, in fact, bring with it some ridicule. There might be glances and whispers from others but still Lady Frederica was, of course, determined.

"It would be a shame to miss such a fine afternoon," she murmured as Lady Frederica cast her a quick smile before climbing down from the carriage. Louisa could not pretend that there was not a small flicker of anxiety within her own heart as she climbed out and walked alongside Lady Frederica. The sun was warm, and Lady Frederica took out her parasol as they walked slowly through the park, enjoying the scent of the flowers, the warmth of the afternoon sun, and the beauty of the park that surrounded them. Many others were walking also, but much to Louisa's relief, none of them said a word to either her or Lady Frederica. In fact, there were only pleasant smiles and murmurs of greeting which only served to encourage Louisa and chase away her fears. The more they walked, their conversation light and cheerful, the more her heart lifted free of the worry and the anxiety that had filled her heart as they had left the carriage.

"Good afternoon, Lady Frederica."

The conversation that both Louisa and Lady Frederica had been enjoying came to an abrupt end as Lady Christina came directly into their path. Louisa bobbed a quick curtsy and murmured her greeting but then fell silent, knowing that it was not to she that Lady Christina had spoken.

"Good afternoon, Lady Christina." Lady Frederica smiled and dropped into a quick curtsy although Louisa could not help but feel a little confused as to Lady Christina's sudden interest in Lady Frederica's company. Had Lady Frederica not said that they had only shared an introduction at some point? That the conversation had not gone further than that?

"You look a little perturbed, Lady Frederica."

Lady Christina's voice was high-pitched and filled with an arrogance that her gentle smile could not hide. Her eyes were bright and fixed upon Lady Frederica, but a coldness was there that Louisa did not miss—and it sent a shiver down her spine.

"It is only that I am surprised that you remember me, Lady Christina," Lady Frederica replied with a quick smile. "We have been introduced, certainly, but that is the only conversation I believe we have shared together."

"But simply because we have only been introduced does not mean that I have forgotten you," came the quick reply. "Indeed, how could I forget, given now the rumors that I hear about your..." her cold eyes flicked toward Louisa, "your companion, who I see is still beside you now."

Louisa's stomach tightened. She looked up directly across at Lady Christina, her chin lifting despite all the swaths of emotion that filled her. Lady Christina's nose wrinkled in evident disgust and she looked away as though Louisa was not even worth her attention.

"Why you should keep such a...*person* as your companion, I cannot imagine," Lady Christina continued, turning her face away from Louisa just a little. "If I should be permitted to give you even the *smallest* piece of advice, it would be to cast aside your companion and find yourself a lady without such a *despicable* past."

In an instant, hot tears filled Louisa's eyes, but they did not come from upset, but rather from anger. To be spoken of in such a way, as though she were not standing directly beside Lady Frederica, brought a fierce anger to her heart that she feared could not be hidden.

However, Lady Frederica spoke before Louisa herself could say a word.

"As much as you might wish to give such advice, Lady Christina," she began, her voice sharp, "pray realize that I have not once requested your thoughts on the matter."

Lady Christina laughed harshly, her eyes narrowing just a little. "But surely you will be glad of such guidance," she answered, her voice tinged with a sickly sweetness that Louisa knew was not genuine. "After all, surely you cannot imagine that to remain with a companion who has such a terrible history—"

"If I might, Lady Christina?" Louisa knew that to interrupt the lady was very rude indeed for a companion, but she simply could not prevent herself from speaking, not when the lady was being so very harsh with her words. She did not wait for permission from the lady to continue speaking but went on regardless. "The rumors that are being spoken are nothing more than that. I am honored and privileged to have Lady Frederica's unwavering trust and support in this matter."

"And not only mine but the Duke of Ellsworth's support also," Lady Frederica interrupted, her chin lifting a notch as Lady Christina's expression tightened into a cold mask of distaste. A mask that Louisa was certain hid a good deal of anger at both Louisa's and Lady Frederica's response.

"I would ask, therefore," Lady Frederica continued, "that you do not judge either my own or Lady Foster's behavior based solely on what is nothing more than rumor."

"For I can assure you," Louisa added as Lady Christina flicked a hard glance toward her, "that I had nothing whatsoever to do with the death of my husband. Should you wish to ascertain that for yourself, might I suggest that you ask those who found him? They will inform you as to where I was when they found my late husband and I am certain that you will realize the truth of the matter then."

Lady Christina snorted in evident disbelief at Louisa's explanation, her expression still one of cold disdain. "I am certain that you could convince anyone to believe whatever you wished, Lady Foster, given that you appear to have convinced the duke of your innocence." Her eyes glinted with a hint of steel. "I wonder what your intentions are as regards the duke, since it seems he is more than willing to defend someone such as you."

The shocking words that came from Lady Christina's mouth delivered such a blow that Louisa felt herself go entirely numb. She stared at the lady in utter disbelief, whilst Lady Frederica stuttered in an attempt to find a response.

"I can see that my *kind* attempts to aid you, Lady Frederica, are entirely unwelcome," Lady Christina continued, turning her head away. "It seems that Lady Judith was correct."

She did not say more but stepped away from them both, her head held high and her back ramrod straight. Louisa closed her eyes tightly against the wave of tears that threatened, somewhere between upset, anger, and shame. For the duke to be spoken of in such a manner brought her such a great deal of embarrassment that she wanted to drop her head low, feeling ashamed over something that she had not done.

"Well!" Lady Frederica exclaimed, her hands on her hips. "I do not think that I have ever been spoken to in such a manner. The very nerve of Lady Christina." She turned to Louisa, her eyes blazing fire. "How could she—"

"I—I am sorry," Louisa found herself saying, managing to open her eyes and hide the tears that still threatened. "I have never wanted either you or your uncle to become affected by such rumors, but now it seems that I—"

Lady Frederica took a step closer, one hand reaching out to rest on Louisa's shoulder, her anger fading into immediate concern.

"You should not feel any shame, Louisa," she said firmly. "You are not at all to blame for what Lady Christina said."

"But to have such suggestions made about the duke," Louisa replied, searching Lady Frederica's face. "Surely that must bring its own embarrassment to him? And for my sake, I cannot imagine that—"

"I will not hear any more," Lady Frederica said, her fingers pressing into Louisa's shoulder gently. "The duke has made his position quite plain. He is determined to find the person responsible for such rumors, just as I am also." She tilted her head, a slight frown suddenly appearing between her brows. "In fact, I believe that something Lady Christina said may, in fact, be of use."

Louisa blinked away the tears that had come into the corners of her eyes and took in a deep breath. "Oh?"

"Indeed," Lady Frederica replied slowly. "She stated, just before she stepped away from us, that Lady Judith was correct." Her brow furrowed all the more. "Whatever could such a thing mean? What was she right about?"

Swallowing hard, Louisa tried to set aside her upset and the fears as to what the duke would say when Lady Frederica related the conversation with Lady Christina to him. "Lady Judith?"

"Do you not recall?" Lady Frederica asked, a spark of excitement in her eyes now. "Lady Judith is daughter to Lady Prestwick. She has attempted to befriend me, if I recall, although I was less than inclined to do so." A small flicker of a smile caught the corner of her mouth. "Lady Prestwick, I believe, is very eager to push her daughter in the direction of my uncle and has no real interest in developing a friendship between myself and her daughter."

"So what, in particular, would Lady Judith be correct about?" Louisa asked, and Lady Frederica shook her head. "What has been said to her that Lady Christina now believes?"

"I cannot imagine," Lady Frederica replied with a triumphant smile on her face. "But I am quite determined now to find out."

11

Nicholas looked up from his papers and called for the person he presumed was the butler to enter. The moment he saw Lady Foster, however, his heart began to quicken, heat pouring into his chest and rising up his neck as he rose quickly in order to greet her.

He had not forgotten how he had felt in the library, when she had sat there so quietly and so forlorn. The way that she had spoken, the things she had said, and the way he had begun to feel had not left him, for he had done nothing other than think of her. To see her now, stepping into his study, just reinforced the truth of how he felt, and Nicholas welcomed such emotions. There was no fear in feeling such overt affection, such abounding tenderness. Rather, it seemed to be quite right for him to feel such things. Whilst he was not yet certain what he wished to do, what the future might look like for both himself and Lady Foster, there was now a certainty that she would remain in his life for some duration.

"Lady Foster, do come in."

She bobbed a curtsy, gave him a quick smile, and stepped inside, the door closing behind her.

"Forgive me for interrupting you, Your Grace," she began, but Nicholas quickly waved her apology away.

"You are always welcome," he said warmly, aware of how she flushed. "Please, do sit down."

Nodding, she did so at once, smoothing her skirts with fractious hands. Nicholas frowned. There was a manner about her that spoke of anxiety and worry. Was this about their conversation in the library? Or was there something more?

He moved forward from behind his desk and came to sit near to her, scrutinizing her face. Lady Foster looked back at him, her brown eyes wide and searching as she studied his face. There was no sense of discomfiture from her, no evident urge to hide her true expression from him but rather an awareness that he could be trusted.

"Your Grace, I must speak to you about what happened earlier this afternoon."

"Oh?" He leaned forward, concern rising up within him. "You were out walking with Lady Frederica?"

She nodded. "We met Lady Christina," she explained as Nicholas' brows rose in surprise. "You will recall that Lady Christina is one of the young ladies we—you, that is—intend to speak to."

"Indeed," Nicholas replied as Lady Foster nodded slowly to herself, as though confirming her own thoughts. "I thought to speak to her this evening."

Lady Foster's lips pulled into a tight smile. "There may be no need, Your Grace," she answered quietly. "Lady Christina mentioned something in the conversation that I thought might be of pertinence."

He wanted to lean closer to her, to take her hands in his, but he resisted the urge to do so. He could not imagine what the conversation between Lady Frederica, Lady Foster, and Lady Christina might have been about, but he was certain that it had not been a pleasant one given the look on Lady Foster's face.

"She stated that 'Lady Judith was correct'," Lady Foster continued, speaking a little more quickly now. "Both Lady Frederica and I have discussed what such a thing might mean but cannot be quite certain at present. However, we do believe that it would be wise to—"

"To speak directly to Lady Judith," he finished as she nodded. He frowned hard, looking away from Lady Foster for a moment as he thought. Such a remark from Lady Christina suggested that Lady Judith had been the one to speak of Lady Foster in the first instance. It was not definite, of course, but certainly something that Nicholas knew needed to be considered. He had to speak to Lady Judith as soon as possible. "That certainly is an interesting remark."

"And one that I believe Lady Christina did not understand the significance of," Lady Foster added. "Although why Lady Judith would be speaking of me in such a manner, I cannot understand."

Nicholas nodded slowly, rubbing his chin for a moment. "Nor can I," he agreed. "I believe that she will be present this evening at the ball." His eyes alighted on her again. "Then perhaps there is no need to dance and converse with these other ladies. Perhaps we need only consider Lady Judith." Reaching out one hand and despite his own hesitation, he pressed his hand over hers and instantly saw the change in her expression. "There was more said by Lady Christina, I believe."

Her eyes widened and she began to stammer, only for Nicholas to shake his head and give her a small smile.

"It is clear in your expression that more was said, but your good heart will not allow it to be expressed—either for her sake or to spare me," he continued as she dropped her gaze and blushed furiously. "Was she very discourteous?"

A heavy sigh came from Lady Foster's lips, her expression remaining troubled. "She was," she admitted quietly. "But it was not only I who had to bear the brunt of such rudeness. The way she spoke to Lady Frederica and what she suggested about you also, Your Grace, was deeply upsetting."

Nicholas found himself on his feet in an instant, his hand gently tugging Lady Foster upwards. She rose also and looked up at him, a dusting of pink in her cheeks as he continued to hold her hand in his.

"Lady Foster," he said softly, "do not permit what was said of either myself or Lady Frederica to become a burden that settles upon your shoulders. Continue to recall that this matter has not anything to do with your own conduct or behavior but rather is entirely because of another's cruel thoughts and determinations." Holding her gaze, Nicholas found his other hand lifting, brushing gently across her cheek. "I cannot have you bearing any responsibility that is not your own."

He saw her swallow hard, saw how her gaze dropped and her head turned, and knew in his heart that, despite what he had said, she still felt such a great sense of responsibility. A flare of anger burned in his heart, all the more determined to discover just who had been speaking of her in such terms and uncover the truth of why they had done so. No longer did he want to see such worry in her eyes, such upset written across her face. He wanted her to be free of it all, to know a new happiness that he fully intended now to give her.

"Lady Foster," he said as she looked back up at him. "I—" Not quite certain what he was attempting to say, he dropped his head, his free hand now settling gently on her waist. Hearing her swift intake of breath, he looked back at her suddenly, ready to step away, ready to move back from her should she wish him to, only to see the sparkle in her eyes and the color that rose all the more in her cheeks. As he held her gaze, he was astonished to see how she moved forward just a little as though eager to be closer to him. Nicholas' heart roared with both delight and hope and he tried to speak once more, to express the truths that were now so very obvious within his heart.

"Lady Foster, I—I want you to know that I have every intention of making your future here with us a very happy one indeed," he found himself saying, closing his eyes and shaking his head as he attempted to express himself clearly but found himself doing the precise opposite. Taking a breath, he opened his eyes again and saw her still looking up at him, a slightly quizzical expression now etched across her features. "That was poorly expressed." With another breath, he took a moment to gather his thoughts, feeling the weight of what he wanted to express now settling upon his heart. "That is, when this matter is at an end, when the truth is discovered and laid bare for all to see, I have every intention of—"

"Uncle?"

He sprang back from Lady Foster, who quickly sank back into her chair, just as the door opened and Lady Frederica stepped inside.

"Oh, you *are* here, Lady Foster," she said, sounding greatly relieved. "Forgive me for intruding so, Uncle, but I had to make certain that Lady Foster was quite all right."

"I have not run away, if that is what you fear," came the gentle reply as Lady Foster smiled at her charge although her cheeks were still rather warm. "I came to tell the duke what occurred."

Lady Frederica looked triumphantly back at Nicholas, who had managed to make his way back behind his desk without any particular difficulty whilst hiding the great swell of awkwardness that now rose in his chest.

"Then you are in agreement?" she asked. Nicholas lifted one eyebrow in question, causing Lady Frederica to sigh in exasperation. "You agree that we need only speak to Lady Judith?"

Nicholas harrumphed in order to clear some of the tension from his frame and nodded, not daring to look at Lady Foster for fear of what Lady Frederica might see in such a glance. "I do," he agreed quietly. "And we shall do so without delay."

"When?"

He spread his hands. "This evening, of course," he stated unequivocally. "For I am just as eager to bring this to an end as you are, if not all the more so."

Lady Frederica smiled and Nicholas did not miss the glint of steel in her eye, finding himself rather proud of his niece's determination.

"Good," Lady Frederica replied as Lady Foster rose to her feet.

"Let us hope that Lady Judith is able to give us the answers we seek."

"Indeed," came Lady Foster's quiet reply as she glanced at Nicholas before looking away again. "Now, we should permit your uncle to continue with his work." She managed a quick smile in Nicholas' direction, and he felt all the more frustrated that he had not managed to finish his conversation with her before Lady Frederica's arrival. "Good afternoon, Your Grace. And I thank you."

"Good afternoon," he murmured, his eyes remaining fixed on her until the door closed and she was gone from his sight.

"I MUST SAY, this is more of a crush than I had expected."

Nicholas grimaced as he led Lady Frederica and Lady Foster a little further into the ballroom, finding himself practically rubbing shoulders with the other guests. Whilst he enjoyed balls, he disliked the fact that some of the *ton* did all they could to invite as many guests as possible, simply so that the great number they had invited would be spoken of the following day. It meant that their name would be spoken of far and wide amongst the *ton*, even if only for a short time, and that, it seemed, was something that some gentlemen and ladies were very eager for indeed.

Nicholas did not appreciate it.

"However are we to find Lady Judith?"

Nicholas resisted the urge to turn around and tell Lady Frederica to lower her voice, knowing full well that she could shout in a most unladylike manner and it would not be noticed even by those around them, such was the busyness of this evening. Spying a quieter corner, he quickly led them toward it, finally feeling as though he could breathe a little more easily as the crowd thinned.

"In answer to your question, Frederica, I do not know," he said heavily as he looked all about him in a futile attempt to locate Lady Judith or her mother. "This evening is much too busy."

Lady Foster glanced up at him, her eyes holding a good deal of worry as she looked back at him for a moment. Nicholas attempted to give her a reassuring smile, but it was not one that lingered on his own expression for there was nothing more than frustration within his own heart at present. He could be here for many, many hours and still never find Lady Judith.

"Her dance card will be filled very quickly indeed, I am sure of it," Lady Frederica muttered, shaking her head to herself. "After all, with so many gentlemen present, there will be many eager to make certain that they have danced with as many eligible young ladies as possible."

Nicholas let out a long breath, his lips twisting hard for a moment. "I believe you are right," he stated, only for Lady Foster to put a hand on his arm.

"Is that not the answer?" she asked quickly, looking up at him. "The first dance is due very soon, is it not? If you were to step out with Lady Frederica—or with any young lady of your acquaintance—might you not be better able to spy Lady Judith? After all, she is an eligible young lady and her mother, I know, is very eager indeed to see her daughter do well. Therefore, surely she will push her toward dancing every dance."

Nicholas' heart lifted free of its frustration. "You are quite right, Lady Foster," he agreed, just as the first dance was called. "Then I must step out at once." He held her gaze for a moment, wishing that he could ask her to stand up with him, but knowing he could not. She smiled softly, perhaps aware of the desire in his heart but instead then turning her gaze to Lady Frederica.

"Then *do* come on!" Lady Frederica exclaimed, clearly eager to do as Lady Foster had suggested and being entirely unaware of what was silently passing between Nicholas and Lady Foster. "Let us go at once."

Nicholas nodded, offered his niece his arm, and stepped forward, glancing back at Lady Foster, who stood quietly with her hands clasped lightly in front of her and a small smile on her face. No matter the difficulty, no matter the hardship, it seemed that she always had a smile ready for either him or Lady Frederica and it was that smile that Nicholas carried with him as he stepped out with his niece. He would see her smile again, free of the burden that these rumors had brought. And what a glorious smile that would be.

～

"Have you seen her?"

Nicholas bowed low, sweeping up and taking Lady Frederica's arm again. "You need not hiss so, Frederica," he said, a small smile playing about his mouth. "But yes, I have seen her. Shall we make our way after her?"

Lady Frederica nodded and together, they managed to walk in the very same direction as Lady Judith and the gentleman who had danced with her. His heart was beating rather quickly, although whether that was merely from the dance, Nicholas could not say. It was a little more difficult to keep his gaze fixed upon the lady given the number of guests, but Lady Frederica was quite determined, it seemed, for she practically dragged him forward, her steps sure and her hisses of frustration at those who delayed them making him smile despite their circumstances.

"And you danced so very wonderfully indeed."

A swell of satisfaction filled Nicholas' heart as he heard Lady Prestwick's loud voice catch his attention, glancing across to see Lady Frederica's eyes widen for a moment. They could not simply barge forward now. They had to make it appear as though they came across Lady Judith and Lady Prestwick entirely without intention. Nicholas slowed his steps and shot a warning look toward Lady Frederica, who, thankfully, seemed to understand his plan. Their steps now a good deal slower, Nicholas forced himself to look from left to right in the most nonchalant manner possible, as though looking for good company to converse with. He did not have to wait for long.

"Ah, Your Grace! Your Grace!"

He hesitated, then stopped, looking around him for a moment

before finally allowing his gaze to alight on Lady Prestwick, who was beaming at him with great delight. The gentleman that Lady Judith had been dancing with grimaced and then stepped away, perhaps aware that his presence was no longer required.

"Good evening, Lady Prestwick." Nicholas bowed low as the lady bobbed a very quick curtsy. "And good evening to you also, Lady Judith."

The young lady's cheeks were already flushed—mayhap from the dancing—and she curtsied also before greeting both him and Lady Frederica.

"It is very busy indeed this evening, is it not?" Lady Frederica asked with a small shake of her head. "It is quite stifling."

Lady Prestwick trilled a laugh and waved a hand dismissively, making a spark of anger jump into Lady Frederica's eyes.

"I do not think it overly so, Lady Frederica," Lady Prestwick said as Lady Frederica's smile became rigid and fixed. "There are just so many acquaintances to meet this evening. Why, they are everywhere you look." She laughed again and Nicholas had to hide his smile, almost feeling the waves of irritation that came from his niece.

"And you, Lady Judith?" he asked, drawing attention away from Lady Prestwick. "Are you finding it as busy and as oppressive as Lady Frederica?" He allowed a teasing note to come into his voice and, whilst this brought a sharp look from his niece, Lady Judith merely smiled and dropped her gaze for a moment.

"I find it a little busy, certainly," came the quiet reply. "But I do not think it overly so."

"Very good," he replied quickly, before Lady Prestwick could say anything. "And I see that you are dancing this evening." He smiled at her again as she looked up at him, clearly surprised at his remark. "Might I enquire as to whether or not you have any dances remaining?"

Lady Judith looked helplessly at her mother, who again let out a laugh that sent a tremor of irritation down Nicholas' spine.

"Of course you have, my dear," Lady Prestwick replied as she took the dance card from her daughter's hand and looked down at it with sharp eyes. "There must be one here that—"

"If there is not, then pray, do not trouble yourself," Nicholas began, only for Lady Prestwick to let out a small cry of triumph.

"There is the supper dance, Your Grace?" she asked as Nicholas glanced toward Lady Judith, who was blushing furiously and looking away, clearly a little perturbed. "I am certain that you will be glad to—"

"If I might, Lady Prestwick?" He did not wait for her to answer but rather took the dance card from her fingers in one quick movement, his eyes drifting down it and seeing, much to his disappointment, that every dance was taken—including the supper dance. Lady Frederica glanced at it also, before looking back at Lady Prestwick, who had now gone rather pale indeed.

"It seems I am a little late this evening, Lady Judith," Nicholas said, handing back the dance card to her and resisting the urge to shoot a hard glance toward Lady Prestwick, who, it seemed, had been all too willing to pretend that her daughter's supper dance was free when it was not. Lord Aynesworth would have been most displeased to have found himself displaced by Nicholas, he was sure. "Perhaps you might care to join my niece and me for a short walk in Hyde Park tomorrow instead?"

He saw the look of shock in Lady Judith's expression and did not need to hear the whisper of encouragement from Lady Prestwick to know that she would accept him.

"Oh, do walk with us," Lady Frederica said, reaching out to settle one hand on Lady Judith's arm for a moment. "It will be a very fine afternoon, I am sure, and I would be glad of the company."

Lady Judith swallowed, her gaze darting toward her mother before she nodded, although Nicholas noted that her smile was a little lackluster.

"I should be very glad to indeed, I thank you," she answered as Nicholas let out a small sigh of relief. "That is a very kind invitation."

"Tomorrow, then," Nicholas replied triumphantly, taking Frederica's hand and beginning to guide her away. "I do hope that you enjoy the rest of the evening, Lady Judith." He inclined his head quickly. "Lady Prestwick."

"Thank you, Your Grace," Lady Prestwick seemed almost exultant as she bade him good evening, her eyes sparkling, her face flushed, and her hands clasped together at her heart. "Until tomorrow."

"Until tomorrow," he replied, a sense of triumph building in his heart as he led Lady Frederica away.

12

"Of course you will join us."

Louisa hesitated, then picked up her bonnet for what was now the third time, already feeling the urge to set it down again and insist that it would be best for her to remain here. "I am certain that both you and the duke will do very well without me," she said, only for the duke himself to step into the drawing room and smile at them both.

Louisa's stomach lurched.

"Are you both ready to depart?" he asked, and Lady Frederica nodded before gesturing toward Louisa.

"I am attempting to convince Louisa—that is, Lady Foster—that she is to join us this afternoon, despite her determination to remain here," she said as Louisa dropped her head in embarrassment, having caught the duke's astonished look. "It seems that she is convinced that Lady Judith might speak more freely without her presence."

"But you *must* join us," the duke said firmly. "I insist, Lady Foster."

Louisa dared a glance up at him and saw the determination in his eyes, knowing that there was no use in arguing with him. "Very well," she replied, settling the bonnet on her head and quickly tying the silk ribbons. "As much as I wish to be involved in this matter, I am afraid that Lady Judith might remain silent if I am present."

The duke came toward her as Lady Frederica waited by the door.

"I think your presence may unsettle her," he agreed, looking down into her eyes as the confidence in his gaze began to fill her heart also. "But that, my dear lady, is a very good thing indeed." One hand reached out and tipped up her chin just a little so that she held his gaze, seeing the gentle smile on his face. "Come."

She blushed furiously at his touch but, from the look on Lady Frederica's face, her charge seemed quite contented—and even pleased—that there had been such an exchange between Louisa and the duke. When he offered her his arm, Louisa had no hesitation in taking it, although she was all too aware of the heat that seemed now to dissipate from her. A new confidence began to fill her heart as the duke led her from the room, a sense of hope that very soon, all this might be at an end and that somehow, Lady Judith would be the one to give them the answers they so desperately required.

∼

"I DO HOPE you are not unsettled by Lady Foster's presence."

Lady Frederica laughed as Lady Judith glanced over her shoulder toward Louisa, who walked beside the duke as they made their way into the park. Lady Prestwick had joined her daughter at first and had made it quite clear, in both her looks and her remarks, that she was greatly displeased with Louisa's presence, but both the duke and Lady Frederica had ignored such remarks entirely. Lady Prestwick had, in the end, been forced to give up her grumblings and had urged her daughter on ahead, stating that she was rather tired and would wait for her return in the carriage.

Louisa gave Lady Judith a small smile which was not returned.

Instead, the lady sniffed indelicately and looked away, a cold haughtiness covering her features.

"Lady Foster has, of course, been through a very great trial indeed," Lady Frederica continued as Louisa's heart began to beat with a little more speed. "There have been terrible rumors spoken of her which have, in turn, made their way all through the *ton*."

"I am surprised that you have remained so steadfastly in her defense, Lady Frederica," came the reply, and Louisa stiffened, hearing the haughtiness in Lady Judith's voice. "You ought to have stepped away from her at once, regardless of whether such rumors were true."

"Come now, Lady Judith, that is a little unfair," the duke replied as Lady Judith looked back at him in surprise. "Are you stating that one must toss aside every friendship, every acquaintance, if there is even the smallest hint of something untoward?"

Lady Judith's eyes held the duke's for a moment as she turned around, coming to step in between Louisa and the gentleman.

"I think," she replied as Lady Frederica came to stand by Louisa so that the duke and Lady Judith might walk together, "that it is wise to always protect one's reputation first, regardless of what others might feel."

"I see." The duke looked back at Louisa and gave her a small smile, which she returned without hesitation. "These rumors, however, are quite untrue. I cannot think that it would be wise to toss Lady Foster aside based solely on the fact that such lies are being spoken of her."

Louisa found herself speaking before she could prevent herself from doing so.

"And I have been very fortunate indeed to have not one but two such persons willing to trust me," she stated, aware of how Lady Judith did not so much as glance back at her. "Their determination to aid me further has been of the greatest significance."

Lady Judith sniffed but said nothing.

"In fact," Louisa continued, before the duke or Lady Frederica could say any more, "such has been their eagerness that something of significance has come to light recently. Something that Lady Christina spoke of." She could not see Lady Judith's face given that she was a step or two ahead of her so could not surmise what she might be feeling at this present moment. "Something that was said of you, Lady Judith."

Her words cut like a knife through the pleasant afternoon air, seeming to whip a coldness about the group that made Louisa shiver. Lady Judith stopped immediately, no longer walking but seemingly unwilling to turn to look at Louisa.

"I do not wish to speak to your companion any longer, Lady Frederica," she said tightly. "Perhaps we might—"

"Then might you speak to me?" the duke asked, stepping forward as, finally, Lady Judith turned around. She did not look at Louisa but made it more than obvious that she was ignoring her entirely by turning her head firmly away from Louisa, her whole frame stiff with tension.

"Of course, Your Grace," came the reply, although Lady Judith's voice had lost none of the tightness that had been there a few minutes ago. "I should be glad to."

"Good." The duke put one hand out and rested it on Louisa's shoulder, bringing an expression of wide-eyed shock to Lady Judith's face. "Then you can begin by telling me precisely what it was you said to Lady Christina about Lady Foster."

Lady Judith, who clearly had been expecting the duke to talk of something else and, in doing so, to bring Louisa's conversation to a sharp end, stared at him in disbelief, her face draining of color. Her eyes roved from the duke's face to where his hand rested on Louisa's shoulder, clearly all the more astonished at this display of favor.

"Lady Christina was in conversation with me, Lady Judith, and stated that it was *you* who had told her of the rumors as regards Lady Foster," Lady Frederica interjected, coming to stand a little closer to them all. "Is that so? And if it is, then why should you do such a thing?"

Lady Judith took in a long breath, her shoulders lifting just a little as she turned her attention to Lady Frederica. "Everyone is speaking of Lady Foster," she answered with an evident attempt at indifference as she waved one hand about aimlessly. "Why should I be any different?"

The duke shook his head, his hand still resting on Louisa's shoulder. "But that is not quite the truth now, Lady Judith," he said calmly, although Louisa knew that what he would say next was merely an assumption on their part. She prayed that Lady Judith would believe it, that she would accept what was being said to her.

"What do you mean, Your Grace?"

"I do not want to have to speak sharply to you, Lady Judith, but I will speak plainly," the duke replied, his hand dropping from Louisa's shoulder as he took a small step nearer to Lady Judith, whose eyes flared at once. "Lady Christina has said that the source of these rumors, of these whispers, is you." His eyes narrowed just a fraction. "Is that the truth?"

Lady Judith's eyes widened all the more, and Louisa saw a hint of fear in them now, rather than the clear determination to keep the truth from them all. She did not say anything for some moments, her mouth opening and closing as she wrung her hands. The duke remained where he was, his eyes fixed to Lady Judith's and a severe line playing about his mouth. Louisa felt her heart twinge with a little sympathy for the young lady, seeing the trepidation in her expression and realizing just how horrible this situation must be for her.

"We only want to know the truth, Lady Judith," she said, speaking as gently as she could. "I do not understand why you would say such things about me."

"It was not I."

The words burst from Lady Judith's mouth before she clamped one hand over her lips as though to keep herself from saying more.

"What can you mean?" the duke asked as Lady Judith's eyes began to fill with tears. "Is Lady Christina incorrect in what she said?"

Lady Judith shook her head, closing her eyes for a moment as her hand fell to her side. "She is not incorrect," she whispered, and

Louisa glanced toward the duke, seeing how he caught her gaze for just a moment. "Lady Christina did hear such a thing from me. But it was only because I was informed of such a thing from another."

Letting out a long breath, Louisa tilted her head and looked at Lady Judith. "You spoke of my late husband, Lady Judith," she said, speaking calmly but with great clarity. "You suggested that I might have somehow been involved in his death. In addition, remarks were made about the duke. Lady Christina stated that she had heard such things from you, and now you say that you were not the one to speak of them in the first place?"

Lady Judith did not look at Louisa directly but spread her hands. "I do not wish to tell you from whom I heard them, Lady Foster," she whispered, a single tear running down her cheek. "It is of the greatest embarrassment."

Louisa frowned, seeing how Lady Frederica folded her arms across her chest in a defensive gesture.

"I must know," Louisa replied patiently. "If I am to free myself of these rumors, then I must know the truth."

Lady Judith shook her head mutely and Louisa's heart sank. Nothing would come of this conversation, it seemed, given that Lady Judith would not speak to her of the matter. It was clear that she knew exactly who it was that had said such things in the first instance but was refusing to speak of this person to them.

"Lady Judith," the duke began, his voice low. "Let me make certain I understand. You were among the first to speak of Lady Foster in this manner, repeating stories that were quite untrue and did a great deal of harm to Lady Foster. Is that so?"

A barely perceptible nod came from Lady Judith, her head beginning to hang low as the afternoon sun blazed all around them in sharp contrast to the cold and tense discussion between them.

"You know who began these rumors, but you will not speak their name," the duke continued quietly. "Is that also true?"

"It is."

Lady Frederica's frown began to lift, and she looked at Louisa with wide eyes, clearly able to see something that Louisa herself could not.

"And you will not speak their name for fear of the embarrassment and shame that will befall you, should you do so?" the duke finished, and Lady Judith lifted her head just a little, nodding toward the duke although her gaze remained low. "You know that if you tell us the truth, you will be the one to suffer?"

Louisa slowly began to realize exactly why Lady Frederica had appeared so astonished. It was beginning to become quite clear to her just who had spoken of such a thing to the lady. She knew now why Lady Judith did not want to speak her name, did not want to reveal the truth. There *would* be a great deal of shame and mortification, a good many questions that would be flung at them both and, mayhap, a good deal of damage done to Lady Judith's reputation.

"It is your mother, is it not?" she asked, before the duke could say another word. "Your mother has been the one to start such whispers."

It was a statement rather than a question, which Lady Judith was required to answer. The young lady broke down then, tears seeping from her eyes as she searched helplessly for a handkerchief. Lady Frederica obligingly handed her one, and Lady Judith wiped at her eyes as Louisa let out a long breath, turning toward the duke, who was watching the situation with an expression of grim distaste settling onto his face.

"Why has she done so?" Lady Frederica asked, speaking with a great gentleness rather than a hard anger. "Lady Foster has done nothing to upset her, surely?"

Lady Judith hiccupped and shook her head. "It is to do with you, Your Grace," she replied, her voice shaking and broken. "It was perceived by my mother that there might be a...a growing intimacy between Lady Foster and yourself. My mother did not wish for such a thing."

"Because she wanted you to catch the duke's attention," Louisa said slowly, and Lady Judith nodded, her face flaming furiously. "And I was in the way."

Lady Judith sniffed, her tears abating just a little. "I agreed to the scheme simply because I—I wished for the same thing," she admitted, although she was no longer looking toward the duke. "I did not ever think that someone would realize that it was both my mother and I who began such rumors."

There was a moment or two of silence as the duke looked from Louisa to Lady Judith and back again. Louisa herself did not know what to say, for given that there was now a distinct possibility that informing the *ton* that Lady Prestwick had been entirely responsible for the spreading of such rumors would impact badly on Lady Judith's reputation, there was an uncertainty as to what they ought to do next.

"I must speak to Lady Prestwick," the duke said eventually. "These rumors cannot be allowed to continue." He shook his head for a moment, rubbing one hand over his chin. "And Lady Judith, there will never be anything of importance between us. Of that, I can assure you."

Lady Judith hung her head, although Louisa could not be certain as to whether her embarrassment came from having to reveal the truth or from a true sense of regret. She presumed it was the former, given just how much Lady Judith had been determined to continue on as though everything was just as it should be.

"Let us continue walking for a short time," Lady Frederica suggested as she turned back toward the path. "Lady Judith, shall we?"

Lady Judith did not nod or speak but instead turned toward Lady Frederica and fell into step with her, leaving Louisa to walk alongside the duke. They said nothing for some moments, only for the duke to hesitate, stop, and turn to face her.

"Lady Foster," he said quickly. "It occurs to me that now might be the best opportunity we have to speak to Lady Prestwick." His eyes darted back toward the carriage where Lady Prestwick waited. "Should you wish to accompany me?"

Louisa was about to nod, but then gestured toward Lady Frederica. "But my duty is to remain with Lady Frederica," she said quickly, her heart torn in two directions. "To leave her unchaperoned…"

The duke nodded, bit his lip, then hurried after Lady Frederica, leaving Louisa standing alone. He spoke to her rapidly, with Lady Frederica nodding in understanding, before making her way to sit down on a bench near the side of the path. Lady Judith hesitated, but a hard look from the duke soon had her scurrying after Lady Frederica.

The duke returned.

"They will wait until they see us emerge from the carriage," the duke said, his breathing a little quicker now that he had hurried back. "Come, Lady Foster. Let us go at once." He offered her his arm and, with a great quickening in her heart, Louisa took it, turning herself in the direction of Lady Prestwick's carriage. The end of her torturous difficulties was, it seemed, very much at hand.

13

"Your Grace." Nicholas grimaced as Lady Prestwick waved her hand at him from inside her carriage.

"You are returned without my daughter," the lady protested, her head now out of the carriage door. "I pray that all is well?"

"Very well," he replied, forcing himself to remain calm in his speech and his manner. "Lady Frederica wished to speak to Lady Judith a little longer—and I had something of importance to say to you also."

Lady Prestwick looked a little surprised, but that astonishment faded in an instant as she smiled brightly and instructed the tiger to open the carriage door a little wider so as to welcome him in. Nicholas knew all too well what the lady was thinking, clearly believing that there might be a purpose in his eagerness to speak to her—a purpose that would involve her daughter. He would strike that spark dead in an instant, he determined, looking down at Lady Foster and seeing the paleness in her cheeks but the bright determination in her eyes.

"After you, Lady Foster," he murmured as the smile faded from Lady Prestwick's face. "I insist."

She did not hesitate but climbed inside at once, sitting down opposite Lady Prestwick just as Nicholas joined them. He cleared his throat and looked directly at Lady Prestwick, aware of how the anticipation had disappeared entirely from her expression.

"Lady Prestwick," he began stiffly. "I have heard something of great interest from your daughter. Something that she has not expressed in its entirety, but that I have been able to surmise without too much difficulty." He tilted his head, his gaze fixed and determined. "You have spread rumors about Lady Foster, simply because you feared that there might be something of an intimacy between myself and the lady. You did so in the hope that I would remove myself from Lady Foster entirely so that my gaze would rest solely upon your daughter." He saw the color drain from Lady Prestwick's face and felt a flare of both triumph and of anger burn in his heart. "Is that the truth?"

Lady Prestwick did not say anything for some moments. In fact, she sat so still and so quietly that Nicholas began to wonder if she would ever speak, given the shock that was now written across her face—but, eventually, she began to stammer.

"I—I do not know— I cannot imagine what Judith has been saying," she replied, trying to smile but failing entirely. "Young girls can so easily become overwhelmed by your company, Your Grace, that they—"

"I will not have untruths from you, Lady Prestwick," Nicholas interrupted, doing his utmost to keep a grip on his temper. "You have done enough damage already, I assure you. At the present, I have kept the truth of what Lady Judith has said entirely to myself, but if required, I will speak of it to the *beau monde,* in the full knowledge of what it will do."

This threat seemed enough to bring the truth tumbling from Lady Prestwick's lips.

"Pray, do not injure my daughter, Your Grace!" she cried, no longer stammering or tripping over her words. "I told her what she was to say, and she said it. It was not meant to injure you or Lady Frederica in any way, I assure you."

"Because," Lady Foster interjected as Nicholas looked toward her, "you expected both His Grace and Lady Frederica to remove me entirely from their company. You thought that only I would be grievously injured by your remarks."

"Yes, that is it precisely," Lady Prestwick declared eagerly, as though this was, in some way, a satisfactory explanation. "Lady Foster would be gone from society, and you might then look toward my daughter instead of to her."

Nicholas closed his eyes and let out a long, heavy breath. The way that Lady Prestwick spoke, the sheer cruelty of how she simply disregarded Lady Foster, sent a shard of pain straight through his heart. He wanted to reach across and shake the lady, to make her aware of what she had done, but instead simply remained where he was, his hands clasped tightly together as waves of tension tore into his frame.

"You are mistaken if you believe that I am so easily swayed, so quickly turned toward disloyalty, Lady Prestwick," he grated, looking across at her once more and seeing the shock ripple into her features. "Lady Foster has done nothing wrong. She has not been involved in any way in the loss of her late husband. How dare you even *think* to suggest such a thing?" His voice rose but he did not hold himself back, speaking with all the wrath that now tore through him. "She is entirely innocent and due to your cruelty, due to your lack of feeling, you have forced her to suffer. Suffer solely in the hope that you and your daughter might benefit. Well, I declare to you now that it shall not be. It shall *never* be, Lady Prestwick."

The carriage itself seemed to tremble with the weight of his wrath. Lady Prestwick was now pressed back in her seat, her eyes wide, her cheeks pale, and her hands grasping at her skirts as though she might find some defense there.

And then, Lady Foster put her hand over his. Nicholas turned his head and looked at her, seeing the gentleness in her expression and knowing precisely what it was she was saying to him. He had said enough. He had expressed enough. There was no need for any further anger.

"You will speak to all those you told such rumors to, Lady Prestwick," he said slowly as the lady stared back at him with wide, frightened eyes. "You will inform them that you were wrong. That you were mistaken. Lady Judith will do the same."

Lady Prestwick shook her head. "I cannot!" she exclaimed, her voice weak and thready. "To do so would bring the greatest embarrassment."

"Then I shall state the truth to those that *I* am acquainted with," he replied swiftly, seeing the horror rush into Lady Prestwick's eyes. "Make your choice, madam. But either way, this matter comes to an end."

∽

"My dear Louisa."

Nicholas reached out his hands as Lady Foster rose to her feet, having been waiting for him in the drawing room. Lady Frederica had gone to her room to rest for a short while, claiming to be tired after the events of that afternoon, but Nicholas had wondered whether or not she had known that Nicholas wanted to speak to Lady Foster alone.

"Your Grace."

Nicholas smiled and shook his head. "You must not be so formal with me," he said softly, his fingers twining through hers. "Surely you must see that? There is such an intimacy between us, such a depth of feeling that..." He could not find the words to speak, lifting her hand to his mouth and kissing it gently.

He heard her sigh contentedly and knew that now was the time to be honest with her, to state all that he felt without hesitation.

"It is at an end, then," she said, before he could speak further. "There is nothing more that we need do."

Nicholas smiled at her tenderly. "It will take a little time for the rumors to dissipate," he said quietly, knowing that she already understood. "But I believe that something else will capture the attention of the *ton* all the more."

"Oh?"

Her eyes were searching his, her hands lying contentedly in his. Nicholas had never thought her more beautiful, knowing all too well just how much she now meant to him. He could not imagine stepping away from her, and her resigning herself to life as a companion for the rest of her days. In his consideration, he would never find another lady like her, not even if he searched throughout the entirety of the *ton*.

"You are remarkable, Louisa," he began, praying that Lady Frederica would not decide she had recovered and accidentally walk into the room at the most inopportune moment. "I have seen your struggle and yet, from that, there has come a determination and a courage that has pushed you forward, has encouraged you to speak up and defend yourself in the face of great opposition." He shook his head, still overwhelmed by all that he knew of her. "I find myself in awe, Louisa. Even when we were speaking to Lady Judith, I heard the quiet sympathy in your voice. You were eager to find the truth, but you seemed to understand the difficulty that she would face should she be forced to speak of it. The gentleness of your heart astonishes me, Louisa. It encourages me to improve my own considerations, my own conduct. And most of all, it urges me toward you, to cling to you for fear that I might lose you altogether, should I let you go."

Neither shock nor astonishment was visible on her face, but rather a gentle flush of her cheeks that spoke of embarrassment that he should speak so well of her. Nicholas smiled to himself as he let go of one of her hands so that he might gently cup her chin, marveling at the beauty before him. "I shall continue to speak in such a manner for the rest of my days, Louisa," he finished quietly. "If, that is, you will accept me."

There was no mistaking her swift intake of breath. Lady Foster blinked rapidly, the color in her face rising all the more as she looked up at him steadily, but Nicholas only smiled, remaining precisely where he was.

"You—I..." She closed her eyes, a little embarrassed. "Might I ask you to speak clearly, for I fear that I will misunderstand you."

"There is no misunderstanding," he said pointedly. "Louisa, I have come to care for you with such a deep affection that it is all I can do even to speak of it. I am convinced that to be without you will injure me for the rest of my days. I love you desperately and I must beg of you to accept my hand." His thumb brushed across her cheek before his hand dropped to her waist, pulling her just a little more tightly toward him. "Say you will be my wife, Louisa, for I cannot bear to be without you."

Louisa said nothing for a moment or two, and then her hand lifted to rest lightly against his heart. Her smile was one of both wonder and joy, her eyes filled with a new light as she moved closer to him.

"Your heart speaks to my heart," she said softly. "For I am certain I love you in return."

Nicholas closed his eyes and let out a long breath of relief, his whole being practically alight with joy. "Then you will marry me?" he asked, looking down at her again, his head already beginning to lower. "You will become my bride?"

"I will." Her answer was nothing more than a whisper, her hands around his neck as he pulled her close and sealed their agreement with a gentle kiss.

"Your Grace?"

Nicholas looked up at once, stopping his pacing for a moment as he stared blankly at the maid who had stepped into the room.

"Your Grace, the duchess seeks your company," she said, bobbing a quick curtsy. "And might I congratulate you also."

Nicholas' heart beat so quickly that he could not find the words to speak, nodding to the maid as he passed through the door. Taking the stairs two at a time, he reached Louisa's bedchamber and, after a moment, pushed the door open quietly.

"My love."

Her voice was not weak, as he had feared, but was rather filled with delight and strength.

"It has all gone very well, Your Grace," murmured the doctor, emerging from the shadows of the room. "Your wife is strong and will, I am sure, produce many hearty children."

Nicholas forced himself to speak, rasping a "thank you" to the doctor before slowly making his way across the room. He could hardly breathe, looking down at his beautiful wife and then, after a moment, at the bundle in her arms. His heart, which had been so filled with love for his wife, now seemed to explode in his chest as he found that love redoubling as he looked down at the child.

"My love," he whispered, his hand resting lightly on her shoulder, his lips brushing across her forehead. "You—I..." He did not speak of his fear and his anxiety that had come alongside her labor pains, but by the gentle touch of her hand on his, Nicholas knew that she understood.

"I am quite well," she said, looking up into his face. "I am well. I will recover quickly. You need not worry."

He nodded mutely, a catch in his throat as he looked down at the tiny child cradled in Louisa's arms.

"Here," she murmured, lifting the babe carefully out toward Nicholas. "Hold your son."

Nicholas swallowed hard, uncertain as to what to do, but in a moment, he found himself cradling the baby, looking down into his face and marveling at the gift he had been given.

"My son," he whispered as Louisa let out a long, contented sigh and closed her eyes. "I have a son."

"And you will love him just as much as you love me," Louisa murmured softly. "I am certain of that."

Nicholas smiled down at the child, brushing his finger lightly down the baby's cheek. "What a gift I have in both you and him," he answered quietly. His eyes rested lightly on his wife, his heart swelling within him all over again. "I love you, Louisa."

"And I love you."

THE ELIGIBLE EARL

HEIRS OF LONDON BOOK FIVE

The Eligible Earl

Text Copyright © 2021 by Joyce Alec

All rights reserved. This book or any portion thereof may not be reproduced or used in any manner whatsoever without the express written permission of the publisher except for the use of brief quotations in a book review.

This book is a work of fiction. Names, characters, places and incidents are either the product of the author's imagination or are used fictionally. Any resemblance to actual persons, living or dead, or to actual events or locales is entirely coincidental.

First printing, 2021

Publisher
Love Light Faith, LLC
400 NW 7th Avenue, Unit 825
Fort Lauderdale, FL 33311

1

"This must be a little strange for you."

Frederica embraced the duchess. "No, indeed not," she laughed as the duchess smiled back at her. "You were my chaperone last Season and this Season, you *remain* my chaperone—albeit as the duchess rather than a paid companion." Her heart filled with happiness as she recalled how, a few months ago, she had been present at the wedding of her uncle, the Duke of Ellsworth, to Lady Foster, who had been Frederica's paid companion. To see the clear and deep affection between them had made her yearn for such a thing herself and she hoped that, with this being her second Season, she might find a suitable gentleman of her own.

"Well, our first ball is this evening," the duchess reminded her, "and you have new gowns to try on this afternoon."

Frederica sighed contentedly and turned to look out of the window, down at the quiet London street. There were only one or two carriages at present although soon, Frederica knew that there would be many afternoon callers coming and going—although none for her yet, given that they had only arrived in London the previous day.

"Are you looking forward to the Season?" the duchess asked, coming to stand beside Frederica. "It is your second one, but neither the duke nor I want you to feel any burden when it comes to matrimony. Your father and mother are of the same mind."

"Yet I find myself eager for such a thing," Frederica replied, thinking fondly of her parents, who, at present, remained back at the estate with the rest of their children. "Last Season, I learned a good deal about society and the like."

"How could you not, given all that occurred?" the duchess asked, a wry smile on her lips.

"Indeed," Frederica laughed, "but now that all is settled between you and my uncle, let us hope that this Season will be a good deal simpler than the last."

"I am sure it will be," the duchess replied, smiling. "And I insist that you continue to call me 'Louisa'. We are just as dear to each other as we were before I wed the duke, are we not?"

"We are," Frederica replied, reaching to embrace the duchess once more. "And I look forward to having your guidance and care during this Season also."

～

Taking in a deep breath, Frederica lifted her chin and stepped forward into the ballroom, with the duke and duchess by her side. The music and the hubbub of conversation and laughter seemed so very familiar, and Frederica could not help but smile, finding herself quite glad to be back amongst society again.

"I am sure you will have many acquaintances greeting you this evening," the duchess said, slipping her arm through Frederica's. "There will be many who will remember you."

"And I am sure that many will greet you also," Frederica replied with a small smile. "After all, marrying a duke will bring with it a great deal of interest."

The duchess laughed, her eyes bright. "But I shall direct all the attention toward you, have no doubt. I am sure that you will find many gentlemen eager for your acquaintance."

"But I should not like to wed a gentleman that is only considered suitable," Frederica replied, speaking honestly and knowing that she could do so given the deep friendship between them. "I have seen the love and the friendship between you and my uncle, and I have decided that that is also what I myself seek."

The duchess said nothing for a moment, although there was a gentleness in her eyes that Frederica knew came from the mere thought of the duke. "That is wise, I believe," the duchess said eventually. "Although I fear it may take you a little longer to find such a gentleman."

"I am willing to wait," Frederica replied firmly, looking out across the sea of guests and finding her determination growing all the more. "I do not think I would be satisfied with a marriage of convenience."

"Good evening, Lady Frederica."

In a moment, Frederica was drawn back into society as gentlemen and ladies approached her, speaking to her, the duke, and the new duchess. In only a few minutes, Frederica found her dance card already half full, her enjoyment of the evening growing with every moment.

"Might I beg to make an introduction, Lady Frederica?"

She turned to smile up at the Earl of Greenford, with whom she was already acquainted. "But of course," she said, seeing the gentleman standing beside him, who was already bowing. "I should be very glad to meet any of your acquaintances, Lord Greenford."

Lord Greenford, who was a very amiable gentleman, if not something of a fop, given his penchant for dressing in an ostentatious manner, turned to the gentleman beside him and gestured toward him, twirling his hand as he did so. "Lady Frederica, might I present the Earl of Wetherby. Lord Wetherby, this is Lady Frederica, daughter to the Marquess of Dewsbury and niece to the Duke of Ellsworth."

Frederica smiled and dropped into a curtsy as Lord Wetherby

bowed for what was the second time. "Good evening, Lord Wetherby," she said, lifting her eyes back to him. "I am very glad to make your acquaintance."

Lord Wetherby smiled back at her as Frederica took him in, seeing a somewhat square jaw, dark green eyes, and dark hair that he had evidently attempted to place into a neat style but that, unfortunately, had already become a little disheveled.

"As I am glad to meet you," he replied, smiling broadly. "Is this your first Season, Lady Frederica?"

"My second," she replied swiftly. "I am very happy to be returned back to London, however, Lord Wetherby."

"And you are here with the Duke and Duchess of Ellsworth, I understand," the gentleman remarked, casting a quick glance toward the duchess, who was engaged in conversation with another lady.

"Yes, my parents remain at home and the duke and duchess have been kind enough to take me back to London with them," Frederica explained as Lord Wetherby nodded, looking more than a little interested. Frederica wondered silently whether the gentleman was truly interested in making her acquaintance or if, as she had said to the duchess earlier that evening, he merely wanted to make certain that he was now acquainted with the new Duchess of Ellsworth. Frederica would, of course, have to introduce them both at some point. "I greatly appreciate their willingness."

Lord Wetherby smiled, his eyes darting back toward the duchess for a moment. "But of course," he said, before looking back at Frederica. "Might I ask, Lady Frederica, whether or not you will permit me to dance with you this evening? I do hope that there are some dances left on your dance card, although, given just how many of the guests have come to speak to you this evening, I fear I have been much too tardy."

Frederica pulled the silk ribbon from her wrist and handed it to him. "But of course, Lord Wetherby," she replied as he accepted it from her with an inclination of his head. "Thank you for your consideration."

He wrote his name quickly and then handed her back the card. "The quadrille, Lady Frederica," he said as she thanked him. "I do hope that I can remember all the steps. It has been some time since I have danced."

"As it has been for me, Lord Wetherby," Frederica replied with a small smile. "And now, might I acquaint you with the Duchess of Ellsworth?" She turned toward Louisa, who had finished her conversation with the lady, and quickly made the introductions, seeing Lord Wetherby's eyes light up as he bowed. Sighing inwardly, Frederica felt her shoulders slump just a little. It seemed that Lord Wetherby was more interested in furthering his own situation than being truly interested in Frederica's company but, Frederica considered, he would not be the first gentleman to do so, or the last. To be known to the Duke and Duchess of Ellsworth, on their first Season in London as man and wife, was something that could be spoken of with great pride and would certainly elevate one's status a little.

"Our dance, Lady Frederica."

Lord Greenford bowed low and then offered her his arm. "The cotillion."

"Indeed, Lord Greenford," she smiled, throwing aside her irritation at Lord Wetherby's behavior. "I thank you."

*

"I AM QUITE FATIGUED."

The duchess laughed and handed Frederica a glass of ratafia. "You have danced almost every dance this evening," she said as Frederica smiled wearily. "I am very glad that all has gone well, however. It is an excellent return to society, my dear."

Frederica took a sip of her ratafia and looked down at her dance card. "I am to dance with Lord Wetherby next," she said, one eyebrow lifting. "Although I must say that he was more than eager to meet *you*, Louisa."

The duchess looked surprised. "Oh?"

"He will be able to tell all of his acquaintances that he has now been introduced to you," Frederica replied, a little wryly. "Not that such a thing should matter to me, of course."

With a small smile on her lips, the duchess patted Frederica's arm gently. "I am sorry."

"It is not your fault, by any means," Frederica cried, not wanting her friend to feel at all guilty. "He will not be the only gentleman who, being acquainted with me, will then seek to be acquainted with you also." She lifted one shoulder in a half-shrug. "I will hope that his conversation will not be solely about my acquaintance with both you and my uncle, else I shall be very put out indeed."

The duchess laughed, only for her smile to become fixed in place and her eyes to round as she looked beyond Frederica and toward someone or something that she could not see.

"Lord Wetherby," she murmured, now standing a little more stiffly than before. "He has very dark hair, does he not?"

"Yes, he does," Frederica replied, frowning as she looked back at the duchess. "Is something the matter?"

The duchess pressed her lips together tightly. "Then I do hope that the dark-haired gentleman approaching is *not* Lord Wetherby, for I fear that he will not be particularly well able to dance."

Frederica turned sharply, hearing the alarm in the duchess' voice and aware of her own heart quickening with concern. To her horror, she saw the newly acquainted Lord Wetherby coming toward her slowly, his steps slow as he swayed this way and the next, clearly already in his cups. Frederica caught her breath, her hand fluttering near her heart as she stared at the approaching gentleman. Surely he did not expect her to stand up with him now, not when he was in such a state as this.

"Lady Frederica." Lord Wetherby bowed low, staggering forward and only just managing to right himself in time before he fell to the floor. "I apologize if I am tardy." A broad smile settled across his face, his eyes glazed. "The dance is to be ours, is it not? Although, I confess that I have entirely forgotten what it is to be."

A swell of anger rose in Frederica's chest. "Lord Wetherby, I hardly think that you should even be considering dancing in your present state," she said firmly, lifting her chin as her jaw tightened. "You surely cannot think that I will be at all willing to stand up with you."

Lord Wetherby frowned, his smile fading. "Why ever not?" he asked, spreading his arms wide and accidentally hitting another gentleman across the back, although he did not once turn to apologize. "My name is on your dance card, is it not?"

"It is," she agreed tersely.

"Then you have already consented to dance with me, Lady Frederica," came the triumphant reply. "Why should you now refuse?" He tilted his head and smiled at her, as though she ought to relish the fact that she was to dance with him, as though he fully expected to be able to do so without any difficulty.

"Lord Wetherby," Frederica replied as the duchess looked on, her brow furrowed. "You are foxed."

"I am not," Lord Wetherby demanded, only to sway forward and backwards again as he did so, frowning hard as he attempted to right himself. "I may have had one or two—"

"I may have your name on my dance card, Lord Wetherby, but nothing could induce me to stand up with you at present, given that you will, most likely, stumble, fall, tread on my feet, or fail to recall any of the steps that are required of you." She spoke with calmness, her voice steady and her expression fixed even though a deep anger was filling her heart at Lord Wetherby's drunken state. He was not behaving at all as a gentleman ought and she was becoming weary of his determination to dance with her regardless. "Therefore, despite the fact that I *do* have your name on my dance card, I cannot accept a dance from you. I will remain here, Lord Wetherby, and despite the fact that you might consider me somewhat rude, I will refrain from accepting your offer."

Lord Wetherby's frown deepened, and he made to say something more, only for Lord Greenford to step forward. He put one hand on Lord Wetherby's arm, clearly aware of just how foxed his friend was and how difficult the situation was for Frederica at present.

"I think the lady is correct, Lord Wetherby," he said kindly. "Remain here and I will take your dance for you." He smiled at Frederica, who closed her eyes for a moment with relief. "That is, Lady Frederica, if that would be amenable to you?"

Frederica opened her eyes and smiled back at Lord Greenford, a sense of relief in her heart. "Thank you, Lord Greenford, I should be glad to dance with you again," she said as Lord Wetherby muttered something under his breath and looked away. "You are most understanding."

"But of course," Lord Greenford replied, his hand falling from Lord Wetherby's arm as the gentleman turned away entirely, stumbling off into the crowd. Frederica's eyes followed him for a long moment, her brow puckered as she shook her head to herself, thinking that Lord Wetherby was the most ridiculous of all the gentlemen she had been acquainted with thus far.

"Forgive Lord Wetherby," Lord Greenford said, evidently seeing the direction of her gaze. "He will regret his actions and his words come the morning, I am quite certain."

"If he recalls them," the duchess added, making Frederica smile and chasing the frown from her forehead. "Thank you for stepping in in such a manner. You are very kind."

Lord Greenford bowed and offered Frederica his arm. "It is my honor to do so," he said as Frederica accepted him. "Shall we dance, Lady Frederica?"

"We shall," Frederica replied contentedly as she made her way out with Lord Greenford, relieved beyond expression that she would not have to stand up with Lord Wetherby. Silently, she promised herself that she would never again accept a dance from Lord Wetherby, thinking quietly to herself that a gentleman such as he had already shown her the true depths of his character. If he could not remain in control of himself, if he could not do anything but indulge his own desires, then what did that say of his character?

Giving herself a slight shake, Frederica took her place and smiled back at Lord Greenford, before dropping into a curtsy, as was expected. Lord Greenford bowed and then the music began, encouraging Frederica to think only of the dance and to push all thought of Lord Wetherby from her mind. Yes, she had been a little insulted and yes, he had behaved in the most ridiculous fashion but there was no need to consider him any longer. Lord Greenford had come to her rescue and Frederica was quite certain that the rest of the evening would be quite splendid. With a smile on her face and a contentedness returning to her heart, Frederica stepped forward into her dance with Lord Greenford and forgot all about the ridiculous Lord Wetherby.

2

Percy let out a loud groan as he opened his eyes, feeling a great heaviness settling upon him.

"My lord," the butler said again, his voice sounding as loud as thunder and searing its way right through Percy's head. "You did ask me to inform you should you have any afternoon callers."

A groan escaped Percy's mouth as he ran one hand down his face, realizing that he had fallen into a deep sleep, most likely as a consequence of being greatly fatigued from last evening's exploits.

"Who is it?" he grumbled, pushing himself up a little more in his chair as the butler pressed his lips together, a slight air of anxiety around him. "A lady?"

"Lord Greenford," the butler informed him, and Percy groaned again, slumping back in his chair and letting his eyes close tightly. "What shall I say, my lord?"

Percy grimaced. Lord Greenford was someone he considered a friend, certainly, but he did not appreciate being woken from his slumber merely to entertain him. Had it been a young lady come to call on him, then Percy might have been grateful for her arrival and her interruption of his sleep but, as things stood, he would have much preferred to remain in the depths of his slumber.

"Very well, very well," he muttered tersely. "Show him in."

"And refreshments, my lord?"

"Coffee," Percy grumbled, his eyes straying to the whisky and glasses that sat on a table in the corner of the room. He could not even think of liquor at present, and even the sight of it made his stomach twist. "Although should Lord Greenford wish for something else, then I will ring the bell."

The butler inclined his head. "Very good, my lord," he said, before departing from the room. Ignoring the pain in his head, Percy forced himself to rise out of his chair and, grimacing as he did so, walked to the mantlepiece so that he might look at his reflection in the mirror that hung above it.

The reflection was not a particularly pleasant sight. There were dark smudges beneath his eyes, his hair was entirely disheveled, and there was a paleness to his skin that spoke of his fatigue. His cravat no longer sat as perfectly as it had done before, and his jacket needed to be straightened.

"At least it is only you, Lord Greenford," Percy muttered as his friend was shown into the room. "You will have to forgive my appearance."

Lord Greenford chuckled and sat down in a chair, propping one leg up on the other knee. "I did think you would be a trifle unwell today," he said as Percy turned from the mirror and went to sit back down in his own seat. "It appears I was quite correct."

Scowling, Percy shrugged. "I may have indulged a little too much last evening," he admitted, frustrated by Lord Greenford's grin. "But it was my first ball of the Season, that is all."

"You do recall what occurred, do you not?" Lord Greenford asked as the refreshments were brought in. "I should not like to remind you of the events that occurred if you already know what I am going to say."

Percy waited until the staff had departed before he spoke, feeling a tight nervousness swathing his heart as he looked back uneasily at Lord Greenford. "What occurred?" he asked as Lord Greenford nodded. "You mean to say, something that *I* did that I do not recall?"

A spark of mirth came into Lord Greenford's eyes. "Yes, indeed," he replied, clearly aware that Percy had no understanding of what he spoke of. "It was with Lady Frederica?"

"Lady Frederica," Percy repeated, musing over the name as he attempted to recall the lady. "I—oh yes, she is the niece of the duke, is she not?"

"Yes," Lord Greenford replied, taking the coffee from Percy with a nod of thanks. "You were introduced to her and then requested her dance card."

Screwing up his face, Percy tried his best to recall. "I did?" he asked, having only a vague recollection of the young lady. Had she seen him in his inebriated state? "I recall dancing a few dances, however, but none with her."

"You did attempt to, however," Lord Greenford said slowly. "You truly do not recall?"

"No!" Percy exclaimed, growing a trifle frustrated with Lord Greenford's seeming reluctance just to tell him the truth of what had occurred. "I did dance with her, then?"

"You were somewhat inebriated by that time," Lord Greenford told him as Percy froze in place, his hand halfway to his mouth as he held his cup of coffee. "You seemed to be aware that you were to dance with Lady Frederica, and thus made your way toward her." The gleam that had been in his eye began to fade, a seriousness coming into his expression. "I could not help but follow you, for you were stumbling rather badly and at one point, looked as though you might fall."

Percy closed his eyes with embarrassment, having very little recollection of such a thing. "I see."

"You then went on to practically demand that Lady Frederica dance with you," Lord Greenford continued, making Percy's embarrassment grow all the more. "She refused, of course, for to agree would have meant that the mortification that would follow might have been severe."

"I see," Percy said again, letting out a long breath and passing one hand over his eyes, reaching to set down his cup of coffee. "I would not have been able to dance well, from the sounds of it."

"If at all," Lord Greenford added, although no smile lingered on his face. "I, therefore, insisted that you remain as you were and instead took Lady Frederica onto the floor for the dance."

The tightness in Percy's heart grew steadily as he realized just how foolishly he must have behaved. "I can only thank you for doing so," he told his friend as Lord Greenford sipped his coffee. "I do not remember doing any such thing and to insist that Lady Frederica stand up with me when I was in my cups is more than a little mortifying to hear."

"She was rather insulted," Lord Greenford said gently. "I came to call upon you to suggest that, even if you do not recall it, it might now be wise to speak to the lady and apologize for your manner."

Percy passed one hand over his eyes and nodded, swallowing hard as he did so. He had not meant to indulge in so much liquor but discovering the whisky and the brandy in the card room had meant an evening of far too much extravagance. "I will have to apologize, yes," he muttered as Lord Greenford nodded sagely. "I thank you for coming to inform me of it. And for taking Lady Frederica to dance in my stead. I am certain I was not very gracious toward you last evening for doing so." One look at his friend, at his raised brow and the wry smile on his lips, told Percy that he was correct in his estimation. A sigh left him as he rubbed one hand over his eyes, irritated that he had made such a fool of himself. "I apologize."

"It is quite all right," Lord Greenford said waving his hand in a dismissive manner. "I did remain near to you for the rest of the evening, I confess, simply to make certain that you would not do such a thing again—but you only appeared eager to make your way back to the card room where you remained for some time."

"And drank a good deal more, no doubt," Percy muttered, knowing that he could not even recall returning to his house.

"You went into the gardens at one point," Lord Greenford replied with a shake of his head. "Although you were not alone. Lord Faraway and Lord Blakely accompanied you, although neither were as much in their cups as you, I am afraid. I did follow, to make certain that all was well, but you appeared to be quite at ease. Lord Blakely was absent for a few minutes but soon returned."

Percy winced again and shook his head. "I should never have let myself get into such a state," he told Lord Greenford. "I shall not do so again. As disagreeable as this may sound, I do hope it is only Lady Frederica that I have insulted?" He searched Lord Greenford's expression, worrying now that he had done something more to some of the other guests, but much to his relief, Lord Greenford shook his head.

"I believe you will find yourself a little lacking in coin, however," Lord Greenford said, a little uncertainly. "I know that you were busy playing cards last evening and there were a few vowels exchanged—but I confess I did not know precisely what had occurred."

"I will find out," Percy promised, not wanting to remain in debt to anyone. "But now, I suppose, I should make myself as presentable as I can and make my way to the Duke of Ellsworth's townhouse." He pushed himself out of the chair with an effort and went to the mirror once more, grimacing as he looked back at his reflection. He would have to ring for his valet to come and fix his cravat and certainly he would have to do something about his hair.

"I will see you this evening, perhaps?" Lord Greenford asked, now also on his feet. "Are you to attend Lord Merseyside's soiree?"

"I am," Percy replied, promising himself silently that he would not touch a drop of liquor that evening. He turned back toward his friend. "I thank you, Lord Greenford."

Lord Greenford smiled and inclined his head, although there was a slightly weary look in his eyes that Percy did not miss. "But of course."

"And I shall give you no cause for alarm this evening, I promise you," Percy said as Lord Greenford chuckled. "Any whisky or brandy or the like offered me will be soundly rejected."

"I will see you this evening, then," Lord Greenford said, walking to the door. "And might I wish you the very best of luck with Lady Frederica." He chuckled and Percy grimaced as he glanced back at his reflection once more. "I fear you are going to need it."

∼

WALKING INTO THE DRAWING ROOM, Percy took in a deep breath and set his shoulders, his hands clasped lightly behind his back as he took in the scene before him. Both Lady Frederica and the Duchess of Ellsworth had risen at the same time and had now dropped into a curtsy, which, of course, Percy returned with a bow. However, when they both lifted their gaze toward him, he could not escape the dislike that lingered there, or the distrust that was so very evident on their faces.

"Good afternoon, Your Grace," he began, "and to you also, Lady Frederica. I am grateful to you both for being so willing to permit me into your presence."

"Please, Lord Wetherby," Lady Frederica replied, looking back at him with a gentle coolness in her expression. "Do be seated."

Percy sat down with relief, glad that he was not about to be thrown from the house in disgrace, even though they had every right to do so. "I thank you," he said as Lady Frederica reached to pour the tea that had been brought in the moment he had entered. "I know that I have behaved rather poorly and should very much like to apologize for my actions, Lady Frederica."

Lady Frederica said nothing for some moments. Instead, she focused entirely on pouring the tea for the three of them and in setting it out, one after the other. Percy was grateful for her consideration, of course, but found that, such was his anxiety, he could not even think of drinking the tea at present. All he wanted was for both the duchess and Lady Frederica to hear his apology and know that he was sincere. He had made nothing but a fool of himself and that, he was certain, was plain to them both.

"I thank you," he murmured as the tea was set down before him. "You are very kind, Lady Frederica."

The look in her green eyes was a trifle unsettling. There was a coldness there that he could not pretend was not present and her smile, although apparent, did not reach her eyes. She was, he realized, a rather lovely creature, with her golden curls and emerald eyes, but the lack of warmth in her expression certainly did not encourage him toward her.

But that is all entirely your own doing.

"I confess that I do not recall all that I did," he continued, before either the duchess or Lady Frederica could speak. "I was, I presume, very rude." He picked up his teacup. "You were, I am certain, very gracious, Lady Frederica." Taking a sip of his tea, he felt the silence fall between them and his heart twisted in his chest. Were they to say nothing at all? Were they just to leave him as he was at present, struggling to find the words to say whereby he might improve the situation between them all?

"Lord Wetherby," the duchess looked back at him steadily, her brows low, "you were very rude indeed to Lady Frederica last evening. She, of course, had the strength of character to rebuff you and chose to do so without hesitation." A tiny smile flickered about her lips although it was gone in a moment. "You did not take too kindly to such a refusal, however, which was why we were both all the more grateful to Lord Greenford."

Percy dropped his head. "Lord Greenford is an excellent gentleman," he agreed, embarrassment searing his heart. "It was he who came to inform me of what I had done, else, as I have said, I would have been entirely unaware of it."

Lady Frederica let out a sigh, shaking her head as she did so. "You were foxed, Lord Wetherby," she stated calmly. "You expected me to dance with you and appeared most agitated when I refused. To have done so would have only caused great embarrassment, and that was not something I was willing to endure."

"But of course," he replied, setting his teacup back down in the saucer with a rattle. "I came not to express any sort of irritation toward you, Lady Frederica, but rather only to apologize for my own foolishness and arrogance that was so obviously displayed last evening, as well as to beg your forgiveness for any embarrassment that was brought to you. If there is anything that I can do in order to improve matters in any way, then please only speak the word and I will do it at once."

Lady Frederica held his gaze steadily, her eyes calm and unwavering as she listened to him. Percy sat back just a little, his words at an end as he found nothing further to say. Lady Frederica picked up her teacup and took a small sip, setting the cup back down and then exchanging a glance with the duchess.

"I appreciate your eagerness to apologize," she said quietly. "It is a little frustrating that you cannot recall for yourself all that you did, Lord Wetherby, but I must hope that you will not behave so toward either myself or any other young ladies again." She gave him the smallest smile possible, although her eyes remained very cold indeed. "I am grateful to you for your willingness to attempt to reconcile."

Feeling as though he had been given a stern talking to, Percy dropped his head and closed his eyes for a moment. "I can assure you that I will never behave so again," he promised her, lifting his head and seeing the doubtful glance shared between Lady Frederica and the duchess. "One such evening is more than enough for me. I have seen the error of my ways and feel such a great shame that it is almost more than I can bear. I am very grateful indeed to Lord Greenford and have told him so without hesitation." He rose to his feet, feeling that his visit was now at an end. There was very little more for him to say. "I shall not impose on your kindness any longer, Your Grace, Lady Frederica." He bowed low, just as they both rose to their feet. Neither of them protested that he did not need to depart so soon. Instead, they both appeared to be more than contented to see him leave their company. "I do hope that you have a pleasant afternoon."

"Good day, Lord Wetherby," Lady Frederica replied, before the duchess made her own farewell. "And I thank you again for your willingness to come and apologize in such a manner."

"It was the very least I could do," he told her before turning smartly on his heel and walking from the room.

3

Frederica let out a sigh of relief as Lord Wetherby quit the room, then looked toward the duchess, who was finally taking her seat again.

"Well," she began, slumping back in her chair. "That was an unexpected visit."

The duchess laughed softly, her eyes twinkling. "Not too unexpected, I think," she said as Frederica's brow lifted in surprise. "Lord Greenford, I knew, would inform Lord Wetherby of what had occurred, for he appears to be an excellent gentleman, and of course, in order to stay in both your own and society's good graces, Lord Wetherby would do his utmost to apologize just as quickly as he could."

Frederica shook her head to herself, picking up her teacup so that she might take another sip. "It is frustrating that he did not remember a single thing about his foolish behavior," she said as the duchess nodded. "I should have preferred it if he had recalled what he had done, for then the apology would have been a good deal more sincere."

"I do not think it lacked sincerity, Frederica," the duchess replied as Frederica finished drinking her tea. "The gentleman was clearly ashamed to know of what he had done and what he had demanded of you and has resolved never to do such a thing again." She looked back at the vacant chair where Lord Wetherby had been sitting. "When he spoke, I was certain there was nothing but earnestness in his words and his expression. It was clear to me, at least, that he meant every word."

Considering this for a moment or two, Frederica eventually conceded. "I suppose that it must be so, if *you* have seen such a thing in him, Louisa," she replied, a wry smile on her lips. "I confess I am still a little angry and therefore inclined to judge him more harshly."

"At least you are able to admit such a thing, although certainly I do not blame you," the duchess replied, smiling back at her. "I doubt very much that Lord Wetherby will have any great intentions of seeking out your company again, however. You gave him something of a set-down."

"I did, yes," Frederica replied, a giggle escaping her as she recalled how sharply she had spoken and how Lord Wetherby had dropped his head. "I did not mean to add to his shame, but I did want to speak openly about what had occurred, especially given that he had no recollection of it himself."

"I think you spoke very well," the duchess replied, just as a knock came at the door. "Come now, let us set all thought of Lord Wetherby aside. It appears you have another afternoon caller, my dear."

Frederica chuckled and sat up a little straighter as the duchess called for the butler to enter. This afternoon had been already quite busy with various callers and she had to confess that she had enjoyed it all thus far. Even Lord Wetherby, she reflected, as she rose to her feet. Something in her had been glad to see him, had been contented to know that he had been unsettled in hearing what he had done and had, therefore, come to apologize profusely. Not that she intended to have anything akin to an acquaintance with the gentleman, of course. As far as Frederica was concerned, Lord Wetherby had proven his character to her already and she did not think him either a reliable or a suitable acquaintance. Many other gentlemen in London would be much better suited to her company and her acquaintance. That thought brought Frederica a good deal of contentment.

～

"Good evening, Lady Frederica."

Frederica smiled back at Lord Merseyside as she rose from her curtsy. "Good evening, Lord Merseyside," she replied as her host beamed delightedly at her. "I thank you for your very kind invitation. This evening will be quite wonderful, I am sure."

Lord Merseyside, an older gentleman with grey at his temples and kind, blue eyes, smiled all the more at her compliment. "You are most kind, Lady Frederica," he told her. "I do hope that you might be convinced to play for the guests later this evening?"

"I am certain you will be able to convince me," Frederica replied, before taking her leave of him and making her way to where the duke and duchess were waiting.

"You have made an excellent impression upon Lord Merseyside, it seems," the duke said, a twinkle in his eye that immediately put Frederica on her guard. "He is a little old, perhaps, but I am sure that your father might be more than willing to be convinced."

Frederica resisted the urge to nudge her uncle with her elbow, seeing how he grinned back at her. "I hardly think I should consider Lord Merseyside," she stated as the duchess chuckled. "Why, he is almost as old as you."

At this, the smile faded from her uncle's face, making both the duchess and Frederica laugh, the sound mingling among the conversations and laughter that came from the other guests at the soiree.

"Very well, very well," the duke muttered as his wife took his arm and squeezed it gently. "I shall not tease you, Frederica, given that your tongue is razor-sharp."

"And I know very well how to respond to such teasing, Uncle,"

Frederica replied with a smile of her own. "After all, I have been your niece my entire life."

This made the duke laugh and Frederica exchanged a delighted glance with the duchess, glad to see her uncle in such high spirits. Last Season had been a particularly difficult one for both the duchess and him, and Frederica was all the more glad that they had found such contentment and happiness together.

"Oh, goodness."

The duchess' quiet murmur caught Frederica's attention and she glanced over her shoulder, only to see Lord Wetherby greeting their host.

She turned back to the duchess and shrugged. "It is to be expected," she said quietly. "It is not as though he will refrain from entering society."

"No, indeed," the duchess agreed softly. "But it will prove to us this evening whether or not the gentleman is true in his desire to restrain himself so that he does not behave as he did before."

The duke, who had heard all that had taken place, including Lord Wetherby's calling upon them that afternoon in order to apologize, let out a huff of breath.

"In my estimation, it will take a strong character to make entirely certain that one will not behave so again," he said, and Frederica considered his remark carefully. "We will have to simply wait and see."

Frederica lifted one shoulder in a half-shrug. "I care not," she said as the duchess smiled. "Lord Wetherby is not a gentleman I intend to acquaint myself with further in any way." Seeing a young lady that she recognized, Frederica gestured toward her quietly. "Might I go to greet Lady Sarah?" she asked, and the Duchess nodded, turning around so that they might walk together. The duke excused himself and the two ladies set out across the floor, with Frederica leaving all thought of Lord Wetherby behind.

"And then it seemed as though we should never get to London."

Frederica caught her breath, staring wide-eyed at Lady Nottingham. "But you must have done so, in order to be present this evening," she said as the small group of guests seemed to lean in closer in order to hear what Lady Nottingham said next. "What happened?"

Lady Nottingham gestured to her daughter, who had, thus far, stood rather quietly, her head low and her hands clasped in front of her.

"My daughter was, of course, very frightened," she explained as Frederica nodded in understanding. "It was growing late and, what with the stories of highwaymen and the like, we were both becoming very anxious. The driver had not returned, and the tiger was standing by the side of the carriage, waiting for his return." She smiled then, an expression of relief filling her features as though she had only just recalled all that had occurred. "Another carriage approached and Josephine clung to me desperately, fearing that we should be stolen from or..." She shuddered, leaving them all without doubt as to what the young lady had been worried about. "However, much to our relief, it was not highwaymen. Instead, it was none other than Lord and Lady Sinclair, come from Scotland to London."

A murmur of relief ran around the group as everyone listened intently.

"We were already acquainted, of course, and I could not have expressed my relief upon seeing them any more than I did," Lady Nottingham continued, reaching across to squeeze her daughter's arm. "Within minutes, we were settled aboard their carriage with only the very most important pieces of our luggage taken with us. The rest remained with our tiger, who stayed with our carriage until the driver returned with whomever he had found to fix the wheel. When I told all to my son, Lord Nottingham, he was very upset indeed."

"I am sure you are now very glad to be back in London, Miss Chalmers," said someone near to Frederica, and the young lady lifted her head and nodded, although no smile pulled at her lips. "What a great ordeal that must have been."

Something flickered in Miss Chalmers' eyes as she nodded again, saying nothing but clearly either still distraught about what had occurred or simply choosing not to speak about it at all. Frederica watched her closely, wondering why the young lady had not said a word about the events that had transpired. Was there something more to the situation that Lady Nottingham either did not want to speak of or had chosen deliberately not to mention again? Or was it simply that the matter had been so very frightening that the young lady did not even want to *think* of it?

"A terrible situation indeed," she heard someone say, recognizing the voice but being uncertain as to whom it might be. "We are, I am sure, all very glad that you are returned to society again."

Frederica lifted her brows in surprise as the change in Lady Nottingham's expression was both immediate and obvious. Her eyes narrowed just a fraction, her lips thinned, and when she responded, there was a tightness to her voice that had not been present before.

"I am grateful for your concern, Lord Wetherby," she said, catching Frederica's attention all the more. "My daughter is, as you can see, still a little shaken by the experience."

"But of course, that is most understandable," Lord Wetherby replied, making Frederica realize why she had recognized the voice. "I do hope you recover yourself soon, Miss Chalmers. A few more days in society and you will have forgotten all about it."

Someone else began to ask Lady Nottingham something more about what had occurred, and it was only then that Lady Nottingham's dark expression began to ease. Frederica watched with interest, wondering at the change and, in particular, wondering why it seemed that Lady Nottingham appeared to be so at odds with Lord Wetherby. Had he done the same to Miss Chalmers as he had done to Frederica? Perhaps there was a dislike there, an awareness that he was not the very best of gentlemen, and that was why Lady Nottingham did not much want to continue speaking with him.

Why are you thinking of Lord Wetherby again?

The quiet voice in her head berated her severely and Frederica turned her interest back toward what Lady Nottingham was saying, glancing across at Louisa, who seemed just as intrigued as she.

"Lady Frederica?"

Her head turned and she smiled at Lord Livingstone, who was bowing toward her. "Good evening, Lord Livingstone."

"Good evening," he replied, drawing her into conversation and away from Lady Nottingham. "Might I enquire as to whether or not you are enjoying the soiree thus far? I have heard," he continued, a twinkle in his eye, "that you might soon be convinced to play the pianoforte for us, which, I am sure, would be very gratifying indeed."

Frederica laughed and, seeing the duchess watching them with a gentle smile on her face, continued on with her conversation without hesitation.

The rest of the evening passed in much the same manner. Frederica spoke to various ladies and gentlemen and *did* end up playing the pianoforte for the guests, as one of many young ladies who were asked to perform. When she caught Lord Wetherby's eye, she smiled gently and nodded at him before turning her head away and making no attempt to converse with him. She also noticed that he had a glass of brandy in his hand and felt herself relieved that she had chosen not to further their acquaintance. It was not that she wanted to give him the cut direct or to do anything so cruel, but rather to simply make certain that he was aware there could never be a friendship between them. Not that such a thing mattered, given that she was convinced that his interest in being introduced to her was simply to make certain he could say that he now knew the Duke and Duchess of Ellsworth.

"You enjoyed this evening, then?"

"I did, very much," Frederica replied, sitting back against the squabs as the duke and duchess sat opposite. A contented sigh escaped her as the duke rapped on the roof, telling the driver that they could move away. "It was a very pleasant evening."

"And you have continued to make an excellent impression, my dear," the duke replied kindly. "I have not heard anything but praise for you, and your performance at the pianoforte was lauded by many."

Frederica smiled to herself as the first fingers of dawn began to wrap themselves around the night sky. "I was very grateful for the compliments that followed," she said quietly. "There were a good many young ladies who played this evening. I think all of them very fine players indeed."

The duchess smiled back at her, her features only just illuminated by the lifting of the night's darkness. "Miss Chalmers played well, I thought," she said as Frederica nodded. "Such a quiet young lady."

"Of whom are you speaking?" the duke asked, with the duchess then going into a long explanation of who the young lady was and the difficulties both she and her mother, Lady Nottingham, had endured as they had attempted to make their way to London. Frederica listened with only half an ear, her eyelids already drooping with tiredness. A small frown caught her brow as she heard what sounded like more horses' hooves coming along the road, only to hear the driver curse loudly.

"Good gracious."

Frederica was forced to brace herself as the carriage pulled sharply to the left, with both the duke and duchess searching for purchase as the carriage came to a sudden stop. A hackney rushed by them, so close to their own that had the driver not pulled them away and into the side, then Frederica was quite certain there would have been the most dreadful accident. The whinny of horses broke through the air around them, leaving Frederica panting for breath with the shock and the fright that had caught her.

"My greatest apologies, Your Grace."

The driver appeared at the window, his eyes wide.

"There came a hackney from behind us," he explained as the duke righted himself. "Thought they would have gone into us."

"I think they might well have done," Frederica replied as her uncle nodded slowly. "You did well."

The driver's expression of worry returned to one of relief as he clasped his cap in his hands, twisting it this way and that. Frederica looked pointedly at her uncle, who, after a moment, nodded, his jaw tight.

"That is understandable," he said as the driver let out a breath of relief. "You have done well. I thank you."

"Thank you for your understanding, Your Grace." The driver nodded his head and then turned to climb back up to his seat, leaving the three of them in the carriage to catch their breaths, with Frederica's heart still pounding furiously.

"Whoever was driving like that was utterly foolish," the duchess said as the duke nodded gravely. "They could have caused an accident."

"It is just as well your driver is as aware as he is," Frederica replied. "For I am sure that the hackney might have knocked into us completely, had he not taken such action."

"Indeed," the duke stated, sounding still rather upset and angry. "If I should ever find out who was driving that, I will—"

"You will not be able to do so," the duchess interrupted calmly. "Be still, now. Do not allow what has been a remarkably pleasant evening to be spoiled by a fit of pique at someone else's foolishness."

Frederica smiled to herself as she sat back against the squabs once more, her fright leaving her entirely as tiredness once more washed over her. She was eager to retire, eager to rest her weary head down upon the pillow. Aside from that very unsettling incident with the carriage, this evening had been very pleasant indeed.

∽

FREDERICA SAT UP STRAIGHT, her bedsheets pushed down all around her as her heart began to clamor furiously. What was it that had awakened her?

She frowned and swung her legs to the side of the bed, wondering what time it was. Making her way to the window, she pushed back one of the heavy curtains, wincing at the sunshine that shone in at her cheerfully. Turning her bleary eyes toward the clock on the mantlepiece, she read it as just after ten in the morning, meaning that she had plenty of time to rest before afternoon calls would begin.

But what woke me?

The question would not leave her, and Frederica frowned hard, rubbing one hand across her eyes as she turned back to look around the room. Nothing was unsettling in her bedchamber, nothing that would have startled her from in here. So where else had the sound come from?

Pulling on her dressing gown, Frederica rang the bell and sat down in one of the chairs by the fireplace, which had a very small fire beginning to burn itself out already. Evidently, the maid had decided that there was enough of a chill in the air this morning to merit a fire and Frederica was grateful for it.

"My lady." The maid bobbed a quick curtsy before closing the door behind her—but not before Frederica had heard a great hubbub of conversation coming from the hallway.

"I have your morning tea," the maid continued, setting it down in front of Frederica. "Might I fetch you something else? Do you wish to break your fast in the dining room or should I bring you something here?"

Frederica hesitated, then looked up at her maid. "Is there something wrong?" she asked as the maid's cheeks began to color. "Something woke me this morning and as yet, I am not certain what it was." She held her maid's gaze steadily, seeing the young lady drop her eyes to the floor.

"I am very sorry if it was I that woke you, my lady," the maid said hastily. "It is only that I got something of a fright this morning." She shook her head and spread her hands. "I can only apologize."

"What was it?" Frederica asked, pouring her tea into her china cup and watching in satisfaction as steam began to rise from it. "What was it that frightened you so?"

The maid said nothing, opening her mouth to speak and then closing it again, her eyes darting all across the room as though she was not certain whether or not to speak of what had scared her. Frederica said nothing but let her brows knit together as she turned her eyes back to the maid, making it quite clear by her appearance that she *would* be given an answer to her question. Eventually, the maid's shoulders slumped, and she shook her head again.

"My lady, I do not want to trouble you," she said abruptly, "but there is a gentleman in the bedchamber next to your own."

Frederica's mouth fell open, her hand poised with the teacup close to her mouth as the maid nodded fervently, as though to encourage Frederica to believe what was being said.

"A gentleman?" Frederica repeated, astonishment rolling through her. "Are you quite certain?"

The maid nodded. "I could not find the poker in your room, my lady, and so I went into the guest bedchamber that is a little away from your own. When I went inside, there was a gentleman lying on the bed!" Blinking rapidly, she placed one hand over her heart. "I got such a fright, I think I must have screamed."

"I am not surprised," Frederica replied, getting to her feet. "And is that what is being discussed at present?"

"The butler is not certain whether or not we should waken the master," she said as Frederica hurried to the door. "But the gentleman is still sleeping—my scream did not waken him at all—and so the staff are not sure what to do."

Nodding, Frederica walked to the door and pulled it open, seeing the butler, the housekeeper, two footmen, and a maid standing congregating together a short distance away. They all jumped to attention the moment they saw her, although Frederica did not feel any irritation or anger at their standing around.

"I hear we have an unexpected guest, Mister Jamieson," she said, speaking to the butler. "Might I ask what has been done thus far?"

The butler inclined his head. "My lady, I do apologize if we woke you," he said as Frederica shook her head. "There is a gentleman asleep on the bed in the guest bedchamber. It is only by chance that Mary found him, and even though she let out a very loud scream indeed, it did not appear to waken him."

Frederica turned her eyes toward the door, which was only a little ajar and not open wide enough for her to see into. "A gentleman, you say?" she asked, and the housekeeper and the butler nodded. "How can you be certain?"

"By the cut of his clothes, my lady," the housekeeper replied, her eyes wide with the evident shock of finding such a gentleman present. "And his boots, which, I must say, have been placed very neatly by the fireplace."

Not quite certain what to make of this—for what sort of gentleman would make his way into another's townhouse, take off his boots, and then lie down on the bed?

Frederica frowned hard.

"My uncle has perhaps invited someone to stay with us," she suggested, although this brought a heavy frown to the butler's lined forehead. "I confess that I would be very surprised if he *had* done so, however, given that he has not mentioned it to me."

"Or to me, my lady," the butler replied, spreading his hands. "I was not certain whether or not to waken the duke, but given the situation, I think it best to do so."

Frederica hesitated, then nodded. "Lock the door," she said firmly, taking control of the situation at hand. "I myself will dress and then will return to wait for the duke to attend. Of course, he must be the one to step inside and to speak to the gentleman within, for there is no telling as to what state this fellow might be in."

The housekeeper's eyes widened all the more and she hastily pulled out the keys from the pocket of her dress. Quickly pulling the door shut, she had the door locked in a moment.

"Excellent," Frederica said calmly. "Now, if someone will waken the duke, I shall dress and return here to keep vigil until he arrives. The rest of you may go about your duties."

The housekeeper nodded and stepped away, ushering the footmen and the maid to do the same.

"I will speak to His Grace at once," the butler said as Frederica turned back to make her way to her own bedchamber. "Thank you, my lady."

Frederica smiled back at him before she stepped into her own room, unable to pretend that she did not find a great deal of curiosity rising in her chest as she thought about the gentleman in the guest bedchamber. Just who was he? And for what possible reason had he come into her uncle's house, uninvited, only to make himself comfortable in one of the guest bedchambers? It was a very odd situation, and Frederica had to confess a great excitement in finding out the truth.

4

"I should rouse yourself hastily, if I were you."

Percy frowned hard as he struggled to open his eyes, wondering which of his staff had the audacity to speak to him in such a manner.

"At once, sir!"

"Hold up there!" Percy exclaimed, his voice rasping and his throat sore as he rubbed one hand across his eyes. "How dare you think to speak to me in such a way?" Opening his eyes, he looked around the room, only to focus on the sight of a tall gentleman standing to one side of the bed, his arms folded across his chest and a deep frown settling across his brow.

Percy caught his breath, pushing himself up quickly and looking all about him, only to realize—with horror—that he was not in his own bed.

"Lord Wetherby!"

Lady Frederica's shocked voice ran across the room toward him and Percy dropped his head into his hands, letting out a loud groan as he did so. Last evening was something of a blur and yet again, it seemed, he had imbibed a little too much.

"I presume there is some reason as to why I find you in my

house this morning?" the duke asked, his tone ringing with authority and making Percy cringe all the more as he dropped his hands and pushed himself into a standing position. His head screamed with pain, but he did not move or cry out. Whatever he had done, he had truly made a fool of himself this time.

"I cannot say at present, Your Grace," Percy replied heavily. "My thoughts are somewhat clouded."

"I can see that," the duke replied, grimacing as Percy glanced at him. "Well, we cannot throw you from the house at present, for fear that someone will see you and, in turn, begin to speak and whisper of what they have seen. No doubt many rumors will begin to fly around London because of your presence here, should you be returned to your house at present." With a heavy frown still settled over his brow, the duke cut the air with his hand. "You will remain here, Lord Wetherby. My staff will see to your clothes and you will make yourself more presentable and then join us at the dining table for breakfast."

Dark clouds settled over Percy's heart as he hung his head, confused beyond measure as to why he was here in this house and what he had chosen to do last evening. "You are very kind, Your Grace."

"I am doing what I believe is best for my own family and situation," the duke snapped, clearly angry with Percy's behavior. "As I have said, join us when you are ready. Come, Frederica."

Percy's eyes snagged on Lady Frederica, who had been standing just inside the door, staring at him as he had risen from his bed. Her eyes were wide, her face pale with shock. Watching her turn away with the duke, Percy felt his shame pour all through him as he was left alone with only a maid and footman ready to aid him in whatever he required. He dared not think about what he looked like, quite certain that he was entirely disheveled, which only added to his disgrace.

He groaned and rubbed one hand over his face.

"I will fetch you some water, my lord," Percy heard the maid say, before the footman asked if there was anything he could do to assist Percy in some way. Removing his cravat and peeling off his shirt, Percy handed the latter to the footman and asked him to find a way to remove the creases, so that, at the very least, he might appear a little more presentable. Being left alone for the first time since he had woken, Percy made his way to the mirror that hung on the wall and looked at his reflection, seeing the bags under his eyes and the dark shadow around his jaw.

Just what have I done?

~

IT WAS some time later before Percy felt able to join the duke, the duchess, and Lady Frederica at the dining room table. He had not wanted to keep them waiting, not after what he had endured himself, but the pressing of his shirt and, indeed, the removal of one or two stains had taken a good deal longer than he had expected. His courage almost failed him as he approached the dining room, having been directed there by the butler, but Percy forced himself to lift his shoulders and to step inside, knowing precisely what was to face him.

The duke, duchess, and Lady Frederica sat together at the dining room table, having clearly already broken their fast. The duchess was busy pouring tea for herself and Lady Frederica stopped as he entered, rising to her feet to greet him although Percy felt as though he deserved no such respect.

"Do be seated."

The duke's voice was low and severe, leaving Percy inclined to hang his head in shame. He went to sit down at once, feeling three sets of eyes on him and knowing that they would be seeking an explanation—an explanation he was not certain he could give.

"Well, at least you look a little more respectable," Lady Frederica remarked, her words sharp. "Would you care for some tea?"

Taken aback by her offer, Percy lifted his head to see Lady Frederica waiting for him to answer, one eyebrow arched.

"I—I would be very grateful," he answered, and she rose from her chair to pick up another china cup and handed it to the duchess, who poured the tea at once. Percy could not help but watch with astonishment, having expected to have been bombarded with questions and then thrown from the house without so much as a morsel of kindness. He did not deserve any such thing from them, not when he had behaved so.

"Here." She set it down before him, her eyes meeting his for just a moment before she turned to seat herself once more. Percy dropped his gaze to his steaming cup of tea, his heart quailing as he prepared to speak.

"I am sure there is nothing I can say that would recommend itself enough to be a satisfactory apology," he began, keeping his head low. "Indeed, if there was, then I should say it at once."

The duke cleared his throat and Percy looked up.

"How did you manage to make your way into my house?" he asked, and Percy shook his head. "And *why* did you do so?"

Percy closed his eyes, his brow furrowing. "I do not recall a good deal about last night, Your Grace," he said honestly, knowing that such an explanation was not at all satisfactory. "Which, I confess, I am a little perturbed about given that I did not drink more than one glass of brandy."

A quiet laugh came from Lady Frederica, which, in turn, caught everyone's attention. Three sets of eyes turned to her and a slight flush came into her cheeks as she gestured toward Percy.

"Are you quite certain of that, Lord Wetherby?" she asked, her tone entirely disbelieving. "It may be that you believe yourself to have had only one glass, but given your penchant for—"

"I am quite certain." Percy spoke without thinking, rudely interrupting Lady Frederica. His tone was hard, but he did not want her to think even for a moment that he had managed to get himself into the same situation as he had done before. "Forgive me for interrupting you, Lady Frederica, but I am quite certain that I drank nothing more than that. I was quite determined, you see, and therefore took great care."

Lady Frederica still appeared to be rather disbelieving given that she gave him a miniscule shake of her head and turned away, but Percy knew in his heart that he was correct. He *had* been cautious. He had only drunk a little brandy and even that had tasted foul, most likely because he had still been enduring the effects of too much the night before.

"My memory is very clouded indeed," Percy admitted. "I have been struggling to recall anything about last evening, even though I am quite certain I was not in my cups." He spread his hands. "As for why I found myself in your house and in your guest bedchamber, Your Grace, I cannot understand."

The duke sighed heavily and passed one hand over his eyes. "It is very strange," he muttered. "None of the staff heard your arrival. Most of them, of course, had already retired to bed, but those who waited for us to return heard nothing."

"Might I ask," Percy said, a little hesitantly, "whether or not the front door was unlocked?"

The duke shook his head. "It would not have been," he said without hesitation. "The butler was informed to lock it tightly and that I should knock when I returned. It is a habit that I have formed for many years and the butler would not have deviated from such instructions."

"Then I must have entered through the servants' entrance," Percy murmured, half to himself and half to the duke. "And, as you have said, if they were all abed then—"

"Then no one would have noticed your arrival," the duchess interrupted, her own brow lowering into a small frown. "But that surely must mean that you were not in your cups, Lord Wetherby. For if you had been, then I would expect that you might well have made a good deal of noise upon your arrival and surely someone would have woken and heard you?" She looked toward the duke, who, after a moment, nodded.

A sheen of relief washed through Percy, his forehead beading with sweat. He did not want the duke or the duchess to believe that he had been foxed for what would have been the second time and yet did not have any real explanation as to why he had been found in the house.

"It must be a trifle unsettling for you yourself, Lord Wetherby," the duchess continued, turning back to look at him. "To have no recollection as to why you were here must be somewhat upsetting."

"I am only ashamed," Percy told her truthfully. "If I had some explanation, I would share it with you at once, Your Grace, but as it stands, I am without anything to say."

Lady Frederica sat up straight in her chair, her eyes bright as she swung her head toward him. "Your driver," she said excitedly as Percy stared back at her. "Would your driver not know of what occurred? Surely if you had your own carriage, you would have—"

"I would have had it driven here and requested them to leave me nearby," Percy finished as Lady Frederica nodded fervently. "Yes indeed, Lady Frederica, that may well be so. My driver might..." He frowned and shook his head as a memory slowly began to return to him. "I recall, however, that I was not in my carriage," he continued, speaking slowly as it came back to him a little more, hazy and uncertain. "I do not know why but, for whatever reason, I recall that I found a hackney." He shook his head, lifted one hand, and pinched the bridge of his nose. Closing his eyes, he remembered how he had climbed into a hackney which must have been some distance away from Lord Merseyside's house given that the streets near to his townhouse would have been filled with carriages. "Why should I have done that?"

"Would you have spoken to your driver?" Lady Frederica asked as Percy dropped his hand back to his side. "Would you have informed him as to why you were taking a hackney?"

"I doubt it very much," Percy replied, shaking his head. "There may be something he can tell us, but it will not be as we had first hoped."

The duchess suddenly caught her breath, her eyes rounding as she stared at Percy. No one said anything for some moments, looking back at the lady as one and waiting for her to speak.

"I recall," the duchess breathed, turning her gaze back toward her husband, "that last night we found ourselves in some difficulty when our driver had to pull the carriage to the side in order to avoid—"

"A hackney," the duke said at the very same time as his wife. "Yes, of course. How could I not recall such a thing?" He turned his gaze back to Percy. "We were forced onto the side of the road by the careless, reckless driving of a hackney," he explained as Percy listened wordlessly. "If that was you in there, Lord Wetherby, then it suggests that either the driver himself was foolish or there was some reason that he was going as fast as he was. Perhaps to avoid someone or to escape from something?"

He spoke as though he expected Percy to remember what had occurred, but Percy could only shake his head. "I am sorry that such a thing happened to you all and can only apologize further if I was the cause of it," he said as the duke's brow furrowed once more, "but there is nothing I can say that will give any sort of explanation. I do not know why I went to the hackney. I do not know why I told the driver to drive in such a ridiculous fashion, if that is what I did. And I certainly do not recall why I then decided to climb into your house and make my way to a guest bedchamber, Your Grace." He spread his hands, wishing that his memory would return. "In time, I might recall a little more, but for the present, there is naught but shadows and whispers in my mind, Your Grace. Forgive me for that."

The duke, who clearly believed that Percy would remember something more should he only tell him about the carriage, sighed and nodded. "I understand," he said eventually. "You say that you were not in your cups, Lord Wetherby, and, whilst I would be inclined not to believe your words, I shall, for the moment, trust them to be true. Which only goes on to beg the question—why do you recall so little?"

Percy threw up his hands, feeling a great sense of frustration flood him. "Would that I could say, Your Grace," he answered honestly. "You find me greatly ashamed this morning, greatly ashamed. I have woken to find myself in a room and a house that I ought not to be in, with no understanding of how I came to be here or what my intentions were. It is to my everlasting shame that I have done such a thing." He glanced to Lady Frederica, who was watching him with sharp eyes, her lips in a thin line as though she could not quite bring herself to believe anything he had to say. "And I can only apologize all the more for what I have done, wishing desperately that there was more I could say by way of explanation."

Lady Frederica sighed and looked toward her uncle, who, after a moment, nodded.

"Pray, take something to eat," he said, gesturing to the side where a good many dishes stood waiting, their silver trays hiding them from Percy's view. "There is no point in you sitting here with us without breaking your fast." He himself rose from his chair and made his way to the door. "Thereafter, perhaps you would be good enough to send a note to your driver requesting that your carriage be brought here during the time for afternoon calls?"

Percy nodded, his stomach twisting this way and that. "But of course."

"That way, you can depart without raising the suspicions of anyone," the duke said, looking pointedly at Percy, who felt heat climb up his spine, embarrassed beyond measure. "My staff will say not a word to anyone, for if they do so, then they are already aware that they will leave my employment without a reference. Therefore, both your reputation and that of my own house will be protected."

"You are very kind, Your Grace."

The duke waved a hand, brushing aside Percy's words. "Not at all," he answered softly, looking first to his wife and then to his niece. "There is something of a mystery here at present, I believe, and if it is merely that you *were* a little drunk, then I *shall* find it out and will bring that particular piece of news to you, Lord Wetherby." His eyes were hard as he looked back at Percy, who, in turn, lifted his chin and held the duke's gaze steadily, quite determined that he had *not* been so. "However, if it appears that it is as you have said, then there is a good deal more for us to understand."

"And understand it, we will," the duchess added, reaching out one hand toward the duke, who took it at once, pressing it lightly as he smiled at her.

"I cannot imagine that you and Lady Frederica would be contented to leave things as they stand," he told the duchess as Percy looked on. "I shall speak to Lord Merseyside this afternoon and discover if there is anything he can tell me about last evening as regards you, Lord Wetherby."

"I am grateful," Percy replied, rising respectfully from his chair as the duke made to take his leave. "I will, of course, do anything I can to be of aid to you, Your Grace. I swear on my very life that I was not overcome by liquor last evening, however. I know for certain that Lord Merseyside will be able to confirm it."

The duke looked back at him steadily for some moments, then nodded. "Very well," he stated as Percy inclined his head in gratitude. "Do send word to your driver as soon as you can, Lord Wetherby. And now, if you will excuse me."

The duchess smiled up at her husband before he took his leave, with Percy making his way to the side of the room in search of something to eat.

"You will find us in the drawing room, Lord Wetherby, when you have finished breaking your fast."

Percy turned to see Lady Frederica and the duchess moving away from the table. Lady Frederica bore no smile on her face, although, at the very least, there appeared to be no anger or irritation settled there.

"But of course," he murmured, bowing. "I quite understand."

"You are more than welcome to join us," the duchess continued as Percy listened quietly. "Or, if you should wish for solitude, then the library or the parlor is available to you. We shall not be insulted if you choose the latter, so pray, feel no obligation."

Percy bowed low. "I thank you for your generosity, Your Grace," he replied as a small smile graced the duchess' lips. "I will, I think, find a quiet place to reflect and consider, in the hope that something will return to me."

"A very wise idea," Lady Frederica remarked, making it quite plain that she did not wish for his company, for her lips bore no smile as the duchess' did and, indeed, her eyes were sharp and cold. "I do hope that you will find some answers, Lord Wetherby."

"As do I, Lady Frederica," Percy replied fervently. "As do I."

5

Had the *ton* known of what had occurred with Lord Wetherby, then surely all of London would be abuzz with the news. Gossip would be threading its way through the streets of London, everyone would be whispering of it, and Lord Wetherby himself would not have any opportunity to so much as lift his head in public.

However, that had *not* occurred, Frederica considered as she walked alongside the duchess. Lord Wetherby had spoken to his driver at length but nothing of importance had been revealed. The driver had stated that, for whatever reason, Lord Wetherby had flung himself out of the carriage and had told the driver to return home before hurrying off into the night. That was all that had been said, and the little that had been given to them by way of explanation was, Frederica thought, more than a little frustrating. The duke had returned from speaking with Lord Merseyside later that same day but had been entirely unable to confirm what Frederica had always believed—that Lord Wetherby had again imbibed far too much and, as such, had found himself in a drunken state. Lord Merseyside had apparently told the duke that he had bid Lord Wetherby farewell and that he had thought him fatigued, certainly, and that he might have had a few glasses of brandy but that he had not been foxed. Thus, Frederica had been forced to admit—only to herself, of course—that Lord Wetherby had not been as she had believed. Not that she had any intention of apologizing to the gentleman, however, for he had done more than enough already and, had he not been discovered, might have caused both her and the duke's name a good deal of damage.

"You are very quiet this afternoon."

Frederica looked toward the duchess as they walked quietly through St. James' Park. "I am thinking," she said by way of explanation. "And yes, I am thinking of Lord Wetherby. It seems very strange indeed to have discovered him so and for him to have so little recollection about why he was present."

"I would agree," the duchess replied, one shoulder lifting gently. "But we cannot know the truth of the matter and Lord Merseyside has made it clear that Lord Wetherby was not as we suspected him."

Frederica let out a long sigh, finding her heart still heavy despite the beauty of the day and the many acquaintances that they had already stopped to greet.

"You would like to know the truth, however," the duchess continued, a note of teasing in her voice. "I know that you are always inclined to such considerations, my dear, but in this regard, I do believe that it is best to simply leave things as they are."

"Perhaps," Frederica replied, not wanting to give up her curiosity yet, or to forget her many, many questions. "It is all so very strange, I must admit."

The duchess sighed. "We do not need any further rumors haunting us," she said, reminding Frederica of the difficult time the duchess had endured the previous Season. "I know just how trying they can be, and I would not like the same for you, my dear."

Frederica nodded but said nothing, aware of what the duchess was saying, and how she clearly wanted to protect her, but still finding a great, almost inexplicable urge to discover the truth.

"You should be focusing solely on acquainting yourself with the *beau monde* and enjoying the Season," the duchess continued firmly. "There are many gentlemen who will seek to call on you, I know, and I am certain you will be very glad of their company soon enough." She smiled at Frederica, who returned it. "Once you have gentlemen calling on you, once you are caught up in the whirlwind of balls and the like, I am sure you will have every cause to forget Lord Wetherby entirely."

Biting her lip, Frederica tried to force herself to remain silent but found she could not. The words seemed to burst from her, pushing her forward as she spoke.

"Do you accept his explanation?" she asked as the duchess looked back at her, startled. "That he was not in his cups, as he is so determined to prove?"

The duchess hesitated. "I do not know," she said quietly, looking away from Frederica for a few moments as she thought. "That does seem to be the most reasonable explanation, but Lord Merseyside said that he did not believe him to be so. And Lord Wetherby did seem quite certain that he had not drunk more than he ought, clearly wishing to make a better impression than he had done before."

Frederica twisted her lips, a line forming between her brows as she attempted to work out just what else might have aided Lord Wetherby's lack of memory.

"Perhaps he is lying," she suggested as the duchess' brow lifted. "Mayhap he *does* know all too well what he was doing in the duke's townhouse and simply does not want to say." As the idea grew all the more, Frederica found herself becoming a little more excited. "Yes, that may be it. He did not mean to fall asleep but accidentally did so and, thereafter, had no other excuse than to say that he could not recall what had occurred."

The duchess let out a long sigh, making Frederica all too aware that she was not particularly pleased about having to discuss matters such as this. "Frederica," she said sternly, "what possible motivation could Lord Wetherby have had to encourage him to do such a thing? He had already shamed himself greatly in front of us both and sneaking into the duke's house for some reason would only have increased that embarrassment." She shook her head. "No, I cannot think that he is lying. There is no motivation for him to do so."

Try as she might, Frederica could not cling onto the idea any longer, feeling it slip away from her like sand running through her fingers. The duchess was quite correct. There was no reason for Lord Wetherby to do such a thing, and the thought that had only a moment ago seemed so wonderful now began to slip away.

"You must forget about Lord Wetherby," the duchess insisted as they came across a small group of acquaintances. "It is not worth your time to think of the matter so. Leave it be, Frederica, for your own sake."

There was no time for Frederica to respond, for the group of ladies and gentlemen who had congregated together on the path now turned toward them both, clearly eager to have them join their conversation. Frederica greeted them all in turn and allowed herself to be drawn into the group, doing her utmost to push all thought of Lord Wetherby from her mind but finding that he still lingered there, regardless.

"I see that you are well acquainted with Lord Greenford," one of the young ladies said, her eyes twinkling as Frederica looked back at her steadily, wondering what the remark might mean. "He is an *exceptional* gentleman."

"I do not know him particularly well," Frederica replied quickly. "We have only recently been introduced."

"That is not what I have heard," said another, laughing just a little as Frederica tried her best to remain outwardly calm. "Lord Greenford is very keen to call upon you, Lady Frederica. I do hope you will welcome him."

Frederica felt a ripple of dislike run through her frame as she looked steadily back at Miss Templeton, whose mother was saying nothing to her daughter when, in Frederica's opinion, she ought to be quietly reminding her daughter not to be impertinent in making such comments.

"I am not particularly well acquainted with him, as I have said," she replied, seeing how the duchess frowned at Miss Templeton, who, upon seeing the expression on her face, immediately blushed furiously. "And as for whether I will either continue or develop such an acquaintance is entirely up to myself, Miss Templeton."

Silence ran around the group at Frederica's words, but she did not care. The young lady had been very foolish to make any sort of remark, and Frederica had never been shy when it came to speaking as openly as was permitted. In her opinion, it was best to put even the smallest hint of a rumor to bed before it grew and spread across society and, just as she had done here, Frederica felt quite justified in her behavior. Having seen just how poorly society had treated the duchess before she had wed because of rumors that were being spread about her had reminded Frederica of just how cruel the *ton* could be—and she was not about to permit whispers to be spread about her either.

"You are also acquainted with Lord Wetherby, I believe," said another young lady, changing the subject entirely. "I have not seen him these last two evenings, however." A slightly disappointed look came into her eyes. "I do hope he has not returned home."

"Why ever should he do such a thing?" another lady asked, dismissing the question with a laugh. "He is always in London for the Season and remains here for as long as he can."

Frederica listened with interest, allowing the conversation to flow around her without feeling any sort of need to engage with it.

"Do you think this will be the year that he will find himself a bride?" asked another, sounding a little wistful as she spoke. "I do hope so."

"I doubt it," came the reply. "He is always here solely to enjoy the Season and never seems to have any interest in such a thing as matrimony."

A small sigh escaped from one or two of the ladies whilst Frederica watched on quietly. She was learning more about Lord Wetherby's character simply by listening and allowing others to speak instead of engaging him in conversation herself. It seemed that he *was* as she had suspected—all too eager to further his own status and place in society rather than consider what he ought: matrimony and producing an heir. No doubt his enjoyment of society was precisely the reason that he drank to excess and now made such a fool of himself. In her own mind, Frederica was now quite convinced that, despite his protestations, Lord Wetherby *had* been in his cups the night he had come into the duke's house uninvited. There really was no other explanation.

"Lady Frederica?"

She jolted in surprise, realizing that she had become quite lost in thought and therefore had not been paying any attention to the conversation. "Yes?"

Lord Rainer grinned and cleared his throat. "I was merely wondering, Lady Frederica, whether or not you intend to dance at my ball this evening," he asked as Frederica smiled. "I am very pleased that you accepted the invitation, I must say, although I will now hope that you will be willing to stand up with me at one point in the evening."

"I shall be very glad to indeed," Frederica replied, quietly thinking to herself that Lord Rainer was a very amiable gentleman. "I thank you for considering me, Lord Rainer."

"Lord Rainer considers *everybody*," said another as Lord Rainer dropped his head, giving the impression of deep embarrassment. "You need not hide your face so, Lord Rainer, everyone knows your character to be so."

Frederica smiled to herself as the gentleman brushed aside the compliment once more, thinking that the duchess was quite correct in her guiding words. It was better for Frederica to consider her acquaintances and those around her at present, rather than let her thoughts return to Lord Wetherby over and over again. Here was Lord Rainer, who, whilst only a viscount, appeared to have a very charming manner. He clearly wanted to dance with her at the ball this evening, and Frederica had no reason to refuse him. To give her time and her thoughts to Lord Wetherby was ridiculous. She would have to make an effort to quell her curiosity and fling aside her unanswered questions if she was to make any progress in the Season this year. Had she not told the duchess that she wanted to make certain to find a suitable gentleman this Season? If she continued on as she was at present, lost in thought about Lord Wetherby, then surely that would only detract from her search.

"I look forward to this evening, Lord Rainer," she said as he smiled at her. "I am sure it will be a most enjoyable evening indeed."

∼

THE BALL WAS, as Frederica had expected, an excellent affair. The orchestra played marvelously well, the food and refreshments were of a higher standard than she had expected, and the company was altogether wonderful. Frederica had spent the evening talking, laughing, and dancing with a good many acquaintances and had even been introduced to a few more. Any time she caught herself looking for Lord Wetherby, she would force her eyes away from the crowded room and look instead into the face of whoever was by her side, whether that was the duchess or another acquaintance. And should her thoughts turn to him, Frederica made certain to think of something entirely different almost at once, simply so that she would not permit him to linger there. It took something of an effort, certainly, but Frederica was quite determined to continue doing so.

"Ah, Lady Frederica."

She turned, smiling, her eyes alighting upon Lord Greenford.

"Good evening, Lord Greenford," she replied, bobbing a quick curtsy. "Have you been enjoying the ball this evening?"

"Very much," he said, bowing low as the duchess came to join them. "Might I enquire as to whether or not your dance card is available for me to peruse?" His eyes twinkled. "I am a little tardy this evening and fear now that I have lost my opportunity."

Frederica laughed and slipped it from her wrist, trying her best to ignore the memory of those two young ladies talking about Lord Greenford in such eager terms. "I have three remaining," she replied as Lord Greenford took it from her with a murmur of thanks. "Thank you, Lord Greenford. You are very kind."

"Not at all," he replied, putting his name in not one but two spaces. "I look forward to dancing with you this evening."

Frederica smiled and took the card from him, thanking him as she did so. They talked for a few minutes longer before Lord Greenford begged to be excused, stating that he had arranged to dance the country dance with Lady Diane.

"Then I suggest you find her," Frederica laughed, and he inclined his head, grinning as he did so. "For the room is very large indeed and the dance will soon begin."

Both she and the duchess watched Lord Greenford walk away, with Frederica tilting her head just a little as she observed him. Lord Greenford dressed in a somewhat flamboyant manner—although it could hardly be said to be exaggerated—but Frederica considered that he did have an excellent character.

"Might I ask, Frederica," the duchess began, turning so that she now stood directly in front of Frederica, "whether Lord Greenford is someone you might consider?"

Frederica laughed, her heart squeezing gently. "I do not think so, Louisa," she replied as the duchess listened carefully. "I have said that I wish very much to find a gentleman for whom I have an affection. I can never have such an affection for Lord Greenford, even though he is a remarkably kind gentleman."

"No?" the duchess asked softly, and Frederica shook her head. "You feel nothing for him?"

"Nothing other than a gratitude for his friendship," Frederica replied truthfully. "That is not enough, I fear."

"Not if you are seeking something a good deal more intimate," the duchess conceded. "I do hope you will forgive me for asking you such a thing, Frederica."

Frederica reached out and pressed the duchess' hand. "I am *glad* that you feel able to do so," she answered honestly. "We have a very dear friendship, you and I, and there should be that openness between us."

The duchess smiled. "Good. I am glad."

"Lady Frederica?"

Her smile still lingering, Frederica turned her head only to see the somewhat shamefaced Lord Wetherby standing there, only just rising from his bow. Her heart slammed into her chest in shock and it took her a moment to curtsy, blinking rapidly as she did so. It had been two days since she had last seen Lord Wetherby, two days since he had appeared in her uncle's townhouse without explanation and then departed in his own carriage without speaking to her further.

"Good evening, Lord Wetherby," she managed to say, surprised that he had come to seek her out.

"Good evening," he said, before turning to the duchess. "Good evening, Your Grace."

"Good evening," came the gentle reply. "And how are you, Lord Wetherby?"

A kindness was present in the duchess' voice that was entirely absent from Frederica's heart, and Frederica felt a sharp sting of guilt at her lack of compassion.

"I am well," he replied, although his expression remained somewhat grave, his eyes no longer holding any sort of brightness and his brow lined. "I have come, Lady Frederica, to ask if I might be permitted to dance with you this evening?" His brows knotted together, and he dropped his gaze, spreading his hands as he did so. "I know that I have no right to ask you such a thing, given that I behaved so foolishly the last time I sought a dance from you, but I hope that, on this occasion, I might prove to you that I am not the gentleman you must surely believe me to be." His eyes lifted to hers, his hands still spread. "If you wish to refuse me, then I will, of course, understand."

Frederica swallowed hard, glancing at the duchess but seeing the tiny shrug that was returned to her. It was Frederica's decision and remained solely hers. She could lie, she thought, pretend that she had no dances remaining and therefore was unable to offer him her dance card despite his very kind offer—but the thought of being so false left a bitter taste in her mouth. Lord Wetherby was looking back at her steadily now, clearly waiting for her to say something, to agree or disagree, to accept or refuse.

She took in a quick breath.

"That is most generous of you, Lord Wetherby," she said carefully, realizing that her heart was still quite uncertain as to what she ought to do. "I fear that I do, indeed, think a particular way when it comes to you. However," she continued quietly, seeing how he looked away from her again, his lips tight, "I do have only one dance remaining."

Lord Wetherby lifted his eyes to hers and looked back at her with such an uncertainty in his eyes that Frederica felt her heart twist painfully. Was he uncertain as to whether or not she was offering that particular dance to him? Did he think that she would be so cruel as to tell him what dance she had remaining, only to refuse to permit him to take it?

"Here."

She slipped off her dance card and handed it to him and, much to her astonishment, Lord Wetherby let out a heavy sigh of evident relief before he took it from her.

"You have a forgiving spirit, Lady Frederica," he told her, putting his name in the only remaining space. "I am most grateful."

Frederica looked into his eyes and found herself smiling back at him gently, as though she wanted there to be no more difficulties between them. "But of course," she said softly. "There is no wisdom in holding a grudge, I suppose."

He said nothing more but bowed low, more formal than she had ever seen him before. She returned it with a quick curtsy, whilst the duchess watched on with interest. And then, he had turned on his heel and made his way from her, clearly only willing to return to her company once their dance was at hand.

"I think that was a wise decision, my dear."

Frederica glanced at the duchess before returning her gaze to Lord Wetherby's retreating back. "I must hope so," she said, a niggle of doubt in her mind as she looked down at her dance card. "Let us hope that this time, he is not in his cups when he comes back to find me."

"I am certain he will not have touched even a drop of liquor," the duchess replied firmly. "I think he is a little more aware than that."

Frederica smiled and made to say more, but then she saw Lord Stephenson approaching and realized that he was to be her partner for the country dance. Once more, she pushed all thought of Lord Wetherby from her mind and fixed her attention slowly to Lord Stephenson. Lord Wetherby would have to prove himself and that time was yet to come. Frederica could only pray that he would not break the fragile trust she had placed in him.

6

The relief that Percy felt as he made his way from Lady Frederica's side was all-encompassing. He had forced himself toward her, had dared to ask her if she would accept a dance from him, and had instantly seen the doubt that had jumped into her eyes. The lady had been uncertain as to whether or not she ought to accept him, but he had told himself that, regardless of what she decided, he would accept it without question. Having fully expected her to refuse, to hear her offer him the final dance that remained on her card had been more than astonishing, and it had carried him from her side with both delight and gladness.

Perhaps he might be able to improve the situation between them both, in time. She was a very lovely young lady, certainly, but it was not her beauty that made him eager to improve his acquaintance with her. Rather, it was the sheer embarrassment that had washed over him time and again as he had thought about all that had occurred and all that Lady Frederica had endured from him. He still could not explain the reason for his appearance at the Duke of Ellsworth's townhouse, could find no real reason for anything he had done that night, but certainly, he was the only one to blame when it came to his lack of consideration for Lady Frederica the first night they had been introduced. That, at least, was something he could improve upon. Whether or not she would accept him, Percy had told himself that she would know of his desire to improve matters in the hope that such a thing alone would encourage her to think a little less poorly of him than she did at present.

"Not that I do not deserve it," he muttered to himself, making his way through the crowd and to a quieter part of the ballroom, where he knew he might find Lord Greenford. The gentleman grinned as he saw Percy, holding up a glass of brandy as though to say that he had acquired one for Percy himself.

"I thank you, but no," Percy replied as Lord Greenford's smile faded. "I am entirely without this evening."

"Why ever for, old boy?" asked Lord Venables, whom Lord Greenford had been talking to. "There's nothing wrong with it. I think it a very fine brandy indeed, although it is certainly not up to what I *myself* have at home."

Percy smiled. "I am sure it is excellent," he replied, "but I shall not permit myself to drink it, I am afraid. I wish to remain fully aware and awake at all times this evening." He shot a quick glance toward Lord Greenford, who merely shrugged and set the second glass down on the table near to them. "Besides which, if I am to dance, then I will need to remain fully competent."

Lord Greenford's brows rose. "You are to dance?"

"Indeed," Percy replied, feeling a sense of pride well up in his chest. "With Lady Frederica." He chuckled as Lord Greenford's eyes widened in evident astonishment. "You will understand now why I cannot take your brandy."

"I do, I do!" Lord Greenford answered hastily. "Lord Venables, you must forgive us for speaking so—but it seems that Lord Wetherby is to dance this evening."

"And must remain entirely sober throughout?" Lord Venables asked, sounding a little astonished. "Well, if you wish to do so, Lord Wetherby, then I suppose I cannot condemn you for it."

"I thank you," Percy replied, grinning.

"And you are only to dance with one lady in particular?" Lord Venables asked, and Percy nodded. "Why, do you have intentions toward her?"

"None at present," Percy replied firmly, fully aware of what stepping out with only Lady Frederica would mean to the *ton*. Perhaps he ought to find another young lady to dance with also. A quick glance around the room told him there were many young ladies to choose from and, if he wished, he could ask one of the wallflowers that draped themselves along the side of the ballroom. They would not refuse to dance with him, and it would not cause a great deal of interest either. Satisfied, he looked around him again, only to see Lady Haseltine sending him back a look of her own, before pointedly glancing at her daughter, who stood beside her.

Percy turned away, feeling more than a little embarrassed to have been caught looking around the room in such an obvious manner. Lady Haseltine would have no doubt as to what he was seeking and, in looking at her daughter in that pointed way, he was being given a clear indication that *she*, at the very least, might be willing to dance with him should he ask.

Clearing his throat, Percy turned back to Lord Greenford and Lord Venables. "And are you to dance this evening, gentlemen?"

"I am already engaged for another of Lady Frederica's dances," Lord Greenford told him. "And I have a good many additional dances also." Pulling out his own little card, he ran his gaze over it. "I have already danced with four different young ladies," he said, puffing out his chest just a little as though this was some magnificent achievement. "And am due to dance with another three."

"I care nothing for dancing," Lord Venables said with a roll of his eyes. "Although I have been told that the young ladies of the *ton* find it very important. Therefore, if I am to secure any particular interest from any of the young ladies present, then I shall seek to do so," he said with such a heavy sigh, it was as though he greatly regretted having to stand up to dance. "I find no enjoyment in being in their company when we dance, however, for they cannot really converse with me and I find myself somewhat dulled by their company. However, I have a few dances that are yet to take place but none for the present moment, thank goodness."

Percy laughed and shrugged his shoulders. "I am sure you will enjoy them regardless, Lord Venables."

"I doubt it," Lord Venables sighed, only to straighten and then bow to someone just behind Percy. Turning his head, Percy stepped aside as Lady Preston and her daughter, Miss Addington, came to join them. His brow lifted as he saw Lord Venables flush as though he were a little embarrassed to be in the lady's company. A small smile tugged at Percy's lips as he bowed, wondering if Lord Venables was just as unaffected by the lady as he claimed to be. He had been introduced to Miss Addington some time ago but found her very quiet. She was a lady who seemed to cling to her mother, although Lady Preston tended to speak over her daughter even if she was inclined to speak. From what he knew, Percy recalled that her father, Viscount Preston, had been something of a drunkard and had pushed his family perilously close to disaster. That had been some years ago, however, although the rumors of it still remained. She was not a particularly beautiful young lady and her quiet nature made her all the less visible to the *beau monde*.

Percy glanced toward Lord Venables, fully expecting Lady Preston to address him first. However, when Lady Preston spoke, it was not to Lord Venables or to Lord Greenford. Rather, she turned directly toward Percy and smiled at him, although it did not light up her eyes and was, in fact, a little tight.

"Good evening, Lord Wetherby," she said as Miss Addington dropped into a curtsy, her head remaining bowed as though she did not dare look into his eyes. "I do hope that you are enjoying this evening?"

"I am indeed," Percy replied quickly. "And you?"

Lady Preston's smile remained fixed. "Some of it has been enjoyable," she said vaguely, keeping her true meaning hidden. "Now, are you to dance this evening, gentlemen?"

Percy hesitated, seeing how Lady Preston looked from him to

Lord Venables and back again, wondering why she seemed to be so very eager for him to step out with her daughter. He found himself rather reluctant, not at all certain that to be pushed into dancing with the lady was something he desired.

"I should be glad to, Miss Addington," Lord Greenford replied, bowing quickly and then holding his hand out for her dance card. "I fear that I do not have very many remaining, but I am certain we can find one that will suit us both."

A little relieved that his friend had taken Miss Addington's dance card, Percy cleared his throat and, much to his relief, found another old acquaintance nearby. Excusing himself, he went to speak to the gentleman and left Lord Venables and Lord Greenford to write their names on Miss Addington's dance card. He had no desire to do so himself. It was a little extraordinary, he reflected, that a lady such as Lady Preston should be so very forward in seeking out dance partners for her daughter. Normally, a gentleman was the one to make requests of the young ladies, with a mother or chaperone looking on. To be so pressing was very unusual. Mentally shrugging, he greeted his old acquaintance and fell into conversation with him, continually reminding himself that he could not be tardy for his dance with Lady Frederica.

~

"THANK YOU."

Percy bowed low as his dance came to an end, finding himself more than relieved that he had managed to make his way through the dance without a single misstep. There had not been much said between him and Lady Frederica, but at least they had danced together. She had been waiting for him just after the dance had been announced and the relief on her face when he had stepped forward had been unmistakable. It had been with a sense of deep contentment that he had offered her his arm, knowing that he was in complete control of himself and would not make a ridiculous remark or a foolish gesture. The dance had gone very well, and

Percy had found himself enjoying it, even though he had not shared much conversation with Lady Frederica.

"I thank you, Lord Wetherby." Lady Frederica rose from her curtsy and, after only a moment, accepted his arm again. "That was most enjoyable."

He beamed at her. "I am glad you found it so," he replied quickly. "It will not make up for my foolishness or my insult to you at our first meeting, but I do hope it proves that I am determined not to do so again."

Her eyes met his and, much to his delight, he saw a warmth in her green eyes that had not been present before, as well as a gentle smile.

"You certainly have done so, Lord Wetherby," she replied as they approached the waiting duchess.

"And I know that I still cannot explain my strange appearance at your uncle's townhouse," he said hastily, wanting to say a little more before they reached her. "But for that, I can only apologize."

"As you have done many times," Lady Frederica replied, a smile on her lips as she glanced up at him. "Let us say that it is nothing more than a mystery and leave it at that."

Percy let out a long breath, finding his spirits lifting. "Thank you, Lady Frederica," he said as they reached the duchess. "I am glad that we were able to reconcile somewhat."

Reaching the duchess, Percy dropped Lady Frederica's arm and took a small step back, his hands now clasped behind his back.

"That was very well done," the duchess said, smiling at him. "Have you enjoyed this evening, Lord Wetherby? Are you to dance again?"

"Not as yet," he told her, aware of just how Lady Frederica looked at him sharply as he spoke. "It was my intention to dance with Lady Frederica this evening so that I might improve upon my last attempt."

The duchess laughed and Percy found himself smiling back at her, thinking that the Duchess of Ellsworth was a remarkable lady who clearly held no grudge against him and was glad to see him attempt to reconcile with Lady Frederica. "I think you have done so," she said kindly as Percy inclined his head. "Now, if you could only remember what you were doing in my husband's townhouse."

"I am attempting to do so," he promised, a little wryly. "I assure you, I fully intend to do so."

"Lord Wetherby?"

He glanced behind him, surprised to see Lady Preston and Miss Addington standing there. Excusing himself from Lady Frederica and the duchess, he turned around a little more and greeted them quickly.

"You were to dance with my daughter, Lord Wetherby," Lady Preston said, frowning. "The cotillion."

"I—I beg your pardon?" Percy asked, looking at the young lady and seeing how she dropped her head, her cheeks filling with color. "Without wishing to be rude, Lady Preston, I think you are mistaken. I have not written my name on your daughter's dance card."

"I am aware of that," Lady Preston snapped, catching the attention of the duchess and Lady Frederica, who, being careful not to turn about and look at the lady, were clearly well aware of all that was being said given that they were within earshot. "But you stated that you would dance the cotillion with my daughter, did you not? I know that you were distracted by your other acquaintance—something I will state *was* a little impolite—but the promise still remained."

Percy blinked rapidly, not at all certain what to say. From what he recalled, he had never once promised to dance the cotillion with Miss Addington. In fact, he had made quite certain to step away from the lady, so that he would not have to agree to dance with her at all.

"And then we see you stepping onto the dance floor with Lady Frederica!" Lady Preston exclaimed, gesturing toward the lady, who, having heard her name, turned to politely smile at Lady Preston. "Whatever is the meaning of that?"

"Again," Percy insisted firmly, "you are mistaken, Lady Preston. I did not agree to dance with Miss Addington. Indeed, I wrote my name on Lady Frederica's card before you and your daughter came to speak to me, Lord Greenford, and Lord Venables."

Lady Preston let out a muttered exclamation and shook her head, clearly indicating that she did not believe what he had said.

"I do apologize if I had something to do with this unfortunate situation," Lady Frederica said quietly as Percy shook his head, not wanting her to involve herself in this matter for fear that she would only think poorly of him again.

"You have done nothing wrong, Lady Frederica," Lady Preston said sharply. "It is only that Lord Wetherby promised to dance the cotillion with my daughter but instead chose to dance it with you. I do not hold you in any way responsible, Lady Frederica."

Lady Frederica threw Percy a glance and he shook his head gently, one shoulder lifting as he did his best to communicate that he had no knowledge of what the lady was speaking about.

"I see," Lady Frederica murmured, frowning as she looked back at Percy before turning her head to speak once more to Lady Preston. "Lord Wetherby is correct to state that he requested a dance from me before he moved to speak to you, however." Her voice was a good deal firmer than Percy had expected, her tone measured but decisive. "I am afraid that there must have been a mistake of some kind."

This seemed to throw Lady Preston somewhat, for she opened her mouth to respond to Lady Frederica, only to close it again as she saw the duchess frowning also.

"I am sure it is a matter that can be easily rectified, however," Lady Frederica continued quickly. "Lord Wetherby, I do not mean to speak on your behalf, but might you consider dancing another dance with Miss Addington? I am not certain how many are left but I do hope that you have one or two free?"

Percy considered for a moment, seeing the expression of hope on Lady Frederica's face and realizing what she was trying to do. In placating Lady Preston and her daughter, he would make certain that nothing untoward was spread about him through society. He grimaced, feeling a little manipulated by Lady Preston but aware that to do as Lady Frederica suggested was the wisest course of action.

"But of course," he said after a few moments. "If there is another dance that you should like me to fulfill, Miss Addington, I should be more than glad to do so."

Miss Addington, who had remained entirely silent thus far, now glanced up at him. Her face was very red, and there was something in her eyes that seemed to speak of embarrassment. Percy felt his heart soften just a little, realizing that this was all Lady Preston's doing and, for whatever reason, she was bringing a great deal of trouble, not only for him but also for her daughter.

"I thank you," she murmured, handing him her dance card. Her gaze dropped to the floor and she stood quietly as he quickly looked over her card. There were three dances remaining and he put his name down for one, making certain not to claim the supper dance. He did not want Lady Preston to have any particular impression of his interest in her daughter. "There," he murmured, handing it back to her. "I hope that has contented you, Lady Preston."

Lady Preston lifted her chin and turned her head away, looking at Lady Frederica.

"I am sure that both Lady Frederica *and* my daughter are both a little put out by your lack of awareness, Lord Wetherby," she stated, before linking arms with her daughter and practically dragging her from Percy's side. Percy was left standing alone, staring into the faces of Lady Frederica and the duchess, both of whom appeared uncertain as to where they ought to look. Much to Percy's disappointment, Lady Frederica did not immediately denounce Lady Preston's final remark and once more, Percy felt a great weight settle over him as he looked back at them both. Evidently, despite his very best efforts, he had convinced Lady Frederica that he was not a gentleman of good character. First, he had appeared entirely foxed when he came to demand a dance from her, then he awoke to find himself in her uncle's townhouse, and now, to her mind, it seemed as though he had chosen to dance with her and then given his word to another. More than a little frustrated, Percy bowed his head and chose to take his leave.

"I do hope that you enjoy the rest of your evening," he said, thinking that there was nothing more for him to say that might improve his standing with them. "Do excuse me."

"But of course, Lord Wetherby," the duchess murmured as Lady Frederica said nothing, choosing only to incline her head. "Good evening."

7

"I did think that Lord Greenford was very attentive to you last evening."

Frederica chuckled as her uncle lifted an eyebrow at his wife's remark.

"You will be glad to hear, Uncle, that I have no inclination toward Lord Greenford," she said as the duke let out what appeared to be a long breath of relief. "He is attentive, yes, but I believe he is so with many other ladies also."

The duke nodded his head and picked up his cup of tea. "That is quite so," he agreed, throwing a look at his wife, who only laughed. "And yes, I confess that I should not be particularly pleased if Lord Greenford was the one you considered, Frederica. As kind as he is, he is not at all inclined toward business matters, from what I have heard."

"I have heard that he spends a good deal on his clothes," Frederica replied with a grin. "More than some of the ladies."

"That would not surprise me," the duchess replied with a smile of her own. "Might I ask if there are any gentlemen who have caught your attention as yet?"

Frederica shook her head, ignoring the fact that she was, for whatever reason, continually thinking of Lord Wetherby. She had done very well for a day or so in making certain not to think of him, but since then, had struggled terribly to remove all thoughts of him from her mind. Given the strange nature of what had occurred last evening, those thoughts had lingered all the more.

"There is Lord Blakely," she said after a moment. "I do not know him particularly well, but he certainly appeared to be eager for my company."

"Lord Blakely?" the duchess mused, only for her expression to clear. "Ah, yes, I recall him. He was very tall, was he not?"

Frederica smiled. "Yes, he was rather," she agreed, laughing quietly to herself as she recalled just how she had found dancing with him to be a little difficult. "Although he did express his regret that he *was* so very tall compared to me and that our dance was a little more...trying than it might have been." She picked up her teacup and took a sip, thinking quietly to herself about just how much she had enjoyed both her dance and her conversation with Lord Blakely. "He did ask if he might call upon me at one time and I agreed without hesitation, certainly."

The duchess' brow lifted. "Indeed?"

"I do not think that he will do so anytime soon," Frederica replied hastily. "It was meant as a kind remark, I think, that is all."

The duke chuckled and made to say something, only for a knock at the door to interrupt him. Calling for the butler or footman to enter, Frederica watched in surprise as a footman appeared with a bouquet of flowers.

This was not a remarkable or surprising thing, however, given that she had received a few gifts such as these after balls or soirees and indeed, three had arrived already. She had not expected another, however. It was almost time for afternoon calls.

"My lady."

The footman set down the bouquet beside her and handed her the card that had come with it.

"Goodness, that is a very lavish one," the duchess commented as Frederica opened the card. "Someone must think very highly of your company, Frederica."

"Why should they not?" the duke asked, a teasing grin on his face. "Who has sent it, Frederica?"

Frederica read the note quickly, finding herself a little surprised at the name there. "It is Lord Blakely," she replied, her brow knotting together as she saw the duke and duchess exchange a glance. "He hopes to call this afternoon."

"Just as he said," the duchess remarked, a knowing look in her eye. "It seems that Lord Blakely wishes very much to continue his acquaintance with you, Frederica. That bouquet states it."

"It is just as well that I will be glad to further my acquaintance with him, then," Frederica replied, knowing that there was no reason to be coy with her aunt. "I do not know him particularly well, as I have said, and this shall be a good opportunity to further our acquaintance."

The duke nodded, his smile no longer teasing. "That is wise, Frederica," he agreed, reaching to pour himself more tea. "Take your time when it comes to the gentlemen of the *ton*. I will not be likely to simply accept the very first gentleman that shows an interest in you, my dear, simply because he wishes to."

"Nor I," Frederica laughed, gently touching one of the roses, already able to smell the scent that came from them. "I assure you, I shall be considerate and careful in all these matters, Uncle." Her smile softened. "Just as you were when it came to Louisa."

∼

FREDERICA COULD NOT HIDE the frisson of excitement that ran through her as she sat expectantly, waiting for Lord Blakely's arrival. She had not thought more highly of him than other acquaintances she had made the previous evening. However, now that he had sent such a beautiful bouquet and had expressed such an eagerness in coming to call upon her, Frederica wondered if there was a genuine interest in her from him. That was, of course, much too difficult for her to know for certain but it did make her feel a little more interested in his arrival.

She had already had visits from three other gentlemen and, thereafter, one Miss Brownly and her mother, Lady Salford. Surely Lord Blakely would arrive soon, else the afternoon would be over.

A knock at the door announced the next of their afternoon callers and Frederica sat up quickly, calling the butler to enter before the duchess could say another word. The butler did as he was asked and handed the duchess a card, which the duchess took, read, and then handed to Frederica.

Her heart lifted, only to fall once more as she read the name on the card.

"Lady Preston?" she queried, looking at the duchess, who nodded. "And her daughter, I presume."

"Miss Addington," the butler intoned. "Shall I send them in, Your Grace?"

There was no reason for the duchess to refuse and so, with another quick look toward Frederica, she nodded.

"How very strange," the duchess said quickly as the butler quit the room. "I am not well acquainted with either of the ladies and our conversation last evening was not exactly friendly."

"No, indeed," Frederica replied, a little confused. "In fact, I do not think that Lady Preston spoke even a word to you, Louisa. She was much more inclined toward throwing angry words toward Lord Wetherby."

The duchess frowned. "A strange circumstance," she murmured, just as the door opened, and both she and Frederica rose to their feet, ready to greet their guests. Lady Preston and Miss Addington walked in one after the other, and Frederica was struck by just how different in appearance they were from last evening. Instead of the angry expression that had clouded Lady Preston's face, she was now smiling gently, the hard lines on her forehead now smoothed. Miss Addington, who had appeared nervous and upset, appeared almost serene as she curtsied, standing tall and with an uplifted face rather than lowering her head as she had done yesterday.

"Good afternoon, Lady Preston, Miss Addington," the duchess said, and Frederica murmured a greeting also. "Thank you for calling upon us."

"But of course, Your Grace," Lady Preston replied, her voice thick as honey. "After our conversation last evening, I thought it best to come to speak to you again this afternoon. After all, there was so much that was not said yesterday that I should very much like the opportunity to clarify."

The duchess glanced at Frederica, who rang the bell quickly for tea, before gesturing for their visitors to sit down. She had no idea what Lady Preston had meant by what she had said but, nevertheless, it appeared that they were going to soon discover it.

"Last evening was a most enjoyable one, I thought," the duchess began as Frederica took her seat. "Did you have a pleasant time, Miss Addington?"

The young lady started gently, as though she had not been expecting to be spoken to directly.

"Yes—yes, of course," she said quickly as Lady Preston smiled gratifyingly. "It was an excellent evening."

"And did you dance often?" Frederica asked, wondering if this was to do with Lord Wetherby and the situation that Lady Preston seemed to have taken upon herself to create. "I think I danced almost every dance and was rather fatigued by the end."

Miss Addington's smile was so brief that had Frederica blinked, she would have missed it entirely.

"I danced some, yes," she replied, her voice a little thin. "Not as much as I should have liked, however."

"Well, it is only the very beginning of the Season," Frederica replied cheerfully. "I am certain that we shall both be heartily sick of balls come the end of the summer." She laughed, as did the duchess, but Miss Addington barely smiled whilst Lady Preston looked at Frederica as though she were the most ridiculous creature in all of the world. Frederica's laughter died away, the sound fading and making her feel a little embarrassed as she looked toward the duchess, not certain what she ought to say next.

Thankfully, the maid arrived with the tea and refreshments, meaning that Frederica herself had a responsibility now to pour the tea and make certain that their guests were taken care of. The duchess quickly picked up the conversation, talking about the ball that she and the duke intended to host in a few weeks' time and making Lady Preston's eyes round with excitement and anticipation.

"We must hope that there will not be a repeat of Lord Wetherby's behavior then, must we not?" Lady Preston asked, clearly now warming to the subject that she had come to speak about. "I must apologize profusely, Lady Frederica, for the way in which it all came about. There was some misunderstanding, certainly, but I am sure it was not on the part of my dear daughter."

Frederica put a small smile on her face and picked up her teacup. "There is no requirement for any apology, Lady Preston," she replied, finding the entire conversation a little bizarre. "There was no harm done."

Lady Preston's expression darkened, as though the sun had just been covered by a thick, grey cloud. "I am afraid there was, Lady Frederica," she said, her voice now holding some anger. "My poor Tabitha was left standing alone, having expected Lord Wetherby to attend her, only to see him dancing with you."

Feeling a little attacked, as though Lady Preston held her entirely to blame for the matter, Frederica set down her teacup gently. "As I have said, Lady Preston, there is no need for any apology in this," she stated, as calmly as she could. "I do hope that your dance with Lord Wetherby was quite perfect, Miss Addington," she finished, smiling at the young lady.

"Yes," Miss Addington said, just as her mother drew in a deep breath, her shoulders lifting as though she intended to explode with whatever it was that frustrated her so. "It was most satisfactory."

"But his behavior was not!" Lady Preston exclaimed, making

Frederica look at the duchess, seeing how her brow was furrowed in much the same way as Frederica's was. "I do hope, Lady Frederica, that you do not intend to continue developing an acquaintance with that particular gentleman. He is not at all the sort of gentleman I think any young lady ought to consider."

Frederica hesitated, wanting to tell Lady Preston that she did not think that such a matter should be of any importance to her, but chose to remain silent rather than speak, thinking that to do so might only infuriate Lady Preston all the more.

"Lady Frederica is always careful when it comes to her acquaintances, I assure you," the duchess said softly, finally garnering Lady Preston's attention. "However, in matters such as this, I think that there was nothing more than a momentary confusion and therefore, we do not think poorly of Lord Wetherby."

Lady Preston put one hand to her heart. "You mean to say that you do not think his action deliberate?"

"Deliberate?" Frederica repeated, all the more astonished and unable to keep her surprise to herself. "No, indeed not, Lady Preston. Why ever should he do such a thing?"

It seemed that Lady Preston could not answer Frederica's question, for try as she might, she could not give any response to her. Her mouth opened and closed, she looked toward Frederica and then away from her, and still, no answer was given.

"Now, do tell me, Miss Addington," the duchess continued quickly, changing the subject from Lord Wetherby to something entirely innocuous. "Are you to attend anything of interest this evening? A dinner party, mayhap?"

Miss Addington, whose cheeks had faded to a dull pink, turned to the duchess with what Frederica presumed was an attempt at a smile. As she spoke about the small soiree she hoped to attend, Frederica could not help but glance at Lady Preston. The lady was now a little hunched as she sat, her hand holding her teacup and her shoulders pulled forward. Her eyes were fixed to the table before her, her lips thin and her eyebrows low over her eyes. She appeared to be muttering to herself, as though the conclusion that Frederica and the duchess had come to was not at all satisfactory.

Why should she wish to keep me from Lord Wetherby? Frederica asked herself, sipping the last of her tea and praying silently that the visit would soon be over. *Why should she wish me to think so poorly of him?*

There came no easy answer and Frederica was forced back into the conversation, smiling at Miss Addington warmly in the hope that the poor creature would not feel as though she herself was being badly thought of. Thankfully, after some more minutes, Lady Preston rose to her feet and made to take their leave, thanking the duchess graciously—just as a knock came at the door.

"Do excuse me," the duchess murmured, calling the butler to enter. He came in with another card held in his hand, which he handed to the duchess at once. Frederica did not miss how Lady Preston's eyes followed the card, noting that the lady was overly interested in all their goings-on.

"It is our next caller," the duchess smiled, looking up from the card and handing it to Frederica. "Thank you both for calling and please do so again."

Lady Preston did not move. "I do hope we have not intruded on your time and that your next...*visitor*—" she looked pointedly at the card in Frederica's hand, "has not been waiting long."

"Lord Blakely has only just arrived," Frederica replied quickly, growing all the more irritated with Lady Preston and choosing to speak his name aloud in the hope that this would hurry the lady's departure along. "I do hope to see you again, Miss Addington."

Miss Addington, however, had gone a very pale shade. Her eyes were fixed to the card in Frederica's hand, her lips a slash of red against the greyness of her cheeks. Frederica found herself rather startled by the change in the young lady's appearance, wanting to ask her whether or not she needed to sit down again.

But then, Lady Preston turned about and took her daughter's arm, pulling her along toward the door. Miss Addington stumbled once but Lady Preston held on doggedly, making Frederica all the more concerned for the lady's welfare.

"Good afternoon," Lady Preston cried as the door was opened for her. "And thank you again for your hospitality."

With the door closed behind them, Frederica turned to the duchess and stared at her in confusion, blowing out her breath in exasperation. "Whatever was that?" she asked as the duchess laughed and shook her head. "Most extraordinary."

"Quite ridiculous also," came the reply. "To think that she can come to speak to you and practically demand that you leave Lord Wetherby's company?" She shook her head as Frederica laughed. "Foolish *and* foolhardy."

"I do wonder at her vehemence," Frederica replied, sitting back down even though she knew she would have to get up again in a moment. "It was very odd. I know that she appeared to be most upset with Lord Wetherby, but I am certain that he could not have agreed to dance with me and then gone on to make the very same arrangement with Miss Addington."

"Indeed," the duchess replied, smoothing down her skirts just as there came another knock at the door. "I do not think that such a visit will be repeated again, however. Now, do smile and get to your feet. Lord Blakely has arrived."

Frederica threw her aunt a smile and did as she was told, finding that the anticipation that had once filled her about Lord Blakely's visit was now somewhat diminished given the strangeness of Lady Preston's conversation. However, she lifted her chin a notch, clasped her hands in front of her, and prepared to meet Lord Blakely, hoping that his visit, at least, would be a much greater success than that of Lady Preston's.

8
———

"Good evening, Lady Nottingham."

Percy smiled at the older lady as he rose from his bow, seeing a gleam in her eyes as he did so. His smile dropped just a little, wondering whether or not she had heard about the strange incident with Miss Addington and her mother. The story would likely have been spread by Lady Preston and, without a doubt, Lady Nottingham would have listened eagerly.

"Good evening, Lord Wetherby," she replied, tipping her head in a birdlike fashion. "I see that you are presentable this evening, at least."

"Presentable?" he repeated as Lady Nottingham's eyes narrowed.

"Indeed, Lord Wetherby," she replied, glancing across at her daughter, who had, thus far, remained entirely silent. "You do not recall?"

Percy shook his head, entirely uncertain of what Lady Nottingham was referring to. "I am afraid I do not, Lady Nottingham," he replied, a great unease beginning to twist his stomach. "I can only apologize if I said or did anything untoward."

Lady Nottingham did not laugh, lifting her head so that she

stood straight once more. "You were entirely *unpresentable*, Lord Wetherby," she stated coldly. "And most improper. You may claim to have forgotten it entirely, but I am sure that you have simply chosen to ignore what occurred. I am glad, however, that you appear to be a little more presentable this evening." She tutted and looked away from him. "My son should *never* behave in such a way."

Clearing his throat, Percy nodded. "But of course," he said, turning to Miss Chalmers. "Good evening, Miss Chalmers. Are you to dance this evening?"

Miss Chalmers, for whatever reason, went very pale and shook her head, her eyes looking away from his.

"What a pity," he said quickly, regretting that he had stopped to speak to Lady Nottingham at all. "Good evening to you both. I do hope that you have a pleasant time here at the assembly."

Hurrying away from them, Percy let out a long breath of relief, his stomach twisting this way and that with the uncomfortable conversation that he had just endured. Whatever he had done, it seemed that Lady Nottingham had also borne the brunt of his outlandish behavior, as well as Lady Frederica. He had not wanted to delve into the details of what he had done but once more took the opportunity to remind himself that he would never permit himself to become so very inebriated again.

The evening assembly was always an exceptional evening and Percy had every reason to expect to enjoy himself, although he certainly did not wish to speak with Lady Nottingham again. Wincing inwardly at the thought of every lady in all of London knowing of his supposed mistake with Lady Preston's daughter, Percy closed his eyes for a moment and drew in a long breath. This Season was not going as well as he had expected and, thus far, he had made something of a poor show of things.

"Lord Wetherby?"

Opening his eyes, he blinked rapidly in order to clear his vision, only to see Lady Frederica coming into view.

"Lady Frederica," he stammered, all the more embarrassed to

have been seen in such a ridiculous state. "Good evening. Your Grace, good evening."

The duchess smiled. "Good evening," she said as Lady Frederica frowned, looking at him curiously. "Are you quite well, Lord Wetherby?"

"I am," he said quickly. "Forgive me. I was lost in thought for a moment."

Lady Frederica said nothing for a moment or two, before she took a small step closer to him.

"Lord Wetherby, might I speak candidly to you for a moment?" she asked as the duchess moved a little further away, turning just a little so that Lady Frederica and Percy might talk together.

"What do you wish to say to me?" Percy asked, a little confused. "I pray I have done nothing more to upset you."

Lady Frederica smiled and shook her head, relief flooding Percy. "No, indeed not," she said quietly. "However, I did wonder whether or not we might speak of Lady Preston for a few moments?"

"Lady Preston?" Percy asked, and Lady Frederica nodded. "You wish me to speak of her?"

"I—I had a very unusual visit from her this afternoon," Lady Frederica continued, a small frown catching her brow. "She was most upset about her daughter and the dance that you were to take with her."

Rather irritated at this remark, Percy shook his head. "I confess, Lady Frederica, that I was a good deal confused by the situation," he said as Lady Frederica held his gaze steadily, perhaps searching for truth in his eyes. "But I promise you that I did not go immediately to Lady Preston and Miss Addington and request the very same dance from her that I had just agreed on with you."

"I believe you, Lord Wetherby," Lady Frederica said and, much to his surprise, placed one hand on his arm for just a moment. "However, for whatever reason, Lady Preston called upon me this afternoon with the seeming sole intention of ensuring that my acquaintance with you did not continue." Her lips pressed together for a moment as the smallest flush of color came into her cheeks. "Might I ask if there is anything that should justify Lady Preston's remarks?"

Percy paused for a moment before he replied, finding that he was both a little embarrassed and, at the same time, very grateful for Lady Frederica's openness.

"I would be honest with you, Lady Frederica," he began carefully. "I know that I made a very poor first impression and that is, of course, why you now ask such a thing. However, I can assure you that I have never once done anything to either insult or upset Lady Preston or Miss Addington. I became acquainted with them both last Season and do not think that I have even *spoken* to them until a few days ago."

He looked desperately into Lady Frederica's eyes, praying that she would believe him even though he had given her very little cause to do so. Her emerald eyes glittered as she looked back at him, her lips gently pursed. Some moments passed and Percy held his breath, feeling his heart pound furiously.

"Very well, Lord Wetherby," Lady Frederica said eventually, and Percy closed his eyes for just a moment, relieved beyond explanation. "Then if that is the case, can you think of any particular reason that Lady Preston would come and speak to me in such a manner?"

"None," Percy replied truthfully, spreading his hands wide. "I believe that there was a mistake in her thinking, and for whatever reason, she has now cause to think me of very poor character indeed." A wry smile tipped his lips. "Whereas you, Lady Frederica, have every reason to think so poorly of me."

She laughed, a light coming back into her eyes as she smiled. "Indeed I do, Lord Wetherby," she agreed. "I presume, as yet, you have not had any real recollection as to why you were found in my uncle's townhouse?"

"I have not," he replied, seeing her smile slowly disappear. "I am sorry, Lady Frederica. I have made a very poor impression—I am fully aware of that—but I will do all I can to improve it, should you be willing to give me another opportunity."

A line appeared between Lady Frederica's brows as she looked back at him. "But of course," she said slowly. "Despite Lady Preston's warnings, I am willing, Lord Wetherby. Although, might I suggest that there is something a little more..." She trailed off, her eyes darting away for a moment as she sought the right word or expression before sighing and returning her gaze to him. "It does not matter," she finished with a smile. "Thank you for speaking with me so openly, Lord Wetherby. I am grateful."

"As am I," Percy said truthfully. "It is not every young lady who is so forgiving, Lady Frederica." He glanced toward the duchess, who was smiling gently to herself, clearly aware of what they had been speaking of. "Might I hope that the Duke and Duchess of Ellsworth are also in agreement with our renewed acquaintance?"

"They are," Lady Frederica replied, her eyes twinkling as Percy found himself smiling back at her, a strange warmth in his heart as he felt all awkwardness and tension disappear completely. He had meant every word that he had said to her—it was not every young lady who would be as willing or as magnanimous as she. It spoke well of her character, certainly, and as Percy looked back into her eyes, he felt his breath catch. She was particularly lovely this evening.

"Do you wish to dance this evening?" he asked, and she quickly pulled the card from her wrist. "I must hope that, this evening, we shall have no difficulties whatsoever, either before the dance or after."

"Indeed," Lady Frederica laughed, handing it to him. "Thank you, Lord Wetherby."

∽

WALKING along the path that led through the gardens, Percy drew in a deep breath of fresh air and let it out slowly. He had come outside to take a few minutes to himself, away from the crowd and the hubbub of laughter and conversation in order to gather his thoughts. Things with Lady Frederica had gone very well, and he was glad that she felt so able to ask him the questions she had done.

The path was lit with a few lanterns although the moon was very bright. Smiling to himself, Percy made to return indoors, only to come across Lord Greenford, who was standing with two other gentlemen.

"Greenford!" he exclaimed as his friend greeted him. "Good evening."

Lord Greenford's features were lit up by the lantern light and, much to Percy's dismay, he saw a thin line pull at Lord Greenford's mouth. "Good evening, Lord Wetherby."

Percy said nothing more, frowning at his friend and wondering at his change in expression.

"I see that you and Lady Frederica appear to be much better acquainted."

His head lifted as Percy studied Lord Greenford carefully, wondering if he heard a small note of jealousy in his friend's voice. Lord Greenford had turned away from the other two gentlemen now, allowing for them both to have something of a private conversation.

"We are," he said, having only just returned Lady Frederica back to the duchess after the first of their two dances. Had Lord Greenford seen him dance with her? Was he, for some reason, envious of that fact? "That is to say, Lady Frederica has been willing to accept my acquaintance again, for which I am very grateful."

"I can imagine," Lord Greenford replied, a little ruefully. "I would have thought that she might have rejected you entirely."

Chuckling wryly, Percy shook his head. "You sound somewhat disappointed that she has not done so," he said, speaking honestly. "I am sorry that she has not done so."

Lord Greenford sighed and looked away from Percy for a moment, no smile etching itself across his face. "I have a great respect for Lady Frederica," he said as Percy listened with interest. "I had thought myself a little drawn to her, I confess."

"You are drawn to a good many young ladies," Percy replied, finding himself a little unsettled at the thought of Lady Frederica being courted by Lord Greenford, although he could not explain why. "What is it about Lady Frederica that is so very different?" He watched Lord Greenford's expression change, seeing how he frowned.

"I could not say," came the reply. "You are quite right to say that I find myself intrigued by a good many ladies, but Lady Frederica has an exceptional character, I think. She is not afraid to speak openly and yet does so with gentleness and consideration."

"And she is rather beautiful," Percy added, before he could stop himself. "I am well aware of what you mean. I am sorry that she has not rejected me as you might have hoped."

Thankfully, Lord Greenford chuckled at this remark, making Percy smile in return. The dark expression on Lord Greenford's face faded and he seemed back to his usual self, allowing Percy to let out a sigh of relief.

"Doubtless I shall find another young lady to dote upon," he said as Percy nodded his agreement, his eyes drifting away from Lord Greenford and across the gardens. "What other young ladies might you recommend?"

Percy chuckled ruefully. "Given that I have made a very poor impression upon not only Lady Frederica, it seems, but others also, I am hardly the best person to ask," he said as Lord Greenford's brow rose in surprise. "Oh yes! I have managed to insult Lady Preston and her daughter, Miss Addington, as well as Lady Nottingham and her daughter, Miss Chalmers." He groaned and threw back his head for a moment, his eyes closing tightly. "And worst of all is that I do not recall precisely what it is that I did as regards the latter."

"I doubt that it matters," came the reply. "After all, you now know simply to avoid her company and, in doing so, will improve yourself heartily to her." He chuckled as Percy winced, knowing that Lord Greenford was only being half serious.

"I think I shall return inside," Lord Greenford continued as Percy nodded. "Are you to dance again this evening?"

"I will join you," Percy replied as they began to make their way back toward the ballroom. "Yes, I am to dance again with Lady Frederica, but it is not for some time." He smiled to himself at the thought of taking Lady Frederica onto the dance floor, thinking about how improved their acquaintance had become these last few days. "Although certainly, I should not like to be tardy."

Lord Greenford chuckled. "I am sure you will not be late," he stated, the path twisting first to the right and then to the left. "Indeed, I think that—"

Much to Percy's astonishment, a hand suddenly grasped his arm and pulled him sharply away from the path and into the shadows of the gardens. Lord Greenford continued speaking, clearly unaware of what had happened to Percy, who, despite his shock, had not let out a single exclamation.

"Lord Wetherby."

A hushed voice spoke quietly to him, the hand that had pulled him in still holding his arm.

"You *do* recall the last time we were in such a place, do you not?"

Alarm swam through Percy's mind and he took a step back, only for the hand to tighten once more.

"I know nothing of what you speak," he hissed, hearing Lord Greenford calling his name. "Unhand me at once!" He did not want to forcibly remove himself for fear that he would drag both himself and this unknown lady into the lantern light. What would happen then? Would the lady be seen by another member of the *ton*? Would Percy then be forced to engage himself to her, in order to secure her reputation? He did not want to even *think* of such a thing, and thus chose to speak and act very quietly indeed. "Release me at once, madam."

The quiet laugh from the lady made the hair on the back of Percy's neck stand on end.

"I know that you pretend," she said as her other hand settled on Percy's shoulder, making his heart beat furiously. "You are not as reluctant as you seem. Although why you will not wed me, as you promised, I do not know."

"Wed you?" Percy shook his head in disbelief, reaching up with one hand to push away her hand from his shoulder. He did so quickly, managing to release himself somewhat. "My lady, you are entirely mistaken. I have never once stepped into the gardens with any young lady and certainly have not spoken of matrimony."

The fingers on his arm began to curl, biting into his skin.

"You look at me as though you and I are not particularly well acquainted," she breathed, anger surfacing through her words. "When we meet, you do not greet me with any of the warmth I would hope for. How can you expect me to continue in such a way when I know what we have shared, when I know what you have promised me?"

"I have promised you *nothing*," Percy replied firmly, pulling her hand free from his arm. "You are mistaken, my lady. I am not the gentleman you require."

The lady let out a hiss of breath and threw her arms about him, and it was only in his panic that Percy realized she was trying to kiss him. It seemed that none of his protestations meant anything to this particular young lady. Given that he did not know anything about her true identity and that she had spoken of his supposed promise of matrimony, Percy knew that the only reasonable thing to do was escape from her without making a scene. Surely, she could not intend to follow him into the ballroom, to demand that he wed her without any real reason for him to do so.

And then, as he tried to pry her hands from around his neck, turning his face to the right, Percy felt quite certain he saw another figure emerge from the gloom. His mind bellowed for him to escape, realizing now that the young lady in question had brought with her someone who would witness Percy's evident affections toward this young lady and, thereafter, call for him to wed her. With an effort—and not at all gently—he unwound the young lady's arms and pushed her back, before turning around and rushing back toward the path.

Lord Greenford's eyes widened in surprise. "There you are," he began, just as Percy grasped his arm. "Whatever is the matter? Where did you go?"

"I must hasten inside," Percy said hurriedly, throwing a glance over his shoulder. "And thereafter, I must go home. If anyone should ask for me, you will inform them that I have had to return back home and did so some time ago." Stepping back into the ballroom was something of a relief, although Percy knew he was not safe as yet. The young lady and whoever else had been with her might then march into the ballroom and demand to know where he was gone. If Lord Greenford could state that Percy had returned home and had, in fact, done so some time ago, then the *ton* would not start calling for him to wed whoever the young lady was. If he remained here, however, there was always the chance that she might do precisely as he feared.

"Home?" Lord Greenford repeated as Percy nodded. "Why should you do such a thing? And where did you disappear to in the gardens?" He frowned and rubbed at his brow, his eyes puzzled. "I was certain that you—"

"I will explain all come the morrow," Percy replied, diving into the crowd and searching desperately for Lady Frederica. "Pray forgive me, Lord Greenford, but I must leave you now."

He did not wait to hear his friend's reply but, keeping his head low, weaved his way one way and then the next, needing to find Lady Frederica and telling himself that he could not leave without bidding her farewell.

Thankfully, he finally caught sight of both her and the duchess speaking quietly together near the back of the ballroom. His heart flooded with relief as he made his way nearer to her, bowing low as he did so.

"Lady Frederica." She turned to him, smiling warmly as she did so.

"I must beg your pardon," he continued, before she could

speak. "But there is a somewhat desperate situation, and I am forced to return home."

Her smile faded immediately, and she frowned hard, looking back at him with cool, green eyes. "Return home?" she repeated as he nodded. "Goodness, Lord Wetherby, whatever has happened?"

Hesitating, Percy shook his head. "Would that I could explain," he said, glancing over his shoulder. "But if I am to protect myself, then I must take my leave. Please forgive me for missing our second dance together, Lady Frederica. It is not what I would wish, but in the circumstances, I—"

A sudden pain slammed hard into his head and Percy pressed one hand to his temple as he grimaced. He could hear Lady Frederica speak his name, could feel the duchess' hand on his arm but, squeezing his eyes tightly closed, could do nothing but endure the pain that now sliced into his forehead.

And then he saw it.

He was stepping into his carriage, only to see a young lady sitting there, waiting for him. She tilted her head but, with his blurred vision, Percy could not make out her face. He stumbled back from the carriage, turning quickly and rushing away from it, clearly desperate to escape from her—just as he was at present.

The pain faded and Percy opened his eyes, his chest heaving with exertion as though he had just run very far indeed.

"Lord Wetherby!"

Lady Frederica and the duchess were both staring at him with concern, but Percy knew he had no time to explain.

"I—I have remembered something about the night I found myself at the duke's townhouse," he stammered, passing one hand over his eyes as sweat began to run down his back. "Forgive me—might I call tomorrow, Lady Frederica? Your Grace? I am sure that I can explain a little more then."

"But of course," Lady Frederica said quickly, before the duchess could reply. "If you must leave, Lord Wetherby, then I certainly will not prevent you from doing so."

He nodded, stepped back, and, without another word, turned

on his heel and hurried toward the door. Panic still clutched at his chest and it was all he could do not to run toward it, so eager to depart that desperation took a hold of every part of him. This evening had been yet another disaster and Percy was all the more frustrated that he had been required to step away from Lady Frederica, unable to stay at the ball so that they might dance their second dance together.

Who was that lady in the garden?

The thoughts and questions that poured into his mind as he waited for his carriage to appear began to pain his head all over again. Pinching the bridge of his nose, Percy closed his eyes and drew in a deep breath. Whoever it was, they had clearly mistaken him for someone else. Someone who had already, it seemed, taken advantage of that particular young lady and had promised her matrimony—most likely in the hope of stealing a few kisses from her. Her reputation had not been ruined, that much was certain, but clearly, she now expected this gentleman to do as he had promised.

Except that gentleman is not I.

Relieved that his carriage had come to the front of the house, Percy hurried forward and climbed inside without waiting for the steps to be brought. Closing the door tightly, he rapped on the roof and, almost at once, the carriage rolled away, leaving the ball and the young lady, as well as Lady Frederica, far, far behind. Percy settled his head back against the squabs and let out a long breath of relief, his eyes closing tightly. Whatever had occurred, at least he had escaped. Nothing could be demanded of him now, nothing could be said of him that might then force his hand. For the moment, at least, he was safe.

9

Frederica bit her lip and tried not to sigh aloud as Lord Morningside continued to drone on about his many, many horses that he had back at his estate. It was not that she could not ride, or that she had no interest in horseflesh, but rather that she had been able to think of nothing and no one other than Lord Wetherby since last evening.

Even now, she found herself thinking of just how he had looked as he had approached her. His face had been grey, his eyes, normally so vivid, were nothing more than a dull green. They had not looked toward her but, instead, had turned this way and that, as though he feared being seen by someone. Quite who that someone was, Frederica had very little idea, but her heart had filled with concern for him. For the rest of the evening, she had found herself wondering what had occurred and why he had been forced to leave so hastily, although no one else seemed to notice he had departed. She had not heard anyone asking for him, wondering where he might have gone. Even Lord Greenford, when she had spoken to him about Lord Wetherby, had merely brushed her question aside by stating that Lord Wetherby had simply had to return home and had done so some time ago.

It was all very strange, and Frederica was eagerly looking forward to the earl's arrival, so that she might make sense of it all. It was strange, she reflected as Lord Morningside launched into a description of one particular gelding, that she now felt a good deal more for Lord Wetherby than before. Given just how much he wanted to improve her impression of him and the lengths he had gone to, she found herself quietly respectful of his efforts. Yes, not all had been successful and, indeed, matters with Lady Preston and her daughter might well have turned things on their head all over again had she allowed them to, but, on the whole, Frederica knew that he truly was attempting to express his true sorrow over what he had done and to impress upon her that he was *not* that sort of gentleman. It seemed, she considered, tilting her head to one side as she thought, that he was doing all he could to improve himself and that, certainly, spoke well of him.

"And with that, I fear that I shall have to take my leave."

Relieved—but making certain to hide it well—Frederica rose from her chair and curtsied. "Good afternoon, Lord Morningside," she said as the duchess smiled at him. "Do call again."

Lord Morningside beamed and Frederica hid her amused smile, aware now that the gentleman hoped for nothing more than another opportunity to talk about his horses. Perhaps she had made a mistake in making such a remark.

"I thank you, Your Grace," Lord Morningside said, bowing toward the duchess. "And you also, Lady Frederica."

She kept her smile fixed in place until Lord Morningside had quit the room, only to tumble back into her chair in a flurry of skirts.

"I do not think I could have endured another minute of listening to his description of his horses," she said as the duchess laughed and sat down a good deal more carefully than Frederica had done. "Perhaps I should not have encouraged him to return."

The duchess chuckled softly. "I fear he may," she warned. "But then, we have had a very pleasant afternoon." One eyebrow lifted in Frederica's direction. "Lord Blakely was very glad to see you again."

Frederica nodded but was surprised that there was no stir of awareness in her heart. Lord Blakely had called, yes, and indeed had sent a very large bouquet of flowers for her for what was now the second time. Their conversation had been pleasing enough, certainly, but Frederica had not been as attentive as she ought. Her thoughts had struggled to depart from Lord Wetherby.

"And Lord Wetherby is still to call," the duchess continued, and Frederica looked up, seeing the twinkle in the duchess' eye. "You are eager to see him, I think."

"I am," Frederica replied, not hiding her true feelings. "I should very much like to know what occurred last evening to make him depart in such a hurry."

"It was very good of him to come and find you," the duchess commented as Frederica nodded. "Otherwise you might have been standing quietly and waiting for his arrival."

"Which would never have come," Frederica agreed softly. "Yes, it was good of him to do so." Her eyes turned back to the duchess, who was sitting quietly but watching her closely. "I believe that, despite his first appearances, Lord Wetherby is a considerate gentleman."

"It would appear so," the duchess agreed, glancing at the clock. "Although if he does not come to call upon you soon, then it will be much too late and—"

A quiet rap on the door prevented her from saying any more and Frederica rose to her feet, her heart beating a little more quickly as the butler came in to announce Lord Wetherby. The duchess had already informed him that Lord Wetherby was to be shown in at once and so he entered the room close behind the butler, stopping to bow before he came any closer.

"Lord Wetherby," Frederica murmured, dropping into a curtsy. "Good afternoon."

"Good afternoon." There was a tiredness about his eyes now, a weariness that had not been there last evening. His smile, whilst present, was lackluster and when he lifted his head from his bow, it seemed as though he was a little hunched in his stature.

"Please, do sit down," the duchess said, gesturing to Frederica to ring the bell. "Might I say, Lord Wetherby, that you appear rather fatigued this afternoon."

Lord Wetherby did not take insult at this but instead gave the duchess a small smile and, after a moment, let out a heavy sigh.

"I am fatigued," he admitted. "Last evening, something untoward occurred which, thereafter, brought to mind something that happened the night I set foot in this very house." He looked back at Frederica, who found herself leaning forward in her chair, feeling a great swell of tension rising up within her. "I am, as you know, deeply sorry that I was forced to remove myself from the ball last evening in such haste, Lady Frederica. I would have very much liked to step out with you again."

Frederica smiled quickly, not wanting him to think that she was at all angry or upset. "I quite understand, Lord Wetherby," she assured him. "In truth, I was a little concerned for you. You appeared to be quite distressed."

"I was," Lord Wetherby replied honestly. "I would be glad to share with you what occurred, should you wish to know?"

Seeing the duchess nod, Frederica quickly expressed her consent. "Yes, of course. If you are willing?"

Lord Wetherby nodded, although waited for some minutes until the tea had been brought in and served. Once the maid had left the room, he took a deep breath and began.

"I beg you not to think ill of me as I say this, Lady Frederica, Your Grace, but it is the truth. Last evening, after our first dance, Lady Frederica, I went to the gardens and found Lord Greenford. We talked for a while and then decided to return to the ballroom." He cleared his throat as a flush of red crept up his neck and into his face. "As I made my return, someone pulled me from the path and into the dark shadows. I confess I did not let out any sort of exclamation and left Lord Greenford in a great deal of confusion."

"I can imagine," Frederica replied as Lord Wetherby took a sip of his tea. "Who was it that pulled you away in such a fashion?"

Lord Wetherby set his cup back down carefully and then looked up at her, his gaze steady. "I do not know," he said quietly. "It was a lady of the *ton*, certainly, who told me without hesitation that not only had I evidently done such a thing before, but that I had also promised her matrimony."

Frederica went very still, looking back at Lord Wetherby and finding a swell of uncertainty rise in her chest.

"I could not have done so when I was in my cups, given that I was with Lord Blakely and Lord Faraway, I believe, as well as being under the watchful eye of Lord Greenford," Lord Wetherby continued, referring to the time when he had first been introduced to Frederica. "I told the lady repeatedly that she was mistaken, but she was most insistent."

"Could you not simply have stepped back from her?" the duchess asked, speaking the question that had formed in Frederica's mind. "Returned to Lord Greenford?"

Lord Wetherby grimaced. "If I had been able to, I would have done so without hesitation," he stated, his jaw tense. "But the lady had a very tight hold of me, and if I attempted to remove myself from her by force, I feared that I would draw attention to myself."

A tremble shook Frederica's frame. "And, in doing so, force you into a situation that required matrimony as the only satisfactory conclusion," she said as the earl nodded. "Good gracious. I have heard, of course, of *gentlemen* seeking to do such a thing—although their intention is not matrimony, I should not imagine—but I have never heard of a lady lying in wait for a gentleman."

"You are as astonished as I," Lord Wetherby replied, grimacing. "I shall not go into particular detail, but I did, eventually, manage to extract myself—but only when I had seen another person approaching us. Someone who, I believe, intended to supposedly catch us together and, thereafter, make certain that this promise of marriage I had supposedly made was then fulfilled."

Frederica swallowed hard, not quite certain what to make of such a remark, and instead looked toward the duchess, who was also sitting with an expression of shock rippling over her features.

"Thereafter, I recalled something about the night I made my

way to this house," Lord Wetherby continued, only for the duchess to rise suddenly.

"Might I ask the duke to step in?" she asked as Lord Wetherby looked up at her in surprise. "I am certain he will be more than interested to hear what you have to say, Lord Wetherby."

The earl nodded. "But of course," he answered at once, spreading his hands. "I have nothing to hide from anyone present."

Frederica watched him closely as the duchess quickly spoke to one of the footmen that lingered just outside the door. Lord Wetherby had run one hand over his eyes a good many times these last few minutes and the lines on his forehead were a constant presence, given just how often he frowned.

"You do not doubt me, Lady Frederica?"

The way he looked up at her, the hope and the fear mingling in his expression, made Frederica want to reach out to him, to take his hand in hers and to press it hard so that he might feel nothing but reassurance.

"Lord Wetherby," she said gently as the duchess continued to hover by the door, "I accept your words without hesitation for, as you have said, there is nothing about this lady's expectations that could have come from you. If you were in company, then why would you have stepped away? And with Lord Greenford being such a considerate friend, I am certain that he would have stepped in to make sure that you did nothing improper."

The relief that poured into Lord Wetherby's expression made Frederica smile. The lines lifted just a little and his jaw no longer remained as tense. In fact, a tiny smile lifted one corner of his mouth and Frederica could not help but smile back at him, knowing just how reassured he must now feel. She spoke honestly, for there was nothing in her that encouraged her to consider him guilty of what he had told her. The concern in his expression, the worry in his eyes, and the doubt in his voice had expressed his fear that she and the duchess would instantly believe the lady's demands of him, that they might then think him just as terrible a rogue as this unknown lady thought him to be. If Frederica could have done so, she would have reached out and touched his hand in order to reassure him further. Indeed, the desire to do so increased all the more as she looked into his eyes, but Frederica was prevented from doing as she wished by the return of the duchess and, a few moments thereafter, the appearance of the duke.

"Lord Wetherby."

Lord Wetherby rose quickly. "Your Grace," he said, inclining his head. "I did not mean to disturb you from your business, but I have recalled something about the night I was here. Something that, for whatever reason, will now no longer leave my mind."

The duke sat down near to his wife and nodded. "Pray, continue."

"The evening I left the soiree," Lord Wetherby began quietly, "I made my way to the carriage and, seeing the door open and waiting for me, stepped inside. I sat down contentedly, thinking that the evening had gone very well, only to become aware of another in the carriage itself."

Frederica caught her breath, her eyes widening. "Someone was waiting for you?"

Lord Wetherby nodded, his eyes catching hers for a moment before darting away, fixing themselves to the floor as he continued to speak.

"I cannot recall her face or her voice," he said as Frederica gasped, realizing that it was a lady who had been sitting within. "All I remember is the fright that filled me as I realized she was there, followed by my demands that she quit my carriage."

"But she did not?"

Lord Wetherby shrugged. "I cannot say, Lady Frederica," he replied quickly. "What I do recall is practically throwing myself from the carriage and telling the driver I would make my own way home."

A measure of understanding lodged itself in Frederica's mind. "And thus, you sought out a hackney."

Lord Wetherby nodded before passing another hand over his eyes. "I did," he said quietly. "But as I climbed in, I saw another carriage coming behind the hackney and waiting for it to depart. Not quite realizing what was occurring, I climbed inside and instructed the hackney driver to drive to my townhouse. It was only a short time later that I realized the carriage was following me. Thereafter, I encouraged the driver to make his way a little faster along the London streets—which, I know, upset you all greatly."

Frederica looked at her uncle, who had now reached across and taken his wife's hand in his own.

"The hackney," she heard him breathe as Lord Wetherby's tight smile caught his lips. "We were nearly run from the road."

"I can only apologize," Lord Wetherby replied, one hand pressed to his heart. "I was doing all I could to lose the carriage, evidently afraid that the lady who had been sitting in my own was now following me." A loud groan issued from his lips as he shook his head. "Would that I could recall her face."

"That does not explain why you stopped at my townhouse," the duke said quietly. "You did not want to return home, I presume?"

"I dared not," Lord Wetherby answered, his expression now pained. "From what I now recall, I told the hackney driver to stop abruptly, paid him hastily, and gave him a little more to continue driving through the London streets for a few more minutes, in the hope that the carriage behind me would not know that I had left it. Given that I dared not return home, I found my way through to the servants' entrance and made my way into the house." Rising to his feet abruptly, Lord Wetherby threw up his hands. "Why I decided to sleep, I do not know," he said heavily. "When I try to remember more, my mind refuses to give me anything but darkness. I am quite certain that all I have said thus far is quite true, but to try and recall any more seems quite impossible."

Frederica let out her breath slowly, letting herself think carefully about what Lord Wetherby had said. She frowned hard, looking down at her clasped hands and trying to understand what exactly had occurred.

"It was by chance that you arrived here," the duke said slowly, and Lord Wetherby nodded, still pacing up and down in front of the fireplace. "And given that you are struggling to recall a good many things and that your memory is so very fragmented, we are left with only two possibilities."

"Oh?" Frederica looked up, seeing her uncle nod, his own brow furrowed deeply.

"One," the duke began, ticking them off on his fingers. "You were entirely inebriated, Lord Wetherby, which I know that you claim you were not."

"I will insist upon it, if I have to," Lord Wetherby replied firmly. "I am quite certain that I only had one glass of brandy that evening and that, since then, have barely touched a drop of liquor." His eyes turned back to Frederica, who smiled at him tentatively. "I wished very much to improve the poor impression that had been made upon Lady Frederica in particular."

"Which you have done," Frederica told him, making a glimmer of a smile appear. "What is the other option, Uncle?"

The duke cleared his throat. "The second option is that something was added to your brandy, Lord Wetherby. Something that might make you more compliant, more willing to go along with whatever was set before you."

Frederica blinked rapidly, her heart picking up its pace as she saw how Lord Wetherby froze in place, his eyes widening as he took in the suggestion.

"There are plenty of things that could have been surreptitiously added," the duke continued as Lord Wetherby stared back at him, clearly having never thought of such a thing. "Perhaps the person in question hoped that you might drink a good deal more but, when you did not, added this to your brandy so that their plan would succeed."

"Their plan?" Frederica repeated as the duke nodded. "You mean to say that someone clearly wished for Lord Wetherby to step into the carriage and by doing so, be forced into matrimony?"

"The very same person who met you in the gardens last evening, Lord Wetherby," the duchess said quietly. "They clearly believe that you promised to wed them and have since made no effort to do so. They cannot simply stand up in society and state that you have done so, for who would believe them?"

"Precisely!" Frederica exclaimed, also getting to her feet. "Therefore, believing that you have compromised this young lady, whoever she is, they are now attempting to force you into the very situation they believe you promised to her."

Lord Wetherby ran one hand through his hair and blew out a long breath, dropping his head low as he did so.

"That would make a good deal of sense," the duke said, looking down at his wife. "First by making certain that you were discovered in the carriage with her and, since that ploy failed entirely, to then discover you in the gardens with the very same lady."

"But I am quite certain I did not make any such promise," Lord Wetherby explained, throwing up his hands. "Lord Greenford would have made certain I did nothing foolish or untoward that night of the ball and, thereafter, I *was* in control of myself...or," he continued, now looking a little doubtful, "as much in control of myself as I could be."

Frederica moved toward him, seeing the confusion and the doubt on his face and finding herself eager to encourage him. "It is clear that you did not drink as much of the brandy as perhaps the perpetrator had expected," she said as he lifted his head to look into her eyes. "Mayhap they thought you would take one drink after another and thought to add more of their concoction so that, when you finally came to stepping inside the carriage, you would be entirely unaware of the lady sitting there."

"Until it was too late," Lord Wetherby muttered, closing his eyes and appearing very distressed indeed. "I had not expected such a thing, I confess. But now that we have discussed it, I can see that the conclusions reached are viable."

Frederica did not know what to say, looking from Lord Wetherby's somewhat forlorn expression back toward her uncle and aunt, who sat quietly, looking at Lord Wetherby with concern flickering in their eyes.

"I am sorry, Lord Wetherby," she found herself saying, as

though it was she who had put him in this position. "If there is anything that I can do to help this situation, then—"

"The difficulty is, Lady Frederica, that I do not know what *can* be done," Lord Wetherby replied, lifting his gaze back to hers. "I have no knowledge, not even a single thought, as to who might be behind these dark intentions and, as such, cannot think as to what I might do."

The duchess rose. "What you will do, Lord Wetherby, is stay for dinner," Frederica said practically. "Uncle?"

"But of course," the duke agreed as a faint smile lifted Lord Wetherby's expression. "This is clearly a lot to accept and I am sure that a hearty meal will improve matters."

Lord Wetherby let out a heavy sigh but smiled in gratitude.

"I thank you," he said, bowing toward the duchess. "You are both very kind, particularly when I know that I have no cause to turn to you for assistance in this matter. I came only to explain why I found myself present in your house and yet the generosity you have shown me is more than I have ever expected."

The duke and duchess shared a look and Frederica could not help but chuckle.

"You will find, Lord Wetherby, that the duke and duchess themselves have had a difficult foray through society," she said as Lord Wetherby's eyes rounded in surprise. "And, indeed, we would not turn away from you now, not when you are clearly in some distress. This is a most extraordinary situation, and it would not be right to permit you to traverse it alone."

Lord Wetherby pressed one hand to his heart and inclined his head. "Then I am all the more grateful," he told her quietly. "I do not feel as though I deserve such consideration."

"Then you are mistaken," Frederica told him, smiling into his eyes and finding that her heart seemed to lift as he returned it with one of his own. "For in the midst of difficulty, everyone surely deserves kindness and generosity."

"Perhaps they do," he replied as the duke rose to pour two glasses of brandy and the duchess rang the bell so that she might relay her orders about their additional guest for dinner. "But not everyone is willing to give it, Lady Frederica. You are one of the most generous young ladies I believe I have ever had the pleasure of knowing and I am greatly appreciative of your kindness, your goodness, and your willingness to come alongside me in this." He reached out and took her hand in his, lifting it for a moment as he bowed—his action hidden from both the duchess and the duke, who were busy with their own tasks. "Lady Frederica, I am very grateful indeed."

10

The sheer nervousness that flooded him as he stepped into Lord and Lady Ambrose's drawing room was so great that Percy wanted nothing more than to immediately turn on his heel and make his way from the room. But, lifting his chin and putting a smile on his face, he greeted Lord Ambrose quickly before bowing over Lady Ambrose's hand.

"Thank you very much for your invitation this evening," he said, pushing aside his fear that he would find himself in a difficult situation once more and that, this time, he would have no way of freeing himself. "And what are we to expect this evening?"

Lady Ambrose blushed furiously, her eyes twinkling as she looked back at him. "There is to be a performer this evening," she told him as Lord Ambrose greeted their next guest. "A wonderful conjuror—or so I have been told."

"How very intriguing," Percy said, his brow lifting as Lady Ambrose giggled. "I look forward to that performance, Lady Ambrose." Seeing the other guests coming into the room, he took his leave of the lady and stepped away, looking around the room but finding that, instead of feeling his usual interest and eagerness to greet and converse with anyone in his acquaintance, he was now a good deal more reluctant. He knew a good many guests here this evening, and some were already smiling at him in welcome. Yet Percy felt no such delight or encouragement. Instead, he was aware of the tension that coiled in his stomach, that seemed to wrap around his bones as he looked all about him. Just which of these acquaintances was attempting to coerce him into marriage?

"Lord Wetherby, good evening."

Seeing Lord Greenford, Percy let out a quiet breath of relief, pasted a broad smile on his face, and made his way to join his friend. "Good evening, Lord Greenford," he said, before looking around the others that stood in the small group. "And Lady Simmons, Lord Willerton, and Lady Prudence." He bowed. "Good evening to you all." A little surprised that Lady Prudence stood without her chaperone, Percy waited until they had all greeted him in response before he continued to speak. "And are you all looking forward to seeing this conjuror?" he asked, and Lady Prudence laughed, her eyes bright. "I take it, Lady Prudence, that *you* certainly are."

"Indeed, I am," Lady Prudence said, just as her chaperone moved back beside her, having perhaps been required to step away for a few minutes. "I have never seen such a thing before."

"I have heard there are some well-known ones on the continent," Lord Greenford said as Percy found himself listening with a little more interest than before. "I am not at all certain about the ones here in London. I presume that Lord Ambrose has found the very best, however. This evening's performance will be sure to take our breath away." He chuckled as Lady Prudence giggled, her eyes dancing as Lord Greenford grinned at her. Percy's brow lifted as he looked on, wondering quietly to himself whether or not Lord Greenford was aware of just how much he clearly enjoyed Lady Prudence's company. Lady Prudence was something of a flirt and giggled far too much for Percy's liking, but she would find a good match in Lord Greenford—of that, Percy was quite certain. Perhaps he would suggest to Lord Greenford that he continue his acquaintance with her, in place of the apparent affection he had for Lady Frederica.

"The performance is to begin very soon, from what I understand," said Lady Simmons, looking rather excited. "I do wonder what will occur. I have never seen such a thing before."

"It will be *most* enjoyable," Lord Greenford said commandingly. "Lady Prudence, might I ask if you would give me the pleasure of your company during the performance itself?"

Percy's brows rose, looking from Lord Greenford back to Lady Prudence, who was, once more, giggling delightedly, her hand at her mouth. It took her some moments to answer in the affirmative, but she did so without hesitation, leaving Lord Greenford appearing very pleased.

"I did not know that you had an interest in Lady Prudence," Percy remarked as the group disbanded. "I was about to suggest to you that I thought her an excellent match for you, but it seems that you have already come to that particular conclusion."

Lord Greenford chuckled. "I think her very pretty and enjoy conversation with her," he stated, looking back over his shoulder toward the lady. "I am glad that she has agreed to sit with me, however. I was not certain she would." He looked back at Percy, his smile drooping just a little. "Although I do hope that you will not find yourself seated alone."

Percy grinned. "I will be contented to sit alone, if I must," he said as Lord Greenford frowned. "But I am sure that I will have an acquaintance here or there that I might choose to sit by." His own smile dropped as he recalled the precise reason he was being cautious. "Although," he continued slowly, "I will choose such a person with the greatest care."

"And why would that be?" Lord Greenford asked, giving Percy something of a startled look.

Hesitating, Percy considered for a moment before he began to explain. He told Lord Greenford everything, keeping his voice low and seeing how Lord Greenford's eyes widened in shock.

"I must ask you," Percy finished, looking fixedly at his friend, "whether you are quite certain that I did not do anything untoward that night of the ball. The night when I was so very foxed that I treated Lady Frederica with such inconsideration."

Lord Greenford's brow was lowered, and for a few moments, he did not speak. Percy wanted to close his eyes and groan aloud, fearing the worst, only for Lord Greenford to shake his head.

"I am quite certain that you did not go into the gardens and pull a young lady with you, if that is what you are asking," he said as a sheen of sweat formed across Percy's brow as relief coursed through him. "Being, as I am, the most excellent of friends, I remained close to you for the rest of the evening, making sure that you did not do any such thing again. Knowing that you would have to apologize to Lady Frederica for your ridiculousness, I thought it best to spare you from having to do so with a good many others also."

"Then you are quite sure of it," Percy confirmed, seeing Lord Greenford nod. "I did not do as this lady—whoever she is—now believes."

"I am certain you did not," came the reply, and Percy closed his eyes and dropped his head, entirely reassured. "This must be a mistake."

"But I cannot tell the lady so," Percy replied, frustrated. "I do not know who she is, and even if I were to claim that I did not do as she believes, I am not at all certain that she would accept that to be the truth."

"I see," Lord Greenford muttered, his frown increasing all the more. "That is most extraordinary. Whatever are you to do?"

Percy shook his head, a scowl on his face. "I could not tell you," he stated as Lord Greenford grimaced. "I spoke with the Duke and Duchess of Ellsworth as well as Lady Frederica last evening, and for the moment, the only thing that we could think to do was to continue on as before, but to make certain that I was being very cautious."

Lord Greenford nodded slowly, his eyes darting away, looking from one side of the room to the other. "It could be anyone here," he said surreptitiously. "Is that not so?"

"Indeed it is," Percy replied as Lord Greenford continued to look around the room. "That is why you find me a little out of sorts this evening, although that does not mean that I expect you to sit by me during the performance." He grinned at Lord Greenford. "Especially when you have Lady Prudence joining you."

Lord Greenford smiled but it did not quite reach his eyes. "I will do all I can to assist you," he said, leaning a little closer so that Percy had to strain to hear him. "I will be on my guard. Watching so that you are not as alone as you might feel."

"I appreciate your willingness," Percy replied, truly grateful for his friend's support. "Let us hope that nothing untoward will occur this evening."

∽

"You appear to be a little more relaxed than you were last evening, Lord Wetherby."

Percy found himself smiling at Lady Frederica as she came toward him, leaving the duke and duchess a short distance behind as they continued their conversation with another guest. "Good evening, Lady Frederica," he replied, smiling at her. Her beautiful green eyes were warm and filled with light, her smile delicate, and her golden curls tumbling down from the back of her head, with a few brushing her temples. Percy's breath hitched in his chest as she came closer, finding himself a little overwhelmed by her beauty this evening.

"You are a little improved?"

"I am," Percy replied, aware of just how much strain he had been under last evening. His mind had been filled with all that they had discussed, realizing that there was a good deal more to his situation than he had first anticipated. What had concerned him the most was the awareness that he had no idea who this particular lady—or ladies—might be and thus, he was to be left entirely in the dark, fumbling around in the hope that he would be able to find a chink of light. Thankfully, the evening had slowly improved with the conversation that he had enjoyed with the duke, duchess, and Lady Frederica. He had found Lady Frederica in particular to be very engaging, and there had even been laughter toward the end of the evening.

"I am glad," Lady Frederica replied softly. "I had wondered if you would find this evening something of a strain, but it seems that you are doing very well thus far."

"I have spoken to Lord Greenford," Percy told her as Lady Frederica's eyebrows lifted in gentle surprise. "I have told him all and he, in turn, has stated that he will be as much on his guard as I." His smile lifted the corners of his lips. "I am certainly not alone in this."

Lady Frederica held his gaze. "No, you are not, Lord Wetherby," she said solemnly, a great deal of meaning in her words. "Nor shall you be for the remainder of the Season—or until you find yourself betrothed."

"Betrothed?" Percy choked, only for Lady Frederica to laugh, her eyes twinkling.

"I meant, by your own choosing," she said as Percy closed his eyes with relief. "Not that you would be forced into such a situation."

"I see," he replied, laughing now at his own foolishness. "I confess that I have—"

"If we might all consider coming through to the music room?"

The voice of their host caught Percy's attention and he looked away from Lady Frederica, seeing Lord Ambrose lead the first of his guests through to another room. Turning back to Lady Frederica, he offered her his arm. "Should you like to join me, Lady Frederica?" he asked, his heart lifting all the more as she accepted immediately. "Have you ever seen a conjuror before?"

"I have not," Lady Frederica replied as they made their way toward the music room, the Duke and Duchess behind them. "I am very excited, I confess."

"As am I," Percy agreed, feeling a good deal more at ease with Lady Frederica beside him. There was nothing more for them to do but sit down together and watch the performance, so surely nothing untoward could happen then?

~

"Goodness, that was one of the most remarkable things I have ever seen."

Percy chuckled as he led Lady Frederica back through to the drawing room. "It was rather magnificent," he admitted as Lady Frederica shook her head in evident astonishment at what she had seen. "I should very much like to go and ask him how certain things were done, but I do not think he would tell me."

"I should think not," Lady Frederica laughed, her eyes twinkling. "For then what employment could he get if he told you all of his methods?"

"Lord Wetherby, Lady Frederica. Might I ask what you thought of the performance?"

Percy stopped and inclined his head toward Lord Ambrose. "My congratulations on an excellent evening, Lord Ambrose," he said, seeing how his host beamed with pleasure. "We were only just speaking of how wonderful that was."

"I am very glad to hear it," Lord Ambrose replied with such a look of relief that Percy wanted to laugh. "It was something of an unusual engagement, but if it has gone well then I am very contented indeed."

Lady Ambrose drew near and began to engage Lady Frederica in conversation. Percy, seeing that his time with the lady was at an end, took his leave of them both and did not miss the way that Lady Frederica held his gaze for a long moment before she turned back toward Lady Ambrose. His heart soared, making him fully aware of just how much he had come to appreciate Lady Frederica's company. She was, as he had said to her himself, one of the most extraordinary young ladies of his acquaintance and he was very glad indeed to know her a little better. Meandering around the room for a short time, he nodded and smiled at a few acquaintances.

"Will you come join us for cards, Lord Wetherby?" Lord Taylor clapped one hand on Percy's shoulder, making him turn around. "We are to set up a few games in the library."

Pleased to have been asked, Percy nodded. "I should enjoy that," he agreed, turning toward the door. "The library, you say?"

The gentleman nodded and stepped away. "I will join you in a moment," he said as Percy made his way toward the door. "I must also ask Lord Fothergill if he wishes to join us."

Making his way back out into the hall, Percy hesitated for a moment, his steps slowing. He had not given a moment's thought to stepping away from the rest of the guests, for a card game was usually the done thing at a soiree. But a niggle of uncertainty entered his heart as he continued to make his way toward the library, not quite certain whether or not he was doing the right thing.

The library door was ajar and Percy stepped inside, only to stop dead as he realized the room was entirely empty. Where were the others?

Perhaps Lord Taylor is the one seeking to set up the game, he told himself, taking a small step inside and ignoring the thrill of dread that ran up his spine. *You are being overly cautious.*

A small sound came from behind him and Percy turned around at once, expecting to see someone there.

A sharp pain seared across the back of his head and blackness began to surround him almost at once. Groaning aloud, he pressed one hand to his head and felt himself begin to sway. His vision blurred as he put his other hand out, seeking desperately for something to hold onto.

Someone grasped his arm and the next moment, Percy felt himself falling backwards, fearing that he would hit the floor and knock himself out entirely, only to land on something soft. Try as he might, his vision simply would not clear and, although a figure moved about in front of him, he could not make out their face.

"What are you doing?" he tried to say, only for his words to come out in a garbled mess. Closing his eyes against the pain that now ricocheted through his head, he tried to find some strength to sit up, to push himself away, or to stand and make his way from the room, but weakness poured through him like a river.

He could see nothing, finding it too difficult to even open his eyes. He heard sounds but they seemed to come from very far away. And then, someone touched his forehead, their hand cool against his skin.

"Lord Wetherby?"

Percy recognized the voice but could not seem to speak a single word.

"I think he is bleeding," he heard someone say. "We should return him home at once."

"No," said another voice. "To our townhouse. Quickly now."

Somehow, Percy found himself being raised to his feet, his head drooping down so that his chin practically rested on his chest. Blinking rapidly, his vision still blurred, he managed to take a few steps forward, being supported by someone on his right.

"Come, Lord Wetherby," he heard someone say—someone he was sure now was Lady Frederica. "You are quite safe now."

"Safe," he muttered, the word falling from his lips. Another person came to support him on his other side and, trusting now that he would be helped in whatever way he required, Percy allowed them to lead him wherever they intended to go.

11

Frederica bit her lip as she paced up and down the drawing room, her heart quailing with anxiety. The duchess watched her with a concerned expression, having already begged her to be seated but having been met with refusal.

"He will be quite all right," the duchess said, not for the first time. "It was an injury to the back of his head. The doctor will be able to clean it and make certain he is well."

Frederica swallowed hard, turning to the duchess. "He was so very pale," she said, her heart constricting as she remembered the sight of him lying on the chaise longue as they had entered the library. "The way he could not lift his head, the way he tried to speak..." She closed her eyes tightly, dragging in a shaky breath. "It was most distressing."

"He will be well," the duchess said firmly. "I know you are anxious, my dear, but trust the physician to do as he is trained to do. I am quite certain that Lord Wetherby will, himself, walk into this room unaided and you will see that he is recovered."

Wanting desperately to believe this but not fully able to do so, Frederica nodded, turned, and resumed her pacing. The memory of walking into the library and seeing Lord Wetherby lying there still plagued her. It had only been by chance that she had seen him depart and, after a moment, had found her worries increasing given that no other gentleman appeared to be doing so. A quick conversation with a footman told her that Lord Wetherby had made his way to the library, although he did not know why. With the duchess and the duke by her side, Frederica had hurried toward the library, throwing the door open wide. It had only been a moment before the two ladies that they had discovered within had fled from the room, running around the furniture until they had escaped through the doorway, their skirts billowing. She had not even had a thought about going after them, looking only to Lord Wetherby and realizing that he had been injured.

The door to the drawing room opened and, as Frederica turned toward it hopefully, she saw that it was only her uncle. Her shoulders slumped as the duke came forward, although she prayed that the serious expression on his face did not speak of something all the more concerning as regarded Lord Wetherby.

"He will join us in a few minutes," the duke said quietly. "I have sent some staff to his townhouse to collect items he will require, given that he should stay here for the present."

Frederica blinked rapidly, one hand settling against her heart. "He is recovering?"

The duke nodded. "A blow to the back of his head," he told her by way of explanation. "There was some bleeding, but it was not severe. The doctor has cleaned the wound and has declared that he will be back to his usual strength in a day or so. However," he said, sitting down next to his wife and taking her hand in his, "I have insisted that he remain here until tomorrow at the very least." His expression was serious, his eyes narrowed as he rose from his chair and went to pour two brandies. "This is certainly now becoming a little more serious."

"If only we could have found those two ladies," the duchess said, regret in both her expression and the way she shook her head. "I know that it was right for us to ensure that Lord Wetherby was quite well, but I feel as though we have done him an injustice in being so close to identifying them but permitting them to leave."

Frederica gave her aunt a brief, encouraging smile. "We had no other choice," she said, one hand thrown up carelessly. "Lord Wetherby needed our help, and evidently, we arrived a few minutes before they had fully prepared the scene." When she had thrown open the door and walked in, one of the ladies had been bending over Lord Wetherby, with the other standing by her. With only a few candles lit around the room, Frederica had been entirely unable to make out their faces and, thus, as they had escaped from the room, she had not had even a flicker of recognition.

"It is frustrating, I admit," the duke agreed, sitting back down again with both brandies now set on a table near to him. "However, we did what was required. To remove Lord Wetherby from the house was of great importance. We do not want the *ton* to be aware of what occurred, for then all manner of rumors might begin."

Nodding, Frederica again began to pace up and down, her anxiety a good deal more settled now that she knew Lord Wetherby was well on his way to recovery. The strain of the evening had begun to take its toll, for she found herself very fatigued even though, had they remained at Lord Ambrose's soiree, she would not have had a thought to return home as yet.

"Ring for tea, Frederica," the duchess said gently. "I can see that you require some refreshment and both the butler and the housekeeper are still attending to their duties, given that we are to have Lord Wetherby reside with us."

She nodded and rose to do so, and as she rang the bell, she saw the door handle turn and push open slowly.

Her heart jumped into her throat as Lord Wetherby stepped into the drawing room, looking all about him as though he was not at all certain what sort of welcome he would receive.

"Lord Wetherby!" Frederica exclaimed, hurrying toward him, unable to keep the relief from her voice. "You are recovered?"

Lord Wetherby smiled weakly and, even in the candlelight, Frederica could see the dark shadows underneath his eyes and the lines of strain that ran across his forehead. Before she could stop herself, she had found his hand and, clutching it in both of her own, looked into his eyes. "You are a little better, then?"

"A little better, yes." His voice was thin and rasping, his fingers cold. "I am very grateful indeed to you all for what you have done." He placed his hand on top of Frederica's, his fingers pressing hers. "I heard your voice, Lady Frederica, and knew that I was safe from whatever danger had pulled me into its grasp."

Frederica swallowed the ache in her throat and looked back at him steadily. "I am only glad that we were there in time," she said quietly. "It seems that the ladies who have been attempting to force you into matrimony have gone to greater lengths than before."

"Indeed." The duke raised his eyebrows and Frederica let go of Lord Wetherby's hands at once, stepping back as the duke held up a glass of brandy in Lord Wetherby's direction.

"Please, do be seated, Lord Wetherby," she said, hastily returning to sit down herself. "You must be very tired."

He did so at once and accepted the brandy from the duke gratefully. "I am greatly fatigued," he admitted, "although the doctor states that it is increased due to what has occurred. I will be vastly improved come the morrow; I am sure of it."

"I do hope so," the duchess replied, just as the door opened and the housekeeper stepped inside. After requesting tea and something to eat for them all, the duchess dismissed her housekeeper and turned back to Lord Wetherby. "You were very pale when we found you, Lord Wetherby. That must have been a very painful blow."

Lord Wetherby winced and reached up to touch the back of his head, grimacing as he did so. "It seems that I was struck rather hard," he said, dropping his hand. "The doctor thought it was perhaps a poker or some such thing."

"Something that could easily have been wielded by either of the ladies present," Frederica said as Lord Wetherby's eyes widened.

"Do you mean to say that there were *two* ladies present?" he asked, and Frederica nodded. "Whatever for?"

"One, I suppose, to strike you and the other to guide you to the chaise lounge," Frederica replied. "You were placed there, I presume?"

Lord Wetherby frowned and rubbed at his forehead. "I do not recall precisely," he replied, grimacing. "I remember falling back into something soft, with my head feeling as though it were burning with an intense pain."

"I believe," Frederica said as the duchess reached to pour the tea, "that the two ladies intended to stage it as though you were in something of a compromising position with the young lady—whoever she may be. When others came in to join the card game, they would find you there and thus, all would be as they intended."

Lord Wetherby nodded, closing his eyes for a moment. "I do not understand their desperation," he said eventually. "Why should they be so determined? Why should they not just speak to me in a quiet manner and ask if I am to fulfill these supposed obligations so that I might then inform them that they are mistaken?"

"I do not think they would believe you, even if they did as you suggested," Frederica replied as Lord Wetherby sighed and took a sip of his brandy. "They appear to be quite certain that it is your hand they intend to force."

The duke rose to his feet, wandering across the room as he gestured, one hand held out in front of him. "You must have said something to them, Lord Wetherby, that has made them believe you have no intention of marrying this young lady," he said slowly. "Therefore, they must, as Frederica says, force your hand."

"It is just as well that you came to find me when you did," Lord Wetherby replied, his eyes turning back toward Frederica. "If you had not..." It seemed he could not finish his sentence, shaking his head to himself and looking away from her.

"It was Frederica who noticed your absence," the duchess replied quietly. "It was she who then asked one of the footmen where you had gone. It is to her that you owe your thanks."

A flush of heat began to creep up Frederica's spine as she looked first at the duchess and then toward Lord Wetherby. The look in his eyes was unfathomable, as though there was a great deal he wanted to say but simply could not find the words. Her heart began to quicken, her whole body seeming to burn with heat as Lord Wetherby leaned a little closer to her in his chair.

"I can say nothing that will express my true depths of gratitude, Lady Frederica," he said softly, as though it were only the two of them in the room. "Had you not been aware of my absence, had you not been so concerned for my wellbeing, then I might now be at home with a drink in my hand, attempting to accept my fate."

Frederica did not know what to say. She did not think that she *could* say anything, given that her mouth had gone very dry. Instead, she merely smiled and sat back in her chair, fully aware of the look that passed between the duke and the duchess. Her chest was tight, feeling as though her awareness of Lord Wetherby's presence, his words of thankfulness, and the deep intensity of his eyes as he gazed at her were much too overwhelming to bear.

"It does beg the question of what we are to do now," the duke continued after a few moments, allowing Frederica to breathe a little more easily as she glanced toward the duchess, who was smiling knowingly. "There is a greater concern for you now, Lord Wetherby. There is clearly a desperation there, a deep, unsettling fear that is being pushed to the very fore of these ladies' minds."

Lord Wetherby finished his glass of brandy. "There is nothing I can do, save to be on my guard," he said heavily.

A sudden idea slammed hard into Frederica's mind, making her catch her breath. Her eyes widened at the audacity of it, knowing that she would be risking a great deal should she do so. It might mean that her second Season would end just as the first had done. It would ask her to set aside her own intentions for the Season, her hopes and her dreams for what might have come to pass, and all for the sake of Lord Wetherby. Her brow furrowed and she leaned forward, rubbing her fingers lightly over her forehead as she thought, worrying her lip with her teeth.

"Frederica?"

She looked up, seeing the concern in her uncle's eyes as he came nearer to her.

"Are you quite well?"

Frederica drew in a deep breath, feeling herself tremble as she nodded. "I—I have a suggestion," she said slowly. "It is one that should, I would hope, protect Lord Wetherby to some degree and, mayhap, find out who precisely is behind all of this." She looked first to Lord Wetherby and then to her aunt, seeing the duchess frown, her eyes holding a good deal of worry as though she knew what Frederica was about to suggest.

"I would be glad to hear any suggestion you might have, Lady Frederica," Lord Wetherby said, looking back at her eagerly. "I do feel a little uncertain about what else I am to do, other than continue what I have been doing at present."

"And not making your way into any libraries, regardless of what you have been told," the duchess added wryly.

Lord Wetherby chuckled. "Indeed," he replied, before looking back at Frederica.

She tried to speak, but the levity displayed by the duchess and Lord Wetherby himself seemed to have thrown her thoughts into disarray. She could already see the duchess' reaction, wondering what the duke himself would say. Both of them, of course, would insist that it was a very poor idea and Lord Wetherby would outright refuse, stating that she could not give up so much solely for him.

"Frederica?"

The duke sat down in a vacant chair and looked at her steadily, making Frederica's nervousness grow all the more. "Do you have any thoughts?"

"I do."

Her voice was shaking, and Frederica forced in a long breath, steeling herself as she did so. Three pairs of eyes were watching her, waiting for her to speak, and still, Frederica could not find the words to say.

"If there is something distressing you, Frederica, then—"

"I should court Lord Wetherby."

The words were flung from her before she could prevent them, and she closed her eyes tightly as heat poured into her face.

"What I mean to say is," she continued, unable to look at anyone for fear of their reaction, "that Lord Wetherby and I should court, albeit as a façade."

Her voice was still weak and a little shaky as she forced her eyes open, looking around and seeing the three expressions on the duke, the duchess, and Lord Wetherby's faces. The duke was frowning hard, his lips pulled tight, whilst the duchess' eyes were wide with surprise, her mouth forming a perfect circle. Lord Wetherby, however, was already beginning to shake his head, his brows knotting together as he looked back at her.

"You cannot, Lady Frederica," he said, his voice low. "I can see that your kind nature is encouraging you to do such a thing for me, but there is no need. I could not bear it should you be drawn into this without explanation."

"I am already a part of it, Lord Wetherby," she told him, her voice a little firmer now that she had begun to speak. "It would encourage the person responsible to leave you be, would it not? If you are seen to be courting someone other than their daughter, then they might realize that their attempts have come to naught and will continue to do so." Taking in a deep breath, she continued before anyone else could speak. "Given what has occurred this evening, I think that something more needs to be done in order to protect you."

"But that does not mean that it has to be something that you yourself are involved in, Lady Frederica." Lord Wetherby rose to his feet, staggering for a moment as he attempted to gain his balance. Frederica watched him closely, seeing the reluctance in his eyes and knowing that it came from a place of concern. "If you do this, then you might very well be throwing away any other opportunity that could be yours come the rest of the Season. The *ton* will speak of our courtship. Everyone will know of it. And to what end? So that, should the courtship come to an end, you are left precisely where you are at this moment, only with the *ton* now believing that you are left without?"

Frederica nodded. "I believe it would be worth it, Lord Wetherby," she said, fully aware that he had spoken about *if* their courtship had to come to an end, rather than *when*. Yes, it was only for his own good that she had suggested this particular course of action, hoping that it would bring him a little more safety, but at the same time, Frederica felt a small surge of hope in her chest. Hope that there might yet be a happiness found between them that could never tear them apart.

"It is dangerous, Frederica." The duke cleared his throat, looking past Lord Wetherby and directly toward Frederica, his brow low. "You think that it might prevent these ladies from continuing along their chosen path. But what if they do not?"

She frowned. "I do not understand what you mean."

"What if, instead of doing as you expect, they go on to say to themselves that you are simply someone that must be removed from Lord Wetherby's side? What then?"

It took a moment or two for Frederica to understand what her uncle meant and, when realization came, it brought with it a cold sheen of fear that ran straight through her.

"His Grace is quite correct," she heard Lord Wetherby say, her frown remaining fixed in place. "It is too dangerous for you, Lady Frederica. Why, should they do something like this to you—" he gestured to his head, "then I should never forgive myself."

"But it would not be your doing or your responsibility," Frederica replied, lifting her gaze back to Lord Wetherby. His eyes were wide as though he feared that she would continue on with her idea regardless, his hands spread wide as he attempted to convince her not to do as she believed to be best. "I know that you are thinking only of my safety, and believe me, I well understand what you and my uncle are suggesting. However, if there is even the smallest chance that this matter can be brought to a swift conclusion, then I am determined to take it. And, if all goes as my uncle believes, if they *do* seek to pursue me and remove the acquaintance between us in some way, then is that not yet another opportunity for us to discover them? To see their faces and finally be able to know who they are?" She looked toward the duchess, seeing how she frowned but knowing that, from the look in her eyes, she would not prevent Frederica from following this course of action. The duchess had been quietly determined last Season to find the truth and, in the very same way, Frederica was now in exactly the same position.

"Let us all think on the matter." The duchess rose to her feet and came toward Frederica, settling one hand on her shoulder. "There is no need to make any decisions at present. To think of doing so when it is so very late in the evening is, perhaps, something of a foolish thought in itself." She smiled down at Frederica, who knew that the duchess would wish to speak to her about her intentions privately, so that it all could be discussed without the duke or Lord Wetherby's presence.

"Very well," Frederica replied, just as Lord Wetherby nodded and sank back down into his chair.

"A wise thought, my dear." The duke smiled at his wife and Frederica rose from her seat, smiling back at her uncle.

"I think I shall retire," she said as the duchess nodded. "Do excuse me. I do hope, Lord Wetherby, that you gain all the rest you require and that your head is a good deal less painful come the morning."

His eyes seemed to glow as he looked back at her, getting to his feet once more. Frederica caught her breath, a swirl of uncertainty settling in her stomach as she looked into his eyes, not certain what it was that he was thinking or feeling. Was he angry with her for what she had suggested? Upset that she wished to become involved? Or was there even the smallest sense of hope that she had now within her heart?

"Good evening, Lady Frederica," Lord Wetherby murmured, bowing low. "I thank you again for your kindness, your generosity, and your consideration. As I said earlier this evening, I do not think that I would be here with you all without it."

Frederica smiled at him and, after a moment, the corner of Lord

Wetherby's mouth lifted just a fraction, stealing some of the solemnity from his face. Without another word, Frederica bobbed a quick curtsy in his direction, nodded to her uncle, and then made her way toward the door, with the duchess stating that she, too, intended to retire before following after Frederica.

"I know that you wish to speak to me about my suggestion, Louisa," Frederica said quickly, the moment the door had closed behind them. "I am aware that there are dangers and uncertainties involved in the matter but—"

The duchess put one hand on Frederica's arm, her gaze a little stern.

"Frederica," she said, interrupting her. "I will only ask you about one particular matter."

Frederica nodded. "Please."

"I must ask you whether or not you have considered what this 'courtship' might mean," the duchess said, dropping her hand. "What if Lord Wetherby finds that he is enamored with your company and he wishes to continue the courtship with you? What if you find yourself desperate for your courtship to go on, to further itself into something more? Something...*permanent?*"

Dropping her head, Frederica was all too aware of the flush that made its way into her cheeks. It was not something that she wanted to hide from the duchess, but she still felt a good deal of embarrassment mentioning it to her.

"Louisa," she began, choosing her words with the greatest of care. "That is something that I have considered, I assure you." With a deep breath, she looked back at her aunt. "I will not pretend that I feel nothing for Lord Wetherby, for to say so would be quite untrue. I have no doubt that I might come to wish that our courtship continues and yes, that perhaps I would begin to think of something akin to matrimony. However," she continued as the duchess' eyes widened, "I also step forward into this in the full awareness that Lord Wetherby might not feel the same. If he decides that our courtship is to come to an end, then I will accept it."

"But you might very well be filled with great distress because of it," the duchess exclaimed. "Is such a thing worth enduring?"

Frederica hesitated, biting her lip for a moment. "Yes," she said, determination rising up in her chest. "Yes, Louisa. Despite the difficulties that may arise, despite the pain that may follow, I truly believe that it will be worth it in the end."

The duchess pressed her lips together and searched Frederica's face for a few moments, before sighing and turning away.

"I do hope you are right, Frederica," she said gently. "I will let you retire now. Good evening."

Frederica smiled at her aunt, grateful that she would not be prevented from doing as she had suggested. "Good night, Louisa."

12

As Percy climbed out of the carriage and then turned to offer Lady Frederica his hand, a deep, unsettling anxiousness flooded his heart. He had not been certain that agreeing to this courtship had been a wise idea, but given Lady Frederica's determination and the duke's apparent acquiescence, Percy had decided to accept the suggestion. Now, he and Lady Frederica were to go out walking together, with the duchess joining them, of course, but to walk in Hyde Park during the fashionable hour was certain to gain them a good deal of attention.

"Are you quite certain, Lady Frederica?"

She smiled at him, her eyes dazzling in the afternoon sunshine. "I am quite determined, Lord Wetherby," she said as he nodded and looked away, finding the urge to protect her growing steadily. "You do not think that I will change my mind, I hope?"

He looked back at her and saw her smiling face, her twinkling eyes, and the glint of steel that was held within them. "No," he answered, a trifle ruefully. "No, Lady Frederica, I do not believe that you will be convinced either way."

"Good." She laughed and took his arm before he had even offered it, her touch seeming to send his heart into all manner of delights given how quickly it beat. "I confess, Lord Wetherby, that I am more determined than perhaps is apparent. I do not like the idea that you should be left to this difficult situation alone, and therefore, I am all the more eager to come alongside you and make certain that you are not so badly injured again." Her head turned toward him as a stray curl bounced gently across her cheek. "How are you feeling at present?"

"Much improved," he promised her, seeing the relief in her smile. "I will not say that my head does not ache somewhat, but it is certainly nothing compared to yesterday."

Lady Frederica winced. "I can only imagine the depths of pain you were in," she said, looking back toward the path they were to take as they stepped away from the carriage, leaving the duchess to follow a short distance away. "That must have come as a great shock."

Percy grimaced and shook his head. "It was my own fault, Lady Frederica," he told her, regret filling him. "The moment I stepped into the library, I knew something was wrong. I was expecting it to have at least one or two other gentlemen there, with the card table ready and waiting for us. To see the room so empty and quiet sent a great warning ringing around my ears."

"But you stayed there anyway?" she asked, no judgment in her voice but a flicker of surprise in her gaze. "Would it not have been best to return to the drawing room?"

"Yes," he admitted quickly. "It would have been very wise indeed, Lady Frederica. But I told myself that I was being foolish, that there was nothing to concern myself with. And then…" He gestured to his head. "I should speak to Lord Taylor," he added as an afterthought. "He was the one who told me that there was to be a card game in the library."

Lady Frederica's hand tightened on his arm. "And there was not?"

"I do not know," he told her honestly. "There may well have been, but it would have occurred after I had been injured. The ladies who attacked me must have been expecting others to come and join me in the library, else what would have been the point of doing as they did?"

A frown touched Lady Frederica's brow. "That is true," she mused quietly. "Although mayhap Lord Taylor was asked to seek you out *first* and encourage you to make your way to the library just as soon as you could. That way—"

"Lady Frederica!"

They were prevented from speaking further by the loud and somewhat obnoxious voice of Lady Warrington, who was gazing at Lady Frederica with wide eyes before she turned them toward Percy. Knowing that Lady Warrington was inclined toward gossip and that, within minutes of them departing her company, she would begin to tell everyone within earshot of what she had just seen or discussed, Percy felt his stomach tighten uncomfortably. He did not want Lady Frederica to be in any danger and yet this was precisely what he had agreed to, was it not?

"Good afternoon, Lady Warrington," Lady Frederica began as the duchess came to stand beside her charge. "It is a very pleasant afternoon, is it not?"

"It is," Lady Warrington replied, looking first at Percy and then at the duchess. "Oh, and good afternoon to you also, Your Grace. And to you, Lord Wetherby."

Percy cleared his throat and bowed, aware now that Lady Frederica's hand was still on his arm. "Good afternoon," he muttered, but Lady Warrington was already speaking again, although her eyes continued to dart between Lady Frederica and him, as though convincing herself that what she was seeing was quite real.

"And so you are out for a walk together this afternoon?" Lady Warrington asked as Lady Frederica smiled blandly. "It is a very fine afternoon, as you yourself have said, Lady Frederica."

"It is," came the reply. "And how is your own daughter, Lady Warrington?"

The conversation continued in such a vein for some time until, finally, Lady Frederica managed to extract them all from Lady

Warrington's eagerness and, stepping away from her, bid her farewell.

A heaviness settled over Percy's heart as he made his way along the path once more, his brows knotting together.

"If you continue to frown that way, Lord Wetherby, then no one will think that you are actually enjoying my company," Lady Frederica's voice was light, but there was a touch of anxiety in her words. "Is something the matter?"

Percy hesitated, wondering whether or not to be truthful. "Lady Warrington is something of a gossip, is she not?" he asked, just as Lady Frederica laughed.

"She is a *terrible* gossip, Lord Wetherby," came the reply. "Although that is precisely what we are hoping for, is it not?"

He wanted to say yes, wanted to agree that this was *precisely* what he wanted, but found that the words simply could not come from him.

"I am concerned for you, Lady Frederica," he said, choosing to speak honestly. "I know that I have agreed to this courtship, that I have said that I will consent to all that you yourself have planned, but in doing so, I realize now just how much danger I am placing you in. What if Lady Warrington tells the ladies that seek to force me into matrimony with one of them?"

Lady Frederica frowned, stopped walking, and turned to face him. "But Lord Wetherby, that is exactly what we want to happen," she said, sounding confused. "Are you now saying that you have changed your mind?"

"No, no," he repeated, screwing his eyes closed tightly for a few moments. "My concern is your wellbeing, Lady Frederica. What if something so terrible occurs that I—"

"Lord Wetherby."

Her gloved hand had taken his and, in that one single instant, Percy felt his heart turn over in his chest, his breath catching as he looked down at their joined hands.

"You are very considerate," she said softly. "I know that you are concerned for me, but you know that I have discussed the matter at length with both the duke and the duchess. I will not be moved from this. No matter what may befall us, I will not permit you to face such difficulties alone." Her smile faded. "The next time, they could be entirely successful and then what would you do?"

For whatever reason, the thought of being forced to marry another, to have to step away from Lady Frederica, never to see her again, was something that Percy could not even bear to consider. It was as though a knife had lodged itself in his heart at the mere thought of it, his chest tight as he looked back into her eyes.

"Very well," he murmured as she released his hand. "I will not say that my concern for you has disappeared," he said as she turned to take his arm once more. "But I shall accept that this is to be our position at present." His gaze slid across to her. "I only hope that I will be able to keep you safe."

"GOOD AFTERNOON, LADY NOTTINGHAM." Lady Frederica smiled warmly at the lady before turning to her daughter. "And good afternoon to you also, Miss Chalmers."

Lady Nottingham greeted Lady Frederica quickly, although her eyes turned toward Percy almost at once, bright and calculating in the afternoon sunshine.

"Good afternoon, Lord Wetherby," she said as Miss Chalmers remained entirely silent. "You have taken Lady Frederica out for an afternoon stroll, I see."

This was not a question but a rather obvious statement to which there was no simple reply. Miss Chalmers glanced toward him and then lowered her gaze to the ground, her head dropping forward just a little.

"I—I have, yes," Percy replied, turning to look behind him for a moment. "The Duchess of Ellsworth is with us also, of course."

"She is just speaking to Lady Montgomery," Lady Frederica explained, gesturing toward her aunt.

"My son is here also," Lady Nottingham said, looking directly at

Lady Frederica rather than toward Percy. "You are acquainted with Lord Nottingham, I believe?"

Lady Frederica nodded. "We have been introduced," she said, before looking toward Lady Chalmers. "Do you enjoy the fashionable hour, Miss Chalmers? I confess that I find it something of a crush."

"I am surprised that you chose to step out into it, given your dislike of the crowds," Lady Nottingham said, before her daughter could answer. "Although, given that you are walking with Lord Wetherby, perhaps you had no other choice but to do as he demands." Her lip curled gently. "I feel that you, Lord Wetherby, are a gentleman solely inclined toward his own interests."

This was something of a strange remark and Percy found himself frowning and glancing toward Lady Frederica, who also appeared to be very confused, given the way her brow furrowed.

"I—it was I who suggested it, Lady Nottingham," she told the older lady, who let out a small exclamation of evident disbelief. "As much as I might dislike the crush of the fashionable hour, there is always some interest in attending, is there not?" Her frown lifted and her smile returned, although Percy was quite certain it was forced. "And are you to attend the ball this evening, Miss Chalmers?" she continued quickly, obviously trying to change the subject of their conversation. "Lord Blakely has told me that it is to be an exceptional evening."

Lady Nottingham tilted her head, ignoring her daughter entirely. "Lord Blakely is an *excellent* gentleman, Lady Frederica," she said, without so much as glancing at Percy. "I had wondered if there might be anything of particular note between you both, but it seems now that I was mistaken."

Lady Frederica laughed as Percy's stomach tightened, wondering whether or not Lady Nottingham spoke the truth. If it was true, that meant that he had pulled Lady Frederica away from what could have been a very happy situation for her indeed. His mind began to turn over the possibility that Lady Frederica might have been interested in furthering her acquaintance with Lord

Blakely and now had given that up for the present, so that she might come to his aid instead. She had such a good heart that it was entirely the sort of thing that Percy knew she would have done willingly but would never have told him about. His heart grew all the heavier as he looked back at the lady and saw that her smile still did not reach her eyes. Perhaps Lady Nottingham was right.

"I am sure we shall meet again this evening," he heard Lady Frederica say, realizing that their conversation with Lady Nottingham and Miss Chalmers was now at an end. "Do excuse us, Lady Nottingham. I should return to the duchess."

Percy quickly took his leave of the two ladies and made his way across to where the duchess stood, although they were only a few paces away and very easily able to converse quietly together.

"Lady Frederica?"

She turned and smiled up at him, making his heart ache all the more. "Yes?"

"Lord Blakely," he said, without even thinking about what he was attempting to express and realizing that he was not managing to do so very well at all. "That is to say, what Lady Nottingham suggested, I..." Scowling, he looked away for a moment, taking in a breath and letting it out slowly. "What I mean to ask is whether or not I have pulled you from something that might well have brought you a lot of joy?" His eyes turned back to hers, searching her face carefully. "If there was ever any interest between you and Lord Blakely, which I have clearly interrupted, then I must beg of you to throw aside any concern for me and, instead, return to whatever it was that was beginning to grow between you."

Lady Frederica smiled gently, her eyes glowing with a tenderness that Percy felt flood his entire being.

"My dear Lord Wetherby, you are so very concerned for my welfare, are you not?" she said, her hand reaching out to brush down his arm for just a moment, so quickly so that no one else would notice. "In answer to your question, no, there is nothing between Lord Blakely and me. I will not pretend that he was not eager to call upon me at one time, but such an interest had evidently ceased."

"That may be because he had very little encouragement," Percy replied quickly. "If you were holding yourself back for my sake, I—"

Her hand squeezed his fingers before she finally let go entirely. "I assure you, I have not done anything of the sort," she answered as Percy nodded slowly, wanting to believe her and yet fearful that she was keeping the truth of her feelings and intentions from him so that he would not feel at all guilty for it. "Lord Blakely is not someone who ever occupies my thoughts, Lord Wetherby. I can assure you of that."

Percy looked back into her eyes and found himself lost. All manner of warmth was in her expression, her clear desire that he believe what she had to say shining out from her eyes. His heart was thumping a little more quickly than before, the urge to take her hand once more in his growing steadily within him. Everything around him seemed to fade, as though the crowds, the laughter, and the conversations about him were no longer there. All there was before him was Lady Frederica, her beauty calling out to him so that he could not turn away.

"Lord Wetherby?"

He dropped Lady Frederica's hand at once, pulled back to the present abruptly. Clearing his throat, he bowed hastily toward Lady Preston.

"Whatever are you doing with Lady Frederica?" she asked, her brows knotting together as anger filled her voice. "Are you attempting to coerce her in some way?"

Percy blinked rapidly, astonished at the red heat that poured into the older lady's cheeks as she glared up at him, one hand on her hip as her unfortunate daughter, Miss Addington, stood a step or two behind her mother.

"I do not know what you mean, Lady Preston," he said, as quietly as he could, fearful that there would be some sort of scene created by the lady's obvious fury toward him. "Forgive me if I have upset you. I—"

"Lady Frederica, you must come away from this gentleman at once."

Lady Preston beckoned to Lady Frederica, who remained precisely where she was, one eyebrow lifting.

"I am sure that the duchess would not be—"

"Lady Preston?"

The duchess turned around from where she had been finishing her conversation with Lady Montgomery, seeming to startle Lady Preston by her presence.

"I am here," she said, coming to stand by Lady Frederica as Percy looked on, feeling more and more confused by the situation at hand. "Is there something the matter?"

Lady Frederica shook her head. "No, there is not," she said as Percy looked at the duchess with wide eyes, lifting both hands in a gesture of uncertainty. "Lady Preston was, I believe, concerned for my welfare, but there is truly no need for it, Lady Preston, although you are very kind indeed to be so watchful."

Lady Preston lifted her chin and turned her head toward Percy, her eyes glinting angrily. "*That gentleman,*" she said sharply, pointing one long finger in Percy's direction, "was taking Lady Frederica's hand in his own." She glared at him for another moment before turning her head back triumphantly toward the duchess. "No doubt he wished to encourage her into some ill-thought-out scheme and right behind your back, Your Grace." She smiled in evident satisfaction, clearly believing herself to be in the right in this situation, whilst Lady Frederica frowned hard, her eyes narrowing. Percy looked at Miss Addington, who had dropped her head so low that it appeared as though she was trying to hide herself away. Clearly the girl was embarrassed by her mother's outburst but could do nothing about it.

"Lady Preston," the duchess began, speaking gently but with a great firmness to her words. "You are treating Lord Wetherby with the greatest unfairness. He is not, as you might have thought, attempting to take Lady Frederica anywhere. As you can see, I was standing just behind Lady Frederica and would have noticed if she had decided to leave my side. Lady Frederica *herself* would not have done so, for she knows what is expected and would never have stepped outside the bounds of propriety."

This seemed to embarrass Lady Preston somewhat, for her anger faded just a little and she dropped her hand from her hip. "But of course," she mumbled. "Although," she continued, her head lifting once more, "just because Lady Frederica would have been so very wise does not mean that Lord Wetherby was not intending to cajole her in the most improper manner."

"I was not doing anything of the sort, Lady Preston," Percy replied firmly. "I can assure you of that."

"Then why did you have her hand in yours?" she demanded, her voice catching the attention of one or two others who stood nearby. "I cannot imagine—"

"Because we are courting, Lady Preston," Percy interrupted loudly. "Forgive me for showing a little of the affection I feel for Lady Frederica. It was not meant to be noticed by any, but given that you have seen it, and felt it was your duty to come and demand that Lady Frederica depart from me, I can only apologize for doing so." He spoke freely, his voice louder than he had intended but with no hesitation whatsoever. "Does that now satisfy you, Lady Preston? Are you now quite convinced that I have no intention of stealing Lady Frederica away from her aunt? I assure you, I am not that sort of gentleman."

Lady Preston stared back at him, her eyes wide and her mouth a little ajar. The color pulled itself from her face just as hastily as it had arrived, leaving her looking rather tired. The anger had gone entirely, the fury fading from her eyes as she continued to look at him, as though she could not believe what she had heard.

"As I have said, Lady Preston," the duchess added gently, "I think you misjudge Lord Wetherby a little too harshly. He is not a cad or a rogue or any such thing as that. Both the duke and I are quite certain of it."

Blinking rapidly, Lady Preston turned back to the duchess and, as Percy watched, dropped into a very deep curtsy.

"I can only apologize, Your Grace," she said, her voice very quiet. "I thought the worst and—"

"And you came to the aid of Lady Frederica, which is not something to be dismissed lightly," the duchess replied, showing more grace than Percy himself might have done, had he been in her place. "Please, Lady Preston, think nothing more of it. I am grateful to you for your willingness to step forward in such a situation, but as I have assured you, there is nothing to be set to rights here." She smiled but Lady Preston did not return it. Instead, the lady nodded, begged to be excused, and stepped away from them almost at once, leaving her daughter, who had remained precisely as she had been when Percy had first looked at her, to follow after.

Percy watched the lady depart, noticing that she made her way directly to Lady Nottingham, who had, evidently, been watching the situation with great interest. He could almost feel the sharpness of her gaze when she looked back at him, although he deliberately turned his head away so that she would not have the impression that he had any real interest in what was being said.

"Most extraordinary," the duchess murmured, turning her back on Lady Preston and Lady Nottingham as she began to walk once more, clearly eager to step away from the situation and from those who had overheard what had been said. "I am afraid all manner of whispers will be starting about you both now."

Lady Frederica laughed, though Percy wanted to groan aloud over what had occurred. Startled, he looked across at her, only for her to slip her hand into the crook of his arm and smile up into his eyes.

"But that is what is to be expected, is it not?" she reminded him as Percy tried his best to throw aside his frustration and upset at what had just taken place. "I will not pretend that the conversation was a pleasant one, however. You must have been a little insulted, Lord Wetherby—but at least the story will make its way through the *ton*." Her smile was a satisfied one and Percy found that his own heart began to lose some of the anger that had filled him only minutes before.

"I suppose you are right, Lady Frederica," he said as she walked alongside him. "Although whomever we are to speak to next, might they be someone who does *not* think so ill of me?" His lips twitched with wry humor as Lady Frederica looked up at him sharply, only for her to stop walking entirely.

"*Why* do they think so ill of you, Lord Wetherby?" she asked as the duchess came to stand beside Percy so that their conversation remained as private as they could manage. "Lady Nottingham and Lady Preston both seem equally inclined to think very badly of your character. Is there some reason that they might do so?"

Percy considered the question, recalling what had occurred with Lady Preston and her daughter at the ball some time ago. "You will remember that Lady Preston was most upset that I had danced with you rather than her daughter, Lady Frederica?" he asked, and she nodded slowly, her eyes searching his. "For whatever reason, even though I stood up to dance with her daughter at a later time, she has never thought well of me since."

"But that is a ridiculous reason to hold any sort of grudge," the duchess said as Lady Frederica nodded in agreement. "It was a mistake, was it not?"

"A mistake on *her* part," Lady Frederica said firmly, before Percy could say anything. "She seemed to think that Lord Wetherby had promised to dance the cotillion with Miss Addington, even though he had only just written his name on my dance card." She shook her head, waving one hand as though dismissing Lady Preston's concerns entirely. "As you have said, Louisa, it is a foolish reason indeed to now think so poorly of Lord Wetherby, which does make me wonder..." She said nothing more, her lips twisting for a moment before she looked back at him. "And Lady Nottingham?"

A little embarrassed, Percy shook his head. "I am afraid I do not recall," he said honestly. "Lady Nottingham and I spoke some days ago where she informed me that I had behaved in a most improper manner toward her daughter."

Lady Frederica caught her breath, her eyes wide. "When did this occur?"

"The night that I so badly insulted you also," Percy told her, closing his eyes for a moment in an attempt to clear the embarrassment from himself. "But Lord Greenford had assured me that I did *nothing* to shame any other young lady in any other way. He was with me beforehand and then, once I had done such inordinate damage to our acquaintance, he felt he had no other choice but to remain near to me for the rest of the evening. I have asked him repeatedly whether or not I went near to Miss Chalmers, whether I did something or said anything that might have caused her distress, but he is certain I did not."

This seemed to bring a great deal of satisfaction to Lady Frederica, for she smiled triumphantly and settled one hand on his shoulder for only a moment.

"Then might I suggest that we consider both Lady Nottingham and Lady Preston a little more?" she asked, her hand now back by her side. "If Lady Preston has no real anger against you, and as she did today and on other occasions, sought to push me far from you, then what is the reason for that?"

"I—" Percy stopped speaking almost at once, realizing with a frown that he had no real understanding as to why Lady Preston considered him so poorly, or why she was attempting to push Lady Frederica from him.

The duchess took a small step closer, leaning forward as she spoke. "And Lady Nottingham?"

"Why does she seem to despise you so?" Lady Frederica asked as Percy shook his head. "She speaks of an insult to her daughter that you do not recall. What was it? And is she attempting to improve matters between her daughter and you in the belief that *you* are the one who insulted her in some manner, even though you do not believe you did?"

Percy rubbed one hand over his eyes. "They are both eager to keep their daughters away from me, Lady Frederica," he said, opening his eyes to see her looking back at him with that small smile still on her face. "Why, then, would they seek to set up a situation where I would be forced to wed one of them?"

Lady Frederica tilted her head. "Because as much as they may dislike you for what they *believe* you have done, there may be more to their disfavor than we recognize at present." She moved a little closer to him. "What if Lady Preston believes that you stole her daughter into the gardens at the ball, promised her matrimony, and then did not fulfill it? What if Lady Nottingham believes that she saw you encouraging her daughter in some improper manner and then promising to wed the girl in order to bring a satisfactory conclusion to the matter? Despite their dislike and distrust of you, they view their daughters now as being somewhat spoiled. Therefore, regardless of how they themselves might feel, they will seek to force marriage upon you for fear of what might occur otherwise."

The duchess spoke up. "They may fear that someone will have seen their daughters and you—I mean, whichever gentleman was with them—and are merely biding their time before they speak of it," she said quickly. "In attempting to encourage you away from Lord Wetherby, Frederica, they do so in order to make certain that it is *their* daughter that will end up marrying him."

Percy considered this and found himself suddenly a little more convinced than he had expected. Lady Frederica's suggestion made sense. The night he had been in the gardens with Lord Greenford, had not the young lady spoken of what he had promised her? Had she not made it seem as though this was not the first time they had been in such a situation?

And then a sudden recollection had him shaking his head.

"It cannot be either of them," he said heavily as Lady Frederica looked at him in surprise. "The young lady that spoke to me in the gardens that evening was confident, well spoken, and had a great deal of determination." His eyes lifted sorrowfully to Lady Frederica's. "Neither of which would describe Miss Addington or Miss Chalmers."

Lady Frederica tossed her head, clearly dismissing the idea at once. "That does not mean that it could not be either of them," she said firmly. "Miss Addington is clearly under the control of her mother, but perhaps there is a part to her character that is very well hidden. A part that seeks to release herself from her mother's grip and to speak with her own words."

"And Miss Chalmers is certainly not as quiet as she appears," the duchess added with a slightly rueful smile. "I know that Lady Nottingham is something of an overwhelming character and, when she is present and busy discussing matters, it seems as though her daughter remains entirely in her shadow. But I can assure you that there have been times when I have heard Miss Chalmers speak openly and directly to others, with a confidence that I confess surprised me a little—but it has been only when her mother has been entirely absent."

"You see?" Lady Frederica beamed, a brightness in her eyes that lifted Percy's spirits. "It may be one of them, Lord Wetherby, and if it is, then this matter will be resolved very quickly indeed."

"But what can we do?" he asked, feeling a flare of hope in his heart as he looked into Lady Frederica's eyes. "What can be done to prove it is one of them?"

"I am not certain as yet," Lady Frederica replied as they began to walk back toward the waiting carriage, knowing that they could not discuss the matter further at present, given the company that surrounded them. "But something must be done, Lord Wetherby, and soon. We are so very near to the truth."

13

"Has Lord Wetherby arrived yet?"

The duchess laughed and slipped her arm through Frederica's. "Not as yet," she replied as they made their way to the drawing room, ready to await his arrival. "You look very well, my dear."

"I thank you." Frederica smiled at her aunt. "I feel a good deal more at ease, I confess, even though we have not yet made any decision about what to do next."

"That is because you have an intimacy building between you and Lord Wetherby," the lady replied. "I know of what you speak because I have experienced such a thing myself. It is a comfort, is it not?"

"It is," Frederica replied quietly, considering what the duchess had said. "And to see the hope in Lord Wetherby's eyes also brought a good deal of happiness to me."

"Let us hope that whatever conclusion we reach this evening will be something that we can act upon at once," the duchess replied, patting Frederica's arm before she let go. "And then, mayhap, you will be able to discuss with Lord Wetherby the truth of how you feel."

Frederica stopped and turned to face the duchess, her heart suddenly ricocheting against her chest.

"I do not think that there is any need for me to do so," she said, as calmly as she could. "Surely he must know that I have an…affection for him." The word seemed to stick in her throat, but she forced herself to say it regardless, not wanting to have any awkwardness between her and her aunt. "Is that not displayed?"

The duchess smiled. "Of course, I would say so," she said quietly, "but that is because I know you very well and can see the effect that Lord Wetherby's presence has upon you. When he is in the room, you can barely look anywhere else. Your conversation is directed, on the whole, toward him and the smile on your face is always only for him." She lifted one shoulder in a half-shrug. "But that is, of course, to be expected and certainly not something that I would ever dream of bringing up in conversation with him." Smiling, she turned to open the door to the drawing room, leaving Frederica to follow after her.

"There is still the possibility that he might come to refuse me entirely," Frederica admitted, feeling a tight knot of fear in her stomach as she spoke those words. "If he does, then I have already promised you that I will accept it without complaint or question. And yet I am fully aware that my heart will be very pained indeed if such a thing occurs."

The duchess nodded and sat down, leaving Frederica to meander around the room, unwilling to seat herself as yet.

"I can only pray that it will not be so," she continued quietly. "We have only just begun this courtship and yet I find myself so delighted with his company that I want nothing more than to continue on as we are."

"I do not believe that it will occur," the duchess answered. "I have also seen how Lord Wetherby looks at *you*, Frederica. Given the way that he wants nothing more than to defend you, to protect your good name, and to make certain that you are entirely uninjured by whatever you endure together, I should say that he is quite taken with you."

Frederica sat down heavily, her heart torn between hope and her determination to remain quite sensible. "I can only hope that such a thing is true," she replied wistfully. "I will prepare myself for either eventuality."

"What eventuality might that be?"

Frederica turned her head sharply, seeing Lord Wetherby and the duke standing framed in the doorway, with Lord Wetherby smiling broadly at her. He appeared much more at ease this evening and bowed toward her before he came any further into the room. The duke smiled at his wife and then at Frederica, greeting them both warmly.

"Please, do be seated," the duchess said, gesturing to an empty chair. "The dinner gong will ring very soon."

"I thank you for your kind invitation," Lord Wetherby replied, seating himself close to Frederica. "Might I hope that you are both well this evening?"

"Very well," Frederica replied, glad that she would not have to explain what she and the duchess had been discussing. "How is your head?"

It had been three days since Lord Wetherby had been injured, and Frederica was relieved that he had continued to make a quick recovery.

"It does not pain me at all, Lady Frederica, I thank you," he told her, passing one hand over the back of his head as though to prove that what he said was quite true. "I am quite at my ease now, I assure you."

"I am glad," she answered, just as the dinner gong sounded.

Frederica rose to her feet. "Shall we make our way through for dinner?" she asked, and Lord Wetherby nodded, coming to offer her his arm as the duke took the hand of his wife. She smiled up at him as they walked together, feeling her heart full of contentment and hope that one day, perhaps one day very soon, they might be free of this difficulty for good. And who could tell what would happen then?

"If we suspect Lady Preston and Lady Nottingham, then there must be something that can be done to reveal their true intentions entirely."

Frederica nodded, lines forming across her forehead as she frowned. Their dinner had been a most enjoyable evening, with a good deal of laughter and excellent conversation. Now, however, the duke and Lord Wetherby had taken their port to join the ladies with their tea in the drawing room and matters of importance were coming into play.

"I confess that I have very little idea of what to do," the duchess said as Frederica picked up her teacup, sipping her tea carefully. "I know that we must find a way to prove that it is they who have been pursuing Lord Wetherby, but how we might go about it without—"

"Could we not use the ball?"

Frederica had not meant to interrupt and hastily apologized, only for the duchess to wave a hand and encourage her to continue.

"There is to be a ball here in two days' time," Frederica said as the duchess nodded. "Lady Preston, Miss Addington, Lady Nottingham, and Miss Chalmers have all been invited, have they not?"

"They have," the duke replied as Lord Wetherby listened carefully. "You mean to say that you think we could set up some sort of situation where we might prove for certain that it is one or the other?"

"Or that it is neither," Lord Wetherby replied, grimacing, although Frederica knew that such an outcome was quite possible.

"Yes," Frederica said, setting her shoulders. "That is precisely what I am thinking."

There was silence for a moment as the others looked first at each other and then back to Frederica. Frederica searched her mind for what they might arrange, but nothing immediately came to her. All she knew was that the ball that evening would be an excellent time to put *something* in place.

"Very well," the duke said gruffly. "We have the ball. What is to happen next?"

Lord Wetherby took in a long breath. "They both are aware now, of course, that I am courting Lady Frederica," he said as Frederica looked back at him, praying he had some sort of idea. "They will expect me to dance with her." Hesitating, he paused for a moment before continuing. "Lady Preston will be just as eager, no doubt, to push me away from Lady Frederica. Perhaps, Lady Frederica, you ought to listen to her and let her speak to you as she wishes. You could pretend to be concerned by what she had to say during the fashionable hour and beg of her to tell you more as to why she is so very concerned."

A frown crossed Frederica's brow. "I do not wish to speak ill of you, Lord Wetherby."

"But it would only be as part of our façade," he said hastily. "Lady Preston might think, therefore, that she has been somewhat successful."

"And might then seek to push you toward her daughter once more," Frederica finished as Lord Wetherby nodded. "Although, again, we could not be certain as to what she might do."

Lord Wetherby frowned, rubbing his chin for a moment. "Mayhap I could join your conversation with the lady," he said slowly, his eyes running all over the room as he spoke his thoughts aloud. "State my anger and my upset and tell you that I am to go out to the gardens to quieten my temper before it becomes too great."

"Thereby setting up a situation for Lady Preston and her daughter to do as she has done before," the duchess said as Lord Wetherby nodded. "It is something of a risk, however, for she may choose to do nothing."

"And it does leave Lady Nottingham also," the duke added. "What about her?

Frederica let out a long, slow breath and tried to put her thoughts into coherent order. "We must do the very same thing," she said quietly. "If Lady Nottingham is the one who sent her daughter to the gardens to coerce Lord Wetherby, then *she* will be the one who appears. If it is Lady Preston, then she will step forward. However," she continued quickly, "I think we should not use the gardens as the place for you to go, Lord Wetherby. It must be stated, very clearly to both Lady Preston and Lady Nottingham, that you are to make your way to the small parlor near to the duke's study. You will know of it, given that you have called upon me before and have joined us for dinner. Perhaps with Lady Preston, I might suggest that you go there in order to quieten your temper, and with Lady Nottingham, you could state that this was where you were going."

The duchess sat forward, her hands clasped but her elbows on her knees as she looked back intently at Frederica. "You will have to have both conversations, one after the other," she said as Frederica nodded. "How will you manage such a thing?"

"Mayhap that is where you and I can play a part, my dear," the duke replied as the duchess' brows lifted in question. "Mayhap you could strike up a conversation with Lady Nottingham at the very same time that Frederica speaks to Lady Preston. Make sure you are close to each other and, as you speak to Lady Nottingham, share with her one or two concerns you have about Lord Wetherby and his courtship of Frederica. No doubt, Lady Nottingham will have something to say on the matter, and as you leave Lady Preston's side, Lord Wetherby, you could overhear something being said."

Frederica bit her lip. It was all very precarious indeed and yet there was still a chance that it would all fall into place. After all, given that it would be the duchess herself talking to Lady Nottingham, Frederica knew all too well that Lady Nottingham would not reject the opportunity to speak to her. And Lady Preston was certainly more than eager to disparage Lord Wetherby, should Frederica give her even the most meager of opportunities

"It sounds as though we have a plan," she murmured as Lord Wetherby nodded, his expression rather grave. "I will, of course, make my way to the parlor soon after you, Lord Wetherby, in the hope that whoever comes to join you will reveal their intentions openly."

"As will I," the duchess added as the duke nodded his agreement. They all looked to Lord Wetherby as one, waiting to see what he would say about this particular consideration.

Lord Wetherby rose to his feet, his eyes still holding fast to Frederica's and his forehead puckered.

"There is a great deal resting upon it," he said quietly. "And yet I am most profoundly grateful for all that you have suggested, for all that you now wish to do." He looked to the duke, then to the duchess, and then, finally, to Frederica. "Your willingness to help me when I am nothing but an acquaintance to you has been overwhelming. I can only pray that our plan will go as well as we expect, so that the truth might be discovered."

"Here, here," the duke murmured as Lord Wetherby smiled, a faint hope shining in his eyes.

"I shall take my leave of you now," Lord Wetherby finished, turning first to bow to the duke and to thank the duchess before he turned to Frederica. "I have had the most wonderful of evenings. I have felt myself contented, free of worry, even for a short time, and I cannot thank you enough for that."

Frederica found herself on her feet in a moment, seeing the surprise leap into the duchess' expression but praying that she would be permitted to do as she now intended.

"I will accompany you to the door, Lord Wetherby," she said, seeing how her uncle frowned, only for the duchess to reach up and press his hand, her face upturned toward his. "Perhaps we can make arrangements to meet again tomorrow, in order to continue our courtship?"

Lord Wetherby glanced to the duke, who nodded his assent, before turning back to smile broadly at Frederica.

"I should be very glad if you would do so," he said as Frederica made her way to the door, her heart hammering furiously in her chest. "Thank you, Lady Frederica."

They walked together in silence for a few moments, the door closing behind them as they stepped out into the hallway.

"Lord Wetherby," Frederica found herself saying, feeling a deep urge to express something more of her heart but finding it almost too difficult to do so. "I do hope—that is to say, I pray that you will find your freedom very soon in this matter. I know that it cannot have been easy for you to struggle all this time." It was not what she had wanted to say, and Frederica felt a great irritation seize her, pushing her to say more. "You shall soon be without any difficulty, I am sure, and will be able to resume your life such as it was."

"And what if I do not wish to?"

Her breath caught and she turned to face him, seeing how he looked deeply into her eyes, his nearness so close to her that she could barely breathe.

"We have only been courting for a few days," he continued quickly, "but I find that even the thought of stepping back from you and bringing our courtship to an end is so very painful to me that I cannot even think of it."

Frederica swallowed hard, unable to look away from him, caught by the deep intensity of his gaze.

"If you would be willing, Lady Frederica," Lord Wetherby continued, speaking a good deal more quickly now as though he was desperate to say everything that was on his mind all at once, "I should very much like to continue our courtship, even after the truth has been found."

Certain that Lord Wetherby could hear just how loudly her heart was beating, Frederica put one hand over it as though it might muffle the sound. "You wish to continue courting me, Lord Wetherby?" she asked, aware of the almost wistful tone of her voice. "Truly?"

A smile pulled at his mouth. "It is my heart's desire, Lady Frederica," he told her as Frederica closed her eyes in utter relief. "I have found myself becoming all the more grateful for you, have found myself in awe of your beauty. Your character is one that I am certain I could never find again and thus, given the affection for you within my heart, given that I find myself drawn to you time and again—each time, with a stronger hold—I must hope that you would be willing to accept my courtship once more." His hand reached out and ran down her arm until their fingers met. "Although this time, it would not be a façade," he finished, his voice low. "What would you say, Lady Frederica?"

She opened her eyes and looked up into his face, seeing the question lingering there. Her smile was broad, her hopes lifting all the more as she pressed his fingers.

"My own heart has been calling for you, Lord Wetherby," she told him as his smile slowly returned. "I would be more than glad to accept such an offer, given that it is the only thing that I have found myself longing for," she said softly. "We have grown very close, have we not? Why, then, should I want to cause myself a great deal of pain by separating myself from you?"

For a moment, she thought he might lower his head and kiss her, such was the intensity of his eyes and the way that he moved closer to her, but instead, he lifted her hand to his lips and kissed it gently. The stirrings of her heart grew all the more, her joy abounding in such great swaths that she did not think she would ever be able to contain it.

"I should take my leave," he murmured, reluctantly letting go of her hand and stepping back. "I will call for you tomorrow, if I may?"

"I am already looking forward to your arrival," she answered, watching him walk away from her and feeling as though her heart would burst with the sheer amount of happiness and delight that tore through her. This was more wonderful than she could ever have imagined.

14

Percy made his way into the ballroom with Lady Frederica by his side. The knowledge that this was to be the evening they attempted to uncover the truth about either Lady Preston or Lady Nottingham ran around his mind a great deal, rendering him a little more nervous than he would usually be.

"This is truly magnificent," he murmured, looking all about him and taking in the sheer splendor of the ballroom itself. Of course, he should have expected as much given that this townhouse belonged to a duke and duchess, but the additional decorative touches added to the opulence. Percy was quite certain that no expense had been spared. There would be no watered-down wine this evening, he was sure of that.

"I am sure that the duchess will be glad to hear that you approve of all that she has planned," Lady Frederica replied as he smiled back at her, making sure to remain in sight of the duchess herself. "It is a wonderful evening." She sighed contentedly, as though she had forgotten all that was to occur. Percy looked back at her and felt his worry begin to drift away, realizing just how truly blessed he was to have her by his side. When she had offered to walk with him to the door two nights ago, he could do nothing but accept without hesitation, finding himself overwhelmingly delighted at the prospect of being alone with her for even a few minutes.

What had come from those few minutes had made him want to leap for joy. He had spoken to her of what was in his heart, having realized that the thought of leaving her side and stepping back from their courtship was more than he could tolerate. There was an awareness in him that Lady Frederica was unlike any other young lady of his acquaintance and that to step away from her would be one of the most foolish things he could do. On top of which, having been so overcome by her kind nature, generous spirit, and beauty of both face and character, Percy had realized just how much he cared for her.

He did not want to be without her. He wanted her to be a part of his life. No longer did he see their acquaintance as being simply that. Instead, there was now a consideration of their future, of what could be for himself and Lady Frederica, if she would agree to consider their courtship again. And the moment she had done so, the moment she had looked into his eyes and smiled with such vibrancy, he had felt his heart lift with a renewed happiness that he was certain could never be taken from him.

All that had to be done now was to remove this burden from his shoulders and then he would be free to court Lady Frederica without any worry about what might happen next. As much as Percy wished for it all to be at an end, he was also a little anxious about whether or not all would go to plan. If it did, then by the end of the evening, he might know the truth in its entirety. If it did not, then nothing would change and they would have to start looking at things all over again.

"Are we to dance this evening, Lord Wetherby?" Lady Frederica asked, her eyes twinkling at him as he quickly fumbled for her dance card, which she held out to him.

"Of course," he said, quickly putting his name down for the supper dance at the end of the evening, as well as for the quadrille

The Eligible Earl

which would begin very soon. "You know that I would take all of your dances for myself, if I could."

"But that would be *entirely* selfish, Lord Wetherby." Lord Greenford came to join them, greeting them both warmly before begging to peruse Lady Frederica's dance card. Glad that there was no animosity between them due to Percy's now pointed interest in Lady Frederica, Percy fell into easy conversation and the next few minutes passed easily enough.

"Ah, it is to be our dance, Lady Frederica," Lord Greenford cried as the announcement came for the country dance. "Shall we go?"

Lady Frederica laughed and accepted Lord Greenford's arm, although she threw Percy a warm smile as she did so, leaving him to watch her stepping out onto the dance floor with Lord Greenford. A small niggle of envy settled within him, but Percy pushed it away with an effort. Lady Frederica had no interest in Lord Greenford, and he was certain that Lord Greenford had now moved on to consider Lady Prudence. A sigh escaped him as he watched them take their position on the floor, glad that Lady Frederica would soon be returned to him.

"You do not deserve that young lady's acquaintance."

Percy turned sharply, looking to see Lady Nottingham standing there, glaring at him with hard eyes.

"I beg your pardon, Lady Nottingham," he said with a tight smile, "but I do not believe that I have asked for your opinion. Lady Frederica is more than contented to court me and I am very glad for it."

Lady Nottingham's eyes glittered. "I witnessed just how poorly you treated her that night," she said, making Percy realize she spoke of the night he had been so foxed that he had practically demanded that Lady Frederica dance with him, despite his inebriated state. "My son would *never* behave so."

"Forgive me, but I am not particularly well acquainted with your son, Lady Nottingham," Percy replied, growing a little angry. "Therefore, I cannot make a comment as to whether or not he has ever been inebriated before. Thankfully, however, Lady Frederica is inclined toward forgiveness and I am very grateful to her for being so." Glancing behind Lady Nottingham, he saw the duchess quickly approaching, and bowing quickly, made to take his leave. "Do excuse me, Lady Nottingham," he said, speaking a little more sharply than before. "I do believe there is nothing more for us to say."

He turned and took a few steps away from Lady Nottingham so that he could await Lady Frederica's return. He did not need to look over his shoulder to know that the duchess had taken this opportunity to speak to Lady Nottingham, given that the sharp tone of Lady Nottingham's voice could be clearly heard. Percy gave himself a slight shake, forcing his anger to die away as he waited for Lady Frederica's return, knowing that now was their opportunity to find Lady Preston and speak to her also. His eyes strayed across the remaining dancers, wondering if Miss Addington would be dancing this evening.

There!

He spied the lady curtsying to her partner as the dance came to an end. Rather than look to Lady Frederica, he trained his gaze on Miss Addington, recognizing the gentleman that she had been dancing with and watching her carefully as she was returned to her mother.

"I thank you, Lord Greenford," Lady Frederica said as she came back to join Percy. "That was most enjoyable."

It took a few minutes for Lord Greenford to extricate himself from their conversation, with Percy's eagerness and tension rising steadily. The moment Lord Greenford stepped away, he turned to Lady Frederica, reaching out to grasp her gloved hand in his own.

"Lady Preston is just over there," he said, indicating her with a nod of his head. "The duchess is already speaking to Lady Nottingham." He wanted to tell her what had been said but knew that there was not much time. "Might you be able to make your way to Lady Preston at this very moment? I will come to join you and state that it is to be our dance."

Lady Frederica nodded, her smile gone and replaced instead with a look of great determination.

"Let us hope that all goes to plan," she said softly. "Know that I care deeply for you, Lord Wetherby." Her fingers tightened in his. "I can only pray that this will soon be at an end."

He nodded, pressed her hand once more, and then released her, watching her as she turned on her heel and made her way toward Lady Preston. Percy turned to glance back at the duchess, seeing how her eyes darted toward Lady Frederica for a moment, only to return to Lady Nottingham. He drew in a long breath, settling his shoulders and pushing aside his apprehension. In a few minutes, he would have to make his way to Lady Frederica's side and begin to act out their plan. He could only hope that everything would go as they anticipated.

∽

THE PARLOR WAS VERY QUIET, pulling Percy away from the noise of the ballroom. He walked up and down for a few minutes, the action helping push away the lingering tension and the anger that had filled him. Lady Preston had spoken with great frankness and clear dislike, telling him directly that he ought not to be courting a lady who was so uncertain about his character. Lady Frederica had played her part well, dropping her gaze and looking very uncomfortable, whilst Lady Preston was almost overcome with delight at the chasm that seemed to be growing between him and Lady Frederica. It had been Lady Frederica who suggested that he might wish to calm his temper a little before they spoke any further and who had directed him to the parlor where, she said, she might consider joining him for a discussion, so long as she had either the duke or the duchess with her. Percy had turned on his heel and left her side at once, stalking away with great anger burning in him—not at what Lady Frederica had said but at Lady Preston's remarks.

When he had made his way past the duchess, she had spoken his name in a manner that had made it appear as though it was not to be overheard, but he had stopped, turned, and demanded to know what she was saying of him. Lady Nottingham had done precisely as he had expected and had told him the truth about what she thought of him, stating, as she had done so many times before, that her son would never behave as he had done. She had then turned to the duchess, taken her hand in her own, and, with a sympathetic look in her eyes, told her explicitly that she thought the match between Percy and Lady Frederica was a mistake. A mistake that both Lady Frederica and the duchess herself would come to regret.

The way the duchess had listened and then turned her head toward him and looked at him thoughtfully before sighing and shaking her head had almost made Percy believe that she had taken in what Lady Nottingham had suggested without hesitation. He had stated to the duchess that he thought it best that they speak privately about any matters pertaining to Lady Frederica, and she had suggested that he wait in the parlor where he might first calm his temper before she even *thought* of coming to speak to him.

And now, all he had to do was wait. His heart was quickening with every minute that passed, half hopeful, half in fear. If someone *did* come to the parlor, then what would he say to them? That he knew what they had been trying to do? That their scheme was now at an end? Would he demand the truth or simply ask quietly why they had done such a thing?

Before he could think of anything more, the door opened slowly, and as Percy rose, he saw none other than Lady Frederica step inside, with the duchess close behind her.

"We made certain to come quickly," Lady Frederica said, hurrying toward him and taking his hands in hers. "Lady Preston believes that I am now with my uncle, feeling quite bereft and heartbroken."

"And Lady Nottingham believes that I will leave you here for the rest of the evening, if I must," the duchess added, picking up a lit candle and using it to light a few more. "She has had me agree that to engage your company any further would be nothing more than a mistake. I have conceded that she may be right in her consideration of you." Her head tilted as she looked from Percy to Lady Frederica. "Although my suspicions are that it shall not be Lady Nottingham who arrives, Lord Wetherby."

"Oh?"

"I believe Lady Nottingham has intentions for her son and Lady Frederica," she stated, choosing to sit in a chair far from where the lit candles now illuminated the room. "That is why she has been attempting to push Lady Frederica from you, Lord Wetherby. She seeks to compare you to her son, in the hope that Frederica might realize that he is a much greater prospect."

Percy blinked rapidly as Lady Frederica murmured her astonishment.

The duchess chuckled. "A mother's motivation, I think," she said as Percy shook his head to clear some of his astonishment away. "Come, Lady Frederica. You must seat yourself and wait."

Lady Frederica reached up and brushed her fingers lightly down Percy's cheek, making his breath shudder out of him at the way her touch seemed to ignite his heart all over again.

"I am sorry for what was said and for what you had to listen to," she murmured as he shook his head.

"It was what was required," he told her softly. "You played your part very well, Lady Frederica."

"I hated every moment of it," she replied, a wry smile on her lips. "Let us hope it was not in vain."

Pulling her hand from his, she made her way past him and sat down somewhere near to the back of the room, leaving Percy to sit alone again. Minutes ticked by and a great tension began to flood the room, forcing Percy to his feet as he began to walk up and down in front of the empty fireplace.

And then, the door opened.

"Lord Wetherby."

Lady Preston swept into the room, pulling her daughter behind her before slamming it shut again.

"You will be glad to know that I have asked my *dear* friend, Lady

Pettigrew, to come to the parlor in only a few minutes' time," she said as Percy stared at her in shock. "My word will be no good, of course, for you could easily state that I am being utterly ridiculous and attempting to force your hand. However, if you are discovered not only by me but by Lady Pettigrew also, then you will have no choice but to do as you have promised."

"I have no knowledge of what you speak!" Percy exclaimed as Miss Addington came a little closer to him.

No longer was she the quiet, reserved young lady that he thought he knew. Instead, her lips were pulled into a curling smile that spoke of nothing but triumph and satisfaction, her eyes fixed to his as she came all the nearer. Percy expected her to stop at once but instead, she flung her arms about his neck and pulled herself close to him. It was only when the door closed that he realized that Lady Preston had stepped outside again. Evidently, her plan was to walk in with Lady Pettigrew by her side, only to come across this particular scene. He attempted to push Miss Addington away again, but she continued to come toward him, until he was trapped against the wall, with no means of escape.

Percy unwrapped her arms from his neck for what was now the fourth time and shook his head.

"Enough, Miss Addington," he said, all too aware that both Lady Frederica and the duchess were witnessing this. "Whatever are you doing?"

She tipped her head and smiled at him, her eyes burning with a dark light. "What I must," she said plainly. "I am not a particularly beautiful young lady. My father was a drunkard and a gambler. Rumors about him continue to this day. There is no dowry to speak of. My mother insists on treating me as though I am a delicate creature with not even a single thought in my head. She speaks over me, speaks for me, and had every intention of making certain that I wed a gentleman of her choosing. But I have never once agreed to such a thing."

Percy caught his breath, realizing in an instant that Lady Preston was not the one to have been manipulating the situation.

Whether she had realized it or not, it was none other than Miss Addington who had done it all.

"My mother and Lady Pettigrew will enter in only a few minutes," Miss Addington continued, standing near to him but no longer attempting to embrace him. "There is no opportunity for you to escape this time, Lord Wetherby. Although I shall strike you, as I did before." Her lip curled. "Something my mother was not expecting, I confess."

"Why should you have done such a thing?" Percy asked, knowing that the duchess and Lady Frederica were listening. "What have I done to you that would force you to behave in this manner?"

Miss Addington laughed. "Because *you* did the very same to me, Lord Wetherby," she said firmly. "The night you were so very foxed, you stole kisses and promised that you would wed me. I may have encouraged you a little but, of course, when I told my mother, she was caught between anger and elation. However, when you did not come to announce our engagement, I knew then that I would have to do whatever I had to in order to force your hand. After all," she continued, one hand trailing up over his shoulder again, "it is not your fault that you were so very drunk and, therefore, cannot recall what you did or said."

"That is quite enough, Miss Addington."

The sharpness of Lady Frederica's voice caught Miss Addington entirely off guard. She gasped and turned to stare at her, allowing Percy free of her attempts to entangle herself with him. He made his way toward Lady Frederica, who slipped her arm though his, just as the duchess came to join them. Miss Addington's eyes widened, her hands falling to her sides as she stared at Lady Frederica.

The door then flew open, slamming hard against the wall as Lady Preston and another lady whom Percy took to be Lady Pettigrew stood there. The smile on Lady Preston's face shattered in an instant as she took in the scene, clearly astonished to see both Lady Frederica and the duchess present.

"Lady Pettigrew, if you might leave us." The duchess stepped forward and gestured for Lady Preston to sit down. "We have much to discuss."

Lady Preston stared in utter shock at her daughter, clearly horrified to realize that the duchess herself had overheard what had been said.

"Sit down, Lady Preston."

The duchess' voice was a little harder now and, after a moment, the lady did as she was asked, just as Lady Pettigrew left the room, pulling the door closed behind her.

"We heard everything, Miss Addington," Lady Frederica said as Lady Preston closed her eyes tightly, her pallor very grey indeed. "You and your mother sought to entrap Lord Wetherby into matrimony. However," she continued, looking to Lady Preston, "it seems that your daughter has been manipulating you more than you might realize." She arched one eyebrow at Miss Addington, who, it seemed, had now returned to her quiet, demure persona.

"It is *you* who are entirely to blame in this, Lord Wetherby," Lady Preston lifted her head and tried to speak with great firmness in her voice, only to glance at the duchess and drop her head a little. "I believed my daughter to be in the company of her friend and her chaperone, only to discover that, in the interim, she had somehow lost her and instead had been taken into the gardens and treated most improperly." She looked up at Percy, her eyes hard. "*You* were the one to do so, Lord Weatherby. And then to promise matrimony, only to brush my daughter aside!"

"Lady Preston," Percy interrupted, speaking with great firmness. "I have done nothing of the sort. Lord Greenford will confirm it. The night I spoke to Lady Frederica with such a lack of decorum, he took it upon himself as my friend to remain near to me to make certain I did nothing more. I never once stole away with your daughter." A sudden thought struck him and he turned to look at Miss Addington. "Although," he said slowly, "I do recall that Lord Greenford stated that Lord Blakely disappeared from my company for some minutes."

Miss Addington jerked visibly, and Lady Preston gasped in horror, staring at her daughter.

"It was not Lord Blakely," Lady Preston breathed as Miss Addington slowly lifted her head and looked at her mother. "Tell me it was not him."

Sighing, Miss Addington rolled her eyes. "It was Lord Wetherby, Mama," she said firmly. "He cannot remember because of his drunken state."

"Miss Addington." The duchess rose to her feet and Lady Preston covered her hand with her mouth, her eyes wide with shock. "This is of the greatest importance. You *will* tell me the truth and you will tell it at once. Was Lord Wetherby the gentleman who stole away with you that night?"

Percy's chest tightened as they all turned to Miss Addington, seeing how she sighed and closed her eyes for a moment. He knew in his heart that he was not the man responsible, but whether or not she would tell him so, he could not be sure. The duchess' voice had been filled with authority and even Lady Preston had quailed beneath it, leaving them all waiting for Miss Addington's response.

"Very well, Your Grace." Miss Addington lifted her chin. "No, it was not Lord Wetherby. He was with Lord Blakely and another gentleman I did not know. However, try as I might to encourage Lord Wetherby to step away from his friends, he did not. Lord Blakely did, however."

"Then why did you state that it was I who had done such a thing?" Percy asked, hardly able to believe the sheer audacity of the lady. "Why encourage your mother to think so? Why do whatever you could to force my hand for what was now the second time?"

Miss Addington's lip curled. "As my own dear mother has stated, if I had cried that *you* had taken advantage of me, it would have done nothing but ruin my own reputation, for there was no proof of it. Had someone come across Lord Blakely and me in the gardens, as I intended they should, then I would have been contented to wed him. However, he stepped away much too quickly and I was presented with another, improved alternative."

"Because Lord Blakely is a viscount but Lord Wetherby an earl," Lady Frederica breathed, staring in horror at Miss Addington. "You chose to pretend it was Lord Wetherby simply so that your status might be improved."

Miss Addington spread her hands, no sign of regret in her features. "Indeed, Lady Frederica," she said, her voice filled with spite. "But it seems that, despite that, I have failed."

"Yes, Miss Addington," Percy responded, drawing Lady Frederica a little closer to him. "You have failed and failed entirely. Thanks to Lady Frederica's devotion and dedication to my cause, you have been discovered and the situation brought to an end." He drew in a deep breath and felt a burden fall from his shoulders. "And I swear to you at this moment, Miss Addington, that I shall never be in your company again."

EPILOGUE

"I cannot quite believe it."

Frederica shook her head as she and Lord Wetherby stood together in the drawing room, having been permitted a few minutes alone before they were to return to the ball. The duke had joined them shortly after Miss Addington's admission and now he and the duchess were speaking at length to both Miss Addington and her mother.

"We were all taken in," Lord Wetherby said, his hands clasping her shoulders gently before running down her arms so that he might twine his fingers with hers. "Even Lady Preston."

"I confess, I do feel a good deal of sympathy for her," Frederica replied, looking up into Lord Wetherby's face. "She did not know the truth, although she certainly ought not to have done as she did."

"Indeed not," came the reply as Lord Wetherby smiled ruefully. "But it is at an end. It is over and now all we need do is think of what might be ahead of us."

Anticipation rolled down Frederica's spine. "Ahead of us?" she repeated as Lord Weatherby moved a little closer to her, his eyes searching hers. "Might I ask what your intentions are, Lord Wetherby?"

"Marriage," he said without hesitation. "That is my intention, Lady Frederica. I want nothing more than to marry you, to make you my bride and my wife. I love you desperately." One hand lifted to her face, his fingers gently tipping up her chin. "The moment Miss Addington confessed all, I felt such a freedom in my heart that I wanted nothing more than to take you in my arms and offer you my hand." He chuckled softly. "But I did not think it wise to do so then."

Frederica closed her eyes for a moment, feeling her heart yearn for all that he had just offered her. "My uncle might have been a little upset had you done so," she admitted, teasingly. "But once you speak to him, I beg you to ask me what you wish." Opening her eyes, she smiled up into his face. "You must surely be able to discern my answer, Wetherby. Surely you can see that the love you speak of abides in my heart also."

His hands slipped around her waist as his head lowered. "I must hope that you will say you agree, Frederica," he breathed as her hands tangled around his neck. "Will you say yes? Will you be my bride?"

"Yes, Lord Wetherby," she whispered, before reaching up to kiss him.

∼

MORE STORIES YOU'LL LOVE

If you loved reading this book, discover other clean romances that will warm your heart.
London Temptations: Historical Regency Romance Collection
Mysteries abound in this sweet collection of historical regency romances.

Ladies, Love, and Mysteries: Historical Regency Romance Collection
Rogues, Mystery, Suspense, Secrets, and Romance.

Brides of London: Regency Romance Collection
Four romances to make you fall in love with the lords and ladies of Regency England. Discover love, mystery, suspense, and scandals in this heartwarming collection.

Weddings and Scandals: Regency Romance Collection
Four Regency romances filled with mystery, suspense, and surprising twists.

Seasons of Brides: Regency Romance Collection
Would you give up everything for the one you love?

LOVE LIGHT FAITH

Receive a FREE inspirational romance eBook by visiting our website and signing up for our mailing list. Click the link or enter www.LoveLightFaith.com into your browser.

The newsletter will also provide information on upcoming books and special offers.

Made in United States
Troutdale, OR
04/13/2024